It was the poor gardener's teeth that Assistant Magistrate Dee Jen-chieh could not forget. Had it not been for those discolored protuberances, Dee might never have become suspicious that an innocent man was moving toward an untimely and expeditious death . . .

Other Avon Books by
Eleanor Cooney and Daniel Altieri

THE COURT OF THE LION

DECEPTION

A NOVEL OF
MURDER AND MADNESS
IN
ANCIENT CHINA

ELEANOR COONEY
& DANIEL ALTIERI

AVON BOOKS  NEW YORK

AVON BOOKS
A division of
The Hearst Corporation
1350 Avenue of the Americas
New York, New York 10019

Copyright © 1993 by Eleanor Cooney and Daniel Altieri
Published by arrangement with the author
Library of Congress Catalog Card Number: 91-47985
ISBN: 0-380-70872-8

Published in hardcover by William Morrow and Company, Inc.; for information address Permissions Department, William Morrow and Company, Inc., 1350 Avenue of the Americas, New York, New York 10019.

First Avon Books Printing: July 1994

AVON TRADEMARK REG. U.S. PAT. OFF. AND IN OTHER COUNTRIES, MARCA REGISTRADA, HECHO EN U.S.A.

Printed in the U.S.A.

RA   10   9   8   7   6   5   4   3   2   1

To the memory of
Michael Harwood

"He was a man, take him for all in all,
I shall not look upon his like again."

ACKNOWLEDGMENTS

Special thanks are due to family and friends:

Especially to our parents, to Gwendda, to Donna, to Lesli Houser and Marcelee and Sharon Gralapp, Jeff and Joan Stanford, and Lettie Cowden.

And special thanks to Carolyn Morrow for so much in the past two years.

And for aid and research in the preparation of this manuscript we wish to acknowledge:

Western Washington University and the Center for East Asian Studies.

Harvard University Press and the President and Fellows of Harvard College.

Bruce Levine, Telion Software, and Wordstar International.

Special thanks to MicroSolutions.

And last but not least, all the other friends and beasts we have not mentioned: to Linnis and to our four-footed companions: six-toed Frankie, Pekoe and Timmy, we will miss you.

And to the valiant defenders of the last of the old-growth forests in the Pacific Northwest: the authors wish to salute your brave efforts against the corporate rapers who so arrogantly take the sustainable resources from our lands and the jobs from our loggers and millworkers.

AN APOLOGIA

The authors wish to make it clear that the intent of this book is not to cast aspersions of any sort on Buddhism, which, in its many extant forms and in its highest expression, they consider to be the most advanced system of thought yet devised by the human mind to address the mystery of existence. As with any philosophy, religion, or system, Buddhism is unfortunately subject to corruption due to human weakness and greed: It is the charlatans and opportunists who were so common in China in the era of our story who are the targets of the authors' disapprobation, and not the practitioners of the true Buddhist faith.

A LIST OF THE MAIN CHARACTERS, WITH PRONUNCIATION GUIDE

The Romanization system used for Chinese names and words in this book is a combination of the Wade-Giles system and the old Yale Romanization system. The modern pinyin phoneticization system, though used in all present-day scholarly works, has been avoided here in order to present Chinese names in a form that the authors feel is more familiar to Western readers.

The names below are those of real people who actually lived in T'ang China.

Ti Jen-chieh, or **Dee Jen-chieh** (*dee-run-chee-éh*): An assistant magistrate in the city of Yangchou

Kaotsung (*gow-tsúng—first syllable rhymes with "cow"*): Emperor of China, son of the late Emperor Taitsung

Wu Tse-tien (*woo-tsóotie-en—rhymes with "sooty wren"*): Former concubine to the late Emperor Taitsung

Madame Yang (*yahng*): Mother of Wu Tse-tien

Shu Ching-Tsung (*shoe-ching-tsúng*): Personal historian to Wu Tse-tien and Madame Yang

Wu-chi (*woo-chée*): Adviser to Emperor Kaotsung

Hsuan-tsang (*swan-tsáhng*): Peripatetic scholar and translator of Buddhist texts

Liao (*lee-oŵ—last syllable rhymes with "cow"*): Abbot and close friend of Wu-chi

Hsueh Huai-i (*sweh-why-eé*): Tibetan monk and magician

PROLOGUE

Yellow light the color of old bones glowed from flickering oil lamps in the corners of the room and on the altar. A dusty shaft of sun slanted down from a high, tiny window, warming and illuminating the side of Dog Boy's head where he knelt on the floor. Dog Boy stared down at the single black hair that grew from a mole on his forearm. The voices of one hundred monks droned a funeral chant in the smoky air, the open throats resonating the sounds of Creation: deep, guttural, atonal, inhuman. The great horns brayed, the bells clamored, and bone clattered against bone with the rhythmic beating of the funereal skull-clappers.

He fixed his eyes on the hair, refusing to blink, until everything in his peripheral vision, the musty shineroom and the kneeling monks all around him, crackled and dissolved. His eyes grew dry and demanded relief, but he ignored the burning and continued to stare. The hair and the plump brown mole that nourished it became the exact center of the universe, the monks' voices enclosing him, pressing him deep into that infinitesimal point. When the monks chanted, time changed, like a lump of cold butter heated over a fire. The monks' voices were the fire, heating up time so that it melted, ran, yielded its recalcitrant form.

The dead monk's soul, they had told him, would naturally be seeking to avoid rebirth. This was an interesting idea to him, and he wanted to discuss it further. But with whom? Someone getting ready to die soon would be ideal. Old Left Foot was old—very old. It was difficult for a lad of twelve to comprehend the years that the old monk carried, but he knew that he must be very, very close. Dog Boy felt that death was such a distant event for himself that it would simply never come. That

---

*A traditional Tibetan Buddhist monastic compound.

was what he told himself when he examined the polished yellow-brown skulls of departed monks, their black eye sockets the infinite void of the universe, lined up on the shelf in the shineroom: death was so far away, it would never come.

Old Left Foot was perfectly willing to talk to Dog Boy about his own impending death.

"Yes," he said, "very soon now. I know exactly how many heartbeats I have left," he said proudly. "I am counting backward all the time. Listen carefully to me sometime when I am not talking or eating. You'll hear it." They were slowly negotiating the rocky path that led down from the monastery, which sat atop a high crag thrust into the blue mountain sky.

"And when you die," Dog Boy asked, "are you going to have to struggle against being born again?"

The old man snorted.

"Born? I won't have to be born unless I *want* to." He pressed a finger to one side of his nose and forcefully expelled debris from his nostril.

"And do you want to?" Dog Boy asked.

"Creaky bones, a body that shits and pisses and demands to be fed all the time? It's a lot of trouble, Dog Boy. A lot of damned trouble. But it has its uses. No, I don't think I want to be born again. It's too much damned bother, starting at the beginning. Infancy. Childhood. Feh! I have no patience. No, I think I'll do it a different way this time."

"You're just bragging," Dog Boy said. "You don't know where you're going next."

"Oh, don't I?" the old man retorted. "Is that the studied opinion of the young master?" He laughed. "The choice is all mine, my precocious sage, I assure you. All mine."

"So what will you choose, Left Foot?" the boy asked over his shoulder.

"I think I'll find someone fully grown, with plenty of bad habits already quite well established. Someone ambitious, selfish, and overwhelmed with prurient greed. I will sneak in, like a burglar in a great house, and graft my soul onto that person's soul, and transform that person into a benign and enlightened being. Not that I care particularly about goodness," he added quickly. "I could just as easily do it the other way around. I just think it will be more of a challenge this way. More interesting."

Dog Boy listened intently. He was getting an idea.

"Left Foot," he said, inspired now, "I can do what I want, too. I'm going to find you. I'm going to find you where you are hiding, and I will undo your influence. While you are working to turn that wicked person into a good one, I will be working to make that person even worse than before!"

Left Foot stopped walking and laughed up at the sky.

"Is it a wager you want, then, my Ascended One? And how much are you willing to stake? And it had better be plenty, or you can forget all about it. How will you pay me when you lose the bet?"

"I won't lose, Left Foot. You will lose. It is you who will have to decide how to pay *me*."

"No, boy, it is *you* who will pay. And the currency will be something valuable, valuable enough so that each of us will be highly motivated to beat the other."

Dog Boy knew better than to mention money or jewels. He knew that the old man was daring him to be stupid, so that he could heap scorn on his head. He knew better than to go for the bait. But he could not imagine what else could be used to pay off a wager.

"Name the price, Left Foot," he said warily. They walked for a few moments without speaking, Dog Boy waiting for Left Foot's answer, Left Foot counting softly, under his breath, as their sandaled feet crunched along the rocky path: *Five million, one hundred eighty-four thousand, six hundred seventy-two . . . six hundred seventy-one . . . six hundred seventy . . .*

"Lifetimes, my canine friend," the old man said then. "I will settle for nothing less than lifetimes. I should enjoy seeing you pay for your insufferable cheek by living several long, un-pleasant lifetimes in succession. How would you like to be a legless cripple, begging on the streets of some great city on a little board with wheels? And after that, one of those men help-lessly compelled to satisfy his lust with farm animals? And then, just to make sure you are properly humbled for your audacity, a long, long life as an idiot. One who is kept mired in his own excrement on a chain in some dark cellar so as to prevent embarrassment to his family. One hundred lifetimes as a pig being fattened for the knife. Eh? What do you say, boy? Do you agree to the terms of the wager?"

"Of course!" Dog Boy replied eagerly. "Because it will be *you* who will be paying!"

"And *I* agree because it will be *you* who will be paying. They call you Dog Boy now; but there will come a time when you will truly know what it is to be a mute, suffering creature on four legs at the mercy of cruel humankind," Left Foot said pleasantly.

"No, Left Foot," said Dog Boy with delight. "I will make the person you have invaded so completely reprehensible, causing you to lose the wager so thoroughly, that before you even get to be a cripple or an idiot tied up in a cellar you will first enjoy a thousand lifetimes as a chicken with its head on the butcher's block, smelling the blood of your compatriots. And each time will be new, the terror fresh and real. How will you like that?"

"I will like it very much," Left Foot replied. "Because *I* will be the butcher, and *you* will be the chicken. Eh? Are you ready to take me on? And don't forget, on the astral plane there is no welching on a bet. We *will* find each other. There will be no avoiding the reckoning."

Dog Boy listened to Left Foot's slow old feet behind him on the path. Ahead, in glorious diminishing perspective, flat-bottomed white clouds casting their shadows on the snowy peaks below hung in perfect geometric order in the sky. He felt time stretching in front of him to infinity, and he felt the springy power and resilience of his young bones and muscles as he descended the steep mountain path with ease and agility.

"I am ready!" he said, jumping from a high rock and landing squarely and surely on his feet. Behind him, Left Foot's voice had dropped to a soft, almost loving inward murmur.

Five million, one hundred eighty-four thousand, four hundred ninety-seven . . . four hundred ninety-six . . . four hundred ninety-five . . .

PART ONE

Uneasy sits the King
Let Him beware His Ruin
For beneath the axle of the Wheel
We read the Name of Hecuba

—Carmina Burana

1

A.D. 653
in the Reign Period of Yung Hui (Perpetual Excellence)
Yangchou, a mercantile port city on the crossroads of the
mouth of the Yellow River and the Grand Canal

It was the poor gardener's teeth that Assistant Magistrate Dee
Jenchieh could not forget. Had it not been for those discolored
protuberances, Dee might never have become suspicious that
an innocent man was moving toward an untimely and expeditious death.

For Dee, few things were such poignant reminders of the
common mortality of humankind as the teeth—or lack of
them—in a man's mouth. Teeth were like stone; not really part
of us, but lent to us, bits of mineral from the earth itself lodged
in our heads, harder even than our bones. How often had he
observed, say, the pathetic protruding yellow teeth of a man
while he talked to him, and had to force his concentration back
to the exchange of words rather than lose himself in the contemplation of the other's gruesome fangs? Fangs which, if one
were to exhume the man's skeleton in one hundred years,
would look exactly as they did now peeking out from behind
his lips as he spoke. It was at such moments that Dee felt most
keenly a sense of compassion for his fellow creatures, caught
as they were—himself included—in the dilemma of being.

There was no suffering that quite compared with the pain
of a bad tooth. In the courtroom, Dee's attention had first been
drawn to the prisoner's mouth by his prominent, fascinatingly
ugly teeth. Dee had watched the prisoner answer questions,
and had winced empathetically as the poor fellow spoke. How
well he recognized, from his own wretched experience, the
slightly slurred speech and the tender, solicitous care he gave
to the right side of his jaw. The man, though he tried to conceal
it, had been in agony with his teeth, while striving to answer
questions on which his very life hung. It was then that the first
unpleasant little doubt had sprouted in Dee's consciousness.

7

But he had said nothing. He was, after all, only a newly arrived assistant magistrate in the court of the oldest and most respected senior magistrate in the city of Yangchou. He had held back, telling himself that his lurid imagination was leading him astray. It was not until the execution, which occurred with bewildering speed following the pronouncement of guilt and the sentencing, that Dee experienced his dreadful moment of realization, and the gardener's teeth fastened themselves to his mind and soul. If his awful suspicion was correct—that the prisoner's mouth had been crumbling and had been an unrelenting focal point of pain during all his waking hours—and if certain other hypotheses put forth at the trial were also true, then he could not possibly have been the one who committed the murder.

It had been the morning after the trial. The prisoner stumbled under the weight of the heavy wooden cangue that hung around his neck while the deputies of the court pushed him roughly through the gates into the bare courtyard. He was not screaming or crying, as some condemned men did, nor was he defiantly silent; he was speaking, rapidly and quietly to himself, his eyes tightly shut.

Dee Jen-chieh had seen many executions before, and thought he had seen every possible sort of behavior on the part of men about to die. Some strutted arrogantly, others called for their mothers while wetting their trousers. Several had laughed. But he had never seen a man carrying on a conversation with himself in an everyday tone of voice.

The prisoner progressed across the courtyard a few steps at a time; when he stopped, a shove from the guards propelled him forward again. Magistrate Dee politely but determinedly moved to the front of the ranks of officials as the doomed man approached and passed by; for a few moments, his words were plainly audible, though Dee doubted that anyone other than himself had paid attention to them.

"But my children, my wife," the man was saying in a soft, reasoning, persuasive tone. "What are they to do now? They will have to eat, and they will have to live . . . but they will eat and breathe shame, shame and scorn. . . . It will not be at all good . . . and my dead mother, my dead father . . . their spirits will drift in the darkness of eternal disgrace. . . . It is scarcely what they deserve . . . it will not do, not at all. . . . "

The guards forced the prisoner to his knees, and his

words became softer, a whisper. He rocked gently, his eyes still shut tight. Dee imagined that any last wild hope for a reprieve was extinguishing itself at that moment; surely the man was feeling the door closing behind him with finality. Not just a door—a wall, obsidian and black, ten thousand feet thick, through which no sound or light would ever pass. In the few moments it had taken for the prisoner to move stumblingly from the gate to the center of the small courtyard, Dee had felt the weight of death that now pressed the wretched fellow to the ground.

The iron bolts of the wooden stock were unfastened and dropped to the stones. The executioner and two assistants lifted the cruel device from the prisoner's neck and wrists. Dee observed a patch of bare, raw skin on the back of the man's head where the rough wood had worn away the hair. The deputies forced his hands behind his back and bound them tightly with a thick rope.

The prisoner's eyes opened, startling Dee. They darted here and there, searching the courtyard, as if possessed by some awful and anxious ghost who had never seen this world before, and who now looked about desperately as if to find something to grab hold of.

In the next moment, as he was lifted to his feet again and forced toward the rear wall of the courtyard, Dee saw the ghost take its leave from behind those eyes, abandoning the doomed body the way a fisherman flees a sinking bark. The poor man's eyes were now stilled, empty and lost.

"Tell my children it is not my fault!" the prisoner cried out abruptly in a dreadful, high-pitched voice. "Let them *know*! Tell my children they . . . "

The deputies pushed him again, causing him to fall squarely and with his full weight to the ground on both knees. Dee winced at the sound of bone coming down on rock. Now the prisoner's eyes were focused on the high wall atop the gate. Dee thought that he understood: surely the eyes must have been searching for one final picture of this world—and they could find only the grimy top of a brick-lined wall. Nothing better than a gray wall.

"Tell them that they are wrong! That they are wrong . . . they are *wrong*!" the prisoner shouted again.

The executioner wound the two ends of the braided leather garrote around his hands so that only eighteen inches of free cord stretched from the knuckles of his right hand to those of his left. He snapped the span rigid. Satisfied with the cord's strength, he nodded to the two deputies, who forced the prisoner's head to the ground. The man pressed one side of his face to the cold stones as if there might be some solace there; the deputies stepped aside and bowed toward the elderly senior magistrate standing at the front of the group of somber-faced officials. The old man removed a small slip of paper from a silk folder.

The executioner moved into place above the condemned man, crouching down and straddling the shoulders with his knees. He slid the garrote between the ground and the gardener's cheek, then with a sudden, violent movement impelled the head upward so that the eyes were now forced to gaze at the gray circle of sky.

"For crimes committed against the Son of Heaven and the national realm, for crimes committed against the prefect of Yangchou and the Province of Huai-nan . . . " the elderly senior magistrate called out, apparently reading from the paper, although Dee noticed that he was not really looking at the document, nor did he raise his eyes to look at the man who was about to die. " . . . for the crime of robbery, exacerbated by greed, resulting in the brutal and untimely murder of the revered and honorable Minister of Transport . . . "

"You think that you cannot make mistakes," the gardener said with the last bit of breath the poised cord left him, his voice a strangled whisper. "The civil authorities . . . " he choked. "Spirit of my mother . . . my father . . . "

"Quiet him *now*, executioner," the senior magistrate ordered.

"*You* are the murderer . . . " the man managed to gasp before the executioner jerked the cord again, cutting off any more words.

The executioner placed one knee between the prisoner's shoulder blades, forcing the upper torso toward the ground; at the same time, in one smooth, practiced, reflexive motion, he tightened the garrote while pulling the head back toward him. He held that position for a moment, then pulled the head back even farther while twisting the garrote tighter. The executioner's hands were white-knuckled with strain; Dee could hear the officials around him softly sucking in their breath. For a long, excruciating moment the executioner held his awful stance over the dying man, the sinews and tendons of his wrists and arms in high relief like those of a painted wooden statue. The prisoner's eyes bulged from his purple face while his mouth opened and closed spasmodically, making Dee think of a dying fish.

A horrible, insulting way to die, Dee thought, closing his eyes. Much worse than decapitation. All the nonsense, the prejudice against the desecration of the body by separating the head from it before burial; it was as nothing compared to this absolute insult to body and soul. Against his will, his eyes opened again.

The strangling man's legs flailed outward, then thrashed and twitched in violent spasms, the sharp rhythm of the death dance, while the arms involuntarily struggled against the silk ropes. As the executioner tightened the cord in one final effort, the head twisted to one side. Then finally, mercifully, the garrote was released and the gardener's body collapsed to the ground, a rattle sounding from the throat. Dee knew that it was simply the expulsion of *ch'i* and ether from the inner vessel of the lungs forced through the blood and mucus that vibrated like the thin head of a *weir* drum. It was not the rattle of an angry soul forced to depart the body.

Dee remained where he was until the senior magistrate had finished with the pronouncement of death and they had dragged the body out of the courtyard. He watched his fellow officials as life and purpose appeared to flow into their beings again. A few moments ago, it had seemed to him that they were feeling vicariously the executioner's knee between their own shoulder blades and the garrote tickling their own necks; now their murmuring voices were relaxing, the exchange of routine conversation was resuming, reasserting itself with its ordinariness. But as they filed from the little courtyard, Dee saw more than one man unconsciously raise a hand and caress his throat while trading some reassuring banality with a colleague.

The next morning, before the rest of the household was up, Dee flattened the paper on his desk before him with one hand while dipping his brush into the well of the inkstone with the other. He blotted the excess from the tips of the bristles and contemplated the unsullied sheet before him.

His grandfather had kept a journal for most of his life, leaving behind a formidable and detailed record so heavy that it had taken two strong servants to carry it from Grandfather's house to Father's house when the old man died.

Dee sighed. He had tried before to emulate Grandfather's form of chronicling his thoughts in difficult moments. He had faced plenty of problems in the past, but nothing as painful and complicated as what faced him now. He did not really believe what Grandfather always said about the clarifying value of detailed self-expression. But he felt particularly gloomy and helpless now. He had been in the Grand Canal city of Yangchou for less than a week since his transferral from Pienchou, and already he was heavily burdened, haunted by oppression and uncertainty. He had to do something.

Written into the journal of Dee Jen-chieh, in the Hour of the Hare, on the fifth day of the tenth month of the second year of the Reign Period of Yung Hui—Perpetual Excellence—of our Divine Sovereign Son of Heaven the Emperor Kaotsung:

I awoke this morning feeling weighted and useless. Today is the day after a poor gardener was executed: a man who had served the estate of Yangchou's Minister of Transport as a salaried tradesman. In the last few weeks prior to my arrival, the esteemed minister was murdered, and although the circumstances surrounding this murder are far from clear, the gardener was summarily tried. Yesterday being the fourteenth day since the annual Autumn Assizes convened before the highest judicial body in the capital, this father of six small children was put to death by strangulation. In truth, I doubt that this most worthy and noble body of councillors even deemed it worthy to review such a lowly case; the poor gardener's fate was never taken out of the hands of the Yang-chou court. The tragedies of the poor always slip unnoticed through wheels that are far too big.

I cannot get the gardener's face out of my thoughts. What did I see there? Though I circle around the truth, desperately trying to avoid it, I know with oppressive certainty what it was that I saw: utter betrayal. It cannot be feigned. At least, not at the moment of death, when only truth prevails. And who, or what, betrayed the innocent gardener? The answer is too terrible to contemplate: the world. Life itself.

I comfort myself somewhat with the fact that old

Judge Lu is due to retire soon. If not for that, I would petition the throne for a transfer.

The old man's attitude constitutes a dangerous, unheeding sloppiness, and by rushing through vital decisions, he holds unwarranted power over men's lives. I want no more to do with old Magistrate Lu and the horror of yesterday's execution. But . . .

There was also something about old man Lu that told me that this had not always been the case. I had sensed from my very first day as assistant to the magistrate's office that he had once been a very conscientious official. I have perused the records of his cases, and I have found that notion to be fairly well confirmed. But time has obviously worn him down. Time, and certain temptations of life that become too intolerably strong when we find that we have so little of it remaining. Many people say that we get wiser as we get older. Perhaps. But we also can become tired. And corruption and bribery can be like a pillow placed beneath the unpadded, arthritic bones of the old.

Besides, there remains the simple algorithm which surely explains at least one aspect of the speed and sloppiness of the trial: *someone* had to die for the Transport Minister's murder. Otherwise, the biggest and most important case of old man Lu's career would remain unsolved in the final days of his tenure. "Bury the corpse before it smells," the old adage says. Something is very wrong here, and although I might wish to, I cannot give it up.

I am compelled to establish that my instincts about the gardener's teeth were correct. The only thing for me to do, though I dislike having to cause her any more grief, is to pay a visit to the widow.

Pushing his writing tray aside, he felt overwhelmed by a very immediate sense of failure. His neck and shoulders hurt. The stiffness was worse than usual this morning; he shrugged, and turned his head this way and that, hearing as he did an unpleasant clicking of the small bones in his neck. He thought of the gardener's neck for a moment, then put it out of his mind.

Not only had he failed in the larger world outside his

gates, but he had failed at home as well. Hadn't he fallen short in his obligations to his progeny as father, as teacher, and, especially, as moral disciplinarian? The last was clearly the worst, because now Dee felt that had he succeeded as father and teacher first, the third problem would not have happened at all. But matters had reached such a state of decay, it would seem, that Dee had only to leave his household, as he had early on the morning of the execution, for everything to fall into chaos. It was Confucius who said that "if the master himself is upright, all will proceed well even if he is not present to give orders. But if this master is himself not upright then it is of no consequence that he gives orders; they will be ignored."

And where did this choice bit of moral teaching leave him, he of the disorderly household and unruly children? The magistrate who cannot order his household first should probably not even show his face in public. Indeed, such a magistrate can hardly delude himself that he has a place serving in the halls of government; nor can he possibly provide a worthy civic example for anyone. Dee's children obviously had no respect for the example that he had once assumed he set for them so clearly. In his absence there was nothing of the princely gentleman in either of his little boys; rather, they had become like swarming demons from hell.

He swung his legs over the side of the day couch. He was very hungry. He would have to deal with the two boys, but not until he had had tea and cakes and fruit. The little ones could not resist fruit.

The servants brought lightly spiced orange-and-rose tea, sesame cakes, and fruit to Dee in his garden pavilion. They moved around their young master on silent feet without a word of their customary cheerful banter. When they set the tray down, they took unusual care not to clatter the dishes and bowls. Dee watched their averted faces, wondering if his gloomy mood was so obvious. What did they think? That he was going to have his sons executed for their transgressions?

When the servants had cleared all of the plates but the bowl of fruit and were about to leave the garden pavilion, Dee pushed his stool back from the table and rose.

"Now bring my little problems to me," he said tiredly. The second servant turned and bowed, acknowledging him. "Two moments of pleasure, and look what it has cost," Dee muttered and shook his head. The first servant responded with an uncomfortable half-smile, then bowed slightly and hurried to catch up with the other.

Dee pushed the bowl of fruit across the table toward the two little boys who stood opposite. Neither evinced the slightest interest in the offering.

These are my own children, he thought. The elder refuses to look at me at all, but keeps his eyes fixed firmly on the floor while he sullenly clenches and unclenches his fists. The younger, clinging to the elbow of his brother's jacket sleeve, simply stares at his father.

Where did they acquire such unrelenting stubbornness? It was not from his side of the family. Nor was the ability to nimbly evade responsibility a legacy of his. The elder, at barely nine years, could dissemble with breathtaking ease, with such wounded ingenuousness that even his little brother, barely six, who had just conspired with him and perpetrated an act, believed in their mutual innocence. The elder was a lesson in wiliness, while the younger was a lesson in unwavering loyalty, a child with but one function and one desire, a being perfectly and wholly dedicated to pleasing his elder brother.

Upon his return late the previous evening, Dee had learned from his nearly hysterical second wife the nature of the boys' misdemeanor: some unspeakably rude prank played with an incontinent pig in one of the bedchambers early on the morning of the execution.

As the father and his two sons confronted each other, Dee found himself at a definite disadvantage, having to shade his eyes from the sun in order to keep his gaze on the boys.

Dee moved so that the sun would not be directly in his eyes. As he did, the boys moved too, maintaining the distance between themselves and their father. Dee's long, penetrating stare had no effect; the elder tested his father with a quick insolent look from his downcast eyes. But it was long enough for Dee to see that there was not even the smallest saving trace of remorse in him. In the meantime, the younger returned Dee's fixed stare without so much as a twitch. His little features remained perfectly flat and fearless; Dee was certain that the three of them might well have remained locked in this stubborn triangle until the clypsedra struck the late-afternoon watch, had he not decided to speak:

"Master Yung," Dee said, moving to their end of the table. This time the boys stayed where they were. "I am speaking to you. You will look at your father when he addresses you." He put his finger under his older son's chin and slowly tilted the head upward. "You will look at your father when he addresses you," he repeated. The older boy's eyes now looked directly at his father's. "You are the instigator of trouble when I am away and at my duties in the city. I am right, am I not?" How feeble and stilted this interrogation sounded. "What is it that Confucius tells us: 'Let there be no evil in your thoughts.' Someday you will serve the government as I do. But how, young man?"

The boy's eyes narrowed ever so slightly as if closing like the gates of a fortification for a long siege. Dee pulled up even more firmly on the little chin, feeling against his fingers the delicacy and shapeliness of the bone and detecting a slight but pronounced resistance.

" 'Those who in private life behave poorly toward their parents and elders, in public life show clear disposition to resist the authority of their superiors. . . . And as for such men starting a revolution on the . . . ' " He stopped. This was a mistake. He could see a faint twitching at the corner of Elder Son's mouth. The boy was fighting to suppress a giggle!

Next to him, the younger one snorted. Dee removed his fingers from under his elder son's chin, but the child kept his head in the same upturned position—an act of raw, undiluted defiance. What I would like to do, Dee thought, is to simply walk away and leave these two worthless pups standing where they are. But that is a luxury not allowed me.

Dee placed his hands on the table before him and appeared to examine his splayed fingers. He sighed, and turned his attention to the younger one. "Remember . . . the Master said, 'A gentleman is not an implement to be used by another of *inferior principle.*' " Dee leaned forward, putting his weight over the table. "Do either of you understand what I am saying?" He waited. All at once, he felt something give way. He had reached the end.

"Answer me!" he demanded fiercely, bringing his hand down hard on the table, startling himself with his own vehemence. But he was gratified to see both boys jump.

"I don't know, Father," the older son said at last, almost whispering, consternation finally coming to his eyes.

" 'I don't know, Father'?" Dee echoed, seizing the advantage of his momentary upper hand. "What kind of answer do you suppose that is?" The boy's eyes were now wide and pleading as if searching for the answer.

"Honesty is the beginning." Dee paused and gave him time to think. Then he spoke slowly and deliberately: "Who is responsible for the foul mess in the west-wing bedchamber?" There was a long silence during which the boys alternated between looking at each other and then down at the floor. At last, Elder Brother spoke out:

"We did not make the mess in the bedchamber," he said finally in a brave little voice.

"And just who did?" Dee raised his eyebrows.

"The pig did."

Later, when he had dismissed the boys with a stern admonition and a "sentence"—they were to take orders from the house steward for one week, assisting with the menial chores of running the home—Dee's hand still stung faintly from the force with which he had brought it down on the table. And where had *that* come from? He stared at the palm of his hand. He was not altogether certain, but he had a strong feeling that if this interview with his sons had taken place before the execution and not the next day, things would have been very different. I would probably still be standing in the pavilion croaking platitudes at their smirking little faces, he thought with disgust.

But he was equally disgusted with what he had done instead. Was this how he would be dealing with his errant sons from now on? Shouting and banging on furniture?

Yangchou led its life on the water. Situated at the confluence of the Grand Canal and the Yangtze-Kiang at the end of the great river's 9,500-*li** seaward journey across China, the city's countless crisscrossing waterways bore the commerce of river, canal, and ocean. For Dee, the odors and the din of the water traffic and the attendant trade and commotion were pure exhilaration after Pienchou, a dry, sedate city by comparison where he and his family had lived for the last ten years. When the opportunity for transfer came up, Dee had taken it without hesitation, but it was not until he saw and smelled Yangchou that he understood how weary he had been with his old surroundings.

---

*3,200-mile.

As a young assistant magistrate still in his early thirties, Dee's job entailed the handling of lesser civil cases, those not quite important enough to warrant the attention of his superior. The pursuit of the details of and precedents for some of these small cases—inspecting census records, tax rolls, and the like, or occasionally visiting the homes of people involved— gave Dee plenty of opportunity to get out of his offices and into the streets of the city. Most magistrates, lazy and chair-bound, sent their young assistants on these missions, but not Dee. He much preferred to go himself, to walk and explore.

Today, he was not on official business, strictly speaking. It was scarcely his place to pursue a closed case. To reopen it, to override his superior, would mean a petition and a long, complicated process. But there was nothing to stop him from going on his own to satisfy himself. If I must reopen the case later, he thought grimly as he crossed a bridge over a sluggish, littered canal, then I shall worry then about proper procedure.

The canals and alleys he walked along became narrower and dirtier and the smells less familiar as he descended into the impoverished western ward. The gardener in his cell await- ing execution probably dreamed of these very streets with longing on the night before he died, Dee thought.

When he found the widow's home and presented himself, she directed at him a look of ill-concealed hatred. How else could she look upon official robes of any kind after the loss inflicted on her by the judicial system? Though he keenly wished to do so, he refrained from telling her the true purpose of his visit.

And so, standing humbly in the face of her pain and an- ger, receiving it full on as if he stood in front of an open win- dow in winter letting the wind blow over him, he asked her about her husband's teeth. Now she looked at him in astonish- ment, no doubt wondering what new outrage was about to be visited on her—a tax, perhaps, calculated according to the number of teeth the breadwinner took with him when he was forced to leave this world? Then her astonishment gave way to fresh grief as a sharp memory overtook her.

"They hurt him so," she cried, shaking her head. "Every day. That poor, poor man. His teeth hurt him every day." She raised her eyes to Dee's, the unashamed tears flowing. "I pre- pared his food for him as if he were a little baby. I mashed it and ground it so that it would be soft, so that he could eat.

Sometimes," she said softly, her face crumpling, "I even chewed it for him myself."

She gave herself up then to oblivious weeping. Dee thanked her, though he doubted that she even heard him, and took his leave. He had no further wish to intrude on her sorrow. Now he was filled with purpose and impatience. With the vision of the widow's grief-distorted face before him, he covered the distance to the judicial offices almost as quickly as if he had been riding in a carriage.

He did not encounter too much trouble getting his hands on the transcripts of the trial. As one of four assistant magistrates under old Magistrate Lu, it was not exactly irregular for him to examine court records, but being new and lacking a letter from the chief magistrate himself, it was necessary to work his way through clerks and assistant clerks of varying degrees of officiousness. When he finally found the way to the clerk specifically in charge of the transcripts he was looking for and made his request, the man gave him a sour look, but led him up three flights of stairs past dozens of scribes and clerks and judicial assistants to the transcript library. The man opened the door and stepped aside, giving Dee a look that told him he was an intruder in his domain. Mindful of obtaining the man's discreet cooperation, Dee indulged the clerk, thanking him elaborately, allowing him to feel that he had some sort of authority with which Dee was duly impressed. This softened the fellow up considerably; in the end, Dee found himself seated comfortably at a reading table while the clerk solicitously located the papers and laid them before the magistrate. Dee accepted his offer of a bowl of hot tea, and set to work.

He noted the important facts. The Transport Minister had met his fate in his office, bludgeoned from behind as he ate his customary afternoon snack of tea and sweet cakes. The corpse was found sprawled face up on the floor, and crumbs from the sweet cakes lay scattered about the carpet. A vivid verbal picture had been painted at the trial of the callous murderer rolling the victim over with his foot and then standing above him, greedily finishing off the dead man's sweet cakes, carelessly and disrespectfully letting the crumbs fall onto the body and the surrounding floor.

Would a man whose teeth hurt him so badly that his speech was affected, whose wife chewed his food for him so that he could take nourishment, voluntarily eat a cake glazed with honey? Only a fellow sufferer such as myself, Dee thought, one who had on occasion contemplated cutting off his own head to stop the pain, could answer that question unequivocally and unhesitatingly: no. He would not eat such a cake. The only circumstances under which he would eat it would be if someone were to hold a knife to his heart and order him to eat it. Plainly, if it was true that the murderer had stood over his victim and devoured the cake, then that person could not have been the poor gardener who paid with his life for the crime. The question, then, was whether or not the basic hypothesis of the greedy murderer eating his victim's food was correct.

He thought of the crumbs. It was only because of the crumbs that this supposition had taken form at all. There were crumbs around the body, the report had said, and on the front of the man's robes. The picture of the murderer fresh from doing his vile deed devouring his victim's afternoon snack was an irresistible one, to be sure; it had enjoyed the ready and unquestioning belief of every man in the courtroom. If I had not personally suffered as I have, Dee reflected, I might have been tempted to believe it myself. It had been established as fact—and the evidence was indeed compelling—but he knew that the deciding factor had ultimately been people's desire to believe it. Such is our imaginative human appetite for morbid romanticism, he thought.

If the body had been facedown and the crumbs had been on the victim's back, then there would have been no question; no matter how careless a man might be in his habits, he cannot spill crumbs down his own back. But he is certainly capable of spilling them down his front, and onto the floor around him. Therefore, if Dee was to establish the innocence of the executed gardener, he would have to prove absolutely that the crumbs fell from the uncouth lips of a murderer and were not the victim's own untidy residue. He knew what he would have to do if he was to establish the gardener's innocence beyond question in his own mind. He thanked the clerk and left the judicial offices, leaving word with two of his own assistants that he would return shortly.

When Dee arrived back at his office, he carried two parcels. One was fragrant-smelling; inside it were cakes from the same bakery that the Transport Minister had patronized. The cakes were identical to the ones that the murdered official had

had brought to him on the afternoon of his death. In the other parcel, he carried a somewhat macabre item—the robe the Transport Minister had been wearing at the moment he had died. Dee could not quite believe his luck in obtaining it. He had stopped at the mortuary where the body had been taken to be cleaned up before being returned to the family. He had asked the custodian if the robe was still on the premises, fully expecting the answer to be no; he had been overjoyed when the man appeared a few moments later and put it in his hands. An official robe, it had been taken off the body and put away in a chest in case the family should claim it. Weeks had gone by, and they had not, and so there it lay. Dee had given the man a few coins and thanked him profusely.

Now Dee took the robe from the parcel, and shook it and brushed it carefully so that it was completely free of debris. He dressed himself in it, trying to ignore the unpleasant knowledge that he was sliding his arms into sleeves where a dead man's arms had recently been. Enlisting the help of one of his young assistants, he arranged the furniture in his office so that it was positioned exactly as the Transport Minister's had been; then he sat in a chair, his back to the door, with the cakes and tea on his desk at his elbow, and pretended that he was a middle-aged high-level bureaucrat enjoying his midafternoon repast after a day of diligent work, his head full of figures and statistics.

Reluctantly, he bit into the cake. The tooth that had caused him so much grief had been pulled from Dee's poor head over a year before, but the creature who has suffered pain will hang on to protective habits long beyond their usefulness. Gingerly, he chewed, but soon found that the tooth physician had done his job well. There was no pain, so he was able to relax into his role as Minister of Transport and eat the sweet cake as casually and in just as relaxed a manner as his predecessor no doubt had. It was quite delicious; he soon found himself finishing the first and reaching for a second.

He took a sip of hot tea and glanced down: crumbs had descended to his chest and into his lap, clinging to the brocade of the robe. He relaxed even more, allowing himself to eat as sloppily as if he were one of his own sons raiding the kitchen at home. The crumbs fell freely, like gentle snow in a valley. He looked at the floor. No crumbs had fallen there. They seemed to prefer the brocade of his robe, where they clung fast to the metallic embroidery.

"Now," Dee said to his young assistant, "please be so kind as to bludgeon me to death." Obligingly, the "murderer" raised his weapon, a club fashioned of rolled-up paper, and struck a glancing blow to the back of Dee's cranium.

He toppled forward, landing on his knees first, then collapsed, sprawled and facedown, onto the floor. The "killer" then came around to where he lay, rolled him over with his foot, and gazed down into his face to be sure that he was quite dead. Carefully, Dee raised his head and examined the floor to either side of his body, and then his clothing: the crumbs, which were quite moist because of the freshness and quality of the cakes, were flattened onto the front of his robe, and still clung fast. They had not scattered onto the floor around him. The murderer, a small satisfied smile playing at his lips, stepped over the body then, picked up the remaining cake from the plate on the desk, and standing over his victim, but slightly to one side, the most natural position for him, ate it. The crumbs rained gently down, settling on Dee's face and on the floor.

Dee was satisfied, but saddened: just as he had thought, it could not have been the gardener who murdered the Minister of Transport. He knew that his findings would scarcely be embraced with gratitude or enthusiasm.

What had been presented to the court as the ultimate damning evidence meant nothing at all. A few valuable trinkets belonging to the murder victim had been found at the executed man's home—some ivory carvings, a few small but fine porcelain vases. The prisoner had told the court that he had found them while digging in the garden around the building. His story was dismissed as a lie, of course, but Dee saw that it was perfectly possible, and even probable, that he was telling the truth. How simple for someone to pilfer these objects from the Transport Minister's office without his even noticing the loss, then bury them in a flower bed where the gardener would be sure to stumble across them and take them home. Then, when the time came for murder, the pieces would be discovered in the man's possession, and he would be blamed.

Why is it, Dee wondered as he undid the ties of the Transport Minister's robe, that a man is considered more likely to be capable of murder if he is a common sort of fellow, a roughhewn worker who uses his hands to earn his living? Why does blame attach itself so effortlessly to a man with dirt under his fingernails? What is the source of our suspicion and secret contempt? Interesting questions, but secondary to the central issue, which was the identity of the real murderer. He had no ready theory, no hypothesis at all, however remote. He knew that he would have to begin, therefore, by acquainting himself further with the other unfortunate dead man in this drama, the one whose robe he now shrugged from his shoulders. He held the garment up, looked at it for a moment, then brushed it hard with his hand, and watched the crumbs dance on the carpet.

Dressed in the clothes of a well-to-do merchant, the assistant magistrate moved along the crowded thoroughfare next to one of the city's largest and busiest canals. Traffic was heavy this late afternoon; the barges, bow to stern and gunwale to gunwale, sat deep in the oily black water with the weight of their cargo: teak, aphrodisiacs, iron, salt, grains, fruit, silk, linens, teas, bamboo, bricks, fine mahogany lumber, lacquer, ginseng, and spices.

Dee shouldered his way with care through the noisy crowd of pedestrians navigating the eastern ward stretches between the locks. Here and there, impeding the flow, people had stopped along the banks of the canal to shout directions and suggestions to the barges, vehemently waving warnings and casting their unheeded opinions about. Aboard the overloaded craft, the harried crews shouted at one another and pushed with pole oars in a futile effort to avoid collisions. The same people shouting instructions from the safety of the pavement were hoping, Dee knew, for a bit of entertainment, a minor disaster, perhaps, a mishap involving one of the top-heavy barges. It was always exciting to watch the confusion as the wooden hulls crunched into each other, causing some weighty cargo to tip and slide out from under its netting and into the filthy water while the bargemasters cursed and shouted their threats to heaven.

This was Dee's world now, the choking commercial reality of Yangchou with its web of interconnecting waterways. Ten thousand *li* of commerce fed into and out of the great city, rife with corruption and ripe with every possibility under heaven.

On the canal, a fight was breaking out. Two barges were at a standoff, each refusing to yield the right of way to the other. Voices rose dangerously as a wave of excitement moved through the crowd on the banks. With their crews gathered behind them, the bargemasters glared at each other, waving their arms in broad, threatening gestures and exchanging insults. The onlookers pushed and jostled for a good position, choosing up sides instantly as if they knew the two contenders and held some great stake in the outcome of the contest. Dee hurried on, grateful that his cap of office was hidden away in his sleeve and not sitting on his head, inviting someone in the crowd to call out, "Magistrate, Magistrate!" and oblige him to intercede.

What he was doing today was not exactly unethical. There was no particular reason why the officers at the Ministry of Transport, which was where he was going right now, should not let him examine records or simply look around. He was not wearing the garb of a businessman and moving anonymously through the crowds in the waning afternoon because of some illicit tinge to what he was doing; rather, it was because his instincts told him, quite simply, to keep his head down. For one thing, the old judge did not need to know that someone in his office was looking into a closed murder case; for another thing, the Transport Minister had undoubtedly led a complicated life. How could he not have, Dee asked himself as he regarded the seething tangle of trade all around him that had been the murdered man's domain. To think that we are supposed to believe that such a man was killed for a few stolen trinkets, Dee thought. No, whoever relieved him of his life was undoubtedly still watching. There would be no advantage at all in attracting undue attention to himself. A tingle of adventure, in equal parts pleasant and disagreeable, shivered along his backbone as he stepped into the cooler, darker air of the alley that would lead him eventually to the back entrance of the Ministry of Transport, which he knew would be virtually deserted at this hour.

His heart beat thickly against his ribs. He could only attribute this new excitement to a sudden and unexpected sense of freedom. What was it? It felt suspiciously like exuberance. Even the memory of the poor gardener's death could not dampen the feeling. Now he identified the feeling: it was the freedom to pursue the truth that caused his heart to live its own life in his chest. I was not much help to you when you were alive, my poor friend, he said to the dead gardener, but I may be able to help you in death. Your family and your name can be saved and your ancestors requited.

He turned the corner into an even smaller, grimier alley.

A woman chased an aggressive rooster from her doorstep in a flurry of feathers.

This area of town defined by the lower end of the canals and locks was a maze of tight alleys and dusty cobbled court-yards. Not the best place to walk alone at night, Dee reflected, though the shadows within the high narrow walls around him told him that very likely that was exactly what he would be doing later. There was only one more block to walk before he reached his destination.

He had already sent a message asking the custodian to be ready to let him in at the rear gate. He had told the custodian, too, not to expect to see him in his magistrate's robes. Musing on his subterfuge, he wondered for a moment if his disguise as a merchant was even necessary. Who knew what sort of complex connections the Transport Minister had cultivated? Perhaps the sight of an official in his magisterial cap and robe was already commonplace here.

He crossed a small paved courtyard and pulled the bell rope that disappeared into a hole in the wall next to a heavy wooden gate. It was a strange feeling, pulling a silent rope, feeling the responding resistance in his hand that told him that somewhere deep in the building a bell was being tipped, its clapper reverberating against the metal sides, but too far away for him to hear. He waited, making an effort to calm his thoughts, which were jumping about like fleas.

It was the Hour of the Dog, and Dee sat alone in the dead Transport Minister's second-story office, his elbows on the minister's ornate rosewood desk. Who had the man been who had sat in this place for so many years?

It was nearly twilight. He remained motionless, transfixed by the dimming silhouettes of exotic sculptures around the room. Occasional noises drifted up from the streets nearby. He rose from the desk and stood at the window for a moment, looking at the deserted courtyard below. Then he closed the shutters and proceeded to light several of the minister's lamps. In the intricate dancing shadows, he examined the full-relief wooden temple carvings that lined the upper perimeters of the room: sensuously twisting and embracing bodies, male mem-bers erect, the females open and receptive, breasts swollen and rigid in the extremes of sexual excitation. He picked up a lamp and held it over his head so that he could examine the pieces more closely: they were all carved in old, dried, cracked, dirt-colored wood of the sort that Dee associated with ancient, distant sacred places. Leaning against the wall nearest the door was a large strangely inscribed wooden wheel with eight spokes; it was cracked in several places. He moved the lamp so that he could peer behind it. The side nearest the wall was raw and chipped, as if it had been pried loose, vandalized, stolen from a permanent location.

These sacred objects could only have been removed from the walls of temples, some of them hastily and by force. Surely they would not have been given up easily by the priests and monks charged with their stewardship. Or could such people be bribed? He thought about it. Naturally, there would be, even among the devout, one or two tainted with normal human greed. Whatever the means, the pieces in the minister's room spoke strongly to Dee of some form of illicit trade. But that, he told himself, is only an assumption at this point. Nevertheless . . .

He moved the lamp so that he could examine the pieces on a table in the center of the room and on ornate stands here and there nearby. These were the ones that interested him the most. He picked one up and considered it. He knew what it was, for he had seen others like it before—but certainly never so many all at once in one place: a lingam, a carved stone phallus of Indian origin. A powerful symbol of the divine life force. He put the lamp down and picked up another of the lingams and compared the two. The first, in his right hand, was much cruder than the other, only suggestive in its shape and form; the one in his left hand, which he had just picked up, was unpleasantly realistic, right down to the turgid veins carved in sharp relief along the erect shaft. He put it down quickly with a small shudder of distaste. The other he decided to take with him. He put it in his carrying pouch, feeling like a thief as he did so. You are merely confiscating evidence, he told himself sternly. Picking up the lamp, he turned his attention to some of the other icons the minister had placed so lovingly about his office. How, Dee asked himself, could the man have concentrated on his work with all of this surrounding him?

These other pieces which drew Dee's attention were even more peculiar than the lingams. In these, rendered in gilt bronze, two figures were clasped in a sexual embrace. Dee arranged three of the small oil lamps in a semicircle so that he could study the pieces in detail.

The brilliant surfaces seemed almost animated: tiny female figures straddled the waists of their oversize male partners, who sat cross-legged upon their lotus stands; the females entreated their male partners with all manner of strange symbolic objects cradled in their outstretched arms. The giant male figures seemed to writhe in counterpoint rhythm, gigantic craniums adorned with elaborate headdresses composed of skulls and human viscera, the symbolic aspects of their Tantric magic; their faces were demonic and in their hands were strange scepters and bells. Swaying and dancing in some cabalistic fixation, their meaning throwing itself in the face of reason and rationality, these joined figures had a quantity he could not add.

By themselves, one at a time, they were strange enough. Artifacts of a distant land, an exotic cult. But all that was foreign, especially Indian, seemed strange; different symbolisms, different metaphors mirroring a different universe. That was the given, Dee thought, absentmindedly rubbing his chin. But there were so many of these figures and phalluses that their effect was quite overpowering, their exoticism no longer just an isolated curiosity, but a compelling current pulling him in.

The sounds of men's voices and the rumble of wooden wheels from outside brought Dee out of his deeply pensive state. He realized that he had been very far away. He felt vaguely disoriented, the way he used to feel years ago waking up from the heavy sleep of childhood fevers, when he would have to struggle to remember where he was—what room, what place; and, indeed, who he was. Those fevers made you dream so heavily, a physician once told him, because they were the gates of death. For a few moments, he had nearly allowed the minister's obsession—if indeed that was what it was—to become his own.

Dee rose from the table and went to the easternmost window and pushed the shutters open. He put his head out and took a deep breath of the cool night air. He looked out through the space between the pillars of the second-story balcony in the direction of the canal. He craned his neck, idly wondering if even a thin sliver of water would be visible from the Transport Minister's office.

He pulled his head back in. He felt awake and alert again, revived by the night air. He closed the shutters and crossed the room to stand by the minister's desk. He looked around him one last time, the flickering lights playing on the sculptures and wall carvings. He began to extinguish the oil lamps, until the only flame remaining was a single lamp he now held above his head.

The room and its contents had taken Dee a few steps out of his ordinary world. Was that all it was? he wondered. Had he become so narrow, so insular, that he reacted with near-peasant suspicion to anything exotic and out of the ordinary? He thought about it. No, it was not that the objects were strange or foreign, or even that there were so many of them that they created an atmosphere where one could scarcely breathe without taking in their essence. They were exotic, yes: Hindu, Buddhist, Indian, Tantric. All of that, of course. He concentrated, searching for a finer distinction. Then he understood: what disturbed him was not what they were, but where they were. The simple fact that they were *here*—dispossessed, displaced by thousands of miles, their meaning distorted by removal from their ancient, distant context. And what had they meant to the Transport Minister?

He made his way to the door, blew out the final flame, and made his way down the hall toward the staircase. He hurried along, acutely conscious of the empty space behind him.

The custodian, a lantern raised high in his right hand, quietly escorted Dee out. Dee had planned to warn the man against saying anything about his visit here this night. But as he stood there on the cool bricks, he made a decision. Perhaps it would not be such a bad thing to leave a faint trail; just enough, say, to draw forth the hidden element, the person or persons who might be watching. Dee thanked the old man, gave him a coin, and walked out into the dark alley as the ancient gate swung shut with a clang.

2

Dee merged into the flow of humanity moving along the main boulevard, walking quickly. He had slept fitfully the night before, impatient for daybreak, full of curiosity and anticipation. He had had his calling card delivered to the steward of the Transport Minister's household staff yesterday, and they had sent word back within an hour that they would receive him in the morning. It was not until sleep eluded him that he understood the extent to which this first case had got under his skin and into his very soul—and now he was about to go deeper. He moved along briskly in the pleasant morning air, easily outdistancing his fatigue. He left the main boulevard and turned onto a wide street, alive with vendors and activity.

Preoccupied as he was, he did not notice right away that he was being followed. A scrawny little dog was keeping pace with him, its head at his heels, nails clicking along. Experimentally, Dee slowed down, then walked even more quickly than before. The dog, a pathetic creature, unbeautiful by any standard, stayed right with him, its short legs a blur of effort. Dee continued this way for nearly another half block before giving in at last and turning to face the animal. He crouched, extended a supplicating hand, and made soft clicking sounds, entreating it to come closer.

He could see that a great war raged within the creature. It wanted to come to him, but could not bring itself to make the leap of courage. Instead, it lowered its tail between its legs and slunk away, casting anxious glances over its shoulder with its sad eyes. After several tries, Dee gave up, rose to his feet, and resumed walking. His thoughts had turned back to murder, a gardener's teeth, and strange temple carvings when, after one hundred paces or so, he realized the dog was at his heels again. He stopped and looked over his shoulder.

"So you want something to eat, do you?"

The dog stopped too, and cowered, tail curling between

its legs, head down. But this time it did not back away as long as Dee held his position.

"You win. I will find you something to eat." He looked around, scanning the vendors' stalls on either side of the street. His own stomach contracted; he realized that he was hungry, too. "You know, you remind me a great deal of my sons." Dee poured a few coins from his purse into his hand. "This will not be much different from taking breakfast with them. They, too, are at Father's heels as long as he can keep them in food. That is about the extent of it."

Later, after they had both eaten, Dee proceeded on his way, with the dog keeping its measured but determined distance behind him. Dee indulged himself in a private little daydream, a fantasy, in which he saw his two boys crawling to him, dirty and cold, very hungry, and very, very polite after having been tossed into the streets a fortnight earlier.

Standing in one of the spacious gardens of the Minister of Transport's vast and luxurious estate, Dee let his eyes follow a group of four young girls, graceful as deer, who walked together about one hundred paces away under the brilliant autumn foliage of a giant tree.

"The master was indeed a connoisseur," the house steward was saying. "He was interested only in the very finest of everything. Goods of dubious quality simply did not interest him," he finished importantly. Dee, his eyes still on the group under the tree, was aware of the man's face, a featureless plane turned toward him expectantly in his peripheral vision waiting for Dee's approval of his dead master's excellent taste.

"I am sure they did not," Dee said, forcing his attention back to the steward.

"No doubt when I brought you through the house you noticed the quality of the furnishings," the steward continued earnestly. "The master allowed only a select few of us to care for his furniture and artifacts. He required us to wear silk gloves whenever we touched anything."

"I notice that he particularly fancied imported goods," Dee said. "He seemed to have quite an eye for . . . unusual foreign pieces."

"Oh, yes," the steward said proudly. "It was my special job to care for the really rare things. I was to see to it that the polishing mixtures of oil and wax were fresh, unadulterated, and that the right one was used on the right piece. That was important, you know. My instructions were to shine the table-tops so that we could see our faces looking back at us."

"Fascinating!" Dee exclaimed, putting an interested look on his own face, though it was scarcely tabletops he was thinking of. "What pleasure it must have given you! And no doubt the statuary required special attention as well," he said encouragingly. "Especially the very old pieces."

"Oh, yes," the man replied. "He trained me himself in their care. Of course, he did not keep the really old, extremely rare works out on display."

"Really!" Dee exclaimed. "Such pieces must have been rare indeed!"

"He had a special room for them," the steward said with pride. "Would you like to see it?"

"Thank you," said Dee. "I certainly would."

They left the garden and walked along a pleasingly ornamented stone path. As they neared the entrance to the house, two young children, both girls, stood to one side holding hands and watched the impressive stranger pass by. They were about the same age as his sons. Dee smiled at them. One returned the favor coquettishly, her little mouth a perfect rosebud, while the other remained solemn. Daughters are what I need, Dee thought, smiling back over his shoulder at the child and her pretty dimples. Sons try your very soul.

Inside the house, they passed through the cool, dark, rich-smelling rooms of the dead Minister of Transport. Stillness reigned in the perfectly ordered, exquisitely tasteful and harmonious interior; even Dee, an outlander, could feel the distinct and permanent absence of the master of this domain. Their feet on the thick carpets were virtually silent.

"The room is at the far end of the complex," the steward said in a hushed voice. "It occupies a space actually enclosed in rock on three sides, so it is always cool and of a consistent temperature." As he spoke, a beautiful young woman crossed the corridor in front of them, passing from one room to another; before she disappeared, she looked momentarily at the two men while the steward bowed his head to her.

"You see," the steward continued, "if extremes of temperature occur too frequently, it is not healthy for the pieces. Especially the ones made of wood. They dry out, they crack, they lose their luster."

"Indeed," Dee replied, striving to maintain a note of lively interest in his tone. "That is so true." The young woman had left a delicate scent of flower water in the air that they passed through; Dee stole a glance to his left through the doorway where she had gone, hoping to catch another glimpse of her. "In caring for objects of great antiquity, we charge ourselves with a very real responsibility," he added, craning his neck, disappointed to see only another empty corridor.

Dee was treading lightly, being as oblique as he possibly could. Though he wore the cap and robe of a magistrate today, and had introduced himself as such, he had not said anything about his suspicions or the strange and undoubtedly illicit collection he had found in the minister's office. Instead, he had chosen an indirect route that he hoped would lead into the appropriate territory, speaking in a general way of things stolen from the minister's office at the time of the murder, furnishings, inventories, and so forth. But he would have to exercise a firm hand; the conversation had already shown a strong tendency to stray into cul-de-sacs of irrelevance. Dee had the feeling that he had only just steered them away from an exhaustive discussion of the virtues of different formulae of polishing wax.

They left the main house and passed through another garden, the sun brilliant after the nearly gloomy interior of the house. Dee heard children's voices singing a nursery tune. Shading his eyes against the light, he looked in the direction of the song, and made out six or seven shiny little heads just showing above the low ornamental shrubbery surrounding a small clearing. Little girls, singing together in a bright, secret garden spot. Dee was charmed. Did his sons ever sit and sing together? No. They sat and conspired to produce mischief and chaos.

"The little ones, of course, are not held to the decorum of mourning," the steward said apologetically. "They do not really comprehend that Father will not be returning."

"Of course not. How could they?" Dee said sympathetically. "Why spoil their fun? They will find out soon enough about the sorrows of this world."

They were inside again, and presently came to an impressive wooden door. The steward lifted the latch almost reverently, as if they were entering a temple. The room was dark, a cave, really; the steward lit a lamp and smiled at Dee.

"These are his special treasures. Very old. Very rare."

Dee looked around him. There were carvings of horses and riders, elephants, and all manner of monkey demons. They were old, obviously rare and choice, and of foreign origin, most of them Indian. But there was none of the mysterious temple erotica.

The steward held the lamp high, possessive pride on his face. Dee moved into the room, inspecting individual pieces and making approving sounds so as not to disappoint the man.

"These Indian pieces are exceptionally fine," he ventured. "Exceptionally fine. I am quite partial to Indian art," he said, as if he had just at that moment realized his preference. "I believe I saw others that must have been of Indian origin. At the minister's office. A most interesting collection. Are there more of that kind here?" Dee asked. "More . . . deeply hidden works, shall we say? Of the truly exotic sort?"

The steward's happy expression tightened into a look of reproval. It was obvious that he understood precisely what Dee was talking about.

"Sir," he said, "I am sure you understand. The minister was a worldly man, a connoisseur of many things. His interests were wide. But with his daughters, he could hardly keep such . . . art under his roof. It was only here long enough for us to separate it from the other things and pack it up to be moved. It would not do at all for young girls to look upon . . . those things," he finished lamely, embarrassed.

"Ah! Of course!" Dee interjected quickly. "That is why he kept them in his office. Of course, of course," he said, as a question occurred to him, something curious indeed which he had not articulated even to himself until this moment. "How many daughters did the minister have?" Dee had seen at least ten young girls so far during his short visit. And the young woman in the corridor?

"Thirty-seven," the steward answered with pride.

"Thirty-seven!" Dee was astonished. "And how many sons?"

"None, Magistrate. Only daughters."

"Thirty-seven daughters and no sons!" Dee said incredulously. "How is that possible? How many wives did he have?"

"Only two wives, sir."

"Two wives, thirty-seven daughters, and no sons? The women must be half dead from childbearing," Dee said. "And not one male birth. Forgive me, but it is all very strange indeed!"

The steward was looking embarrassed again. "Well, you

see, actually, there have been no births at all. The minister is . . . or was, I should say . . . without issue of his own. His daughters are all adopted.''

"He was without issue, and he adopted only daughters?" Dee was thoroughly confused now.

The steward shrugged. "He preferred them. It was a matter of taste. He found it pleasant to be surrounded by females."

Dee considered, remembering his own thoughts when they had been coming through the garden and had heard the sweet little voices singing. It was not impossible to understand. Of course, he had not been entirely serious; his sons sorely tried him, made him old beyond his years. But they were his sons, his most precious commodity. Weren't they?

"Well, the orphanages must have been exceedingly grateful to him," Dee said. "Thirty-seven of them! It is not easy to place girl children—and in such a fine home as this!"

"Oh, he did not get them from the orphanages," the steward replied. "A gentleman brought them."

"A gentleman? What sort of gentleman?"

"A gentleman of . . . color," the steward replied awkwardly.

"What do you mean, a gentleman of color?" Dee asked. "Was he an African, a Moor?"

"Oh, no, no. He was an Indian, I believe. He came two or three times a year with a most exquisite selection of little girls, some only infants, none of them older than one or two years. Ten or twelve of them. The Master would look them over carefully, and choose. Sometimes one, sometimes three, sometimes none at all."

"And the ones he didn't choose?"

"They left with the Indian gentleman. We do not know where they went, or what became of them."

"And where did they come from?" Dee pressed.

"We do not know that either. The master never mentioned anything to us, and we never asked."

"And you do not have any notion of who the Indian gentleman was? His name? Anything about him? Did he appear to treat the children well?" The questions were pouring out of Dee now, his pose as an official taking inventory of furnishings forgotten.

"No, no," the steward replied, flustered. "I mean, yes, he treated them very well. With great solicitude, actually. They were clean and pretty and well fed, that was obvious. And he spoke to them kindly. But no, I do not know his name or anything about him. He simply appeared, went into the master's private rooms with the children, and then left. Once, twice, occasionally three times a year. That is all we know."

"But you saw him," Dee said. "You know what he looked like."

"Forgive me," the steward replied, "but to me, one Indian is indistinguishable from another." The man shrugged. "Perhaps he was connected to one of the monasteries of the city. Many Indians are," he added weakly.

Dee was exasperated. The man was no help to him at all. He wondered at people's complacence and utter lack of inquisitiveness. He was quite sure that if he himself had been a member of the minister's household staff, and a strange Indian appeared twice a year with a batch of little girls for the master of the house to select from, he would have found out everything he could, if for no better reason than sheer curiosity. If only the children themselves had not been mere babies, they could tell him themselves where they came from.

"Was he old? Young? Fat? Thin?" he persisted. "How many years did this go on? Some of the girls appear to be quite grown up now."

The steward made an effort to remember. "He was neither old nor young. He was not thin, but you could not call him fat, either." Excellent, Dee thought, though he said nothing. That is most helpful. "He wore Chinese clothes, if that is any help," the steward continued. "And it went on for . . . at least ten years. It may be a longer time, but I have been here only ten. Yes, the master's eldest daughter is seventeen now. So I would venture to say seventeen years."

"I don't suppose you have any notion as to the minister's sources for his collection of Indian art that he kept at his office?"

"Certainly not, Magistrate," the man replied stiffly, disapproval showing on his face again. "Nor did I want to know."

Leaving the minister's house, Dee passed through hallways, rooms, and gardens once again. Inside the house, he heard giggling and the sound of small running feet; in the garden, the children were still singing.

The little dog was waiting exactly where Dee had left him. He raised his head sharply when he saw Dee come through the gate, then rose and trotted after him.

Where do I go, Dee asked himself, to find out about an Indian gentleman, neither young nor old, neither fat nor thin, who has passed through the city for at least seventeen years? He thought for many paces, the dog's toenails clicking on the paving stones behind him. An idea came to him. Perhaps the steward had not been entirely unhelpful after all. At least it was a place to start.

Dee shifted his weight. His backside was very sore. The ungraceful oxen-drawn cart jarred his bones so that a series of small, precise pains traveled up his spine to his neck. He braced himself against a load of firewood, struggling to maintain a position that was not too painful while trying to keep pieces of wood from toppling onto him.

Rustic and unluxurious as it was, the farmer's cart was still preferable to walking the final five *li* outside the city's western gates to the Golden Cloud Monastery. His feet could not have taken him much farther today. All the while, the little dog trotted tirelessly just behind and to the side of the great rumbling right rear wheel. Sometimes Scoundrel—that was the name Dee had decided to confer on the creature—would disappear from sight, and Dee would fully expect to look back and see his crushed little body in the road; but in the next instant, the dog would reappear unscathed, his short legs moving as fast as ever to match the speed of the wagon.

After leaving the Transport Minister's house the morning before, Dee had gone home, changed his clothing, and, acting on the one slim lead the steward had provided, spent the rest of the day trekking across the city to four different Buddhist monasteries, all disagreeably placed in the farthest and most inaccessible corners of the city. So far, he had turned up nothing at all except a growing feeling that his search was a futile one.

And these small monasteries proved to hold something else in common: they were all drab, dreary, unmaintained places of peeling paint and cracked plaster, of faded altar cloths and shabby icons dulled with age and too much handling.

The monasteries had yielded nothing for Dee other than a close look at the process of decay that comes about through neglect and indifference. The people he had encountered, perfunctorily going about the daily rituals of these crumbling temples, had not known anything about a foreigner. None of them had so much as lifted an eyebrow or twitched even slightly at his circumspect line of conversation, into which he had dropped, with what he thought was exquisite nonchalance, a mention or two of a gentleman of color, an Indian. Dee could not always tell when people were hiding something, but he believed he could almost certainly tell when they were not.

What the steward had suggested was correct—many Indians in China came there under the auspices of some Buddhist establishment. If the man Dee sought was not an exception, then it was more than likely that he came under the sponsorship of a monastery that could afford to pay his way and his fees for some exotic and esoteric purpose having to do with the religion: to carry new learning, to restore some ancient relic, to uncover new texts, to translate sutras, all of which, Dee knew, was currently fashionable. Whoever the Indian was, he must have started somewhere before the inception of whatever clandestine arrangement he had entered into with the deceased Transport Minister. After what he had seen of the tired little monasteries in the city, he decided that he was not looking in the right sort of place. Rather than waste any more time on the remaining small temples within the city, he decided to make the journey out into the countryside to the Golden Cloud Monastery, which, according to various people he had consulted today, was quite a bit larger and better endowed.

Of course, he thought, as the old, bent tree that marked his destination came into view ahead on the dusty road, there was the possibility that this elusive gentleman of color had nothing at all to do with Buddhism and Dee's footsore wanderings today would come to naught.

The driver shouted to his beasts to stop, and Dee slid off the back of the cart. He thanked the man, gave him a small tip, and stood and stared down into the valley as the cart rumbled away. Indeed, the Golden Cloud Monastery was visible from the road, just as the farmer had told him it would be. But after what he had seen today, he had not expected anything like this.

It was vast, its stately compound sitting in the midst of cultivated grounds stretching from one end of the long, tree-lined valley to the other. From where Dee stood at the side of the road, ornate rooflines, like those of a palace, peeked out here and there from the trees. Beautiful red-and-gold footbridges spanned rocky streams. The whole of this enormous and elaborate Golden Cloud was fashioned by man, but so exquisitely as to be an improvement on nature. A most pleasant and geomantically auspicious place, to be sure. A path wound invitingly down in front of him. Slapping the dirt and grime from his robes, he began his descent, Scoundrel at his heels.

It was extraordinary, Dee thought as he and the dog walked toward the Golden Cloud Monastery, that he had spent his life oblivious, for the most part, to this Buddhist religion— a religion that, although once foreign, had so completely entered the mind, heart, and very mythical fiber of China that it had woven itself into her tapestry so as to be totally inseparable: a system, or a multitude of systems, as Dee had come to understand, that in some way shaped the thoughts, actions, manners, and lives of vast numbers of Chinese people. Considering this prevalence of Buddhist institutions all over the Empire, Dee had had remarkably few encounters with any of it. It was always just there. Thinking about it, he realized that he rarely noticed whether or not someone's house held the usual Buddhist icons on the family altars. Like stones in a field or leaves on an autumn path, such things were so commonplace as to be virtually invisible to him.

Before entering the compound of the Golden Cloud Monastery, Dee stopped and sat on a bench under a stand of roughbarked old trees. The dog waited at his feet, panting, his long pink tongue hanging from his mouth. Looking through the monastery's main gate, Dee was struck by something else: in contrast with the others, this place was full of activity. Scores of monks passed into his view, moving from hall to hall. There were small groups, talking and laughing, and there were many lone devotees walking about with bowed heads. In all this activity it would seem that something was being worshiped, some deity being revered; though Dee did not know very much about Buddhism, he knew that this was not so.

Scoundrel raised his head warily, ears alert. Someone was approaching them; a round figure in a saffron robe strutted out along the path that led away from the monastery's tiled gate.

"Are you hungry, pilgrim?" the man called out before he was within fifty paces of the magistrate and his dog. Where the other devout he had encountered today exuded humility and abstemiousness, this one exuded officiousness and proprietariness the way a fish left out in the sun gives off an aroma. Dee rose to greet him. As the man approached, he clucked disapprovingly with his tongue. "Your clothes! Ahh! You are in such a state!" Shaking his head, he came closer: a pompous, compact, round-faced fellow comporting a broad, unctuous grin. The little dog rose to his feet and retreated behind Dee. "Your clothes are filthy, traveler. You are in need of fresh clothing. Perhaps a bath?"

Only then did Dee realize just how grimy he was from all his hiking about and kneeling in dusty shrines before innumerable images of bodhisattva-saviors seated upon their elephants and lions. Good! His simple street disguise was that much more convincing. But it seemed odd that this ascetic would be so concerned about Dee's appearance. Dusty, weary pilgrims would certainly have been very common to so large and apparently wealthy a monastery as this enormous Golden Cloud complex. Especially considering its out-of-the-way position along this rural road some distance from the center of Yangchou. Why was Dee such a curiosity to this man, then? He had yet to even enter the monastery grounds.

"Have you come far?" the man continued with scarcely a pause. It was not kindness alone that modulated his voice; a superficial veneer of concern lay unconvincingly over a pointed and unmistakable nosiness.

"I thank you," Dee said, "but I am quite fine. A bit tired, you must understand. I have walked a great distance in the past few days to offer my prayers and to burn this . . . this . . . " Dee fumbled around in the pocket of his outer waistcoat, produced a crumpled packet of cheap incense, and displayed it in his extended palm. " . . . this incense before the altars of the all-merciful bodhisattvas." Dee allowed his hand to tremble a little and put a note of anxiety in his voice. This was a ruse that must not be overdone, Dee warned himself. Subtlety was all-important.

"You seem distraught," the man said with a concerned tilt of his shaved head. "Is there anything that I might do for you?" There was a short silence in which Dee stood looking at the ground as if deciding whether to speak or not.

"No . . . " Dee said uncertainly, at last.

"Nothing! Nothing at all?"

"It is only that I am afraid that I shall fail my friends."

"That you shall fail your friends? How might this be?"

"I have come such a long way. My journey has cost them most of their household money so that I might offer prayers at the Golden Cloud Temple."

"These friends of whom you speak have sent you on a mission?"

"Yes."

"But certainly there are other Buddhist temples nearer your village?"

"There are," Dee replied, "but I was told that my prayers at the Golden Cloud Temple might be more . . . how shall I say it . . . "

"Efficacious?" the other broke in enthusiastically. "Is that what you were trying to say?"

Dee nodded wordlessly, his eyes humbly studying the ground again.

"Come inside to the Great Hall to pray," the man said, taking hold of Dee's arm. "I am the abbot of the Golden Cloud, and I welcome you." Dee docilely allowed himself to be ushered inside the gates.

"Your little dog is also quite welcome," the abbot said. "He will need something to eat too, no doubt."

"Thank you. Yes," Dee said, pocketing the meager bag of incense. When they had passed through the ornate tiled gates, the abbot released his grip and Dee followed him into a magnificent Buddhist rockery. Undulating paths wove through clusters of twisting pine; sandy rocks and stands of softly rattling bamboo reflected in the black pools. The Four Celestial Kings, guardians of the four cardinal points of the compass, were tucked neatly into the dark piney shadows of the far corners of the garden. In the center of the garden, turned so that he faced the entrance and whoever passed through there, sat the mirthful Maitreya—the Future Buddha—on his raised lotus dais, ancient gnarled cudgel in hand, with laughing face and great pendulous belly. Clambering over the laughing Buddha's great shoulders and rippling belly were scores of Arhats, disciples, represented as tiny children. As they neared the rear of the rockery, a great wooden Kuan-yin covered with rich gold leaf reclined in sybaritic splendor alongside the meandering course of an artificial stream. Dee recognized these personages of the Buddhist pantheon from the bit of research he had done before setting out today. It was one thing to see them as drawings accompanying a text; it was quite another to see them alive, as it were, in this very compelling setting.

"Just what, if I may inquire, is the nature of this prayerful mission?" the abbot asked at last.

Ah, my friend, Dee thought, I did not think that you would be able to resist the question much longer, but I would have given you at least another hundred paces or so.

"I have come to pray for the little daughter of the dear friends who sent me here," he said. He watched his companion for any small reaction, any hesitation or gesture at these words. But if the abbot was surprised in any way, he appeared to have admirable control.

"Is this poor child very ill?" he asked without a pause, his voice still full of concern. As they neared the hall's entrance, the cloyingly sweet perfume of burning incense assailed Dee's nostrils, cutting through the rich earthy smell of pine and damp rocks.

"We do not know her condition."

"You do not know if she is ill?" The abbot put his arm around Dee's shoulders, his features assuming a mixture of great concern and consternation as he spoke. "Is the child perhaps . . . possessed by demons?"

"No, no—certainly not," Dee said. "We hope not! It seems to be nothing like that. She is missing. She has been kidnapped."

"Kidnapped?"

"She was barely two years old, you see."

"Barely two," the abbot echoed, shaking his head ruefully. "A mere infant."

"Yes," Dee said sadly, "a mere infant. Who would want a child so young? And of what use would a female child be for someone's prosperity . . . an infant, a useless female child?" Dee looked sorrowfully down at his hands.

"It is at times a strange and cruel world, is it not?" the abbot said sympathetically. "Quite remote from and indifferent to our sensibilities as decent moral creatures." Dee nodded sadly at the abbot's words, raising his eyes to the man's face occasionally. "Although this world is but a material illusion, it is a most convincing one, and we are its long-suffering inhabitants," the abbot went on as they climbed the Great Hall stairs. "If this is the dream world, then it is most substantial and rich, is it not? But you come here to be free of the harsher realities . . . to have your soul uplifted . . . "

"To pray for the safe return of the child," Dee corrected firmly.

"But of course. The true purpose of your prayers goes without saying. The child . . . the infant female. The merciful bodhisattvas will understand what is in your heart. You have only to invoke them." The abbot swept his hand in a broad gesture that took in the magnificent interior of the hall.

The sumptuous display of the Great Hall's wealth was startling beyond anything Dee had seen before. On the grand altar, running the length of the rear wall, sat four enormous gold gilt statues—the four great bodhisattva saints of China: Kuan-yin, Wen-shu, P'uhien, and Ti-tsang. Behind each of these resplendent cross-legged deities was a gigantic aureole of hammered silver and gold. And each of these radiating semicircles of precious metal was alive with elaborate repoussé scenes of demons and angels, legends from the life of the Buddha and his saints. And set around these scenes were hundreds of tiny carved flower symbols, like the many depicted flames of divine enlightenment, their raised leaves and petals encrusted with countless rare gems.

Across the Great Hall, within a railed enclosure, sat the three incarnations of the sacred Buddha—past, present, and future, their mouths curled in enigmatic, devilish grins beneath wild bulging eyes on fire with unattainable knowledge. In the midst of this overwhelming symbolism, Dee plainly felt the abbot's pride of possession, as unmistakably as if he were being shown through the fine, expensive house of a rich man. Which, in a sense, he was.

As Dee and the abbot entered, a few monks passed in front of them, heads lowered reverently, voices droning just below the level of comprehension. They crossed the floor of the Great Hall and disappeared into a rear chapel door between the four enormous bodhisattva images, toward which the abbot gestured lovingly.

"*They* will listen to you. But tell me, from whom did you first hear of the Golden Cloud Monastery?" The abbot's hand was once again on Dee's shoulder. "We think of ourselves as remote . . . not so much in distance, but in our minds and hearts. We are a contemplative monastery, a place of study and learning. A preserve. We support a very great library of ancient texts and sutras and maintain a museum reliquary for rare artifacts."

"Then you do not see many pilgrims or devotees?" Dee asked, interested by the abbot's last words: reliquary and artifacts, he had said. Considering all he had seen, it was interesting.

"It is rare," the abbot replied. "An occasional weary traveler like yourself is all we ever see out here. It is seldom that those who do not *belong* to this monastery . . . well . . . " The abbot shrugged. Belong? Dee recognized that this man's pressured and artificial attempt to be cordial had pushed his tongue too far. "You will be needing warm water and fresh clothing," the abbot said then, as if making a concerted effort to reestablish his gracious manner.

"No, I will make my offerings and invocations and then go on my way, but I thank you for your most kind offer," Dee said humbly.

"Then you have somewhere to go from here, my friend?"

"My brother-in-law and his family reside in Yangchou. They have graciously offered to take me in. He is a furniture maker. A member of the guild. Very fine cabinetry. I, also, am slightly skilled with woodworker's tools. I shall apprentice myself to him; I am hoping that I might be able to earn my way in his household. He will be needing assistance. His business is quite good now." Then Dee added for good measure, "There is no want of work here, I have heard. There are so many wealthy people of late building their houses in Yangchou. Are there not?" he asked, as if seeking reassurance.

"Indeed!" the abbot responded happily. "The canals have brought with them a flourishing trade. Many people have benefited under the merciful eyes of the gentle bodhisattva Kuanyin. But tell me," he asked determinedly this time, fixing Dee with a direct look, "how did your grieving friends—the ones for whose infant daughter's safe return you now pray—come to send you to this monastery? How did these unfortunates first learn of us?" Here was Dee's opening. He took a breath and plunged ahead.

"An Indian gentleman," he replied, watching the abbot's face closely. "They can remember the day that they encountered him—it is quite rare that we see any foreigners, and rarer still that we see a gentleman of color, from so far west, in our tiny village. We tend to be distrustful of foreigners of this type, different as they are from us. But, as I have said, these acquaintances are quite lost in their grief for their infant daughter."

"An Indian gentleman?" the abbot repeated, as if musing over an interesting but irrelevant piece of information. "And this Indian gentleman . . . mentioned *this* monastery? Have you also seen this particular . . . foreigner . . . yourself?"

"No, I only heard about him through them."

"But he suggested that the family seek us out?" the abbot asked patiently, as if he were trying to solve a clever, perplexing riddle.

"He told us to go to the Golden Cloud Monastery for deliverance from this burden of pain. They needed something in their distress. To proffer offerings and prayers." Dee's whole tale today had been concocted of fragments, a plausible-sounding creation, he hoped, composed of salient bits and pieces of the mystery with which he might draw forth something tangible. "This Indian gentleman took a definite interest in the children," he said. "He had a special fondness for girls, it seemed. And, quite specifically, he said that at this place, prayers for the child would definitely be heard."

"Oh, indeed! And he is not wrong. It is most certain that they will. Most certain." The abbot seemed distracted now, a trifle distant, as if he was letting his mouth go on while his mind worked on something else. "The mercy of the Four . . . their mercy is ultimately all-enduring and powerful. They hear all prayers, whether they are the prayers for children or . . . the prayers of children. . . . " His voice trailed off. "But you must pardon me now. I should leave you to your meditations and offerings," he finished, his indulgent patience gone now, like that of a man who has tarried too long and now wants only to get away. Dee could not resist a direct question.

"Do you know such a man as this Indian?" he asked.

The abbot shook his head absently. "I should leave you to your meditations and offerings," he repeated. "Since you will not be staying here long, then you will wish to get back to Yangchou before nightfall. It is very dark along the road."

Dee looked at the abbot. Though there seemed something unsettled and disturbed in the man's demeanor, Dee cautioned himself against reading too much into it. What appeared to be significant abstraction fraught with hidden meaning might very well be nothing more than the man's rumbling stomach reminding him that the dinner hour was approaching. Dee's assessment of the plump, complacent abbot was that he was a man lovingly fond of his little habits and routines.

"I wish you luck," the abbot said with a pleasant smile, and turned to leave.

Dee removed the incense pouch from his pocket while his eyes followed the abbot out of the hall. Did he actually seem to be in a hurry as he left? Or was it merely the same officious, self-important gait that Dee had first noticed? He sighed. He knew no more now than when he had set out this morning. He himself was hungry now. The abbot's offer of food, so ingratiatingly made earlier, seemed to have been forgotten. Tired and discouraged as he was, though, he could not leave just yet.

He knew that he must continue with the appearance of the offering and prayer. He must assume that as long as he remained on the monastery grounds he was under scrutiny. He found a small bronze incense burner fashioned in the shape of an ox at the foot of the bodhisattva Kuan-yin. He removed the top and blew out the dust and arranged all but one of the small perfumed cones in a semicircle inside the base. He touched the tip of the cone that was still in his fingers to a candle flame and then used it to transfer the fire to the others. Then he blew the flames out so that all of the tips glowed like a semicircle of distant campfires. He replaced the final cone of incense into the arrangement and lowered the heavy bronze top back down. Colored smoke curled out the nostrils and rose from a tiny row of holes placed in the decorative pattern along the animal's back. Without looking around, Dee dropped dutifully to his knees and began to send softly muttered nonsense heavenward on the smoke.

Dee lifted one of the temple carvings from the crate, studied it for a moment, and placed it high on a shelf over his desk. Several other crates lay on the floor.

He had had the Transport Minister's collection carefully packed and brought to his own office. Clearly, there was no place for the pieces at the Transport Minister's house, and his successor, who was taking over the dead man's office in the coming week, had expressed a desire that they be removed immediately. And, Dee told himself, the carvings still qualified as evidence.

But the most important reason was that his curiosity was aroused since his rounds of the monasteries. He wanted to know more about the mysterious mind of India, where the sacred and the profane seemed to be intertwined.

Dee lifted the straw out of an open crate, revealing a section of a carved frieze. A series of bodies tumbled in riotous confusion, embracing, copulating fore and aft, kneeling to perform fellatio. In their midst, a man coupled with a horse. Dee looked at it for a while before lifting it from its packing and propping it against a wall. It was interesting, but it did not have the same power for him as the carvings of couples, which he found much more compelling.

In one of these, a broad-shouldered man of heroic proportions embraced a delicate, voluptuous woman who pressed her breasts to his chest while a graceful leg wrapped around his torso. He supported her leg with one hand and cradled her chin with his other, tipping her head back, looking down into her upturned face. Dee looked at some of the others, studying hands caressing legs, arms, and breasts with delicacy and tenderness, lovers gazing into each other's faces. The gestures in these pieces were so . . . human. Dee could think of no other way to describe them, and they moved him profoundly. He glanced back at the frieze leaning against the wall; it projected an indiscriminate, orgiastic, almost ritual sexuality, a force unleashed and out of control. But the pairs of lovers suggested a sweetness and graceful dalliance, a focused eroticism, that was much more to his taste.

It was not as if Dee had not seen plenty of erotic art before in his life. Chinese painting masters frequently turned their attentions to the graphic and colorful depiction of the act of love. He was even familiar with the idea of sensuality as a form of religious meditation; he had heard of the tantalizing esoteric practices of certain sects of Taoists, who immersed themselves in the vast unceasing flow of the river of life, so they said, through sex. But they were often reviled as cultists and societal outsiders, detestable opportunists wallowing in concupiscence, satisfying their carnal appetites under the guise of spiritual contemplation. Dee's feeling was that it was altogether different in India. It was truly as if the artists who had made these carvings had succeeded in tapping into a vein of divine inspiration. He lifted a piece of carved wood to his nose and inhaled its faint fragrance, imagining for a moment that he was smelling the air of India itself.

Perhaps he would even travel there one day. From what he had heard, frank eroticism permeated every level of Indian society. He wondered if what he had heard was true—that one could scarcely draw a breath in India, eat a bite of food, or gaze at a cloud passing in the sky without an acute consciousness of its being a dimension of eros. It seemed that vigorous sex, and plenty of it, was practically an obligation if the world order was to continue. Early Hindu writings were filled with references to lusty earthly sex serving to stimulate the deities into having sexual relations with their goddesses, charging the universe, like the sky during a thunderstorm, with divine power, which then flowed directly back into the affairs of human beings on the earth. A most expeditious exchange, Dee thought.

The artists who had made the pieces in front of him had been truly inspired. Dee recognized in the gestures and embraces of the carved men and women his own ideal desires and fulfillments, the rare moments in his life when lovemaking had been sublime, transcendent, harmonious. Yes, he understood the source of the carvings' power. And yes, he was beginning to understand why there was something wholly appropriate about a temple of worship calling forth these emotions in the worshiper.

He lit a lamp and placed it on his desk. It was not quite dark yet, but it had been a cloudy day, and the late afternoon was already dying. Carefully, he pried the lid from another crate and lifted the packing away; lingams of all shapes, sizes, and degrees of refinement or crudity lay nestled in the straw. He lifted several out and set them on his desk so that they pointed heavenward in a most realistic way.

The lingam really told the whole story of the mind of India, he thought, studying the bold audacious upward curve of one. China had its yin and yang, the female and male principles of the universe intermingled and embraced. But compared to this, the Chinese form was so dry, so removed, so . . . abstract. This Indian-Hindu symbol was ardent, passionate, imbued with power. The lingam was actually a symbol of a symbol—because the erect human organ that it imitated was already considered to be a representation, fashioned in flesh, of divine potency.

A scholarly Indian monk had once told Dee that there were devotees in that far-off land who did not bother with the secondary symbol, the lingam, but merely worshiped their own erect organs. The same monk had told him of special rooms attached to temples where hundreds upon hundreds of lingams were placed on display. And no household, the monk had said, was without its lingam on the family altar—where it was worshiped, attended to, and anointed with melted butter and garlanded with flowers. There were even places in India, the monk had whispered to Dee, where it was customary for a bride to be deflowered not by her husband, but by a ritual lingam—so that she would belong first to the deity, then to her husband.

Well, Dee thought, the Transport Minister had certainly displayed his own collection of divine phalluses in a way worthy of a temple. And Dee himself could attest to their overwhelming effect. But he still wondered about the dead man's

interest in the objects, and the rest of the erotic art as well: *had*
he been susceptible to their power? Had he kept the pieces
around him because they stimulated him, excited him, made
him dream? Or had the meaning of the pieces been limited
strictly to their value as rare, exotic curiosities, undoubtedly
worth plenty in cash, and imparting special prestige to their
possessor? He lit another lamp and turned back to the splendid
temple carvings.

Apsarases. That was the word for the women in the carvings, the monk had told him. They were rather like divine
courtesans, whose beauty, desirability, and skill in the art of
love were as far beyond earthly women's as a god's wisdom
and span of life were beyond mortal men's. The *apsaruses*, so
it was said, dwelled in the afterworld, fairly languishing with
desire for the virtuous dead, wanting nothing else but to reward them for all eternity. And the rewards began on earth, it
would seem; it behooved a man to be a master of the art of
love while he was alive if he wanted to find himself in the
arms of *apsarases* forever and ever.

He knelt over a carving that still rested in a crate. An
apsaras, full-bodied and voluptuous, stood alone with one sensuously rounded hip thrust to the side, the shape of her impossibly uplifted breasts delineated by a necklace that traveled,
clinging to every curve, down to her belly, where gentle horizontal lines suggested a luxurious distribution of fat emphasizing the deep triangle between her legs. She was nude but
for her elegant jewelry, which decorated her arms, feet, ankles,
and head; on her face she wore a small, cryptic smile. Her
whole stance suggested that she was waiting . . . and ready.
The heavenly courtesan, indeed. He blurred his eyes a bit, trying to see her not as old, carved, dry wood, but as living flesh.
He endeavored to see her smooth brown skin, the gold of her
jewelry flashing against it, her black hair and eyes. He smiled.
In the soft lamplight, it was not a difficult feat of the imagination to achieve. For a moment, he really saw her. She had
the same skin as the courtesan a young male relative of his had
obtained for him on his fifteenth birthday, unbeknownst to the
rest of the family. She had been an Indian, and her skin had
smelled of smoke and patchouli. It had been a long, feverish
night for the youth; he could still recall the minute details of
those hours with perfect clarity.

He started to lift the piece, thinking that it deserved a
special place of honor by itself, and several rolled-up pieces of

paper dropped to the floor, as if they had been tucked into the back of the carving. He set the sculpture down on a stool and retrieved the papers. He smoothed one out on his desk near the lamp and read:

> . . . her thighs form a sacrificial altar; the hairs between them the sacrificial grass where a man kneels; her skin is the sacred liquor a man drinks to become intoxicated; the two lips between her thighs the place where the rubbing stick makes holy fire. Truly, the world of the man who practices the art of love knowing this is as exalted as the world of him who performs the sacred strength-libation sacrifice. . . .

Dee raised his eyes as a rush of warm blood moved involuntarily through his body all the way up to his face. These were some sort of translated holy Indian writings, it would seem; obviously, the dead Transport Minister was interested in verbal pictures as well. Heavens, but these were even more powerful than the carvings. Those had done nothing like this to him. Here he stood, alone in his office, feeling very tangible pangs of physical arousal, his face hot and his pulse and breathing quickened, because of words on paper.

He thought of his wives. He would go to one of them tonight. But which? His second wife held the prerogative at the moment. She had a right to receive his attentions next, and indeed, he was obligated to her. But his first wife, a more flexible, imaginative woman, would be more likely to go with him where he wanted to go tonight. If he went to his first wife tonight, he would have to be sure to make it up to his second wife, and soon. He closed his eyes and allowed tantalizing pictures to flit through his mind. He felt strong. He sorely needed the relaxation and revitalization. He could, perhaps, go to both of them tonight. Yes, of course. Why not? He lowered his eyes to the page again. " . . . the place where the rubbing stick makes holy fire."

If he had not heard the smallest creak of a floorboard behind him, the blow would have landed squarely on the back of his head. But his body reacted before his mind had time to comprehend. He twisted to one side and caught the full force on his right shoulder. His hand shot up at the same instant and caught hold of a piece of rough, splintery wood and held it. Flailing behind him with the other hand, he seized and held tight to a piece of his attacker's clothing. In this strange embrace, unable to see each other's faces, they whirled around, knocking over furniture and carvings, making a terrible din. Dee pulled as hard as he could at the club, the angle awkward and strengthless, splinters digging into his flesh, his assailant's breath hot on his neck. Then he backed up toward the wall and slammed the other's body against it hard—once, twice, a third time, until whoever it was let go of the club. Dee flung it across the room, and still gripping the piece of clothing, turned to face his attacker, pinning him to the wall with an arm across the neck.

The utter surprise at what he saw stopped him for perhaps three heartbeats. A boy—no more than twelve or thirteen, scrawny and wiry, with short, bristly hair—stared back at him with wild eyes, gasping for air, feet barely touching the floor. Dee relaxed his grip so the child could get his breath. Those few seconds' lowered vigilance were all the boy needed. He sank his teeth into Dee's arm, ducked under him as the magistrate howled with pain, and headed for the door to the balcony before Dee knew what had happened. He lunged, but something under his feet rolled, pulling the floor out from under him. Down he went, landing hard on his back. By the time he stumbled to his feet again and out to the balcony and looked over the rail, the boy was gone.

Trembling, his back throbbing, Dee went back into the office. The carving of the beautiful *apsaras* lay facedown on the carpet. Lingams had been knocked to the floor and had rolled in all directions. That was what he had slipped on, of course: a holy phallus had brought him to the ground. It was a miracle he hadn't cracked his skull. With shaking hands, he began to set things aright again, afraid that something might have been damaged. Nothing was broken, though, merely scattered, just as surely as his mood of a few moments ago was scattered irretrievably. He picked up the *apsaras* and looked at her. Her little smile had not changed. No earthly scuffle, no mortal struggle, could ruffle her eternal, untouchable hunger.

In a far corner of the room, where he had hurled it, he found the club meant for the back of his head: a rough, heavy piece of wood, half as long as a man's arm and just as thick, perfectly suited for delivering a deathblow while he sat absorbed and oblivious—precisely how the Transport Minister had died. He felt almost certain that he held in his hands the very weapon that had killed that unfortunate man. And the little demon who had fled over the balcony? Without a doubt, Dee had also had his hands on the true murderer for a few brief moments.

He looked at his palms. There must have been one hundred splinters embedded in the one that had gripped the club. It was beginning to sting and throb mercilessly. When he went to one of his wives tonight, it would be to ask her to search out with her infinite feminine patience each and every murderous sliver, pull it from his flesh, and rub soothing balm into the wounds with her own cool, soft hands.

JOURNAL ENTRY

The bruised bones in my shoulder and back and my bandaged hand and arm feel to me like the dead gardener demanding my attention. Now he is with me every waking moment. I hobble about like an old man; whether I am painfully rising from my bed, bending stiffly to put a slipper on my foot, or even lifting a brush to write, I feel his outraged spirit in every ache and twinge. All I have accomplished is to confirm my theory, because in my blundering about, I have obviously drawn the attention of the true killers.

The boy who very nearly dispatched me, whose tooth marks I carry about on my arm? I scarcely believe that he is the lone perpetrator; the complexity of the Transport Minister's life, though it is only a looming, undefinable shape in the dark for me, tells me that the child is no doubt a paid killer, an agile, lethal monkey able to move with impunity and invisibility, slipping through cracks, climbing balconies, and scampering over rooftops.

I am unable to devote every waking moment to this case, much as I would like to. There is other business aplenty for me to attend to, for I have been promoted to the position of first assistant to the chief magistrate. There are even some other murder cases. After what I have seen, I know I must apply myself to the latter with special diligence. I cannot allow any more innocent men to face the executioner. My bruises and wounds will heal, and the gardener's hungry ghost will most likely retreat a bit, but I will not forget him. And I will watch the crowds for the face of the murderous child. I certainly will not forget him.

I will listen more carefully for boards creaking behind me, for doors opening softly, for a breath on the back of my neck.

What if he had succeeded, and they had found my poor corpse sprawled on the carpet? Would they have found another gardener to blame, or would they have diligently sought to uncover the truth? I fear the answer to that question.

3

A.D. 653
Loyang, the eastern capital, center of the Imperial government and site of the Royal Palace

The light that filtered through her bedchamber curtain must have been playing tricks with her reflection this morning. That was the only explanation. It turned Madame Yang's youthful image into a haggard and prophetic statement. Worn and tired, the eyes that looked back at her were an old woman's eyes, sunk in the shadowed hollows of their bony orbits. It was not at all difficult for her to see the skin of her face sagging from her high cheekbones and her marble complexion mottled with liver spots and the stray hairs that old grandmothers sprouted on their chins. That is what you are now, she told her reflection: an old grandmother. At least you will be one shortly. Then inspiration came to her. Here, obviously, was the reason for this unusually severe and persistent manifestation—it was a sign that the birth was imminent.

She tilted her head and regarded the hag in the mirror. She had become her mother, overnight. So—it was true what everyone said, that little by little you did become, in some fashion, the image of a parent. But she had not expected it to be so sudden and startling.

In the hallway to the reception room the polished mirrors caught and multiplied the same image. It was, of course, only a trick of an unflattering light, she told herself. A prophecy without any substance. Something that Madame Yang only imagined. But prophecies, she knew, became self-fulfilling if one gave them credence, breathed life into them. She tried to push that unsettling notion out of her mind. She turned away, then turned back sharply as if trying to catch her multiple reflections off guard. This time there were four. They faced her again. But now they were slightly older, and if she was not mistaken, a tiny bit more exasperated than before. As if *they* had grown tired of *her!*

Raising her brows and widening her eyes, she brought her chin up smartly; she switched profiles in the mirror, turning her head first this way and then that. She knew that she was, in reality, still young and beautiful, and not her mother at all. But the aging effect, this trick of perception that had become increasingly troublesome to her of late, was particularly difficult to dispel this morning. Yes, she told herself, it could only mean one thing. The time was very, very near. Nearer than she had thought! She drew herself up, alarmed. Perhaps it was too late already! Perhaps this was the reason why Daughter was late this morning!

She could not sit still. She paced back and forth relentlessly. She was a jangle of nervous energy. She went as far as the day couch before turning around and passing through the hall again. This time, trying to ignore her carping and critical reflections, she went straight for the window and pulled aside the heavy brocade curtains. She looked out through the spaces between the narrow wooden shutters. The courtyard was empty.

She strode out of the reception room, but was only halfway down the hallway to her antechambers—for one heartbeat those weary and obstinate old faces were at her again—when she turned back toward the front room again. The curtain had barely stopped swaying from her most recent touch; this time, she grabbed it and pulled it completely back along its elaborate wooden rod. She pushed open the delicate little shutters, baring the room to the bright, indiscriminate light.

Outside, the courtyard was still, sun-drenched, and defiantly empty. No promising sounds came from the street beyond the high wooden gate, no distant clatter of hooves, nothing. She sniffed the air, impatience whistling in her nostrils. The massive gates looked lifeless and obstinate, as if they would never swing open again.

In the next instant, she turned from the window and

called to the servants. Purpose and life flowed into her being, displacing the dead, dry, stunted feeling of frustration and stalled time. She shouted to the servants outside the reception-hall doors. In that moment, she had felt her daughter's presence.

Daughter Wu arrived seated in a curtained palanquin carried aloft by eight men. She arrived as all members of her family did, spared always the common and unenviable compromise of effort. All work was common and vulgar, Mother Yang had told her frequently. Surely if a thing did not come easily and without strain then it was not intended for her daughter.

Of late, though, Madame Yang had had to adjust her position. The family's once exalted place under the earlier Sui Dynasty and the T'ang's first Emperor, Kaotsu, had slipped somewhat. Under Kaotsu's usurper, Taitsung, the late Emperor and father of the present Emperor, Kaotsung, the family had, thanks to Daughter, regained some of its former status. Daughter had been the old Emperor's favorite consort—young, bewitching, and imaginative. Now, with Taitsung dead and his son Kaotsung on the throne, circumstances were ripe for full restoration of the family to its proper place. Daughter had been only a consort under Taitsung—but with Kaotsung, her role was limitless. But not without considerable effort and sacrifice. The work that lay ahead for herself and Daughter would be hard, but it would be thoroughly noble and worthy. Mother knew that her late husband, Wu's dear departed father, approved. When we *must* work, she told herself, there is no one better than ourselves. She and Daughter would show the world what hard work really meant.

Daughter Wu stepped down onto the sun-warmed cobblestones of the courtyard, her long-nailed fingers settling gently into the supporting palms of her flanking handmaidens. Madame Yang eyed with relief and approval her daughter's full-term belly, still bulging under the shining silk of her gown. Good. There was still time.

No sooner had Daughter placed a dainty foot to the stones than a massive fringed parasol rose and was held over her head to protect her from the sun and a band of richly colored carpet was rolled out in front of her. The eyes of mother and daughter met. *Think as a queen. Behave as a queen. Be a queen.* Madame Yang had instructed Daughter Wu to invoke these words in her mind every day, just as the Mahayana Buddhist nuns invoked the names of a myriad of attendant saviors. It was all pure realization. This was what the Buddhists meant by transcending the material with thought. She understood it perfectly.

Mother and Daughter sat alone at the big table in the shade of the garden pavilion. Mother had sent the handmaidens away to assure the two of them absolute privacy. The six women dallied now by the reflecting pool, safely out of hearing, giggling and talking softly among themselves. Mother poured daughter some cool wine as they dined on fried ginger pork and honeyed fruit.

"He is still pleased?" Madame Yang, mouth full, gestured with her chopstick toward her daughter's belly.

"Greatly pleased," Daughter replied with a smile. "Everything pleases him." She took a healthy bite of food. "You were right, of course, Mother."

"Tell me what I was right about," Madame Yang demanded pleasurably, spearing a piece of meat.

"You know that he has inherited the predilections of his father." Wu ran the flat of her hand sensuously over the rounded corner of the table. "But in the son, they are more than predilections."

"Breeding is breeding, whether it is with horses or men. All characteristics will tell in time," Madame Yang replied, and raised a portion of savory pork to her lips. "The predilections of the father will ultimately become the habits of the son. With some cultivation, of course," she added, and put the food in her mouth. She waited, addressing herself unconcernedly to her plate and her wine cup, enjoying the pleasant suspense, the tacit understanding between them that the details, all of them, would be forthcoming in good time. Daughter stretched her right hand out languorously upon the shining tabletop. Madame Yang saw that there were only four long, manicured fingernails on the hand; the middle finger, the longest, wore an exquisite cloisonne cap on its tip. Mother and Daughter smiled at one another.

"Certain things that the father enjoyed the son enjoys as well," Daughter said. "But in the son, these tastes are—shall we say—more profoundly developed."

"More fully realized," Madame Yang offered.

"With my help, of course," Daughter Wu added. She held

up her right hand with its jeweled fingertip and leaned across the table toward her mother. "Emperor Kaotsung is driven mad by this finger," she whispered.

Madame Yang put her head back and burst into laughter. It was contagious. They laughed together, rocking in their seats, attracting the attention of the handmaidens across the way, who looked at them in alarm from their distant perch at the pond. Madame Yang put her utensils down and wiped the tears from her eyes. Daughter rested her chin on her hand and studied her mother's pleasure.

"It is true, Mother," Wu-chao said, trying to regain a shade of seriousness. "The Empress will do things for him, but perfunctorily, with no pleasure, and only because it is her wifely duty. She is bound to do what her Imperial husband requests. But he senses it, and he tells me that her attitude dampens his lust. I, on the other hand. . . ." She shrugged. She did not need to finish. She proffered the finger again, and removed the cloisonné cap from the tip. She held the finger up for her mother's scrutiny. "I have had the Imperial physicians remove the nail surgically so that it will not grow back." Mother Yang grimaced at her daughter's pronouncement. Wu picked up the little cap and admired it. "I have had many such accouterments commissioned—different colors and shapes. They protect the sensitive tip of my finger. And, of course, the sight of it serves to remind him constantly. . . ." They both laughed again, and she placed the cap back on with an exaggerated, sensual suggestiveness that caused Mother Yang to smile slowly with appreciation.

"I have developed for him a very subtle technique, Mother, which I have practiced, and which renders his passions quite beyond his control. It is the total abnegation of his will. His member becomes so rigid that it goes from 'sandstone to jade.'" She caressed the talented finger lovingly.

"No sacrifice is too great," Mother Yang remarked.

"The pain and the excitation reach such a level of superb torment and ecstasy that he is absolutely helpless. Absolutely helpless! Like an infant for the tit. Were I to leave at that moment, I believe he would go mad. He becomes a plaything . . . a toy with a rock so hard between his legs. . . ." Daughter's voice trailed off for a moment, her thoughts turning inward as she contemplated the memory of the Emperor's helpless lust.

"It is most exquisite torture," she continued. "The flow of *ch'i* through the lower vessels of his body is virtually blocked so that his juices are backed up inside him. He is quite unable to release the pressure that builds within him. Unless . . . " She paused. "Unless I release him. Do you know, Mother, that many times I have worked him into that state, then abandoned him—just to tease him! I have driven him to this wonderful hardness, then tied his hands—most playfully, you understand"—Wu demonstrated, spreading her arms—"to the canopy posts of the bed with the silk sash from my robes." She sighed with pleasure, and speared a morsel of gingered fruit, her eyes turned demurely down.

"And then—and this is the part that is most fun, Mother—I dance for him, lifting my skirts way above my knees; and then there will be times when I will simply roll around enticingly on the couch. I writhe and fondle myself. He cannot *stand* it. He tells me that none of the others can bring him to this state. He tries to get to me, or so he pretends. That is much of the excitement for him. The restrained predator. He tries to chew his way through the sash like a wild animal, shaking and rattling the posts so that I expect the entire bed to collapse at any moment. I think he could escape if he really wanted to. But he does not. He always stops short of injuring himself or pulling the furniture apart. The game only serves to arouse him to insanity; he loves the indulgence, his jade stalk throbbing and swollen to the point of bursting . . . the head of his 'turtle' is as red and glistening as the vermilion pillars of his porch."

"No doubt he saw that teasing wickedness in you when he was just a Crown Prince watching you from afar. Something in him, unconscious and unformed, drew him to you. He scarcely understood it himself. But I knew. I used to watch him watching you. Even then, you had him.

"At first he did not know what was happening to him in your presence," Mother Yang continued, as if telling her daughter a story about some long-ago, faraway people. "He might have mistaken it for simple lust, simple arousal that would be quenched when he had finally bedded you. But of course, he would not be able to do that while you were still a consort to his father. So he had to drive the mere thought of it from his mind, since there was nothing he could do about it. But then there came the moment when he saw that the way was clear, that *you* were an agent of fate. *You*." She pointed at her daughter, shaking her finger. "You he could not chase from his mind." Daughter Wu sat upright, raptly absorbing every word of the oft-told tale of her ascendancy. She never grew tired of it.

"It is true, Mother. He cannot take his eyes off me, even when the Empress is present. She is tolerant. I suppose that she thinks of it as just his temporary interest in another. Or that, perhaps, we shall simply share him—she as Empress, and I as First Consort." She leaned back then and narrowed her eyes. "She is tolerant. But the Court . . . that is another story. Taitsung's six old councillors whom he left behind to watch over Kaotsung like six fussy old nursemaids are the worst of the lot. It is just not done, they all say in stupid unison, wagging their heads. It is just not proper decorum, they say. Those old aristocrats think that I, or any woman who was part of Taitsung's life, should simply be relegated to some distant palace, or a nunnery. To live out our lives in perpetual mourning. With the death of an Imperial husband we are supposed to be through, dead ourselves. They have made it clear that this is what they would prefer. My presence is just barely tolerated, and only because I have given Kaotsung the spine to stand up to them. As long as I am not too conspicuous, as long as I am kept in the background, as long as he traverses the back staircases to get to me, then they do not make too much of a fuss. But they don't like it, Mother. They don't like it at all. Well, I don't like them, the damnable old meddlers!" She paused, savoring her righteous indignation. "What nonsense, Mother! That six old men who should have been in their graves long ago share nearly *equal* power, equal *responsibility* in ruling. It is nonsense . . . *nonsense!*"

Wu brought her open palm down sharply on the table, making the crockery dance. "They should all go to hell, Mother!" she exclaimed loudly, again attracting the attention of the handmaidens by the water. "They are old and they should *die* before they stand in my way!"

"You are done?" Mother Yang asked calmly, her manner quiet and controlled, her tone reflecting long experience with her daughter. "There will be another moment, perhaps." Mother Yang smiled suggestively. "The moment when my daughter learns that the Court does not matter! What they want, what they wish for the young Emperor and his consort, simply does not matter."

Looking at her mother's beautiful face and listening to her calm words and assured tone, always a balm to her incendiary temper, Wu relaxed again. She could always, always depend on her mother.

"You almost have him, Wu-chao," Madame Yang said then.

"What do you mean, I *almost* have him? What are you saying, Mother?"

"I am saying, my dear, that you have not conquered him yet. You have only just netted the *beast* within him. But you have yet to toss the *man* himself into the trap." Madame Yang brought a single emphatic finger up to the level of her nose. Closing one eye as if evaluating a piece of jewelry, she regarded her daughter. "You do not have his total devotion yet. You have been with Kaotsung only a very short time. Too short a time to tell, and, of course, there is still Kaotsung's Empress. She is in your way.

"Also, although they are the least of your problems, this Council of Six. They tell him what he can and cannot do. Who he might marry. They would probably like to tell him when he could breathe or evacuate his bowel, if he would allow them. And should it come to that, I am not so certain that our young Emperor possesses the will to resist them. . . . " Madame Yang shook her head and let her voice trail off.

Daughter Wu waited, rapt, for her mother to continue, her chin resting solemnly in the heels of her hands, her fingers curled to her lips. Then, quite suddenly, and without any warning, Mother Yang grabbed hold of her daughter's wrists, pulling her arms out from under her. "You have the opportunity to change all of that! You have one perfect, precious opportunity," Mother Yang declared vehemently.

"What is that?" Wu was taken aback.

"You have something that pleases Kaotsung. Something that pleases the Emperor greatly. He is very proud of the child he will have by you. This child," she said, reaching over and putting her hand on her daughter's abdomen, "is the instrument of fate we have been waiting for." Daughter looked down at her mother's hand where it touched her, then raised her eyes to meet her mother's.

"What are you saying, Mother?" Wu asked.

"I am telling you, my daughter, that you must *appropriate* the moment," Mother Yang whispered. She withdrew her hand. "An opportunity presents itself to bring Kaotsung to you completely, body and soul, over the objections of the Council of Six, and at the same time to remove the minor encumbrance of the Empress from your path. Everything done swiftly . . . and expediently." Mother Yang paused long enough to assess her daughter. "You have little trouble with what I am saying?"

Daughter Wu nodded her head. "I have no trouble, Mother," she said slowly. "Shortly after my child is born . . . "

"No longer than a fortnight," Madame Yang said peremptorily. "No longer."

Wu said nothing, but sat and nodded her head thoughtfully.

"You should know," Mother Yang said, dropping her voice again and leaning forward, "your father came to me again last night. He says that he will not rest until he has done everything that he can do for you." She gestured widely, taking in the entire grounds. "His spirit should have gone on to be a part of everything here: the stones, the walls, the trees, the ponds, the fish. But instead, he waits. Pulling himself together out of the ether, he holds himself for moments in tentative and transient form, a delicate balance of the real and the unreal, of material and immaterial, of being and nonbeing, of substance and shadow, of *anatta* and *atman*—and he does it for his daughter. For you." Mother leaned across the table, whispering again. "The Hinayana Buddhist texts have helped me to understand this process. It is all there in the Diamond Sutra. But of course, the Tibetans take it many steps further. . . . "

"Mother, what precisely did he say to you?" Wu asked impatiently.

"He can see both past and future. There is no ponderous linear time for someone, like your father, who has passed beyond these rudimentary material bonds. All time is like a silk ribbon for him, you see. You can gather both ends and make a loop, like so." Yang picked up a silk napkin, made a loop, and pinched the narrower ends together. "There." She studied her handiwork with pleasure. "Past and present converging. And to one standing in the middle"—she held the model up for her daughter to see—"all time is equally visible, all events equally visible. Invisibility is only a concept held on to by the blind. There is no difference, no distinction at all between the having happened, the happening at present, the about to happen, and the not yet having happened. They are all the same to the one who stands in the middle."

Dusk was descending on the courtyard garden, the changing light lending an air of transfiguration and strangeness to Madame Yang's words. The groundskeepers and handmaidens had long since retreated into the house, and the servants knew to stay away. Here and there nightbirds tested tentative songs—pale, shy notes that would blossom into full composition under cover of dark. Insects whirred their grating tunes in the tall grasses by the carp pond, frogs croaked, and the darkening air was cool and charged.

"Sometimes his apparition wavers as if it has not quite fixed itself upon this material plane," Mother continued. "Other times, it is quite substantial. At those times I am more than certain that I will be able to feel the warmth of his breath," Yang said fondly. "He has seen the future and the birth of your child," she added.

"Will it be male or female, Mother?"

"He did not say."

"And you did not ask?"

"One does not ask a soul in such a state of passage. One simply listens," her mother said with the certain dignity of a scholar correcting a textual error. "But he said it: you should wait no more than a fortnight. Opportunity presents itself like a door in a windowless mansion of solid granite walls," Madame Yang went on in her soft, compelling tone. "And only the very brave take those doors when they appear."

"Never mind, Mother," said Wu bluntly. "I will take care of matters." She did not necessarily believe in her mother's visions, but she believed in the infallibility of her words.

"And the rest will follow. That is his . . . "

"Prediction?" Wu finished for her.

"Heavens, no, child, predictions are for the blind," Madame Yang corrected her as she rose from her seat. "Your father makes statements of fact. He makes *proclamations*."

Lady Wu sat in the early-morning light of the nursery, her newborn daughter on her lap. She looked with wonder on the miniature perfection of the infant's features: the tiny, delicately sculpted curved lips, the shiny eyelashes lying along the cheek, the translucent skin with blue veins running like tendrils beneath. She opened one of the diminutive fists and spread out the fingers, examining the whorls on the palm and fingertips, and turning the little hand over, inspected the impossibly small but perfectly complete pink fingernails, like chips of mother-of-pearl. The infant lay on her back in the strange state of torpor peculiar to newborns: not asleep, but not awake, either, arms and legs jerking like a dreamer's and a troubled frown between the brows, as if concentrating on some inner discomfort. Wu put her forefinger between her daughter's eyes and smoothed out the worried wrinkle there; the baby tightened her hands into fists and waved them about.

She opened the front of her robe, and sitting in the shaft of early sunlight, nursed the child for a while. She watched the small face, the opaque eyes that opened occasionally as the infant fed. When the baby had had her fill and began to doze, Wu rose, taking great care not to wake her, and laid her down on her bed.

Lady Wu listened. There were no voices nearby, no footsteps in the hallway. She was quite alone. She picked up a thick quilt and walked over to where the baby lay; she looked down on her daughter, memorizing the sleeping infant features. You are going to help to make your father great, she whispered, then put the quilt over the child's face and pressed down with all her weight.

Much later, she felt as if she were waking from a dream. She opened her eyes, saw that the baby had stopped moving, and lifted her weight off the quilt. She turned the baby over onto her belly, arranged the limbs in a natural sleeping position, and pulled the coverlet up.

She lay in her bed, the pillows arranged behind her, her hair loose and disheveled as if she had just awakened. She listened to Kaotsung's approaching footsteps, his polite knock on her door.

"My lord does not need to knock on my door," she called out, just as she always did, and he put his face around the door, just as he always did, and smiled at her before entering the room.

"I thought perhaps you might want to rest for a longer time this morning," he said solicitously.

She watched him cross the floor. She knew that general consensus held that he was a weak young man who walked perhaps a shade on the irresolute side of life, not at all like his father, Taitsung, beloved and practically worshiped as a god; but the youthful Emperor's comeliness and physical symmetry made a satisfactory outline of manly strength in her eyes. The rest she could fill in. She had strength to spare, she knew, and she was about to make a gift of some of it to him. He was about to become a much stronger man. She smiled.

"I am feeling quite well!" she said, taking his hand as he

knelt at her bedside. "I am a very happy woman." She let go of his hand and pulled his head toward her, compelling his face into the still-soft flesh of her belly. "But I fear I have disappointed you," she said in a sad voice.

"Disappointed me?" he cried, raising his head. "That would not be possible. How?"

"Well," she said, "the baby is very beautiful . . . "

"The most beautiful thing I have ever seen," he declared.

" . . . but the baby is a girl. I wish I had given you a son."

"I don't want a son," he said fervently, kissing her hands. "I want daughters, from you, who will grow up to be just like you."

"What a thing to say," she said, smiling and shaking her head. "An Emperor saying he doesn't want sons. You are just trying to spare my feelings."

"No. I mean it," he said, his voice muffled in the bedclothes.

"Then you love her?" she asked.

"She is part of you, and part of me. I love her," Kaotsung said with feeling.

"Let's look at her together," Wu said, as if the idea had just occurred to her. "Let's have them bring our daughter to us so that we may look at her perfection. And you can tell me everything about her that pleases you."

She rang the little bell that called the handmaiden, and dispatched the girl to the nursery to fetch the baby.

"Make sure she is clean and sweet," she called after the servant. Looking at Kaotsung, she smiled. "Tell her her father wishes to see her."

The sun slanted across the bed. Kaotsung, still on his knees, sprawled his top half across Wu while she caressed his neck and shoulders. He pulled himself up a little farther so that more of his weight rested on her, and ran his lips over the skin on her neck.

"How much longer . . . ?" he whispered.

"Oh, at least a fortnight," she answered. "Perhaps longer." He moaned with frustration.

"But it has been ten days already since the child was born," he protested weakly, breathing onto her collarbone and pressing his pelvis against her ever so slightly.

"If my lord wishes it, then it will be sooner," she said in a humble tone. "I will risk injury if his need for me is so great that he cannot wait."

"No, no, no!" he protested. "No. I can wait. If I must. But . . . "

She pulled his head up by the ears and gave him a conspiratorial smile.

"But don't worry," she said slyly. "You will be taken care of. I am nothing if not a very . . . *resourceful* woman," she finished, and put her tongue onto one of his eyelids. "There are many other tortures that I can inflict on you, are there not?" she whispered then. "Why, I can think of all sorts of things." She moved her hands down and gave him a dig in the flesh alongside his rib cage, causing him to writhe and laugh, his face buried in the sweet-smelling quilts.

"Madame?" A tremulous female voice from the direction of the doorway caused Wu to abruptly cease her tickling and Kaotsung's laughter to die on his lips. They both looked up to see the handmaiden standing on the threshold, a bundle in her arms, her face white with fear.

The servants tiptoed about, in awe of Lady Wu's terrible grief. She had wailed and cried without stopping for a day and a night now. Long, piercing screams of agony were followed by low, gravelly moans of mortal anguish. The voice would rise again, keening and sharp, before disintegrating into sobs. Then the screams would start again, hoarse and powerful.

Where did she get her strength? they asked one another. For she was also tossing furniture about, breaking things, kicking the walls. She sounded like an elephant on a rampage.

She had called for her mother the day before, and Madame Yang had been fetched from her home in the city. Immaculately dressed and made up as if for a grand occasion, rustling with self-importance, she had arrived at the palace yesterday afternoon and gone into her daughter's chambers. Now it was morning, and Madame Yang was still in there with her. Some of the servants whispered to one another that they believed they could distinguish two different voices screaming and wailing in turn. Some of the other servants rejected the idea as ridiculous; what mother would actually encourage her daughter to grieve so intemperately, so exhaustingly and agonizingly?

When Madame Yang had swept into the palace the day before, they had all been startled at the resemblance between mother and daughter. And not just that—the two women also looked as if they were the same age. Lady Wu, as everyone knew, was twenty-seven years old; her mother did not look any older. She is forty-one, Lady Wu's handmaiden had whispered; she was only fourteen years old when Lady Wu was born. They are practically the same person.

And where was the Emperor? Pacing the halls, helpless, shattered, dazed. He appeared from time to time, his face white, and knocked and pleaded, but the two women behind the closed doors ignored him, and the wailing continued. The sounds were pure torture to him, that was obvious. He covered his ears and groaned, his face a mask of impotent misery. He would leave, only to return and try again later.

A terrible, terrible thing, the servants told each other, to shut him out like that. He would do anything for her. Did the women think that he did not grieve, too? some of them asked. Yes, but a mother's grief, others said . . . it is always worse. No one can know a mother's grief.

Toward early afternoon, the crying stopped abruptly. The door to Lady Wu's chambers opened a short time later, and Madame Yang emerged, looking as immaculate as she had the day before when she arrived. Without a word to anyone, she swept out of the palace, silks rustling and jewelry tinkling.

Kaotsung held both of Lady Wu's hands tightly and gazed at her ruined, swollen face. Her hair hung down, tangled into clumps, and there were long self-inflicted scratches on her arms and chest. Her face was vacant, her eyes dry and exhausted. The room was a shambles. The curtains had been torn down, vases smashed, tapestries and quilts ripped into shreds, furniture splintered and overturned, and food thrown against the wall. Lady Wu's robes hung in tatters from her body. She sat, saying nothing, eyes half closed.

"Please," Kaotsung whispered. "Tell me what I can do to make you happy again. I am begging you." She raised her eyes and looked hard at him.

"Bring my firstborn back to me. Restore her to life and put her in my arms."

"I would if I could," he cried. "I would do it a thousand times!" He put his head down and began to sob.

"Or . . . " Lady Wu began in a small voice. He raised his head eagerly.

"What? What? Anything. I will do it."

She looked at him.

"Make me your Empress," she said.

Kaotsung sat back, mouth open, unable to reply.

"But . . . " he faltered.

"Make me your Empress, and you will give me joy. Nothing will ever take away this pain. It will live, coiled like a snake inside me for the rest of my life. But that is one joy you could give me."

"But I already have an Empress," Kaotsung protested weakly. "You know that. Chosen for me by my father. I cannot—"

"You disgust me," she said then. "You say you will do anything for me. Here is a simple thing, and you say you cannot do it."

"But it is like asking me to bring the infant back from the dead," he protested. "It is impossible. It cannot be done. I . . . I would have to depose the Empress, overturn every precedent, cause terrible grief, go against the will of the Council of Six and my own dead father! And the family of the Empress would turn against me and all my descendants. Probably for generations! What you are asking would tear me in two!"

She said nothing, but lowered her eyelids, let her shoulders sag, and looked down at the floor.

"Very well," she said softly. "Very well." Kaotsung was on his feet, walking back and forth helplessly, desperately.

"Please," he begged, arms spread supplicatingly. She said nothing. Kaotsung stopped pacing and looked at her. Then he found the only object in the room that had not been destroyed, an empty chamber pot peeking out from under the bed. He picked it up and hurled it against the wall.

The old men of the Tsai-hsiang, the Council of Six, looking like a group of wise and venerable turtles, the wrinkled and sagging flesh of their faces furrowed with disbelief, consternation, and outrage, sat facing Emperor Kaotsung.

"We cannot permit it," said Sui-liang, the oldest of them, the loose folds under his chin quivering. "Your father charged us with a sacred duty, to watch out for you, to be his eyes after his death."

"You would not even think of doing this if it were your father sitting before you," said Wu-chi. At sixty he was the youngest of the Council members. "To defy us is to defy your father. Why, we *are* your father!" he declared, raising his hands and shaking them at Kaotsung. "She is a perfect Empress. Your father loved her. The people love her."

"She lacks all of the worst female traits," said old Han-yuan. "She is an innocent. She is not ambitious, or vain, or scheming. She is not jealous. She is graceful and modest. She is beautiful. And she has given you a son!" he finished, his cracked old voice rising in agitation. "What can you be thinking of?"

Kaotsung said nothing, but sat nervously chewing the inside of his mouth.

"I should not have to answer to anyone," he said finally. "If I want the Empress deposed, I should not have to explain my reasons. It should be enough for you to know that I *have* my reasons."

"You young fool!" cried Lai-chi then. "Look on the face of your father and say that! Do you care nothing for posterity? For the Empress's family? Do you wish to make enemies of them for generations to come? What do you think the stability of good government rests on? The wishes of one selfish young man?" he said with passion.

"At least think of the people," Wu-chi said in a more kindly tone, placing a placating hand on his colleague's trembling arm. "They are like . . . like children, in a sense. They need to know that the lives of those who govern them are firm, are not subject to the vagaries of human indecision and fate the way their own lives are. You are responsible to them!"

"In another sense," said Min-tao, shaking his head, "your life is not your own. You would do well to remember that. You belong to the people, to your father's memory, to history."

"Wait," said Ho-lin, who had said nothing at all until now, but had sat with his wary old eyes trained on Kaotsung. "I have a question for the young Emperor. Does he have . . . a replacement in mind? Is he trying to remove the Empress because of some shortcoming of hers, or does he wish perhaps to put someone else in her place?"

Kaotsung shifted in his seat.

"It is personal," he said tersely, not meeting the old men's eyes.

"I think you had best tell us," said Ho-lin.

"Yes," said Lai-chi, his voice still angry but quieter now. "You had best tell us everything."

"It is Wu Tse-tien," Kaotsung answered reluctantly. "Lady Wu. I wish for her to be my Empress." The six old men could not have looked more appalled if he had told them he wished to marry his mother.

"Wu Tse-tien!" cried Han-yuan, looking around in disbelief. "But . . . but she was a consort of your father's! It is quite disgraceful enough that you have bedded her. It is already a terrible scandal. But to make her your Empress! To destroy a sacred marriage vow in order to elevate a tainted liaison, for the sake of your . . . your . . . intemperate passions . . . your selfish, vulgar needs . . . your . . . " he spluttered, unable to finish.

"It would be incest, pure and simple," said Min-tao, in a voice flat with finality, rising to his feet with effort. "You may as well go to your father's mausoleum and urinate on it. I will hear no more," he said, turning and leaving the room. The others, muttering and shaking their heads, also began to rise from their chairs.

Kaotsung rose and shoved his own chair roughly back in exasperation. Sui-liang came around the table and seized his arm. The oldest of the ministers looked up at the younger man with his watery ancient eyes, bright with fervor.

"Think about what you are doing," he said urgently. "Remember you can tell me anything. Anything! That is why I am here! I am your friend before I am anything else!" He leaned closer and spoke in a confidential tone. "I was not always the shriveled old carcass you see before you now. I was a young man once, too."

Kaotsung looked at the old man for a moment as if he could almost believe such a preposterous claim, but the look did not last. The younger man could not speak. The face of his father's old friend was so earnest, so imploring, so full of confidence that the young Emperor would come to his senses, that Kaotsung found himself paralyzed. All he could do was shake his head sorrowfully. Wu-chi walked to old Councillor Sui-liang's side and put his hand on his shoulder. Sui-liang released the Emperor's arm and looked into Wuchi's eyes and nodded.

"Sui-liang is right!" Wu-chi now said. "And you can talk to me, too. You will come and visit me privately, eh?" he said. "You will come and tell Wu-chi everything before you do anything rash. I know you will." And he gave Kaotsung an affectionate squeeze on the arm before taking his leave.

Miserably, Kaotsung sat down again. He saw that the old men were right. It was impossible. The pain and upheaval that lay ahead if he proceeded would be terrible indeed. Wu would have to settle for other consolations. She could be promoted in rank—perhaps to Most Favored Consort. He would even build her her own palace if she wanted it. And she could have more children. The shock of losing her firstborn had obviously unhinged her. But with time, she would get over it. He was resolved: he would tell her it was impossible.

But he did not go right away; he sat for a long time, unable to exert the will to move from his chair, feeling like a sleeper who wants to wake up but cannot make his arms and legs obey him.

Lady Wu listened very calmly and with perfect composure while Kaotsung told her of his decision. Her chambers had been restored to order, and she herself was groomed and whole again, her long sleeves covering the scratches on her arms.

"We must think of my father," he said. "We both loved him, did we not? For a Confucian, it would be the worst kind of filial ingratitude on my part, an unforgivable insult to his memory to wait until he is dead and buried and then undo his work."

He relaxed as he spoke. She was listening. His words sounded right. He was being firm and sensible. She would see that what she asked was out of the question. "I know that you would never ask me to insult my father's memory," he finished. "I know you loved him too." He waited, holding her hand, rubbing it tenderly.

"I know who killed the baby," she said then.

"What are you talking about?" he said, startled and alarmed. "No one killed the baby. It simply died. The physician said so. They do that sometimes. Their life force is fragile, not firmly rooted, and they . . . they simply die!"

She raised her eyes. He felt all his strength and resolve drain out of him at that moment.

"My baby did not 'simply die,' " she said in a voice that chilled him. "She was murdered."

"But . . . but . . . who?" he asked lamely, his heart thudding panic. She regarded him for another moment before answering.

"It was the Empress."

"What?" he cried, dropping her hand. "You are mad!"

"It is true," she said, then lowered her voice to a whisper. "I have proof. She was *seen*."

Kaotsung rose and stalked to the end of the room and back again.

"You are turning the world inside out for me," he said. "You are making me think I have lost my mind! The Empress a killer!" He sat again, shaking his head dumbly from side to side.

"I have proof," she repeated. "But I am prepared to spare her." Kaotsung looked up in disbelief. "I have thought of a way to hide the fact that she is a murderess. I, too, am thinking of your father's memory. It would not do at all to have this get out. It would be the worst possible scandal. And I am prepared to make the sacrifice. Much as I would like vengeance for my child's death," she said, her voice tightening with sorrow, "I will do this thing for you." She lowered her face humbly.

"But I cannot comprehend it . . . " he began again helplessly.

"What we will do," she said, "is make a pact between us. We will keep this ghastly knowledge to ourselves forever. The Empress must be deposed, obviously, but we will tell the world something else entirely. Something that will cast no aspersions on your father's memory, that no one can argue with, and that will remove her with a minimum of disgrace and conflict."

"What would that be?" he asked, shaken.

"It is so simple," she said, taking his hand and pressing it to her bosom. "You will make a simple public declaration. You will say that you have developed a physical aversion to the Empress."

"Oh, now I am completely mad," he said, pulling his hand away. "I am sure she would rather be called a murderess! She does not deserve such a terrible insult!"

"A murderess does not deserve an insult?" Wu said fiercely. "She deserves death, but not an insult? The woman who killed my daughter—*your* daughter—does not deserve an insult?"

"But I cannot believe that she is a murderess!" he shouted.

"Hush!" Wu said, covering his mouth.

"I cannot believe it," he said in a low, rasping voice.

"You do not know what a jealous woman is capable of," she said sadly. "I do." She picked his hand up again. "Now it is my turn to implore *you*. Think of the ignominy. Your father's choice for Empress a killer. His memory defiled. Your family in disgrace. I will spare you all of it." She moved his hand up and down on her breast. "Otherwise, I will be forced to tell the truth, because I cannot let a murderess remain on the throne. My conscience will not permit it."

Kaotsung stood stunned and wordless, chewing his mouth, his eyes wild.

"Make the declaration," she said soothingly, "and it will be over easily and quickly. But let me make a suggestion, something that will make it easier for you and for her."

"What?" he said stupidly.

"Go and tell her yourself, first."

Wu-chi walked quietly and pensively by Kaotsung's side, holding his arm affectionately. The fatherly touch of those fingers made Kaotsung want to tell the older man everything, then give it all up and run and hide. He could not get the sound of the Empress's soft sobbing out of his mind. He had heard it through the door after he had left her: a low, steady, spasmodic sound that had bewildered him, because for a few moments he had mistaken it for laughter. He had pressed his ear to the door, and immediately realized his error. He had slunk away, full of shame and confusion, because somehow he had come to believe what Wu had suggested. He had actually felt a mild aversion to the Empress as she sat before him listening to his words. Her pain and humiliation had been odious to him, and he had thought that he really did not care to touch her ever again.

He had then gone to Wu-chi, because he did not know where else to go, and now they walked in the old man's private garden.

"In love, it is the wrong tactic to give a woman everything she wants," Wu-chi was saying sagely, reasonably. "Your father knew that. I know that. I am sure that somewhere inside, you know it too. Give her what she wants, and her respect for you will be eroded. Keep her just a little bit hungry!" They walked in silence for a few moments. "You may think that you are making Wu Tse-tien happy by giving her what she wants, but you will be wrong. You will actually be contributing to her discontent. She will want more. And what can you give her beyond making her Empress? Eh? There is nowhere else for her to go. So you see, you would be giving her a life of frustration rather than a life of contentment."

At the mention of Wu's name, Kaotsung felt Wu-chi's words the way a rock might feel water flowing over it. He felt dense and impervious. The more Wu-chi talked, the more the feeling grew. The desire to confess was leaving him. He felt himself solidifying.

"If you want to make her happy," Wu-chi continued, "show her a firm hand. It is what she really wants. Women are contrary creatures. They lack a man's simple directness. If you fail to grasp that fact, you will be swept into the tortuous convolutions of feminine thinking, and—"

"It is too late," Kaotsung interrupted, abruptly cutting off Wu-chi. The older man looked at him sharply.

"What do you mean? How is it too late?"

"The Empress has told me that she wishes to step down voluntarily." Wu-chi stopped walking and stared at him. "She does not wish to be my Empress any longer. We have ceased to be . . . physically compatible." He looked away from Wu-chi's eyes.

"You young fool," Wu-chi declared sorrowfully, all the patience and solicitude gone from his voice. "Then you leave us no choice. I had hoped to avoid this. I had hoped to appeal to your reason and judgment. Now I see that you have none. Therefore, we must protect you against your own stupidity, just as your father would have done. I and the other members of the Tsai-hsiang," he said, releasing the young Emperor's arm, "will be taking direct censorial action against your decision."

"There is nothing you can do, Wu-chi," Kaotsung said. "You cannot petition the throne. I *am* the throne."

"Your father, Taitsung, is the throne!" the old man retorted.

"My father is dead."

"His body may be dead, but I assure you he still lives. He knew you well. He left a set of provisions against just such an eventuality as this."

"He is dead," Kaotsung repeated.

"Not as long as I am still breathing," Wu-chi declared in an angry voice. "If your father stood before you at this moment and told you to cease and desist, you would do it."

"But he cannot," Kaotsung said patiently.

"Yes, he can! He is in me! His will is alive in me! On his deathbed, he transferred his responsibility for you to me. I have a document, in his own handwriting, a letter from him to you, his son. The letter says that you must obey me as if I were Taitsung himself!" He looked hard at Kaotsung to see the effect of his words. The younger man stood mute, taken aback, looking at Wu-chi as if perhaps he actually saw the face of his father in the old man's features. They stared at each other for several tense moments. Then Kaotsung let his breath out.

"No," he said at last. "No one, not even my father, can extend his will beyond the grave. My father's document has value only if I allow it to. His will lives only if I believe it does. Without my belief, my compliance, it is only a piece of paper. I am the Emperor now. My father is dead!"

Wu-chi was looking at him closely.

"Where did you acquire such stubbornness? I have never seen you display such strength of will before, boy," he said. "Never! What a shame that it is pointed in the wrong direction! What a shame that it is going to destroy you!"

Kaotsung turned to leave, but the voice of his father's old friend followed him out of the garden.

"Min-tao was right. You might just as well go to Tait-sung's mausoleum and urinate on it."

On the day that the Empress was to leave the palace, Kaotsung made sure that he was far away, on a hunting expedition in the Imperial preserve. His heart was not in it at all, though, and after letting several clear shots at whirring pheasants go by, he handed his bow to his steward and simply rode his horse along the shaded trails.

He had not liked the blank face that his steward presented that morning. Usually, the man was talkative and sociable; today he averted his eyes when the Emperor looked in his direction. And so it had been for many days with all of the servants and staff. His eunuchs hardly spoke at all, and he noticed that the eyes of many of the female servants were red and swollen. All of the females in the palace seemed to be similarly affected. He had listened at the entrance to the women's quarters in the Hall of Consorts the night before and had been annoyed to hear snuffling and weeping. Everywhere he looked, he encountered empty, sorrowful faces, absent gazes, and eyes that slid away from his.

The only eyes that met his directly were Lady Wu's. As the removal of the Empress proceeded, she had turned her undivided attention on him. I am healing, body and soul, she had told him just that morning, and had trailed her long nails down the side of his neck, causing him to shiver with anticipation. The festering wound of my grief is drying up, she had whispered. And you have done it. You are such a strong man, you have done it for me. He closed his eyes now, his horse rolling rhythmically beneath him, imagining her speaking those words to him, and pleasurably recreated for himself that same shiver of anticipation. Let them weep and avert their eyes, he thought; let them implore and reason.

Let them present petitions, too. Two days before, Wu-chi and the rest of the Council of Six had solemnly presented him with a long list of names of respected high ministers, most of them men who had been members of his father's government. Below each name was an eloquent paragraph, expressing that particular minister's opinion of Kaotsung's action. Impressive and eloquent, these memorials had conjured every possible consequence, from the erosion of unity within the governmental body to discontent—even rebellion—among the common people. Frightening pictures had been painted of his own moral disintegration, the dire effects of which would not be diluted to harmlessness for generations to come.

They had all been disturbing enough, but one of them, a particularly terse contribution by an old retired minister, had simply spoken of his father's heartbroken ghost trying in vain to lay his phantom hand on his errant son's shoulder. That one had made Kaotsung freeze inside. Only Lady Wu's touch had been able to free his joints, muscles, and will from seizing up completely. And she had said to him in the midst of it that he would do well to remember that Taitsung had been especially fond of her when she was one of his consorts. He liked to be touched, too, she had whispered. Like this. Surely the father could not blame the son for loving what he himself had loved, she had said, impaling him on a sharp point of ecstasy.

Later, he had retrieved the Council's document, squashed and wrinkled and stained with his own sweat, from among the tangled bedclothes. He had smoothed it out and rolled it up. One day he would bring it out again, and show them how wrong they were.

The afternoon shadows were growing long. He would ride for another hour or so, and then, under cover of twilight, return quietly to the palace. The Empress would be gone, and the new Empress waiting for him.

Empress Wu Tse-tien was elated at times. At other times she found herself full of anger. She could not always distinguish between the two feelings. Anger, carefully fanned like the flames of a fire, could be a source of pleasure that suffused her whole being with an intoxicating intensity of aliveness.

She could cultivate resentments inside herself, allowing them to fester to dangerous ripeness. She did not regret her anger. Rather, she was proud of it. It was a glorious thing: her power and her treasure.

The Empress Wu sat at the end of her day couch and felt refreshed. She had an appetite this morning. For what? She was not entirely sure. She had slept surprisingly well. She sat back, leaning on her hands, the sun warming her face, and indulged herself in the memory of some of her choicer rages. She was serene now, but she allowed herself a small surge of invigorating anger, a mere trace.

There was a last obstacle in the way of her happiness; for the night hours she had forgotten about it, entertained and distracted as she had been by her dreams. But now that obstacle returned to her. Six obstacles, to be precise—six very annoying old men who had no place in any dream of hers. They would have to go.

Wu Tse-tien rose from her couch and hastily yanked on a robe. There would be no more languorous basking in the sunlight for her this morning. Her movements became purposeful and deliberate. She went to the door and called for her handmaiden, and then, before the poor girl could respond, she shouted for several more servants of the inner household staff. Find my husband, she shouted to them. Now!

The sound of her own voice stimulated her to restless impatience. She must talk to him immediately. What she had to do required *him*, and it burned inside her worse than any impatience she had ever felt. She would conduct a search. She would turn the palace and the Halls of Government upside down; she would tear them apart if she must.

It was well after the time of the daily Morning Audience's dispersal from the Hall of Grand Harmony. It was nearly noon, was it not? Where *was* he?

When word was brought back to her that he was still at Morning Audience, she was furious. His place was with *her*. The session had gone on much longer than usual. She remembered that last night, as she had been drifting into sleep, Kaotsung had been talking about problems with granaries, or flooding, or some such matter in Kiangsi Province, but it had not made much of an impression on her at the time. Of course, she realized now, this was what was keeping him.

With each passing moment she became angrier. She

stormed around her apartments. It was not just the minor irritation of his absence at this moment—it was a growing conviction that when Kaotsung was not by her side, he was
ignoring her. There were only two places the Emperor of China
could be: by her side, and not. And the latter was definitely
an annoyance, and becoming by gradual degrees inexcusable.

She thought about Morning Audience: the sea of old men
in robes, surrounding him, faces earnest and full of importance,
each with a long, tedious memorial in his wrinkled old claw
of a hand, to be read, item by time-consuming item, then argued over, debated, dissected word by word. Her wrath was
building to a fine, heady, satisfying pitch.

Her eye roved about. Objects were beginning to irritate
her. Chairs, lamps, vases, statues; their stupid, inanimate cheer-
fulness fairly begged for punishment. She knocked some
bronze incense burners and candlesticks out of her way; they
made a great metallic clatter when they fell, bringing the
household servants rushing into the room. Only then did she
know what to do.

"Tell the Emperor that I am quite ill!" she ordered,
steadying herself against a table with one hand while pressing
the other to her breast.

"But . . . madame . . . he is in Morning Audience! Perhaps
the physicians should—"

"The physicians be damned!" she growled. "The physicians can go to hell riding on the backs of their dead mothers!
I don't care *where* he is. Tell him his queen is *dying!*"

"Yes . . . of course . . ." The chief household steward,
badly frightened, backed away from her with the others
crowded behind him. She advanced on them menacingly, a
heavy vase of flowers in her hands.

"Get him *now!*" she shouted. "Send runners to the Hall
of Grand Harmony. Tell them to bring him to me *now!*" The
servants crowded through the door, jostling one another in
their panic. She hurled the vase to the tiled floor as they fled
ahead of the madwoman's words: "Get him! Get him *now! I
am dying! Do you understand?*"

Never in recorded history had the sacred Morning
Audience—the solemn sea of hundreds of turquoise-, purple-,
and golden-robed magistrates standing in the perfectly
graduated rows of their ranks of office—been interrupted, not
even in times of war. Even the ultimate news of the ruling

household's demise waited until the veiled removal of the Emperor from his Peacock Throne and the final dismissal of the Audience of Ministers.

Eunuch servants of the Inner Household staff relayed the unbelievable words of the impending tragedy to the incredulous chief of the Inner Household staff, who informed the high advisers in the Imperial waiting chambers. The unfortunate messenger bolted breathless up the three tiers of steps to the Hall of Grand Harmony and burst through the great doors into the long central aisle, where he dropped immediately onto his hands and knees; facing the Son of Heaven from across the long expanse of the crowded hall, the messenger brought his forehead respectfully to the floor. Far down the long central aisle of the hall on his throne an astonished Kaotsung whispered to his councillor. The councillor then descended the stairs of the dais, passing the kneeling figure of a minister who had been in the process of delivering a memorial to the throne, and ordered the prone messenger at the far end of the hall to approach the Emperor. As all faces turned to follow this lone figure, the rustle of silks was accompanied by a wave of murmuring spreading through the Audience—a deep hum of speculating voices.

"The Son of Heaven commands you to speak. Our Divine Emperor is most curious to discover what news could be so important as to interrupt Morning Audience!" the councillor intoned.

The messenger fell to his knees again. The Emperor shook his head in disbelief and the councillor motioned for him to rise. The man stood up again, his eyes fixed firmly on Kaotsung's feet. "I have come to tell our August Son of Heaven that his Most Revered Empress is dying. . . . "

"The Court is in an uproar," Kaotsung said at last, quietly, tiredly, sitting on the edge of the couch where Wu lay.

"An *uproar*?" she asked from her prone position, as if she did not quite understand the meaning of the word.

"As soon after the funeral of my child and the deposition of my first Empress . . . "

"Your first what?" she said, as if this were another mysterious term, unknown to her.

"My first Imperial wife," he corrected himself. "You are the only true Empress, of course. But I am having a difficult time understanding what you want of me," he said patiently, sitting down again.

She sank back onto the cushions.

"All that matters is that I am ill," she said. "I need you by my side. The events of the last few months . . . " She let her eyes fill with tears. He picked up her hands and pressed them to his face, tears starting in his own eyes. She released a ragged sigh. "But you spend all morning at Audience, as if I do not even exist."

"The floods in Kiangsi . . . " he began feebly, his voice full of sorrow.

"But I . . . I am flooded with grief," she cried, putting her arms around his neck.

"There is much suffering," he said into her hair. "The people are dying by the thousands . . . flood dikes have given way from the rains . . . "

"Peasants can only die once," she said. "Theirs is an easy death compared to my heart's. The suffering of the great is deeper, commensurate with our place in the universe. That is our burden as ascended creatures. . . . I could suffer forever under your father's ruthless old councillors." She drew back and gazed at him sorrowfully.

"What would you have me do?" he asked helplessly. "Relinquish the Mandate? Relinquish the Council of Six, who share my burden? I am at a loss."

"You would as soon relinquish me, would you not?" she asked sadly, tears running down her face now. "You would toss me away, just as easily, just as arbitrarily, as you did the poor Empress. Merely because you found her physically objectionable?"

"Because *I* found her physically objectionable?" Kaotsung was stunned.

"Heaven has granted you ears like every other animal. Use them."

"*I* found the Empress physically objectionable? Am I mad? Those words originated with you!"

"Oh, so it was *I* who found her physically objectionable. *I* who developed a distaste for her flesh. I suppose it was *I* who was sleeping with her. Is that what you are implying?"

"But . . . " he began, but got no further.

"And I suppose it was I who sent her away? Will history record that a mere consort sent an Empress away, because she smelled bad? Future generations will not believe that the lowly wielded such power over the great Son of Heaven." She shook her head. "The great Kaotsung, history will say. A woman and six old men told him what to do. 'Such events,' historians will intone, 'are truly staggering in their mysterious implications.' "

Kaotsung rose yet again, clapping his hands to his head. "You are twisting everything out of recognition! I cannot keep up with you!"

"You are forgetting my anguish and pain. You only talk of your own." Tears welled again.

Kaotsung walked desperately to the window and back again, not knowing where to turn, rubbing his sweaty palms up and down his thighs. "What do you want of me?" he asked at last. "Please, tell me what it is you want!"

"There is no need to raise your voice at me, my husband," she answered almost meekly. "I want only what you want. I want what is best for the Empire."

"And what is that?"

"To get rid of your father's Council of Six," she answered matter-of-factly. "Those six ugly old turtles. Those old men who do not accept me as the rightful Empress. The ones who do not want me at your side," she added sadly.

"They are merely a cautious body," Kaotsung said apologetically.

"They are a *meddling* body," she shot back. "They poison the Court aristocracy against me." She paused and composed herself. "But that is not the reason that they must go. No. They must go because it is a rite of passage that your father requires of you! To prove to him that you are a true Emperor!"

"My father . . . ?" he began, utterly confused now.

"Did he not force his own father to abdicate?" she demanded. "Now you must do the same. You must force your father's ghost to abdicate." She took his hands and began to back toward the day couch. "And your father's ghost resides not in one place, but in six," she whispered, pulling him down with her.

They came from all over the city and even the province beyond: artisans, responding to a general call put out from the palace by the new Empress, Wu Tse-tien. They crowded against one another at the palace gates.

Each man believed that this was the opportunity that could change his life. If only his designs caught the fancy of the Empress, if only *he* was chosen. The notice she had put out

several weeks before had sent some of the artisans scurrying
to the libraries of Buddhist monasteries to educate themselves
as quickly as possible. Others, of course, were already quite
prepared from lifetimes of study. What the Empress wanted,
and what each man so fervently hoped to provide her with,
was a design, unique, original, never before seen in the world,
for a stupa—a Buddhist memorial shrine.

The rumor was that the shrine was to be for a member of
her family. No, said others, they had heard that it was in honor
of the late Emperor Taitsung, who himself had commissioned
the construction of many stupas, in honor of the men who had
fallen in battle helping him to achieve victories in war. No, said
others, it would be a travesty for her to be building a stupa for
the late Emperor. His ghost must already be seething, probably
ready to return to the moldering bones in his mausoleum, raise
them up again, and stalk furiously into the palace. Hadn't she
mocked and dishonored Taitsung himself by becoming Empress?

No one could quite believe it when the announcement
finally came. A design for the stupa had at last been selected
from among hundreds. The fortunate man whose work had
been chosen had been told for whom the memorial was to be
built. In the tradition of Emperor Kaotsung's late father, Taitsung, who built his memorial shrines for the brave dead who
gave their lives on the battlefield, a grand and glorious stupa,
bigger than that of any man, was to be dedicated to a nameless
ten-day-old female infant: Wu Tse-tien's firstborn, who had
died in the cradle.

They shook their heads, and asked each other the same
question over and over. Who *is* this woman?

4

The missive arrived one morning several months after the completion of the stupa. It bore the official seal of the Office of Historical Records; otherwise, Wu might not even have bothered to look at it.

She slit the seal with one of her long fingernails and flattened the parchment on her dressing table among the bottles of cosmetics and perfumes. She read slowly and carefully, almost laboriously. She was improving all the time, but she still had a frustrating sense of being shut out from the possible stray hidden nuance or subtle innuendo. She examined each character with a fierce, determined eye. Nothing would escape her.

To the Most Exalted, Rightful, and Worthy Empress of the Great T'ang, Wu Tse-tien, May She Live One Thousand Years:

The advent of the True Queen has inspired this humble Servant to seek the Truth of Truths embedded in the layers of History the way Gold lies in the Earth waiting to be freed by the hands of the Miner. This humble Miner-Servant believes that the comparison of Truth to Gold may be extended even further. What is Gold? It is the most Difficult of Metals to Obtain from the Stubborn, Protective earth, jealous at Giving Up her Treasures; but once it is Obtained, at Great Expense and Effort, It is shining, precious, dazzling, inspirational, and yet the most Malleable and Workable of metals, the Artisan's delight. It can be Worked to a Thickness No Greater than the Wing of a Moth, or it may be sculpted in Huge, Heroic proportions to rival the Light of the Sun. Its Nature is to Serve. And so it is with Truth.

Wu put down the letter and rubbed her eyes. She was intrigued. If she was not mistaken, this letter had nothing at all to do with the art of metallurgy. Her eyes returned eagerly to the page before her. She read the last line again before continuing:

> . . . And so it is with Truth.
>
> Why do we maintain Meticulous Historical Records? So that Posterity may Know us, we who Went Before Them. Obviously, we cannot leave anything so Vitally Important to Chance. Would Her Majesty consider allowing her Royal Gowns to be fashioned by Blind Seamstresses? Would she allow Herself to be dressed in the Dark for a State Occasion, with no knowledge at all of the Colors or Designs adorning Her? Of course not. And so it should be with the words Future Generations will read about us.
>
> Madame, no doubt you have hairdressers, seamstresses, and makers of jewelry to Serve You, to carry out your wishes and Valuable Perceptions. Similarly, I, Shu Ching-tsung, a Great Admirer of the True Queen Wu Tse-tien, Wish To Be Her most Attentive, Perspicacious, and Imaginative Personal Historian.

She raised her eyes from the paper and looked at her reflection. She almost laughed. Whoever this man was, he had practically read her mind. She had, in fact, been entertaining herself with a certain fantasy lately. People at court were still making her feel unwelcome, still whining and complaining, still comparing her to the first Empress with every breath. She had thought of many possible ways to silence them; her favorite idea had been to produce "evidence" that would compromise the Empress's virtue. Perhaps, she had mused, it would be possible to hire a man to step forward and declare that he had been the secret lover of the Empress. Someone lowly—even, perhaps, a servant. But she had discarded the idea; she could not, she knew, pay a man enough money to claim for himself a transgression punishable by forced suicide.

She rose from her dressing table, taking care with her bulging belly, six months heavy again with child. A personal historian. She turned the concept over in her mind. She had heard quite a bit from her husband's lips about "history," had she not? His discourses on Confucian filial piety invariably came around to the proper reverence for one's ancestors, the honored dead. She herself could see no reason to assume that the dead were better than the living simply by virtue of being dead; but ancestry was, apparently, everything. If so, then the opportunity was before her now. It would be well and good to prove that the Empress had been a whore or something along those lines, but with a bit of thought, a bit of planning, Wu knew she could do even better than that.

She sat down again, turned the historian Shu's letter over to its blank side, and seized her brow-painting brush. Dipping it into a pot of watery black eye paint, she began to write. Slowly, painstakingly, for her knowledge of the written language was not thorough, she constructed the characters for "first Empress" and "father." Carefully, she added the rest of the words which she thought would satisfactorily convey her wishes and the information he would need. If this man Shu was what he seemed to be, he should have no trouble interpreting her message. She felt the infant inside her moving, like a fish nibbling at her insides. It pleased her that this one was showing a marked tendency to respond to her thoughts, kicking, poking, and grabbing when her mind was most actively engaged. To her, these were the secret signals of an intimate conspirator. This one, she had decided, felt like an ally.

When she was finished, she rolled the paper up again and wrapped it in a piece of silk. She would send it back to Shu Ching-tsung immediately. She hoped that his response would be prompt; if there was one thing in this world she could not tolerate, it was to be kept waiting.

The handsomely bound pamphlet circulated the Court with the speed and thoroughness of a rumor of war.

Every hushed conversation that old Wu-chi happened to overhear was about the pamphlet. If he stood still and listened, he could almost hear a low murmur rising from everywhere in the Court and the city itself, and every voice spoke of one thing only—the pamphlet. He felt an unpleasant current running through his bones.

Now he sat in his office holding a copy of the pamphlet. He had determined that he would retreat to a quiet place where he could read it carefully and in privacy. A bowl of tea sat at his elbow; a bird sang on a branch outside his window. He made an effort to steady his hands.

He noted the stamp, plainly authentic, of the Office of Historical Records. The silk brocade in which the pamphlet was bound was expensive, the very best; so was the paper it was printed on. No cost had been spared. That fact alone increased his dread. He closed his eyes for a moment, then took a sip of hot tea, opened the pamphlet, and smoothed the paper. The first thing he saw was a name, and a title. Who was this Shu Ching-tsung, calling himself president of the Office of Historical Records? He began to read.

A CORRECTIVE BIOGRAPHY OF WANG CHU-I, FATHER OF THE RECENT EMPRESS WANG

Sad and Troubled in our Hearts as we may be over the recent Deposition of the Empress Wang, we may take Comfort in the fact that we are only witnessing History Righting itself, a natural process for which we should be grateful. It is the same Miraculous Process by which the body, in its Infinite Mysterious Wisdom, heals itself when it is sick or wounded. The Departure of the Empress was, Very Simply, Nature Itself correcting an Ailment. The Ailment lay in the Royal Lineage. We should be Glad in our Hearts that Nature moves so Quickly and Expediently to Correct an Ailment in the Royal Lineage, for it Demonstrates to us that Royal Lineage is as Real, as Necessary, and as Decreed by Nature as the blood that flows in our Veins, as the Sun which rises and sets, as the Rivers which flow to the Sea.

The Ailment Troubling our Exalted Line of Succession grew from a case of Misrepresentation. As we all know, an Empress is like a Blossom on a Tree. In order for the Blossom to be flawless in its Beauty, fully formed and Sweetly Scented, the Tree, from which grows the Branch, from which grows the Twig which bears the Blossom, must be Sound. In the case of our Departed Empress, it is no Fault of her Own that the Branch that bore the Twig was less than Perfect and True.

The "biography" went on to assert that recently discovered journals of the deposed Empress's father revealed that though he was remembered as a worthy and trusted minister of Kaotsung's father, Taitsung, he was hiding a sordid past. Though it was true that he came from the Wang household, he was not related by blood to that noble family, the "biography" sadly revealed, but had been the offspring of a common household servant. It described his ambition as he grew up and went forth into the world, succeeding in many business endeavors, some of them less than scrupulous, and some of them downright traitorous. The text asserted that the sturdy war chariots used by traitorous forces seeking to oppose the revered Emperor Taitsung, and which carried death and bloody conflict against the T'ang itself, were made of wood procured from the western provinces by none other than Wang Chu-i.

The tale described how he grew rich from his enterprise, caring little about the erosion of land caused by the careless cutting of trees for his timber enterprise, and when the T'ang had finally vanquished its enemies, he inveigled his way into a high position in the new regime by adopting the good name of the household where he had once been only the son of a servant.

The final lines of the story asserted that it was little wonder that young Emperor Kaotsung had developed a physical aversion to the departed Empress Wang. He had no way of knowing it, but it was simply "Nature correcting itself."

Wu-chi closed the pamphlet. He had not known that she was capable of such thoroughness. His hands were shaking hard now, and the dread moved to his solar plexus and coiled there like a snake. The dead, the living; to the Empress Wu, they were the same. She would raise a pile of bones if she saw fit, or put the living in the ground if it suited her. She could look at a living man and see him as a corpse. And where did he, Wu-chi, dwell? Among the dead or the living? He did not know. He did not know at all.

He looked at the heading of the preposterous essay. Shu Ching-tsung. Who in Heaven's name was he?

Historian Shu was a diminutive man. Madame Yang liked that; it made him seem to belong to her, like a lapdog. And like a lapdog, he had a sort of pointy-eared attentiveness, his very being quivering with an alert, energetic readiness to comply that pleased her very much. She smiled. She could barely suppress an image of herself hurling a stick and Historian Shu racing after it, robes flapping, feet kicking up dirt and grass. She felt comfortable with him right away.

No one had the slightest bit of information about Shu's past. No one could recall a single thing about his appointment.

He was the sort of invisible little man whom no one noticed—until this moment, when he had burst out of total anonymity into being chief historian, president of the entire Board of History, a position that came with a handsome salary. They certainly noticed him now, she thought with pleasure.

He claimed to hold both the Ming Ching and the Chin Shih degrees, but Madame Yang doubted this could be true. After all, the final rite of passage administered to those who successfully passed the grueling three-day written civil service examinations was an interview by the Board of Examiners and Appointments. It was here that they considered other, less tangible qualities than academic excellence: demeanor, comportment, self-assurance, even the quality of the voice—all components of the man who would assume the honored robes of officialdom in the greatest government between heaven and hell. Listening to Shu's high, comical little voice and watching his scurrying, obsequious gait, Madame Yang doubted very much that the Board of Examiners would have granted him the full degrees.

But the truth about Shu was irrelevant, she knew. There was certainly no need to pursue it any further. What did it matter? The fluid, flexible nature of truth was what they were here to discuss today anyway, was it not? If Historian Shu could reshape others' pasts, then he could do the same with his own. It was sufficient to know that he had come to her daughter, the Empress Wu, through his own enterprising and imaginative spirit. That was recommendation enough for her.

Madame Yang was gratified by the rapidity with which Shu's household steward had returned his master's calling card to the Yang family compound that afternoon. Of course, Shu Ching-tsung could hardly afford to ignore an invitation from his sponsor's household and the mother of the Empress. Still, Madame Yang felt that Shu's promptness and enthusiasm were genuine. He had an intensity and sincerity that pleased and flattered her. She knew that theirs would be a productive relationship.

And it took them no time at all to get down to the subject at hand: the nature of truth.

"It is a most grand and elegant courtyard, madame," the high-pitched voice said, its owner striving to keep up with his hostess. Madame Yang was a tall woman, as was her daughter, and in her enthusiasm to show Shu the next magnificent thing on her property, she unconsciously relaxed back into her long, easy stride, causing the little man to struggle to keep up. "It is true that one can tell the quality and breeding of the master, excuse me, in your case, Madame Yang, the mistress of an estate by the excellence of placement. Each object in perfect, sensitive balance. Each shrub and stone, each statue and tree . . . " Shu was breathing hard as they reached a delicate bridge arching over a miniature waterfall. Madame Yang slowed down just long enough for him to catch up with her.

"The greatness that you see is the inheritance of my deceased husband. It was his desire," she said, and paused thoughtfully, "to reflect in his house and grounds the nobility and greatness that is everywhere evidenced around us."

"Ahhh . . . the late Master Wu Shih-huo . . . the Empress Wu's most august father." Shu nodded thoughtfully. "Of course. Of course!"

"I am merely my husband's caretaker, if you will allow that," Madame Yang said with false humility.

They turned into a long pillared corridor and made their way back from the rear gardens toward the estate's elaborate reception gallery. "Master Shu, I must tell you that I am feeling quite comfortable with you. It is as my husband told me. He said that you would be a most compassionate ally."

"Excuse me, Madame Yang. But did you say that your husband spoke to you of me? He has been dead for . . . "

"Ten years," Madame Yang replied.

"Ten years," Shu repeated. "I regret that he could not possibly have known me; I have been here no more than seven years . . . " He had to stop talking for a moment to hurry after his hostess. Her chin was raised dreamily, a serene little smile on her lips. " . . . though it is my deepest regret that he and I could not have known each other—"

"Forgive me, Master Shu," she interrupted. "Perhaps I neglected to explain everything to you earlier." She stopped in the middle of the corridor and turned and faced him. "It is a terrible oversight on my part. You see, it was my husband who invited you here."

"But, madame, your husband is dead," Shu said carefully, watching her face.

"To some, Master Shu. But to others who grasp that there are alternate planes of existence . . . "

Shu's face relaxed with these words, and he smiled.

"Then you are a devout Buddhist, Madame Yang?"

She ignored Shu's question and continued.

"It was my husband who first directed your literary and historical talents toward my daughter." Shu remained silent, waiting. "You may have thought that you acted independently in presenting your services to my daughter. But that was only an illusion." Yang walked over to the balustrade and ran her fingers over the smooth wood of the rail as she stared absently out into the courtyard.

"Perhaps I do not understand everything as clearly as I should, Madame Yang," Shu said with careful diffidence.

She turned and smiled compassionately. "Such an understanding of these things can rarely be expected even of the most devout."

"Of course."

"Everything you see around you, Master Shu, all the greatness and beauty of this house and its grounds, the furnishings, the family's Buddhist oratory, the rockery, the great reception hall ... everything that you have so graciously admired is, in fact, *not* a reflection of my husband's family but rather that of the once great household of Yang. *My* family. A household that extends back to the Sui Dynasty before the founding of our T'ang, and to the Northern Chou before that, and to the great families that sponsored the Buddha's teachings."

Madame Yang moved away from the rail and began to walk again, slowly and reflectively this time. Her eyes were clouded with sadness now. "Unlike the Yang clan, my late husband's memory is lost to history, Master Shu. The Wu clan, although tracing itself back to the Wei Dynasty three centuries ago, is not numbered among the national aristocracy. His only hope was in marriage and an alliance with our great family name of Yang. But the time has come for *him* to be great. He is an Empress's father. It would not do for my daughter's enemies to point to the 'unsuitability of her birth.' The name of Wu must share greatness alongside the name of Yang. My husband, Wu's father—Wu Shih-huo—must be a great man. He begs for a new life, Historian!" She said with forceful conviction. "Can you understand that?"

Now Shu was smiling broadly.

"I *quite* understand, madame."

"You have been singled out by forces beyond your understanding. You have been brought to us by the good fortune of a universe that understands that history must be refashioned to fit our multiple realities. That is the task—no, I should say the destiny—of the one who is chosen to prepare our names and lives for posterity, who sets our names into eternity with his indelible inks."

Shu squared his shoulders with obvious pride and joined Madame Yang at the balustrade. He looked admiringly at her profile. She was an elegant and beautiful woman, like her daughter; the difference in their years was barely noticeable. She had expressed much of his own feelings regarding the nature of truth. Who was to say that what could have been was any less true than what had actually been? And if what had actually happened was obviously an error, or if it was not colorful or fascinating enough, or if it led in an obviously unsuitable direction, was it not our responsibility to repair it? Do we build a house upon a dilapidated foundation, or do we repair that foundation first, make it sturdy, make it fit the rooms we intend to build above?

Together they looked out over the carp pond in silence; the reeds above the water joined with the reflected images below to form the strange angular lines of some mystic script.

Shu spoke in hushed tones as if Yang's words had suddenly brought him into a new and powerful reverence for everything around him.

"Yes," he said. "I understand perfectly. But may I ask, madame," he began, making an effort to phrase his words in his most diplomatic manner, "how is it that your husband—"

"He comes to me often in my dreams, Master Shu," she answered before he had finished his question. "He has transcended the barriers between the worlds."

Shu nodded. "Death is certainly the ultimate transcendence, madame," he said vaguely, not quite sure what it meant, but wishing to keep the conversation going.

"Hardly the ultimate, Master Shu. Only the first stage," she corrected politely. "About those things, Master Shu, I should enjoy talking with you. It is all in the Divine Sutras of the Vijnanavadin. We will have much time later to speculate on the philosophical and the ontological . . . much time. But the work before us is urgent. My husband appeared to me because he no longer wishes to be remembered as he was."

At these words, the little historian immediately assumed an interested, professional air.

"Madame Yang, what is the . . . forgive the expression . . . *truth* concerning the late Wu Shih-huo?" he asked now with the same candor with which she had spoken.

"That he was nothing," she offered without a moment's hesitation. "At least in terms of the sort of family connections befitting the father of an Empress. That are *required* by tradition, by custom, by consensus."

"Then he was not . . . a hero of the founding of the T'ang as the Empress Wu would like us to believe?"

"Hardly. My daughter has almost convinced herself that it is so, but not quite." They had entered the great gallery by now, and stood in its vaulted space. She spoke with amused forbearance, as if the facts she related were mere inconveniences soon to be set right—which they were. "Wu Shih-huo did not aid Kaotsu in the founding of the T'ang against Yang-ti, the mad Emperor of the Sui. In fact, Master Shu, far from playing a role in aiding Kaotsu and Taitsung in restoring the land to unity and peace under the T'ang, my late husband had earlier aided mad Emperor Yang-ti by selling him the timber for the construction of two hundred thousand war chariots with which to battle the T'ang. No, he was scarcely a founder of the great T'ang," Madame Yang said, turning away from Shu and toward the gardens, laughing. "In fact, he made the fortunes that kept this great house alive—and keeps it alive to this day—in supplying the Empire's enemies."

Now Shu was positively beaming with admiration.

"Quite so, madame, quite so," he said. "And was it not so that your esteemed husband also . . . *adopted* the family name of Wu . . . ?"

"Quite so, Historian Shu," she answered, and smiled back at him. "Quite so. Oh, and Historian," she said then, gazing out over the grounds, "not all of your work for us will be of such a grave nature. My daughter and I have another project in mind after this one has been completed. One which you might call a *reward* for your serious efforts."

"Excellent, madame," Shu said with a bow. "I am nothing if not a fun-loving fellow at heart."

Councillor Wu-chi stared across his desk at Kaotsung. His old eyes were bright and black as they studied the young man across the table, who sat fidgeting, folding and unfolding his arms. Between the two men lay three finely bound pamphlets, each with a silk ribbon around it. Wu-chi pushed one across the table, propelling it away from himself as if it were a rotten fish.

"What do I tell you now, son of my good friend?" he said,

shaking his head. "You do know how to read, I presume? Yes? Then surely you have perused these literary masterpieces and have an opinion!" Kaotsung avoided looking directly at the pamphlets or at Wuchi's face.

"I have not had time to read them, Wu-chi," he said.

"You have not had time?" Wu-chi replied matter-of-factly. "No doubt, then, you have had one of your advisers study them and summarize them to you. Yes?"

Kaotsung shifted his feet unhappily.

"Well, then, allow me," Wu-chi said, reaching for the pamphlet nearest him.

"Wu-chi, please," Kaotsung said irritably, turning his face away.

"This first one is most interesting," Wu-chi continued, unabashed. "A 'biography' of the deposed Empress Wang's father, Wang Chu-i. Fascinating reading. One can learn so much at the hands of a skilled wordsmith. And just when one thinks that there is nothing left in the universe to learn, behold! Another great work of historical significance!" He held up a second pamphlet, his eyes fixed on the Emperor, and untied the silk ribbon. "A 'biography' of Wu Shih-huo, father of the Empress Wu Tse-tien." He tossed the pamphlet so that it skittered across the desk and came to a halt against Kaotsung's arm. The Emperor made no move to pick it up. "I am *fascinated* to learn that Wu Shih-huo, and not Wang Chu-i, was the honored close friend, the invaluable ally, of your father, Taitsung. That it was *he* who performed such valuable service in defeating Yang-ti and consolidating the T'ang, and that Wang Chu-i, the man that *I* knew, was nothing more than a usurper and an opportunist! It is extraordinary how one can know a man well for years, and work with him, and then find that one knows so little about him!" he finished with heavy sarcasm.

"What does it matter, Wu-chi?" Kaotsung said weakly. "They are both dead. They will never read these pamphlets, these silly stories."

"I can scarcely believe that I am listening to a Confucian telling me that it is acceptable to defame dead men," Wu-chi said, shaking his head. "The truth, young Emperor Kaotsung, is almost too embarrassing to speak aloud. That you are *afraid!*" He spoke these last words with fierce emphasis. Then he dropped his voice to a near-whisper, leaning forward to speak. "Afraid of your *wife!*" he hissed. "Why?" Wu-chi asked quietly. "Why do you not stand up to her?"

"We do not know that she had anything to do with this," Kaotsung said with no conviction in his voice. Wu-chi only looked at him.

"Please," the older man said. "Let us not waste any more time in self-delusion. You know quite well that she is behind all of it. She and her witch-twin, Madame Yang. Fables. Historical transgressions. Spurious appointments!" With these last words Wu-chi's anger began to rise again. "At least tell me that I am wrong about *that*. That the Emperor of China has not allowed a woman to encroach upon his authority. That you appointed this . . . Shu Ching-tsung yourself. A bad choice, but your choice nonetheless. One that you can reverse!"

Kaotsung considered lying, telling the old man that he had indeed appointed this anonymous spinner of tales to the presidency of the Board of History. He began to open his mouth to speak, but desisted at the last moment. He looked back at Wu-chi, and saw that the other man had seen everything that had passed through his mind in those few moments.

"At least I do not lie to you, Wu-chi," he said tiredly.

"I am grateful for that, anyway," Wu-chi replied. " 'Chief Historian' Shu Ching-tsung! As if official positions were a joke, a game, a child's box of toys . . . no, a *woman's* box of paints and bangles, awaiting her frivolous pleasure." He stopped then, quieting his shaking voice and lowering himself back into his seat. "No. It is quite wrong to call her frivolous. These are not acts of frivolity, but deadly serious acts of war. War against this ruling house. War against this court. War against myself and my colleagues."

"Against you? But . . . but the tales were not about you," Kaotsung began.

"That is right, my young Emperor. They are tales about 'dead men,' as you so aptly put it. But you have not read them. I have told you what is in the first two pamphlets. But I have not told you anything about the third," he said, pushing it slowly and deliberately across the table. "I am not going to tell you anything at all about it. I am simply going to let you read it for yourself. And I agree with you on one point: they are all stories about dead men. Never mind that my colleagues and I are not quite in our graves. We *are* dead men."

Kaotsung took hold of the other man's arm. "I will speak to her, Wu-chi. I will reason with her. I promise that I will."

"You do not reason with witches," Wu-chi declared, twisting his arm free from Kaotsung's grip in firm defiance and rising from his chair. He came around the table, picked up the pamphlet, and dropped it into the Emperor's lap. "Not while you are under their spell."

Much later, when he was quite alone, Kaotsung finally brought himself to open the pamphlet. His stomach churned as he did so; he burped and swallowed, tasting the sour juice that rose in his throat. This reaction of his gut to an official document was not unusual; of late, everything that came to him—petitions, memorial drafts, civil appointment schedules, retirement and transfer requests—caused griping in his stomach or pressure in his head.

Last night the gingered fish, a longtime favorite, had turned on him. Fruit had always agreed with him before; this morning, however, it had caused a great heat in the center of his breast, which the Imperial physicians had carried away with adept circular massage. But now that that unpleasantness was gone, he could still taste the bean curd. Distressing. Food was the nurture of the body; eating and digesting should be a harmonious experience.

He closed his eyes and thought with longing of the hot sun on his back, the leaves caressing his face, the soft thud of hooves on a pine-needle-carpeted forest trail. Anything but this, he thought, opening his eyes again to behold the insidiously attractive and tastefully designed object in his hands. His stomach gave a long, low growl like faraway lions.

Kaotsung untied the silk ribbon and opened the cover. The paper was finer even than he had expected; the text, which had been set into print, was carefully and professionally done. The title was on a page by itself—an unusual arrangement: *A Tale of Six Fools*. On the next page, he read a brief admonishment: "*A Tale of Six Fools* is merely the contrivance of the author of this document—the president of the Board of History— and this work does not have any parallel in reality but has been written only in order to serve as an amusing parable."

Kaotsung took a deep breath and held it, then released it with a long sigh. He turned to the next page: *A Tale of Six Fools* appeared; this time, set beneath it in tiny characters, was an emendation that stated: "Perhaps should be read as *A Tale of Six OLD Fools*." He gently massaged his chest, imitating the motions of the physician that morning. His eyes began their forced journey down the page.

There were six men, whether they had been friends from birth or had been acquainted with each other from early family connections is not known. But they were already old during the flagging days of the previous corrupt dynasty, and then much older when the new dynasty was founded. From the very beginnings of their inessential lives they were useless, dull-witted men. All of them had strange afflictions that affected the eyes and the Sea of Marrow. In short, they were either partially blind or totally muddle-headed.

These six men had paired themselves into three couples in an attempt to compensate for their physical deficiencies and mental failings. It was not successful. In the first couple, there was one man who could see things clearly at a distance but could make out nothing clearly close by and the other who could see things close by but hardly anything at a distance. In the second couple there was one who could see only those things for which he had a name: if he could not put a name to something he would then fail to see it; failing to see it, he would then fall over it until someone might name it for him. The other one continually forgot the names of everything he saw and then might think that everything was something else. If he saw a candlestick he might well take it for a tree; and if he saw a goat he might well take it for his neighbor's wife, of whom he was most fond. But at least he could give a name to things (albeit a wrong name) in order that his partner might see them. Then there was the third couple. The first man could see everything clearly and although he knew what everything was, he was completely unable to speak and write. And then there was the other, who in all ways seemed most normal. But anything that he might experience became quite confused in the retelling.

They were all six gathered in a wineshop in Loyang one day to discuss the nature of the world and the uses to which they might, at last, put themselves. They had no need of food and shelter, as the local residents always took pity on them. Nevertheless, they desired employment. When they had been in the wineshop some time and the drumtowers had rolled out the evening curfew, they were already very drunk with rice wine.

They began to make their way home but soon discovered that they were lost. They had managed to stagger drunkenly down to the canal, where they sat upon a parapet. But in their confusion, they were quite certain that they had wandered down to the River Lo and were now seated on her grassy banks.

In their drunken state and half asleep, they waited patiently by the canal, which they thought to be the River Lo. After some time they saw a pretty young girl with double topknots dressed in poor and ragged but immaculately clean clothes holding a small wicker basket in her hand. She was evidently making her way home from the market before the last light of dusk. But this is not what they saw. As she passed them she nodded courteously and greeted them with a few pleasant words for the evening, possibly assuming that they were six venerable scholars from the Imperial Academy. But this is not what they heard.

After she had left, the six fools engaged in a long and considerably heated debate regarding her identity. They had all seen and heard different things and could not concur on anything. But at last, the one who seemed perfectly normal, but who would ultimately confuse everything in the retelling, made the final pronouncement for all six:

From her appearance, he proclaimed, she must be the Goddess of the River Lo. After all, was she not dressed in the clothing of a classical queen—wearing head ornaments of gold and kingfisher feathers and her bodice adorned with glittering pearls—as the ancient records state? And are we not sitting on the banks of the River Lo? They all concurred confusedly, nodding their heads and sighing. And did we not ask her what we should do? Again they agreed. And did she not speak to us and tell us that we had best serve the Emperor as high advisers and councillors of state? And surely, the Goddess of Lo, the daughter of the Great Fu Hsi, could not be wrong! Once more they all nodded in unison. Though indeed, not a single one among them knew that only a peasant girl had wished them good evening. The next morning these six blind and stubborn old fools found their way to the palace. And it was certain that wherever they went they would surely spread confusion.

Kaotsung let the booklet slide from his hands onto the floor. He could read no further. He bent over double, squeezing his eyes shut against the pain. There was only one thing in the world he wanted right now, and that was Wu's hands on him. Her touch could dissolve knots and put out the fire. Despite the dull knowledge existing somewhere in his mind that she was responsible for starting the fires in the first place, he could not help himself. He thought of her hands, cool and silky, moving over his flesh, and the pain in his gut released just a little bit. Still bent over, he cracked open his eyes. The booklet lay on the floor, inches from his nose, the elegant brocade cover glinting in the afternoon sunlight.

Her mother held one of the infants, and she held the other. She glowed with pride and self-admiration. She knew that it was munificent Nature making her a lavish offering, restitution for the sacrifice of the girl child. Not one son, which would have been compensation enough, but two!

She sighed, letting herself sink deeply and indulgently into the warm, smug, animal contentment of the female whose bloody travail, now finished, has produced male progeny for her lord.

She looked at her mother, who was taking the extraordinary event in stride. Madame Yang held one of the infants up and looked at it with a shrewd, appraising eye, as if it were a goose she was considering for her table.

"This one," she said, "is your true heir. He is the one who carries your spirit."

Wu could not see whatever it was that Madame Yang saw in the squirming, pinkish, ugly creature she dangled in front of her. But she took the pronouncement as the truth, since it came from her mother. A red silk ribbon was tied around the infant's wrist to distinguish it from its brother.

"That one is named Hsien," she told her mother. "The new Crown Prince. At least," she added, seeing her mother's questioning look, "he will be before long. And this one," she indicated the bundle in her lap, "is named Hung. He is my fail-safe. In case anything happens to the first one." The two women looked at each other and smiled. "Oh, Mother!" Wu said then, settling back happily. "I feel strong. I feel as if there are one hundred sons in me waiting to come out!"

"There are," her mother replied. "But don't let them all out. Keep some of them in." She leaned forward and spoke in a conspiratorial voice. "Keep some of their life force for yourself. That is what I did."

They looked at each other then, and put their heads back and laughed heartily. Without question, life was good. Very good.

The Emperor gawked at the two sleeping infants as if they had descended directly from heaven and into the gauze-covered cradle where they lay. The Empress stood beside him on the breezy, flower-scented veranda, leaning against him as if for support. His tongue felt paralyzed, but he forced himself to speak.

"My dear," he began with deep reluctance, "there are some things that have come to my attention."

"Yes?" she answered quietly. He gazed down at the pink, wrinkled heads of the infants, took a breath, and continued.

"Councillor Wu-chi is very concerned about certain . . . writings that are circulating in the court and the city."

"Which writings?" she answered unconcernedly, reaching down through the gauze to fondle the sparse black hair of one of the little princes. Kaotsung sighed.

"The writings of one Shu Ching-tsung, who is calling himself chief historian. That is a position that has not been officially active for many years."

"He need not be concerned," she answered. "They are merely entertainment. Amusing tales. Nothing more. They have nothing at all to do with him or his friends."

"He feels that they are something more. That they are . . . a veiled satire on himself and the other Council members."

"Well, he is only calling attention to his own foolishness if he sees a resemblance between himself and the old fools in the stories. They are nothing. They are cautionary tales illustrating the folly of bad government, designed to be entertaining as well as enlightening. I cannot help it if Wu-chi and the others see themselves in that mirror. And," she added, "Shu is calling himself chief historian because I told him that he should. Of course, it is not official. That is up to you. But I believed that you would be pleased with his work. He is a most talented little man, and will be of great help to us."

"Pleased with his work?" Kaotsung asked, incredulous. "What of the . . . the . . . 'corrected biography' of the former Empress's father?" He despised the weakness, the apologetic tone, that had crept into his voice.

"What of it?" she replied. "It should be very obvious to you what it is. It is all for you. All of it." She turned squarely toward him, eyes intent. "I am saving face for you. It is as simple as that. The people will learn that she was never meant to be Empress. They will accept her removal. And they will be distracted ever further from the truth about her. That secret will remain ours alone."

The idea of the former Empress as a killer existed as a blank space, an empty windowless room in Kaotsung's mind. He had no words.

He directed his eyes down toward the cradle as Wu was now doing. He was surprised in the next moment to see a teardrop splash onto the silk netting.

"What is the matter?" he asked quickly, looking up at Wu's face with alarm.

"It is nothing," she said. "Only that I fear that my sons are doomed."

"Doomed!" he cried. "Their lives have just begun! They will live for a hundred years!"

"My daughter lived for ten days," she said in a sad voice, and raised her brimming eyes to his. "Or have you forgotten?"

"No," he said, releasing his breath with weary resignation. "No, I have not forgotten. But who would . . . " he began, confused and reluctant. "I mean, the Empress . . . "

"Yes, she is gone," Wu replied. "But that does not mean that her influence cannot extend itself. After all," she said, dropping her voice again, "it is her son, Jung, who is the Crown Prince. He is still here. And those old men. They are here, too."

"You cannot mean what you are saying," Kaotsung said weakly, feeling his gut contract sharply as he spoke.

"These babies are as good as dead," she said with heavy resignation. "I might as well kill them myself right now, and spare them the ignominy of dying by a stranger's hand."

Kaotsung seized her arms. "Don't talk that way," he said desperately. "I cannot bear it. Nothing will happen to these babies."

She collapsed gently against him and spoke into his shoulder. "All I want is to make you great," she whispered. "It is all I ever wanted. And I ask for very little in return."

Kaotsung was defeated. He felt every line of resistance collapsing and his tongue readying itself to speak whatever words she wanted to hear.

"What?" he said flatly.

"Guards," she said, her tone becoming abruptly firm and authoritative.

"Guards?" he asked, not understanding.

"I want two—no, four—guards to follow each of the Council of Six members wherever they go, every hour of the day and night. They must never be unwatched."

"But that is insane!" he protested, but she cut him off.

"Insane? You think it is insane to protect your newborn sons from meeting the same fate as my daughter?"

"But . . . I cannot incriminate and humiliate honored gentlemen that way."

"The old men and Prince Jung must be guarded closely every moment. Every moment!"

"Prince Jung, too?" he asked, amazed. "But . . . but he's just a child."

"Prince Jung, too!" she echoed fiercely. "We will take no chances! He is the disgraced son of a disgraced Empress."

Kaotsung cast his eyes miserably about, as if looking for assistance from the placid sky or the birds twittering about on the branches of the trees.

"I do not know what I would do," she said then, softly and seriously, "if anything happened to these infants. I simply do not know. It would probably be the end of me."

"No, no, no," he said, shaking his head. "I cannot listen to such words from you. I cannot. As you wish, then. Guards. As many as you want."

"And there is one more thing," she said, pressing her head against his shoulder again. "It is nothing at all. A small favor to me that will help me in my work." He said nothing, waiting. "Make the appointment of Shu Ching-tsung official," she said. "Give him the legitimacy of being appointed by the Emperor he so fondly wishes to serve."

Kaotsung did not answer immediately; he was fighting down a wave of bilious nausea rising from his churning gut. He closed his eyes and felt a fine, cool sweat on his forehead. When he opened his eyes again, he felt as though he were returning from somewhere far away; she was looking at him with a satisfied, pleased expression, as if he had given his consent but had no memory of it. He wondered if in fact he had. He felt profoundly disoriented.

"You are wonderful," she said happily, not waiting for him to answer. "I will tell Shu this afternoon." She took both his hands fondly and raised them to her lips, kissing and caressing the fingers. "We are working on some wonderful stories," she said conspiratorially. "You will be most pleased. Who says there is no room for humor and levity in government? We will spread joy and laughter among the people, all the way to the far corners of the Empire."

He pulled himself away from her abruptly as another rush of nausea rose sharply. "Please excuse me, my dear," he said, and walked to the railing. He leaned over it, thinking that he might actually vomit, but nothing came up and the feeling gradually passed. He closed his eyes and rested for a moment, letting his head hang over. He heard her come up behind him, then felt her cool fingers stroking his forehead, soothing the last of the sickness out of him.

"The people will remember you, and love you for it!"

Kaotsung stood very still among the dappled shadows of a grove of ornamental fruit trees, listening to his name being called in the distance. He hoped that if he stood very still he might not be found.

The voice belonged to Wu-chi. It was loud and vigorous, and even at this distance, Kaotsung could tell, very angry. He looked into the branches over his head; it would be easy to scamper up into the tree and spend the rest of the afternoon there. They could search the entire Imperial Park and the palace and never find him. Tentatively, he reached up and grasped a limb. It could easily hold his weight.

The voices were close now, as was the sound of heavy, tramping, booted feet. He felt a small thrill of terror, the feeling every hunted creature must feel. He did not move. He stood holding the branch, and waited, his divided will paralyzing him. Wu-chi appeared at the bend in the path, shouting Kaotsung's name. He ceased in abrupt surprise when he saw the young Emperor standing only a few paces away under a spreading tree.

Wu-chi was not alone. The heavy footfalls belonged to the four expressionless guards who flanked Wu-chi. Kaotsung and Wu-chi stared at each other for one astonished moment. Embarrassed, Kaotsung dropped the hand holding the branch.

"So there you are," Wu-chi said in a flat voice. "If you will do me the favor of relieving me of my overzealous lovers, there are pressing matters I must discuss with you."

Kaotsung ordered the guards to stand at a distance. They

hesitated at first, but the fierceness of the Emperor's tone made them retreat to a distance of one hundred paces.

"Did you see that?" Wu-chi said. "They very nearly didn't obey you, the Son of Heaven! They have received their orders from someone else whose authority impresses them more."

"Nonsense," Kaotsung said. "They simply did not understand me at first." Wu-chi raised a cynical eyebrow and sat down on a stone bench.

"Have you read this?" Wu-chi asked quietly, extending a bound pamphlet toward Kaotsung. The Emperor started to answer, but Wu-chi interrupted him. "I am not talking of the original *Tale of Six Old Fools*, or even the fascinating story of the great celebrated hero of the T'ang, Wang Chu-i. No, this surpasses them all." The calm, dangerous tone of Wu-chi's voice unnerved Kaotsung.

"The Six Old Fools, it seems, have not yet finished their amazing exploits. You have not seen it? I am surprised. Everyone else in the Court and in the entire city knows it intimately. They can even recite passages of it by heart." By now Wu-chi was trembling perceptibly. Seeing that the Emperor was showing no sign of taking the pamphlet, Wu-chi began, unsteadily, untying the ribbon himself. "Very well," he said. "I will read them to you. Where shall I begin?" he asked himself, flipping through the pages. "It does not matter. I can start anywhere. Sit," he commanded. Obediently, Kaotsung sank to the ground and listened as Wu-chi selected a page and began to read in a voice cold with rage.

" 'Typical of the Old Fools was old Lame Donkey, whose unbecoming lust far exceeded his discretion. Many was the time his office steward would find him, robes up around his head, trousers dropped to his knees, sweating and grunting while striving to force his way into the "unripened peach" of a young serving girl who would have no recourse but to give in to the demands of a high-grade government official . . .' "

Wu-chi looked up and was startled to see an expression of twisted agony on Kaotsung's face. He was holding a silk handkerchief to his mouth, eyes tightly shut. He knew the Emperor had been having trouble with his stomach; he was gratified to see that the story was having some effect on him.

"This is preposterous," Kaotsung whispered painfully through his handkerchief. "How could this happen?"

"Oh, but there is more," Wu-chi said. "Listen to this.

" 'Failing to attend the funeral of his father, old Lame Donkey returned some time later to the family farm to look after his sister. But being that his greatest desire was not her welfare but his lust for her, he chased her around the house. However, his inability to distinguish led him to fornicate with a goat, which he had mistaken for his sister. The local authorities would have caught him in the act of sodomizing the animal but for the fact that they, too, were familiar with old Lame Donkey's state of confusion. When confronted with the old man in the yard with his robes pulled up over his head and his silken trousers falling down around his skinny legs, they assumed he was merely looking for a place to relieve himself . . . The old man was most happy to support their story, knowing that if he had been found out the Imperial Court would force him to take his own life.' "

While he read, Wu-chi had heard uncomfortable grunting sounds coming from Kaotsung. He raised his eyes. For an instant, he thought that the Emperor was weeping, so red and contorted was his face. Spasmodic gasps came from beneath the silk handkerchief and tears stood at the corners of the squeezed-shut eyes. It took Wu-chi a long, strange moment to comprehend that the Emperor was not crying, nor was he suppressing a gastric onslaught of some sort.

He was laughing.

Wu-chi sat, mute with disbelief, for three or four heartbeats before he leaped to his feet.

"I am glad that you are so amused," he shouted. "As no doubt everyone in the Empire who reads this vile slander will be!"

Kaotsung struggled to regain composure. He held up a hand, the other hand still pressing the cloth to his mouth. His shoulders shook.

"I am sorry, Wu-chi," he said. "I am sorry, I am sorry, I am sorry." But he was lost in a fresh peal of laughter.

"Then perhaps you will find this amusing as well!" Wu-chi said coldly. "This morning Min-tao and Ho-lin instructed me that they had submitted their formal resignations from the Tsai-siang, the Council of Six."

Kaotsung's eyes were glazed now. The fit of hysteria had taken away the pain in his stomach. He stared stupidly at Wu-chi.

"And," Wu-chi said with fierce emphasis, "Ho-lin is ready to commit suicide. He was preparing a letter to his family last night." With those words, Kaotsung's laughter was extinguished as abruptly and thoroughly as a fire doused with water. Wu-chi pressed his advantage. "I have asked Master Sui-liang to intercede, to inform him that your actions will put an end to this. I have assured him that you will do what is right."

"I am appalled . . . I cannot even speak—" Kaotsung began.

"There are more parts to the tale," Wu-chi said, cutting him off. "There are still four other old fools to be 'examined.' Shall I go on?" Wu-chi asked. "The circumstances differ in each tale. The author has shown a most commendable inventiveness. But the one consistent element is the utter degradation, the humiliating posture of the Old Fool: with robes yanked up around his head and trousers dropped to his knees. Perhaps you would enjoy another good bout of laughter!"

"No . . . no more is necessary, Councillor," Kaotsung said, pulling himself to his feet and mopping his brow and face.

"It must be stopped by Imperial Decree, the tales renounced, and Min-tao and Ho-lin returned to their seats on the Council," Wu-chi said slowly and emphatically. "You are the only one who can do it. The only one who can restore the Council of Six to its rightful place and punish the offenders." He paused in order to appraise the effect of his words. "The only one who can save the life of Ho-lin," he added. "I will leave you to think on these things," he said then, and prepared to leave the grove. The guards, who had been standing at a distance, closed ranks around him, their faces blank. Kaotsung watched the incongruous group walk away from him; Wu-chi did not give even a backward glance.

The pain, which had eased during his intemperate fit of laughter, tightened its fist again. It was dark and blunt, but with an edge of red fire to it, a tiny little searing point that had begun to pierce through the dull throb. He thought of Wu, and tasted the faintest trace of blood in the back of his throat.

She caught him by surprise. He had waited for her all morning and had finally given in to an insistent drowsiness. Now she was bending over him and smiling. He had the sense right away that she had been standing there for a while; it was obvious that she was enjoying being the first thing his eyes should behold.

He jumped up quickly. You had best be on your feet for what you have to say, he told himself. At the same moment that he stood, she sat down on the bed. He looked at her. It was curious: the rigors of childbearing and birth seemed to agree with her. Unlike other women he had seen, who lost a little bit of luster with each parturition, Wu seemed to thrive on it. She fairly exuded potent vitality today.

"I have had a most excellent visit with my mother," she said. "But I could not wait to see you. I hope you do not mind my coming to you this way." She smiled up at him. "I was *so* impatient!"

Speak quickly, he told himself, or all will be lost. He felt an intent in her bent on satisfaction. He stepped back.

"You have gone too far," he said quietly. "The joke is out of control. It is causing real suffering. I am going to have to put a stop to it."

She smiled her wickedest smile at him. "Then you liked it," she said. "I knew you would."

"Liked it!" he said, exasperated. "Two of my father's oldest and most trusted friends are ready to commit suicide. Ministers and officials are looking at me as if I were quite insane."

"Has it occurred to you," she said in the same calm voice, "that there is a reason why these old men take my innocent stories so personally?" She looked at him roguishly. "It could only be that at some point in their long, useless lives, they have committed the offenses of the old men in the stories. Why else would they be so sensitive, and protest so loudly?"

"I have made a promise to Wu-chi," he pushed on, determined. "I promised that the stories would stop. And they will!"

"Wait a moment," she said then, fixing her eyes on him and tilting her head to one side. "Are we sure we are talking of the same stories? Let us be certain, so that there is no confusion." She rose and advanced toward him. He stepped back, unsure of what she meant to do, but sensing deep mischief. "Are we talking of the story wherein the old men get drunk in a wineshop and then stagger down to the canal?"

"You know quite well that I am not referring to that story," he answered, holding his ground.

"Not the story where the Old Fools sit by a canal and think that they are on the banks of the River Lo?"

"No, not that story," he said nervously as she took another step toward him, her eyes darker still, causing a faint giddy feeling in his chest and stomach.

"Not the one where they encounter the beautiful peasant girl and mistake her for a goddess?" she said, her voice low and compelling, her hands extending themselves toward him. He raised his own hands defensively; it was absurd. He was terrified that she was going to start tickling him!

"You know very well which story I am talking about!" he repeated, fending off her fingers as she feinted toward the sensitive spots on the sides of his chest and under his arms. He felt a ludicrous smile tugging at the corners of his mouth. He grabbed her hands; she firmly pulled them away, grabbing both of his in one of hers, and with her free hand began to dig him here and there on his flanks. The more he fought the smile, the more insistent it grew; she was smiling broadly, poking him, tickling him, eyes dancing.

"Oh, now I think I know which story you are talking about!" she said, releasing his hands, her fingers beginning a leisurely walk down his chest. "Let me think," she said, her fingers moving down, her eyes holding his while she talked. "You could only be referring to the story of the Old Fool who is caught in his office with the young serving girl. Am I right?"

He could not answer; a fit of giggling was rising like floodwater. "The Old Fool forcing his way into the girl's . . . 'unripened peach,' " she said, enunciating the last two words with suggestive emphasis.

By now he was giggling helplessly. She had lowered herself slowly while she talked, eyes still holding his, her hands moving down until they held the hem of his long robe. "And the Old Fool is caught with his garment hiked up over his head and his silk trousers down around his ankles. Like this!" she cried, yanking the robe up and over his head and in practically the same motion pulling his silk trousers down to his knees. She bunched and tangled the robe around his head so that he was quite unable to see, and tickled his naked flesh while he laughed wildly and staggered about, blundering into furniture, trying to escape her relentless fingers, his face hot in the black, airless confines of the heavy silk.

"Or was it the story of the fool lusting after his sister, chasing her around the house?" he heard her say, her hands all over him now, compelling him this way and that while he writhed, convulsing and gasping, until she had him against the bed, where he collapsed headlong. "And who mistakenly sodomizes a goat, thinking that it was she? Are those the stories we are talking about?" she asked, laughing too, climbing onto him and pinning him down. "Are they? Tell me!"

"Yes, yes, yes, those are the ones," he gasped from within his brocaded prison, laughing and struggling, ashamed and helpless, grateful for the darkness that hid him.

A.D. 657

She was the greatest mother the world had known. That was what the people were saying about the Empress Wu. They assembled now by the hundreds and even thousands to participate in the grand event that she had prepared. Her coronation was also a commemoration of the second birthday of her sons, the cherished little Crown Princes Hung and Hsien. And the brilliant volume of her robes did nothing to hide the proud fact that she was once again with child.

Wu had become nothing less than a goddess of motherhood. In the eyes of her subjects, she could do no wrong. Her nurturing, succoring extravagance was a model to all. Women of means looked to her example of lavish attention to her children, attempting to emulate it for their little ones whenever possible. In their mock imitations of royal festivities, wealthy households held sumptuous parties to celebrate birthdays amid magical garden settings.

If the saying was correct that as the twig is bent so grows the tree, then Wu would have nothing less, they predicted, than perfect and honorable princes—paragons, as was their mother, of filial nobility. They would be sons who would revere their mother's extraordinary humane ideal, who would take her well-displayed virtues as their own. And tiny Prince Hsien, his little pudgy hands now grasping the crown that he delivered to his mother's head, was her most perfect reflection.

5

A.D. 657
Yangchou and environs

Everyone in the village recognized the little man who climbed reluctantly down from the carriage that had rumbled into the square and halted by the well. His face was set in an uncharacteristic expression of sour distaste that startled them into awed silence. Over his shoulder he held a bulging, clinking sack. Two armed constables followed him from the carriage. He stood and fussily smoothed his abbot's robes with his free hand, then trudged down the street under his burden, his eyes haughtily avoiding any contact. An official in magisterial robes and cap stepped from the carriage then, and walked after the first man and the constables. People began to follow at a polite distance.

The man with the sack on his shoulder turned a corner and proceeded into a dead-end lane of small run-down houses. When he stopped in front of one, people nudged one another and whispered. He cast an imploring look at the stony-faced constables, then raised a hand and tapped on the door so gently that it scarcely seemed as if anyone within would hear it. But the door opened and an old lady stood there. Confused at the sight of her visitor, she dipped her head respectfully over and over while he lowered his burden to the ground with a grimace. Muttering and cursing under his breath, he reached into the sack, groped around, and pulled out an ornamental box flashing with silver and inlaid mother-of-pearl. He looked at the beautiful object sorrowfully for a moment, then straightened his back and held the box toward the old woman. He addressed her, speaking to the space just above her head, avoiding her eyes, humbly downcast though they were.

"My true name is Chang Feng-tsui," he said in his familiar high, supercilious voice. "I am not a true abbot of the Buddhist church, and I am unworthy of being thought of as such. I ..." He cleared his throat, reluctant to go on, while people exchanged incredulous looks. One of the constables prodded him in the upper arm with his stick. He shot a poisonous glare

107

at the constable and continued, speaking through his teeth now: "I am a thief, and a promulgator of false sutras. I have robbed you and everyone else in this village. I have . . . preyed upon your simple faith for my own profit and comfort. I wish to offer . . ." His eyes fell with regret to the brilliant box in his hands. "I wish to offer this to you as restitution, inadequate though I know it to be."

People stared at the sumptuous object. It was easily worth a decade of crops; it would pay taxes for a lifetime. Embarrassed, the woman dipped her head still lower, refusing to take it.

"Please take it, madame," the magistrate said then. His voice silenced everyone. "It is owed you. It is yours. For once, he is speaking the truth." She looked around with a pained expression. The box stayed where it was in her visitor's extended hand, inches from her face, his own face set with the grim determination of one who has vowed to endure.

"I . . . I will hold it for you. For safekeeping," she said, taking the box and backing through the door into her house. The visitor's hand sank slowly down to his side as he released a long, exasperated breath.

"All right," he said to no one in particular, hoisting the sack again, his voice sharp with petulance. "Let us get on with this *farcical* little performance, shall we?" The entourage moved down the lane to another door. He raised his hand and knocked.

Well after dark, Dee asked the driver to drop him off several blocks from his house so that he could get some fresh air after riding in the carriage since early morning. Chang Feng-tsui and his two guards had been deposited at the constabulary. Tomorrow, and possibly the next day, the prisoner would fill up his sack and go forth to repeat his speech at various doors throughout the countryside and the city, the sack growing lighter and his greedy, acquisitive heart growing heavier with every passing hour.

Dee patted his cap, making sure it was securely in place. His wives were not at all happy about his bald head. A week before, he had reclined in the garden, closing his eyes against the ring of faces above him—his wives' fretful ones and his sons' impertinently smiling ones—while the steward reluctantly lathered his master's head and scraped away the hair with the sharpest knife in the house.

Over the years, Dee had found it useful and informative to adopt various identities for ease of movement through the streets or when he wished to satisfy his curiosity. He was good at it, and comfortable with it. As a youth, he had had an uncle, a much younger half brother of his mother, who occasionally took him on exploratory adventures in their home city of Ch'ang-an. They would slip away from the great family home and dress as beggars, farmers, or foreigners, and go forth to see what they could never have seen as wellborn young men of the upper class.

As a grown man and a magistrate, he had taken his disguises no further than clothing—a merchant's robes, or peasant garb and the like. His wives tolerated it, but had never quite approved. It embarrassed them. They said it compromised his dignity as an official—more so since his appointment two years before as senior magistrate after the retirement of the elderly Magistrate Lu. But there was more to his wives' objections—his first wife had told him once that it removed him from them, that it made him into a stranger. He recognized the truth in that. It did make him feel like a stranger, but he did not always dislike the feeling. It was pleasant and instructive to lose oneself, to become a different person for a time.

Certainly he had never before done anything so drastic as shaving his head. Gazing upon his naked skull that day in the garden, his wives must have felt that they did not know him at all. He had been sorry about that, but it could not be helped. From the moment he realized that his old "friend" Chang Feng-tsui—known more appropriately in some circles as Diamond Eyes—was at work, Dee had had little choice but to run him to earth, and to do so, it had been necessary to turn himself into a monk. It had been an exhausting but infinitely satisfying week wherein Magistrate Dee Jen-chieh had walked countless *li* in crude leather sandals that rubbed his poor feet raw, had raised blisters on his hands at backbreaking physical labor, had worn his poor knees down to the bone at endless droning prayer, and had brought a criminal to justice, devising a punishment for him so fitting that Dee had laughed with delight when he thought of it, a punishment directly adapted from the wise and comprehensive legal code of the T'ang.

It had started two weeks before with a tax case. Or rather, many tax cases, and all from the same rural village on the outskirts of the city. It was a time of great abundance, with carts and barges in the city fairly groaning with produce, yet seven farmers had been unable to pay their yearly tariff. The bags of "grain" they had turned in had been filled with sand and hay with a thin layer of produce on top of that.

There had been something very familiar about the interview with the farmers when they came before his bench. For sheer evasiveness, it reminded him of the many interviews he had conducted with his sons. The difference was that the farmers were naive and charming, and unlike what he felt about his sons, he did not believe that the farmers had any real criminal intent. Their utter lack of sophistication and their crude method of deferring payment made that plain. And throughout the interview, the farmers invoked the name of the Blessed Maitreya and the Blessed Amitabha, as well as other religious names and terms. Dee was aware that it was not at all uncommon for rural peasant folk to adhere to Mahayana Buddhism, with its central concept of salvation. But the men seemed to be unusually . . . *immersed.*

Curious, Dee sent the farmers away for a few hours while he set his assistant to a bit of investigating of census records and the Registry of Temples. How many people lived in the village? Was it a generally prosperous one? Was any particular monastery in proximity to it? If so, what was its name, and how many monks did it have? While the assistant was gone, Dee hauled down off the top shelf in his office an enormous volume that he had been meaning to study in depth ever since the unsolved murder of the Transport Minister four years before, with its mysterious sacred and profane overtones of India. He looked at the daunting title page, and remembered afresh why he had put off his intended careful study of the contents: *Translation from the Sanskrit of Sacred Mahayana Buddhist Texts: the Sukhavati-vyuha-sutra, The Vagrakkhedikka-sutra, The Pragna-Paramita-hridaya-sutra, The Amitabha-dhyana-sutra.* Lacking a better idea of where to begin in the vast text, he decided to turn to the Sukhavati Sutra; that was a term not entirely unfamiliar to him from his past studies, and it had come up at least twice when he had been talking to the farmers.

He had been reading for the better part of an hour, utterly absorbed, when his assistant returned. He looked up from the page, his lips still forming the last line he had read, for he had been whispering the extraordinary words aloud to himself. The assistant told him what he had found: that about three hundred people lived in the village, that it had never had any particular tax problems before, and that there was a new temple in the vicinity, built only about two years before, that it was called the Land of Bliss, and that the abbot was a man whose name had once been Chang Feng-tsui.

Dee repeated that name aloud, looking down again at the words on the page before him, and leaped to his feet in astonishment. In the next moment he was out the door and rushing through the streets. An hour later he was back, bearing a load of valuables that he had hastily grabbed from shelves, tables, and dressers throughout his own house while his wives followed him from room to room uttering little expressions of horror as each piece disappeared into his bag.

Then he called each of the farmers individually into his office, disarming them by invoking the name of the merciful Kuan-yin, and begging each of them to allow the bodhisattva to act through him. The men were astonished enough to hear the name of Mahayana's most potent deity issuing from the lips of a high Confucian magistrate, but what he did next rendered them speechless. He gave each of them a treasure from his house: a silver lizard, gold-and-ruby hairpins, a carved ivory elephant set with precious stones, a brooch that had belonged to Dee's grandmother, silver plates, hair ornaments, and a pearl-and-cloisonné jewel case more than six hundred years old.

Take it, pawn it, and pay your taxes, he said solemnly to each stunned man. Keep the rest for next year's taxes. But, he added in a low voice, it must be our secret. Hide it in your pouch or in your clothes. Do not even tell your fellows what has passed between us. Tell them that I have imposed a stiff fine on you.

He looked intently into each man's eyes, endeavoring to forge a bond sufficient to carry him through that one promise, but no further. He was counting on the men's will to break down after that. He watched with a twinge as the irreplaceable treasures disappeared, one by one, down shabby shirtfronts or into tattered bags, and tried to reassure himself that if his plan worked as he hoped, the pieces would inhabit their proper places again. And he sighed, and asked himself what it was that the Buddhist sages had said about attachment to the material plane.

He waited. The walk out to the Land of Bliss Monastery a week later—his head shaved and the coarse fabric of his robe scratching his skin—was a long one, and he covered the entire twelve *li*** on his two legs so that he would arrive at his destination appropriately dusty and footsore. Though it was not twenty years of wandering, it might put him in the right frame of mind. While he walked, he mumbled bits and pieces of holy writings he had read: form is emptiness, emptiness is form . . . emptiness is not different from form, and form is not different from emptiness . . . perception is emptiness, conception is emptiness, and knowledge is emptiness . . . here in this emptiness there is no form, no perception, no name, no concept, no knowledge . . . no eye, no ear, no nose, tongue, body or mind . . .

Before long his feet began to sting and blisters to rise; it was strange to walk along the road—grit in his eyes and teeth, smelling the aromas of manure and flowers on the wind while farmers driving oxen and women carrying water and vegetables passed by him—and deny that any of it was real.

He discovered the Land of Bliss Monastery to be so new that it was as yet unfinished, with monks and peasants busily working everywhere, digging, hauling, moving rocks and dirt in barrows. He moved about, observing, chanting the sutra of form and formlessness to himself, recognizing among the workers at least two of the men who had come before his bench. Farmers, who should have been out working their fields, engaged in gardening and landscaping. And Dee's sophisticated and imaginative eye saw that the raw, as yet unfinished terrain would soon be transformed into a restful oasis of carp ponds, shade trees, elegant stone walls, and fountains: a personal pleasure garden. Formlessness at its most tasteful and well ordered.

And precisely what he should have expected.

To make himself inconspicuous, he offered to help a group of workers moving big rocks. After some time, the monks working nearby had put down their shovels and barrows and moved toward the door of the temple. One of them nodded politely in Dee's direction in a way that seemed to indicate that he could join them if he wished. Inside, in a dimly lit, nearly windowless prayer room, with tallow candles flickering in holders on the walls, he knelt, the gloomy light and droning voices of the monks casting a strong, inviting spell.

---

*Four miles.

He spoke the words of the prayer, following only a fraction of a syllable behind:

" . . . called Amitaprabha, possessed of infinite splendor; Amitaprabhasa, possessed of infinite brilliancy; Asamapta-prabha, whose light is never finished; Asangataprabha, whose light is not conditioned; Prabhasikhotsrishtaprabha, whose light proceeds from flames of light; Sadivyamaniprabha, whose light is that of heavenly jewels . . . "

When they adjusted to the light, Dee raised his eyes for a moment and caught a glimpse of a glittering array of small, bright objects on the altar.

And the prayer droned on, Dee's head reverberating with the names of the Sage of the Western Paradise:

" . . . Abhibhuyanarendrabhutrayendraprabha, possessed of light greater than that of the lords of men and of the lords of the three worlds; Srantasankayendusuryagihmikarana-prabha, possessed of light which bends the full moon and the sun . . . Abhibhuyalokapalasakrabrahmassuddhavasamahesva-rasarvadevagihmikaranaprabha, possessed of light which bends all the conquered gods, Mahesvara, the Suddhavasas, Brahman, Sakra, and the Lokapalas . . . "

The monks moved on to the Sukhavati Sutra, the one Dee had been reading in his office on the day the farmers had come before him. Sukhavati: the Land of Bliss, the jeweled paradise, and the inspiration, he was sure, for the name of the monastery.

" . . . Oh, Ananda, that world Sukhavati is fragrant with several sweet-smelling scents, rich in manifold flowers and fruits, adorned with gem trees frequented by tribes of sweet-voiced birds . . . and oh, Ananda, those gem trees there are of gold, of silver, of beryl, of crystal, of coral, of pearl, of diamond . . . and oh, the beings who will have been born in that world Sukhavati will be endowed with such enjoyments of dress, ornaments, gardens, palaces, and pavilions . . . and if they desire such ornaments as head ornaments, ear ornaments, neck ornaments, hand and foot ornaments, diadems, earrings, bracelets, armlets, necklaces, pearl nets, jewel nets, nets of bells made of gold and jewels, then they see that Buddha country shining with such ornaments that are fastened to ornament trees . . . "

The long prayer ended with a passage that seemed familiar and unfamiliar to Dee at the same time. It was an exhortation to those who wished to see the ornament trees of crystal, beryl, coral, and diamond, and who wished to wear jewels upon their arms and legs and to walk along the pathways of ornament trees listening to the singing of sweet-voiced birds while smelling the perfumed wind that stirred the jewels hanging heavy from the trees like fruit and playing heavenly music against one another, and who wished to bathe in the rivers of warm, sweet emerald-and-sapphire-colored waters. If they wished to see these things, then they must build a staircase from the earthly realm. A staircase of earthly jewels and treasures, which would, of course, appear as pieces of rock and mud when compared to the heavenly jewels of the Land of Bliss.

Then Dee rose on numb legs and moved forward with the rest of the monks toward the altar and its mysterious, glinting array, a display of jewelry and treasures that seemed to rival the wares of Sukhavati. With a start, he recognized among the pieces his own silver lizard that he had given to the farmer a week before. But as he got closer, he saw that something about it was not quite right. The emerald eyes were flat and dead, the scales crudely rendered. In the next moment, it was as if a thin layer of grime were lifted from his eyes. He saw clearly what was before him: every piece on the altar was a fake—cheap street-market-quality counterfeits, the jewels garish glass, the ivory painted wood, the pearls polished pieces of seashell. In the candlelight, to an unsophisticated eye, the collection on the altar would resemble an Empress's treasure.

And where were the real pieces? Back outside, he blinked in the bright sun, then moved toward a group of men struggling with an enormous ornamental boulder, levering it with long poles and blocks of wood. He smiled ingratiatingly and put himself next to one of the men, placing his shoulder against the stone. Together, they heaved and balanced the huge stone. Dee felt the cool solidity of the rough granite against his cheek, and thought that this was the perfect paradigm for earthly life. In this realm, he reflected, giving a mighty push and feeling the stone roll a few more inches, it is flesh against stone. There are no pleasure gardens without the painful effort of muscle, bone, and sinew. No fields of grain and rice, either.

Head down, still straining with all his might, Dee heard two voices approaching. One of them sounded utterly familiar to Dee, though it had been more than ten years since he had heard it last. He listened as the voice held forth fantastically on the poor qualities of spotted carp versus solidly colored ones. The second voice murmured ingratiating agreement now and again, addressing the first speaker as Your Holiness. The two speakers stopped and stood to one side of the group of sweating, grunting men.

The voices were now a mere three or four paces from Dee, who, with his head discreetly down and his shoulder to the great stone, found himself looking directly at a pair of immaculately pedicured sandaled feet protruding from beneath a saffron robe. You men must take care not to injure yourselves, the voice that Dee knew so well said in a kindly tone. You must think of this work as a meditation, every little push a prayer, the weight of the rock the weight of lives.

Dee had been unable to resist. Reasonably certain that his bald head, many elapsed years, and the sheer incongruity of where he was would protect his identity, he raised his eyes and looked into the round, congenial face of the head of the Land of Bliss Monastery. It was exactly the face he had expected to see, but what caused him to stare for a moment longer than prudence dictated was the jeweled brooch, with two flashing rubies in a setting of fiery gold, unmistakably genuine, that was pinned at the neck of the man's robe.

Dee's grandmother's brooch.

While His Holiness prattled on about how the stones would be placed just so—to resemble great listening heads, as he had put it—Dee smiled an idiot's smile at him and lowered his face. The next day, Chang Feng-tsui was arrested.

Dee had almost felt sorry for interfering with the arrangement between Chang and the villagers. It had been satisfactory for both, providing purpose and comfort to the peasants while maintaining Chang in a life to which he was accustomed and to which he sincerely believed he was entitled. For Chang Feng-tsui—or, as Dee had once known him, Diamond Eyes—life without luxury, without fine houses, fine clothing, fine art, was not worth living. These items *were* life, more important for survival than food or air.

It was when Dee was a young assistant magistrate over a decade before in the western capital city of Ch'ang-an that he had first encountered him. Chang Feng-tsui had been a well-born, well-educated fellow from an old but lately impecunious family. In the final stages of an education that would have eventually procured for him a well-paying position, he threw it all off in a fit of impatience, turning instead to the cultivation of friendships among the very wealthy. For years, he moved as a highly successful collector and dealer of objets d'art in the insular circles of their society. And his greatest love, where all of his adoration for the rare and beautiful converged and was concentrated, was fine jewelry.

One evening, he was caught leaving a party at the home of a wealthy minister with his sleeves full of the minister's wife's jewelry. It all came out then—jewelry and other treasures stolen over the years from his wealthy friends had provided him a brisk and pleasant livelihood of trading and selling; pieces he especially fancied, he kept. He had been arrested, and eventually sentenced to several years at hard labor even though many of his friends whom he had robbed had petitioned for clemency. One day a few months into his sentence, he disappeared from his work gang. It had been generally supposed that one of his rich and powerful friends had arranged for his escape. His disappearance had made him something of a legend; it was after his departure that his picturesque sobriquet had been bestowed upon him.

The moment of realization for Dee had been the moment his assistant had returned to the office on the day Dee had interviewed the seven farmers. It so happened that Dee had been reading the Sukhavati-vyuha Sutra, the description of the jeweled Land of Bliss; nearly stupefied by the dazzle, Dee had raised his eyes from the page to hear the assistant utter the name of the man for whom such a land might have been personally designed. And what else would he call his monastery but the Land of Bliss?

Dee recovered his family's treasures, including his grandmother's brooch, when Chang Feng-tsui's quarters were searched on the day of the arrest. But the night before, after Dee had returned weary and footsore to his home, he had reread the Sukhavati Sutra and had found that part of what the monks had been chanting in the prayer room that afternoon was not in the text. Diamond Eyes had apparently turned his versatile hand to sutra-writing, inserting an authentic-sounding but quite spurious passage into the ancient, revered scriptures: they must build a staircase from the earthly realm, and they must build it of gold and jewels. . . .

Upon this unassuming but powerful phrase he had built his little empire. With the sweat and labor of his monks and peasants he had built a fine home for himself. With goods and cash given to him by the farmers, having convinced the people of the village that he could thus help them get to the jeweled paradise, he found himself happily back in the business of acquiring, buying, and trading rare treasures. It had been a clever system: when a peasant brought him an offering, he used it to purchase a valuable item that he fancied. Then he would show the piece to the man, telling him that it belonged to the peasant and his family, and that it would take a permanent and exalted position on the altar. The more lavish the altar, the more expeditious the intervention of the merciful Kuan-yin, assuring them plentiful rainfall and bountiful crops and the rest of it— and eventual access to Paradise, of course. In the meantime, a worthless duplicate of the item would be made, and it would sit on the altar in perpetually dim light while the genuine article either went into Diamond Eyes' personal collection or into his inventory, to be traded or sold.

Dee had not known the specifics of this when he gave his personal treasures to the farmers in his office, but he had been wagering that by some route they would end up in the possession of their "spiritual leader." He had relied on Diamond Eyes' hold on the men being stronger than any temptation they might have had to keep the objects, or to pawn them and pay their taxes. That had been the riskiest part of his plan, but he had been right.

Years of hard labor, though Chang Feng-tsui deserved it sorely, would have accomplished little toward chastening such a man. So Dee had devised a punishment much more painful and difficult: returning the treasures and making a public apology. Dee could think of few things more reprehensible than the manipulation, for personal gain and comfort, of hardworking peasants' hopes for paradise.

Dee had enjoyed his good long walk since the carriage had dropped him off this evening. It was with gratitude that he turned onto his own quiet, deserted street. Passing the large, comfortable estates secure behind their tall gates, he thought of how the common folk were always so exposed—to weather, to the vagaries of nature, fate, and politics, and to whatever superstitious dogma might be abroad in the land.

The gatekeeper was waiting for Dee. The man ushered him through, a lantern held high to light the way. What hope was there, Dee thought as he stepped into the secure confines of his garden, for a just, rational, moral society when men were always looking beyond this world, lured by chimerical visions of the next?

And what forces shaped an unscrupulous sort like Diamond Eyes, so willing to take advantage of their weakness?

In the outer vestibule that led to the reception hall, Dee surprised his sons in the midst of a furtive conversation. Their heads came up abruptly and their whispering ceased when he entered. Their school bags lay on the floor behind them. The boys lined up side by side, facing their father like two little soldiers.

Dee attempted conversation with them, asking them what they had learned at the academy today and such, and received perfunctory answers accompanied by ill-concealed smiles. Apparently, they had not got over their amusement at his appearance. Patting them on their shoulders, Dee maintained a patient demeanor, then took his leave. He was aware, even with his back turned, of the whispered resumption of the conversation.

"What is this?" Dee stood in the center of the reception hall and looked from one statue to the next. "I have been gone for one day, and this is what I come home to?" His gaze rested on a large standing figure of a Buddha by the planter that divided the long, spacious room.

"If my husband does not want these statues here, we can put them in our quarters with the others," said Dee's first wife firmly.

"The others?" He looked at the two women. "Do you mean that there are more?" Dee moved across the reception hall toward the corridor that connected the library and sleeping chambers. But he stopped dead before mounting the stairs when he saw an odd assortment of booklets and pamphlets scattered about the tops of the low decorative tables that lined the walls, the covers glowing woodblock ink prints of lotuses and seated Buddhas along with rows of Sanskrit and Chinese characters.

"And these books? What are these books?" His inflection rose in bewilderment. First Wife hurried to put her hands protectively over the pile.

"Popular sutras and prayer books," she explained quickly. "They came with the statues." She paused, then added cheerily as if it would help matters, "At no extra cost. It was a priest from the Glorious Flower Monastery who came to the house. They make everything there. Such craftsmanship."

"Oh, that is fine," Dee said with heavy sarcasm. "Very fine. The prayer books did not cost me anything. I am so very pleased." He shook his head. "To think that I allow the steward and servants and cooks to haggle with the merchants over the price of food to the kitchen. Surely I should allow *you* to bargain instead. I did not know you were so talented. I had no idea. So the books cost me nothing. Then you should not mind my doing this," he said, pushing the booklets off onto the floor.

"They are only there for the comfort of passing mendicants," Second Wife protested.

"What is this? A monastery?" Dee implored. "A way station for contemplatives? The next time I return to my home, will I find wandering ascetics with begging bowls sleeping comfortably in my bed? I will not have it!" With that, he strode toward the sleeping quarters.

He stood in First Wife's bedchamber and looked around. He became aware of giggling behind him; he turned to see his two sons peeking in the doorway. He leveled a warning look at the smiling boys. "I have quite enough trouble with my sons. Now it is my wives, too," he said, gesturing toward the icons carefully placed here and there around the room.

"Leave those alone," First Wife warned as Dee approached the dressing table. "What are you doing?"

Dee stood at the dressing table, carefully moving every item on it to one end, freeing the large square of decorative silk on which the items had been resting. He seized two small Buddhist statues, piled them onto the piece of silk, then carried the bundle to another table and set to work there, too.

"Those are Lohans and Lokapalas," Second Wife squealed. "Our disciple saints and guardians!"

"I am quite aware of what they are," Dee said, dropping two more statues into his cloth. "I don't believe that there is a piece of iconography that I have not seen somewhere in this damned city." He twisted his hands away from Second Wife's grasp as she tried to seize the bundle.

"Put them back," she said angrily. She reached for the cloth again. Dee yanked it away. The statuettes clattered inside. "You are going to break them if you are not careful," she cried.

"I am going to do more than just break them. I am going to throw them into a great pile along with rosaries and prayer books and burn all of this claptrap."

"No, you are not. Definitely not." Now First Wife was on the other side of him, grabbing for the cloth. "They are comforting and helpful."

"They are nothing but hollow promises," Dee said, jerking the cloth.

"That hurt my hand!"

"Good. Sacrifice hurts." He moved toward a figure of the goddess of mercy, Kuan-yin, on a window plant shelf. Second Wife caught his glance and rushed over to it.

"No. You will not touch her. She is our morning blessing."

"Give me that bit of foolishness!"

She cradled the statue in her arms like a baby. Dee caught hold of the goddess's head; she pulled away sharply, and the rosewood neck snapped off cleanly.

"Look what you have done," she wailed. "Now you have angered me, my husband!"

"I will not have them in my household!" he said, tossing the head into the cloth with the rest. Snickering and scuffling caused Dee and both of his wives to turn toward the doorway; the household steward came up behind the two boys, took hold of their arms, and pulled them away from the scene.

"They are not in your household," First Wife scolded. "They are in our chambers. You do not even have to know that they are here."

"But since I already know it, it is too late."

"Then pretend that you do not."

"There is a whole city out there wanting me to do the same thing. To turn away. I cannot! I will not! And I cannot allow you to give yourself over to all of this. Not under my roof. My father did not allow superstition under his roof, either. That was the problem with my mother. 'A respectable household is a Confucian household,' he said. 'The Buddhism is for the servants.' How would it look? This . . . this foreign religion," he sputtered. "It is a religion for eunuchs and old ladies!"

"And we shall be old ladies soon enough," Second Wife declared. "It is quite harmless, husband! Just a little comfort! Would you deny us that?"

Later, in his study after an inconclusive parting with his wives, during which he had apologized for hurting First Wife's hand and reluctantly agreed to allow them to keep a few small icons within the confines of their bedchambers, Dee sat, intending to make a journal entry. He rose again at the sound of scratching and opened the outer door that led to the garden.

Scoundrel bustled in with an air of having accomplished a great deal that day and flopped down, panting, in his place beneath Dee's table. Dee knelt and scratched the dog's ears and head. The only member of the family who did not contribute to the general household disharmony, he thought, and straightened up tiredly.

Dee had taken his second wife ten years ago. There was nothing at all unusual about a prosperous Confucian official having two or even three wives. It was all part of maintaining proper outward appearances. But Dee had done the socially correct thing for quite different reasons; he had done it not because he believed particularly that it was the necessary thing for a man of his rising status to do, but because his mother had insisted on it. He had taken his second wife for no other reason than to appease his mother!

To be sure, appeasing his mother was a major part of his duty as a filial Confucian. Mother had persuaded him to take as his second wife the daughter of an aristocratic and very wealthy childhood friend of hers. At the time of the second marriage, Dee already had a small son by his first wife; within a year, his second wife produced a son, and it became evident very quickly that the two boys had been destined for each other by Fate itself. From the time the littler one could toddle around, he and his brother were a virtual inviolable unit of two, looking at the world through the same eyes, speaking the same language. Dee well remembered the first incident wherein the little one—at no more than three years of age— had demonstrated the fierce loyalty in his heart to his brother; the older one had told him to eat a cricket—to actually chew and swallow it—and he had, without hesitation. Not much later, the boy had told his little brother to take the coverlets from their beds and stuff them into the chamber pot, and he had happily obeyed.

There was some quarreling between Dee's wives after that, each woman claiming that the other's son was the instigator of the pranks. But when they were not quarreling, the women tended to draw together. On occasion Dee felt that between his sons and his wives he was a presence tolerated in the house, but not a great deal more. Tonight had been an excellent example of that attitude.

Dee's mother was an extremely persuasive woman, even from the distance of many hundreds of *li* that separated the coastal canal city of Yangchou from the western capital of

Ch'ang-an where she resided. Her letters arrived with great
regularity, full of admonishments, warnings, and advice. She
had never agreed to live with him, as was expected of an aged
parent, and that was something of an embarrassment. But Dee
was secretly very happy with the arrangement, and so were
his wives. Though Mother had vigorously approved of Dee's
first marriage and had personally chosen his second wife, she
claimed to be unable to get along with either, and so lived with
other relatives in Ch'ang-an. Thank the gods, Dee had whispered to himself more than once.

Dee sighed and picked up his brush. There was a knock
at his study door. Wearily, he laid the brush down.

"Enter," he called out. Timidly, the steward creaked open
the door and put his head through.

"Visitors, master," the man said.

"I am sorry to disturb your evening, Magistrate," said
another voice. Dee looked up and recognized one of his district
constables. "But we have a bit of a problem." Behind the constable stood an old man, who kept his eyes firmly fixed on the
floor.

"This is old wood carver Ling. He has a small shop in the
next district." The old man began to attempt to prostrate himself, clutching his thick wooden staff as he sank on his good
knee. Dee waved the unnecessary effort away. The old man
stopped, and then bowed his head slightly, but he would still
not look up at Dee.

"Surely this old man has not committed any crime for
which we cannot forgive him!" Dee said, but it did not produce
a smile on the constable's lips.

"Magistrate, Master Ling has not committed any crime.
He has suffered one."

"Has Master Ling suffered a loss?"

"Yes, Magistrate. There has been a robbery at his wood-
carving shop. He tells me that some small items were pilfered.
It was done in the usual way. One thief distracted Master Ling
while the other helped himself."

"Do we know who the culprits are?"

"Yes, Magistrate. I think that we do." There was a long
pause while the constable chose his words. "They were two
young boys. One appeared to be nine or ten years old. The
other was about thirteen or fourteen. Both clean and well-fed
children." Another pause. "They were followed to . . . this
neighborhood."

Dee stared at the constable and the old man for a moment, remembering his sons standing in front of their book bags in the vestibule. Blocking his view.

He flung his brush to the carpet, strode to the door, and shouted their names into the empty hallway.

6

A.D. 658
Loyang

Wu-chi was seriously concerned for old Sui-liang. On this tenth grueling morning of hearings, which were plainly intended to exhaust and grind down the old councillors and break their spirits, Wu-chi saw that his friend was in pain. He had gone quite pale earlier and had needed Wu-chi's assistance to support his unsteady walk up the stairs and down the long aisle to his seat in the Hall of the Court of Revisions.

Wu-chi took hold of the dry aged hand that rested on the lap of the old man to his right. He gave it a small reassuring squeeze. He felt the bones, frail as a bird's, collapsing like a paper fan under his gentle pressure. Wu-chi saw that there were tears on Sui-liang's withered cheek, but he pretended not to notice. Wu-chi patted his friend's hand as he looked politely away.

At eighty-four, Sui-liang was the oldest of the councillors, and Wu-chi knew that his friend would not see eighty-five. He no longer walked the leafy paths in the Imperial Preserve—walks that had given him such pleasure and solace. And he had not played the sixteen-string *chin* for a long, long time. This magnificent lute had been the gift of his son some thirty years ago, and playing it had given him his greatest pleasure. "Music produces a pleasure without which human nature cannot survive," Sui-liang had once quoted to his great-grandson. Wu-chi remembered the old man tuning the strings and reciting from the Book of Rites while the child looked on. "Virtue is the sturdy stem of the tree of human nature," he had gone on to say, smiling at the rapt little boy who stared, full of wonder, at the miraculous instrument, "and music is the blossoming of virtue." And now, the disappearance of Sui-liang's music was for Wu-chi a poignant prophecy—like the disappearance of an animal that knows it is time to die.

Virtue and honesty: those were the qualities that summed up the old man. Of course, the same was true of Han-yuan and Laichi, too, his other colleagues in the Council of Six. They sat stoically this morning on the row of benches to his left in the Court of Revisions. This was the final day of the formal hearings that had gone on without a break and the day in which the final deposition—the decision of the court's "findings"—would be announced and read.

Who could ever have foreseen this? They were no longer even the Council of Six. So great was their despair and humiliation that two of them had already salvaged their honor in the only way left to them—they had killed themselves.

Wu-chi did not recognize the newly appointed vice president of the Censorate who crossed the hall in front of them. In the flood of incomprehensible events of the last few weeks, this was just one more extraordinary thing. He had never even seen this man who was vice president, even though he, Wu-chi, was supposedly the president of the Supreme Censorate, a position he filled full-time along with his part-time service on the Council of Six. Or he had been, until just two weeks ago, when the "charges" against the surviving four members of Tsai-siang first appeared.

The Censorate was the highest judicial and investigatory body between the Imperial Department of Punishments and the Court of Revisions. If anyone were to judge another for slander or treason against the government, it should have been Wu-chi himself. But everywhere, the hand of the Empress Wu and her pet historian, Shu Ching-tsung, was evident. In the last week Wu-chi had discovered the presence of at least one more person central to all of this: Lai Chun-chen, recently "appointed" head of the Ministry of Civil Appointments and Wu's Secret Police. An interesting combination, Wu-chi reflected. No doubt this Master Lai was responsible for the selection of civil servants—filling the halls of the three judiciary bodies with those who possessed the proper "understanding," and the correct "point of view."

Now a stout man pushed himself across the hall with slow but purposeful motion, carrying a roll of official-looking documents. His labored breath whistled in his nostrils as he moved to seat himself before the hall with the other members of the assembled judiciary. Wu-chi did not recognize this man, either. Han-yuan and Lai-chi returned his quizzical look.

Keeping his hand low, Wu-chi made a surreptitious gesture to Lai-chi, trying to tell his friend not to give up. And he needed to tell him something else, though he feared it was too late.

When the hearings began ten days earlier, the four had been taken into house arrest. The charges were insane: they linked the surviving four members of the Tsai-siang, the Council of Six, with a vague and implausible "matriarchal conspiracy" to rally a coup d'etat against the Emperor Kaotsung around the figure of the deposed Empress Wang's son, the thirteen-year-old ex-Crown Prince Jung. But this state of "house arrest" was most odd; it was unlike anything Wu-chi had ever heard of. They were treated like princes.

A lavish palatial compound was at their disposal. Each of them had private apartments and a staff of servants and personal physicians. From their rear doors, each of the four elaborate apartments gave way to a large and beautifully ornamented central common garden where the councillors could meet and talk freely.

The guards that had escorted them everywhere for nearly a year dropped from sight. At first, Wu-chi wanted to think that their persecutors were, in small degrees, coming to their senses. After all, how very implausible were these accusations of conspiracy against the throne! And what could four arthritic old councillors do? It was a cautious bit of optimism that Wu-chi had nursed along. But that small, slim hope had been dashed as soon as the "charges" had been announced. On that morning, everything had become very clear.

The fat magistrate clearing his throat and unrolling the parchment caused the already quiet room to fall into a deadly, attentive silence. The man began to read:

"On this fourteenth day of the seventh month of the second year of the Reign Period of Lin Te, Moral Excellence of the Female Unicorn, in the reign of Emperor Kaotsung of the House of Li . . . "

Finally, it had begun. The fat man intoned:

"The decision of the Greater and Lesser Judiciaries of the Three High Courts are in concurrence regarding the actions of the four councillors of the Tsai-siang. It is the decision of this court that the four councillors, servants of his August Supreme Son of Heaven the Emperor Kaotsung, and loyal and valued councillors of state to his father before him, the late Divine Emperor T'ang Taitsung, are innocent of all charges of plotting against the government; are innocent of any and all charges of collaboration with Prince Jung, noble son of the retired and virtuous Empress Wang; and are innocent of any and all machinations regarding a 'matriarchal conspiracy' with the Empress Wang, living now in peaceful seclusion on a state pension . . . "

What sort of deadly trick was this? Wu-chi turned his stunned eyes toward his colleagues, who sat as if carved from stone.

"Good joke," Sui-liang hissed to Wu-chi. In a futilely protective gesture, Wu-chi reached over and clasped Sui-liang's hands, now tightly clenched into bloodless fists in his lap. The deposition reader stared out into the hall for a moment, then resumed:

" . . . nor are they, singularly or in union, in any way guilty of any attempts to undermine the well-being of the state or to overthrow the Peacock Throne and thereby wrongly attempt to supersede and usurp the Divine Mandate of Heaven. They are innocent on all counts of wrongdoing, and further . . . "

A small white bubble of spittle oozed out from between Suiliang's tightly pressed lips. Wu-chi's first reaction was to spare his old friend the humiliation; he brought the back of his hand up toward his colleague's chin, but at the same moment, Sui-liang's head began to drop forward. Wu-chi's eyes, unwillingly following the other's slow trancelike fall, came to rest at last upon the fabric of the old man's lap, which was soaked dark and shining. A warm, acrid smell touched Wu-chi's nostrils. His embarrassment for his friend was doubled. How foolish, he thought, annoyed and astonished—why has old

Sui-liang pissed all over himself? Crazy old man. Then, eyes wide open, Sui-liang slumped forward in his seat, as if he meant to rest his forehead on his knees, and annoyance and embarrassment were displaced forever by the rush of knowledge engulfing Wu-chi's every sense. Sui-liang was dead.

Wu-chi pushed his friend's shoulders back, preventing him from sliding off the chair. All he could think about was the resounding thud old Sui-liang's body would make if it hit the wooden floor, and that it must not happen. As he pushed against the bony upper chest, the loose folds of skin that hung at Sui-liang's neck rested on his hand. The mottled flesh was soft and warm, and Wu-chi knew that he was feeling the last bit of life as it abandoned the old man's body.

Still holding the corpse upright, he twisted himself around to face Han-yuan and Lai-chi: Han-yuan was nearly expressionless as usual, but Lai-chi smiled and nodded. In the front of the room, the magistrate read on, unperturbed, while heads turned and a murmur spread through the crowded rows of clerks, scribes, and officials. The attention of every person in the hall was divided: their eyes, stunned by the sudden spectacle of death, stared for a moment in confusion, then dutifully snapped back in the direction of the presiding magistrate's bench. The unrelenting voice droned toward the conclusion of the deposition as if nothing at all had happened.

" . . . It is the ruling of the Three High Courts that the four councillors of the Tsai-siang were incapable of treason against this throne and were incapable of any and all attempts at conspiracy and any and all attempts at abetting with such conspirators due to the most serious and severe sufferings of mass delusion and insanity that they have shared for the last year since the self-inflicted deaths of two of their members one year ago. . . . "

Servants appeared and made their way down the rows toward Wu-chi and Sui-liang. Reluctantly, Wu-chi released his hold as they lifted the corpse. One of the servants carefully wiped the puddle from Sui-liang's seat. Necks craned and the scraping of the benches and whispering and the rustle of robes swelled as the body was hastily borne up and over their heads.

" . . . In this regard, and for their exemplary services to this throne, the surviving four councillors—correction, *three* councillors; note that the record has been here stricken to read *three* surviving councillors . . . "

With these words, Wu-chi at last felt the full shock of what had happened. With one slash of the heartlessly expedient brush, one drop of ink, even while his lifeless body was being carried from the hall and without even a moment's respectful pause, Sui-liang had been eliminated. And the magistrate—the piglike, winded, pompous bastard—merely continued to read, on and on without mercy, as Sui-liang's limp body was borne, arms dangling gracelessly, down the broad central aisle, the magistrate's voice echoing as if in a great cave.

" . . . shall be permanently relieved of all obligations and enjoined against any and all further service to this throne, ensconced and provided for in a luxurious manner appropriate with their high positions and great service, and they shall be maintained in this manner for the remainder of their lives. . . . "

Now the hand of the Empress and her "civil servants" was clearly ungloved. The deposition would be sent up from the Lesser and Greater Judiciary Assemblies to the Emperor for his approval. And of course Kaotsung would approve. What other action would a man held in a spell by two witches be able—no, he corrected himself, *allowed*—to take?

Kaotsung. It was no longer the name of an Emperor, but of a frightened man—a man reduced by a woman.

Wu-chi also understood that the rest of their lives did not amount to much at all—that his expectation, at sixty-one years of age, of another two decades or so like his father before him was quite irrelevant. Now he might have a few months at the most. Enough time to allow the news of the trial to settle, and. . . .

Han-yuan and Lai-chi had shown no emotion: the death of Suiliang and the reading of the final deposition were all the same. Again, Wu-chi tried to capture their attention with his eyes, but they stared straight ahead. Now, more than ever, Wu-chi felt the urgent necessity to speak to them before evening.

The fat magistrate's voice labored on; now and again, he brought the cuff of his robe up to wipe the beads of sweat from his broad pasty forehead as he read:

" . . . In order that the functioning of a well-ordered bureaucracy shall continue without interruption, it is deemed necessary that the Three High Courts shall honor the interim substitution appointments as follows, until such time as more worthy and permanent replacements can be found: President Shu Ching-tsung, whose great accomplishments in the Imperial Board of History toward the writing of the *Veritable Records of the Emperor Kaotsung* have already been fully noted, shall assume the additional duties of Lord Secretary of the Chancellery— the full-time position held by the former councillor Hanyuan, now relieved of civil obligations after having been deemed invalid and incompetent to continue in this position; and President Lai Chun-chen of the Ministry of Civil Appointments and the Empress's Secret Police shall be granted the position in the Censorate judiciary position formerly held by the former honorable councillor Master Wuchi, no longer capable of fulfilling . . . "

Surely it would be impossible to hate all of my accusers, Wu-chi thought. Most of them were simply caught up in the web of the Empress's machinations. Would any of them consider himself a murderer? Could they understand that in some small way each of them was responsible for the death of an old man pushed to the limit of his strength in the ten days of "hearings"?

There were clerks and scribes and guards and a great number of lower-grade ministers of the Court of Revisions and the Censorate who simply thought that they were doing their jobs—and they were. It never would have occurred to them that they themselves were criminals. And yet as he studied the faces, he imagined that he could pick out signs here and there that a minor cleric or a functionary sensed that something was indeed wrong—it might just be the set of a man's eyes, an involuntary twitch in the muscles of the jaw, a sucked lip, the chewing of a finger. Someone who would, however, push the disagreeable notion away before he sat down to his evening meal, before he allowed his eyes to meet his wife's or his children's. Because Wu-chi was certain that most would simply lie to themselves; that was the nature of men. That was their vulnerability.

And the nature of evil was the ease with which one could allow oneself to flow into it. Evil was the herd. Evil was ordinary, commonplace. It was what a man ate for breakfast. This was the frightening truth that marked him a dead man.

The deposition was completed with the final statements regarding the vacancies created by the departed councillors. The members of the Three High Courts were escorted out of the hall. The waiting servants made their way slowly toward the surviving three old men.

Outside, the air was crisp and cool; the pine trees of the Imperial Park were a startling green against the blue, cloudless sky. Was this the last of the world that Wu-chi would see? Beneath his feet, miraculously beautiful clusters of grasses and weeds pushed through the pavement cracks, growing outward in spiraling circles of ever larger blades and leaves. Breezes stirred the crowns of the conifers with soft hissing sounds, rustling the hems of his robe and fluttering the tassels on the decorative skirts of the waiting palanquin. Clusters of brown pine needles were caught up in swirls on the cracked pavement, and the air was fragrant with their resiny scent.

Han-yuan and Lai-chi had been carried off toward the compound, their palanquins vanishing from sight around the dense copse of trees. In the courtyard, Wu-chi's eight bearers hoisted the conveyance and waited patiently; he complained of an arthritic knee that had flared up. He walked slowly, hobbling and wincing as he put pressure on that knee coming down the stairs. His young servant was polite, nodding in sympathy, supporting the councillor's elbow despite Wu-chi's protests.

Once he stepped into the palanquin, all would be lost. Though he remained outwardly collected, his blood raced and his thoughts tumbled over one another as he moved slowly toward the waiting servants. Then, for no apparent reason, he recalled an image from *A Tale of Six Old Fools*: the lascivious old councillors, the robes hiked up over the old men's heads. Why did he think of this preposterous thing now? But in the next moment, he knew why.

"I am most sorry for the sudden passage of your friend,"

the servant said, interrupting Wu-chi's thoughts.

"The world has suffered a great loss, but there is little sense in grieving now. Master Sui-liang was wise to have been born before the rest of us. And wiser still to have left the fools who remain here today. He will have some distance. We shall have to face it without him." He choked, suppressing a spasm of grief. "It was not that we did not expect his death." Wu-chi stopped and placed his hands on the railing. The grief moved in his chest, a persistent rising pressure, until he felt for the first time the tears brimming in his eyes. He tilted his head back and brought the tips of his fingers to his cheek to brush the tears away. He felt the warm sun and soft green breeze on his face—it was cool where it touched the tears. Sui-liang's autumn music playing for him one last time.

"Does the acupuncture help the pain and stiffness, Master Wuchi?" the servant asked, embarrassed, attempting to change the subject.

"It has helped somewhat," Wu-chi said brusquely and resumed his exaggeratedly painful climb down the stairs, wincing sharply each time his foot touched the stone. Now he was certain of what he had to do. Had it been old Sui's ghost bringing the image of the Old Fools and their hiked robes to mind? He turned to the servant and spoke in a low, discreet voice. "But it is the diuretic that the most 'helpful' physician has chosen to administer to me that has caused me the greatest problem . . . surely you understand. It has been a long morning. . . . "

At first, the servant did not appear to understand, but then he gave Wu-chi a look of pained sympathy.

"Of course, Councillor. Of course. I understand," he said, lowering his eyes. "We are fortunate to border the park woods."

"Most fortunate," Wu-chi agreed. "You will, of course, allow an old man a bit of time. My vessels no longer possess the vigor of youth."

"Certainly, Councillor. I will wait by the palanquin." The servant walked back to the bearers and gestured for them to take a rest. They lowered the elaborate chair to the ground with a great deal of grunting and muttering and straggled toward the grassy verge.

Wu-chi moved slowly at first, knowing their eyes might still be on him. He turned around cautiously, and saw that the servant was sitting unconcernedly on the pavement propped against the ornate chair, absorbed in a paper puzzle Sui-liang had made for the boy the week before. He thanked Master Sui's munificent ghost, and promised to make an offering to the old man's departed spirit. I may be a man who ignores my own father's funeral, he thought, remembering the spurious tales, but I will not soon forget you.

He moved into the corner of the trees and began to run. Small branches caught and tugged at the hems of his robes and waistcoat; he ducked from one, but another snatched his starched cap from his head. Good! Let the woods have the useless thing, he thought, picking up speed, the pain in his knee forgotten. His gray hair fell ungracefully around his face. He pushed deeper into the woods, leaping and running with newfound nimbleness over ancient mossy logs and up rocky slopes.

He tried to recall the layout of the Imperial Park. He remembered the outings of many years ago and how this thick tumbling stretch of woods opened onto the more level farmlands some distance north of the capital. It was just shortly past noon; therefore, he should keep the sun at his left shoulder. And above all, he must avoid the riding trails. The smell of decaying leaves and rich forest earth warmed by the sun took him back as he ran, awakening memories of happier times long ago.

The sound of voices and the pounding of hooves startled Wu-chi out of his reverie. He had wandered too close to the trail. He quickly moved away, but now found that the ground had begun to slope steeply downhill, and ahead there was an open patch of sky, as if there was a large clearing in the trees. From far below came the sounds of a stream. He remembered: the ravine! A deep, rocky depression of twisted pines and tall ferns cut across the park like an immense scar roughly from the eastern to the western boundary; and at the bottom was a small stream that would be more mud than water this time of the year. If he could have stayed on the trail, he would have had a convenient bridge to negotiate the ravine. But for him, there was only one way across—down and up the other side.

Wu-chi stumbled down the rocky slope, grabbing for branches and shrubs to check his momentum, his feet turning up piles of small stones and sending them bouncing down into the thick vegetation at the bottom of the ravine. He slipped, his legs flying out from under him, and fell painfully on his tail, sliding downhill for a few yards. He grabbed at a branch and pulled himself to his feet again. The branch cracked, and rocks clattered against one another. The noise in his own ears was terrible. It crossed his mind that his escape might not be successful if he made this much noise, but he told himself he was probably far enough away from the trail; it was also probable that no one was even looking for him yet. There was no helping the noise he was making. But of course, the woods were full of deer and other creatures that crashed away at the approach of men; anyone hearing him would assume he was hearing a frightened animal. Which I am, he thought.

Wu-chi slid down into the boggy grove of ferns, the stream trickling over the rocks just a few feet beyond him. By the time he had picked his way across the water and struggled up the other side of the ravine, he realized that the forest had taken its toll not only on his strength but on his clothing as well. For a moment he stood in the warm sunlight on the ridgetop and assessed his appearance. His robes were torn here and there, burrs clung to the hems, and his slippers had been sucked from his feet by the thick mud, which was drying like plaster between his toes. He felt his hair; it was a tangle of pine sap, needles, and twigs and was sticking out from his head like a madman's.

He stood trembling. Now where? Who would take a poor madman in? Where in the city would it be safe for him to go? Nowhere—considering that the Empress's agents would no doubt be searching for him before nightfall. A family was out of the question—his presence would be a danger to anyone kind enough to give him shelter.

Wincing with the pain that now spread from his tailbone to his hips, Wu-chi tried to tidy himself up, pulling futilely at his clothes, raking his fingers through his hair, but stopped as inspiration came to him. A madman. What better disguise? He knew who would take a poor madman in—especially a poor madman who could not even remember his own name.

A.D. 658
The Pure Lotus Monastery, north of Loyang

Wu-chi had lost track of the precise time, but it had been well over a month since he had been given lodging by the compassionate monks and nuns. He now resided within the enormous Buddhist monastic compound of the Pure Lotus, north of the Imperial Park, some ten *li* beyond the northern gates of Loyang. Within these walls, time passed and flowed serenely.

When he had first arrived, it was not that way. Time dragged into eternity like the ceaseless droning of the chanting monks. Even the solicitousness of the nuns with their infinite compassion for this poor lost soul who told them he could not remember his past or his own name had seemed overweening and trying to Wu-chi. There were the endless bells and flutes and stone chimes that announced calls to prayer and meditation in the Great Hall, forever breaking the day into unmanageable blocks of time. The lingering sun took forever to stretch the shadows along the drab walls of his cell.

And then it changed. Wu-chi gradually let loose the ardent Confucian zeal that had accompanied him throughout his life, relaxing into what the good Buddhists called a higher state of being. No longer the councillor of state overwhelmed by the immensity and importance of his Imperial duties, Wu-chi at sixty-one had gradually found time regaining the wondrous infinity of childhood on a hot summer day. The buzzing sounds of insects, their beauty and complexity, the sunbaked green smell of trees and grasses and flowers, then the chill breath of autumn; nothing passed without his notice and appreciation. His loss of memory, a tale he had told them as a way of deepening his disguise, ceased to be entirely fiction. There were days when he hardly thought about his past, though he took care not to forget entirely.

He had made very good friends with the abbot, Master Liao, a learned fellow close to his own age who was exceedingly eager for news of the outside world. He studied the day-to-day news from the capital with the same intensity, Wu-chi imagined, that he must have once devoted to the sutras. Wu-chi claimed a similar interest. As far as the abbot knew, his guest remembered only sparse fragments of his past life. Wu-chi seemed to remember that he had once been a minor provincial magistrate, or something like that. Perhaps only a clerk in a distant civil office—but a very literary one. At first Master Liao said that this interest might shatter his bliss, that news of the world outside might bring back unpleasant shadows of the past for his confused friend. But Wu-chi convinced the abbot that whatever peeks he took at his own past would not separate him from his bliss, which was now profoundly rooted and centered at the base of his divine chakras. Besides, Wu-chi knew that the old man was eager to have an intelligent partner with whom to discuss the increasingly strange developments in the Imperial politics of the capital.

The first bit of news that Abbot Liao brought was Wu-chi's own obituary. It seemed that the remaining three councillors from the defunct Tsai-siang had committed suicide, though all care had been taken for their comfort and well-being.

> ... The sudden madness that had struck down the first two councillors over a year ago seemed to be infectious. The three surviving honorable lords, Masters Han-yuan, Lai-chi, and Wu-chi, were found dead in their separate apartments, apparently having taken their lives by their own hands. ... No malaise or discomfort was sensed by any of their servants prior to the tragic series of events, leading the court physician to rule that madness had finally taken them all. ...

Wu-chi mused on all the possibilities. Had his escape ever been reported at all, or had there been an elaborate cover-up to keep the Empress from knowing that he had escaped? Wu-chi thought with a pang of regret of the young servant who had kindly allowed him to go into the woods to pass his water. No doubt his fate had not been a pleasant one. But what choice had Wu-chi?

And what had Empress Wu Tse-tien told Kaotsung about the poor old councillors? They were crazy, she would have said. So deluded, their Sea of Marrow so dried up that they must have suffered profound hysteria and hallucinations. And he, poor, useless Kaotsung, would have pleaded with her that there was nothing at all wrong with the old men. ...

Then Wu-chi wondered whose body had stood in for his at the scene of his supposed death. What poor old soul had had the misfortune to resemble him? And his old friends Lai-chi and Han-yuan. Tears blurred his vision as he prayed that their deaths had not been too hard.

Wu-chi's thoughts kept him awake late into the night. When he drifted off it was to dire images chasing up and down through thin, permeable layers of sleep. By early morning he was exhausted, and only then did he fall into a deep, dreamless sleep.

By early afternoon he struggled to wake. The bedclothing,

infinitesimal details of the walls and ceiling, even his own spotted hand, motionless on the bed by his face, were all visible to him in a bleak gray overcast light, but he could not quite bring himself to their side. Fatigue and oppression sat on his chest so heavily that he thought he might never rise again.

He was a criminal. He could never return to his life, because he had none.

But he had the abbot. The two found a strong friendship growing up between them.

A.D. 659

"You are late with my breakfast this morning," Wu-chi said to Master Liao as the abbot entered his quarters carrying a food hamper. Wu-chi did not look up. He was drafting a letter.

"Well, I am quite sorry to be late, old Councillor, but there are simply too many hungry people on the street out there waiting for us each morning." He released a deep sigh of exasperation. "We feed a hundred dirty little beggars each day. For each that we feed, there are a thousand more clamoring for our food and our mercy. In that order."

"Food alone, without the mercy, would suffice. That is all they want. Let us be honest. The good Buddhist can expect no more from the suffering people he helps. The suffering people do not wish to be preached to; just give them their food and they have what they need from you," Wu-chi added, his eyes still on the page.

"Excellent," the abbot said. "You are becoming as cynical as I am."

"I do not think I am being particularly cynical." Wu-chi put his brush down and looked up now. "Food is the earthly work of this monastery."

"More likely our earthly penance. No doubt we were all fat sated pigs in another life. This is our reward."

"Speaking of satiation, where is *my* breakfast, old priest?"

"Here is your breakfast," the abbot said patiently, putting the basket on the desk. "And," he grunted as he leaned over to extract something from the food hamper, "I have brought you a special treat this morning."

"I do not want a special treat," Wu-chi said crankily. "I do not care for your culinary surprises. I want my regular breakfast. The dry rice cakes! That is all I eat! You know my finicky digestion." Wu-chi rooted in the food basket. When he lifted his face it was not with pleasure. He brought out several greasy soy cakes. "These soggy greasy things are no surprise. They give me gas."

"No, no. You misunderstood me. There are no surprises in the food basket, Councillor," Liao said soothingly. "The surprise I speak of is quite indigestible." He opened a small package and began to unfold some papers.

"I doubt if it could be more indigestible than these," Wu-chi grumbled, peeling back the damp translucent wrapping.

"Do not bet on it, old man. It is *dreams*. Not something you would want to sink your teeth into. I think you would have to spit it across the room if you were to put it in your mouth, my dear friend."

"Not unlike this breakfast."

"Dreams," Abbot Liao continued, undaunted, "from our great Empress Wu. Published dreams circulated throughout the capital to demonstrate to all her subjects the awesome truth of her divine greatness." The abbot spoke through his mouthful of cake. "To show to us poor nonbelievers her place in the grand scheme of the universe."

"Please go ahead," Wu-chi said, attentive now.

"Well, it seems that our little historian Master Shu Chingtsung—president of the Imperial Board of History and Lord Secretary of the Chancellery—has added to the Veritable Records of Our Poor Beleaguered Emperor Kaotsung a few more things. Omens and portents. Just when you think that you have heard it all, our ever prolific Master Shu discovers something else that somehow got left out of the Veritable Records of Kaotsung's father, Taitsung. Such an oversight. How do these things happen?" He looked at Wu-chi.

"Why are you eating the soy cakes when you say they will upset you?"

"Oh, never mind. Go on."

"The first dream," the abbot said, rustling the papers, "is attributed to the Empress Wu's father—Wu Shih-huo."

"Ah, yes, Wu Shih-huo. One of the great founding fathers of the T'ang."

"According to this, Wu Shih-huo had a dream that foretold his daughter's destiny. This part reads: " . . . and during his long and selfless service to the Divine Kaotsu's father, the August Emperor Taitsung, the honorable governor-general of Ching-chou, Duke Wu Shih-huo—"

"Ahh! So now father Wu is a Duke, too."

"—Duke Wu Shih-huo had a dream in which he found himself floating on a perfumed cloud."

"Of course! Nothing else!"

"Essentially," Liao said, his eyes skimming down the rows of characters, "it says that Father Wu was taken up into the heavens to fly around the constellations. Once up there, he touched the sun and the moon with a golden staff. And, supposedly, touching the moon first meant that the founder of the new dynasty would be yin, female. And touching the sun next would imply that she would be imbued with yang, or male potency."

"So Wu will found a new dynasty. I had not been aware that the old one, the T'ang, had fallen. This has more consequence than the rebirth of the Buddha." Wu-chi almost laughed, wiping his greasy fingers nonchalantly on the front of the abbot's jacket. "But I should not be too surprised."

"Odd that you should speak of the rebirth of the Buddha," Abbot Liao said, turning over the pages. "It seems that poor Kaotsung's father, the Emperor Taitsung, also had a tendency toward prophetic dreaming, or, as it says here, to 'disembodied voices,' singing or whispering nonsense in his ear, telling him that a great Martial Prince would come to overturn the T'ang Dynasty. This prince would found another dynasty that would last a thousand years with the blessings of the all-seeing Future Buddha Maitreya and his earthly representatives the vigilant bodhisattva Avalokitesvara/ Kuan-yin: two forms, male and female, of the same bodhisattva savior. This he/she implying, so it says, male blood coursing through female veins. So the prince who will rule incarnate, beloved of the people, is actually a female assuming the role of a male." The abbot looked up from the page. "And who might that be, do you suppose?"

"So," Wu-chi said at last. "So the T'ang, or whatever it will be called, will be under a new ruler, a being who will be a freak of nature. Of that we are already certain," he finished bitterly.

The Empress's mother was dressed in a very handsome, almost austere robe this morning, with her hair done up in a sleek, plain knot that was most flattering to her features. She wore only one or two simple, tasteful ornaments, and her perfect skin was free of cosmetics. Historian Shu thought that she was the most beautiful woman he had ever seen in his life.

She sat in her newly appointed meditation room in her house in the city, with Shu and her daughter. She had had all the elaborate furniture, artwork, and knickknacks cleared out. Only an elegant carpet remained on the floor, and several plump embroidered silk pillows faced an altar where a small but very fine gilded Buddha sat in perfect repose, eyes closed in contemplation of infinity, flanked by two flickering oil lamps. The walls were bare, and the odor of freshly oiled wood mingled with the perfume of the lamps.

Madame Yang knelt in front of the altar, her face rapt, her eyes focused intently on the paper charm, which she touched to the lamp flame. She held the charm for a moment while it burned, watching the flame, then dropped it onto a gold dish at the Buddha's feet. The paper blackened and curled, the irregular glowing red edge racing inward, devouring the pure white, then extinguishing. She gazed at the drifting smoke for a moment before turning to her daughter and the historian. She waited a moment before speaking.

"I have had a dream," she announced, though they all knew perfectly well that that was why they were there. The historian had a small, discreet writing desk in his lap and a brush in his hand. Madame Yang closed her eyes for just a moment and then began. "In the dream, I was gazing down into a clear pool of water between two gigantic rocks. I thought it odd that I could not see my own reflection, but only the pure blue sky and white clouds above me. I leaned as far out over the water as I could, but still saw no trace of myself. I found a stick on the ground, and picked it up and held it out over the water: it, too, had no reflection. There was nothing but the sky and the drifting clouds." She paused and closed her eyes again, as if savoring the memory of that dream world. The historian leaned intently over his writing desk, the characters flowing from his agile brush.

"And then the wind began to blow," she continued, eyes still closed, swaying slightly as if she were going into a trance. "I was afraid, because there was debris flying all around me—sticks and rocks and small animals and such, picked up and driven forward by the wind, which became stronger and stronger. I covered my head to protect myself, uttering a prayer for deliverance. I knelt close to the ground, curled up in a ball, my arms over my head, and waited, for I knew there was nothing else I could do. Soon the wind was howling, filling the world with its sound. I could hear nothing but the voice of the wind." She pursed her lips then and made a sound like a fierce wind blowing, loud and strong at first, then subsiding gradually to a soft, thin sound like a whisper. She opened her eyes and looked at her daughter and the historian.

"The wind died finally, and I raised my head and looked around, and saw that the world was empty, clean, and pure like the sky. The wind had blown away all dead and unnecessary matter, leaving only the clean, strong, beautiful rocks. I looked down into the water again, and this time I could see the reflection of the rocky cliffs that rose around me. I looked more carefully, and saw a distant figure sitting high atop the cliff, framed by the blue, blue sky." She dropped her voice to an awed whisper. "Though he was far, far away, I knew right away that I was seeing the Blessed Maitreya, the Future Buddha himself. He was far away because he was not quite ready yet to come into this world. But a little golden frog swam up out of the depths of the pool and fixed me with one green eye. The frog had a perfect little human mouth, and he spoke to me in a tiny, shimmering voice."

The Empress and the historian were leaning forward, taking in every fascinating detail. Shu had filled an entire page with minute characters. He whipped the first sheet aside, not bothering to blot it, and began on a fresh one underneath.

"The little golden frog told me that the Maitreya will be coming soon, and that we will know when that time is imminent because a universal monarch will have come just before and cleansed a corrupt and confused world, making it pure to receive the Future Buddha. Like the wind that swept the world clean, the frog told me. How, I asked the frog, will we know when the monarch has arrived? By the monarch's name, the frog replied. You will know by the name, because it will have the same sound as the word for egolessness, for not-being. The name, the frog said, that had been spoken by the wind." She pursed her lips again and made the sound of wind blowing. Then she let her eyes rest on her daughter for a long, significant moment. "There are several words for not-being. But there is only one that also sounds like the wind blowing: that word is *wu*."

7

A.D. 660
Yangchou

"You see," Magistrate Dee said to his assistant, ignoring the neatly folded paper the other held in his outstretched hand, "I do not turn down these requests for my presence at banquets because I am not an unsociable creature. I enjoy food and talk as much as the next man. No; I decline for a very good reason."

"But you have not seen *this* invitation, sir," the assistant said.

"Nor do I need to. There are too many people who consider the—"

"And you have not seen his calling card, either," the assistant added in a determined way.

"There are too many people who regard the invitation of the senior magistrate of Yangchou to their homes only as an opportunity to corner him repeatedly with their petty demands for his personal attention as the chief judiciary voice of this province, which, too often, take the form of individual requests for their own aggrandizement—"

"I do not expect, sir, that a person of such stature visits Yangchou very frequently," the assistant put in when Dee paused to take a breath.

"—for their own aggrandizement, for special treatment, or worse, for their own profit. It is the reason that the rich get richer and rarely have to pay the full price for their crimes or their greed." Dee was in fine form. It was a lecture that had been crystallizing in his mind for some time.

"And, no doubt, this invitation has been extended because of your growing reputation pertaining to your work in the areas of monastic and clerical abuses."

"Whereas the poor cannot afford to put out the most meager of repasts for even one extra mouth without putting a dreadful strain on their poor households," Dee went on. "It is a shame that the poor must suffer under a legal system that often gives greater weight to influence, wealth, and bribery than to truth."

"It is evident, sir, that you have attracted considerable attention from higher-ups in the eastern capital."

"But there are those of us who cannot be bought, and I want them to know that."

"Especially the attention of such an important and honorable personage as the president of the National Bureau of Sacrifice," the assistant finished quietly, allowing that title to resonate for a moment.

Dee stopped talking and looked up. The assistant proffered the parchment. Dee glanced quickly at the official seal on the envelope and then looked at his assistant with an expression of utter surprise.

"It arrived just today, sir."

"He is here? In Yangchou? The president of the National Bureau . . . ?" Dee stumbled momentarily. "Why didn't you stop my infernal monologue and *tell* me?" He fumbled with the paper. "It is an invitation from the president of the National Bureau of Sacrifice to join him at the estate of one of Yangchou's most influential families. Why do you suppose he would be interested in meeting me?"

"I could not say, sir," the assistant said, clearing his throat. "But it is a *most* impressive honor."

The National Bureau of Sacrifice was the highest Imperial organ of government that oversaw the affairs of all religious practices within the Empire—state-sanctioned worship, as well as the practices, rituals, and festivals of the myriad of non-Chinese, barbarian belief systems. Nondisruptive foreign religions—Nestorian Christianity, Manichaeanism, Zoroastrianism, Islam—were all tolerated under the Son of Heaven's great T'ang, because in truth, the Emperor was also the ruler of the barbarians—though the barbarian nations might not always recognize that fact.

The bureau was the final arbiter of cases, the ultimate punisher of abuses, and the granter and revoker of licenses for all the diverse sects that were allowed to practice within the Empire. Of them all, Buddhism was rising to slow but sure dominance, becoming much more than a functional household religion of hearthside gods, paper charms, and incense sticks. Buddhism had become a force that occupied the mind of a nation and had entered all levels of society. With its thousands of monasteries, its enormous landholdings, its exemptions from Imperial taxations and levies, and its own laws of discipline and regulation, it was becoming a force of political power, and it was the major concern of the National Bureau of Sacrifice. And within that body, the president of the bureau was the highest authority on these matters aside from the Emperor himself.

Why should the president of the bureau request Dee's presence at the estate of his host? There was something that bothered him about all of this.

"Ah. Here it is," the assistant said from behind the disorder of the desk, jarring Dee out of his thoughts. "The president's calling card, sir. With the time and date."

"But doesn't this whole thing strike you as . . . odd?" Dee asked, examining the card and turning it over.

"Odd? Why? You are the presiding authority in Yangchou."

"No. Not odd that the president should call upon me. Odd that he should not make an official visit through this office. Certainly this is where we have all the records of abuses and licenses and all. Why would he want to meet me at a private home?"

"Probably the host is an old family friend," Dee's assistant offered. "No doubt he has a fine estate and the capacity for a very fine party. What have we? A grimy compound of old buildings and a stipend from the district magistrate."

"It still seems somewhat unorthodox that he would not at least come here first."

"Perhaps he intends to another day."

"Perhaps. But . . . " Dee shrugged, perplexed. "Well, why ask questions that will soon be answered?"

Tonight, it would be one rational Confucian to another. There would be solid ground between Dee and the president of the Bureau of Sacrifice. If it was impossible to turn things around, then there might at least be ways to slow the course of events. Surely they might reach an agreement on the number of new monasteries licensed, or at least impose some inoffensive means of limiting begging and proselytizing and almsgiving outside the temple confines. As it was now, the city streets were out of hand. The president would certainly help him to arrive at something to assure that the religion stay "pure" and nonmaterial, as the true Buddhist faith was intended to be. It would be a fine meeting of Confucian minds and hearts. He was looking forward to it.

He had just turned to leave when he heard a familiar scratching at the door from the garden.

Scoundrel entered Dee's study, stiff-legged and panting, and heaved himself down at his well-worn spot under a table. Dee went and rubbed his friend's head; the dog's tongue hung out of his mouth like a long, limp, wet pink ribbon. The hair of his muzzle was gray, his rump was almost completely bald, and Dee had begun to notice a whitish opacity to his eyes when the light caught them at a certain angle. But the dog sat panting, fresh from his prowls, catching his breath, smelling of the garden and the night outside, unsentimental and unlachrymose about his own mortality as only an animal can be.

Dee spoke to his friend as he straightened up and prepared to leave.

"Do you have a particular message you would like me to deliver to the president?"

The household steward received the senior magistrate of Yangchou at the far end of a splendidly lit pathway and walked silently along with him as Dee admired his host's grounds. Delicate bridges spanned a tiny stream alive with lacy foam, bordered by a miniature rock gorge and a forest of bamboo and pine. Leaning in close around the path with rows of tiny candle lanterns in their midst, the gnarled trunks and low branches cast mysteriously flickering, dancing shadows. The exquisiteness of the place was seductive; for a few moments, Dee enjoyed the illusion that he had forgotten why he had come there.

Orchestral music emanated from a small pavilion, the harmonious sounds blending pleasantly with the gurgling of the stream: the gentle rhythmic plucking of the *chin* strings framed an easy melody that was echoed by an elaborate round on the *hsiao* bamboo flutes and the *sheng* pipes. A most pleasant composition, Dee thought, and given his host's very imaginative garden and its fairyland tunnel of pine boughs, it was a melody that lent an agreeably haunting and ethereal quality to the surroundings.

Dee heard voices now. It sounded like a good many people conversing enthusiastically some distance off among the rocks and trees. The steward escorted him over another footbridge and then guided him along a zigzagging pathway of stone through a maze of hedges. Now Dee was able to intercept bits and pieces of distinctly heated and animated conversations going on in the courtyard garden.

" . . . it is not difficult to contend with the size . . . "

" . . . but there are fully six hundred chapters to the Mahaprajnapar . . . "

" . . . as for the Yogacara Stages, other than the initial treatise, I would hesitate to . . . "

"The problem is that the Arabs have closed the western end of the overland routes . . . "

"Hsuan-tsang would be best advised to take heed . . . "

Dee strained his ears, but the steward was moving him on a course away from the lively discussion and closer to the orchestra. Dee knew that soon all he would be able to hear would be the pounding of the *weir* drum and the strumming of the *bi-pas*.

" . . . and yet he has brought some six hundred and fifty-seven sutra items packed in five hundred and twenty cases . . . "

"It would never be possible. One hundred thousand cash could barely begin to cover the cost . . . "

"There are immense problems of translation . . . "

"The problem, of course, with the Abhidhar is the obscure dialect . . . "

The steward was motioning Dee through a second gate and toward a hall that took him in the opposite direction.

" . . . it is all very expensive," said an officious-sounding, distinctly foreign-accented voice. "But if this is not the duty of wealth, what is?"

If *what* is not the duty of wealth? Dee asked himself as the sweet melodies drowned out the voices altogether. He found himself becoming irritated with the lilting strings and echoing pipes. They seemed as shrill to him now as the voice of a bothersome old grandmother.

"Senior Magistrate Dee Jen-chieh, it is so very good that you have arrived at last," said a voice very close to his left shoulder. Dee turned to face a tall, handsome, bearded man supposed to be in his late fifties. He put a smile on his face meant to match the somewhat overly warm grin on the other's face. The steward bowed and left after presenting the bearded man with Dee's calling card. But the man made no effort to read the card, apparently recognizing Dee on sight. Dee realized that though he could not recall ever meeting or seeing this tall fellow before, the man had recognized him.

"Do you not think that the great Confucius would be pleased with our music and garden this evening?" the man said, still grinning.

"Everything is magnificent!" Dee enthused politely, his mind still on the fragmented conversation back in the garden. Why would guests at the home of a Confucian be discussing the costs of translating sutras and the travels of religious pilgrims? He had heard the name Hsuan-tsang mentioned. Dee had heard of him: one of the most influential monk-scholars alive today, a man who had made countless pilgrimages to the far west, carrying back holy writings. Shape up, old boy, Dee told himself, this could prove to be a much more interesting night than even you had supposed. "Truly magnificent—and it is such a beautiful, soft evening," he added.

"Our divine prayers could not have been more amply rewarded," the other said. "Tonight is important to all of us, would you not say?"

"Indeed!" Dee answered noncommittally, not altogether certain what his host meant.

"Forgive me . . . oh, do forgive me, Master Dee Jen-chieh. I have completely forgotten my manners. Such a beautiful evening can make one forget the most basic things. We become like children. It is most reprehensible. Of course, we all know our good and assiduous magistrate from his work in our great city, but how could he know us? It is most inconsiderate of me. I am Lu Hsun-pei, your most humble host this evening and the master of this rustic little estate. And this is—"

"So . . . you are the brilliant young Senior Magistrate Dee Jenchieh," another voice said from behind them. Dee turned toward the stairs of the main hall. A short smiling man in the glistening silk turquoise robes and starched cap of the highest-grade Confucian official bounced ebulliently down the steps and onto the terrace. "I have heard so much about you," the new arrival said. "Such a worthy replacement for your predecessor. An official of such vigor and honesty . . . such integrity! Yes! Master Dee Jen-chieh, we are most fortunate. The great city of Yangchou is proud to have you. And *needs* you."

"I do not know what to say," Dee said, bowing.

The small man waved the formality away. Then he rolled his head from side to side. "Tsk, tsk, tsk! It is *I* who should bow to you, Master Dee," he said, bringing both hands up in supplication. "It is such a difficult world today. So complex. Especially a city such as yours. All the comings and goings . . .

the maritime trade, the canals. All the foreign . . . uh, *barbarian* influences you must contend with. You are a most extraordinary Confucian civil servant. The matters you have had to concern yourself with . . . the sheer number and nature of the infractions. It is unimaginable to those of us who sit in the upper reaches of Imperial office in the National Bureau of Sacrifice; we are, so to speak, shielded from it all. Protected from the little crises." So this was the president of the National Bureau of Sacrifice, Dee thought appraisingly. "It is the day-to-day, the small particular matters that surely must be so overwhelming," the man said, shaking his head in feigned sympathy.

"As you have no doubt gathered, Master Dee, the one addressing you is the Honorable Master Fu Yu-i, president of the National Bureau of Sacrifice," Dee's tall, bearded host said. With the introduction, Dee nodded his head in the president's direction. Neither man would stand on ceremony. Dee appreciated that. Artificial social barriers could be broken through that much more quickly, clearing the way for a truly constructive exchange, he hoped.

"And I have already heard the story from our host of how you, Master Dee, the illustrious city magistrate, have recovered the courts from your predecessor's laxity," the president said.

"I am afraid, gentlemen, that I cannot accept such accolades," Dee demurred. "My predecessor had established a superb reputation and staff within his office. I am only the inheritor of his wisdom." Dee's humility was the necessary response. It would not do, so early in his meeting with these men, to attack old man Lu.

"You are too kind, Master Dee. The embodiment of the ideal Confucian," the president said, then leaned close and spoke. "Senior Magistrate Lu was a corrupt old fool; it is good that he is dead and you are in office. We do not need to play with the truth. At the Imperial level, we see far too many of his kind asking for undeserved promotions or asking for reappointments to other districts when they have worn out their welcome, and . . ."

"Gentlemen, I shall leave you to your discussions of politics and ethics," Lu Hsun-pei said to Dee and President Fu, bowing slightly. "I must attend to our revered guests in the courtyard. You will excuse me."

Dee was intrigued momentarily. Revered guests? The owners of the voices that had tantalized him on the way in, obviously. But he returned his attention to the president, who was still speaking to him.

" . . . always, they are the ones most bribable," the man was saying. "Your old Judge Lu was just such a petty creature. Do not cover for him, Magistrate. It is not necessary for such an exemplary Confucian official as you to trouble himself making apologies for petty and inferior men. We see it all." He lowered his eyes slowly to the ground as if contemplating some sadness in his words, then brought them back up quickly to fix merrily on Dee's. "In any case, Master Dee, your work is gaining you some renown."

Just then the distant honking of geese took their attention. Far off in the darkening western sky, just coming into view over the tops of the courtyard trees, an irregular chevron form moved south, wavering like a spider's thread in a breeze. It was not long before individual birds could be made out, like pearls on a string, as they flew overhead. The treetops swayed, the dark branches of the conifers moving like a dancer's fingers. The two men watched the birds of autumn together for a long moment before the president resumed.

"What interests our host, Master Lu Hsun-pei, and me the most, Magistrate Dee," the president said, the tips of his fingers stroking his smooth cheek thoughtfully, "is your enviable work against these religious charlatans." Dee listened attentively now. The subject of Buddhist clerical abuse and the state was the one Dee had been waiting for. The preliminaries and formalities were over. "Most commendable! Most commendable!" the president said.

"I thank you, Master Fu, but I was only doing my duties in a most unexceptional way. A criminal is a criminal, no matter how devout."

"Unexceptional? Not so, Master Dee. It is most important to ferret out these charlatans among the Buddhist establishment who are preying on the vulnerable minds of the peasantry."

"I agree wholeheartedly."

"But Master Dee, I wonder if you are aware that this work is more important than it might first appear," the president said.

"I never thought of it as unimportant," Dee responded.

"I am not speaking merely of the necessity of separating the good from the bad for the proper ordering of this world," the man said, leveling an unwavering look at Dee. "No. There is much more at stake. There are the higher realms to be considered."

Higher realms? Dee waited, saying nothing. He was more than a little taken aback.

"The church will be unable to do its proper work among us if charlatans are allowed to cloud the righteous paths," the man continued. "The true work of the Buddhist church must not be obscured by these self-seekers, Master Dee. That is why we are here today. Is that not so?" Dee said nothing, making every effort to keep the astonishment he was feeling from showing on his face. The president ignored Dee's silence and continued, "We are here to make certain that the true work of the church continues unobstructed. And that work is going to be expensive."

Expensive? This was interesting indeed. Dee was certain that he had picked the words "expense" and "cash" from the jumble of conversations in the rear gardens.

"Master Dee Jen-chieh," the little man said, assuming now a formal tone, "are you aware of the enormous costs involved in sutra translations from the Sanskrit? Heaven seems to have thrown up incredible barriers—as a test of our resolve, no doubt—between our two languages: one the language of men, the other the language of those higher realms. Ah! And we are not even beginning to speak of other costs. The costs, for instance, of devotees' journeys to and from sacred India. Many of which begin on your very own canals." He paused and allowed his eyes to close as if contemplating the weight of such a task. "Truth is a matter of *patronage*, Master Dee. And patronage is *money*. Staggering amounts." The president opened his arms wide and fixed his eyes firmly on Dee, who smiled in a way that indicated curiosity and growing interest.

"How true," Dee said thoughtfully, pausing a moment and then leaning forward to speak confidentially. "I would be most interested in meeting our revered guests."

"Of course! Of course, Master Dee Jen-chieh! I apologize. All my talk is keeping you from such very enlightened company. Come with me to the courtyard gardens."

It was growing very dark by now. The president called for servants to light the pole lanterns and escort them through the winding maze of bridges and pavilions.

The rear garden and rockery and the lawns and terraces were alive with motion and talk. In the lanternlight, he could see richly dressed men and women moving among the rocks

and pavilions like glittering silken wraiths. There were more
people gathered here than Dee had thought. He caught flashes
of color as they moved, like so many magnificently exotic insects, in and out of the pools of light. Soon Dee's eyes adjusted
and he saw a row of banquet tables along the perimeter of the
garden, laden with delicacies of infinite variety, on plates of
silver and jade. The president took Dee gently by the elbow
and coaxed him into the sea of people like a proud father with
a shy child.

"Come, Magistrate . . . there are many, many people here
who wish to meet their new judge. The masters and great ladies of Yangchou's finest households have assembled here tonight. Patrons, each of them in his own way, to some of the
most profound." He spoke the last word lovingly, savoring it
as if it were a tasty morsel melting on his tongue.

The president pulled Dee into the center of the activity,
where two shaven-headed monks were engaged in a lively debate with a third man. This other was thin and richly dressed,
his fancy brocade robes trimmed with ermine, his gaunt whisk-
ered face partly obscured by the broad brim of his horsehair
hat, which bobbed up and down like an enormous articulating
eyebrow as he spoke. The president guided Dee to the edge of
the conversation, but did not interrupt yet. He stood and listened as if it were a particularly fine piece of music they were
hearing and he were personally and proudly initiating the
magistrate into its delights.

"But the problem, Master Li," one of the monks said to
the wealthy-looking man, "is the enormous task facing the
translator for the rarer sutras. Especially those damaged by the
Godovari River floods and the flooding of the Tapti tributaries
in south central India." It was the shrill, high-pitched, accented
voice full of urgency and self-importance that Dee had heard
when they were approaching. Dee saw clearly now that the
man was dark-skinned and foreign: an Indian.

"My brother would be speaking of the great parchments
of the Elura and Ajanta temples. It is an expense with no apparent vanishing point," added the second monk, who was
Chinese, in his low, calm, steadily droning baritone.

"That is so. And particularly when one considers that the
Sanskrit ligatures can hardly be deciphered because of the
sorry condition of certain of those more ancient sacred parchments," the first monk continued in his thin high voice. "Key
words are shrouded in mystery in each fragment of a sentence

strophe; four or five are entirely unreadable in each strophe. Entire issues of sacred Dharmic Law—the highest matters of Buddhistic nomothetics—are in danger of being lost forever to us, explaining the confusion that our devotees face in China."

Master Li nodded his head and removed his great wide-brimmed horsehair hat with one hand and mopped at his torrid forehead with the other. His troubled eyes expressed his clear sympathy with these problems.

"The Truth is difficult enough to grasp even if it is bestowed upon us in the clearest translations," the Indian continued. "The paths to enlightenment remain elusive enough in the best of worlds," he said, looking around himself and shrugging sorrowfully.

"Then what of the recent materials excavated from our own Buddhist caves at Tunhuang?" asked Master Li.

"Ahhh. The greatest of our blessings is the yield from our own lands!" the Chinese monk rumbled in his deep, confident tones. "But, once again, there will necessarily be great expense involved in restoring and translating." He shook his head and let his words trail off. "Well, you begin to see what we are facing."

Yes, Dee thought, looking at the man's shaved and polished skull and watching him raise a cup of wine to wet his lips after delivering his words, I certainly am beginning to see what we are facing.

This was little more than a glorified matchmaking affair—a gathering of wealthy Buddhist sponsors and their potential protégés. It had been disheartening enough to learn that a highly placed Confucian magistrate was capable of being seduced away from his proper moral and ethical course; now it became clear to Dee that he himself, the senior magistrate of the city of Yangchou, was being courted by them. Why?

The president was positively beaming now, and chose this auspicious pause in the high-minded talk to break in.

"May I introduce you gentlemen to Yangchou's illustrious Magistrate Dee . . . old Judge Lu's most worthy replacement." By this time Dee and the president had been spotted by their tall, bearded host, who came briskly across the terrace to join them. The president turned toward the thin man in the fur-trimmed robes and continued his introductions. "Master Li, this is Magistrate Dee—the watchful eyes of our illustrious city. Magistrate Dee, this is the honorable Master Li, representing one of Yangchou's most prosperous families," the president said enthusiastically. "And two of our district's foremost abbots," he said, indicating the two conversing monks, who protested the compliment, demurely throwing their hands up in front of their faces. Dee nodded politely to them.

"You have no doubt gathered from our conversations, Magistrate Dee, that we are concerned with the inordinate expenses involved in difficult translations, and excavation and recovery projects in flood-ravaged temples and stupas," the first monk said, his voice calmer and not quite so grating now. "The good president of the National Bureau of Sacrifice, with the gracious help of our host, has brought us together for this beautiful evening. I would prefer that my attentions were allowed to remain on the sacred. But this world," he said, pronouncing the word with disdain, "demands to be dealt with. It is *expensive* and quite *real* while we are here."

"Quite real," Dee agreed. "And the obligations of cost are, without a doubt, an essential aspect of this cruel reality?"

"It is so, Master Dee," the first monk said in a voice full of regret. "That is why we are here tonight."

"And is that also why you have come tonight, President Fu Yu-i?" Dee asked.

"At the kindness of our host," the president said, turning to acknowledge the bearded man who now stood just behind him, "we have been given an opportunity to bring the greatest patrons together with the greatest need. The great pilgrim Hsuan-tsang has returned from India with six hundred and fifty-seven untranslated items packed in five hundred and twenty cases." He turned to the second monk, inviting him to elaborate.

"There is the Mahavibhasha—the Great Commentary," the deep-voiced monk began, counting on his fingers as he spoke. "The Yogacarabhumisastra—the Treatise on the Yogacara Stages; the Jnanaprasthana, the Abhidharmakosa, the Trimsika . . . the list is endless, Magistrate." The monk looked around at the others, soliciting their agreement and support. "The work is nearly infinite. And that means great expense. With the overland routes to the sacred land cut off . . . all of this can only add to the enormous costs. I am sure you see what we are up against."

"Indeed I do," Dee replied politely.

"Tonight, Magistrate," his host's voice said behind him, "we bring together wealth and righteousness. Wealthy patrons of the Buddhist church join us to become sponsors, Magistrate Dee."

"That is where our ways must part, Master Lu," Dee said politely to his tall, handsome host. "It is not that this lowly magistrate denies the philosophical brilliance of the higher-minded aspects of Buddhism, or the dedication of the men whom fate destines to contemplate it. But . . . for me, *this* world demands my fullest attention."

"This is a world of suffering, Magistrate," the second monk intoned in a fatherly, almost condescending way. "It is a futile struggle, at best."

Dee's eyes narrowed as he looked at the man. "That may be, but it is the only world we can really know and the only one we are truly capable of dealing with. And the state will continue to support and sanction the church's charities, hospitals, and kitchens, as always."

"Master Dee . . . Master Dee . . . " Their host, Lu Hsun-pei, pushed his way into the center of the gathering and threw up his hands in exasperation. "Master Dee, it is sad. Most sad. Very, very sad," he said, shaking his head in exaggerated grief. "It is not the suffering or the obligations *of* this world or *to* this world that matter at all."

"Master Lu Hsun-pei is correct. Our obligations are to the higher realms of the soul," the president of the National Bureau of Sacrifice exclaimed. He reached up and grabbed hold of the magistrate's shoulders. "And to worlds other than this one," he declared. Dee could taste the odious little president's sour breath on his chin. His dislike of the man was growing by the second. "Master Dee, I give my unqualified support as president of the Bureau of Sacrifice to our host and his efforts at higher enlightenment this evening."

"Master Lu Hsun-pei," Dee said to his host, "you, of course, are free to follow your conscience. But *he* is not!" Dee returned his eyes squarely to the little president's. "Master Fu Yu-i, as long as he retains his office and his title, is not free to be anything but a Confucian official, and that and that alone is the greatest responsibility between heaven and earth. Your obligations are to *this* world, President Fu Yu-i. To your Emperor and to his subjects, all under heaven."

"Really, Master Dee," the president said, looking around him for support. "Confucius was appropriate to his time. But it is a new world! Buddhism is coming to us, embracing us, closing the distances . . . it is indeed a new world," the president repeated, savoring every word, then clasping his hands and turning for approval to their handsome host.

"It does not seem a new world to me, President Fu Yu-i," Dee said wearily. "I see the same tired fools every day. Nothing has changed. I see officials making a mockery of their office." Dee crossed his arms and tucked his hands up under them. His eyes moved slowly down from the president's indignant face to settle on the little man's anxiously tangling hands. Dee nodded with polite finality to the four men and turned away.

Dee was nearly to the steps of the courtyard gate when his host intercepted him, tapping him lightly on the arm. "Master Dee, I should hate to have you leave us like this. Allow me the pleasure, at least, of having you sample some of our extraordinary delicacies." He guided Dee gently but firmly toward a table near the gate, its beautifully polished rosewood-and-teak-inlaid surface reflecting the silver and jade plates in the graceful dancing light of the candles. "Some wine, perhaps, Magistrate? Turfan, chrysanthemum, pepper, mare's teat grape? The finest. Something?"

Dee was exasperated, but the man seemed so genuinely anxious that a guest not leave his house unhappy that he took pity on him and relented.

"Yes, Master Lu Hsun-pei," Dee said, forcing a civil smile. "A cup of wine—pepper, I think—would set most nicely."

The host nodded to the steward, who brought them both a cup. The host raised the cup and then lowered it in the proper ritual salutation before signaling to Dee to sample the wine. "Delightful," Dee said at last. His host then gestured for Dee to follow him to a quiet corner beneath the pines.

They sipped their wine quietly for a few moments, Dee making an effort to appear as if he were enjoying himself at least to that extent. His bearded host spoke at last.

"Magistrate, I understand that you must do your job. But might I ask you to do me a kindness? There is so much at stake here, you understand. So much effort and time . . . the finest families of Yangchou . . ."

"The finest money, you mean," Dee returned shortly. He took a healthy drink of wine and turned to his host, who sat there, a bit taken aback. "I am astonished, but I should not be," Dee continued. "I should not be surprised at all. In a way, I am grateful to you for opening my eyes." His host waited. "I now understand more clearly than ever that religious opportunism knows no bounds. The rich are pitted against each other, to vie greedily for the privilege of having their names attached to this or that great sutra or document, to compete for sacred prestige!" He shook his head, marveling at it all. "An assurance of paradise through more and greater patronage! And all under the guise of what is current, what is *fashionable*."

"Master Dee, my request is simple," Lu Hsun-pei said after a moment, a flicker of deliberate calculation passing across his face. He gently took hold of Dee's elbow and walked him to the interior of a small pavilion nearby. "I can make you a very wealthy man. My resources, like those of Master Li of the great shipping family, are nearly infinite, tied up as they are with the Grand Canal.

"I shall ask you what your price is," his host continued. "And my promise is that once that price is told, I shall not balk at it. One million strings of cash for starters?" He paused. "Two? Three?" Seeing that he was getting no response, he took a breath and leaped ahead. "Then it is *ten* perhaps?" Still Dee said nothing. The host covered his discomfiture at Dee's unreadable stony silence. He pushed on: "I ask only that you confine your brilliant work against clerical abuses to the lower levels of society. Stay there. It is no problem. Prevent the poor, unfortunate peasant from being victimized by the charlatans who would prey on his superstitious nature. By all means. Play the good paternal magistrate. But it would be best for everyone if you would *not* proceed any further. If you would offer no obstructions to *our* work . . ."

"It would depend on what that work is, would it not, Master Lu?" Dee said, studying his host's face. "The poor must be protected from the wiles of the religious charlatan, and the rich must be protected from themselves. That is the irony— both rich and poor promote the same phenomenon, and are ultimately victims of the same delusion."

"That is where you are wrong, Master Dee." Lu Hsun-pei laughed and shook his handsome head. "It is not the same creature that possesses the rich. There is an undeniable fact in this world: the poor, through their impoverished efforts, only promote deeper poverty for themselves. But as you well know, it is a different tale for the rich. They are in the position in life that they are in because they have *won* it. Look around you." Lu Hsun-pei made a broad expansive gesture with his arms. Dee did not oblige his host, but kept his eyes level, his way of telling the man he had seen more than enough. "No. I am hardly such a fool as to be chasing only after elusive, invisible worlds," Lu Hsun-pei said, openly arrogant and boastful now, any pretext of piety dropped. "We are dealing also with the prospects of this very real one as well. There is hard practicality in our sponsorship of great translations and documents and of religious journeys that set sail in our very own canals. Something more than mere self-aggrandizement. Remember, Magistrate Dee—he who pays the piper calls the tune," he said enigmatically. "The poor, in their devout ignorance, have no choice but to grow poorer while the rich have no choice but to grow richer. Why," he said, then, laughing, "the poor will even sell us their daughters if the price is right."

"That is an expression I have never found amusing, even in jest," Dee said to Lu Hsun-pei. "But I am grateful for this small bit of honesty from you, however odious it may be. It is probably the only straightforward statement I have heard all evening. There is another difference between the rich and the poor. The rich possess the means for even greater delusion." The other man bowed as if Dee had paid him the highest compliment.

"What of my offer?" he asked then. "Perhaps you would like to give it some thought."

"Yes," Dee said. "I would like to give it some thought." Dee turned away from his host as if he were about to leave the garden pavilion. "Oh . . . pardon me, Master Lu Hsun-pei, but I seem to have forgotten my manners." With that, he picked his cup off the railing where he had put it earlier. He hefted it, appearing to assess its weight and materials, then raised it into the flickering light, examining the delicate workmanship of the embossed flower patterns and the beauty of the dripping glazes. He moved his gaze from the cup to a group of guests milling nearby. He picked out President Fu Yu-i standing at a nearby banquet table, plainly curious about what was passing between Lu Hsun-pei and Magistrate Dee.

Dee obliged him. "President Fu Yu-i," he called. "Would you do me the kindness of coming here, please?"

The little man's eyes brightened as he put down his silver chopsticks and stepped nimbly over to the pavilion.

"Is this not a beautiful cup?" Dee asked. "I mean," he reassessed, "a most *exquisite* cup!" He held it up for him to look at in the lantern light.

"Well . . . yes. Of course it is . . . but . . . " the president said, still smiling, but guarded now, wondering what sort of game they were playing. "Naturally. All of Master Lu Hsun-pei's appointments are of the finest quality. Most beautiful, Magistrate."

"Would you say it is valuable?" he asked innocently.

"I suppose it is! For a cup, that is, Magistrate!" the little president answered, his eyes a shade worried now, darting from Dee to his host and back again. "But what is this about?"

"It is about nothing, Master Fu Yu-i," Dee replied. "Merely about art and its value."

"Value?" the president asked.

"Yes, I only wondered after its value. You see, Master Lu Hsun-pei, our handsome and gracious and wealthy and artistically sensitive host, has offered me a gift." The little man shot a quizzical look to Lu Hsun-pei, who cautioned him with his eyes before turning his back to Dee and the president and leaning on the pavilion railing to look out over the party. "But the gift was far too generous. Far too generous. It would be a prince's ransom, President Fu Yu-i. Regretfully, I had to refuse it." Dee watched the back of his host's head, which told him as much as the man's face possibly could. "Instead of accepting Lu Hsun-pei's kind offer, gentlemen, I shall keep this cup. Such a beautiful cup. It will more than pay for the ink that I must purchase for the memorial that I am drafting to the throne: a memorial warning against the corruption of supposedly responsible officials and their susceptibility, like the poorest, most ignorant peasant, to the seductive power of a foreign dogma. And I shall not hesitate to use President Fu Yu-i's name as an example of corruption on the highest levels. Sir," he said, bowing to the president, "please be informed that I shall look for clerical abuses wherever they occur. And if they should lead all the way to your honorable office at the National Bureau of Sacrifice, I shall look there, too."

Dee turned to leave on that ringing note, satisfied that he had made a suitable impression on the two men. But before he had stepped out of the pavilion, he heard his host laugh and speak in a voice just loud enough for Dee to hear.

"A memorial to the throne?" Lu Hsun-pei said to the president. "Good. Let us hope that he is as good as his word. And let us hope that he does it soon." The other laughed too, albeit nervously, without the overweening self-confidence of the other. Dee did not turn around, but the strange words followed him all the way out the gate and to his waiting carriage.

* * *

Dee was awakened the next morning by an idea. He had gone to bed simmering and indignant, hearing again Lu Hsun-pei's arrogant laugh and recalling the way he boasted so shamelessly of his wealth and privilege, as if they had been granted him by the gods themselves, making him a different creature from his fellow men, exempt from the rules, godlike himself. Dee's mind must have been working while he slept, because when he woke up, he was no longer angry. Instead, he was full of purpose, curious, and impatient to get to his office as quickly as possible.

His assistant was there when he arrived, as he always was. Dee hurried in, aware of the young man looking up from his desk, his face full of questions. But Dee did not give him time to speak.

"Do you recall the murder several years ago of the Transport Minister?" Dee asked the assistant as he swept by his desk.

"Of course," the young man replied, surprised. "For which a gardener paid with his life."

"And for which *I* nearly paid with my own life," Dee said, sitting down at his desk. "The case that nearly drove me to distraction, slipping from my grasp, eluding me, tantalizing me, leading me down blind alleys and then nearly smashing me over the head in my own office. The case that has been gnawing at me for years."

"You have a clue?" the young man asked, interested.

"Not exactly. But I am thinking of it again. It was a most interesting gathering last night. I met a man with all the proper qualifications to know something that I don't know about the murder of the Transport Minister. He is rich, he is arrogant, and he is quite without scruples."

"That describes a great many people, sir," the assistant remarked.

"True enough," Dee conceded. "'But this man, in the midst of his boasting, mentioned that a large part of his fortune is connected with the transport system of the city. And," he said significantly, seeing the look of alert interest on his assistant's face, "the man has regular contact with foreigners. Indians, to be precise," he finished with satisfaction. He pulled a blank piece of parchment toward him and moistened a writing brush. He dashed off the characters of the man's name and held it out to the young man. "Lu Hsun-pei. A wealthy man. A man of many and varied contacts. I think it would be worth our while to look for any connections he may have had with the dead Minister of Transport. This case has sat dormant for too long. The ghost of the dead gardener has even given up. Drifted away. He flits across the background of my dreams once in a while, but less and less as the years go by." He shook his head. "And that is much, much worse than if he haunted me night and day. Search the trade records, the transport records, the tax records. Look for any places at all where he and the murdered man may have intersected, professionally or personally. I do not know what we will find, if anything. But I want you to do it."

"It sounds as if it was a most interesting gathering," the assistant ventured.

"The world is certainly full of surprises," Dee conceded laconically. "But I kept my eyes and ears open. What I saw surpassed any morality play or metaphorical puppet show I might see in the street bazaars of the city, those hyperbolic dramas that no one is expected to believe but that are designed to teach us, through extreme absurdity, about good and evil," he said, pleased with his comparison. "It *was* rather like an enormous puppet show. Populated with thieves, beautiful ladies, corrupt officials, holy men, and villains offering bribes."

"Holy men?" the assistant asked incredulously.

"Of course. What else?" Dee answered with heavy sarcasm. "Holy men being wined, dined, and courted lavishly. What should I have expected at a party where the guest of honor is a high Confucian official whose sworn duty is to keep superstition from running amok? Though the true guest of honor, the one whose name was on every tongue, was not present. Apparently he is kept busy with his constant and very costly pilgrimages to the far west, where he diligently mines for Truth and then sells it, like so many chunks of precious metal."

"And who is that?" the assistant asked with a smile.

"A traveling monk by the name of Hsuan-tsang, who has contrived to make himself indispensable to the idle affluent of the city. The most influential families. A list of the names at the party would have read like the National Clan Registry. Thank goodness—we would not want them to feel that their lives are utterly useless, would we?"

"Hsuan-tsang," the assistant said thoughtfully. "I have heard that name before!"

"No doubt," Dee said. "Everyone has."

"No. I mean I have read the name. And very recently. Today, in fact." He began to rummage through the papers in front of him. "It is here, Magistrate. Somewhere. It arrived this morning. I did not deem it important enough to show you immediately, what with other matters so much more pressing. But now . . . ah!" He pulled out a folded yellow document and held it up toward the window. The Imperial seal blazed in the morning light. "It arrived enfolded in another letter," he said, holding up a second, plainer piece of paper. "Apparently someone wished to bring this to your attention."

"Give them to me immediately," Dee said, jumping up from his chair. He pulled the documents from his assistant's surprised fingers and stood by the window to read.

"One is a decree from the family of the Empress Wu," he said looking up. "More specifically, from the mother of the Empress Wu, the 'Reverent' Madame Yang. The other is a letter from . . . I do not know who it is from." He began to read:

To Magistrate Dee Jen-chieh:

You do not know me, but it is my hope that we shall become acquainted. I know you through your very distinguished work, word of which has made its way well beyond the gates of your city. I had heard of the past exploits of the criminal called Diamond Eyes through a relative in another city who was once one of his victims, and it made my heart glad to hear that you had put him and his dishonest pose among the devout out of business. And I am aware, like you, that he is not an isolated phenomenon. Knowing your work, it is my belief that the enclosed document will be of interest to you. Until recently, I myself was a government official of not inconsiderable rank. It is my fervent belief that no one is too exalted to bear watching closely.

You may find irony in the knowledge that I sought and received sanctuary under the roof of a Buddhist monastery, presided over by a good and honest abbot, a man who has taught me by example what a charlatan is not. With the passage of time, I have come to trust him completely, and have told him everything about my life.

Since dead men do not need names, I have put mine aside. You may address me simply as

An Old Fool

Dee turned the paper over, examining it closely. Then he held it up so that the light was behind it. "Ah!" he exclaimed. "This man is very, very brave, whoever he is!" The assistant came closer to see what it was Dee was talking about. The magistrate traced three faint watermark characters just visible in the upper left-hand corner of the page. "The name of the monastery. Hidden from ordinary, unobservant men who might intercept his message. But not hidden from me, as he well knew!"

The assistant read the characters aloud. "City . . . star . . . flower." He looked at Dee.

"Loyang," Dee said. "The star city. The capital city. Flower could only mean lotus, the holiest of flowers in Buddhist mythology. We will look for the name of a temple with 'lotus' in it. He has made it possible for me to communicate with him. Wait. Give me a moment," he said, glancing at the letter again. " 'Old Fool' . . . my heavens." He looked at his assistant. "Do you realize who this letter is from?" He could see from the young assistant's blank expression that he did not. But Dee had heard all the ludicrous tales of the Six Old Fools. It had been about two years ago. The elderly officials, senior statesmen left over from Taitsung's reign, had apparently gone mad en masse and entered into a suicide pact in the tales' wake.

He turned the letter over in his hands. Dead men do not need names, it said. At least one of the old officials, then, was not dead, and had opened communication with Dee Jen-chieh.

Excited, he opened the other document and read:

. . . It is with great and ardent fervor and faith that the Holy Mother of our grand and beloved Empress, Madame Yang, welcomes and celebrates the return of the Pilgrims-in-the-Truth, Hsuan-tsang and his disciples, Tzu-en and I-tsing, from the western regions, the Buddhist kingdoms in the Southern Archipelago, and from the Motherland of the Buddha. And that in embracing the knowledge that has been brought back to China, Madame Yang with the munificence of the Empress Wu Tsetien has surrendered all resources of the Court of the Divine August Emperor Kaotsung to render translations of the great Ideational Texts of the Vijnaptimatratasiddhi and the Madhyantavibhagatika. The Reverent

Mother Yang has sponsored the projects, a sixty-volume discourse on higher metaphysics of the esoteric Lesser Vehicle Hinayana School, in one thousand three hundred thirty chapters, in the name of the glorious T'ang, the Emperor Kao-tsung, and Madame Yang's daughter, the Empress Wu Tse-tien; and has done this in the honor of the throne and in the name of the Future Buddha Maitreya . . .

Dee lowered the paper and looked at his assistant.

"Did I mention the wealthy? The upper classes? The idle rich? I may as well have been speaking of dirt farmers and barefoot peasants with manure between their toes." He heaved a long, discouraged sigh. "But of course, I should have known. What, after all, did I expect?"

He was thinking again of Lu Hsun-pei's arrogant laugh, that much more brazen, impudent, and contemptuous in his memory now that he understood more fully what was behind it. And the words he had overheard as he left. "Let us hope that he keeps his promise and delivers a memorial to the throne," Lu Hsun-pei had jeered. "Let us hope that he does it soon."

He must have looked quite the fool, striding off self-righteously at the conclusion of his little speech. He might as well have declared his intent to complain to the Sovereign of the Wolves that he was disturbed by the crunching of bones. Yes, he must have looked quite the fool.

8

A.D. 661
Loyang

The deaths of the six revered old councillors had been, of course, a great shock to the city. For weeks after the news was sadly and regretfully announced in the gazettes, virtually every conversation in the wineshops and teahouses throughout the capital pertained to the mysterious illness that had spread among the six old men like a plague, taking over their minds, driving them to self-inflicted death. Rumors, theories, and speculation flew, and the topic inspired many lively debates. There were those who nodded their heads wisely, saying that such things were not altogether unheard of, that men's minds were subject to communicable sickness exactly like their bodies. Some said that they had heard of whole villages of people who had killed themselves, one after another, until there was no one left. And it usually started with the old people, they said. Had anyone done a count of suicides in the city after the deaths of the councillors? they asked. Anyone who does, they declared, will be sure to note an increase. It was true that there was a brief spate of reports of several old grandfathers ending their own lives in the weeks following the deaths, but much to the disappointment of the doomsayers, it did not develop into the pestilence they had predicted.

And of course, there were those who seized the opportunity to promote themselves and their own peculiar obsessions. One man said that the suicides were a natural inevitability—according to a formula he himself had worked out, based on statistics he had gathered over the years involving rainfall, damage done by rodents in the city's granaries, male births, the migration of wild geese, and the amount of cosmetics being worn by fashionable ladies in any given year. He would be glad to offer his services to the Emperor, he told an amused crowd in a wineshop, if it would help forestall another tragedy.

But most people were philosophical. There are seasons in the lives of men, and in the lives of empires, they said. A particular season had ended, and a new one had begun. Everyone knew about the Empress Wu's great sorrow over the tragedy. She had stepped in to help lift the burden of grief from her husband's shoulders, attending official audiences with him, advising him, lending her support and clear-headed views on important decisions. All this with the invaluable help, of course, of the new Lord Secretary of the Chancellery Historian Shu Ching-tsung, and of the president of the Department of Civil Appointments, Lai chun-chen. Civic programs had been initiated by her and in her name to help feed the hungry and employ the poor. People were excited. Was this not the new-found vigor of the T'ang promised in the late Emperor Tait-sung's dream? And was not the Empress acting in accordance with the directive of compassion required of us by the Blessed

Maitreya? And though abundantly female, producing new princes one after the other, was she not forthright *like a man?* Clearly, it was time to put scandal and sorrow behind and enter gladly into the new era of humaneness and prosperity.

Even in the dawning of a golden age, there will always be unreconstructed cynics and irreverent ways. Facetious, sinister stories concerning the fate of the lost head of Councillor Wu-chi made the rounds with the same speed as the news of the Empress's innovative social programs. It had turned up in a caldron of soup in a restaurant in the eastern ward, one story went. Then it was thrown out with the garbage and was last seen bobbing along the river, telling passersby that it had had quite enough of Loyang and was on its way to the sea, never to return. Is that so, one wise old jokester said darkly; well, I heard that the Empress uses the head of Wu-chi for a pillow, so that she may have sweet dreams.

One winter morning before dawn, a man woke from obscure, uneasy dreams unable to recall who or where he was. He lay in the chill darkness, his open eyes looking up into what seemed to be the infinite night sky, and listened to the sound of his heart thumping and his blood hissing in his head. His body was inert and so distant from him that his consciousness seemed to be suspended in a great void; he was afraid, and wanted to call for someone, but he could not remember any names, or any words at all, and so lay mute for a long time before slipping back down into his dreams. He dreamed of fire, red and searing hot, his heartbeat huge and thundering, filling the universe like a great drum.

When he woke, a woman's face looked down on him, her expression one of fear, solicitude, and impatience all at the same time. She was shaking his shoulders and telling him to speak to her immediately. He knew this woman, he was sure of that. Her face was familiarity itself, but strangely disconnected from any memory of who she was exactly. He tried to smile, and felt warm drool run out of the corner of his mouth, down his cheek and jaw, and onto his neck. This seemed to make the woman even more annoyed. She accused him of playing disgusting games and shook him again. But she must have seen something more in his face, because anger vanished from her features as swiftly as it had come and was replaced by alarm. She said that she was going to fetch the Imperial physician immediately, and ran from the room. He tried to tell her that it was not necessary, but found no words to express the thought. Soon the drool on his cheek and neck chilled. He wanted to wipe it away, and tried to raise his right hand, but found that it no longer belonged to him. He tried his left hand; shakily, it obeyed his command. He wiped his cheek, shivered, and with his good hand pulled the coverlet up over himself and lay in the soothing darkness under the bedclothes.

By afternoon, Emperor Kaotsung had regained the use of his right hand, though it was feeble as a baby's. The physician regarded him with worried eyes, and implored the Emperor to allow him to administer a needle treatment, but Kaotsung refused, communicating his feelings with gestures, because words were still evading him. By now, he knew who he was and that the woman who had hovered over him that morning and who conferred now with the physician in low, worried tones was his wife, the Empress. He knew her name, too, but found that he was unable to move it from his brain onto his tongue. Words and sentences piled up inside his head, but met the same barrier. He had no confidence at all that if he spoke, anything but gibberish would issue from his mouth, so he refrained. It was strange, and quite interesting, and he settled back into himself to explore the phenomenon.

After the physician had left, the Empress came and sat on the bed, took both his hands in hers, and looked at him.

"Speak to me," she implored. He opened his mouth to answer her, but only an inarticulate rush of air, like wind in the treetops, issued from between his lips. It took him by surprise, and he shut his mouth quickly. The Empress started in alarm at the sound. "What is the matter with you?" she said sharply, her voice edged with fear and vexation, dropping his hands as if he had suddenly become odious. He shook his head and looked at her helplessly, embarrassed at the strangeness of it, unwilling to try again. Her eyes grew hard. "You are doing this to humiliate me," she said. He shook his head again.

Then her face softened and she began to cry. She picked his hands up again and stroked them while tears ran down her cheeks. "My poor love," she said then. "My poor, poor love. Don't worry, I will take care of you until we drive out whatever this horrible thing is that has possessed you. I will care for you as if you were one of my own little babies." With that, she pressed her sweet-smelling breast against him and laid her head on his shoulder so that her perfumed hair was directly under his nose. She lay and sobbed softly while he closed his eyes in resignation.

In the next several weeks, Kaotsung found himself sinking deeper into the silence that had taken hold of him. Unable to ride his horse because of the weakness on one side of his body, he took long, slow walks in the park on the palace grounds, gradually and carefully trying to build his strength. On these walks, he spent hours at a time bringing up memories from his childhood, in such detail and with such clarity that he was practically reliving portions of his life. It was truly wondrous what he could remember—whole days of his boyhood, long buried and forgotten, returned to him, vivid and complete. Powerful images of his father came along with these youthful memories. He recalled the day his father sat him down and informed him that he was to be Crown Prince, and would succeed him one day as Emperor.

His father had carefully explained all of his strengths and weaknesses to him, emphasizing that the Council of Six would be there to advise and assist him through the first years. Most of them will be old men by then, his father had said, but they are vigorous and should last for a long time. My good friend Wu-chi, Taitsung had said, the youngest of them, will surely last until you yourself are showing a bit of snow on the mountaintop. Then he had reached out to ruffle the boy's hair.

Well, here he was, in his mid-thirties, his hair still sleek and black as when he was that boy sitting before his father, but feeble as an old man, and Wu-chi was gone. Shame, sorrow, and nostalgia impaled him, filling his eyes so that the woods around him were a green blur.

Sometimes, when he was quite alone among the trees, certain that no one was near and could hear him, he tried out some words. He whispered at first, then spoke. He would walk for miles, talking quietly to himself, occasionally singing a song or reciting a poem. The words would flow smoothly for a time, then jam up like a water duct obstructed by a mass of dead leaves. He would start over again, approaching the word he could not say as if he were on a horse approaching a hurdle. If he was stopped enough times, he would be forced to find a way around the word, searching for another with a similar meaning, which for some mysterious reason he was able to utter when the other word simply refused to come out.

He kept his experiments with speech private. When he

returned to the palace and there were people around him again, he did not speak. The memory of Wu-chi seemed to ride around on his shoulders now, and he began to feel that his own muteness and the isolation it engendered were proper penance for his betrayal.

If he was still and silent, the Empress was in motion and more alive, if that was possible, than he had ever seen her. During his convalescence, she was up at dawn, attending the Morning Audiences, consulting with officials, hearing the various ministers who presented themselves before the throne, introducing laws and legislation. She would come to him then and sit on his bed, and tell him everything she had done. He had to give her his grudging admiration. Her judgment was sound, her ideas innovative, her social programs progressive, viable, and humane. Even Taitsung would have been impressed.

And she never failed to come to him and give him a full report, in an effort to make him feel that he was part of the process. She would stroke his face and watch his eyes while she spoke, her own eyes full of tender concern.

But as the weeks went by, her tender concern grew threadbare. She looked into his eyes in a way that made him think of someone peering into a dark cave with a lantern, determined to know what was hidden in there. At times, he felt sure that she had caught a glimpse of the image of Wu-chi that lurked just behind his eyes, for her own eyes would narrow with annoyance and she would demand again that he speak to her. When he did not, she would rise and stalk from the room.

One evening after one of these episodes, she entered his bedchamber again. He had been asleep, but woke to the feeling of her sitting on the bed. She turned the lamp up a bit; he could see that her earlier anger and impatience were gone. She was sweet and tender. She stroked his face. She lifted his weak arm and moved it over her soft bosom.

"I will give you back your strength," she said. "I will restore your power of speech."

He willed himself to resist. He lay very still and tried to think of Wu-chi and the other old men. He tried to think about his father's angry, disappointed spirit. He tried to think of his own degraded, shameful self. But it was to no avail: he felt himself hardening, rising. She felt it too. She smiled slyly and victoriously. "See?" she said, and climbed onto him, making him draw his breath in sharply, and began to move herself slowly up and down. When he squeezed his eyes shut with the first nearly agonizing rush of pleasure, he saw that Wu-chi and his father and the others were indeed there, watching the whole sorry performance.

The next night, she had the evening meal brought to their private chambers. She was vibrant and animated, a residual effect he knew very well. And just as he had experienced it many times before, her intent filled the room like something alive.

"You look well tonight, my husband," she said. "I think we have stumbled upon a prescription that did not occur to the physician," she added suggestively. He did not answer. He dropped his eyes and took a bite of food. She must have seen something in his expression, for she quickly changed the subject and the tone of her voice. "I myself have been working hard today. There were many interesting pieces of legislation brought up this morning, and I wish to consult you."

She took a healthy serving of food and began to eat. He had always been impressed with her appetite. She did not eat like most women—little dainty bites, and barely enough to sustain a field mouse. She ate as much as he did, chewed it with uninhibited enjoyment, and often spoke with her mouth full. "The general consensus," she said now through a helping of dumplings, "is that incentive, not punishment, should be the basis of our lawmaking." She swallowed. "In every case, we should think first of building a system of encouragement into laws and resolutions so that they will be beneficial to people, and therefore easier for them to comply. The conscription laws, for instance," she said, taking another mouthful and chewing thoughtfully, her eyes on him all the while. "As they stand now, people regard these laws as punishment. Possibly we should work to change the way people think of conscription. Instead of using it to punish, say, tax offenders or those who fail to register with the census takers, perhaps we should begin to work in a system of long-term benefits for the families of those who are conscripted. Workable land, a reduction in taxes, a guarantee of a certain amount of seed for planting—that sort of thing. The benefits will be manifold . . ." Seeing his distracted expression, she trailed off. They both chewed in silence for a few moments. "Then there are the embargoes on imported goods. Should they be raised, in order to encourage

domestic production of the same goods, or should they be lowered in order to encourage the free flow of trade? What do you
think?"

He shook his head. He found it quite impossible to concentrate on the meaning of her words when they had nothing
at all to do with the intent beneath them. "Encouraging domestic production may seem, on the surface, to be the best
thing, but it is my opinion that an Empire cutting itself off from
free trade is an Empire in danger of becoming ingrown," she
went on. "But I realize that the attendant questions are not
simple ones. That is why I wanted to discuss it with you. You
have much experience to draw on."

She took a drink of wine and another bite of food. He felt
his face beginning to go pink. He was striving to make sense
of what she was saying. But the effort to understand, and certainly the effort to frame a reply, was too much for him. Why
should he answer at all? he thought. It mattered little what she
was saying. She was doing everything in her power to draw
him out. To draw him out of himself and into her. He tightened
his jaw. Besides, he did not trust his tongue at all. Best to stay
safe indoors when the weather threatened. Best to stay sheltered. Best to stay safe and dry. He looked at her.

She looked back at him and lowered her wine cup to the
table. She said no more for the rest of the meal. Finally, she
wiped her lips, rose from her seat, and came around to where
he was sitting. She did not touch him yet, but stood silently a
few inches away. He felt his face growing warmer, but kept
his gaze down, looking at his plate and the scraps of food lying
on it. He concentrated on the bits of meat and gristle, the glistening noodles, the pool of amber juice they rested in. She knelt
then, and like a person peering underneath a tablecloth,
brought her face close and turned her neck sharply so that she
was looking directly up at him. His heart was beating thickly,
hammering the inside of his breastbone like a fist. He was sure
she could hear it. His face was as hot as if he stood near a
roaring fire; when she reached out and trailed her fingers along
his cheek, he felt as if he were bursting into flames.

"You are positively blazing, my love," she whispered,
and began to undo the ties to his clothing, opening the front
of his robe so that the soaked skin of his chest was exposed to
the cool air. She blew on him, then brushed her lips over him
so that he put his head back and let all the breath out of his
body. His mind swirled with fragmented, absurdly joined im-

ages of his father's and Wu-chi's faces and his own and the Empress's naked bodies. Then her hand was in his lap. She had found him.

The next evening, she did not speak at all, and she did not even give him a chance to eat before she climbed onto his lap facing him and bent his head back as far as it would go, planting her mouth on his neck as if she meant to devour it. She was merciless, taking his flesh between her teeth, working her hands into the sensitive spots on his body until she had him on the floor and was astride him again, moving slowly up and down while she gazed intently into his eyes, looking more than ever like someone endeavoring to identify indistinct shapes beyond the threshold of a darkened room.

When it was over, she brought a plate of food to where he lay exhausted and ashamed on the floor and tried to feed him little pieces with her fingers.

"I am so lonely," she said finally, her voice startling him. She waited. "Oh, I know, you are thinking that that is absurd—I have my mother, I have Historian Shu, I have ministers and servants and advisers." She laughed. "I have my children. But unless I can talk with you, I am all alone. I need to hear your voice telling me that you love me, that you appreciate the work I am doing for you. I need to hear if you are unhappy with anything I have said or done. I just need to hear your voice. My ears are strained at every moment, practically shutting out all other sounds, yearning for one thing and one thing only, hoping against hope that I will hear your voice again. Where, oh where, has it gone?" she implored, raising her tearful eyes to the ceiling.

She looked down at him. "Sometimes when I am alone I hold imaginary conversations with you," she whispered. "I ask a question, or make an observation, and I answer in your voice. It is a poor substitute indeed, but it is better than nothing at all." He looked up at her uneasily. He did not like to imagine her inventing words for him to say. There was something peculiarly ominous about it. He pictured himself voiceless, and powerless in all his limbs: a full-sized marionette, his numb, lifeless arms and legs jerking while his mouth moved mechanically with the voice of the Empress issuing from it. The bizarre image was so strong that it caused him to sit up sharply, displacing her hand from where it rested on his chest.

"What is the matter?" she said soothingly, pushing him back down and wiping the sweat from his brow. "Rest. There is nothing to fear. Nothing at all. We are together." She passed her fingertips over his eyelids, closing them, her face so close he could feel her breath on his chin.

" 'Yes, we are together,' " she said then in a much lower voice and with a different modulation than her own. " 'And I would be lost without you, my dear.' " He kept his eyes tightly shut, repelled but fascinated by her imitation of his speech. " 'Promise me you will stay with me, that you are not disgusted by my illness,' " she said then in the same low voice. "Disgusted?" she replied in her own voice, injecting a note of incredulous horror. "That would not be possible! Never!"

"I am so happy to hear that," the other voice replied. " 'Love is so subtle and so strange. Passion and aversion are so close, they are barely distinguishable from each other. One can turn into the other overnight, you know, like milk curdling, turning from something sweet and delicious to something foul and rotten-tasting.' "

"No," she answered in her own voice. "That may be true of ordinary love, but not what I feel for you. My love can only turn sweeter."

" 'Then you do not find me repulsive?' "

"Quite the contrary."

" 'I have not become grotesque to you?' "

"You could never become grotesque to me. It is not possible. It is *I* who fear that I have become odious to you, my husband," she said, but this time she did not answer herself. Instead, she waited pointedly for him to reply. He felt her downward gaze through his closed eyelids. The compulsion to open his eyes, to let her look in and see everything, was strong. But he willed himself to lie perfectly still.

They lay as they were, at an impasse, for many long minutes. Then he heard her breath catch in a tiny spasmodic sob.

"Then it is true," she whispered. "You are repelled by me. You hate me." A tear fell onto his face. He opened his eyes and raised himself up, a protest rising to his lips. Her tears were the worst possible thing, the thing he absolutely could not endure. He had to speak now. He had to say something, anything, to stop her tears.

But when he opened his mouth, nothing came out but a dreadful, inarticulate idiot's-breath hissing, just as the first time he had tried to speak. She recoiled visibly, then pulled herself hastily to her feet.

"Don't *ever* make that revolting sound in my presence again," she shouted. "It is *unbearable!* I cannot *stomach* it!" She glared at him, pinning him to the floor with her fury. "You are not a man at all," she said through clenched teeth, her lip curled. She pulled her disheveled clothing around her body. "You *revolt* me!" She turned sharply on her heel and stalked out of the room, slamming the door mightily behind her. He lay where he was for a while, listening to her footsteps, hearing in them her offended pride as clearly as if she were speaking it. He judged that she would not be back that evening at all. He lay still as the room grew quiet around him.

"No," he said then in a voice that was not much more than a whisper. "No, I do not hate you."

The next evening, she left him quite alone. He expected her to return the evening after that, but she did not. Nor did she come for the next several evenings. Word was that she had gone to her mother's house in the city. He ate his meals alone, quite contented, and took long walks in the dusk, speaking to himself, trying out the game that she herself played: he spoke in his own voice, then answered in hers. In these imaginary conversations, she was patient, loving, and understanding, conversing with him in an infinitely soothing way on a wide range of topics unrelated to themselves, his affliction, government, or the nature of love.

When he saw her again, she was not alone. At first, his heart sank several notches, because he thought the woman walking with her in the garden was her mother. As they came closer, he saw that it was not Madame Yang at all, but someone he had never met. When they were close enough so that he could see her clearly, a strange excitement took hold of him. She resembled the Empress strongly, but something was different: her face was what the Empress's face would have been if she were ruled by grace, patience, sweetness, kindness, and generosity. It was a revelation for him, and he stared at her almost rudely before he came to his senses and heard the Empress telling him that this was her half sister, her father's daughter by an earlier marriage, Wu Ssu-lin.

The woman smiled at him, and he felt his face break into a wide, foolish, uncontrollable grin. His hand came up and self-consciously wiped at the corners of his mouth, for he had a sudden terror that he might be drooling. He was wrong, though; all was well, and he stood grinning and staring happily, hearing his wife's voice explaining as if from a distance that Ssu-lin had traveled from Ch'ang-an to visit her sister the Empress and Madame Yang.

"Many is the time that I have looked into the eyes of my lapdogs—silly, ridiculous little creatures though they may be—and asked myself what it is that they see. What do our voices sound like to them? What do our faces look like? How do they perceive the world they live in with us?"

"Yes, yes!" Kaotsung replied happily. "So many times, when I am riding my horse, I wonder what he is thinking and feeling. What does my weight on his back feel like? My feet digging into his sides? And my voice, giving him commands." He spoke slowly, choosing his words with care, but they flowed with miraculous ease from his brain to his mouth without obstruction; like clumps of ice melting, he thought.

"Sometimes I think I can imagine it," the Duchess Wu Ssu-lin said. "Sometimes I feel as if I can put myself in the animal's place and look out through his eyes, hear with his ears. But I know, finally, that I can never really know. It is a mystery from which I will always be locked out."

"But there are people who know exactly what it feels like," he said. "Practitioners of the Tao who adopt animal form. Who travel by night in the form of a cat, or fly over the treetops by day looking out through the eyes of a big black crow." Wu Ssu-lin smiled at this.

"Do you believe it?" she asked simply, with no judgment or mockery in her voice. He thought about it as they walked in silence for a few moments. It was early afternoon. It had rained during the morning hours, and the low gray sky, though spent, still had a swollen, dangerous look. The tall wet grass had soaked the hems of their heavy outer robes as they moved across a meadow in the Imperial Park.

"It is not so much that I believe it," he said. "It is that I *want* to believe it."

"Yes," she answered. "The practitioners of the Tao know the human mind and heart. They know of our fierce curiosity about the rest of nature. They understand our yearning to leave our humanness behind occasionally. So they do it for us, in a sense. They are like emissaries traveling to a foreign land."

"But do they really do it?" Kaotsung asked. "Or do they only imagine or pretend that they do it?"

"It is difficult to say," the Duchess answered thoughtfully.

"It seems that the Taoist has an understanding of what it is to be human that eludes the rest of us. They tell us that to be human is to be every kind of animal, and therefore we can experience the consciousness of them all. That we need only find, and step into, those animal natures that already exist in us, and *be* them—the wolf, the crow, the cat, the snake."

"Or the pig, the ostrich, and the lapdog," Kaotsung said, laughing.

"The weasel, the toad, the flea," she added, laughing too. "Yes. When I think of certain people I have met in my life, I know there can be little doubt."

"But if all those animals live inside us," Kaotsung asked, "what is that part of us which is purely human?"

She smiled at this. "I have thought about that a lot," she answered. "And I think I know what it is."

They walked, their feet parting the wet grass, the air fresh, charged, and sweet after the rain.

"Think of this," the Duchess said. "Think of yourself grooming your horse. You are filled with admiration for the sleek hide, the powerful muscles, the graceful curve of its neck. You look into its great deep brown-purple eye, and it makes you think of fine glass. Think of yourself looking at a mountain range, entranced by the way the light changes when it hits it at different angles during the day. Think of yourself spreading out a bug's wing under the lamplight, straining your eyes to trace the delicate green veins. Then you look at the veins in your own arm, and you see that they are the same pattern, the same structure. So strange and beautiful is it that you make a drawing of the veins in the bug's wing. Your eyes are the eyes that nature made so that it could look at itself. That is the part of you that is purely human!"

"Nature looking at itself," he said in wonder. It was so simple, and so obvious, but it had never occurred to him before. "And why? Why does nature want to look at itself?" he asked excitedly.

"I don't know," she answered. "Perhaps it has no choice."

"No choice," he reflected. "Perhaps it has something to do with the sheer force of beauty. It demands to be seen."

"It does not like to go to waste," she suggested.

"Yes! Yes!" He laughed. "That is it! Our lives, all our struggles and pain and occasional moments of happiness—all of it is because the beauty in nature does not want to go to waste!"

"It is certainly possible," she said.

They had passed from the wild meadow to the long winding stone path that led back into the palace gardens. They had been talking for most of the afternoon. They had discussed the movement of the stars, childhood, the origins of mythical tales, foreign languages, the definition of money, whether or not it was possible to move through time differently than did people around you, insects, dreams, illness, ugliness, death, and horses. When they arrived at the subject of horses, Kaotsung had remarked that there was something unique that passed between a man and the horse beneath him that occurred nowhere else in nature; he said the man's and the horse's minds became one, and that was how a man either controlled a horse when it felt his mastery or it controlled him when it sensed his unease; she had remarked that the man and the horse were designed specifically to complete one another, and he had seen that she was absolutely correct. It was not until they had been walking and talking for more than an hour that he realized that not a single word of his had lodged itself recalcitrantly in the way of the others. But even this extraordinary phenomenon was soon forgotten as they moved on, entering into an extensive discussion of whether or not—if humans were truly every kind of animal—the ability to fly was hidden somewhere inside us.

They passed through the palace gardens, hardly noticing that it had begun to rain again, lightly, but with definite serious intent. And they scarcely took note when servants materialized, approaching the two on silent feet and raising wide silk parasols over their heads, walking skillfully just behind them and a bit to the side so as to be virtually invisible and nonexistent.

Were there not sorcerers and holy men who claimed to know how to fly? he asked. Didn't pilgrims returning from the far west tell stories of yogic masters who raised themselves off the ground and hovered for hours at a time? Yes, she said, she had heard such stories too, but for her their significance lay in the fascination they aroused in the people who heard them. Until I see it with my own eyes, she said, I must assume that accounts of men flying or levitating are a function of our yearning. Yes, he said, but perhaps that yearning is an indication of the unrealized potential within.

Perhaps, she answered.

Yes, perhaps, he said happily.

The rain came down in full force now, drumming on the stretched silk suspended over their heads, running in little dancing rivulets around their feet, and soaking to the skin the wordless servants who walked behind them holding the parasols aloft.

"So they want to fly, do they?" Wu shouted. "I will teach them how to fly. Oh, yes, I will teach them!" She hurled a small jade statue of Kuan-yin against the far wall, but it did not break. Instead, it bounced, rebounding into a collection of ivory miniatures, which clattered violently to the floor. "They will be flying. Oh, yes, they will be flying before they even know what has happened to them!" she snarled, looking around for some other hapless inanimate thing to destroy.

Her mother sat and watched her with impassive eyes, carefully noting the *objets* her daughter picked up to throw. The statue of Kuan-yin was expendable; so were the ivory miniatures. But when she saw her reach for a prized ceramic horse, she quickly rose, put a firm hand on her daughter's arm, and deftly turned her around so that she faced the other direction. Before Wu now was a glazed pitcher and a terra-cotta pug dog. She seized them in both her hands; in the next instant they lay in pieces on the far side of the room.

" 'Unrealized potential within,' " Wu intoned in a sneering, mocking voice cold with fury. "They haven't the smallest *idea* of unrealized potential within! Not the smallest *notion*!" She turned her blazing eyes on her mother; in the next moment, her face dissolved into a mask of sorrow, red and weeping, the tears spilling from her eyes with the suddenness of summer rain. "Oh, Mother," she said, sinking to her knees on the carpet, her voice high and distorted with grief. "He was talking. *Talking!* I heard them. They passed right under my balcony. With me, he is as silent and stupid as some animal, some rock, some revolting mute dead *thing!* With her, he chatters away like some bright little child, some smart little monkey, some precocious, clever, cunning, innocent *creature!* Oh, I cannot bear it," she wailed, and prostrated herself on the floor.

She stayed as she was for a few moments, bent forward, head resting on the carpet, sobbing intemperately. After a time she raised her face and looked at her mother. Her features were slack, wet, and distorted; her black eye cosmetic was smeared down her cheeks, and a long glistening string of moisture hung unheeded from her nose. "How dare he?" she implored in a soft voice. "After all I have done for him. *How dare he?*"

Madame Yang reached forward, and using the sleeve of her gown, wiped the offending string from her daughter's nose.

She had washed her face clean of all cosmetics and put on a simple, tasteful gown. She had let her black hair down, combed it smooth, and secured it with a pin at the back of her head. She sat smiling across the small table at Kaotsung. When he reached for a piece of food from one of the platters, or even looked as though he might possibly be interested in it, she quickly picked it up and served it to him herself. Each time he took a sip from his wine cup and set it down again, she filled it from the pitcher at her elbow.

"I love the rain we have been having recently," she said. "I love the way it sounds at night. I love waking up in the dawn to hear it tapering off, then waking up later to hear it coming down furiously again." She took a drink of wine and gazed up over his head, as if savoring the memory. He did not respond. "And the way the air smells afterward," she continued. "So clean, so new. As if everything in the world were being given a second chance," she said, pleased with this sudden extemporaneous bit of poetry. "It seems to make the birds happy, too. They twitter and sing, and you can see them frolicking in the puddles. Birds must work very hard in their tiny lives, but that is their little holiday," she said brightly, and raised the wine pitcher to fill his cup, which he had just set down.

She watched him chewing his food, the motion of his jaws visible at his temples. He kept his eyes down. She watched his throat move as he swallowed, watched him raise more food to his mouth and put it in, chew, and swallow. His wary eyes flicked up from his plate occasionally, regarded her for an instant, then dropped again. She cleared her throat.

"I should like to be a bird. For a day or two," she said. "Just to know what it is like. Sitting in treetops, swooping after bugs in the air. I suppose I would have to eat bugs, and worms, and caterpillars." She made a little face of disgust, then smiled again. "But then, *if* I were a bird, I would like it, wouldn't I? Bugs and worms would taste as good to me as this wonderful food in front of me does." With that, he pushed his plate away. That was the wrong thing to say, she rebuked herself. Her words had stirred revulsion in him.

"Of course, birds get eaten too," she said quickly. "A cat or a weasel could catch me, or a great big owl, and swallow me in one gulp." She laughed, annoyed with the forced sound of it, and quickly drank more wine. "Birds are musical creatures," she said. "Do you suppose they enjoy the sound of the rain?" she asked. He shook his head and emitted a small grunt. "Yes? You think so? Does it make them happy?"

His throat was moving as if he were swallowing or trying to speak. She knew there was no food in his mouth, so he could not be swallowing. She waited, a cheerful little smile poised on her lips and an iron hand gripped firmly on her rising irritation at the sight of the futilely twitching and bobbing throat.

"Of course it does," she said, still smiling, rising from her chair, coming around the table, and sitting in his lap. "Of course it makes them happy," she said, holding his face in her hands and looking into his opaque eyes. "How could it not?" she asked, feeling his arousal against the backs of her thighs like some little creature nosing about insistently beneath the fabric of his robe.

"Of course it does," she repeated.

They had just been served the clear shark's-fin broth, Madame Yang's cook's specialty, when Wu Ssu-lin's face went white and she put down her bowl with an expression as if she had just remembered something important she had forgotten to do.

Madame Yang looked at her sharply, then resumed her conversation with the ancient Buddhist scholar who was their dinner companion that evening.

"The Era of the Final Degenerate Law is not upon us at all," the old man was saying in his cracked, singsong old voice between loud sips of broth. "The ones who insist that it is are whiners and malcontents. They would accuse the Buddha himself of being an impostor even if he walked into their houses and sat down to tea. This broth, madame, is most exquisitely delicious!" he said, greedily refilling his bowl.

With an abstracted expression on her face, the Duchess had picked her bowl up again and resumed drinking. The old scholar slurped his food with gusto. "I must tell you, madame, that privately, I have never quite approved of the doctrine of Degenerate Law. It seems to me to be something of an insult to the Sage to imply that his influence and teachings can, shall we say, run down, lose their effectiveness merely because time is passing."

"To me," Madame Yang replied, still watching the Duchess, "it represents a wise balance, an acknowledgment of the inevitable weakness of humankind, which will set out with the best of intentions and armed with perfect, inspired teachings, but will eventually corrupt and distort those teachings beyond recognition." The Duchess had raised her bowl halfway to her mouth and held it there, poised, before gently lowering it again. The hand that had held the bowl rested on the table; a troubled furrow appeared on her brow as she sat quietly looking at the empty space between herself and her companion.

"But to say that," the scholar replied, swallowing and smacking his wet lips, "is to tacitly declare that the Buddha's teachings are . . . imperfect. After all, if he cannot anticipate human weakness . . . if he cannot cause us to overcome our innate flaws . . ."

"Perhaps," Madame Yang said, "he was interested to see how far his teachings would go with an imperfect race. A way of measuring our imperfection. Perhaps he intentionally omitted that which would have made us perfect." The Duchess was bending forward now, her eyes wide, her hands tightening into fists.

"That is possible, of course, madame," the old man said, "but of course such a statement also implies that the Buddha is less than omniscient. He would know the height, breadth, and depth of our imperfection intimately. What need would an all-knowing being have with experimentation of any kind?"

The flow of his words was interrupted by Madame Yang's rising very suddenly and unexpectedly from her chair. He blinked and looked around him, noticing for the first time that all was not well with their dinner companion. Her forehead was nearly resting on the bowl in front of her, and her hands were now pressed tightly into her midsection.

"Perhaps it is not an experiment," Madame Yang said, moving quickly to the Duchess's side. "Perhaps it benefits us in some way known only to him, which will be revealed to us when we finally reach enlightenment."

"Perhaps . . . perhaps," the scholar said, distressed and distracted as Madame Yang put her hands solicitously on the Duchess's shoulders. The woman groaned then, and raised a face of agony from the table and looked right at the scholar.

Horrified now, the old man rose from his own chair, knocking it over. "Madame! What is it?"

"It is nothing," Madame Yang said, standing over the Duchess. "She is prone to dreadful bouts of indigestion. It has been a problem all her life. I hold myself fully responsible. I was not careful enough with the menu. I cannot leave these things to my cooks. I must oversee them myself. Next time I will know better. Steward!" she shouted, as the Duchess's hand swept blindly in front of her, clutching at objects on the table. With impressive strength, Madame Yang pulled the woman to her feet and away from the table. The steward appeared, and rushed into the room to offer assistance. "Have her put to bed," Madame Yang told the man. "She will be perfectly all right in the morning. She always is."

The Duchess was doubled over now, unable even to stand. The frightened steward lifted her by the elbows. The scholar stood, appalled and helpless, bits of food clinging to his chin, as the Duchess was carried bodily from the room. Madame Yang saw them to the door, pulled it firmly shut, and turned back to her guest.

"Perhaps we have no real idea what the Sage meant by 'enlightenment.' Perhaps there is something that he must teach us that can only be taught through hard, bitter experience," she said, deftly righting the scholar's chair and moving back to sit in her own. Slowly, the scholar lowered himself back down. He sat dumbly, the back of his hand wiping the crumbs from his lips as he looked at the just-closed door, the empty place at the table across from him, and then at his hostess.

"What?" he said, having lost the thread of their conversation entirely.

"Perhaps 'enlightenment' is something different from what we believe it to be," she reiterated patiently.

"Yes?" he said. "Yes, yes. Quite so, quite so, quite indubitably so," he intoned, with no idea at all of what he was agreeing to.

Madame Yang had picked up her bowl and was sipping her broth contentedly. The scholar, remembering his manners, lifted his own, but discovered that he had entirely lost his appetite.

"Poisoners," the Empress Wu said to Historian Shu. "There are poisoners in our midst, and it is obvious to me whom they meant to kill."

"Do not say it, madame," Shu said, shaking his head. "It is too terrible to contemplate." As he spoke, his brush moved deftly down the page.

"My sister—even though she was only my half sister—resembled me very strongly. She was seen, by persons unknown, leaving the palace that day, riding through the streets to my mother's house. They insidiously found their way into the kitchen there. They got the poison into her food somehow. But how? How could they know which portion would be going to my mother, which one to the scholar, and which to my sister the Duchess?" She was talking quickly, pacing back and forth while Shu wrote.

"In a busy kitchen of a great house, people could come and go virtually unnoticed," the historian suggested.

Wu thought about that for a few moments. "But how did they get the poison into *her* food? You have not satisfactorily answered my question."

"Well, let me think," Shu said, licking the tip of his brush thoughtfully. "Exquisite timing, madame? Such things are certainly possible, you know. Exquisite timing coupled with acute observation."

"Possibly," she said. "Though I find that a trifle farfetched, Historian."

"It would not be so farfetched if you were to consider that possibly the poisoner or poisoners were persons already known to the household staff. Or," he said ominously, his busy brush pausing for a moment, "perhaps the poisoner or poisoners were members of Madame Yang's staff."

"Yes!" Wu said. "Of course that is possible. I suggest that we immediately arrest the house steward."

"And the cook," Shu suggested.

"No," Wu shook her head. "Not the cook. His skills are irreplaceable. My mother would never forgive me."

"The steward, then."

"There is another possibility, of course," Wu said, watching the historian's brush. "She may not have been poisoned at all. She may simply have died of digestive complications. She was never very strong, you know."

"Natural causes," Shu said, starting a fresh page. "Very possible. She was taken ill, and though Madame Yang's household staff did everything they could for her, she died. By the time the physician arrived, it was too late. How sad," he said, looking up. "But it does seem that it was almost inevitable, doesn't it? Given her frail constitution."

"Of course," Wu said, turning to look at the historian, "she may simply have choked on something."

Kaotsung recognized Wu's approaching footsteps. They were particularly eloquent today; he could read them as clearly as words shouted in his ear: brisk, tapping, full of self-important exuberance, with an underlayer of unswerving, uncompromising, single-minded intent. He also detected a note of incongruous cheer. Was it her intent that created her impatience, or did her impatience give rise to her intent? It was a riddle he had pondered often. The answer was no clearer to him now than it had ever been, but he could hear them both now, seeking him out as unerringly as an arrow shot from the bow of the surest hunter.

He rolled to the side of the massive bed and let himself drop down to the floor in the narrow space next to the wall. He lay with his shoulder tightly and comfortably wedged, smelling the dust in the carpet and enjoying the odd perspective of the bed and the carved ceiling as seen from this unusual vantage point, and thought that this would be a good place to lie forever.

He held himself very still as he heard the door open. Her presence immediately filled the room. It was not that she was making a lot of obvious noise, or that her perfume was strong, or that she was breathing hard; it was nothing so obvious as that. It was her intent, tangible and palpable as something alive, that actually displaced the air so that he could feel it pressing against him. At that moment, he decided that it was her intent that came first, then her impatience. He closed his eyes and waited.

He heard the bed creak and the quilts rustle. He sensed the moment when he was no longer alone, when he could feel himself being looked at. He opened his eyes; her face was directly above him, looking over the side of the bed, her dark eyes steady and calm and fathomless.

They regarded each other for a long time. Presently, she moved back out of sight; the next thing he knew, she was pulling the bed farther away from the wall, making more space. Then she came across the bed again and lowered herself down into his hiding place with him. He did not move. She nestled against him wordlessly, her face in his neck so that he could feel her breath.

"You know, of course, that it was I that they meant to kill," she said finally, her mouth right next to his ear. "My poor sister is a heroine. She stood in their way, and took the blow for me. I am devastated. Who would want to kill me? Who? I am so afraid!" She tightened her arms around him. "Let us stay right here together forever. We will hide, and no one will ever find us." She put a leg over him as she spoke, drawing it up slowly so that it moved along his thighs toward his midsection. She let it rest there for a moment, then began to move it gently back and forth.

He was aware of her concentrating, her attention focused on his groin, feeling for his response. When she found nothing, no answering movement of his flesh, she deftly pulled up his robe and opened his silk trousers so that her bare leg, the silky inner surface of her thigh, moved against him now.

She did this for several minutes, varying the pressure, her tongue in his ear or on his neck. He held himself perfectly still. I am a dead king, he thought to himself. I have been lying in my tomb for three thousand years. It has been so long since I have seen the sun or heard another voice or sniffed the air on a summer morning that I cannot remember any of it at all. All I know is darkness, vague memories of faces, and the dank walls of my tomb.

He felt her hands on him, squeezing and kneading his limp flesh. Then her mouth and tongue, resolutely demanding that he rise. A dead king in his tomb, with no memory, no desires, he thought.

She was working with fierce determination now. She had pulled up her gown and was astride him, then moving down to use her mouth again, caressing him with her tongue, raking him ever so gently with her teeth, then her tongue again. She rubbed, squeezed, licked, tickled, and caressed, even tried to press him into her body by force. But there was nothing. He opened his eyes and looked down, and saw her holding what looked like a drowned snake, flaccid and useless as his dead arm had been on the morning of the seizure. The look on her face was one of pure revulsion as she gazed down on the ugly thing in her hand.

9

Magistrate Dee stood yawning in the chill dawn air, gazing down into the oily black water of one of Yangchou's uncounted and nameless backstreet canals. Wavelets lapped gently against the stone abutment where he stood, bits of garbage and refuse bobbing on the surface. The thought came to Dee that water, no matter how filthy and defiled, no matter what sort of vile detritus rode upon it, was always graceful in its motion; innocent. That was what it was, he thought; this foul, evil-smelling water at his feet rippled against the stone with the same carefree innocence as the purest, sweetest spring water.

The wavelets broke with increased frequency now as a small flat barge was poled out to the center of the canal. The handful of onlookers that had gathered around Dee were strangely quiet and respectful as they watched the men on the barge extend a long hook toward the corpse that floated face-down in the water; Dee reflected that if this had been high noon, the streets full and the traffic and commerce of the city flowing, there would have been a noisy crowd, jabbering and shouting—suggestions, speculation, jokes. But the gray, quiet, solitudinous quality of the very early morning, the light fragile and new and the cool of the night still upon them, seemed to cast a pensive, introverted spell over the few people who happened to be out and who now stood and watched.

The hook caught the collar of the corpse's billowing robe. The men on the barge turned the body around, pulling it toward them. When it was alongside, they heaved and grappled it ungracefully on board, the head making an unpleasant cracking sound as it hit the wooden deck. They poled their craft toward the magistrate and the constable who stood next to him.

Dee lowered himself down onto the barge, then knelt and looked at the body: a man in his early fifties, he judged, healthy, well-fed, and prosperous-looking. The robe was expensive, fine-quality silk, of a style and cut that suggested a moneyed member of the merchant class.

Dee sighed. The canal ran through a neighborhood of brothels and wineshops. It was not unusual for drowned corpses to turn up in waters such as these, nor was it uncommon for the victims to be obvious outlanders, visitors to this less savory underside of the city. Dee checked the dead man's clothing. His purse was there, intact, and full of copper cash. There was no sign of a blow to the head. If he had not been robbed, then it was more than likely that he had blundered into the canal on his own, making his way blind drunk through unfamiliar streets and alleys and mistaking the black smooth surface in the darkness for the pathway home. Dee could imagine the man's surprised foot expecting solid ground but not finding it, the vertigo, the single moment of utter clarity in the midst of stupor, the shock of icy water.

Yes, it was easy to imagine, but the picture did not set entirely easily with Dee. He would, without much second thought, have consigned the dead man to the unfortunate category of accidental drowning victim who lost his way in the dark were it not for the fact that the same thing had happened a scant two weeks before only a few blocks from where this morning's forlorn and sodden corpse lay. The other fellow had also been a prosperous businessman, and his purse had been so heavy with cash that the body had been practically pulled down to the bottom of the canal; it had caused quite a commotion when an early-morning farmer poling his way to market saw the pale drowned face peering up at him from a foot below the surface of the water.

The victim had been identified without too much trouble. A trader, very successful, a longtime resident of Yangchou. The verdict had been simple: out drinking and debauching, he had had an unfortunate accident. Within a few days, the man's widow had appeared at Dee's office, complaining that her husband had left her almost nothing in his will. She was virtually unprovided for, and would be turned out of her house within a year. The beneficiary named in her husband's will was a man whose name she had never heard before, she declared with bitterness, but who had been described in the document as being an "adopted son." She had no knowledge at all that her husband had any sons, adopted or otherwise. She herself had been childless, and her husband had had no other wives.

Dee had told the distraught woman that he was not at all

sure of the legality of such an arrangement, and would look into the matter. The inheritance laws favored a son over a wife as the prime beneficiary of a dead man's estate, but usually not an adopted son—unless, he had said as delicately as he could, the wife had violated some code of propriety. The woman had returned a look so genuinely offended that he had not pursued that line of thought any further with her, though he privately intended to investigate the possibility.

Dee had other, more urgent cases that took priority for the time being, so the disinherited woman's case was still pending. Since she was not going to be turned out of her house for a year, Dee had given the particulars to his assistant so that he could research the finer points of the inheritance laws. Dee had promised the woman that he would attempt to contact the "adopted son" and try to appeal to his sense of justice. So far, he had not been able to locate him. The case had not been foremost in his mind—until this moment.

The dripping corpse in front of him now would most likely be identified within a day or so. He looked at the bluish lips and the opaque eyes glinting through the half-closed lids, and had a sense of a secret lurking there, of something being not quite what it seemed. He rose and turned to the constable who waited nearby. A hand-drawn cart had been sent for to carry the body away. The two bearers stood and studied the dead man at their feet; a well-to-do corpse was much more interesting than a ragged, penniless one.

"Take him to the central mortuary," Dee said to the constable and climbed back up onto the abutment. "Have a gazette circulated describing him—his age, any distinguishing features you find on him, his clothing, where he was found. When and if anyone comes forth to tell us who he is, make sure that person is sent to talk to me."

The constable nodded and gave the order to the bearers, who clambered down and picked the body up and heaved it onto the bank and then onto the cart. They covered the dead man with a rough piece of cloth. Dee watched them as they moved down the street, the corpse's feet sticking out behind from under the cloth. He yawned and pulled his cloak tightly around his shoulders. He was tempted to return home and go back to bed, whence he had been hastily roused with the news of the drowning less than an hour before. Instead, he turned resolutely in the direction of his office. He would get an early start on the day's work.

* * *

Dee put down his brush and rubbed his weary eyes. It was early afternoon now, and he was feeling the full effects of the two hours or so of lost sleep. He eyed the low, comfortable chaise against one wall of his office. Why not? he thought, and moved toward it. It had been one of those long, dull, quiet, overcast days, the sky low and heavy, that enervate the body and spirit anyway. A small nap—or just some time with his eyes shut and his mind wandering wherever it cared to go—was exactly what a day such as this called for.

He lay down and covered himself up with his cloak, his grateful bones aching pleasantly. Awareness of his bones led him to think on the subject of bones in general; he thought about them lying decorously in mausoleums, scattered on desolate plains, ornately carved and adorning a jungle chieftain's hut. He thought of the fearsome skeleton puppets that figured so prominently in morality tales. Bones: our solid earthly residue, so vividly picturesque, exciting in us so much fascination, fear, and ceremony, the symbol and focus of all of our unease with the mystery of death. Religion and mysticism were the natural response to our unhappiness about the fact that we must die; an elaborate measure of, and compensation for, the plain animal fear of death. Animal fear of death? Yes and no; he thought of cornered rats he had seen fighting fiercely for survival, the frightened bellows of doomed animals in the slaughterhouses. Didn't animals' instinctive resistance of death, their struggles and white-eyed terror, whisper an ominous message to us about our own prospects for an afterlife? But then he thought of Scoundrel, calm and unperturbed, disappearing into the garden to take care of the business of dying, alone and dignified. Dee had searched for him, and had buried the small corpse exactly where it had lain. Scoundrel's chosen spot. He thought of the small yellow bones enfolded in the rich black earth of his garden.

He was drifting pleasantly, his thoughts welling and gently rising like porridge boiling languidly in a pot, when the sound of a woman weeping and keening snapped him abruptly awake. There was a knock on his office door; he rose quickly, straightening his clothing and rubbing his face. "Enter!" he called out.

The sobbing woman before him had the same prosperous look about her that the corpse in the canal had had. She too was well-fed and healthy-looking, and about the same age as the drowned man. The resemblance was no accident; they had been married for thirty years, she told Dee, her tears streaming. He ordered hot tea for her and made her sit down.

"Tell me something about your husband, madame," he said, offering her the steaming bowl. "His occupation, his interests, his habits."

"He was a good man," she said. "Generous. Kind." She broke off and sobbed for a moment or two. Dee waited. Dead men were always generous and kind. It was an amazing transformation that they went through at the moment of death.

"He was . . . well-to-do, was he not?" Dee probed gently.

"A wonderful provider," she said sadly.

"Tell me more," Dee said. "How did he earn his money?"

"Oh, it is such terrible irony," she wailed. "That he should lose his life to the canal!"

"Ah, so his business was connected somehow to the waterways?" Dee asked, intrigued. The other businessman who had drowned had been a grain merchant, a man heavily reliant on the canal system of the city. But then, virtually anyone in business in Yangchou relied on the canals; it was almost unavoidable. Nonetheless, a part of his mind could not help but note it as a consistency.

"He owned a fleet of barges," she said. "He leased them to farmers and tradesmen. He had worked very, very hard over the years, and had built up his business. He was honest. He was respected. He was fair."

"Then he was not a man with enemies?"

"Not a one in the world!" the woman answered, as if surprised that Dee could even suggest such a thing.

"Was it his habit to . . . frequent that part of the city?" Dee asked delicately. There was usually only one reason for a man to descend into those particular tortuous, odoriferous byways, and though it certainly constituted a masculine prerogative, many men were reluctant to press the point with their wives. The woman raised her head and gave the magistrate an offended, haughty stare.

"*Only* if his business warranted it, sir," she said coldly.

"Of course, of course," Dee answered, reflecting on the futility of getting an honest description of a man's life and habits from his wife. Whatever his virtues, she would be bound to exaggerate them; whatever his shortcomings, she would be bound to do everything in her power to cover them up so that they would not cause her embarrassment. For all he knew, this fellow was a lying, cheating rascal who went drinking and whoring every night of his life after putting in a hard day's work swindling his clients.

"Well, madame," Dee said summarily, "if your husband had no enemies, then he was undoubtedly tending to some business when he accidentally stumbled into the canal. It was an accident, plainly."

The woman made as if to rise from her chair, but she sank back down in resignation. Without a word, she handed Dee a note.

He took it, and read aloud:

"'I, Fang Yu-chih, upon leaving this world, pass my earthly wealth into the hands of one Chang-lo, of Yang-chou Province. He is to collect in one year's time.'"

He lowered the paper and looked at the woman in astonishment.

"I was reluctant to disclose it," she whispered. "I almost did not. The disgrace, the shame. To be passed over by one's own husband could only imply that I was an . . . an adulteress, or worse," she said, barely whispering the words. "I would almost rather starve than have anyone know that he left me penniless. I was not going to show the letter to anyone. But if I did not . . ." She made an empty gesture and let her words trail off.

"If you did not," Dee said sympathetically, "then you would stand no chance at all of recovering some part of your husband's holdings to support yourself in widowhood. I quite understand, madame." Dee leaned forward. "But who is Chang-lo?"

The woman shook her head miserably. "I don't know. I have never heard of him before in my life."

"Tell me, madame," Dee said, suddenly inspired, "do you have sons?"

"No," she answered sadly. "We had two, but they both died as children. It was one of my husband's greatest sorrows."

Dee's household was in an uproar when he returned home that evening. His first wife had shut herself in her bedchamber and was not speaking to anyone, and his second wife was in tears, pacing back and forth in the reception room of the house.

It did not take long to get to the source of the trouble. Any serious disharmony in his house could always be traced to his sons, and today was no exception. And trouble with the two boys—now young men—invariably set his wives against each other. Each was mother to one boy, and each blamed the other for the nefarious influence of the other woman's off-spring on his sibling. And which one *was* to blame? Dee had never satisfactorily answered the question for himself. It would be natural to assume that the elder was the one to lead the younger astray, but Dee did not really believe that it was that simple.

And what was the problem today?

"He is going to bring disgrace on us, and he doesn't care at all," his second wife declared through her tears. "Disgrace and ruin!" She was referring, of course, to the elder boy; the younger was hers. "And *she* will not acknowledge *her* respon-sibility!"

He spoke a few ineffectual words of consolation to her, his words sounding thin and inadequate to his own ears, then went and knocked deferentially on his other wife's door. He waited, listening to her determined silence emanating from the other side of the heavy wood. He knocked again, slowly and steadily. She flung the door open with startling suddenness, and stood glaring at him.

"Your sons," she said evenly, "are going to grow into criminals. I do *not* take responsibility. Simply because my son is the elder, *she* places the blame on him. We have always known that the little one leads the bigger one around by the nose! Goading him into ever bolder acts of daring and defiance! No," she said before firmly shutting the door again, "I absolve myself."

"The only thing that has changed," he said to the two sullen youths who stood in front of him, "is that I am growing gray and tired while the two of you have become strapping young fellows. Other than that, no one would know that this was not ten years ago, that I was not disciplining two obstrep-erous babies." He watched them intently for any signs that they were suppressing a snicker or an impertinent smirk. He was gratified to see that their faces were solemn—but then, that very solemnity gave him an uneasy feeling.

On the desk, lined up between Dee and his sons like so many unasked questions, were a dagger with a carved blade, a painted, feathered monkey mask, a small statue of Kuan-yin, and two jade lingams. The boys did not look at the items at all, as if denying their existence.

"We simply want to know where you got these things," he said patiently. "And I in particular want to know. We are not accusing you. We are simply curious."

"We found them, Father," the elder answered.

"And why did you not show them to me?" Dee inquired.

"Well . . ." the younger began, and shot a look to his brother.

"We thought we would sell them," the elder said.

"I see," Dee replied. "And did it ever occur to you that they might very well be stolen? Did you ever stop to think of how it would be if the sons of Yangchou's senior magistrate were apprehended trafficking in stolen goods?" he asked calmly. His sons shrugged.

He looked at them. They looked different to him today. He realized that for the first time, he was seeing two adult men he did not really know. Their faces resembled the faces of the two infants he had raised, but with the features uncannily enlarged and coarsened into those of strangers. No, he thought, I do not know them at all.

"Would it please you to come up before me not here in my study, where you can ignore my authority with impunity, but before my bench instead?" he said in a cold voice.

"No, Father," the elder said, his voice shaking almost imperceptibly.

"All right," Dee said wearily. "You are to apologize to your mothers. You are to return these things to where you found them, and you are to end this practice of staying out late into the night past the curfew, and returning home whenever it suits you. There has been far too much of that lately, and somehow I cannot but think that there is a connection between that"—he paused and gestured toward the objects on his desk—"and this." He looked at them, waiting for a response. Their eyes shifted and their jaws clenched; they positively seethed with secrets.

He thought about the very real possibility that one day he would be sentencing his own sons in an official courtroom, and he thought of himself playing with them as toddling cubs.

Life was certainly strange. Soon, very soon now, he thought, watching them wordlessly gather up the pieces from his desk, you will both be beyond my responsibility. Your transformation into strangers will be complete. And I will be relieved.

Tired as he was, he slept poorly that night. He could hear arguing voices in other parts of the house: his wives and his sons. The words were unintelligible, but the meaning was clear nonetheless. Unrest and disharmony had settled under his roof.

He covered his ears with a thick quilt in an effort to drown out the plaintive mutterings, rising and falling, receding and advancing, many rooms and walls away. If not for those two male heirs of his, all would be peaceful. He would be far away in blessed oblivion or enjoying a dream excursion to another world. Instead, he was detained in this world against his will, fretful, restive, exhausted. He thought of the weeping widow earlier today, telling him of her husband's sorrow over the loss of his sons. Dare he think it? If I had drowned them as pups, Dee thought irritably, rolling over and covering his head again, I would be sleeping peacefully right now. Just as the dead Transport Minister had no doubt slept, in his cloistered compound of femininity.

The Transport Minister had been much on Dee's mind of late. Thanks to his assistant's excellent work, Dee had established that the murdered man and Lu Hsun-pei, the host at the party the year before last, had been much more than acquaintances. They had known each other as youths, and had been involved together in various business enterprises in earlier days; there was even a connection by marriage between their two families. And of course, Master Lu had many Indian contacts; there were at least three who might possibly qualify to be the mystery gentleman who used to show up at the Transport Minister's home with his selection of little girls.

Dee thought of the two drowned men, also without male issue, floating dead in the very waters that had been their livelihood, leaving their wives with nothing, leaving their money to strangers, questionable adopted sons and such, deliberately excluding the women. Cutting themselves off from femaleness. Not like the Transport Minister, who had surrounded himself with it.

His mind hummed like a beehive as he stretched and turned and fought with the bedclothes. The lingams his sons had smuggled home brought back vividly the Transport Minister's exotic collection; he thought of black-eyed women wearing nothing but jewels, of Indians clad in monk's robes and resplendent silks, and the oily, tortuous waters of the great canal system of Yangchou, snaking its way through the city and through the lives of everyone in it.

At last, Dee blessedly began to drift, like a boat delicately shoving off from the shore, feeling the tug of the current, letting himself be taken. Just before he was carried off, he clearly and momentarily heard the voice of his elder son, raised in a plaintive query:

"Why does he always think the worst?"

It began to rain sometime during the night. Dee had been sleeping for what seemed to be no more than a few minutes when, for the second gray dawn in a row, he was awakened by the hand of his house steward, shaking his shoulder gently but insistently.

"Sir," the man was saying reluctantly. "Sir. Sir!" Dee listened to the drumming rain for a moment, considered feigning deep sleep so that the man would go away, then hauled himself up on an elbow.

"What *is* it?" he asked with infinite weariness.

"Another body, sir."

"A body?" He did not understand at first.

"Yes. Drowned. In the canal."

By the time he got there, a mere two blocks from where yesterday's corpse had been found, they had already pulled the dead man from the water and loaded him on a wagon. The same constable stood nearby; the same two bearers waited patiently in the rain, which came down without pity. Dee climbed from his carriage and raised his parasol. He could see from here that the victim was tremendously fat; the great mound of his belly rose beneath the cloth that covered him. Smallish, almost dainty, slipper-clad feet stuck out at one end. Why, he wondered for a fleeting moment as he approached, nodding to the constable and the bearers, do they always leave the feet uncovered?

He pulled the cloth away from the corpse. It was a not unfamiliar face. He thought for a moment: the man had been in his court within the last year or two, he was quite sure of it. Yes. In fact, Dee had been to the man's home to discuss some of the details of the case—a claims case, something to do with a business partner who owed him money from some enterprise on the canals. He looked at the pale, suety dead countenance: another well-to-do entrepreneur. He pulled the cloth down farther, and saw what he expected to see—an intact purse, bulging with cash. He sighed and covered the face, recalling now the man's agitated animation when he talked of money and what was owed him, chins quivering with sincerity and conviction. Dee had seen many dead men, but it always affected him peculiarly to see someone dead whom he had known, however slightly.

"There will be no need to take him to the mortuary," Dee said to the constable. "We will take him directly to his house."

The widow did not behave as if it was particularly unusual to have her husband returned to her soaked, dead, and lying in the back of a cart. She came out and stood under the covered entryway and looked impassively down at his face as Dee uncovered it for her.

"Where is his purse?" she asked pointedly. Dee pulled the cloth down to show her. "Remove it," she said tersely to her house steward, who stood aghast and staring at his dead master. "Give it to me," she ordered, and took the bag of cash. "He will not cheat me out of this, at least," she declared, then turned and went into the house, indicating to Dee that he was to follow.

"If you will excuse my saying so, madame," Dee said politely, gratefully accepting a bowl of hot tea, "you do not appear to be surprised at what has happened to your husband."

"That is because I am not," she snapped.

"Then you . . . expected it?" he said carefully.

"Let us just say that I am not surprised. Nor am I particularly sorry, except about certain circumstances." Dry-eyed and stolid, she sat very straight in her chair and sipped her tea. Dee was impressed. Two weeping widows, and now one who acted as if it were normal for her husband to come home dead, as if he did it every day.

"Excuse me, madame," Dee began, "but did I hear you mention something about your husband cheating you?"

Now her eyes flashed fire, the first emotion he had seen in her. She put her bowl down.

"He will not get away with it," she said in a flat voice.

"Excuse me for one moment, please," she said, rising and leaving the room. She returned in an indignant rustle of silk, and dropped a rolled document into Dee's lap. "No, I was not surprised. Not after he left the house yesterday afternoon, and I found this in my jewel box."

Dee looked at her expressionless face, unrolled the document, and read:

"My name is Chou Lu-ti. Willingly, and by my own hand, I relinquish my worthless existence, tainted by wealth. I leave all of my earthly wealth and possessions (with the exception of my wife's jewels, which she may keep) to one Chang Fang-chi, who shall collect in one year's time.

"Being set free from the bonds of the prison house of existence, possessing natures perfectly pure, you will attain nirvana. Thou who art conquered by women, go and conquer this earth!"

"Suicide!" Dee said, thinking of the two other drownings, looking up happily, his voice registering perhaps a bit more enthusiasm than might seem appropriate. Despite her impassive demeanor, the woman looked startled at his cheerful tone. "Madame," Dee said quickly as theories and stratagems began to form in his head, "am I correct in assuming that you and your husband have no sons?"

"You are not," she answered coolly.

"No?" Dee said, disappointed.

"Strictly speaking, no, you are not correct. My husband and I have a son. But in another sense, you are correct." Dee waited, fascinated, while she chose her words. "Our son does not live here. He lives in the country with a peasant family. We pay for his upkeep, plus a stipend to the family for caring for him. You see, Magistrate, he has the mind of an infant inhabiting the full-grown body of a man. He is an idiot."

It was still raining mercilessly when Dee got to his office, but he scarcely noticed. He shook his wet cape off and tossed it aside, hurrying up the stairs two at a time. He could not wait to tell his assistant what he had found out.

The young man was there, but it was plain that he had arrived only minutes before Dee. His hair and face were still wet, and he was breathless and enthusiastic himself.

"Another drowning," Dee said before the other could start speaking. "But this one left us something to go on. All the usual things were there," he said, pouring a bowl of tea and rubbing his hands. "A well-to-do tradesman. Dead in the canal with a purse full of cash. The will cutting his wife out of any inheritance. No proper male heir to pass it on to. A stranger named. But now—thanks to corpse number three—we know who killed those men!" he said pleasantly.

"Who?" the assistant demanded, instantly fascinated. Dee smiled.

"At least," Dee amended himself, "we know who killed number three, and I have no doubt that the others died the same way, since everything else matches. Suicide, my young friend," he said with satisfaction. "Those men put themselves in the canals. And it was no accident." He tossed the man's will across the table to the assistant, who picked it up and read it, amazement growing on his face as he did. "And the rest of it is clearly a reference to some sutra or other. No doubt the key to the entire mystery. I should have known that religion would have something to do with this," he declared, taking another drink of tea and a mouthful of pastry from the plate on the table.

"I have found some things out, too," the assistant said, putting down the document. "That is why I did not get here until just now."

"Yes? Anything relevant?" Dee asked eagerly.

"Well, I have ascertained that the beneficiary named in the second will is also an 'adopted' son."

"Yes. Very good. As we will no doubt find with the one named in this one," he said, indicating the damp scroll of paper on the table between them.

"I have researched some of the finer points of the inheritance laws," the younger man continued. "The legality of by-passing one's wife in favor of an adopted son is definitely shaky, definitely open to question. The women and their families would certainly be able to challenge the wills, as long as they could maintain that the wife was above reproach, that she was not a criminal or an adulteress, or disrespectful to her husband's parents or some such thing."

"And is there any evidence of that?"

"Nothing in the records. And it seems unlikely that we will find anything anywhere else."

"Well, then, we can reassure the women that they need not worry about finding themselves in the street! We will locate these 'sons,' and we will inform them that they are not going to have their purses fattened through the deaths of their 'fathers.' We will question them, and search out whatever spurious holy scheme is behind it all. Perhaps we can prevent another deluded soul from frightening the life out of some poor farmer poling his way along the canal in the early morning." He began to straighten the papers on his desk.

"Perhaps," the assistant said. "But there is a problem. The money may not go to the women after all."

"Oh?" Dee stopped his shuffling of papers and looked up.

"I made another discovery at two of the district clerical offices. At the time of their deaths, neither of the victims was a married man. They had both secretly divorced their wives a mere few days before they were found dead."

The rain continued for the rest of the day and into the night. Evening found Dee at home in his comfortable study, warm and dry, the lamps burning cheerfully, hot tea at his elbow, and heavy volumes of translated holy writings spread out before him. The house was quiet as a temple tonight, his sons ostensibly engaged in their lessons and his wives at least temporarily mollified. He had changed out of his wet clothes upon arriving out of the storm, had had a delicious dinner, and had gratefully settled down to his reading. His home, with its gently burning lights, tasteful and accommodating furnishings, harmonious colors, polished brass, and pleasant scents, seemed truly to be a haven, and he was aware of it tonight in a heightened way. From time to time he glanced up from the text and moved his contented admiring gaze around the room.

No doubt the men who had drowned themselves had had pleasant, comfortable homes, too, and soft dry clothes and delicious food. He tried to imagine trading all of that for the dark chill waters of the canal. What force could make *him* get up out of his chair and go out into the night, never to return? It would have to be something strong indeed. Set free from the prison house of existence, the last man had said in his letter, you will obtain nirvana.

Dee's eyes fell to the page he was perusing. *I am not so afraid even of serpents nor of thunderbolts falling from heaven, nor of flames blown together by the wind, as I am afraid of these worldly objects,* he read. *These transient pleasures, the robbers of our happiness and wealth, which float empty and like illusions through the world, infatuate men's minds even when they are only hoped for, still more when they take up their abode in the soul. . . . What man of self-control could find satisfaction in those pleasures, which are like an angry, cruel serpent, which are like snatching up a hot coal, which are like the enjoyments in a dream—which are gained by their recipients after manifold pilgrimages and labors, and then perish in a moment?*

What man indeed? On the other hand, Dee thought, how does one arrive at the absolute belief that worldly pleasures are a vale of lies? Certainly, if the doctrine were somehow proven to be true as a rock, that such mortal pleasures make one a slave to desire and perpetuate the cycle of birth, death, rebirth, and suffering, then one might think twice. But Dee knew that he himself would never be able to take that leap of faith. How can we *know* anything beyond what is in our hands at the moment? he asked himself. And what sort of cruel, sly, conniving and tricky universe would toy with poor susceptible mortal souls by tempting them with comforts that are in reality a bouquet of hissing serpents? Then tell them that the only path to true pleasure is to renounce pleasure, to mortify the flesh? How could a man trust *anything* in such a universe? If it was possible that earthly pleasures were a snare and a delusion, then was it not also possible that religious doctrine was the falsehood, the lie, the mirage, luring men away from the only real pleasures available to flesh-and-blood creatures?

It occurred to him that religious writings drew much of their seductive power from their poetic language. Didn't poetry itself fill a void in the human soul, and couldn't it incidentally carry anything else into that void with it, give it a ride on its back, so to speak? It certainly seemed so to him: *Deer are lured to their destruction by songs, insects for the sake of the brightness fly into the fire, the fish greedy for the morsel swallows the iron hook—therefore worldly objects produce misery as their end.*

There was philosophical logic here, too, also persuasive; the next several verses that he read dealt with the definition of pleasure in an incisive way: *As for the common opinion that pleasures are enjoyments, none of them when examined are worthy of being enjoyed; fine garments and the rest are only the accessories of things; they are to be regarded as merely the remedies for pain. Water is desired for allaying thirst; food in the same way for removing hunger; a house for keeping off the wind, the heat of the sun, and the rain.* Dee could not help looking up again and taking in the solid comforts of his room; was it all merely a remedy for pain, and not a true pleasure in and of itself? He read on: *Since variableness is found in all pleasures, we cannot apply to them the name of enjoyment; the very conditions that mark pleasure bring also in their turn pain. Heavy garments and fragrant aloe wood are pleasant in the cold, but an annoyance in the heat; moonbeams and sandalwood are pleasant in the heat, but a pain in the cold.*

Dee could not agree with this at all. He certainly understood the philosophical point, but he could not see why a true enjoyment should not be relative—rest when the body is tired, or coldness when one burned with fever, or fire when one shivered with cold. Denying that such things were true enjoyments seemed to him a vain attempt to solidify a constantly shifting universe—a failure to recognize the true meaning of pleasure. He glanced at the text, skipping about, until his eye fell on a verse that gave him pause: *I, having experienced the fear of old age and death, fly to this path of religion in my desire for liberation; leaving behind my dear kindred with tears in their faces.* The last words certainly described the grieving widows, with the exception of the lady he had met today.

And what about women? He knew that the doctrine's attitude toward females was complex, to say the least. While women were apparently able to embark on the path to enlightenment as were men, it seemed that they began their struggles from an even less advantageous place. He remembered a significant passage from the Land of Bliss Sutra. He checked his notes, thumbed ahead several hundred pages in the text, and began his search. It had been in the description of Sukhavati. He ran his finger down line after line, skimming the repetitive, singsong, nearly hypnotic verses. His finger halted; he had found it: *O Bhagavat, if, after I have attained Highest Knowledge, women in Buddha countries on all sides, after having heard my name, should allow carelessness to arise, should, when they are free from birth, not despise their female nature; and if, being born again, they should assume a second female nature, then may I not obtain the highest perfect knowledge. . . .*

He looked again at the final words of the document left by this morning's drowned man: *Thou who art conquered by women, go and conquer this earth!* Everywhere in the writings, women—femaleness—figured as a veritable anchor, a dense heavy weight pulling men back down to earth, keeping them from perfect knowledge, keeping them out of paradise. Like earthly goods, offering a delusory and doomed paradise.

He sat and thought for a long time, the rain pattering over his head, the sweetest music in the world—and most conducive to inductive reasoning. Though many details were missing, some of the larger pieces were beginning to fit together quite nicely. He was also starting to feel the familiar excitement that always preceded one of his little forays. He drank the last of his tea, then poured himself some sweet peach liqueur from a decanter and let it slide delectably down to his stomach, where he felt it bloom like a flower. Pleasure is pleasure precisely because of its fleetingness, he thought, taking another sip, closing his eyes, and listening to the rain; and its fickleness as well.

Plans were forming in his mind. He smiled. His wives would not have cause to be upset with him. It would not be necessary to shave his head this time.

The carriage Dee rode in was the most important part of his disguise. If Dee did not wish to, he would never have to set foot to the pavement; it was his prerogative, if he chose to use it, to go everywhere in a carriage or sedan chair. But Yangchou's highest-ranking Imperial magistrate was known throughout the city as an avid walker. It was the only way most people had ever seen him. If details of a case demanded going to far corners of the city, Dee sent the constabulary runners. How they traveled was up to them. But he himself could be counted on to go by foot if it was at all possible and the weather permitted it. Today, the sun was shining and the air was brisk—a perfect day for walking—but instead, he rode in the richly appointed satin interior of the finest carriage he had been able to lease on short notice.

Dee understood that the most important component of any disguise was the state of mind of the person behind it, so the sumptuous luxury of his carriage should serve him well. Rumbling along behind him on the dusty road that led out of Yangchou was a second well-fitted carriage. Inside it was an elegant covered sedan chair and four sturdy bearers who would carry him from the gate of the Golden Cloud Monastery to the main temple; his feet would never even touch the ground. That fact alone would go a long way toward preventing the abbot from associating today's visiting well-to-do merchant with the footsore impecunious traveler of many years before. A different voice and way of speaking, a different facial expression and way of holding his head, the sparse grayish whiskers painstakingly glued onto his chin and upper lip hair by hair, the padding under his robes to lend him a look of prosperous corpulence, and the set of crooked, slightly protruding teeth fashioned from ivory to fit over his own all made him a different person. He was sure of it, because he had tested his disguise out on his own first wife, coming up quietly in the garden behind her, asking her a question, and watching her jump back in shock momentarily at the appearance of a stranger within the family compound.

And of course, he reflected as they approached the final bend in the road, the abbot would most likely be looking at him through a different set of eyes—eyes reserved for wealth, blind to all that was dusty, weary, and threadbare.

When they had reached the perimeter of the great monastic estate, the sedan chair was brought out and the lone merchant, the extraordinarily wealthy "Master Lao," stepped inside.

This time, instead of having to make the precipitous hike of years before, he was carried down the steep trail that led from the head of the road to the valley where the monastery nestled, the four strong men bearing him aloft stepping surely and carefully. It was a strange feeling, allowing other men to walk for you. It required a certain complacence, Dee thought as he gripped the armrests while expecting to be dumped on the ground at any moment, that he was not at all certain he possessed. Soon they were on level ground. He pulled back the curtain, and saw the gate ahead.

Standing under it, as if he had known in advance that an important personage was arriving, and looking even more acquisitively genial than the last time he had set eyes on him, was the abbot of the Golden Cloud. We meet again, my friend, Dee thought as the bearers lowered him gently to the ground and he pulled the curtain back the rest of the way and stepped out.

"Good afternoon, Your Holiness," Dee said in his new voice to the man who stepped forward smiling broadly and welcomingly. "Perhaps you can help me. I am seeking salvation."

10

The servants followed him as he shuffled about the room. One of them attempted to fasten the frogs of his morning robe, which, despite their ministrations, persisted in falling open to the damp drafts. His eyes, dark and alive, hung brightly in the pale wreckage of his face, moving independently of his body's restive, meaningless forays from chair to couch to table to desk to window and back to chair and couch.

He sat, pulling his useless right arm into his lap with the other, heedless of the blanket sliding from his shoulders. The servants rushed to replace the blanket, but before they could get to him he was up again and wandering across the room.

"Can't you fools keep him *still*?" Wu demanded, striking the table where the colorful preliminary sketches were laid out. "How can I show him these plans if you do not keep him *still*?" Her voice was still controlled, but beginning to rise dangerously.

"We are doing the best that we can, Your Grace, but . . . but . . . " The little eunuch was flushed with anxiety.

"But he simply does not appear to be here with us at all," said the older, experienced chief of the Inner Household staff.

Meanwhile, Kaotsung had wandered toward Wu's corner of the room and sat down again on a chair near the desk where her papers lay. He arranged the dead arm in his lap, then let the good arm rest carelessly on the table, wrinkling and displacing the papers as if they were not even there, while his eyes, refusing to fix on hers, seemed to be addressing questions to odd corners of the room.

"His mind is sick," Wu said with disgusted finality. "Strap him there."

"What is it madame wishes?" the chief eunuch asked, as if he had not heard right.

"Strap him to his chair," she repeated, enunciating each word with exaggerated care. "Strap him with the cords from

202

his robe. Anything. So that he cannot get up and wander around the damned room anymore."

"But madame," the attending physician protested, "a man in his condition must be treated most delicately."

"Then you will tie him to his chair most delicately," she said, mimicking the physician's voice with a fierce tone. "And gag that drooling mouth of his shut. I will *not* look at it!" She snapped her head around and glared at the chief eunuch and his attendant. "Do it now!"

"But madame . . ." The man who was personal physician to the emperor felt the need to protest.

"*Do it!*" she bellowed; they all jumped.

While Kaotsung remained seated, the servants began to rush around the room removing all the cords from the Emperor's many scattered robes and even began yanking the sashes from the blinds. They passed the cords, one after another, to the chief eunuch, who muttered his way through the elaborate and unenviable task of tying the stricken monarch to his chair, a task he forced his attendant to share. In the meantime, and without Wu's even noticing, the physician had backed angrily out of the room, absolving himself, with his own shaky conviction, of all responsibility for the heinous crime being perpetrated against the Son of Heaven.

When they had finished with the binding, Kaotsung's good arm was tied to the filigree at the side of the chair, his ankles to the chair's teak legs, his upper torso to the chair back. Only his head was free to move. The servants simply could not bring themselves to gag him, so Wu seized a cloth and tied it around his mouth and jaw herself. The servants retreated while Wu stood over her husband.

She took his head gently in her hands and turned his face toward hers, making him look at her, and rested her softening tear-filled gaze on his.

"You see," she said in a warm motherly voice, "all of this is for your own good. I am only thinking of you. In this state, you are prone to hurt yourself—perhaps to trip over something you do not see, or maybe bark your shins against the sharp corners of the furniture.

"Now!" she said, putting direction and enthusiasm into her tone and flattening out the papers before her. "I will show you what I have planned for the greater glory of the T'ang and for you, my husband, the Emperor. We will have a new Reign Title, and we will rename the palace. We will call it P'eng-lai.

The historian tells me that in the ancient Han Dynasty legends, P'eng-lai was an island of beautiful sylphine immortals and coral trees, somewhere in the eastern seas. A fairyland! And we are going to remake the Imperial City in Loyang into a veritable fairyland!"

For the first time, she seemed to have his full attention: he looked at her, his eyes bright and alert, his body bound in an absurd parody of submission.

A.D. 663

With a diminished husband at her side, Wu Tse-tien appeared suddenly one blazing late-spring morning on an elaborate altar-balcony to christen the four Lokapala Guardian Gates marking the farthest corners of her project with the Temple of the White Jambhala at its center.

Kaotsung, leaning on a massive walking stick, stared out in silence over the assembled ministers gathered in the Palace of the Peacock King. Wu knew that this was the first he had seen of her enormous building projects for the Bureaucratic City. As far as they could see, a world of new buildings spread out before them, and around these were a maze of half-finished walls, forests of bamboo scaffoldings, raw earth, piles of splintered lumber and ragged stacks of smashed paving stones, fields of newly set paving brick, and crates of recently fired tiles and ornamental porcelain and earthenware figures for the eaves and acroteria of the new structures.

Taoism, the traditional ideology for the T'ang, had its age-old iconography of cranes and tortoises and dragons. But what were the surviving officials to make of the great golden Mahasiddhas, the flying Tantric magicians, with their strange ears and misshapen heads? And what of the half-man, half-animal Kirittimukha, the winged Garudas, and the reptilian Makaras? These were part of the Buddha's exotic realm, images appropriate for temples and monasteries. But these things had no place in the traditional centers of Confucian civil government, they told one another—but quietly, cautiously, since the "suicide" deaths of the Council of Six. So they would simply avert their eyes or force their concentration to other matters as they moved past the oddly sensual trunked and tentacled forms with their strangely inexpressible concupiscence.

Wu spoke the blessings of ten thousands years over the assembly, then she blessed the Empire of the T'ang for a *kalpa*—a thousand years—of the Future Buddha's peace. She was remaking the world of men and reshaping the universe. All the while beside her stood Kaotsung in his impassive silence, his useless arm tucked into a sleeve tied to his midriff so that the limb would not simply hang indecorously by his side.

"But it is all one with the universe, Madame Empress," the short, wiry, dark young man said as he spun around gracefully, arms outstretched, his swirling robes revealing well-formed and muscular calves. Although he appeared very strong, he was surprisingly fluid, agile, and light—something Wu had noticed from the outset. "I take from the universe my power and it gives back a thousandfold to me," he said, and stopped quickly, his arms undulating in the air as if drawing a magical charge through the tips of his fingers, his plaited hair snapping around his dusky, handsome features. "And then, my increase adds to its increase, and so I and the universe increase conversely. It is boundless power and stimulus throughout both spirit and bodily vessel." He ran his hands down along his broad chest and stopped at his hips so that the fabric of his robe tightened, briefly displaying a surprisingly ample flaccid proportion.

He flung his arms out again and began to strut slowly and majestically across the room as if occupied with some strange birdwalk ritual. Wu's gaze followed his odd procession, his eyes darting with flashing suddenness from hers to some unfixed and ethereal distance. "We tap into the infinite, madame, we tap into the infinite forms of nature, we move our souls in and out of this world with no greater thought than an old woman picking up a teapot."

He had told her that he was a *gomchen*, a priest of Tantric magic, a Nagaspa—a magician belonging to a very rare and mysterious Tibetan sect, though he himself was an Indian from Ghandara. He also told her that he had come to study at the Imperial Libraries. Though Wu wondered at that, because the Imperial Libraries, although strong in areas of Indian Buddhism, were as yet devoid of any Tibetan-Tantric resources. Wu did not take with great seriousness anything the acrobatic young man said—but she enjoyed the game of discoursing with him on abstruse subjects. And she liked looking at him.

She had arranged for him to visit the library in her apartments several times a week. There he expounded on ancient sacred texts and mystical rituals, the history of this or that seminal *gompa* monastery or legendary adept or *rimpoche* or this or that famous *gomchen* and about phantoms and the mind, hallucinations and reality and the raising of corpses. He conjured worlds of remote mountain vistas, and he conjured scenes of battles with real and imagined demons-though he said there was no difference—taking place against these desolate landscapes.

And he would dance. With the "strength of a tiger and the lightness of a bird," he bragged to Wu without a trace of modesty in his deep luminous eyes. Then he would leap and twirl about the room with so much trancelike fervor that the servants were ordered to push back the tables and bookshelves and roll up the rugs in preparation for his visits. Despite her suspicion that his trance state was a consciously contrived and well-acted dramatic effect, Wu appreciated it. If what she was seeing was a reflection of things that he had seen with his own eyes in faraway, exotic places, then it scarcely mattered whether his "possession" was contrived. Real or not, it fascinated her. But mostly, she found it profoundly flattering that he would go to so much effort to impress her. She felt life and vitality flowing back into her being.

"Madame, I am a *lung-gom-pa*," he announced with artful suddenness between several pert little turns on the balls of his feet. "Do you know what that is?" He arched his neck gracefully and allowed his arms and fingers, extended in front of his face, to follow some private drumming rhythm that only he could hear. His demeanor suggested that he had no interest in any possible response from her, so great was his concentration. Wu did not answer; she smiled demurely and waited. He continued dancing as he spoke: "It is an ancient and little-known practice. I doubt that there is anyone in all of the Empire who may know the answer. But it shall, of course, be revealed to the Empress of China!"

He lunged forward like a swordsman with one arm extended straight, as if thrusting at a demon with his ritual *phurba* dagger. Then, snapping his dagger arm back, withdrawing the "blade" victoriously from the demon's punctured gut, he pushed up and spun around in midair so that both feet were well off the floor for several turns. Wu studied the clear outline of his narrow waist and firm buttocks, and thought again that he was a most pleasant young man to look at.

"The training of the ancient practice of *lung-gom*," he continued, "began in the faraway Shalu Gompa. By extensive and rigorous training, the *naljopa* adept acquires enormous nimbleness and speed, like a horse, madame."

"Ah. A horse," she mused.

"Oh, but with far greater stamina, madame. The one who has acquired the *lung-gom*—the *lung-gom-pa*—can run and leap for days. Can traverse in two days—without stopping—what would take the untrained two weeks. An adept can run in a meditative trance across the grassy plains of Tibet for days and days without stopping—as long as the trance is unbroken. His body becomes so light that his running becomes leaping and his leaping becomes sheer levitation."

"Days and days?" she repeated. "Extraordinary. And there is, no doubt, some great purpose to this?" Wu asked politely, studying her hand with the bright jeweled cap on the middle finger.

"Ah, yes," he said, his eyes fixing intently onto hers. "There is, as you say, a great purpose to it all." Her eyes followed his hand as it traced graceful arcs in the air and then lingered on his chest. "The *lung-gom* runner trains to such physical perfection so that he might perform a most important task: to extend an invitation to the evil deity Shinjed, the Lord of Death, and his demonic minions." The young Nagaspa whirled to a graceful halt and in the same motion came to rest on one of the embroidered stools across from the Empress at the library's long table.

"You see, madame, this is a rite that must be accomplished every twelve years. Shinjed and his disciples would slay every sentient being on the earth to satisfy their insatiable hunger. The early magicians were forced to coerce the god into accepting a substitute dinner of infinite numbers of phantom birds that they would conjure and drive into its mouth. But the deity Shinjed has gathered quite a few disciples in his time, and the runner must travel great distances to the various corners of northern Tibet to invite each of them in turn to the sacrificial dinner of phantom doves. Once they are fed, mankind is safe from the slaughtering demons for another eleven years."

"And the invitations must be carried by runners?" Wu questioned. "A man borne by a fleet horse will not do?"

"It would hardly satisfy demon propriety, madame!" he answered matter-of-factly.

"Hardly!" Wu responded. "And you—you are just such a *lunggom-pa* runner yourself?"

"Yes, madame," he said, drawing himself up proudly. "I am one with extraordinary stamina. It is a practice that comes from learning to control the 'internal air.' I believe the Chinese refer to this 'air' as *ch'i*." He paused and shut his eyes, blissfully drawing in a deep lungful of the life-giving substance. Then he opened his eyes and looked directly into hers. "Once I am standing, I do not lie down for days. I do not break stride. I do not recline at all, but rather remain erect and moving until the job is done and all parties are fully satisfied."

"I am certain that you do. I should most like to see you run." She raised her eyes in a challenge, tracing the outline of her lip with the tip of her finger. "I am sure that it would prove most educational!"

Kaotsung knew that he had lost a great deal of time. Wu had been busy. Very busy. During the time that he had been sick and slow and inattentive, he had not been alert, and Wu had filled all those moments with projects, had made ten thousand decisions without him. And his councillors were gone. But he was not totally helpless. His silence was a formidable weapon, one that he wielded from a place deep within him.

He did not speak at all anymore. Not even when he was alone. It was like a promise, a gift he had made to himself, his silence. It was a luxury, a place he could retreat to, where he had been able to watch what was happening to him and to everyone and everything else from a safe distance.

She hated his silence, of course, but it could not be helped. He did not wish to ever hear his own voice again. It was as if a cord had been cut deep in the center of his being, severing his will from his tongue forever. He found himself growing comfortable with the silence. It was his best protection against her.

Kaotsung no longer thought of her as his wife; she was a thing that had grown out of him and that had to be fought. She was the manifestation of everything he was not, of everything he had neglected. She was strong and powerful because he was not. That was why he had to remain silent: words were the open window, the door standing ajar, the crack in the wall through which she would wriggle and by which she would gain entrance to his hiding place.

He dropped his morning robe to his waist and then let it

fall off him completely and settle to the floor in a soft pile around his ankles. He stepped out of it. He was completely naked. He wanted to study himself in the large polished oval mirror alongside the day couch, wanted to see how weak he had become. His face was dragged; the energy in it had sagged with the muscles. With the tip of his finger, he pulled his lower lid away from the right eye, then the left. The whites of his eyes were yellowed and bloodshot; like the eyes of an old street vagrant, he mused. He thought it lent him a certain gravity and dignity, though the physicians who had come to read the signs on his tongue and in his eyes that morning had assured him that the whites of his eyes would clear.

Although the right corner of his mouth no longer drooped so severely, that side of his face was now permanently lined. Kaotsung did not like his face at all, though the knowledge that he maintained a permanent sneer was strangely satisfying.

His right arm still dangled limp and useless, and a hollow indentation had developed at his shoulder. But his good arm was strong, becoming stronger all the time. He had seen to that, insisting at every possible instance that his stewards allow him to serve his own tea, fetch his own water into the basin, and dress himself, no matter how difficult that might be for the Son of Heaven.

This morning, despite his ravaged face and dangling arm, he felt renewed and purposeful and had dismissed his old *t'ai chi* master early. He wanted to see for himself what was about. And he did not want to be hampered by his Yu-lin Palace Guard escort. If they insisted on following him, then they must stay back and out of his sight. His newfound strength and interest made him feel like a boy on the prowl again. The air was crisp and fresh and whispered to him of things unexplored. And today he was going to explore a world that was new and foreign to him: his own palace.

Though he had been silent, he had not been deaf. Kaotsung had heard many rumors about all sorts of odd religious activities. Of course, he knew about all of the rebuilding and renaming and christening projects. He had been dragged through many of them. It was some of the other stories that interested him—scarcely credible ones about the Empress and her mother and their "spiritual" activities. And there were all sorts of religious ascetics roaming about the Palace City; the grounds were infested with monks, abbots, anchorites, and other devotees moving about with their prayers, their incomprehensible humming and mumbling, chanting and droning in the strange tongues of their litanies. With his councillors gone, it was a different world Kaotsung was walking back out into; it was surely a different palace from what he had known. Wu had seen to that.

As Kaotsung stepped out into the long corridor that connected the Imperial apartments, throne rooms, and private libraries of the royal family, the very air seemed charged and different. He was excited by the prospect of discovery that lay ahead of him. There were thousands of rooms—some that he had not visited in months, many others in years, others not since childhood, and still others never once in his lifetime. But he was about to change that. During the time of his removal from life, his illness and withdrawal, the Empress's feverish activities had seemed to be happening far, far away. but now, today, this morning, he was acutely interested in everything.

Kaotsung stood leaning on his heavy walking stick in the middle of the long corridor, the shining, polished black tile and rich carved wood stretching away from him, and breathed the ancient pungent air. The smell of lacquer and oil that permeated the woodwork and furnishings was the heaviest and the first to reach his nostrils. That odor was the most familiar and powerful one for him, the odor of his very life. He inhaled deeply. But he detected something else, something alien and new; a sweet layer of incense, strangely flattened by a faint essence of mildew. Beyond the odor of mildew, there was something else, so subtle that he would never have noticed it in his days of full health and vigor but that now revealed itself to his heightened senses: the cold, damp essence of stone.

He marveled. The smell of the air said it all. Why had he never noticed it before? It was a complete, perfect metaphor for existence: above, obvious and pervasive, were the bright, interesting, appetizing odors of furnishings and oils—the civilized varnishings. Below that were the not unpleasant odors that whispered to us of the first traces of death, but were still alive and came from life—mildew, mingled with the colored scents of ritual perfumed offerings. That, he reflected, was the human side of death, perceived from the vantage of life. Kaotsung sniffed the air again and concentrated. Then there was that other thing, the lowermost smell, subterranean and profound, like the inside of a tomb: the cold damp smell of eternity, of stone. That was death's side of death.

Kaotsung heard noises coming from behind the Imperial

family library doors. They did not sound to him like the noises of library business. He positioned himself between the two doors that opened onto the corridor, steadying himself with his stick as he listened; he was still a little unsure on his feet. He waited. There were no more sounds for a long time other than distant voices and footfalls a long way off. Then he heard the sounds from behind the doors again: low soft groans, a woman's voice, deeper grunts, a man's voice, shuffling, the grating scrape of wooden furniture legs pushed along the tiled floor, heavy breathing, and more grunting, as if someone was trying to move another heavy object. There was a short silence, which gave way to a woman's high breathy exhalations. Kaotsung listened. Soon the woman's breathing was matched by low masculine groans; then the two sounds were locked in an urgent rhythm, punctuated and labored.

He was both irritated and pruriently intrigued. This was his father's library, and before that, his grandfather's. He put his hand tentatively on the latch. The Yu-lin Guards who were escorting him at a discreet distance had seen his hesitation; they moved forward and quietly flanked the library doors. Kaotsung shook his head and motioned them away, his gesture telling them that it was nothing serious and a gleam in his eyes telling them that the pleasure, whatever it is, was all his. A handmaiden and a servant, perhaps? A high-ranking concubine with access to the Inner Household? Obviously, a servant who was not a eunuch—but who?

The male voice was now strained with effort, while the breathy whimpers of the female bloomed into full-throated cries of agony and delight; something heavy and wooden knocked against the wall in a growing, frenzied rhythmic accompaniment. The male moaned, the woman whimpered.

Kaotsung gently released the latch and silently pushed the door open. The pair were atop a long library table, facing away from the door. He studied the embrace with interest. Narrow dark muscled buttocks contracting and thrusting inward, then releasing and spreading outward again. In, out. The couple were well beyond the point of return; the rhythm told Kaotsung that the lovers would release together very soon. They had not seen him. He would allow them to finish before tossing them both out into the corridor without their clothes. That would be punishment enough.

Soft female legs wrapped tighter around the male's back. Well-defined shoulders heaved upward, then the buttocks con-

tracted again in one final thrust down. The delicate white female feet slid down into the small of the back and locked in a
long concluding shudder. She was spending while the lover's
buttocks continued to contract and release in a graceful arch.
The man was practiced, Kaotsung noted. He knew what he
was doing.

The woman stopped. Her flood was over. Then her hand
slid down her lover's back, and Kaotsung saw color glinting
on the tip of the middle finger; mesmerized, the Emperor
watched the hand move low to stroke the man's "bag of eggs,"
causing the buttocks to clench in sudden excitation, shaping
the flesh into hard wrinkles. With violent spasms that drove
him even deeper into her, he, too, released. Then he collapsed,
spent, onto the woman.

Kaotsung entered the room and walked to the side of their
"couch." In that moment, Wu and Kaotsung found each other
with their eyes. The man, whoever he was, looked no farther
than the Emperor's slippered feet, then froze as if he had been
turned to stone. He kept his face averted, staring steadfastly
downward as if waiting for his head to be severed.

Kaotsung brought his heavy stick down with ferocious
force on the wooden floor, making a tremendous noise. Four
Yu-lin Palace Guards stormed into the library, stumbling into
each other and nearly tripping over their own half-drawn
weapons. They stared with amazement and confusion at the
intertwined bodies on the table. Kaotsung pointed, inarticulate,
his eyes flashing fire.

"Kill him!" the captain of the guards ordered, directing
his lance toward the dark, muscular body of the naked Indian.
But Kaotsung intercepted with his good arm, shaking his head,
his mouth working, trying to speak. He pointed emphatically
at the Empress. What sort of man did they think he was? Did
they think he was like her? You do not kill the man seduced
by the Empress, for he has little choice. Throw him out and
kill *her*, he gestured furiously. They understood.

The guards pulled the Nagaspa's sweaty body roughly off
Wu's and pushed him naked through the door. Kaotsung
heard the sound of the man's feet running, escaping for his
life, down the corridor.

Then he turned to Wu.

Startled, she lay in the position in which her lover had
left her. Kao-tsung's rage engulfed him. The sight of the naked
Empress-legs spread, knees up, her body vulnerable and glis-

tening with sweat—enraged him even more. Wu, looking boldly back at him, pulled her legs together and started to rise to her elbows, but he pushed her back down. She forced herself up again. This time he brought the back of his hand hard across her face. Her head snapped to one side as she dropped back down flat on her back; he slapped her again. She said nothing and offered no resistance. Two thin trickles of blood crisscrossed below her nostrils. He stared. She pulled herself up to a sitting position, her eyes defying his.

"Shall we kill her now, Imperial Father?" the captain of the guards asked, his weapon ready. Kaotsung raised a hand, gesturing for the man to desist for the moment. I have only to tell them, he said with his eyes. One word. And no questions asked of me. There is nothing for me to arrange. No elaborate plans. Kill you or exile you to the farthest ends of the earth for life. It is all the same.

She moved to cover herself with a piece of clothing, but he pulled it from her and stared at the glistening black hair and the soft open flesh beneath it, the perfect white of her inner thighs. His rage burned in his chest, then turned to something else. His anger was moving, driving low in his belly like hot sinking coals. He clenched his fists. His eyes watered and blurred. His breath came rapidly; his body stirred without his willing it. His eyes traveled from Wu's middle back to her eyes; there it was, the challenge, that was always there. In that moment, anger was desire and desire was anger. He stiffened harder than he could ever remember, his breath harsh and grating. He turned to the guards. They stood there wide-eyed, weapons slack at their side, staring down at their naked queen.

Take her off the table, he gestured with a sweeping motion of his arm. The men dropped their lances and dragged Wu up by the armpits and waited. Without warning, Wu lashed out. Her foot flew into the groin of the guard at her left arm. He dropped howling to his knees, his hands clutching at his crotch. She pulled herself free of the other lieutenant, but in that instant a third guard joined the fray and both were on her arms, forcing her back against the unstable bookshelves. With both feet off the ground, Wu kicked out again, but the guards held tight. The injured guard rolled and moaned as the captain raised his lance again, waiting for the Emperor's orders. Kaotsung was galvanized. The sight of Wu struggling naked against the palace guards aroused him to exquisite breathless torment.

"You crippled bastard," Wu yelled at her husband. "Is this all you can do? Have your moronic thugs push me around like an animal? Has your mind gone as limp as your 'old man'?" she jeered.

She lunged out again with her feet, catching the captain of the guards above both knees. The man's lance clattered to the floor. The other two brought Wu's arms high above her head, forcing her wrists back against the bookshelves' highest tier. "An *impotent fool* of an Emperor calls in his trained dogs! They do his bidding because he cannot do anything for himself. Did you think that I would wither away, pining for your sex again? I could not wait for you in your *damned drooling silence!*" Wu shouted to the ceiling.

Kaotsung was dizzy from the blood rushing from his head to the lower part of his body. He pointed to the floor. His meaning was clear.

Wu pushed down hard with her feet, forcing her body backward and bringing the bookshelves, herself, and the two guards down. The men scrambled on top of her as she kicked and fought. They pinned her to the floor among the toppled and scattered volumes. The captain forced her flailing legs apart while the other two, struggling to hold her arms, added their weight, straddling her legs with theirs.

"You filthy impotent *bastards*! You dirty *swine*! You *dogs!*" she howled.

Kaotsung threw aside his stick, dropped his robe, and stood over her naked. His erect member, shiny and purple, twitched with each pulsebeat. He made another gesture, indicating his mouth; again, the guards understood. So did Wu. She spat and glared. The kicked guard, moaning and rocking back and forth on his haunches on the floor, moved to obey the Emperor's wordless command. The man dragged himself up and shuffled in an excruciatingly bent posture toward the day couch, where the lovers' clothing lay in a heap. Grunting with pain, he picked up one of the Empress's sashes and tossed it into the captain's outstretched hand. The captain brought the thick satin sash down to Wu's mouth.

"I'll have every one of you ripped apart! *Ripped apart! Castrated! Drawn and quartered! Fed to the dogs!*" Then she was muzzled, but not before chomping down hard on the captain's hand. The man bellowed and brought the bitten finger to his mouth while the other guard, the one she had kicked, did his best to finish the job of gagging the Empress.

Kaotsung bent down and stuffed the sash the rest of the way into her mouth himself; resting on his good arm, he lowered himself between her legs. With a brutal thrust of his hips, he slid himself fully into her while the guards stared as if their eyes would fall from their heads.

He thrust as hard as he could for a dozen strokes or so, then paused and held himself still, savoring the sensation of her squirming around him, her black enraged eyes boring into his above her gagged mouth, the pleasure building in him to painful intensity. He felt on the brink of spending himself and fought to hold back. Then he spoke. His voice, which no one had heard for months, filled the room, startling himself no less than Wu and the guards, each syllable accompanied by a jabbing thrust. "Clever men build cities, clever women topple them!" he rasped, speaking the ancient words from the Book of Odes.

Then his eyes shut and his face dropped to hers so that he could feel the hot rush of breath from her nostrils on his cold sweaty cheek. Despite herself, Wu's eyes closed too as the warm rage of many long, silent months poured into her.

11

A.D. 662
Yangchou

"Salvation is not such a simple thing, Master Lao," the abbot said, walking slowly and thoughtfully next to his visitor, a solicitous hand on his elbow. "There is no set formula, no infallible ritual, no rote set of words that will assure a man entrance into paradise. It is rather like a suit of clothes. What fits one man might be entirely inappropriate for another. If I am to help you, then you must open your mind and heart to me." He walked in silence for a few moments. "If you are prepared to do that . . . " He let his words trail off as they entered the huge Great Hall.

Dee had remembered that the hall was opulent, but the glitter of gilt was nearly blinding this time. The four bodhisattvas still sat in cross-legged contemplation, but now the wall behind them had been fitted out with countless small niches, in each of which sat a golden Buddha. The other walls had niches, as yet unoccupied, but it was plain that the abbot meant to fill every last one eventually.

"I am quite prepared, Your Grace," Dee said, maintaining an air as if he scarcely noticed the splendor around him. "There will be no secrets." He heard the abbot release a small satisfied sigh of pleasure at these words. Dee glanced curiously at the strange little man as they reached a door that the abbot opened with a sweeping gesture. It was the same door the abbot had disappeared through all those years before, when Dee had traveled out to the Golden Cloud, dressed as a dusty peasant, searching for an elusive Indian following his strange and inconclusive visit to the murdered Transport Minister's home. The last time Dee had set eyes on this abbot, the man had left Dee on his knees to make offerings at the indifferent feet of Kuan Yin.

Seated comfortably in the abbot's private quarters, "Master Lao" accepted tea from his gracious host.

"It simply would not do," the abbot was saying, "to give you a sheaf of prayers, intone some impressive-sounding words, and send you on your way. Which, I'm afraid, is precisely the way some of my colleagues might be inclined to respond. But not I. It is far too serious a thing when a man comes asking for spiritual guidance of any kind. My conscience would not allow me to treat any matter, however small, with anything less than my full attention," he said, pouring himself a bowl of tea, gathering his robes about him, and sitting down.

Unless, of course, my clothes were shabby and my pockets empty, as they were the last time we met, Dee almost said.

"You are a man of great complexity," the abbot went on ingratiatingly. "I can tell just by looking at you. I can see that you have led a varied and interesting life. This is not an ordinary man sitting before me." Yes, Dee thought, and you are a very astute fellow—one who understands that the quickest way to get a man to talk about himself is to flatter him.

"My life has been perhaps . . . too rich, too varied," Dee said sadly.

"Do not hesitate to tell me everything," the abbot coaxed. "I have not always been the simple ascetic you see before you now. I, too, have lived," he said confidentially. "Though I sense depths in you that one such as myself could never know. Living as I do now, surrounded only by men, it is sometimes possible to forget . . . " He shrugged. "I myself never married," the abbot said then. "Though that fact did not deprive me of experience. Yes, I lived. As, no doubt, you have." He looked up then. "You are a married man, are you not?" he asked.

"Oh, yes, quite," Dee answered, wondering at the strange turn the conversation was taking.

"But your experience is not confined to marriage, I assume."

"No, not entirely," Dee answered carefully.

"You see, I have a theory," the abbot said. "Earthly life is a great, deep sea that we swim in. We either move around forever in its farthest, darkest depths, ignoring the light dimly penetrating the gloom from above, or else we want more of that light and begin to swim toward it. In this sea of life," he said, dropping his voice, "we swim the deepest and are the most heedless of the feeble shaft of light from above when we partake of . . . fleshly communion," he finished, licking his lips. "And who can blame us?" he added quickly. "Who can blame us? Aren't those moments of earthly bliss a temporary illumination in the darkness? Don't we believe that the light is shining full on us in those moments? Ah, yes." He sat, seemingly lost in contemplation for a moment while Dee waited. "Tell me, Master Lao, are you and your wife . . . or wives . . . ?" He raised questioning eyes to his guest.

"Wife," Dee answered, remembering that the drowned men had each had only one wife.

"Are you and your wife still . . . shall we say . . . compatible?"

Dee was not sure which direction he should take this in. He thought for a moment.

"When we were young, nothing could keep us apart. But time and familiarity have taken their toll . . . though we are still able, once in a while . . . "

"Ah, yes, time and familiarity. The greatest enemies of earthly love," the abbot said. "But surely you are conversant in the various remedies that have the power to restore passion?"

"Remedies?" Dee asked cautiously.

"Why, yes! Remedies of all kinds—from breaking old habits to infusions of potent elixirs to having a new woman!" the abbot said with enthusiasm. "There are ways, my friend! There are ways! Myself, I was once inclined to simply find a new woman, the way a butterfly flits from flower to flower when he has drunk his fill."

"Indeed," Dee said.

"Of course," the abbot added hastily, "I am speaking of the time before I became a man of the cloth."

"Of course," Dee said dryly.

"Women are interesting creatures," the abbot continued. "A man will believe that he is leading a woman, when in fact it is she who is leading him: I am sure you understand what I am talking about, eh?" he said with an expression that came very close to being a leer.

"Well, I could say that I have found myself . . ."

"She is leading you into the depths, my friend," the abbot cut in, his eyes bright and his lips moist. "Down into the gloom. Away from the light. But it is sweet while it happens, is it not? Yes. Very sweet. That was one of the reasons that I fled the secular life. I was susceptible—very susceptible. But we are not here to talk about me, are we? It is you, my friend, upon whom my attention should be turned." Dee waited, fascinated, for whatever was coming next.

"You are a man of means, that is plain," the abbot said. "May I ask what is the source of your livelihood?"

"I am an importer and purveyor of rare woods," Dee answered. "On any given day of the week, at least ten of my barges move somewhere along the canals."

"Ah, yes," the abbot said thoughtfully. "You have wealth, which means that you are involved with the world and with all worldly things. Unlike me, who lead an austere and ascetic life devoted to contemplation of the infinite," he said, as if they had not just walked through a room so full of the dazzle of gold that one could be virtually blinded by it, and as if they were not sitting in private quarters as comfortable and well appointed as any rich merchant's house.

"It is true," Dee said. "I am rich. But it is riches of another sort altogether that I really yearn for."

"Then we must direct that yearning," the abbot said.

"In fact," Dee said then, "I have been thinking of casting all of it aside and becoming a monk myself. Perhaps to travel to India, to wander, study, and pray." He watched the abbot's face closely for any reaction that might stray across the features, but saw little more than distaste.

"Many have done that, of course," the abbot said almost disdainfully. "But simply donning a rough robe and rubbing ashes on one's head is no guarantee of paradise. It is more difficult than that, I am afraid. There are other ways. I beg you to let me guide you. I truly think that I can help you."

Dee let out a sigh calculated to let the abbot think that "Master Lao" was only too grateful to shift his burden onto the other's shoulders.

"First, let me ask you a question. When you have, ah, shall we say, relations with your wife, does she achieve, ah, complete satisfaction?" Dee felt himself going very definitely pink at such a personal question, even though it was the fictional Master Lao, and not he himself, who was being asked. He looked with ever growing curiosity at the face of the abbot, who waited attentively for a reply. "Do not be embarrassed," the abbot said reassuringly. "I ask for very good reasons. And don't forget, I was once—"

"Yes, yes," Dee said hastily. "A man of the world. To answer your question, I would have to say that it is my belief that she does. At least, on occasion," he finished self-consciously.

"And do you feel a greater surge of interest and response in yourself when she does?" the abbot pressed on.

"Well, perhaps, I would say . . . that is . . . "

"Of course you do. Of course you do. And that is precisely my point." He looked gravely down at his hands as if deep in contemplation. "My friend," the abbot said in a serious tone, "we must begin somewhere. Now that I have got to know you just a bit, I am beginning to discern the path that I must help you cut through the jungle of earthly life. Yes. I am seeing the way," he said, looking up with an earnest expression. Then he rose and went to a shelf of manuscripts. He made a selection, then sat back down and placed the papers importantly on the table.

"I am going to give you some writings that I want you to read and contemplate. And it will be necessary for you to purify yourself—to abstain completely from relations with your wife—or, pardon my saying it, any other woman—for the next several weeks. I want you to come back to see me in ten days. And you must be very careful to keep the writings private, discreet, and to yourself. Very simple! Not so very much to ask, eh?" he said brightly and encouragingly, putting a hand on Dee's shoulder and looking suddenly grave. "I am glad that you came to me. I feel very strongly that the all-merciful Kuan-yin guided your steps to my humble door, and not a moment too soon." The hand on Dee's shoulder exerted subtle pressure with these last words, as if the abbot were trying to drive their mysterious, complex meaning home. "Besides," he said. "I feel that we shall be great friends."

Within the confines of the rumbling carriage, Dee finally allowed his face to relax out of the expression that had been his "mask" for the duration of his visit with the abbot. He had an annoying sense of possibly having wasted a great deal of time and effort. It had been a bizarre experience, to say the very least, to have the strange little man probing so skillfully and insistently for details of intimacy. Dee was certainly not accustomed to speaking of such matters with anyone, and the act of answering the man's questions, even in his role as the merchant Master Lao, had been a strain and an embarrassment.

He looked down at the sheaf of papers in his hand. He pulled aside the window curtain, admitting the last of the slanting afternoon sunlight, and read as best he could with the carriage jolting along the road.

It seemed to be the story of an unusually noble young prince lavishly beloved by his father, a great king. A holy man had told the king about the child's destiny, that he was to be the one who would set the earth free from pain, delivering a distressed world of creatures from the ocean of misery that was life. The tale went on to tell in great detail how the youth led a sheltered and blessed life as a child and young adolescent, with his presence in the kingdom causing prosperity and good luck to smile upon everything. The king himself became a paragon of mercy and virtue, so the story said, exonerating criminals sentenced to death and reforming their characters, laying aside weapons and practicing perfect calm, relinquishing all passions that involved defilement, harming no living creature, and so forth. Then one fine day the young prince decided that it was time to venture out into the glorious forests surrounding the kingdom.

The king, hearing that his son wished to take this little excursion, made fitting preparations—which included the removal from the road of any "afflicted person"; the king did not want the prince's outing to be spoiled by any distressing sights, and so, with "great gentleness," he removed the sick, the decrepit, the maimed, the "squalid beggars" and such, so that the highway would be serene and beautiful for the tender eyes of the prince. But the gods, it seemed, had other plans.

Dee read with interest how they placed a bent, ancient, white haired man along the road for the prince to see; thus it was that the flabbergasted youth learned for the first time of the phenomenon of old age. Next, the gods placed a sick, trembling man there for him to see, and finally, a dead one. Thus it was that the youth learned of old age, sickness, and then death, and the unpleasant fact that all creatures were subject to these afflictions. His reaction when he learned of the inevitable fate that awaited all living things was profound agitation—like "a bull who has heard the crash of a thunderbolt close by." "What rational being," the prince asked, bewildered, "who knows of old age, sickness, and death, could stand or sit down at his ease, or sleep, or far less laugh?" An excellent question, and one he had asked himself more than once, Dee had to admit, lifting his eyes momentarily from the page to the landscape moving by before resuming his reading.

The story continued with the prince, in a gloomy and preoccupied state of mind, eventually reaching the forest grove, where a troop of beautiful women awaited him and did their best to seduce him. There followed lavish descriptions of their "full bosoms," "hips veiled in thin cloth," "red mouths smelling of spiritous liquor," and "eyes like lotuses," and how they contrived to "collide softly" with him, pressing their breasts against him and trying to bind him with garlands of flowers while "punishing" him with words, like "anelephant driver's hook—gentle yet reproachful," while their garments continually slipped down off their shoulders and bosoms and they exerted every feminine wile.

All to no avail; the prince, having learned of old age, disease, and death, was in no mood for any of this frivolity. Instead, he returned grimly to the palace to inform his father the king that he wished to forsake everything and follow the religious path so that he might free himself from the cycle of birth and death. Naturally, the father tried to detain the much-beloved son by confining him to the palace. But one night, the gods decided to intervene, causing all the people around the prince—including the harem women—to fall into a deep sleep. The prince wandered about for a while, looking at the sleeping women in their heedless, unconscious state, mouths open, snoring, limbs sprawled gracelessly this way and that, and thought to himself that he was seeing them as they really were, and felt nothing but scorn, disgust, and sorrow. So much so that he was moved to make a pronouncement before mounting his horse and riding away forever from his father's palace through doors flung open by the gods themselves: "Such is the nature of women, impure and monstrous in the world of living beings; deceived by dress and ornaments, a man becomes infatuated by a woman's attractions. If a man would but consider the natural state of women and this change produced in them by sleep, assuredly he would not cherish his folly, but he is smitten from a right will and so succumbs to passion."

The light was growing poor. Dee put the manuscript down and pulled the curtain shut. It was quite strange, indeed. The uncomfortable feeling left by the abbot's thinly masked prurience still lingered. He felt slightly sullied, remembering the embarrassing questions, the probing, insistent inquisitiveness, and the man's moist lips and bright eyes. Altogether odious, Dee thought. He doubted very much that the abbot read such writings as he had given "Master Lao" with the spirit of detachment of the celibate, scholarly ascetic.

They were approaching the city gates as dusk descended. Dee was tired from the journey and the effort of maintaining his false identity for so many hours, and wondered with growing disgust if perhaps he had expended a great deal of effort only to uncover nothing more important than a debauched old cleric wallowing in his own private lubricity, fed by isolation and deprivation. He could imagine the abbot's personal library of holy writings, with certain pages marked, creased, and well worn. It was not difficult to picture the man behind the closed doors of his quarters, reading and rereading the tales of the women in the garden with their full bosoms and their garments slipping down off their bare shoulders or sprawled helplessly asleep, unconscious and defenseless, and deriving an altogether different sort of inspiration from them than the writers of the tales ever intended.

"It is not that I hold women responsible for their condition," the abbot said. "Heavens, no. Can you hold an animal responsible for not being able to speak, a rock for not being able to move? Of course not. They, like women, simply are what they are."

It was ten days later, and "Master Lao" again sat in the abbot's study with a bowl of tea in his hand. The subject today was the poverty of all earthly things compared to what awaited in paradise—women in particular. The abbot was in fine form, glib and eloquent, mingling what were plainly his own fantasies and obsessions with his personal interpretations of holy writings.

"Poor creatures—it is almost as if they have an instinctive knowledge that if given a chance, the righteous man will naturally gravitate away from them rather than toward them. It is as if they themselves are aware of their counterparts in paradise, the heavenly *apsarases*, next to whom the most beautiful earthly woman is as a lump of rock next to a pearl. Oh, no. They do not want you to see those pearls, Master Lao. They do not want you to see the extent of their deficiency. Tell me, did you follow my directive? Did you abstain from relations with your wife?"

"I did, Your Grace," answered Dee.

"And how did your wife . . . react?"

"I think that it was more difficult for me than for her, Your Grace. I am afraid that the more I studied the writings you gave me, the more . . . interested I became."

The abbot's face became nearly radiant with pleasure at these words, though he adopted an admonitory tone with his next words.

"Well, that is certainly not what I had in mind when I gave them to you," he scolded. "It is up to you to discipline yourself. I trust that the lesson in the writings was not lost on you!"

"Certainly not, Your Grace," Dee answered. "I understood perfectly. It is just that the descriptions of the women were so . . . "

"Delectable. Tantalizing. I know," the abbot said, licking his lips in a way that was becoming annoyingly familiar to Dee now. "My point precisely. It is simply that the sacred words were so masterfully written! And just as you found the women beautiful in the stories, were you not repulsed just as the young prince was when he saw them all sprawled about and unconscious? Did you not go and look at your wife while she slept and feel the same revulsion?"

"Well . . . " Dee began, unprepared for this question. He could only answer truthfully at this point. "I have actually always found the sight of a woman sleeping to be rather touching."

"Oh, my friend, you have a long, long way to go," the abbot said, shaking his head sympathetically. "I am glad you came to me when you did. It is part of a woman's natural negativity to make you feel compassion for her helplessness. It is very similar to the pull of worldly objects. Luxuries, material pleasures. All are designed to distract you from the real world that awaits. Imagine the sunniest, finest, most brilliant day you have ever seen, the most radiant silks, the sweetest music, the tastiest food, the most beautiful woman you have ever laid eyes on, and yourself in the midst of it all at the peak of youth, health, and vigor. And know that compared to a typical day in paradise, you would resemble a decrepit wreck of a man, a pathetic hunchback dressed in rags standing under a murky, ugly yellow sky listening to the screech of buzzards with the smell of putrescence filling your nostrils. And the woman would be like a hideous hag with scabs on her head and sores all around her mouth! That, my friend, is how beautiful paradise is!"

Dee was impressed with the abbot's picturesque description, and would have found it amusing under different circumstances, but was growing impatient. The false beard on his chin itched, the muscles of his face ached warily from maintaining "Lao's" expression, and it was a long journey out to the monastery. He wanted to know before he wasted too much more time on this man if he was on the right trail at all; he would have to make an effort to steer the conversation in some useful direction very soon. He thought he saw a way.

"It would not matter how beautiful it is, Your Grace, if I was not able to see my son again," he said sadly.

"Oh, I am sorry," the abbot said sympathetically. "A son was lost to you?"

"It was a very long time ago. He was only a little child. But I have never really recovered from the loss."

"It can be painful," the abbot said. "But surely your other children have helped to assuage the pain . . . ?"

"I have no other children," Dee answered. "He was my only one." The abbot took this in and sat ruminating for a moment before speaking.

"In a way, you are fortunate," he said. "To have offspring is to be tied to this world. The pull is very strong. It is my belief that offspring can bind one to the cycle of birth and rebirth. It keeps one *involved* in earthly life, attentive to it. When one has children, one worries constantly about them—their health, their welfare, their future." True enough, Dee thought, watching the man. "So perhaps—if you will forgive me—your son's early departure from this world could be taken as a blessing. At least for one such as yourself, an earnest seeker after paradise."

"But will I see him again?" Dee persisted.

"Possibly, possibly, possibly," the abbot said, as if intoning a sutra. "There are various schools of thought on that subject. Myself, I am inclined to believe that you will encounter him. Possibly in some different form. In paradise, you see, we exist in our purest, most idealized, evolved essence. Not as the imperfect beings that we are now. Remember—in some other incarnation, you may have been the son, and he the father!" This sounded to Dee like little more than high-minded evasiveness, but as the bereaved "Master Lao," he put a look of hopeful piety on his face.

"Is your wife still capable of bearing a child?" the abbot asked then, taking Dee by surprise again. One certainly could never predict what the man was going to ask next.

"Well . . . " He hesitated. "Yes. I would guess that she is."

"All the more reason to abstain, my friend. The endless cycle of birth and rebirth—think about it: it is all because of women! They draw a man into their negative space, their . . . their . . . *deficiency*, and what is the result? A birth! Another soul drawn back into the world to live, suffer, and die! It is a woman's nature. She is sweet, she is charming, but she is like the pit dug to ensnare the lion! A dark, dangerous pit a man can stumble into unawares! All of it to keep you earthbound. Beware, my friend!" He shook his head. "This would be a very bad time indeed for you to become more involved," he said. "Don't put it past a woman to know, on some instinctive level, that you are seeking after the Truth and to try to impede you. It is not that she will do it *premeditatively* or even *consciously*. Oh, no. She will do it with the very best of intentions. It is simply that it is her *nature* to impede a man, as it is a crocodile's nature to devour things with one snap of its jaws, or a monkey's nature to scream and chatter and swing from branch to branch." He shook his head ruefully for a few seconds, gazing at his visitor, before standing up in a decisive way that told Dee that the visit was concluded. "I am going to give you further material to read and study," he said, producing a sheaf of papers from a drawer and placing them on the table, then speaking with his hand resting reverentially on the pile. "I believe you are making excellent progress. I truly feel it. Every once in a great while, a seeker comes along who, though ostensibly asking me for instruction, reveals himself to be the true teacher, and I the student."

He stood, hand still resting on the papers as if he were touching a relic of the Buddha himself, eyes closed meditatively, nostrils flared as he drew air deep into his lungs and then rhythmically expelled it from between his lips with a hissing sound, like a yogi performing his breath-prayers. Dee watched, utterly fascinated by the man's performance.

He had stayed later than he had the last time, making it too dark to read in the carriage. It was not until he was at home and had pulled the hairs of Master Lao's beard from his chin that he finally spread the abbot's papers out in front of him and began to read. It was a continuation of the same story, the tale of the prince.

Having gone forth in the woods, abandoning family, friends, and kingdom, the prince was holding forth to his faithful manservant, who had accompanied him there, on the futility of trying to persuade him to delay his departure. What is the use, he told the man, since it is the fate of all creatures to part eventually anyway? Valiantly, the manservant tried to appeal to the prince's emotions and sense of duty by reminding him of the old king, who would surely grieve himself to death, of his mother, whose travail had brought him into the world and given him life, of his beautiful young wife and little son, who yearned for his return. But the prince's resolve was unassailable. To be a lover, friend, wife, husband, mother, father, sister, or brother, he told the weeping servant, is to be invariably bound to come to separation and grief, so what is the use of postponing the inevitable? With that, he discarded his princely garments, cut his hair with his sword, donned a plain garment of rough cloth, and strode forth into the woods without looking back, leaving the servant and his faithful horse in tears. Dee had to smile at the notion of a horse weeping for his lord; most horses, he was sure, would be only too happy to be rid of their human masters.

The poor servant, in the meantime, had to be the one to return to the palace minus the young lord, and to bear the brunt of everyone's dreadful sorrow—from the common people in the street to the king himself. The prince's father and mother mourned horribly, of course, lamenting and weeping, but the worst grief, it seemed, was that of the prince's beautiful young wife. Why, she implored, has he forsaken me? Why did he not take me with him into the forest as the sages of old took their wives? Is it that he hopes to partake of the charms of heavenly nymphs, rather than of me who loves him?

Dee rubbed his tired eyes. This was as far as the story went today. This was what the abbot wanted "Lao" to read and study.

He was not at all sure that he wanted to return to the monastery for a third visit. He had chosen this monastery for reasons that had seemed solid to him, but he was entertaining serious doubts at this point that he was going to learn anything other than the extent of this particular abbot's prurience. His questions were becoming increasingly personal and, Dee suspected, irrelevant.

He reviewed the reasoning that had led him to the Golden Cloud. His first meeting with the abbot years ago had left Dee with a strong impression of the man's well-fed, complacent ambiguity. That alone had been a strong factor in bringing Dee back, but not the most important one. Social parameters in the city were notoriously rigid; it would be a rare thing for a man from the wealthy merchant class, however well-to-do, to have contact with, say, the abbot of a temple that served the official class, and certainly he would never go near one that served the peasant class. No, the Golden Cloud was definitely the one that men of the class and position of the drowned merchants would have associated with.

Of course, there were other possibilities—a lone abbot or holy man of some sort, a maverick unassociated with any particular temple. Farfetched, but not impossible. If the dead men had traveled out to the Golden Cloud, they had not done so in their own carriages and with their own servants. That much Dee had been able to determine by questioning the household staffs. He had assumed that they had, for the sake of discretion, hired conveyances. But perhaps he was entirely deluded. Perhaps they had never been there at all, had had no association with the Golden Cloud.

One more time, he told himself. He would give it one last try, subject himself to the arduous trip and the embarrassing interrogation and bizarre sexual ramblings one last time. If something did not turn up, something substantial that he could work with, then he would have to turn his attention in some other direction. There was only one thing he was certain of tonight as he rolled up the papers—and that was that he knew all he cared to know about the abbot of the Golden Cloud monastery's personal peculiarities.

It was late morning, and Dee was considering leaving his magisterial offices for the rest of the day. The weather was simply too fine, and his concentration suffered because of it. The beautiful blue sky outside was distracting him from the dry and dreary indoor tasks in front of him; he could imagine the tempting aromas of the food stalls and the cheerful chaos of the marketplace, and felt the urge to spend the afternoon walking the streets of the city just to see what he might see. This morning's business had been routine and mundane: a minor tax question, a civil complaint, a case of petty thievery. Surely nothing was going to happen today that his assistants could not handle.

He leaned from the window and sniffed the air. His decision was made. He went to the desk and shuffled the papers he had been reading into a neat pile, bound them with a cord, and prepared to take them with him. There was no reason at all for him to be sitting here.

He began to open the door to his office and was looking for his assistant when he heard the cranky squalling of an infant and a female voice hushing it. He considered ducking back inside, hesitated for just a moment, and then it was too late—he had been seen. A poor peasant family, a husband, wife, and baby, were squatting on the bench in the anteroom; the man and woman had looked up just as the door opened. The woman, holding the baby in front of her like an offering, jumped to her feet and rushed toward Dee with an ingratiating smile.

"We wish to sell this child," she said. "We were told that you would buy her."

Dee stood where he was, one hand on the door, poised to pull himself back into the office. The woman held the squirming infant, who was about one year old, scrubbed clean, and dressed in her best, less than an arm's length from his face for his appraisal.

"And who, may I ask, suggested such a thing to you?" he asked the eager woman.

"A man in our village," she replied with a smile. "He said that you once paid his taxes for him, many years ago."

*   *   *

"Master Lao" and the abbot of the Golden Cloud Monastery strolled meditatively through the magnificently kept temple grounds. Mercifully, the abbot seemed to be steering the conversation in a rather different direction from that of the previous visits. Dee did not find it nearly so embarrassing to discuss the pleasures and pitfalls of wealth as those of sexual intimacy.

"It is of more than passing significance that the prince in the story was the man of royalty, wealth, and stature that he was," the abbot said. "It is most important that we grasp this point with thoroughness. Let me ask you a question, my friend. What is the first thing a seeker after Truth does, if he is in earnest?"

"He renounces material things, things of the world," Dee answered tentatively.

"Exactly!" the abbot exclaimed enthusiastically. "He discards his fine robes, he shaves his head, he sleeps on the hard ground. But I have a much finer point to make than simply to impress upon you the importance of nonattachment."

They had traversed the paths of the garden until they were moving into the sheltered greenery surrounding the main temple itself. Dee could hear faintly the chanting of monks at prayer. The abbot slowed his walking as he talked, occasionally stopping entirely while he held forth on this or that point, then resuming his stroll. Dee took his cues entirely from the abbot, walking when he walked, stopping when he stopped. Now the abbot had halted in a clearing under a tree; his eyes shone and his hands shaped the air as he talked.

"There is a deep significance to the fact of the prince's blessedness and wealth. His was the ultimate earthly wealth, and he gave it all up. Wealth, my friend, is a true blessing. Do you know why?" he asked, and began to walk again.

"Well," Dee ventured, "it makes life more comfortable."

"That it does. But beyond that," the abbot said, "I am speaking of a *spiritual* blessing. Wealth is a *spiritual* blessing. That probably seems like a contradiction to you, does it not?"

"I do not know, Your Grace, but I am most attentive to what you have to say," Dee said, which was certainly the truth.

"It is only a contradiction if one fails to grasp the true meaning of wealth." The abbot halted once again and turned to face his visitor. He spoke his next words with emphatic intensity. "The wealth that a person accumulates, or is born with, is an indication of his *chosenness*. It is the earthly manifestation of the richness and worthiness of his soul. It is no mere accident, my friend. And it is nothing to be ashamed of. There are those who will tell you that wealth is a barrier to true spiritual liberation—but that is true only if you make wealth your *end* rather than your *means*—if you fail to recognize the simple truth that your clothing, your magnificent house, your holdings, are all a measure of the greatness of your soul. Think of it this way. Your wealth," he said, beginning to walk again, "is a magnificent egg from which you will one day hatch!"

They had been moving closer to the temple all the while; the monks' voices carried clearly now into the green copse where Dee and the abbot had been standing. The serenity of the gardens and the droning chant blended in a most compelling way; Dee wondered to what extent their arrival at that spot at that precise time and at that point in the discourse was due to artful planning on the abbot's part. They stood saying nothing for a few moments, Dee appearing to be taking in the abbot's profundities while the abbot looked thoughtfully at the ground.

"I have something rather amazing to tell you," he said in a bemused tone. "I had not been certain whether to bother you with it or not. But I meditated on it, and gave it much thought, and decided you should know. You will, at the very least, find it interesting." He smiled. "Come with me."

He led the way into the temple. They quietly entered the prayer room where the monks sat cross-legged on the floor, chanting, eyes closed, in the manner that was now familiar to Dee.

"Do you see the monk in the fourth row, seventh from the right?" the abbot whispered. Dee counted, and saw an entirely nondescript young man, head shaved like all the others, rocking slightly as he intoned the prayer. "He happened to see you on your last visit here. A few days later he came to me, and confided that he had recognized you."

Dee looked up sharply, though he kept his expression composed. Recognized him?

"From a dream," the abbot whispered. "You see, this young man was an orphan. He never knew his parents. But for years he often dreamed of a man who had been his father in a previous incarnation—his true father, he said, the one who had been kind to him and had not abandoned him as his father in this life had. He had never attached very much importance to the dreams. He thought they were just his mind's way of offering comfort. Until he saw you," he said significantly.

"Me?" Dee asked, momentarily nonplussed.

"You. He said he recognized you as his true father from another lifetime." The abbot shrugged. "Perhaps you would like to meet him."

Dee looked at the abbot. It was all he could do to refrain from breaking out in a radiant smile of gratitude, because at that moment all doubt as to whether he would return to the monastery after today—doubt he had been entertaining until this very moment—vanished as completely as grit on a sill when the wind changes direction.

"Yes," Dee replied. "I would like very much to meet him."

Dee reread the abbot's texts with great care and attention before reading the new material he had been given after today's visit. His brush and ink were at hand, ready to copy down significant passages. Everyone else had gone to bed. The house was utterly quiet.

Dee dipped his brush and copied a single passage:

Since from the moment of leaving the womb death is a characteristic adjunct, why hast thou called my departure to the forest ill-timed? I would enter the blazing fire or the deepest waters, but not my house with my purpose unfulfilled.

The room that the abbot led Dee into was dark, and a rich smell of oiled wood permeated the atmosphere. Waiting for the abbot to light a lamp, Dee stood in the blackness inhaling the pleasant, nostalgic aroma; it made him think of Grandfather's study in the old man's house long ago.

"You are most patient," the abbot said, repeatedly scratching a flint. "I don't mean to keep you standing in the dark forever." There was more scratching, and then a lamp flared to life. It took a moment for Dee's eyes to adjust. For an instant, he had the impression that he had been carried back to the office of the murdered Minister of Transport where he had stood transfixed in the twilight years before. The four walls, from the height of a man's shoulder upward, were lined with a continuous frieze: women, men, and animals locked in every conceivable type of carnal embrace; voluptuous *apsarases* encircling men with impossibly broad chests with their legs, pressing their breasts against them and embracing them with their heads tilted back in utter submission, or standing with a hip thrown rakishly to one side in an attitude of blatant yearning sensuality. The room was twice as large as the Transport Minister's office, with tables, shelves, and altars whose surfaces were entirely obscured by lingams and other exotic Indian statuary. Every corner and every space was filled; here an *apsaras* thrust her breasts forward and pouted; there a legion of lingams pointed rigidly toward heaven. The momentary, ghostly suggestion of Grandfather's study that Dee had experienced in the darkness vanished like a dream.

The abbot stood, smiling proudly and holding the lamp, obviously well aware of the effect of the dancing shadows cast by the flame, and watched his guest.

"My private meditation room," he said.

Dee turned and smiled back at the abbot; his gratitude now knew no bounds.

"These are most handsome pieces of art," Dee said to the abbot, and looked slowly and appraisingly around the room again. "Tell me," he said then, casting his host a sly look, "are any of them available for purchase?"

The abbot pursed his lips for a moment before answering, as if giving consideration to an entirely novel idea.

"For anyone else, I would say no," the abbot replied ingratiatingly. "But for you, an exception could be made. You are, after all, practically a member of my family now."

Dee raised questioning eyebrows.

"I was not going to tell you until later. Do you recall the young monk whom I introduced you to on your previous visit? He was very moved by the meeting. He told me that he wishes for you to make him your son." He smiled again. "He would be honored if you would adopt him."

From then on, all of their meetings took place in the abbot's "meditation room," and always with a single lamp casting its hypnotic moving shadows over the figures. And the abbot began to offer his guest wine. Very fine wine, from his personal supply. Never did he allow Master Lao's cup to be empty. It was the abbot's pleasure to read aloud now. He had an excellent reading voice, and always sounded as if he himself were just discovering for the first time the story or scripture that he read.

Many of the stories were familiar to Dee. The abbot was particularly fond of reading lengthy excerpts from the descriptions of Sukhavati, the Land of Bliss, the jeweled paradise that had been the favorite of poor old Diamond Eyes, who had disappeared from Yangchou after the forced apologies, never to be seen again. Dee had thought about him more than once recently; compared to this man, Diamond Eyes seemed like nothing more than a harmless entrepreneur.

He reread the tale of the prince, with great dramatic emphasis and with a startling range of versatility, adopting a different voice for every character. First he was an old king mourning the loss of his son, then he was a young wife keening and sobbing over her husband who had left her, never to return, undoubtedly hoping to partake of heavenly nymphs rather than her own poor mortal flesh. He ended the story with the prince, his entire being resolved to his purpose, crossing the "speeding waves" of the River Ganges. And he read, in lavish, loving detail, ancient religious writings describing the beauties and sublime skills of the love-hungry *apsarases* awaiting the righteous dead in paradise.

And Dee sat, sipping his wine, listening to the abbot's voice and watching the shadows caressing the temple carvings, remembering himself bewitched in the failing light in the Transport Minister's office by the canal and then in his own office until the creak of a floorboard behind him snapped him to, and began to understand the power of the spell that the man was casting, and had undoubtedly cast before.

"I am going to ask you to prove yourself today," the abbot said at the beginning of "Master Lao's" seventh visit. They were seated in the meditation room, but today the abbot's hands did not hold a bundle of texts. He kept them resting calmly in his sleeves as he spoke with a tone of quiet resolution. "I have no doubt that you now understand the importance of removing oneself from earthly attachments. With the example of the prince before you, and his unshakable determination even in the face of his family's entreaties, I am sure you have grasped the extent of the sacrifice required of the true seeker."

Dee nodded thoughtfully. I am beginning to grasp the extent of the sacrifice that *you* require, he thought, watching the abbot's stern face.

"Today, there will be no reading. Instead, I want you to

write something. I want you to put yourself in the place of the prince who went forth into the forest." He paused, shutting his eyes and taking several yogi-like breaths. "I know what you are thinking. Am I going to tell you to go forth, literally, into the forest? No, my friend. I am going to introduce you to the seeker's sacrifices symbolically. I want you to begin to accustom yourself to such concepts. This will be purely an exercise. A learning experience for a man of the world such as yourself. You will be going forth into the wilderness," he said emphatically. "But it will be in your mind," he said, pointing to his own head. "You will continue your life, but inside, you will know that you are separated from it in essential ways. This, my friend, is your first step."

The abbot pushed a writing tray and brush toward his guest. "Write a short letter, stating in succinct and certain terms that you are renouncing the trappings of this existence. And think: what are the two things that pull you into the world, that keep you here? Women and wealth, my friend. You must renounce both. But remember—this will be your secret, your treasure that you carry around inside yourself, even as you sit with your wife and as you conduct your business. It will be a glorious contradiction, a paradox inside you, functioning like the grain of sand inside the oyster that eventually causes a pearl to come into existence."

Obediently, Dee picked up the writing brush and smoothed a piece of paper in front of him.

"One more thing. You must not word it so that you will feel that you are compensating your family by leaving them with your wealth in your stead. The separation must be total. Remember, your wealth is also your spiritual treasure. You could never leave such a treasure to a woman."

"But Your Grace," Dee asked as ingenuously as he could, "what would I do with my fortune if I were going forth into the forest? Hypothetically speaking, of course."

The abbot smiled for the first time that day.

"Well—perhaps you would bestow it on your new spiritual family." He shrugged. "Your adopted son, for example."

"Your Grace," Dee said to the abbot as they walked in the dusk toward "Master Lao's" waiting carriage, "there is something on my mind that I wish to discuss with you."

"Of course," the abbot replied in a kindly tone. "Anything. Anything at all."

"Well," Dee said, choosing his words with infinite care, "it seems that you were quite right about a woman's innate propensity for obstruction. You warned me, but I admit that I did not give you full credence at the time."

"Yes?" the abbot said attentively, his interest aroused.

"My wife has been speaking in a rather wistful way about children lately."

The abbot clucked his tongue.

"What did I tell you? She senses your spiritual quest. She smells it, without even knowing it consciously." He shook his head. "Be careful, my friend. Be very careful. You know what I mean."

"Oh, indeed, I know," Dee replied. "But I have what I think might be an excellent idea. Of course, it is only an idea. I would never implement it without discussing it with you first." Now he imitated the abbot's own mannerism, stopping and standing still to deliver his next words. "What about a daughter for my wife?"

The abbot looked alarmed for a moment before regaining his composure.

"My friend, you cannot take the chance. What did I tell you about offspring and relations with women? It is detachment you are seeking, not further bonds!"

"But you see, a daughter would satisfy her craving without greatly binding me to more responsibility. It would not be like having a new little son, for whom I would have to plan and sacrifice to assure his future. What is a daughter, really, but a pretty plaything? A little flower?" The abbot stopped walking and faced "Master Lao."

"You talk as if you are certain that she will give birth to a daughter simply because you have willed it. You cannot take the chance!" he said warningly. "You have come too far in your spiritual quest!"

"Oh, but there is a way. The maid of my wife's aunt is acquainted with a certain old woman, a shamaness of sorts," Dee said, relishing what he was sure would be the abbot's extreme distaste for such a creature. "They say that she can provide certain elixirs that will guarantee a male or female birth!"

"And you would take such a chance?" Dee could hear the anger and disappointment the abbot was striving to keep out of his voice. Of course, the last thing he would want, after all his careful work, would be for "Master Lao" to suddenly produce an heir. They had reached the carriage and stood next to it in the fading light.

"The old woman's record is excellent, Your Grace! They say she has never failed! I think it is a fine idea! I have already told my wife to make the initial arrangements. I am absolutely certain that my spiritual quest will not be compromised," Dee said, and turned as if to get into the carriage. The abbot put out a restraining hand and grasped Dee's arm.

The two men stood looking at each other for a moment. Dee could see conjecture and calculation teeming just behind the abbot's eyes; then the man smiled tentatively.

"I have a better idea," he said, making an effort to keep his voice low and pleasant. "What would be wrong with, say, ah . . . *adopting* or *purchasing* a daughter for your wife?" Dee stopped as if utterly surprised at the notion.

"That is an idea not without merit," he said thoughtfully. "But I wouldn't know how to go about such a thing, or even where to begin looking. The old woman says that she does not make mistakes—"

The abbot, still holding "Master Lao's" arm firmly, cut him off.

"*I* have contacts," he said quickly. "*I* will assist you in finding the perfect baby daughter for your wife."

Dee held in his hands the tiniest, most fragile porcelain bowl he had ever seen. He sipped the hot, strangely spiced tea and set the bowl down on a table. Indian statuary surrounded him, and Indian silks and tapestries covered the walls. The strong, sweet, faintly nauseating smell of incense hung in the air, making Dee think of something meant to mask the odor of putrefaction, which, he had heard, was apt to be on the wind in India.

The heavyset man who smiled at him and offered more tea wore Chinese robes, but his face with its spot of red on the forehead was as dark as a moor's and his hair a startling white.

"You are in luck, Master Lao," the man said in his lilting accent. "Not only can I offer you a choice, but I can make it virtually impossible for you to choose! That is how delectable, perfect, and beautiful are the little darlings I will show you this morning." The Indian had deep plum-colored circles under his large dark eyes and spoke in a moist, lascivious way, like a gourmand discussing tonight's repast. It was not difficult for

Dee to imagine the warm camaraderie that no doubt existed between this man and the abbot.

The Indian rose from his cushion with an epicurean smile; each motion of his limbs released more of the overwhelming perfume into the air. He went to the door and clapped his hands, then returned to his seat and settled himself like a pasha.

Four Indian women who looked as if they might be the *apsarases* of the temple carvings come to life entered the room. Each woman held in her arms or led by the hand a Chinese female infant, none more than two years old, who looked with solemn faces at the two seated men while the women kept their eyes cast politely to the floor. Dee was startled by the beauty of the women; at the same time, he could hear the Indian sighing with pleasure at the sight of the children. It is simply the appeal of the foreign and exotic, he thought, turning a smiling face toward his host.

"Do you wish to have them undressed for your inspection?" the Indian said to his guest accommodatingly. "I deal only in perfect goods. I am proud indeed of the quality I can offer."

Dee shook his head. "That will not be necessary," he said. "The child I select today will be a gift for my wife."

"Of course," the Indian said. "But in ten or twelve years' time . . ." He did not finish, but raised his eyebrows suggestively. Dee hid his distaste and looked at the man. The abbot and his foreign friend were truly brothers under the skin. But there was somebody else Dee wanted to connect with his host, someone whose power and influence, his instincts told him, reached far and wide. He lifted his bowl and took a sip.

"No, it will not be necessary," Dee repeated. "Master Lu Hsunpei assured me that you deal only in the finest. I trust his judgment implicitly," he said, evoking the name of his host at the party, the man who had so arrogantly tried to bribe him. He watched the Indian for a reaction, but the man was unperturbed. Either he did not know Lu Hsun-pei, which Dee doubted, or else the soothing balm of flattery overcame any surprise that he might have felt at the mention of Master Lu's name. "He, like you, is a man of impeccable taste," Dee added. The Indian paused only for a moment before answering.

"Indeed he is," he said with a smile.

Calmly, betraying none of his inward excitement, Dee lowered his bowl to the table.

"I believe I have made my choice," he said, raising a hand and pointing at a tiny girl who had been regarding him with unwavering eyes since the moment she had been brought into the room.

"Oh, excellent, excellent," the Indian said admiringly. "She would have been my choice, too. All infants are comely things, but they can grow up to be quite plain, even homely. But with this one, the bone structure bespeaks great beauty in the future. I . . . " He paused. A servant had appeared in the door, gesturing with a hand. "Won't you excuse me?" the Indian said politely, rising from his seat. "There is a bit of business I must attend to. I won't be more than a few moments."

Alone with the children and the Indian women, Dee felt shy and slightly embarrassed. How, he wondered, did they perceive him? Of course, he reminded himself, it was not Dee Jen-chieh before them, but a nonexistent entity known as Master Lao. His musings were cut short by the sound of a discussion in the outer hall. The Indian's lilting cadence mingled with another voice, one whose petulant tone was utterly familiar to Dee. Dee listened for a moment, unbelieving. He caught a few words: the topic was payment for services rendered; the owner of the complaining voice did not feel that he had been properly recompensed, while the Indian was asserting that in fact he had been given twice what he was worth. Unable to stop himself, Dee rose from his chair and moved quietly to the door and partway down the hall so that he had a clear but discreet view of the Indian's visitor, who stood in profile and did not notice the aghast man who stood and stared at him some distance away. There were actually two visitors, but one slouched silently to one side and allowed his compatriot to do all the talking.

Dee had learned many things today, but before him was a bit of unwelcome knowledge he had never anticipated—though in retrospect, his shocked senses told him, he should have. Yes, he should have known, he thought, getting hold of himself and withdrawing his head before one of his sons should happen to glance in his direction.

The abbot leaned heavily on Dee as the two men negotiated the narrow, evil-smelling alley in the semidarkness. Dee could feel the abbot's breath on his neck, hot and redolent with wine, and the man's arm intertwined with his own, steering him firmly in this or that direction with subtle pressures. If I were drunk, Dee thought, which the abbot believes me to be, I probably would not even notice that he is moving me about as if my arm were a rudder.

Dee giggled and stumbled, pulling his partner down with him, the other pulling him up again, Dee reaching out with his free hand to steady himself against the rough wall before regaining his balance. It was strange indeed: Dee feigning drunkenness for the abbot, while the abbot, though he staggered and laughed uproariously, was as sober as he, each man sharply observing the other through a false alcoholic haze. Though the difference, my friend, Dee thought, is that you believe my act.

They had been drinking for many hours, each man artfully avoiding intoxication. When the abbot had invited him on an expedition into the city, instructing him to first place the letter of renunciation in his wife's jewelry box, Dee knew that it would not be an ordinary night and had drunk half a cup of oil to line his stomach, though it had nauseated him to do it. As for the abbot, Dee was not certain what his technique was. The man was able to consume cup after cup of wine, and did an excellent impression of a drunk, but Dee could sense the canny, clear-eyed control behind the charade, and felt it in the comradely arm linked casually but dangerously with his own.

They had been moving, in a zigzagging but determined way, on an easterly course into the most run-down part of the city, pausing at various seedy wineshops. What would seem to a drunken man to be a rambling, random course was leading inexorably toward the area of the lonely stretches of canal where the rich men had drowned, pulled down by their purses stuffed with cash. Dee's hand felt the heavy bag of money tied to his own waist. The abbot himself had been filling it throughout the evening, telling "Master Lao" that he was paying him for every cup of wine he drank, every step he took, because he was moving, so the abbot said, through danger and closer to glory with each.

"We are lowly, disgusting creatures, are we not?" the abbot said, laughing and out of breath, pulling Dee along. "And we are about to descend even lower," he intoned with mock solemnity, coming to a halt in front of a dimly lit door. Dee resisted the impulse to look behind them. He had warned the two constables trailing them at a distance to exercise utmost caution, that the abbot must never sense their presence. They had taken his orders well—too well, Dee thought uncomfort-

ably. What had they done, he wondered—turned themselves
into smoke? He had seen and heard no sign of them for the
better part of an hour. He was sure that they had lost him.

"Tonight, we walk with danger," the abbot said. "For one
night, you leave the safety and comfort of the life you have
known. Your letter sits in your wife's jewelry box. You will,
you think, remove it before she ever sees it. But what if she
finds it before you have a chance to return home in the morning? What if you don't get there in time? You may not, you
know. You may be passed out on the pavement in an alley
come morning. You may be lost, unable to find your way out.
You know the letter is there, in your house, radiating danger.
That danger is your power, my friend. It is your secret, and
you draw on it for your strength. That letter could destroy the
safe, pleasant existence you have known until now, and you
know it. You know it! But you take that risk, and that is your
power. For in your mind, *in your mind*, you are inexorably separating yourself from all of it. It is your way of donning the
sackcloth and entering the forest." He paused and looked hard
at his charge. "And now," he said, "are you ready to go
through another door?"

"Quite ready, Your Holiness," Dee said, swaying a little
and trying to look as if he were making a mighty effort to focus
his eyes. The abbot pushed the door open.

The room they entered was different from the wineshops
they had been stumbling into and out of all evening. It was
clean and prettily furnished, reminding Dee of his wives'
drawing rooms, though the furniture was slightly shabby and
the carpet bald and worn, and the cloying odor of Indian incense hung in the air. A woman rose from a chair smiling as
soon as the abbot was through the door. She was beautiful, her
skin dark as mahogany, her silks flashing.

"This is Master Lao," the abbot said to the woman. "He
wishes to experience the joys of paradise," he added with a sly
leer. He shrugged. "I suggested to him that there is only one
sure way."

"We are happy to offer our humble services," the woman
said in the same lilting speech as the Indian baby-seller. Dee
flushed in spite of himself as she looked at him appraisingly.

"But wait," the abbot said, putting a hand on Dee's arm.
"You are a married man, are you not? It would be . . . most
unseemly, I think, for you to . . . " He smiled. "Ah. But I believe
I know the answer." He turned to the woman then. "A cup of

wine for our friend," he said. "And then, perhaps a visit to the 'Purification Room,' eh?" The woman bowed. A cup of wine was put into Dee's hands. He pretended to take a drink; he was reluctant to swallow anything bestowed upon him within these walls. A canal snaked its way through this part of the city just a block or two away. How easy it would be to drug a man and slip him quietly into the water . . .

"Purification," the abbot whispered importantly in Dee's ear, and began to compel him through the far doorway into a darkened hall. Dee had a formidable dagger secured in his waistcoat, but wished fervently for his two constables as well. In the darkness of the hallway, Dee discreetly tipped his cup and let the wine run onto the carpet. By the time they pushed through another door, the cup was empty, and he held it to his lips as if draining the last drops. Then he lowered it and looked around the room.

A man sat at a small writing table with paper, ink, and brushes at his elbow. He wore an official cleric's robe; indeed, the room had been set up to look as much like an office as possible, it seemed to Dee. The man and the abbot smiled at each other, and the abbot pushed Dee forward.

"This is Master Lao," he told the man. "He wishes to divorce his wife."

Out in the cool air of the alley an hour later, Dee took deep breaths and thought for a fleeting moment that he might actually be sick to his stomach. The close, hot rooms, dense with sweet smoke, had got to him, making his head swim and his innards churn.

If there had truly been a Master Lao, he would have been a divorced man by this time. Dee vaguely recognized the corrupt little official at the desk, from a minor district office, who had performed the ceremony and put his seal on the papers after "Master Lao," with meticulous drunken care, had made his statement and put his own seal there. Never mind that the seal actually belonged to Magistrate Dee Jen-chieh. The little man—and the abbot—would be finding that out soon enough. Then the abbot had congratulated "Master Lao" by making an elaborate show of putting another handful of coins in Dee's purse.

They had gone from the makeshift office back to the room where the Indian woman waited; there, Dee had been compelled to enter a small bedchamber with a very young, fragrant-smelling Indian girl. When the door was shut behind them and she had made a tentative move to undo the ties on his robe, he made a gesture telling her to be quiet and had reached into his purse and given her a handful of cash. He had pointed to his stomach, as if telling her that he was feeling unwell, and had lain down on the bed to rest. He had stayed for the better part of an hour, feeling dizzy as if he were actually drunk, firmly holding the girl's hand all the while so that she could not leave the room. Presently, he had risen, given her another handful of money and a whispered admonishment to be silent, and reemerged, blinking and swaying, his hand ready to grasp his dagger, into the light of the room where the abbot and the woman awaited him; the abbot had grinned and produced another fistful of coins. He had pulled Dee's purse open and ostentatiously dropped the coins in one by one, muttering a prayer with each.

Then they had staggered back out into the night, the abbot's arm heavy on his shoulder. Leaning against the rough wall, Dee filled his lungs and began to sing, a signal to his constables, who were, he hoped, out there in the darkness within earshot. The abbot joined in the song, and they proceeded along their way.

"You are already gone," the abbot said unexpectedly, speaking directly in his ear, interrupting their song. "You are as far from your old life as the prince was when he left the palace forever. You are right in their midst, but you may as well be a million *li* from them. They can smell you," he added in a harsh whisper, "but they cannot find you. Your wife is awakening in her bed right now. She is sniffing the air in the darkness, wondering what the bad smell is that has come into her clean, pleasant chambers. She wonders if someone has placed a rotten fish, or perhaps some offal, beneath her bed as a prank. But it is no prank. It is *you*, my friend. You reek of paradise, and she, with her woman's senses, smells it so keenly that it wakes her from her sleep." He paused, standing still for a moment, drawing the air in noisily through his nostrils like a dog snuffling. "In fact, I can smell it myself," he said. "You smell of the *apsaras*-whore. Her juices are on you. You are anointed. Shorn of worldly attachments, and anointed!"

There was a smell in the air now, but Dee knew that it was not emanating from his person. Rather, it was the ripe redolence of the canal, which they were fast approaching. As they drew nearer, the abbot's voice became a steady drone in his ear.

"You can never wash the smell off. The *apsarases* in paradise can smell you, too, and they are yearning for you. Stretching out their smooth brown arms longingly. But to them, you smell like jasmine, ambrosia, peach blossoms. To your wife, you smell of dung and rotten fish. She lies awake in her bed smelling you; the *apsarases* lie on their soft carpets of flower petals in paradise, beneath the jewel trees, beside the sparkling emerald waters, smelling you, wanting you with all their beings."

Now Dee could hear the water of the canal lapping against the mortar embankment. The abbot's arm had twined itself with his own again as they walked. Dee's other hand fastened itself to the hidden handle of the dagger.

"The little fishes flashing like jewels in the emerald waters of paradise sing their desire for you, too," the abbot went on. "And the birds in the jewel trees, opening their throats, singing out their unquenchable longing. They fly down and light on the jeweled, slender fingers of the *apsarases*, and drink the sweet tears that flow from their huge limpid eyes. Tears of longing for you." They were only a few steps from the water's edge now, the brackish smell tinged with garbage and refuse rising to their nostrils. "The 'speeding waves' of the River Ganges," the abbot whispered now. "The Ganges, India's holiest river. She is brown with filth and carries the ripening flesh of the dead on her broad breast, but her waters are the sweetest, and the purest, for she is the way to paradise."

As he talked, the abbot's arm slid out from Dee's. " 'I would enter the blazing fire or the deepest waters, but not my house with my purpose unfulfilled,' " the abbot whispered, and began to gently compel "Master Lao" toward the water. "Touch it. Smell it. Anoint yourself," he whispered as they stood at the very edge of the canal.

The blow to the back of Dee's legs made his knees collapse, but he twisted and grabbed a handful of the abbot's clothing and together they tumbled over the embankment, Dee giving a mighty shout for help as they went. The abbot hit the water fighting, going for Dee's head, trying to hold it under. Dee delivered a blow with his knee to the man's midsection, which dislodged him for only a moment, and then he was back on Dee's head, brutally pushing him down. Dee groped, found the man's ears, grabbed on, and pulled with all his might. Now the abbot's head was beneath the water too. They hung there in the blackness for a small eternity of heartbeats, then simultaneously released their respective grips and shot gasping to the surface. Dee filled his lungs and gave a second shout before the abbot could push him down again. A knee to his groin just missed its target; he lunged for the abbot and locked his head in a one-armed embrace. Their feet flailed beneath them in the bottomless water. Where was the embankment? He held the abbot's head like a battering ram, thinking that he would smash it against the mortar. But don't kill him, a voice inside warned him. Much as you would like to, don't kill him. You want him alive.

They sank down, the abbot writhing. Dee's head went beneath the water, making him lose his hold, and the abbot twisted free. Dee went down again. The abbot's heavy body was on top of him now, pressing with merciless determination. Dee began to black out, saw an image of his own corpse, weighted down by the purse around his waist, floating in the canal.

And then, just when the image was growing to a certainty, the abbot released his grip like a lover who has abruptly finished. Dee broke the surface, gulping air; water splashed furiously around him. He was no longer alone with his enemy. His two constables were in the canal; one held the abbot in a stranglehold while the other came to Dee and held his head above the water with the same determination that the abbot had shown holding it under. The abbot was emitting hideous gargling noises and pulling at the powerful arm locked around his neck.

"Don't kill him," Dee gasped. "And don't let him try to kill himself!" The constable must have eased his grip just a little bit, for the abbot found his voice again.

"Arrest this man!" he shouted absurdly. "He tried to kill me!"

They subdued him quickly and hauled him up onto the pavement. Soon he lay facedown, panting, arms and legs trussed, the fight gone out of him. Legs quivering with exertion, Dee knelt carefully and spoke in his ear.

"Thank you for showing me paradise," he said. "Now I shall return the favor."

Dee had taken some care with his appearance that morning, putting on his finest magisterial robes and even having the house steward trim the sparse hairs of his beard, for he was on his way to visit a lady. He was feeling a hint of the peculiar little thrill of anticipation that he had experienced in the early days of courting his first wife. And it was odd, because the woman he was going to see had passed across his field of vision but once years before, and then only for a few seconds. And there was an excellent possibility that she was a murderess.

He was paying this visit at the suggestion of the deposed abbot of the Golden Cloud, who had been stripped of his title and who now stood only as the criminal and murderer Ch'u-sin.

Ch'u-sin would not be facing the executioner for his crimes. Instead, he would trade his fine robes for the rough fabric of the prisoner's shirt, and the pickax, the shovel, and the barrow would be the instruments of his expression for the rest of his days. Though he richly deserved to die, he had been spared a death sentence for a variety of reasons.

Well before Dee and the false abbot went on their nocturnal foray that had ended in the stinking waters of the canal, Dee had understood that the man, though supremely clever and greedy, was not a lone entrepreneur, that his venture was but one of many in an interdependent system of criminal opportunism that likely reached to every part of the city of Yangchou and far beyond. After the arrest, certain that he was a veritable trove of invaluable information, Dee had offered Ch'u-sin clemency if he would assist the court.

And he had, thoroughly and without hesitation. Though it was what Dee had been counting on, the readiness with which Ch'u-sin had betrayed his compatriots and other "business" contacts in order to save his own hide had disgusted Dee. But the result was that countless guilty men now lay exposed and writhing in the light, landholdings had been returned to the people and to the tax rolls, and an intricate and extensive web of unlawful, immoral, and lucrative enterprises involving some of the most powerful and influential citizens of Yangchou—both official and clerical—had been shut down. In the process, arrogant men had been humbled and widows saved from disinheritance. And now an old murder case was being exhumed; quite possibly a gardener's desolate ghost was soon to be exonerated and his family compensated monetarily for his wrongful death.

This, of course, was no small part of the thrill of anticipation Dee was feeling today. There was a very good possibility that within the hour, Dee would learn at last who had actually killed the Transport Minister nearly a decade before.

And all of it because of a fateful encounter that had proved to be the stitch that pulled the fabric together for him—an encounter he had nearly missed because of the temptation of a beautiful blue sky on a fine breezy afternoon. He thought back to the day shortly after his second visit to the Golden Cloud, when he was entertaining serious doubts about going back at all. He had been about to escape his desk and his papers and go for a long walk when the peasant couple appeared, hoping to sell him their infant girl. Had he stepped out of his office a moment earlier, he might not be on his way to visit this particular lady right now, and many other criminals might still be operating securely behind their guises of respectability, or piety, or both.

He had not dismissed the couple, but had sat them down and encouraged them to tell him everything. There had been another daughter, they said, a few years before. Of course, they had been hoping for a son. Then an Indian—a "holy man," as they put it—had come through their village and bought the child from them for a small sum. He had left them with what he said was an object of infallible potency, which, along with a special prayer he also gave them, would bring them a male birth. The object was a carved wooden lingam, which they had brought with them and showed to Dee. They had performed the ritual faithfully, they said, only to produce another daughter. Of course, there was no way to find the "holy man" after that. But a farmer in their village had told them how Magistrate Dee from the city had once helped him so generously with a tax debt, and so they had come to him.

Surely, Dee had thought, turning the lingam over in his hands, this had to be the very Indian who used to visit the murdered Transport Minister with his selection of children. The man was obviously running some sort of trade in infant girls, selling them—Dee did not yet know to whom—as slaves, servants, or pleasure objects, he conjectured, acquiring his inventory by preying on the poor. And Dee had remembered something then, while he was still sitting with the distraught husband and wife, that had made him doubt the Indian was operating alone. It was a particularly odious remark that had been made to him by Master Lu Hsun-pei, his host at the party who had tried to bribe him: "The poor will even sell us their daughters." Words that had merely disgusted Dee at the time, but whose true meaning was surfacing at last. It was at that moment that Dee had begun to sense the as yet indistinct outlines of something much larger than a mere private arrangement between the Indian and the Transport Minister. What insufferable arrogance, Dee had thought at the conclusion of his meeting with the couple; very likely, Lu Hsun-pei had been practically telling Dee to his face about his criminal involvements in the same breath with which he had tried to buy him.

Little girls, the Indian, the lingam, the Transport Minister's connections, the temple art from India—without a doubt, the Indian baby trader who gave out carved lingams to gullible peasants was connected not only to the Transport Minister's collection of daughters, but to his collection of temple art as well.

So far, Dee had not connected the abbot of the Golden Cloud with any of this. Indeed, he had almost given up on the man entirely in his quest to solve the mystery of the well-to-do corpses floating in the canals. But he had persevered, and it was one or two visits later that inspiration came to him in a most apt and appropriate manner: the abbot had been working to strike his flint in the dark of his "meditation chamber," and the light had suddenly leaped into the room, illuminating the artifacts and the corners of Dee's mind at the same time.

So. You, too, Dee had thought with a slow inward smile, looking around and marveling, then testing Ch'u-sin by slyly asking if the items were for sale. When the man had said yes, Dee would have been willing to wager his house and everything in it that he too was connected to the Indian and whatever complex business he conducted—and in all likelihood to the Transport Minister as well.

How well Dee remembered the abbot's vagueness and evasiveness on Dee's first visit years before, when he had gone to him with a contrived story about a friend's missing child, and how Dee had been unable to decide if the man was concealing something or merely thinking about his next meal. Well, my friend, Dee reflected as he gazed with pleasure on the abbot's collection in the lamplight, it is unlikely that it was food that was on your mind after all when you disappeared so abruptly through that door, leaving me on my knees with my incense and my empty prayers.

And was it you who sent the murderous child to my office? Or someone else I blundered into that day, the day before, or the day before that? You know, and all of your "associates" surely know, Dee thought while an old excitement stirred in his bones, who killed the Transport Minister.

Inspiration had come to Dee then: he thought of a way to confirm the connection between the abbot and the Indian that would also lead Dee directly to the Indian himself. That was when he had invented the tale of "Master Lao's" wife wanting another child. The abbot, so close to harvesting a rich convert, had risen nicely to the bait.

And so Dee had found himself sipping tea in the Indian's parlor and contemplating the extraordinary structure that was revealing itself. Effortlessly, merely by dropping a remark, he had confirmed his suspicion that Lu Hsun-pei was known to the Indian and was indeed a member of the thriving partnership. And of course, he was to learn more that day than he had ever cared to about the extent of corruption in Yangchou. Dee had been spared the realization of an old, uneasy vision of his: that he would one day sentence his own sons in court. He had been able to assign that task to an assistant magistrate. They received a fair and just sentence that would guarantee that Dee would not have to look upon their faces—nor they upon his—for quite some time. Military service in the far western provinces would ensure that they would be occupied with hard work and vigorous outdoor pursuits, far from the seductive enticements of city life, to which they were so susceptible. Whatever his sons were, whatever their weaknesses, whatever they would become or had already become, and whatever their contributions to the criminal life of Yangchou—all of it, Dee knew, was his shared responsibility. That was the other reason that Ch'u-sin had been spared the death sentence.

"Abbot" Ch'u-sin's revelations were fascinating. He and the Indian were indeed old colleagues from way back. The Indian had run a lucrative two-way trade for many years, importing rare and valuable stolen erotic Indian temple art and other fine pieces into China for sale to wealthy connoisseurs, and exporting infant females to India to become prized concubines to rajahs and such. A few of the girls were sold in Yangchou, to men who liked to groom them from infancy as sexual playthings.

Ch'u-sin assisted in the process of procuring children by using his many contacts among corrupt clergy to steer the Indian toward likely prospects, in return for which he had his pick of exotic art, to keep or sell, whichever he fancied. In return, the Indian assisted Ch'u-sin in finding wealthy, heirless men to "convert" and exploit, receiving a share of the "inheritance." Master Lu Hsun-pei made himself useful by introducing wealthy buyers of art and the occasional Yangchou buyer of a child to the Indian, for which he was compensated with a large share of the business.

And what had been the Transport Minister's role in this alliance? It had been more or less what Dee had thought it would be. The master of the canal system of Yangchou was a contact to every corrupt and bribable official in the city, and saw to it that the illicit goods moved freely and unimpeded along the waterways. In return, the Indian visited him regularly on his way out of the city with his latest selection of little girls, and extended to him the privilege of choosing one or two for himself before they were taken to India. And he did the same on his way back from his journeys to the far west, always allowing the Transport Minister first pick of the imported art.

Of course, these men were the highest-ranking members of a versatile entrepreneurial association, with many lesser members of descending importance under them: a vast, thriving illicit profit structure of businessmen, clerks, foreigners, procurers, madames, courtesans, clergy, and officials.

And at the very bottom of the pile—at the lowliest level of apprenticeship—were messenger boys. It should have come as no surprise that the sons of Yangchou's chief magistrate were part of the organization. In time, they would probably have risen through the ranks. But how far? Would they have become wealthy and arrogant entrepreneurs like Lu Hsun-pei—or would they have risen only so far, like the corrupt little clerk performing divorces in his makeshift office in a brothel in exchange for kickbacks from the abbot? There was no way to speculate. Dee's misplaced paternal pride had taken a beating.

Dee had saved his most important question for last. He asked Ch'u-sin, the false abbot, about the death of the Transport Minister. Surely it was in connection with his underworld dealings, was it not?

Ch'u-sin had paused for a moment, considering.

In a sense, he answered. And Dee had asked: What exactly do you mean by that? And Ch'u had looked up with a sly little grin as he replied: Why don't you go and ask his daughter?

* * *

Waiting politely and discreetly in the reception hall were Dee's constables. Outside, two carriages waited—Dee's, and another for the Transport Minister's eldest daughter. He had come here today knowing that there was a strong likelihood that he would have to remove her from her home. He was not well versed in the etiquette of arresting a fine lady, and so he had improvised, and was improvising still.

The house and grounds were exactly as Dee remembered them: serene, tasteful, harmonious. And after so much elapsed time, there was still a sense in the atmosphere of the rooms and gardens that the master had only recently departed. Femininity still reigned here, too; there were young women and girls here and there in the halls and on the grounds. The only male in the house that Dee could discern was the very same steward who had received Dee on his last visit here nearly ten years before. The daughter herself received Dee today without surprise, as if she had been expecting him for a long time.

Dee sat face to face with the phantom who had flitted across the corridors of his memory countless times over the years. She was still a young woman, for she had been only seventeen that first time he had glimpsed her. Looking at her lovely face and bearing, one could imagine generations of aristocratic ancestors. But her true parents, Dee marveled, could only have been hardworking peasants from somewhere in the countryside.

"You ask why my father adopted only daughters," she was saying. "It was a personal preference—no more, no less. Femaleness pleased him. He grew up with seven brothers."

"I see that you have maintained his tradition," Dee said.

"My sisters and I are very happy here. They may marry if they wish. I do not stand in their way. But most of them have chosen to remain here. We are content with each other. We have no wish to leave our home, and live under the tyranny of a mother-in-law and subjugate ourselves to the demands of a husband."

"Then I take it, madame, that you are the . . . ah . . . *head* of the household?"

"I am," she replied coolly, looking steadily at Dee, causing a faint warmth to rise in him. "My father made special arrangements so that I, his eldest daughter, would inherit everything he owned upon his death."

"Is that why," Dee said with great care, "you had him killed?"

She looked at him for what must have been a full minute. He held her gaze, his heart beating quickly. Then she sighed, and seemed to sag just a bit in her chair.

"I would not have had to do it if he had left things the way they were." She shook her head with regret. "But he decided, quite late and quite suddenly, to adopt a son. Of course, I could not allow that."

No, Dee thought, of course you could not. Your inheritance would have gone to the adopted son instead.

"Tell me," Dee said, an idea coming to him, "did the abbot Ch'u-sin play a role in your father's decision?"

"He did," she said coldly. "He convinced my father that it would be wrong to leave his earthly possessions to a female. He convinced him that he should adopt one of his young monks as a 'son.' Ch'u-sin wanted to take what was mine." She paused. "I was angry at my father, and determined that he should honor the original arrangement."

"And so, before the 'adoption' could occur . . . " Dee said.

"Yes," she replied firmly. "But I have suffered badly for it. My father's ghost sits on my bed at night and weeps. It has . . . detracted from my serenity considerably." With those words, Dee noticed for the first time faint blue circles under her fine eyes, and a drawn look to her face, so subtle that one could easily miss it, and he understood: the woman had not had a proper night's sleep in years.

Setting up the gardener had been a simple matter, of course, especially with the extra assurance provided by a bribe to Dee's corrupt predecessor, old Magistrate Lu. And Ch'u-sin had known that she had arranged for her father's death, but because of her knowledge of the abbot's own vast criminal involvements, had been compelled to keep it to himself.

"Obviously," Dee said then, "you did not dispatch your father with your own hands. May I ask who . . . ?"

"He was no one. An urchin who used to come to the kitchen to be fed. An unusually canny and agile boy who would work for a price."

The one you sent after me when you saw me sniffing about your house, Dee thought. The one who very nearly finished me.

"And where is he now?" Dee persisted.

"I could not tell you," she said, her voice and manner hardening. "I have not seen him for some years."

What did Dee see in her face then? Had this urchin grown from boy to man before her eyes, taken what he could from her in every possible way, and then vanished? Yes. He was certain that this was what he saw.

The murder was solved, but it was not solved. The true killer was still out of Dee's reach. And now—assuming, of course, that he still lived and breathed—he had grown into a young man in his twenties.

The perfect disguise.

A.D. 663, spring

TO MY FRIEND THE OLD FOOL:

Since I know you are not a fool, then I will assume that you are not so old, either. At least not so old that you will not still be alive and breathing four years from now, when I will be traveling to Loyang, and we will meet each other face to face. Because of my recent work, my name is spoken in tones of great esteem; they are calling me a hero, a seeker of justice, a courageous crusader, but it is all quite hollow. I have much more work ahead of me.

I have received word that a great debate will be taking place there, of historical significance. The question that will draw Buddhist clergy and high civil officials from all over the Empire and cause them to polarize into two enormous parties, secular and cleric, is this: Does the Buddhist community owe respect and obeisance to the Confucian civil government—and individuals to their parents—or is it beyond any law but that of its own Dharma?

I do not see how I can afford to miss this event, as I have been honored by leading members of the Confucian civil party to represent the Yangchou metropolitan and prefectural district. I have been wanting to draft a memorial against the excesses of the popular Buddhist church for quite some time—and now I have more reason than ever to accomplish the task. I will, of course, be delivering this memorial before the assembled debate. Even as I write to you, I have already spent much time working and reworking my humble prose for this august body.

The gathering in Loyang already has a name: the Pai Debates.

> Until we meet—
> Dee Jen-chieh

12

A.D. 664
Loyang

Emperor Kaotsung bent and picked up a silk slipper from the garden path, held it under his nose, inhaled, and closed his eyes. He put his fingers inside it and felt the smooth satiny texture. He raised his eyes and moved them around the deserted garden, which was still, blooming, and hot under the spring sun.

He put the slipper in his pocket and moved silently forward, placing his walking stick before him with great care. He halted when the path diverged; on the left, it led him down a gentle slope and toward a stand of ornamental fruit trees. On the right, it wound for a way among flowering shrubs and led eventually to a secluded little stone pavilion. He considered for only a moment, then turned to the left. He examined the leaves and blossoms that hung over the path on either side, then studied the ground for petals that may have been knocked loose by the hem of a passing robe. Ahead, a bluish-white flurry of them lay scattered on the stones.

He moved toward the petals, his eyes scanning the ground minutely. Something sparkled a few paces farther on. He bent and picked up a tiny jeweled hairpin.

He followed the path toward the trees ahead, their crowns a cloud of blossoms undulating with the motion of ten thousand bees at work. The lazy drone of insects could disguise the murmur of lovers' voices, he knew. He held his breath and listened. Had he heard a laugh, low, short, and impudent? He steadied himself against a tree.

The laugh came again, then cut itself off abruptly. He crept in the direction from which he thought the laugh had come, then stopped and cast his eyes warily around him. He turned slowly, the rows of trees marching geometrically away from him in every direction as he rotated. He halted. There, at the end of a line where the trees lost their order and gave way to the true forest: a motion, something in the tall grass, a casual, unreflecting, unconscious movement, of a foot or a hand that does not know it is being watched. Then the low, abrupt laugh again.

He moved down the row, staying as close to the trees as he could, his heart accelerating and a cool sweat starting on his brow. Now the murmur of voices disengaged itself from the hum of the bees, and carried, low and distinct, to his straining ears.

He saw the edge of a carpet, a bundle of clothing, and an elbow, which occasionally straightened itself out into a gesturing arm. A man's arm.

Kaotsung approached, the murmuring conversation unintelligible over his own breathing and the pounding of his heart. He stood, trembling, leaning heavily on his stick, looking down on the two nude bodies lying on robes spread in the grass under the tree.

Wu, lying on her side propped on one elbow, looked up at him then; the dark-skinned man, who lay on his back, twisted his neck around and looked at the Emperor as well, then turned away and took one of Wu's breasts in his hand. Wu smiled and licked the man's shoulder. Kaotsung pulled the slipper from his pocket and raised it to his nose.

Wu caressed the man for another few moments, then looked at her husband. The caressing hand then tapped the prone man on the chest sharply and withdrew. Languidly, taking his time, the man sat up, stretched, gathered his clothing, and rose to his feet. Without even a glance in Kaotsung's direction, he slung the clothes over an arm and strode away naked, scratching himself occasionally or pausing to sniff a blossom on a branch. Wu had rolled onto her back, and now smiled invitingly up at Kaotsung, who had dropped his walking stick to the ground while he pulled and tore at his own clothing, which had suddenly become recalcitrant, obdurate, and unyielding.

"I could cure him completely, you know," the Nagaspa said to Lady Wu. "I could restore him fully, as if he had never been ill for a moment."

"My little sorcerer," Wu said fondly.

"But I would have to compensate for his essential weaknesses, of course. I have observed him closely. Though he would never allow me to touch him, I have often wished that I could measure the precise distance between his eyes, the width of his skull from temple to temple, and the angle at which his forehead rises from his nose."

"And what would you learn?" Wu asked, turning up the flame of the lamp, casting shadows about the large, nearly empty room. It was their room, one of countless forgotten rooms in the palace, the room he had chosen after an elaborate search during which he had read the magnetic oscillations, so he said, and intercepted the vibrational fields. It was the room where they went so that she could renew herself, where they magnified one another's *ch'i*, drawing down the potency of the heavens, as he put it, and causing the gods to laugh and squirm with cosmic delight.

"The soul directs the growth of the bones, madame," the Nagaspa said. "And reveals its purpose, its intent, its karma, by their shape. Especially the head. Ah! The head alone tells us so much! I have held the skulls of dead men in my hands and felt the living, pulsating essences of who and what they were in life—why, I have practically conversed with them!"

"And what, do you suppose, would you learn about my husband?" Wu asked, lighting a stick of incense in the flame of the lamp and placing it on the small altar in front of them.

I have already learned quite a bit simply from observation. Although measurements are desirable for detail and accuracy, one can, with practice, read a man's head just by looking at it. His life essence is not abundant. Part of his soul is already looking into the next world." He shrugged. "Also, he is an incomplete ruler. Part of him is missing, as if he had been born without an arm or a leg. You, madame, have taken the place of that missing part. He could not rule without you," the Nagaspa said, looking into her eyes with single-minded intensity.

He raised appraising hands to Wu's head then, placing his fingers on her temples, so lightly that he was barely touching her skin. Then, making calipers of his thumb and forefinger, he tested the distance from the bridge of her nose to her hairline, the width of her face from cheekbone to cheekbone. He squinted appraisingly as he felt the top and back of her head. She waited for his verdict, looking back into his eyes, a little patient smile on her lips. "It is as I thought, madame," he said, lowering his hands reverently. "You are the one. The one who makes him complete, as a man and as a ruler."

"How can you know so much?" she asked coyly. "For one so young." He straightened his back, shut his eyes, and sucked the air through his nostrils authoritatively.

"Only this body is young, madame," he replied, opening his eyes again. "Like you, I am an ancient soul. And we are here for a purpose. Your husband knows and doesn't know of your greatness of spirit. He himself is not one of the chosen ones."

The flattering words caused a deep feeling of importance and munificence to well inside her. She sighed at the heaviness of her responsibilities while savoring a warm, rich glow of admiration for herself.

"The whole world knows it," he said. "The whole world knows of your greatness. And you make *him* great. A name has come to me in a vision. At first, I was not sure whom the name referred to, but now I know for certain that it was meant for you and your husband the Emperor."

"Tell me the name, my sorcerer," she said with an indulgent smile.

"A name for you and your husband, who are truly twin sages, twin rulers: the Two Holies, my queen," he said, his eyes grave with portent.

She looked at him solemnly for a moment before putting her head back and laughing heartily. The Nagaspa's intent, important expression changed to one of hurt.

"Why do you laugh, my queen?" he asked with a touch of peevishness.

"Because it is too absurd," she said, shaking her head. "Even for me. It is like a woman wearing unbecoming cosmetics, a too-tight bodice, or an ill-fitting hairpiece. I could never utter such a phrase, or hear it uttered, without putting a hand over my mouth to stifle an inane giggle." She set her face into a mock-serious expression, as if she were a court minister delivering a memorial. "The Two Holies," she said, trying the phrase out, but she could not keep a smile from her lips, and she laughed again, waving her hands apologetically at the Nagaspa's discomfiture. "I am sorry, my sorcerer. I do not mean to ruffle your feathers, but it is just too silly. But wait! I have a name for you."

"I am not sure I wish to hear it," he said testily.

"No! You will like it!" she declared. "You," she said suggestively, leaning forward, "are my Divine Monkey."

The young man sitting within the high walls of his cloistered courtyard looked up from the text he was translating and squinted into the sun, unable at first to see who the two women were who stood over him. Even before he could identify them, he saw that they looked almost exactly alike. For a strange moment he thought that perhaps he was having an odd hallucination. Then one of them spoke. With a fright, and though he had not seen her in ten years, he recognized his stepmother the Empress.

Groundbreaking ceremonies were to begin today for the construction of the new palaces honoring the renaming of the city. It was rumored that a contingent of Confucian officials, shocked at the very notion of conferring a Buddhist name on the capital city, were planning to appear en masse and register their disapproval. It was a preposterous name, these officials said, some nonsense dug up during the excavations at the Tunhuang Caves and translated under the patronage of Madame Yang.

Word spread among the populace with the speed of a brushfire driven by summer winds, and it seemed that every man, woman, and child in the City of Transformation was planning to get as close to the proceedings as possible—out of curiosity, of course, and also because state occasions often meant food, drink, and gifts for the common people. But mostly, it was an opportunity to catch a glimpse of the Empress Wu, who seemed to have replaced the sun and moon in the sky for some.

Was the Empress not truly the people's queen? they asked one another. Did she not bring the woman's tender concern to the business of government? Was not her hand on the shoulder of the people like a mother's loving hand on the shoulder of her child? And was she not offering magic and hope with her invocation of a holy name? The gods, the Blessed Maitreya himself, must be smiling on the newly named city, they said.

Some, of course, were a touch doubtful. If she felt compelled to give the city a new name, why did she not draw from traditional Chinese sources? Why was it necessary to use what was, after all, a foreign name for a Chinese city? Could she not equally offer magic and hope with a Taoist name?

Still others were more than doubtful; they were downright cynical, declaring that if she were to pay a personal visit to their homes and offer to scrub the floors, they would not even rise from their chairs to greet her.

When the afternoon of the ceremony arrived, most of the population of the city had pressed as close to the outer grounds of the palace as they were allowed to. Festive music played, and a long line of hundreds of mounted, resplendently uniformed guards looking like Kuan-yin's warriors kept order in the front ranks. Every wall, building, or lamppost tall enough to afford a view was entirely covered with humanity. Those not close enough to see or who weren't fortunate enough to obtain a high perch jostled and stepped on one another in a vain effort to move forward; others waited patiently, knowing that the best they could hope for would be immediate reports from the front, which would travel, practically with the speed of thought, to the farthest reaches of the crowd.

A preliminary report was already making the rounds. A group of elderly officials, no more than twenty-five or thirty in number, were gathered to one side, reading, one by one, memorials protesting the renaming of the city. There were no fiery displays of oration, no stirring invective—just old men quietly, steadfastly, and determinedly reading their protests aloud to whoever would listen. And wasn't the Empress showing her tolerance and forbearance? Though a contingent of guards stood around the old Confucians, watching them, the officials were not ordered to disperse, were not interfered with. They were being allowed to have their say, though their voices and their words seemed as thin and unsubstantial over the music and the excited chatter of the crowd as if they had been reading into a thunderstorm.

When the music swelled and the crowd pressed forward, word travelled back that the Emperor and Empress had appeared in a splendid carriage, and had emerged. The Emperor, though he limped a bit and leaned on a heavy walking stick, walked without assistance, the Empress by his side. A young man was with them, a pale fellow with a confused, bashful expression. Who was he? people asked one another. Was this the fabled Historian Shu? No, he was much too young. And Shu was a cocky, arrogant little fellow, not at all shy; the way this one blinked his eyes and looked around in astonishment made him seem like some poor creature who had just emerged from a dark cellar into the light, someone who had perhaps not had a great deal of human companionship in a long, long time. He looked so frightened that they expected him to turn and crawl back into the carriage at any moment.

But the Empress had a firm grip on his arm, so it seemed, and pulled him along with her to the place where she and the Emperor were to bless the ground out of which the new palaces would spring. Transformation will begin here, the decree had said, and radiate outward through the entire city and beyond; our lives will be new, the sky we walk under will be new, our spirits will be new.

Then a new rumor moved through the crowd, one that somehow people knew to be the truth: the young man was a prince. What prince? One of her sons? No. Not one of hers. He was none other than Prince Jung, once the Crown Prince, the forgotten son of the deposed Empress. Impossible, some people said. Hasn't he been dead for years? Not dead, others said, but locked away as a virtual prisoner, cloistered in a lonely compound in a remote wing of the palace. Difficult to believe that this was the one around whom a traitorous conspiracy had once gathered. Why, he must have been nothing more than a boy when it happened. Plainly, all was forgiven now. Was the Empress Wu not magnanimous, bringing the son of her rival and her onetime enemy out to appear with her before the multitudes?

Was she not truly teaching us the meaning of Transformation?

It was an exceptionally fine spring, with blue skies, warm winds, and a sense of promise in the air. The new palaces grew from the ground almost like something alive. The people of the city often made an expedition of going to observe the progress. And every day, not just the day of the ceremony, meant food and gifts for the citizenry. The unseasonably warm days became hotter very quickly; one morning people woke to find the sweet spring gone and the full, sultry heat of summer upon them. It was not even June yet.

The heat came to stay, sitting upon the City of Transformation like a fat lady on her chair. The carefree mood of spring was quite forgotten as people grew testy and listless, and in the poorer districts, where people must always live that much closer to nature's extremes and where the constant proximity of other humans is an irritant without respite, tempers flared, squabbles broke out, and the constables had their hands full. One woman was reported to have tossed a pot of boiling soup in her husband's face before attempting to fling herself into the river, and at least three "holy men" were known to be wandering the streets claiming to be the Buddha reincarnate, attracting the jeers and unkind attentions of bands of youths.

Still the work on the palace progressed, and by midsummer the outer walls were in place and their huge new silhouette dominated the horizon. The once-copious flow of gifts and treats for the people seemed to be drying to a trickle, though, like the water in the city's many rivers. Some people came away in disgust after being handed a few stale cakes; one man spat his on the ground when he found insect fragments in the one he had just bitten into.

But the bounty of the rivers was unusually good, despite the low, sluggish waters. Fishermen were bringing up an unusual abundance of large red fish, which seemed to be getting larger as the summer wore on. Some thought they made very good eating indeed, though they seemed to have less flavor the bigger they got; some of the huge ones were downright bitter in taste. Soon the fishermen were throwing the really big ones back. But when they started to get as long as a man was tall, some were hauled out merely as curiosities. One enterprising fellow started to skin them, saying that he had found a way to preserve the fragile leather, which he declared he would then fashion into exotic garments for the Empress and become a wealthy, famous, and distinguished man.

Early on a morning in late summer, a crowd of people gathered on the banks of the city's largest river. They stared down into the riverbed, where the brackish water stood in shallow puddles. Here and there pieces of rubbish—bones, pottery shards, old shoes, twisted scraps of rusty metal—lay forlornly exposed in the stagnant muck already sending its perfume up under the hot sun. But it was not these interesting pieces of detritus that had the awed attention of the people on the bank. It was the enormous red fish, as long as three men, which lay gasping and wriggling in the last few inches of water, its gills gaping and closing fleshily and obscenely, its eye looking glassily up to the empty blue sky.

The heat continued into the autumn, until one day in early October when the skies broke and rain hissed onto the paving stones and filled the rivers. That same day, a memorial by Historian Shu appeared in the gazettes circulating the City of

Transformation. The few literate ones among the populace were called upon many times that day to read aloud; people stood under their dripping hats and parasols listening to the lamentable words, shaking their heads and looking sorrowfully down at the glistening pavement. Well, they sighed, it is sad and dreadful, but necessary, for a crisis has been averted, the Emperor and Empress are safe. Let us thank the Blessed Maitreya, they are safe.

THE MEMORIAL FROM HISTORIAN SHU

It is with Deep and Terrible regret that the Emperor and Empress inform us that Disaster has been Narrowly Averted. In the Tolerant Atmosphere of the Court, where Dissenters have always been allowed to Have their Say, a Traitorous Conspiracy has been uncovered, led by the Deposed Crown Prince Jung, who, in his Guilt and Cowardice, has hanged himself. This has been a Particularly Dreadful Ordeal for the Empress, who, as many are Aware, befriended the former Crown Prince. But she draws on her Deep Resources of Equanimity in rising above the Sorrow and Betrayal. Transformation, as we are learning, will sometimes entail Pain, but we must put Sorrow Behind Us, and look only to the Future. So say the Emperor Kaotsung and the Empress Wu, the Two Holies who Watch Over our Lives.

13

A.D. 667, spring
Loyang

"Mother," the young man hissed, looking around him with acute embarrassment, "please take your hands off me!" He peeled her fingers from his worn jacket while he strove to haul her to her feet, but she resolutely refused to stand, letting her legs fold beneath her so that she was dragged along on her knees. Her own clothes were old and worn, and Dee could see the pallid flesh of her bare calves and the jagged course of the bluish-purple veins.

Anger and embarrassment made the young man harsh.

"Off me! Get off me! I have told you where you can go, old woman. I brought you here so you could go with them." His eyes looked anxiously toward the crowds of colorfully robed monks gathering in small conversant groups in the outdoor square behind the great debating hall. "Mercy. That is what they do best. *They* will feed you!"

The old woman sobbed and bowed her head.

"I cannot feed you. I can barely feed myself!" His voice rose with desperation. "You are sick and old. I cannot take care of you anymore! Get away. Go. Go to them." His mother wailed and clung tighter.

A curious crowd, both passersby and Pai Debate participants milling about during the afternoon recess before the final session, had been drawn toward the little drama. They formed a semicircle two and three people deep around the pathetic scene.

"Please don't leave me here. Please don't leave me," she pleaded in her cracked old voice. "I will work. I will bring us food. You will see. Let me stay with you."

"You are too sick. You can do nothing. You know it quite well," he pleaded coldly. He tried again to pry her hands from him.

Now she had hold of the pockets of his jacket. The worn fabric tore, the woman sank to the ground with a handful of shredded fabric in each fist, and the young man was free. "You are all that I have," she moaned. "Please. Please. Don't make me go." She advanced on her knees toward her son, but he backed deftly away from her, and pointed to the gathering of Buddhist holy men looking on.

"No. You have them," he said. "They will take care of you." He darted into the crowd without looking back.

The woman sobbed, her bony shoulders convulsing. The crowd parted as two Buddhist monks made their way forward. An old shaven-headed man knelt and lifted her gently to her feet. She trembled and appeared to be quite unable to stand on her own; the monks supported her on either side and spoke soothing words. Dee had seen that she was also badly bruised around her eyes. Was it possible, he asked himself as the holy men led her away, that a son could beat his old mother? The sad truth was that she would indeed be better off among the monks and nuns. Dee had seen the guilt, confusion, and anger on the young man's face, and knew that his own conscience would probably give him a good beating. For a while, at least. He shook his head. A sorrier scene he had never witnessed. He turned and left the square.

Dee was to be the Confucian party's final speaker, and he would be delivering the concluding memorial of the debates. He had sent up a handwritten copy to the throne as well. He had prepared the work carefully over many long months: a finely honed piece of prose, in a reservedly turgid and parallel style, each and every word selected and placed with the care of a jeweler setting stones, a remonstrance and a historical treatise on the drawbacks of the incursion of a foreign order. It was a piece that could very well survive him, to be published and circulated for generations. He brought the papers of the text out from the leather satchel that swung under his arm and looked at them in the warm light of this Loyang spring day for a few moments before abruptly thrusting them back inside. Something was very wrong.

There was still some time before the afternoon Pai session would resume. There were bakers' stalls not far from here. The thought was tempting; the meager monkish breakfast of dry barley cakes and tea that had been passed around at the debates had not held much pleasure. Following his nose, Dee began to walk to the market.

Thoughts of the unfortunate old woman were with him as he walked, and following naturally, thoughts of himself and how his own sons might treat him when he was old and if he was at their mercy. It was then, as he moved along the river, breathing the fragrant air redolent with the sweet perfume of blossoms from rows of exquisitely manicured plum and peach and cherry trees, that he resolved never to be an old man in their presence. And it would be better, if need be, like an old scoundrel, to go off alone to die.

He made his way through the crowds of pilgrims and ascetics, Buddhist and Lamaist anchorites, Confucian scholars and officials who had flocked to the capital city for the great national Pai Debates, filling the hostels and guest rooms and pressing into the bustling markets. He stood at the edge of a walkway following the course of the river and watched the reflected images of crowds of colorfully and variously robed strangers to Loyang's streets and alleys passing by. Loyang, a city of meandering rivers and tributaries, was also a city of infinite reflections. Though it looked the same as it had when he had visited once or twice in years past, it was no longer Loyang; its mind and soul were afflicted. It would seem that the Empress Wu Tse-tien's odious new name for the beautiful old capital city—the City of Transformation—was beginning to take substance.

Everywhere Dee went, in the restaurants, teahouses, parks, markets, and wineshops, he heard the same conversation in progress on a thousand different tongues, addressing questions that seemed to Dee to be nothing less than an insult to the gracious old city: Did the Buddhist owe respect to the Confucian governmental authorities, and to the Emperor himself? Further, did the monk, once having taken his vows of removal from the society of men, even continue to owe the simplest and most basic respect to the ultimate, fundamental foundation of Confucian order—to his own parents? Or was he separate, by virtue of his religion, from all obligations to Emperor, state, and family, obliged to adhere only to his own "higher law"? Was the Sangha—the Buddhist community of tens of thousands of monasteries—separate from the rest of society, from its reach and its laws? Did the Sangha owe obeisance (*pai*) only to the Dharma, its own inner code of Buddhist law?

The conversations formed and broke apart like the countless reflections in the water flowing under the arched bridges. As Dee made his way through the milling debate crowds toward the market stalls, he felt a new and stronger purpose filling him. When he entered that hall again after the recess it would soon be his turn to speak. He had come to the Pai Debates to deliver the oral version of his memorial. But now he thanked the terrible, unfilial son who had abandoned his old mother to strangers, and he thanked his own sons, too, for they had reminded him of what all of this was about.

When the esoteric veneer was stripped away, maybe there wasn't much difference between religious charlatans and his own sons. Didn't his own sons, and others like them, consider themselves to be exempt from the laws that governed everyone else? And now that he thought of it, couldn't any lawbreaker exonerate himself on "religious" grounds? From his experiences, most criminals seemed to believe themselves inspired by some higher—or at least separate—set of rules. Some had an almost devotional belief in their own right to live outside the law, of that he was certain. What was the difference between the criminal extorter and the false prophet? They were both deceivers, giving false hope, imparting faith in false truths. Each in his own way preyed on hope and will.

Dee took the steep stairs two and three at a time up one side of a beautiful corbeled brick bridge. When he had reached the highest point in the bridge's center, three little barges were gliding noiselessly, one behind the other, along the rippling surface of the water below. They were roped together like a team of pack animals, tarps covering their cargo.

He looked down and studied his reflection in the wake of the last of the barges. He watched the image of the man looking up from the depths reassemble in perfect clarity as the ripples settled. Squinting his eyes, he saw the old man he would one day become looking back at him.

Beneath the externals of this foreign dogma there was something opaque, something subterranean, like the secret hidden seething passion of a very perverse, very clever mind. Yes, there was certainly goodness, compassion, and mercy among the honest practitioners of the true religion. But a system of thought transplanted from a faraway place could not help but bear strange, hybrid fruit when it was cultivated in what was not, after all, its native soil. The weaknesses and defects peculiar to the Chinese as a people, as a civilization, he thought, find expression far too easily in a system of thought meant for another world, another time, another mind. Hadn't he just witnessed a poverty-wearied young man passing his own sick old mother off on the Buddhists? Instead of following the example of compassion set forth by true Buddhist thought and taking care of his mother until her death, and instead of adhering to the Confucian directive of unstinting filial devotion, which would have had the same result, he had fallen between the two in a way that accommodated his own weakness. It is acceptable for me to relegate my responsibilities to others, he was saying. It is possible to surrender responsibility and filial duty.

Looking into the water, he imagined he could feel something moving, rising toward the Empire's placid surface. As he climbed down the far side of the bridge, sufficiently distancing himself from the great hall on the other side of the tree-lined park and its hordes of recessed participants, an idea was forming in Dee's head. It was a powerful and consuming idea—coming together once again as had the swirling fragments of his own reflection. He felt for the soft leather satchel under his arm. The sure folded weight of the parchment that contained his memorial speech inside was comforting to him; he knew what he had to do. Now the words began to take shape, too, a shadow of this new idea.

Dee bought two fried dough cakes from a stall in a narrow market alley, then walked a good distance to a less crowded part of the river walkway to sit down and eat. A leaf-stained stone step flanked by two small marble lions looked inviting, but next to it, a carved bench with a backrest appeared even more comfortable. He was nearly to the bench, carefully balancing the two cakes on an oily piece of paper to avoid crushing them, when he noticed a black obsidian plaque beneath the seat. He stooped for a closer look.

The top of the plaque was incised with the outline of a stupa, and beneath it metered rows of characters were painted in gold leaf. The text extolled the uncompromising virtue and compassion of the Future Buddha Maitreya's earthly representatives and servants: the Divine Empress Wu Tse-tien and her mother Madame Yang, the great patroness of Buddhist sutras and learning. The remaining text bore some nonsense about " . . . and in sitting, one rests, away from a world of strife and suffering, in the Wondrous Realm, each day nearer to the final earthly glories of the coming Great Age of the Future Buddha's Law, the Dharma . . . "

The spring sun, reflecting off the water, was bright on the shiny black stone, and a haze of white spiderweb and dust obscured the date at the very bottom of the plaque. Dee knelt closer and carefully placed the paper with the dough cakes on the bench. With both hands now free he wiped clean the bottom part of the stone with his cuff. The date was what he expected: the plaque and the bench had been erected only a few months before. In anticipation of the debates? he wondered. Was it all done to set the "proper" atmosphere?

There was more to it than that. Wherever Dee had roamed in Loyang the names of the Empress and her mother—also referred to in reverence as the holy mother, Madame Yang, generous and devoted disciple of the Buddha—could be heard. And, Dee supposed, the benches, along with the other things he had seen in recent days, fountains and gardens and the like—were all some sort of visible testament, offerings spread out before the people. Public works—new kitchens, hospitals, and orphanages—abounded throughout the city, and with each one the same revered names were somehow always attached: Wu and Yang and the blessed Future Buddha Maitreya. And testament to this Empress's compassion were her charitable works among the people.

But what, Dee wondered, did Emperor Kaotsung think of all this? Now that he thought of it, he had not heard the name of the Emperor uttered at all, except as it was invoked this morning to begin the debates—whereas the two women's names were practically being sung by the birds in the branches of the blooming fruit trees.

From the vantage of the center of Loyang, from the gardens and markets, from the great lanes and canals and back alleys, it seemed that the Divine Emperor, the August Son of Heaven, was silent. Dee was listening, his ear to the ground as well as to the walls of the Forbidden City, and he heard nothing. He would give anything to have a pair of eyes and ears behind those hallowed walls. The texture of Loyang, the Imperial capital—the City of Transformation, he corrected himself cynically—seemed to be changing right before his eyes.

Dee was now extremely hungry. He had nearly forgotten about the food in his hand. The hunger he felt now, and the imminent promise of satiation, pleasantly eclipsed thoughts of politics and corruption, charlatans and unfilial offspring, at least for the time being. He rose from his crouch in front of the shiny black plaque and dusted his knees, then sank to the bench to enjoy his fried dough dumplings, thankful to the all-compassionate Buddha for this humble resting place. Thankful, indeed, for all of *her* munificence. He took a healthy bite of his dumpling.

He removed the pages of his Pai memorial speech from the leather satchel resting on the bench alongside him. Heedless of his greasy hands, he held up the papers he was to read before the enormous and controversial assembly. A light breeze rustled their edges like invisible fingers flipping through the pages. He took another bite of the pastry. What was it that he had been hearing in this great city, this City of Transformation? What was it that was all around? It was something far more insidious than the depredations of charlatan abbots and their false sutras and spurious promises of divine intervention and salvation. No, it was far worse than that. It was a soft and willing moan.

A marriage was taking place. A marriage between two creatures who should never have met at all, but who, having once met, were drawn inexorably one to the other, to their mutual doom and detriment: Buddhism was the woman, and the Confucian state her husband. She was an alluring and exotic creature drawing him in with her bewitching fragrance, teasing his staid reason with dangerous whimsy. And he, having perhaps gone too far in the direction of dry reason and rationality, was peculiarly vulnerable, was allowing himself to be seduced. The City of Transformation had been misnamed, Dee thought. This gracious city of parks and scholarship and Imperial government, this jewel of the Empire, should have been named the City of Surrender.

Dee no longer had any intention of delivering yet another long-winded memorial at the Pai Debates, as had so many of his Confucian colleagues before him. It was far too late for that. There was so little time.

At this point in its course, the river was swift and deep. In a city of rivers and green parks pressed between narrow crowded market lanes, no one would notice a bit more detritus.

He rose from the bench and walked over to the canal's edge. Here he was again, poised above on the brick and mortar ramparts at the water's edge, looking down, with the old man staring back up from his deep world of roiling turbulence. How fitting, Dee thought. This was the place.

He tore the pages of his Pai speech, pages he had worked over for the better part of a year, pages full of scholarly posturings and rigidly metered prosody and historical allusions, all so vain and irrelevantly self-indulgent, it seemed now—and allowed them to flutter piece by solitary piece into the racing water.

No, he would not be reading his tired speech. Dee resolved to deliver a warning. A clear and unambiguous warning.

In the final moments before he was due to rise, Dee was tense and expectant. He studied the faces in the hall: eyes met his, and seemed suddenly brighter, more alert, ready for something. A palpable current filled the room; a scuffling, a few small coughs, as the participants settled into an attentiveness that said to Dee that they were preparing themselves for something other than another chance to doze through someone's droning. So, Dee thought, it would seem that I have a reputation. When he realized that the entire hall was in a state of suspense, waiting for the delivery of the magistrate from Yangchou, he felt his throat go dry and his stomach flutter like a paper fan. He had only one chance before this assembled body. They fully expected something different from the esteemed and diligent magistrate. Many of them had returned to the afternoon session solely because of Dee, and it would not do to let them down.

With the announcement of his family name and rank, degree and official title, the formalities were over. Dee rose to his feet from his seat behind the row of desks at the rear of the hall and prepared to make the long walk down the central aisle to the speaker's dais. Behind him someone began to rap rhythmically on a tabletop as if beating a tune on the skin of a *weir* drum. Another joined in and they in turn were joined by other groups of three or four around the room, then five and six, eight, ten, and twelve, the rhythmic thumping building until the hall shook with a thundering accolade for the "young" magistrate from Yangchou.

Dee moved quickly down the aisle, observing the crowd in furtive little sideways glances. In the midst of the commotion the clerics were noticeably quiet; their passive expressions made it seem as if they had expected this outbreak. Dee himself certainly had not. A flush warmed him as he climbed the steps of the dais. The drumming rose to a great crescendo, then stopped just as quickly the moment he reached the top step.

He stood and looked out over the room, silent and attentive now so that even the faintest whisper of silk robes could be heard as someone shifted his feet. The strong midday light shone full on the upturned faces at the center of the room. Many shaded themselves with hands, sleeves, and loose sheets of paper; Dee looked out at the assembly, still but for the flutter of fans here and there. Hundreds of eyes, some squinting against the light, were trained on his face. He began to speak, his voice sounding tinny and impostor-like to his own ears.

"I have heard it said that a man's reputation precedes him. That my humble and undeserving reputation has preceded me like the martial drummers of Shensi Province. Well . . . " Dee's face warmed as he groped momentarily for his next words. "It is considerably more than I could have hoped for, or indeed, would ever have expected. I have come with pleasure to this most honorable and revered gathering on this glorious spring afternoon in the most beautiful city on earth. But I have come not to tell pleasant stories, but to warn of a danger to the fabric of society. My brilliant colleagues have, it seems, failed to address the most pressing problem;

they have failed to address the real issues before us and before this Empire today." The hall stirred. He waited a moment, then continued.

"But by ignoring them, we will not make them go away. It is not a simple matter of duty and filial piety." Dee paused again, allowing the weight of his heresy to take hold. A wave of muttering spread across the hall; everywhere, heads were turning around.

Two brightly capped monks—their brilliant yellow feathery headgear suggesting to Dee some esoteric school of Buddhism, perhaps some Tibetan Lamaic tradition—rose from their cross-legged position and abruptly left the hall by the rear entrance without turning around. He waited until they were gone, and continued.

"In speaking of the ills that attack the root of government and law, I must first address the state of human affairs. I beseech our August Imperial Father to have pity on the multitudes of his subjects who are, at this very moment and even while I speak, being deceived and deluded by the tens of thousands, their lives sinking into a deathless oblivion; they are united solely in their naive and unguided desire to follow the dictates of this foreign religion and to succumb before the infinite forms of its idols, abducted on board its 'Precious Raft.'

"Elaborate pagodas and halls rival the grandest Imperial structures, demanding a veneration of human effort and wealth, unprecedented in recent times, that saps the resources of this nation. As for these monasteries and nunneries, many are outside the law, deeming themselves beyond repute or remand.

"As I face each of you personally before this great assembly, I look into your consciences and into your souls and tell you of the true expense that we are forced to endure. There is no magic involved, although there are such members of a clergy who might, at times, wish us to believe that there is. No. There is no magic. Just one simple truth: to enrich the few, they must impoverish the many."

By now Dee could see that the back row of monks lining the farthest wall were rising from their pillows and moving toward the rear gardens.

"If these Buddhists do not wish to injure the masses, and I am certain that they do not wish to do so, then what is it that they seek to do? There is only so much time granted a human life upon this earth, but there seems to be no limit to the expenditure demanded of it, although it is most often the poorest households that are the victims of this seemingly magical and hypnotic mass delusion. A grand deception. A sleight of hand on a scale hitherto never seen. Unable to satisfy the boundless greed of the church, the masses, the worn, tortured, body of the nation, is first seduced and then pushed beyond the painful limits of endurance. And we, my fellow Confucians, my colleagues, scholars and officials . . . all of us seem content to sit back in our complacency, while a nation is pried from our grasp."

"Go ahead," Dee intoned. "*Go ahead*," he shouted, and a rustle of shocked murmurs rippled through the hall. He had them. "Go ahead and dare to look around you. Each and every one of you. I dare you to walk the streets of this grand city and look about you with an untainted vision. You will not like what you see. Wherever you go, the neighborhoods and wards, the streets and lanes and alleys are crowded with every manner of secret Buddhist shrine. Along every wall and beneath every market gate lie the innumerable variety of odd little temples, little houses of the spirits. Little houses to suck out the souls of men.

"And there is another problem, one that has thrust itself upon me far too often. The monastic establishment in providing a refuge for the pure also provides a refuge for the criminal. Those people fleeing the law, criminals, thugs, and miscreants of all sorts wishing to escape punishment, all rush through the welcoming gates of these Buddhist monasteries, secure in the fact that they are safe. How many tens of thousands of nameless criminals have escaped into the waiting arms of this establishment? Close investigations from magisterial offices in the capital and the provinces below have already seized many thousands of those seeking to evade the law in this way. How many others are there as yet unapprehended? And posing as priests and abbots and monks, these criminals—these charlatans—appeal to the baser desires of men's bodies and not to the loftier metaphysics of their hearts and minds, so that bit by bit, soul by soul, rational mind by rational mind, we are being seduced. *Seduced!*" He allowed this last word to reverberate in the air; the rear of the hall responded with a muffle of low angry groans.*

---

*See Notes to the Reader (page 622) for a translation of the actual Memorial delivered by Ti Jen-chieh (Dee).

Outside, the breeze had picked up so that the branches of
trees with their delicate new green churned and dipped; sunlight flashed erratically through the gauzy spaces like the reflections of a wind-played mirror. Now the wave of
dissatisfaction became a fit of coughing that seemed to have
broken out spontaneously in the back row of monks sitting on
their pillows against the wall. It became an infectious taunting
joke, spreading from one cleric to the next until the entire back-
row contingent hacked and wheezed in mockery of the great
Confucian speaker at the dais. The coughing continued for
many long minutes, the monks rocking back and forth and
whacking one another on the back, the sound echoing around
the hall. In the front, someone began to thump on his desk in
a repeat of the accolade that had accompanied Dee to the dais;
the thumping spread as Dee's Confucian supporters sent up
their own defiant barrage of noise.

The thundering and hacking went on, filling the huge hall,
while Dee stood, unbelieving, looking down on the crowd, the
eyes of the Confucians trained raptly upon him as they
pounded the desks and floor. He raised his arms for silence,
but the din went on unabated for many more minutes until the
four monks who had begun the insurrection broke into laughter, coughing and hooting alternately. The four faced their colleagues, then turned to leer comically at Dee before stamping
their feet in some giddy childish dance as they moved toward
the rear door. A wizened old monk sitting nearby spinning his
wooden prayer wheel nodded to each of the four with toothless
glee as they exited. Dee kept his arms raised, imploring the
room to come to order; slowly, the pounding and laughing
receded and the great hall was quiet once again.

"What of the man who does not work, but receives his
sustenance at the expense of others? Is this not fraudulent?
And what of those whose means far surpasses those of the
multitudes and who yet still choose a course of robbery from
those same multitudes? I can only reflect that this realm is indeed a place of pain and suffering just as the Buddhist tells us:
but it is also a realm of false sutras and relics, of false hopes
and promises, which infect us like a plague of virulent sores."

Dee raised his eyes after these last words to gauge their
effect. A little metered prosody never hurt one's argument—
but only a little, only the lightest touch. He studied the hall.
He knew that lessons were transitory; still, there was scarcely
a restless shuffle in the entire enormous room. He had them.

For now, at least. Even the clerics, the ones who had stayed, were quiet now, hanging on his words as if they were learning of the transgressions committed by charlatans in the name of popular Buddhism for the first time. Perhaps they were. Now he must bring his final statements together before he lost any of them. He rubbed his sweating palms against his thighs and stared hard into the hall before continuing.

"We see a nation now in crisis, plunging steadily into a darkening shadow of superstition. All about us the great roads and byways are darkened by the black silk of Buddhist robes. And it seems that there is no one left to assist the state in its time of crisis—because all about us good men are falling prey to this disease of the mind, good men whom we had once relied upon for their rational council.

"If Buddhism is a religion of compassion, then they, the *good* Buddhists, must take that compassion as their universal guiding principle. And they must bring that ideal of compassion down as an example, a paradigm of righteousness for the common people. This compassion must be at the root of their hearts and conduct. If they followed its dictum they would not sway from it. But they do not because the religion is in the hands of charlatans . . . charlatans who follow a law of greed to support their vain and insubstantial adornments."

Dee paused again. The hall still held itself in near-breathless silence.

"If we do not sow the proper seeds now, then we shall bring famine upon ourselves and upon the future. Without the loyal and diligent assistance of our officials, righteousness will not succeed. If we waste the official wealth and if we allow the labors of the people to be exhausted, then no corner of this nation will escape the dire consequences. And it will be too late to save us. Too late. Historians will only speak of the lost glory of the past—the past that was us."

He was through. He looked around the hall; it was plain that the audience expected something more from him, for they did not move or even shift in their seats, but sat steadfastly watching him. His gaze shifted to the doorways at the rear of the hall. In the garden beyond, Dee could see a few seated monks, who appeared to be waiting for someone; every so often they turned their heads in the direction of the trees and the outer gate, then conferred animatedly with one another.

As he brought his attention back to the expectant faces before him, his closing words came to him, the most important words of all. They had begun to take form in his mind a few hours before when he had cleared the debris from the plaque on the bench in the park and read the names of the Empress Wu and Madame Yang.

"Religion is superstition," he said, his voice disarmingly low and soft. "Superstition! And government is the rule of reason and law. The two cannot sleep in the same bed. Not if the state is to remain guided by principles of order and propriety . . . and, yes, above all, reason. As once rational men, we have come to doubt ourselves. We doubt the rule of reason and law. And because we doubt ourselves, we become weak and allow ourselves to become victims. We have allowed ourselves to become both enchanted and entranced. Beware!

"Government cannot be and must not *ever* be subject to the abstract whims of metaphysics, nor must the common good be shaped by the wanton subjectivity of mysterious teachings. Government, for all its inadequacy, is the property of men, and not divinities."

With that, he stepped from the dais; the thunder that rose now threatened to deafen him.

Perhaps it was the famed monk's entrance at the end of the debates that turned the tide so severely against the Confucian party, though Dee had recognized long before his own enthusiastically received delivery that afternoon that the Confucian argument had already been lost: the monastic establishment would be free to go its own way, free from civil obligations to Emperor, state, and parents. But he could never have foreseen the magnitude of their defeat. For Dee, it was a disaster of the first order, an insult to the T'ang and to the millennia of civilization that had preceded it. But the final moments of the Pai Debate had been a display of showmanship of a sort that the Confucians could never have hoped to equal; on that point, Dee conceded absolutely and without reservation.

Before the tribute for Dee had died down after his final words and before he had left the hall, the monks were on their knees knocking their heads on the floor. But it was not for the magistrate from Yangchou that they were prostrating themselves. Three long, deep mournful notes, like the tremendous doleful sighs of the gods themselves, sounded from outside the door, causing all talk and motion inside the hall to halt abruptly. Then a single monk's voice enunciated the venerable name of Buddhism's most illustrious disciple.

The great Hsuan-tsang was brought in then, carried aloft on his peacock-feather throne like a high priest or the Buddha incarnate. And that, Dee supposed, was precisely how he was looked upon. The entire hall, including the official Confucian contingent, fell silent as the famed pilgrim was borne to the speaker's dais. This was the man whose daring travels into barbarian lands, whose arcane translations and historical, cultural, and religious revelations of the mysterious worlds of India and Tibet were on the tongue of every Chinese Buddhist.

The great melancholy notes sounded again from outside; now Dee could see the enormous Tibetan trumpets, fully sixteen feet long, their curved necks resting on the ground, born and bred in the remote high mountains, created to send forth a voice that would travel from lofty peak to lofty peak above the clouds. Here, in the green, civilized, earthbound city garden, the sound they made filled the world.

Dee found himself momentarily shocked at Hsuan-tsang's ancientness. Of course, Dee had heard of the fabled peripatetic monk-scholar, but he had never imagined the white-haired and age-spotted grandfather who ascended the stairs with the aid of two assistants, a frail and venerable figure. Of course, he would not match the image of the black-haired and vigorous man that Dee had held in his mind; after all, word of his distant travels and his great translations had been circulating in China for decades.

Nothing in the elderly monk's clothing or in his behavior indicated that he was anything but a traditional Chinese scholar-gentleman. The monks who had been outside returned to their cross-legged ranks on the pillows along the rear wall. Everyone—monks and officials alike—stared with rapt attention at the old man, who raised one thin, spotted hand in a gesture of blessing. Then Hsuan-tsang began to speak, his voice soft, yet surprisingly full and vigorous, with a controlled strength that suggested the imminent breaking of all constraints.

"We as a people shall become by greater degrees ever more and more enlightened. This is our fate." His breathing was audible in the pause that followed his opening words, his nostrils flaring as he inhaled through his nose and then exhaled from his lips with a peculiar hissing sound. In spite of himself, Dee was fascinated, entranced.

"And by those same gradual degrees we as an empire of men shall learn to negate our egos and in this state enter a world of KNOWING THE BLISS OF OUR OWN DIVINITIES." The voice rose, gathering volume and strength. "WITH THE FUTURE BUDDHA MAITREYA COMING AS OUR GUIDE." The old man's words filled the great hall.

"WE TAKE REFUGE IN THE THREE PRECIOUS ONES," Hsuan-tsang invoked with ardent fervor.

"WE TAKE REFUGE IN THE THREE PRECIOUS ONES," the Buddhists in the hall echoed their leader.

"WE GRASP THE TRIPLE GEM OF ENLIGHTENMENT," the old monk intoned in his huge voice.

"WE GRASP THE TRIPLE GEM OF ENLIGHTENMENT," the devotees chanted.

"I GO FOR REFUGE TO THE BUDDHA."

"I GO FOR REFUGE TO THE BUDDHA."

The unison dirge of the monks' voices was casting the power of its liturgical spell over the vast sunlit room. Dee felt enveloped by the sound, impaled and nearly paralyzed, the vibrations penetrating to the marrow of his bones, immobilizing him where he stood.

"I GO FOR REFUGE TO THE DHARMA."

"I GO FOR REFUGE TO THE DHARMA."

"I GO FOR REFUGE TO THE SANGHA."

"I GO FOR REFUGE TO THE SANGHA."

"I PRAY TO THE FUTURE BUDDHA MAITREYA FOR GUIDANCE."

"I PRAY TO THE FUTURE BUDDHA MAITREYA FOR GUIDANCE."

"I PRAY FOR THE COMING OF THE AGE OF THE LAW."

"I PRAY FOR THE COMING OF THE AGE OF THE LAW."

"I PRAY FOR THE COMING OF THE AGE OF THE LAW."

"I PRAY FOR THE COMING OF THE AGE OF THE LAW."

"I PRAY FOR THE COMING OF THE AGE OF THE LAW."

"I PRAY FOR THE COMING OF THE AGE OF THE LAW."

Somehow, Dee and some of the other Confucians found it in them to break the grip of the spell and leave the hall, the chanting continuing behind them, the oddly ominous phrase repeated over and over, rising to the rafters of the hall and the sky above: not a prayer, but an ultimatum.

14

Magistrate Dee had been a guest in many grand and elegant houses in his time, houses of magnificent proportion and luxurious appointments, but they might as well have been mud huts with earthen floors compared to the opulence enveloping him now. He had ten enormous rooms to himself, a private walled garden with reflecting pools and statuary, his choice of five different huge, soft, fragrant beds to sleep in, chests full of brilliant embroidered silk robes to wear, and servants ready to respond to his smallest wish at any time of the day or night.

The Pai Debates were over, Loyang was in an uproar, and the "brilliant" magistrate from Yangchou had been summoned to the palace. A letter from the Emperor had been put in Dee's hands shortly after the conclusion of the debates, a letter saying that Kaotsung had been most impressed by Dee's reputation, by the memorial that Dee had sent to the throne before the debates began, and most of all by the tumult in the hall when Dee rose to speak, already a legend throughout the city and beyond. The Emperor wrote that he was most anxious to meet the magistrate, and that there was a matter of some importance that he wished to discuss with him. The letter concluded with an invitation.

To say that Dee was confused, intrigued, and filled with curious anticipation was to understate things seriously. Here he was, being received at the palace as a guest of honor, an audience with the Emperor imminent, and yet the Confucian party had been declared the official losers in what was supposed to have been an unofficial debate, with repercussions sure to follow that would be as devastating to the Empire as any flood, earthquake, or tidal wave.

Yes, it was all very curious. At the conclusion of the debates, the final tally of votes had been sent up to the throne in the predetermined form of a petition—five hundred thirty-nine votes for the clerical stance, and only three hundred fifty-four for the Confucian position. The purpose of it all had been—so

it was understood—strictly symbolic, a forum meant to demonstrate the prevailing frame of mind of the nation, the timbre
of considered opinion pertaining to the great question of loyalty to the Dharma versus loyalty to state, family, and Emperor.

Then, with bewildering swiftness and quite unexpectedly,
the Buddhists' exemption from such loyalty was written into
law. Law! Sealed and approved, apparently, by the Emperor
himself. No one could understand it. It could only be the influence of the Empress, people said. Only she could drive him
to such a contrary act. Others dismissed that line of reasoning
as illogical; why would the Empress move to sanction an official policy that strengthened religious autocracy, thereby
causing her husband—and consequently herself—to lose control over such a large portion of the population? And yet, those
who had seen her since the debates and the humiliation of the
Confucian party said that there was a distinctly sly, happy glint
in her eye, despite the clear reduction of her power.

Why, then?

Dee had his own theory. It seemed transparent to him,
and he found it difficult to understand why it was not so to
others. It was very simple: Wu was very plainly enjoying the
setback that had befallen the old, entrenched Confucian system—an ethic that by historical tradition assured that women
would remain in their proper place behind men. And, now, in
this new atmosphere, with her considerable ties to a strengthened Buddhism, she could only become more securely influential. She had lost, but she had really won. It was all very
simple, Dee thought. Of course she was happy. Of course.

He sat at the enormous, ornate desk in the center of his
grand Imperial Palace antechamber, overlooking the exquisite
spring garden. In the solitude of this vast and tranquil room,
Dee filled page after page of his journal with impressions of
the debates and these last several whirlwind days. It was the
afternoon before he was to dine with the Imperial family; the
invitation had finally arrived that morning. He was full of anticipation, and musing on the various stories imparted to him
concerning the eccentricities of the royal family. Surely the tales must be greatly exaggerated, Dee thought, cleaning his
brush and thoughtfully smoothing the bristles. It was human

nature to extend, distort, and embellish. Tonight, he would speak with the Emperor. He would find out the truth.

And of course, he was most interested in meeting the Empress.

🦁 JOURNAL ENTRY SEVEN HOURS HENCE ─────────

I have heard rumors of aberrance, but they cannot touch what I now know to be true. I record what I have seen in the hope that these words I write survive me, and with the clear, certain knowledge that should they be discovered while I still breathe, then that breath would surely be my last.

I have just come from a dinner at the palace. It is an evening I shall not soon forget, the event which marks my introduction to the August Family and the first time that I have had the opportunity to observe at close range the phenomenon that is our Divine Empress Wu Tse-tien, wife of the Son of Heaven. I should mention also that I made the acquaintance, briefly, of the Imperial offspring, who were brought in to meet the "guest of honor" before being removed again by their nursemaids. The Empress has produced no fewer than five princes for the Imperial Father, the oldest of which are a set of very fine twin boys of thirteen years or so who favor the Empress strongly. Though she is a woman of refined and delicate appearance, she seems to have the constitution of an ox, for she is great with child again and in obvious robust health. The children are an indulged, adored flock of little princelings, though I ask myself, in the deepest, most secret part of my mind, if Kaotsung could be the father of all of them. One of the princes, a child of about one year, has a distinctly tawny complexion. But the children were a short-lived distraction, for all too soon, we bade them good night.

It was a small party, attended only by the innermost circle. In addition to the Empress, the Emperor Kaotsung, and the Empress's mother, Madame Yang, there was a certain little wart of a fellow, Historian, Chronicler, and Sycophant Lord Secretary Shu Ching-tsung—who, merely an extension of the brains and tongues of mother and daughter, nodded his approval and chortled with every grotesque antic. And, mentioned here for the sake of historical accuracy, a handful of assorted monks, abbots, and bizarre holy men. These last appear to be part of a no doubt constantly shifting entourage, symbols of the feminine mood, indicators of the particular state of "transcendence" attained that week.

Transcendence or not, it would seem that the Son of Heaven, the Divine Emperor of China, has become incapable of feeding himself without considerable difficultly and mess. How much of this is an act contrived to get the attention of his queen and how much of it is for the purpose of demonstrating to everyone else the sorry state to which he has been reduced, I am not at all certain. The ploy for attention is certainly effective, though I am not sure that the result is always what the Son of Heaven intends, or if he knows what he intends at all. Tonight, I believe the Emperor got the results he desired, for the Empress was responsive indeed.

Although the weather on the day of the dinner had been warm, the Empress stated that she felt chilled that evening and insisted that the eunuch servants light the braziers in the dining hall. Kaotsung, who seems to be always in a state of flush, complained in the tones of a spoiled, self-consumed, sickly child that he was far too warm. His queen informed him that he was mistaken, that it was not at all warm in the dining hall. To demonstrate the extent of his error, she asked the others if they were warm, and they all shook their heads. At this point, the Son of Heaven appeared to resolve to stand up to her. Ignoring the others, he asked her in a demanding tone and with surprising force why she had insisted on lighting the braziers and the brick *kang* heaters.

Now—and I ask that posterity hear me—I witnessed a taste of the Empress's sport: to her Divine Husband's question as to why she had had the fires lit, she declared that she had merely been responding to *his* complaint of a few moments before that he was feeling too cold to enjoy his fine dinner, and looked around herself for corroboration. The others agreed to this order of events with amiable nods and thoughtful grunts. I, being no one but the "brilliant young magistrate from Yangchou," a mere insignificant guest from outside the walls of the Forbidden City, was constrained from saying anything at all.

Our Imperial Father then slapped his one good hand

on the table and insisted that he had never said that he was cold. He was now drooling slightly—from anger, or because he has lost function and can no longer concentrate on two things. Cold? Cold? she responded, jumping up from her seat. The poor dear must be chilled with fever, she cried. Hurry, she ordered the household staff—attend to the heat and cover him with a thick quilt. And the sickness has obviously gone to his mind, because the poor dear cannot even remember ordering the heat. The eunuchs, poor confused creatures, obliged Her Majesty's wishes and began to cover the Imperial afflicted with a quilt. With his one good arm and hand, Kaotsung threw it off and cast it to the floor, where it remained, the eunuchs having backed off submissively at his anger. He now howled (I write "howled" because I can think of no other apt word to describe the sound he made) that he was burning up with the damnable heat that she had caused. She told him that his tone was unbecoming and that it was unfair for him to scold her for trying so hard to oblige him and to assure his comfort. Then he said that he no longer felt warm, but was now chilled. See, she said, turning to the others, the poor dear is in the grip of fever and is totally confused. He goes from hot to cold with the arbitrariness of a pendulum. She rose, put her hand to his forehead, and declared that he was far too warm and must cool off.

But it was what happened next that caused me to question my own objectivity. Did I truly witness it, or was I drunk, or possibly dreaming it? He must cool off, she repeated, and ordered the servants to remove her Imperial Husband's clothing. Kaotsung protested vehemently, throwing the servants into a torment of conflict. Some of the eunuchs simply walked around in circles wringing their pudgy hands and wailing like old women. But Wu was forceful; in fact, the tone of her delivery made the hairs on the back of my neck stand up. If I were a poet, I might say that her voice would cleave the hills asunder and reverse the course of the mighty Yangtze, but since I am not, I will only state that the servants did as they were told. They tugged at the Emperor's clothing, against their own wishes and his. But then I became uncertain of the sincerity of Kaotsung's resistance. He appeared to be struggling valiantly, swatting at them with his good arm like a man flailing at bugs. The others around the table, if they had any reactions or opinions, kept them to themselves, and continued their conversation as if nothing at all untoward were happening in their midst. But I am certain that I detected in Madame Yang's eyes an expression of warm approval for her daughter. And through it all, while Kaotsung struggled, Wu continued to entreat him in tender, kindly tones that the disrobing was for his own good.

In the end the Son of Heaven's clothes lay in a heap on the floor and the man sat perfectly naked at the table. He said nothing more to his Imperial Wife, but proceeded to eat ravenously. The others, having awaited his first divine bites, followed suit. We all began to eat; she, between mouthfuls (she is nothing if not an avid eater, as is her mother; there seems to be nothing dainty about the ladies in any of their appetites), continued to ply him with little entreaties. Do you see how much better you feel now, my beloved? The food will help to flush the fever from you. And so forth, and so on. He simply grunted from time to time; whether these were eating noises or responses to her I could not tell, but he now concentrated solely on his food, and the damaged logic be damned.

The ascetics in the company then began to fill the conversational void, blathering away among themselves with their nonsensical philosophical and speculative chatter, occasionally posing a question, like a sacred offering, to their distinguished patroness, Madame Yang, who had behaved throughout the earlier performance as if what happened tonight was quite in keeping with the royal family's normal activity. I was more than a little bit uncomfortable for the rest of the meal, and found it difficult to eat, but soon the Empress turned her full attention to me and showed a great interest in my career as the "brilliant and outstanding" (her words, not mine) hunter of religious charlatans from Yangchou, and flattered me no end when she was not entreating her husband. Wu Tse-tien, who had taken no notice of my discomfiture of a few moments ago, now went out of her way to make me feel appreciated and at ease. To say that she is a many-sided creature would scarcely do her justice.

I have done my best to faithfully record the events of the evening, but I cannot expect posterity to believe what I put down next as I conclude my tale. But it is what I saw, and so I am obliged to put it on paper with the rest of it.

As the meal wore toward its inevitable conclusion, which seemed as far away to me as the very end of time itself, I thought—no, I am certain—that I saw a clandestine little smile pass between the Emperor and his wife.

I very nearly forgot to mention one thing here, so insignificant does it seem next to the rest of the evening's events: when I finally found an opportunity to take my leave, the Emperor—naked and with his mouth full of food—turned to me and informed me that I was to receive an Imperial appointment. When he told me what it was, I thanked him and retired to my rooms in a state of confusion and incredulity such as I have rarely experienced before.

"Of course, you understand the nature of your appointment," Wu-chi said to Dee, rubbing his upper lip thoughtfully with his forefinger.

"Two appointments," Dee corrected. "There was another one as well." Face to face with the "Old Fool" at last, Dee gazed with awe upon the last surviving member of the late Emperor Taitsung's Council of Six, the man who had escaped the Empress like the animal that streaks from the trap in the moment before the door clangs shut forever. He had told Dee the entire astonishing tale, causing the bizarre royal dinner party of two days before to take on a deepeningly ominous hue in Dee's memory.

"True. But it is the first one that concerns us. You would not have received that appointment if she did not want it for you." The old man looked outside. The gardens of the Pure Lotus Monastery north of the city of Loyang were ablaze with color this fine spring afternoon. A handful of small blue birds squabbled over a bright red patch of berries on a bush. "Your appointment to the presidency of the National Bureau of Sacrifice would not have happened unless she wanted it."

"I assumed that there must be some areas where Kaotsung still holds a remnant of power," Dee replied, but as soon as he said it he knew how absurd it sounded, and he knew that Wu-chi would answer before he even spoke.

"Not unless she gives it to him," the other said flatly. "Surely you did not expect anything else."

"I did not know what to expect."

"Of course not," the old man responded. "But you are coming to know her better, are you not? There was a time when I knew her very well indeed. Very well." His voice trailed off sadly. "Though it has been many years and I no longer have the pleasure of witnessing her ... *determination* firsthand, I know her thoroughness well."

Dee glanced around dubiously. Wu-chi shook his head and smiled.

"There are no spies within these monastic walls. I have been here so long that I know every face and every soul. They are all true, compassionate, and philosophical Buddhists. There are no charlatans here, or criminals taking refuge in this monastery, Dee. Except for me." He laughed quietly. "When I heard that the great Dee was in the city, I knew it was time that we met at last, so I summoned you here using only my Buddhist name. Even Wu's henchmen could know nothing. Your new position as president of the National Bureau of Sacrifice puts you in the unenviable position to receive a thousand petitions from the clerical world, all right under her nose, but I was confident that you would recognize a letter from me."

"Of course," Dee said. "I would have found you myself, in any case. But ... about my appointment. Am I to take it that this was not Kaotsung's doing, and—"

Before Dee could finish the sentence, the old man was speaking in a strong, steady voice, heedless of the open window shutters and the monks walking, gardening, or meditating nearby. His eyes followed the timid dash of a ground squirrel across the open courtyard.

"I know from bitter experience that Wu is the hand that guides the Emperor's every move. She is the puppetmaster and he is the puppet. Even though you, the brilliant young Confucian scholar-magistrate, represent the opposition—the old Confucian power bloc, which has always been set against her—she is charmed by you. That is the only explanation. Tell me—did you not sense the Empress's ... *pleasure* in your presence?" He moved his gaze from the window to Dee.

Dee vividly recalled the Empress's attentive gaze upon him, her eyes deep and unblinking, a vortex into which the unwary could easily stumble, and felt an odd rush—of danger, excitement, confusion. The look on his face, and his silence, must have told Wu-chi everything.

The old man's attention drifted back to the scene outside the window. "I thought so," he said simply. "For whatever reason, she was intrigued by the brilliant magistrate from Yangchou, the man who can uncover a hundred mysteries. On the face of things, it seems most odd," he added, his eyes following two monks engaged in a lively debate as they strolled unwittingly by the tiny squirrel hidden motionless in the root of a great tree. He turned around and smiled at Dee now. "It is very simple, my friend. She *fancies* you." He paused. "Who knows? She may even wish to *bed* you. The point is," he said, seeing Magistrate Dee visibly shudder, "that it could be something as simple as that, or something else known only to her own convoluted reasoning. We can put nothing, nothing at all, past her."

"I do not understand her," Dee responded, shaking his head. "She is a cipher."

"Understanding her will not become easier, I can assure you. If you think that your Wu is confusing now, then consider this. I had waited to tell you. There was a vacancy left by the death of the former president of the National Bureau of Sacrifice, as I am sure you knew."

"Of course. I was appointed to fill that opening."

"But do you know precisely how that vacancy came to be, precisely the circumstance of the former president's death?" the old man asked in a way that caused Dee a ripple of unease.

"The late president of the National Bureau of Sacrifice was an eminently corrupt man," Dee offered tentatively. "I had an encounter with him at a party in Yangchou some time ago. An insipid, odious figure of a man. He was tied into the clandestine activities of Yangchou's Buddhist gangs. And to add to it all, he was a nervous, anxious, ill-at-ease little fellow."

"Yes. All of that is true, Magistrate Dee. But—"

"I was told he hanged himself shortly after my investigations closed in."

"Ahhh . . . Most logical! A very simple explanation! And most credible, too!" The old man threw his hands up delightedly, thoroughly enjoying his game of revelation. "But don't you see, that is precisely what Wu would want you to think," he declared, suddenly becoming serious. "I still have my sources on the inside, Dee, even though much has changed since I was at the palace, and my connections grow more tenuous with each passing year. But I *am* still in touch. The Council of Six still exists as long as I am alive."

Dee nodded distractedly, thinking of the round, unctuous little president, feeling almost sorry for him.

"Her deputies have long since given up the search for me, probably assuming that I am dead. Gone for worm's meat as the others. But I am alive to tell you that when the Empress Wu learned that the great Magistrate Dee Jen-chieh was coming to Loyang for her infamous Pai Debates, she wanted to make a place for him." Wu-chi's gaze fixed on Dee. "Why? We don't know. But obviously, she wanted to inspect you first face to face. Tell me this—exactly when during your evening with the royal family did you learn of your appointment?"

"It was very nearly the last thing said to me after many hours of strangeness."

"Exactly as I thought," Wu-chi said. "At some point in the evening, after she had looked you over, she gave her wordless permission to the Emperor to bestow your appointment on you." He shrugged. "Maybe she liked your eyes."

The old man's expression remained flat and unchanged, telling Dee that he was completely serious. "She is very good at that. She can remove one person and replace him with another with no more difficulty, no more conscience, than a decorator exchanging one vase for another on a rosewood stand. She forced President Fu Yu-i to take his own life because he was no longer useful to her."

"And *I* am?"

"The Goddess works in mysterious ways. Why she should want the assiduous magistrate, the Buddhist hunter from Yangchou, to serve as president of the National Bureau of Sacrifice—or what is left of that body since the clerical victory—is beyond me," Wu-chi said, pausing to follow the little squirrel's furtive dash across the open courtyard to the relative safety of the next tree. "But obviously, her interest is piqued. So it is not ours to fathom her, only to follow as best we can her tortuous trail. And you are now an enviable part of that trail, Magistrate Dee. Now you wear *two* hats," Wu-chi offered. "You are not only president of the National Bureau of Sacrifice, but you are chief civil judge of the Loyang Capital District. That is, of course, *if* you decide to accept the latter position. And I beg you to make your decision only after judicious consideration. Because in that capacity, you will find our fine city a very different place from Yangchou. Far different." He smiled wistfully. "You have a new mistress now. All I can tell you is to court her with great care."

15

A.D. 667, early summer

"You see how these people follow me!" The tall, lanky foreigner's black eyes appeared to be leveled at Dee's when he spoke these words, as if he were addressing him directly. Dee, standing well to the back of the market crowd, knew that it was unlikely that the man had picked him out particularly. Part of a street performer's skill, he knew, was to make each person watching feel that the show was just for him.

"They follow me and flock around me like so many foolish chickens, like lambs following their mother's teat!" With that, the stranger's eyes lingered on Dee's for another fraction of a moment and moved on. They swept the crowds that jammed around him, fixing no one and everyone with a penetrating intensity.

"Like hungry jackals who have caught the scent of carrion on the wind!" he shouted. People stepped back, giggled and chattered. He had them, Dee could see. They were his. He stirred just the right mixture of intrigue and repulsion, scaring them just enough to excite them—but he had no intention of driving them away. The foreigner waved his long arms above his head, the sleeves of his colorful robes riding up to his lanky elbows.

"And if I were to take you by the hand and lead you to that canal there, and tell you to jump in, would you do it? Hm?" A murmur of denial rose from some of the braver ones in the crowd. "No," he said sadly. "I believe that you would. And if I were to lead you to the greatest cave carvings of Lungmen and stand you on the head of Her Majesty's highest Buddha and tell you to jump, I believe that you would!"

When he spoke again, his voice was as loud as a trumpeting elephant's. "FOOLS!" he bellowed. "I don't *believe* that you would! I *know* that you would! But if that were not so, then what place would there be in this world for men like me?"

This one was quite the performer, Dee thought. Hardly the usual street trickster. He had never seen such power over a crowd, nor such an unmitigated display of audacity.

"Move away now." The people pushed backward into one another. "But *you*, boy, stay there . . . right where you are." The foreigner lowered his voice again as his eyes fixed on a shabbily dressed young peasant who stood a few paces back. The young man was transfixed. The crowd around him receded, but he stayed where he was, suddenly alone.

"We know each other, don't we?" the foreigner said, squinting now, looking appraisingly into the young man's eyes and nodding thoughtfully. "Yes. Yes, we know each other well. I am certain. And I can see that you know it as well as I do. Not that we have ever been introduced! No. Nothing so shallow as that. Ours is an ancient knowledge. *We* know each other," he said, his arm moving forward sinuously toward the youth's smiling, frightened face, "the way the mongoose knows the cobra!"

The foreigner's hand, graceful as a temple dancer's, moved in the air in front of the peasant's eyes. "With each good thought," he said, modulating his voice to a low dramatic whisper, "a flower will burst from the paving stones." His black eyes flashed with wicked humor as a gaudily colored paper flower crackled open between the young peasant's sandals. The glazed youth looked down at his feet and jumped back in shock.

"But in the same measure, and by the converse laws of the universe," the tall one intoned, "a swarm of foul, filthy, lice-infested rats will scamper across your bare feet should your thoughts be *evil*." The magician savored his final word as if it were a delectable morsel. With real dread on his face, the young peasant shot a quick look toward his feet, but this time, nothing happened.

"Such is the manifest power of thought," the magician continued. "And . . . " His eyes brightened, as though a lantern shining out through his eyes had just been turned up, projecting a peculiar light. "Sometimes, if we know how to tap those rivers that flow through the invisible universe, to tap the unseen well, then the hidden worlds will reward us with the most unexpected and fantastic displays!"

As the foreigner continued with his performance, the crowd grew. People stopped what they were doing to elbow and push their way into the throngs, which slowly began to close around the magician again. Those in the back rows stood on their toes and craned their necks to get a look at this strange wizard.

Definitely not Chinese, Dee surmised. A street magician and soothsayer from the far west, he heard people say, creating this spectacle for them today in the tiny avenue park. And although it cost them nothing to watch, the price was one copper coin per person to have the magician look into your future: one thin copper coin to peer forward into the tedious gray forward trek of each little life.

"Stand back . . . stand back, please," he implored. "I must breathe. You are drawing the vital essences out of the air with your crowding. And I must concentrate. It is most difficult!" The wizard was very tall and thin and would have been gangly but for a certain powerful grace. His face was angular and handsome, the skin dark and coppery, Dee noted, like that of other western foreigners he had seen. But it was his eyes with their odd light that drew the people to him and held them fixed.

It was the magician's eyes and the way they delivered his pronouncements that held Dee, too. At this moment, Dee would have allowed this man to say or do almost anything. He would have exerted his authority to keep the constabulary from interfering in any way, just so that he could see what the man might do next.

"I must concentrate on the young gentleman who has come before me," the magician said, and swept a hand in an imperious and impatient gesture over the crowd. "And from each of you, I must have absolute quiet in order to *hear* and to *see* into the years that stretch ahead. Not a whisper now. Not a breath . . . please . . . "

The crowd focused its silent attention on the spectacle of the tall, colorfully cloaked man hovering over his short and raggedly dressed subject. The magician seemed to grow. It was like watching a magnificently decorated garden spider closing in on a common housefly. The magician bent down and began to whisper in the man's ear. From where he stood, Dee could see the subject's eyes go from narrow anxious slits of incomprehension to widened astonishment.

Today Dee walked the streets of Loyang as he had walked them in Yanchou—as its chief civil magistrate, but wearing ordinary street clothing and not his official robes of office. And although he was also president of the much emasculated National Bureau of Sacrifice, he nevertheless thought of himself only in his capacity as a civil judge. He had decided, after some agonizing, to accept the latter position and remain in Loyang for a time—a year, perhaps two, perhaps three. The opportunity to live and work in the capital, so close to the workings of government and the great beating heart of the Empire, was not one he could turn down—especially with such a creature as the Empress Wu in ascendance.

As for his other position, the only prerogative left to the government and therefore to the president of the National Bureau of Sacrifice was the right to oversee the laws regarding the ordination of monks and priests, and still, on rare occasions, the ability to defrock the abusive ones. This morning, as civil magistrate, Dee had to preside over a relatively simple squabble concerning warehouse boundaries, but it could wait. At the moment, Dee was far more fascinated by this most engaging fellow before him.

Now the air filled with a thundering and beating and a flash of white; feathers . . . wings . . . *birds*! And then, astonishingly, unbelievably, the magician was gone!

People scrambled in panic, stumbling over each other in an effort to escape whatever was happening. Dee stayed where he was and watched; from where he stood it seemed at first that the street magician himself had simply burst into a fluttering, sunlit, air-beating flurry of white. Dee scanned the crowd. Most of the people were still pushing and shoving their way out of the melee. But then Dee found him. Or he was almost certain that he had. But the clothes were different! He was sure, though; it *was* the magician, unmistakably! How had he changed clothes in the blink of an eye?

Then Dee understood. Under cover of the distraction, while everyone was engaged by the birds, the man had simply stepped aside and adroitly turned his jacket inside out, revealing a different pattern and color. Now he was stooped over, and the transformation was complete. He looked like a confused old man, anxious to get away from the epicenter of confusion.

And the birds? At least a hundred snow-white doves were fluttering all at once over the spot where the magician had been standing.

But how . . . ? Dee began to ask himself, when a final few doves flew in, flapping their way toward the others. Dee looked in the direction they had come from, and understood. It was simple and unimaginably complex at the same time.

Hidden among the shrubs and rocks of the grassy knoll where the magician had set up his "performance" was a series of well-camouflaged traplike boxes. How the magician tripped the boxes from where he had been standing was another question, but Dee had no doubt that there was a rational explanation.

It was ingenious. The magician's illusion was solely dependent upon the predictable reactions of the crowd, the unswerving tendency of people to see only what they expect to see. And the magician's ability to trap their attentions elsewhere for the briefest interval. Brilliant. Positively brilliant. Dee rubbed his chin. The simplest things always were!

The mysterious white flock was dispersing now, flying off to roost in the treetops and the eaves of nearby buildings. Cautiously, the crowd began to reassemble, chattering and pointing at the miraculous doves from paradise, the remnants of the great wizard who had turned himself into a flock of birds.

"BEHOLD! BEHOLD!" a voice boomed out then, causing all heads to turn. A tall, thin figure stood atop the roof of a two-story building. The crowd gasped. "Behold, my poor deceived friends, this unworthy charlatan who stands in your midst!" the magician called. His arms were spread wide, his fists clenched, his jacket turned inside out to once again display the colorful patterns he had been wearing when he vanished. The people gaped as he walked to the edge of the roof and opened one fist, dropping a palmful of tarnished copper coins to the ground.

"I do not have the heart to keep money that I have tricked from your hands and taken away from the hungry stomachs of your children. You have been deceived! I am certain that it is not the first time. Nor will it be the last! But gather up your coins, now! There are fourteen coins, and fourteen faces that belong to them. And I know each face," he warned them. "Come forward! These belong rightfully to you!" He gazed down from his lofty perch. "But in principle, they belong to the man who is clever enough to relieve you of them. And rightly so," he declared. "Let this be a lesson. Pick up your coins and go!" But the people hung back, reluctant to be fooled again, eyeing the coins as if they might burn them or bite their hands.

Dee sat on the grassy knoll and nodded his head in satisfaction. Not all thieves are so unsubtle as to merely knock you over the head and steal your purse, he thought.

* * *

An hour later Dee sat in a small tea garden with the magician, his afternoon appointments forgotten. After the performance was over and the crowd had dispersed, Dee had been crossing a street when he came upon the magician crossing in the opposite direction. Inspired, Dee had approached him, congratulated him on his performance, and introduced himself. The man had been pleasantly surprised and suggested that they share a pot of tea.

Whatever insight he might gain into this unique man was surely worth rearranging his schedule. Dee watched the handsome, animated face.

"There was a time," the tall foreigner was saying, leaning toward Dee and looking around the tiny tea garden before continuing, "when the office of the president of the National Bureau of Sacrifice actually amounted to something, hm? Long before that position was bestowed upon you. And long before President Fu-Yu-i and his gang of pigs corrupted that office—corrupted it beyond recognition. You know, Magistrate, that I was in the hall throughout the Pai Debates, and I followed every word of your brilliant memorial. I, better than anyone, though I am technically a member of the opposing party, appreciated and understood your references to the criminals within the church. I know also of your work in Yangchou, Magistrate, and how you traced their filthy droppings—guised in the sacred name of the Buddha—right to the doorstep of the president of the National Bureau of Sacrifice."

"And beyond. I am most flattered that you would follow my meager work," Dee said, contemplating the tall stranger's features, especially the eyes. Talking to him was a little like walking vertiginously close to a precipice.

It was interesting to study the magician up close after watching him perform from a distance. The dark woody architecture of his face belied the obvious youth and loose, limber strength of his limbs. Deep lines ran from his nose to the corners of his mouth, and more lines radiated from the edges of his eyes. Dee decided he could be anywhere from twenty-five to forty years of age. The face was mobile, to say the least, like the long graceful fingers that flicked and danced along the rough tabletop as he talked. Dee thought that but for his distinctive height, this magician could disguise himself merely by changing his expression if he so chose—never mind turning his coat inside out.

The man did not smell unclean, like a street beggar, but

he did not smell like someone who lived in a fine house and washed with pea soap every day, either. Probably he took shelter in various temples around the city. Dee noted that he ate and drank with a most unascetic gusto.

As they spoke, Dee studied the different visages the man presented, and wondered which was the true one. The magician had told Dee that aside from being what he termed a "passable" street magician, he was also a master craftsman, a designer of temples and gardens, and a master of another sort of illusion—he was a purveyor, he said, of rare cosmetics. He alone, he declared, could obtain exotic lotions and creams that would truly remove all signs of age from a lady's face, and reverse time for her so that she would grow younger with every passing year. It was a good practice, he declared; once he was through a client's gates for the purpose of designing a garden or a pavilion, he was free to appeal to the true power in the household-the vanities of the master's women. "I promise, like the Taoist with his elixirs, to keep them young. The difference is that I can deliver," he said with confidence, thrumming his long, narrow fingers on the rough tea garden tabletop.

But he was, first and foremost, he told Dee, a Buddhist monk, a disciple of a highly esoteric Tantric Tibetan order, and at this stage in his spiritual journey he was required to go forth into the world to seek out and counter the damage done by false prophets of the sacred word. "You and I are doing the same work," he said to Dee. "It is just that I approach it from the west, so to speak, while you approach it from the east." Dee was more than a little bit intrigued. Although everything the magician said had a cryptic quality, Dee could detect no deception.

"If the truth be known," said this Tibetan, who went by the Chinese name Hsueh Huai-i, "I journeyed to this city because of the Pai Debates, and more specifically, to hear the great Dee Jen-chieh. You do yourself a great disservice, Magistrate, hm? Your work is hardly meager. As for those who exploit the weakness and superstitions of the gullible, I can only wish them great unpleasantries in the next incarnation." He squinted, his chin resting in his hand, his long fingers now thrumming against the side of his cheek. "It is sad as well as evil, hm?" This time his odd little interpolation seemed gloomy and questioning.

"I agree, my friend." Dee poured the monk a bowl of hot green tea and then poured himself another.

Hsueh Huai-i sipped his tea and leaned languidly back against the wall, cooing softly to himself as if in agreement with some inner voice, his long arms folded behind his head. Dee could not help thinking of the soft little noises made by doves, and imagined the magician speaking to the birds in their own language, commanding them to fly out of their boxes. The monk rolled his eyes upward toward the rough-hewn beams of the little open-air teashop's ceiling. "This, Magistrate, is how the ceiling of a monastery should look."

"Meaning . . . ?" Dee asked, looking up.

"Simple. Primitive. Without gilded vestiges of earthly wealth. This wealth and power is an earthly deceit, a delusion, a lie, a contradiction to the principles of the true Buddhist faith, and an abomination. Where is the logic?"

"Where, indeed!" Dee responded. The conversation and the man in front of him were both growing ever more interesting. Had the magician not taught the peasants a lesson in superstition and charlatanism today at the same time that he had earned his meager pay? And he *had* earned it. Some of the people had refused to retrieve their coins, and so he had kept them. But a performance like that was worth a great deal.

"And such wealth of monasteries, these gleaming gems, gold, icons, and the like, far from being a metaphor for truth or a reflection of higher realms, only confuse and blind the poor and ignorant."

"And the not so poor and ignorant," Dee began, musing in an ironic tone, but Hsueh did not let him finish.

"I know, Magistrate. It is not just among the peasants that we find the weak and gullible. They come from all social classes, hm?"

"That is certainly true," Dee said, eyeing this perceptive stranger before him. "And all of them clinging to a religion of superstition, a host of gods and goddesses and evil spirits and demons all demanding to be appeased or which must be exorcised."

"Hm. A dreadfully naive and foolish view of the ineffable . . . but the only one that their minds can comprehend," the Tibetan replied, straightening up from his reclining position and laying his hands flat on the table.

Admirably put, Dee thought. "A physician of the soul

might say that the vessels of the chakras were clogged in the ignorant," Dee offered.

"Hmmmm! A crude but useful metaphor, Magistrate. If it helps to visualize it that way . . ." He smiled and settled back again into his relaxed posture, long arms folded behind his head. "The ultimate sin is to manipulate the faith of the naive for gain. There is no room for earthly wealth or advantage over one's fellow creature. *Corrupt* clergy . . . *wealthy* monasteries . . ." His hand shot out and slapped the table indignantly, rattling the tea bowls. " . . . are as incongruous, as unnatural as, say, hm . . . a *flying pig*!

"Master Dee, I will get to the point," the monk said then. "The performance this afternoon was for your benefit. My calling card, if you will. I did not wish to be just another admirer coming forth with praise and adulation, hm? I wanted to gain your attention first. To give you a little, shall we say, *gift*."

Dee shifted his position on the hard bench so that he could take advantage of a warm corner of lingering sun. It was late in the day, and most of the people around them had gone. He thought about this afternoon, and the possibility that the foreigner had set up his performance in Dee's path so that Dee would not be able to avoid seeing it. Was it possible? Or was the man extemporizing because he had Magistrate Dee sitting before him? There was no way to know. Dee smiled. The lecture on gullibility delivered from the rooftop—had *that* been for Dee's benefit?

"Well, Master Hsueh, I am most appreciative," Dee said. "And you *have* my attention."

The monk smiled.

"I have been in the city only a few weeks," he said, "but already I know of at least three unscrupulous abbots. One is promulgating a false sutra and profiting by it. Another is operating a sanctuary for thieves, purchasing them from punitive work gangs and sending them forth in their ascetic garb to pick pockets and commit other petty thefts. The third is presiding over a nunnery that is in reality a brothel. He has convinced his young female recruits that they are performing some sort of sacrament with his wealthy customers. Of course, all the profits go to him. And there are others. Many others." He heaved a great sigh and shook his head. "And with the recent outcome of the Pai Debates, we can be sure there will be a great increase in abusers. The unprincipled will come scuttling forth like cockroaches!"

"Now you truly have my attention, Master Hsueh," Dee said, leaning forward intently. The monk leaned forward as well.

"Think, Master Dee," he said, "of what you and I could accomplish if we put our abilities and resources together. We are on the same mission. I, the monk and magician, and you, the tireless investigator and president of the Bureau of Sacrifice and the chief civil magistrate of Loyang! Your work in Yang-chou was brilliant. Your work in Loyang will be three times as brilliant. The credit will all go to you, though I know it is immaterial to you. My satisfaction will lie solely in accomplishing my spiritual quest." The strange light in the monk's eyes was burning just a bit brighter as he spoke. He hesitated then. "You are planning on remaining in the city for a time, are you not?"

"I am," Dee answered. "For a time, at least. And since the time is indefinite, my family wish to remain in Yangchou." He sat, considering the man's extraordinary proposition. "It will be lonely for me."

"Well, you have a friend now, hm?" the monk said affably. "And a partner and colleague, if you wish." He smiled and lowered his voice conspiratorially. "A spy."

Dee regarded the tall Tibetan.

"Master Hsueh," Dee said decisively, rising from his chair, "it is growing late. Would you do me the honor of taking your evening meal with me? We have much to talk about." The magician stood, unfolding his great length.

"Of course, Master Dee. I am honored."

A.D. 668

After almost a year of separation from his family, Dee missed them when his mind was not directly occupied with his work. But since he was working virtually every moment of the day, he did not have a great deal of time in which to miss them. It was only when he was drifting off to sleep late at night in his plain but comfortable quarters in a guest house in the heart of the city that he indulged in thoughts of his wives, the little daughter he had purchased from the Indian, and even his sons, whom he had not seen for four years now since they had gone west to their military service. He kept in touch with his wives through long, detailed letters. The girl child, almost five years old now, kept them happy and occupied; occasionally he entertained the suspicion that they were quite content without his presence.

But it was just as well that they were far away in Yangchou, for they would never have approved of the amount of time he now devoted to work, and nothing but work. Master Hsueh had been quite right. In the year since the Pai Debates, clerical abuses had proliferated like mushrooms after a heavy rain. They ranged from the petty and minor to the elaborate and masterful, from the marginally profitable to the hugely lucrative. At least a dozen abbots, both longtime criminals and newcomers and scores of their minions, had been defrocked and their monasteries shut down. Hsueh had been right about all of them.

And Hsueh Huai-i had been right, too, about the effectiveness of a partnership between himself and Dee. Hsueh moved with sinuous ease through the society of monasteries and clerics, infiltrating, befriending, and gathering information, with a magician's flair for the covert and devious that incited Dee's admiration. Dee's arrests and trials moved forward with speed and efficiency. No sooner had one corrupt abbot or false holy man been sentenced than Hsueh was onto another case like a hound after a hare. His delight in "purifying" the faith perfectly matched Dee's satisfaction in ridding society of corruption.

Dee found him to be a most satisfactory associate as well—a good friend, but one who respected his privacy, and an excellent intellectual companion. They had many lively late-night debates and arguments. Hsueh wanted to learn as much as he could about civil law, history, and the workings of government. From Hsueh, Dee learned fascinating details about various esoteric sects of Buddhism in the high mountains to the west, and came to have a much better grasp of the tenets and practice of pure Buddhist thought and philosophy in their uncorrupted and unexploited forms.

Dee had not been invited back to the palace, but he did receive several commendations from the Empress for his "distinguished work" in which she declared him a true friend of the faith, a warrior for truth, and so forth. Hsueh was particularly scathing over these missives, saying that she was probably the worst religious offender of them all. There are some utterly fantastic rumors leaking out from behind the walls of the Forbidden City, Hsueh said. According to what I have heard, the woman is carrying on with various "holy men" right under the nose of the poor ruined Kaotsung, appeasing her spiritual and carnal appetites in one efficient stroke. Or should I say many efficient strokes, he had added wryly.

Hsueh had looked very serious then, and declared that *there* was a nest of vermin and maggots he would like to clean out—the false holy men who had made their way to the Imperial inner sanctum where their poisonous juices could ooze down over the rest of society, fouling the pure faith for everyone.

And Dee had said to Hsueh that they had much work to do and should not frustrate themselves with unobtainable goals. Besides, he had said, teasing Hsueh a little, aren't you becoming just a bit *attached* to your war against the charlatans? Was it not you who said that life itself is the ultimate illusion, that the dung on the boot and the pearl in the hand are all the same thing? And Hsueh had smiled, and said that that was certainly so; but did Dee know that there was a special category of enlightened beings who made a conscious choice to step into the midst of evil, put it on like an overcoat, and neutralize it from within? And if they failed, if the evil overcame them, that there was a special place in hell reserved just for them?

Dee and Hsueh had many such stimulating and thought provoking conversations. Between the Tibetan and Wu-chi in his sanctuary north of the city, Dee was able to keep loneliness at bay. He visited Wu-chi and the good abbot Master Liao as often as he could, adhering strictly to the vow of secrecy, not even telling Master Hsueh who he was seeing, though he often wished to. Perhaps eventually, he told himself.

His trips to the Pure Lotus were always rejuvenating. While he was there, his nerves and his restive thoughts seemed to slow for a time, to release their hold on him. He had his own special quarters there, ready for him anytime he cared to escape for a day or two. He enjoyed observing the unique friendship that had grown between Abbot Liao and Wu-chi. The old councillor indulged in a mild testiness and petulance with his friend, who tolerated it with infinite patience and good humor, always willing to do one more thing to assure the old man's comfort and well-being. They were like an old married couple, Dee thought, who thoroughly knew each other's ways and were secure in their little personal arrangements and exchanges.

Dee was grateful to the good abbot and to Master Hsueh for demonstrating to him the principles of pure and uncorrupted faith. It was now much more than a mere abstract concept, and it gave new purpose to his work.

In the meantime, evidence of the Empress's own good works were everywhere, too. She instituted programs to feed the poor, she funded a dozen new orphanages, and she had declared a tax amnesty for the needy throughout the Empire. People loved her. Dee thought a lot about these good works of hers, about the bizarre rumors Hsueh had heard, what Wuchi had told him, and what he himself had seen with his own eyes, and pondered often the enigma who was the wife of the Son of Heaven.

What was she, really?

16

A.D. 668, early winter
Loyang

"Relatives are a bore," Madame Yang said. "One does not choose them, and yet one is saddled with them. They are baggage—unfortunate happenstances of birth." She reclined on a day couch in her garden pavilion, one hand stroking the chin of the great Himalayan cat lolling in her lap.

It was unseasonably warm and sunny this day, though autumn was well past, so Wu and her mother were taking their afternoon repast outside in the small garden pavilion.

Her mother was right. Relatives must be watched, managed, scrutinized at all times. At the moment, Wu was bothered by that unique class of close but discardable relatives: two nephews and a niece.

"Indeed," Madame Yang said, briskly scratching behind the cat's ear so that the animal rolled its head around ecstatically. "History is full of these events. Someday we must have our eager Historian Shu chronicle the cases for us."

"He would need access to an enormous staff, Mother," Wu said idly, without looking up from her foraging among the delicacies on the table.

"So many stories of greedy, useless, dangerous relatives, who, simply for want of their own clear destinies, interfere with others'."

"Unforgivable!" Wu said, her words muffled by a pickled lichee nut. "Inexcusable!"

"Has there been any improvement?" Madame Yang asked pointedly, abruptly brushing the cat off her lap as she sat up.

"None that I can see," Wu replied. "Though the Nagaspa, of course, claims otherwise. But I cannot see that he has exorcised the ghost of my unfortunate deceased half sister, the Duchess. If anything, her presence grows stronger." Pensively, she speared another piece of fruit. "Niece Ho-lan resembles her mother more every day."

"Of course she does," Madame Yang said. "At fifteen she is coming into her own. A young girl inheriting her mother's womanhood."

"No, Mother. It is more than that. Ho-lan's resemblance to my half sister is not limited to mere family resemblance."

"No, it is not," Madame Yang agreed. "And I am pleased that you can see that. You have inherited that perspicacity from me." She teased the displaced cat with a small strip of dried fish. The cat stood up on its hind legs as she lifted the fish in front of it. Then she moved the morsel just beyond the animal's reach, causing it to walk forward on two legs, its front paws tucked away like little flippers. It was a trick of which Madame Yang was especially proud. It never failed to make Wu laugh. It pleased Madame Yang to make her daughter laugh; the child was altogether too serious and sullen at times. She teased the cat forward with the fish.

Wu laughed now; she had seldom seen the cat stay up that long. Yang began to laugh, too. The animal's earnest striving and its unnatural stance were too absurd. Madame Yang lowered the fish tantalizingly, then jerked it away again at the last moment, making the cat lurch like a drunk. They laughed harder, until Madame Yang relented.

"I cannot stand to see my darling suffer anymore," she declared, and dropped the fish to the ground. Instantly back on all fours, the cat seized the fish in its jaws and hurried away. "Relatives are much like that. Greedy little performers, begging for what we hold out to them, and wanting more. But they are not nearly so cute or entertaining." She bent down and looked under the table, where the cat was grooming itself after its

feast. "Are they, kitty? No, they are not," she said in the solicitous little voice she used only with the animal. She straightened up then and looked at her daughter seriously.

"Your father has told me that we would see your half
sister's soul begin to consume her daughter's. By gradual degrees, he said, your niece Ho-lan would *become* her dead
mother." As she spoke, Madame Yang saw her daughter's eyes
darken a shade, like a curtain being pulled across a window,
as they did when certain subjects—such as the deceased Duchess—were brought up. "And that *is* what is happening," she
added.

"That would explain many things," Wu said after a short
pause.

Wu, with a sort of prescient vision, had seen something
in the way Kaotsung looked at the visiting niece, though she
was certain that Kaotsung himself was as yet unaware of the
girl's subtle effect on him. She often saw things before he did.

There was an ingenuous sweetness about the girl, and a
quality of playful intelligence that particularly grated on Wu's
sensibilities. It was all part of the growing resemblance. Ho-
lan was blossoming. A splendid flower, when a weed would
have done just as well. Wu was growing weary of the Nagaspa's spells and incantations, which were obviously useless in
this situation. She put a candied plum in her mouth and
chewed the gummy, too-sweet confection. Nieces were bother
enough in their own particular female way, but what of nephews?

Relatives!

They arrived from the far west, from Szechuan Province.
They had sent a letter to the Imperial Father, but Kaotsung had
never read it because Wu had intercepted it, and had consulted
her mother and Councillor Shu. Together, they had helped her
to draft her reply. After all, this was a family matter and the
two nephews were not part of Kaotsung's family.

They were nineteen and twenty-three, and related to Wu
through her father's first wife. They were really only half nephews, just as Ho-lan was only a half niece. But they were still
relatives, and an annoying reminder of father Wu's other life
before he married Madame Yang. The Empress and her mother
resembled each other strongly, and there was something they
particularly had in common: each resented the fact that the
universe contained things that were outside of her control.

These two upstart nephews were not only reminders of that other life of her husband's—they were inconvenient.

"Relatives are baggage heaped onto an already overloaded wagon," Madame Yang remarked one afternoon shortly after the nephews had arrived. "And distant relatives," she added pointedly, "are a far more excessive burden. It is not even *their* wagon."

"But Mother," Wu said, "might they not be blessings in disguise?"

Madame Yang considered this before answering. "They might be," she agreed. "Just possibly."

The young men ostensibly came to pay homage before the altar of their late aunt, the Duchess Ssu-lin. And although they had been in mourning since her death had been announced a few years before, they had not been able to make the long journey to the capital and the Forbidden City until now.

The nephews were welcomed with gracious extravagance. They were given lavish apartments in Wu's newly expanded west wing of the palace, in the Hall of Buddha's Earthly Mercy. And although Wu made every effort to treat them like long-lost princes—a treatment to which they clearly were not entitled—they were brash and arrogant and disdainful. Though they were formally respectful before Wu, never violating protocol or decorum, it was obvious that they did not approve of her.

Madame Yang, after meeting them but once, had said that she read open contempt for her in their eyes. Wu said that she did not see anything quite that extreme; what she did see, though she kept it to herself so as not to upset her mother, was that they perceived Madame Yang as meddlesome and unnecessary.

The older of the two, at twenty-three, was homely and squat—much like Historian-Councillor Shu but without his charm. With bulging eyes, a flattened fishlike nose, and a pasty ill-complected face, he was unpleasant. And with his lubricious manner of speaking, he became quickly obnoxious. But the younger at nineteen was slender, medium tall and straight, square-faced and almost handsome. It was the ugly one who had more contemptuous eyes, though Wu thought the handsome one was probably the more dangerous of the two.

This younger one had an annoying way of lifting his eyebrows one at a time while listening to someone speak, a habit, Wu declared, that revealed that he distrusted everybody. An insult, pure and simple, the two women agreed.

It seemed to them that these young relatives had come to court for no other purpose than to nose about—to find out what they could about the Duchess. And what was there to learn? Wu said to her mother. After all, people do simply die sometimes. Why should they want to question this? The altogether unpleasant, uncomfortable atmosphere of suspicion they had created was unforgivable and entirely unnecessary. Innuendo and rivalry had been brought into Wu's peaceful domain. It needed to be stopped before it got out of hand.

It was then that Madame Yang announced that she wished to bring the family together for an extravagant dinner.

The party was to be at Madame Yang's estate in the city— a change from the isolation of the palace, and closer to the Duchess's burial shrine. An ensemble orchestra of highly selected Imperial musicians would play as the four dined, in honor of the nephews' long journey to the capital. The Emperor, they agreed, was to be left at the palace. His condition made him bothersome and put a strain on Wu's nerves.

Kaotsung did not realize that the fingers of his good hand were in his mouth, stretching it open to an unnatural width so that spit rolled down his chin. He was not aware of that, either; it was not until he chomped down hard at the words contained in Wu's proclamation in a small unrolled parchment that rested on his knees that he became conscious of the whereabouts of his fingers at all. He yelped and yanked his hand from his mouth, tasting blood.

He caressed the excruciatingly painful finger between his lips. You are becoming one of those foolish old men who dodder about injuring themselves. Oh poor, feeble old Kaotsung, they will say. Where is he? What is he doing? He is biting his fingers. Sitting and biting his fingers, and wetting his trousers, and the old fool doesn't even know it.

He squeezed his throbbing finger hard between his lips and read for the second time the words that had already appeared in a public proclamation and Imperial decree and in the gazettes throughout the capital of Loyang.

December 668

It is with Considerable Regret that the Reign of Buddha's Mercy must be reduced to the Reign of the Angry

Buddha's Revenge. The Divine Empress Wu Tse-tien announces this with Great Sadness, having Delivered for Execution two relatives of the Realm—nephews of the Royal House of Wu once removed—for the Slow Poisoning of the Duchess Ssu-lin, beloved half sister of the Empress, and for the Insidious Murder, by a similar and subtle administration of poisons, of the Duchess's daughter, the Beautiful and Innocent Ho-lan, who had not Yet Seen her sixteenth year.

The motives for the two murders are not Fully Understood at this time, nor is it known whether the nephews were Working in Alliance with Others outside the Imperial Family. Addressing itself to These Questions, the Empress's Yulin Palace Guard Secret Police Investigators will conduct an Inquiry. But as the Duchess was without any Issue other than her Daughter, and as there were no Male Heirs to her Fortune, it is believed that the nephews sought through Deceit and Cruelly Calculated Murder to promote themselves in the line of Inheritant Succession.

We mourn the death of niece Ho-lan, taken in a Moment of Joy at the home of the beloved Imperial Matriarch Madame Yang. But we have Reason to Rejoice, as the sight of a miraculous Snow-White Goose was seen Ascending into the Blue Winter Sky from the Pavilion Eaves at the Moment of the Departure of Ho-lan's Soul. This is a Clear Sign from Heaven that her Soul has Traveled to the Buddha's Pure Land of Bliss.

Dee finished reading and lowered the paper. He looked at Hsueh, who had been listening attentively.

"What does this smell like?" Dee asked the monk. Hsueh pursed his lips pensively.

"It does not smell like peach blossoms," he remarked.

"Indeed, it does not," Dee agreed. "I am most interested to learn more about the death of the Duchess Ssu-lin."

"It was several years ago."

"Years mean nothing to the wrongfully dead, my friend. This is something I know from experience."

"Hm," Hsueh grunted in assent. "There was another death, you know, that did not smell at all right. Not long before you arrived in the 'City of Transformation.' A young one as well. The former Crown Prince Jung."

"Ah, yes. The 'conspiracy.' I did hear about it."

Hsueh shrugged. "And of course, many old men, and at least one president of the National Bureau of Sacrifice."

Dee looked up and smiled wanly. "Only one so far, you mean."

"Hm."

"My friend," Dee said with great deliberateness, "you once told me that one of your wizardly skills is to move among the rich and powerful. How rich, and how powerful?"

Hsueh looked at Dee unblinkingly. "There are none too rich or too powerful. Send me, and I shall go."

Dee smiled back at him, a rare excitement beginning to stir. "Madame Yang is, after all, a great patroness of Buddhism. And you are a monk and a scholar."

"True. She is also a beautiful woman of a certain age," Hsueh said with a sly smile. "And I am also a purveyor of the finest cosmetics in this or any Empire."

"Hm," Dee said, doing a fair imitation of the monk, and they both smiled.

"Master Dee," the monk said then, "did you know that many years ago, the Empress Wu's firstborn, a girl no more than ten days old, was found dead in its cradle?"

Dee looked at him for a moment, then shook his head.

"No. I refuse to even consider it, Hsueh. It would simply not be possible."

Hsueh shrugged. "I merely offer you the information."

Dee thought again. "No," he repeated firmly. "No. It is simply not possible."

17

A.D. 669, January
Loyang

According to those who study the ancient classic doctrines of the Book of Rites, a distinction has always been made between those ceremonies that are feminine and those that are masculine. When it is a question of bringing the participants before the feminine altar or the mas-

culine altar, then these participants have always
conformed to the proper gender: masculine attendants
for the masculine deities; feminite devotees for the feminine deities. Then why is it not so when conducting the
most important ceremony in the maintenance of order
and propriety between heaven and earth—the Feng
Shan? This ceremony—a trip to the sacred peaks where
the Divinity of the Earth can be worshiped—has been
performed by every ruler and his entourage since those
earliest times when all history was recorded on the shells
of tortoises. And yet is this not a ceremony which is essentially a worship of the Divinity of the *Earth?* And is
not this Divinity *feminine?* But nowhere in history has a
woman been allowed to attend. Is this not a great oversight that needs to be corrected? And is it not right that
so great a responsibility should rest alone with the
Daughter of Heaven, the Divine Empress Wu Tse-tien?

"The 'Daughter of Heaven'?" Dee asked incredulously,
tossing the Imperial proclamation down on the table.

Today, Loyang's chief magistrate and investigator sat at
the desk of the president of the National Bureau of Sacrifice.
Wearing his other hat, as the old councillor put it. And because
of his high position in the Imperial bureaucracy, Dee had been
among the initial few to be honored with the Empress's "his-
toric" announcement—that she would be the first woman to
lead a sacred ritual already ancient a millennium before the
birth of Confucius. Dee did not find himself particularly disturbed by this flagrant violation of protocol and decorum, although he knew every Confucian left in the government would
be spluttering with outrage. He sighed. If only the Empress's
audacity were confined to little pranks such as this.

No, he scarcely had the time or interest to give much
thought to the Empress's proclamation. Before him was a map
of the city of Loyang, marked with the location of Madame
Yang's home, where the fatal dinners had occurred. He was
happy to note that her house was in the city proper and was
not part of the Imperial compound.

According to the T'ang legal code, her estate was under
his jurisdiction as presiding magistrate of Loyang; but his investigation, he knew, would necessarily encroach upon the

sanctity of the Divine Imperial Gates. It would be as delicate and dangerous a matter as he had ever pursued. Proceeding would be as touchy and perilous as walking through a darkened room where snakes lay coiled under the furniture.

"Master Hsueh," Dee said, "This will be the singular test of your mettle. Among the Vinhayan Buddhists Madame Yang is treated as a semidivinity; she is, for them, a demiurge."

"I understand fully, President Dee," Hsueh responded with a wry smile and a shallow bow. "A most delicate matter, and a most influential lady."

"Remember, you know nothing, suspect nothing."

"Of course, Magistrate. I understand our position."

"I do not know what you will find," Dee said. "But I have already conceived of the pretext that will bring you to her gates. I have given you impeccable credentials as a holy man from Tibet, so I doubt that you will be turned away. But in case they are not enough, I have given you the most remarkable credential of all.

"You see, Master Hsueh, I have done my studying. In the past several days I have struggled to come up with the perfect reason . . . no, *means*," Dee said, shaping his hands into a tight sphere in front of his face, "the perfect means for you to enter the domain of the Empress's mother. But before I tell you what it is, I want to hear your thickest, most incomprehensible Tibetan accent." Dee smiled. "You can go back to that other, long-ago life, can't you?"

"My life as a boy?" the magician said, bemused. "Hm. It will not be difficult. I will certainly try, Magistrate."

"Remember the most important thing: this pretext that brings you to Madame Yang," Dee said, leaning forward conspiratorially, though the two of them were quite alone, "must not only appeal to her acquisitiveness and vanity, but bring you into one particular room of her house."

"Reverend Father, I have not thought to ask you for your Tibetan name."

"And I am most remiss for not having offered it, madame," "Lama" Hsueh Huai-i responded with a charming smile. "However, it is most difficult for the Chinese tongue to pronounce—the language is capable of such odd combinations of sounds. *Ngogpa*," he said importantly, "meaning the Lama from Ngog, Madame Yang. But there is more." He paused significantly. "Ngogpa Lhag-tongpa-nyid. Lama Ngogpa Lhag-tong-pa-nyid" he repeated in his thick Tibetan tones.

"Meaning . . . ?" Madame Yang eyed him with curiosity and delight.

"Meaning the Lama from Ngog Possessing the Knowledge of Superconsciousness and the Clarity of Voidness of Thought." Hsueh studied Madame Yang's admiring features for a moment. It was plain that he was not failing to make an impression. "That is the best that I can do in translation, madame. So much is, of necessity, lost in words," he said with a shrug. "You, of all people, would understand. I must borrow words from the lexicon of the Taoists. They come the closest, madame, but even they are lacking."

"There is so much that we cannot know," Madame Yang said, shaking her head. "It is truly humbling."

"*All* true knowledge is humbling, madame," Hsueh concurred. "But that brings me to the great gift I have brought to you." He lowered his voice to a whisper. "What I am about to reveal to you is a bit of true knowledge for your eyes and ears only."

Hsueh turned to the table where the decorative box stood; until this point, Madame Yang had been resolutely ignoring the mysterious, tantalizing object. He opened the box, lifted the reliquary chorten, and placed it with infinite gentleness on the table. Madame Yang's face remained impassive, but she felt her heart begin to race: before her was a cylindrical gold container with a deep and richly detailed repoussé depicting flying geese. On its lid the image of the reclining Buddha Gautama—the true historical Buddha—was flanked by the standing images of Indra and Brahma.

"It is indeed beautiful, Lama Hsueh," Madame Yang said with great restraint. "May I touch it?"

"Of course, madame." Hsueh moved the chorten toward her. "But the exterior beauty of this ancient vessel is as nothing compared to what it contains." She lifted it and held it in the sunlight from the window, studying every detail. "It is a copy, madame, of another more ancient vessel: the Great Reliquary of Kanishka from the Votive Stupa in Loriya Tangai in the Swat Valley in Gandhara, northern India. When the Great Buddha died, his followers left his homeland in the Doab region and moved to the cooler valleys of Gandhara . . . "

"Lama Hsueh, what do the flying geese represent?" Madame Yang asked, looking up at him at last, her thumb and forefinger caressing the smooth raised surface of one of the birds' outstretched wings.

"Their flight represents the spreading of the Buddha's Law—his Dharma—to distant shores."

"How wonderfully appropriate for us in the City of Transformation."

"Certainly, madame. But there is something far more magnificent and, as you say, appropriate to the City of Transformation: it is the true reason that I have imposed myself upon you today." She replaced it on the table, but he still made no move toward it.

"It is no imposition, Lama. We are flattered that one of such great learning as yourself would see fit to grace us," she said encouragingly.

Hsueh bowed a shallow bow. "Inside, Madame Yang," he said in hushed tones, "is a secret so great that I dared not bring it to the attention of anyone other than yourself, the greatest devotee of the Buddha Gautama in China." Hsueh began to remove the lid of the reliquary with painful slowness. He slid an earthenware cylinder carefully out from the sacred vessel and placed it delicately on its base. It was blue and red and inscribed around its top with tiny rows of incised Sanskrit ligatures.

"This is a handsome object, too, Lama," she said, enjoying the little game of suspense. She rotated the object on its base, and watched the pleasure on the tall stranger's face. "Very handsome," she repeated, as if that were the entirety of his mysterious gift.

"Allow me, madame." He removed the top of the cylinder. "It is carefully disguised. Clever workmanship on the part of this unknown artisan. Perhaps he calculated that if anyone was clever enough to discover the sacred vessel in the first place, and then got so far as to remove the earthenware cylinder, he would simply stop in frustration, assuming it to be just another inscribed cylindrical prayer wheel. But . . . "

His hand disappeared inside and brought out a transparent blue cube that fit snugly into a square hole inside the deceptive cylinder. The cube was completely clear, smooth, and seamless, like a block of ice. Despite herself, Madame Yang felt her eyes go wide.

"Glass, madame. Beautiful blue glass, introduced, perhaps, from Macedonia into the Indian Motherland by way of the northernmost Gandhara region, by the great conqueror Sikander."* Hsueh extended the cube to Madame Yang with reverent care. "Hold it to the light and look inside."

"It is crystalline . . . beautiful! But . . ." She paused and brought her face close to the cube, furrowing her brow. "But look. There appears to be a flaw deep inside—a crack, perhaps." She squinted into the cube, then held it out toward Hsueh. "There, Lama. In the center."

Hsueh still stood without moving, his arms crossed on his chest, his expression implacable.

"Look closely, madame. I told you that I had brought you the ultimate treasure. I did not deceive the mother of our Divine Empress and our most holy patron of the Dharma. That is not a flaw inside. *That* is the treasure." She looked again.

"It is white. It is . . . a bone?" Hsueh uncrossed his arms at the moment that she raised her startled eyes to his. "Heavens, Lama, tell me that this is only the bone of a great teacher . . . a great Lama or monk, dead for centuries?"

"I *cannot* tell you that, madame."

"But many people lay claim to the fact that they have a true piece of the Great One."

"Many do, madame, that is true." Hsueh pressed his fingertips together. "But, then, these many are the subject of their own folly or the deceptions of others. There is only one true recorded fragment. Only one that the ancient followers knew to be true. When those first followers of the Buddha Gautama left the Buddha's homeland in the sweltering southern Doab region and moved to the cooler north—the Gandharan region—they began to lead a far more settled existence. Great monasteries and stupas were built in the name of Mahayana Buddhism, structures that rose seven and eight hundred feet from the ground, topped with tiers of gilded umbrellas, their interiors lined with rows and rows of colorfully painted Buddhas and boddhisatvas. But only in the wall of the one great Gandharan stupa, now in ruins, was hidden *this* very vessel containing the only true piece of the Master to be recorded in the ancient texts." Hsueh stood back and took a deep breath as if the revelation had taken all his strength.

"My heavens, Lama. But how did you acquire it?" Madame Yang asked, stroking the icy coolness of the sacred cube.

"That is a long story, madame, and one that I have put

---

*Alexander the Great.

behind me. But I will only say that I felt the Gandharans to
have lost the true message, clouding the one Buddha with their
innumerable metaphors of boddhisatva-saints, goddesses, demons. . . . This bone, madame, is the ultimate symbol of the
Law of the one true Buddha, the Dharma, the only Law that
we are ultimately subject to. And I believed that we must go
to any lengths. Any lengths at all," he repeated significantly.

"Are you saying that the taking of life was involved?"
she asked solemnly.

"Perhaps I shall pay for my transgressions in many lifetimes, madame," he said softly. "Perhaps . . ."

"Perhaps what, Lama?" she urged him.

"Perhaps . . . this is a bit difficult," he said, clasping his
hands as if in prayer and looking earnestly into her eyes. "Although the Buddhist has reverence for all life, perhaps one
must make an *exception* when it is a matter of protecting the
Dharma. It may well be the only exception." He dropped these
words like stones into a pond.

"Oh, yes. I believe it is true, Lama," she said without hesitation. "That is perhaps the one exception. I myself have often
wrestled with this most difficult notion. If it is absolutely necessary, even our supposedly unassailable code of reverence for
all life must be secondary to the primary duty of protecting
the Dharmic Law." The Tibetan was watching her closely as
she spoke. She felt as if she could tell him anything. Anything!
She felt a sudden strong pressure of purpose behind her words
which gave new meaning to her past. "The taking of life in
this higher cause would be . . . ultimately . . ." She pleasurably
pursued the right word. "Justifiable," she finished quietly.
When she had said it, the very sound, the echo of the word in
her mind, wrapped her in a warm comfort.

"Perhaps, madame, perhaps. At any rate, I *shall* find out
one day, shall I not? Whatever karmic destiny awaits me, however, will be well worth it if it means that I may lay this gift
at your feet. I would pay with a thousand lifetimes for the
privilege. Now, madame, as keeper of the one certain true remaining fragment of the Buddha's physical being, your position in this Empire and in the earthly realm of Buddha is even
more exalted than before. And, as such, your duties to yourself
and your own household are even greater. I pray that you will
allow me to be of assistance."

"Of course, Lama," she said happily.

"Your house is your temple, madame. It now resides at

the center of the Earthly Buddhist Universe of Jambudvipa. If you will allow me, I will help you to make it an even more perfect haven for the contemplation and exaltation of the ineffable, a more perfect refractory crystal, if you will, of the divine light. It must all be precisely adjusted: the alignment of the very stones in your garden, the angle at which the first rays of the morning sun enter through a window, the subtle gradations of color from one room to the next, the colors used to enhance the already perfect beauty of madame's face." He stopped and looked around him at the sumptuous dwelling, then held up a purposeful finger. "And I would like to begin with your kitchen."

"My kitchen, Lama?"

"We were speaking of the reverence for all living things. You must allow me into your kitchen, madame, so that I may instruct your staff in the proper methods of maintaining a strictly vegetarian table."

"You know, Hsueh, that the esteemed Court Historian Shu is not unknown to me."

"Please do not tell me that he is a friend of yours."

"Certainly not." Dee laughed. "Though it seems that we were destined to be colleagues one way or the other. He is roughly a contemporary; very roughly. In actuality he is a good eight years older than I am."

"And how did you make the acquaintance of this fine gentleman?"

"It was many years ago, when I, along with countless other hopeful young men, came to Loyang during a beautiful spring to submit ourselves to the most intense trial of body, mind, and spirit ever devised."

"Ah. The Imperial Civil Service Triennial Exams," Hsueh said in a tone suggesting that the very concept was a quaint amusement to him.

They were walking in the seclusion of a wild wooded park north of the city on the day after Hsueh's visit to Madame Yang. They were enjoying the unseasonably warm weather of an early January thaw.

"Yes, Hsueh, the Triennial Exams, which determine who will and who will not obtain a government position. Something that you are fortunate to have been able to avoid."

"Do not think that my own training and initiation were not without their trials and rigors," the magician said. "I have been put to tests you could not even begin to imagine."

"Of course, Master Hsueh. Of course," Dee said quickly. "But tell me about Historian Shu."

"I do not know if he remembers me, but I certainly remember him. When I arrived that spring many years ago for the first time, Shu had arrived, too, but it was not the first time for him. It was his third, and last, try. He had failed twice before. Three is the maximum number of times a candidate is allowed to take the exams. If he fails it a third time . . ."

"Then he is forced to draw upon other resources," Hsueh said.

"How succinctly you put it, Master Hsueh. That is exactly so. At any rate, many of us were aware of the slightly older fellows, the anxious-looking ones, back for their third and final try, mingling with the younger ones, doing their best to absorb a bit of our youthful energy, or perhaps that one piece of knowledge that would make the difference this time."

"And Historian Shu was among them?"

"He was. I remember him well because he approached several younger candidates and offered to pay them handsomely if they would take the exams in his place. I was one of the ones he approached. I believe that no one took him up on his offer, tempting though it was, and he was forced to go in himself for the third time."

"And I assume that he failed."

"He did. But as you can see, it has not stopped him. We were speaking of other resources—obviously, Historian Shu has them in abundance."

The magician gave a dry snort. "Indeed," he said.

"So that is how I remember him. It is less likely that he remembers me, for I was merely one of scores of young candidates he approached. What I have not decided yet," Dee said thoughtfully, "is whether it would be to my advantage or my disadvantage to remind him that we have met before."

"You are going to meet with him?" Hsueh asked with sly enthusiasm. Dee shrugged as they paused near a serene and lovely little lake, its surface, frozen for so many weeks now, melting in the warm sun.

"Considering the information you have brought me from Madame Yang's house," Dee said, looking out over the water, "I think that I must." He turned back to the magician. "Now I need what we in the magisterial profession refer to as 'hard' evidence. You recall, I am sure, the Empress's 'Daughter of Heaven' proclamation?''

"I could scarcely forget it."

"Our office was honored. Most others received printed copies, but we received an original, from the brush of Historian Shu himself. His chop mark* was on it. I saw something, Hsueh, something very small, but that makes me want very much to see other of our friend's original pieces of 'art.' ''

"Why, Magistrate Dee, what a most pleasant and propitious surprise!" the diminutive man said, jumping to his feet. "Welcome, welcome!" He made a sweeping gesture and ushered Dee into his office.

Smiling broadly, Dee accepted the gracious invitation.

"No doubt you were expecting me sometime soon, Master Shu," he said. "Surely you have been expecting me to pop in at any moment since we met again at the Empress's most superb dinner party!"

"Met again?" Shu asked, puzzled. "Master Dee, I do not recall that we ever met before that night."

"No, of course you would not remember. There is no reason why you should," Dee said, accepting a comfortable seat near Shu's large, beautifully carved and elaborate desk. "But there is every reason why I should remember you!" He kept his smile warm and his tone scrupulously friendly as he spoke.

"Master Dee, please! I am consumed by curiosity!" Shu said, bustling about and ordering tea from a servant before settling himself in his own chair with much swishing and arranging of the fabric of his robes. He sat with an expectant smile on his lips.

"The Triennial Exams, Master Shu—nearly twenty-five years ago." He watched Shu's smile weaken just a bit at the edges, though the expectant look remained. Dee leaned forward the way a person does who is gathering his memories to tell a wonderful story. "I remember the night when we had all been turned loose from our stalls after three grueling days during which a few of us had had our spirits broken permanently, and many more of us knew perfectly well that we had failed. On that night, though, before any of the scores were posted— they would not be for some time—most of us were mad with

---

*Individual signature seal from a carved stamp usually made from ivory or jade but also popularly made from soapstone or cow horn.

joy and wine, simply because we had at last been let out of our torture rooms. Just to breathe, talk, laugh, and drink like free creatures was all that we cared about at that moment. The noise we made must have kept the entire city awake as we sang and drank and shouted and debated various questions and problems put to us during the days of testing. And you and I, Master Shu, shared a pitcher of wine on that night. It was because of that pitcher of wine that I remember you so well out of the hundreds of scholars around me." Dee smiled and shook his head as if in bemused recollection; Shu waited, mirroring Dee's smile. "You," Dee said, "and you alone, were as calm and serene as a star in the sky on that night while the rest of us were nearly demented. I remember wondering why. Later, I found out."

Dee was warming to his story now, and could see that despite the ghost of guardedness behind Shu's smile, here was a man who was enthralled by a good tale. As well he should be, Dee thought. Dee had made it his business to read everything Shu had written since the man had gone to work as the personal historian of the Empress and her mother. The fellow was nothing if not a master storyteller himself.

"Many weeks later, after the scores were posted, and some of us celebrated and some of us began the long journey home with failure riding our shoulders every wretched step of the way like the weight of death itself, I remember the rumor that flew around the city, leaving us breathless with envy and incredulity." There had indeed been such a rumor that year, though it was never proved to be anything more than a rumor—but Dee was sure that Shu would have heard it too and would remember it. Now he smiled his biggest smile at Shu, as if inviting him to finish the story himself. "I am sure that you recall," he said conspiratorially.

"I am sure I have no idea at all, Master Dee," Shu said with real ingenuousness.

"None of us could believe it. And yet it was, apparently, true. Somebody, one among us, one of the thousands who had ever taken the exams, that spring and over the centuries, had achieved that which was normally reserved only for the gods: perfection, Master Shu. A perfect score on the Triennial Exams. The rumor reached my ears, and the ears of several of my friends, that the man who had done this thing was having a small celebratory cup at a certain wineshop in the city. We kept very quiet, and slipped away, saying nothing at all to our associates because we did not wish to cause a stampede, and went to that wineshop to peer through the window at this creature who had done what no man had ever done or would do again." He gazed at Shu as if he were looking through that window. Historian, he thought, now I am going to present you with the sort of history that you love so well yourself. "I saw him, Master Shu. I saw that man, and recognized him as the serene one, the ascended master I had shared a drink with a few weeks before." He paused, lowered his eyes, then raised them again to Shu. "You have not changed so much that I did not recognize you again when I saw you sitting at the Imperial dinner table here in Loyang a quarter of a century later."

Shu dimpled, blushed, and stammered like a shy maiden. "Oh, no, Master Dee. You are mistaken. Surely you do not believe that it was I," he said unconvincingly, obviously wanting very much that Dee should continue to believe it. "I did well, of course, but not that well," he said, still smiling happily.

"Never mind," Dee said. "I will not press you. Your modesty is that of a true gentleman." He leaned back and eyed the great scholar admiringly. "But I know the truth, even if you will not admit to it. And I can scarcely blame you! People would give you no rest if they knew!" He held up a silencing hand as poor Shu was about to lodge another feeble protest. "Don't worry—your secret is safe with me. I will not breathe a word of it to another living soul. But I will have the satisfaction of knowing to whom I am speaking!"

"Well, Master Dee, I . . ." Shu was so happy that he was nearly giddy. Dee pushed on, scarcely giving him a chance to collect his wits.

"They said that not only was the scholarship impeccable, but the calligraphy was sublime. I myself dabble in the art of calligraphy, though of course I am a mere dilettante. I came here today hoping that perhaps you would do me the honor . . ." He stopped, as if realizing that he was simply asking too much of such a gracious and modest man.

"No! Please! Master Dee, what is it?" Shu said eagerly.

"I came here today hoping that you might perhaps let me see some examples of your elegant hand." Dee knew that Shu did in fact study calligraphy and fancied himself a distinguished practitioner. This milder bit of flattery, closer to something that had at least a slim foothold in reality, produced the results that Dee expected. Shu bounded up from his desk, scurried to a cabinet, and pulled open the doors to reveal shelves of rolled and bound parchments. He gathered up a small arm-load and dropped them eagerly on the desk in front of Dee. He began to unroll them and weight their corners with figu-rines, ornamental boxes, shells.

"You will see that I am no master, Magistrate, merely a competent and earnest plodder," he said with becoming mod-esty.

"What nonsense!" Dee exclaimed, eagerly scanning the documents as they were opened before him. As he had hoped, some of them were the original drafts of the various procla-mations and spurious histories for which Shu was so famous. His eyes moved rapidly over the pile, examining the lower right-hand corner of each. There were poems here, too. Shu the Poet, Dee thought. Incredible. He leafed through the papers reverently, as if they were holy documents, and cursed in-wardly. There was a particular one he wanted to see, but he could not find it in this batch. It simply was not there.

"Aaah," Dee murmured as if he had never seen such matchless work before in his life. "It is as I suspected." The calligraphy was in fact not bad, though scarcely of such a qual-ity as to inspire rapture. But Dee did not let that stop him. Certainly Shu was not going to protest.

"Please, Master Dee, tell me what you see!"

"It is that elusive thing which the calligraphy master cannot teach to his students—he can only bring them to such a level of practiced expertise that if this nameless quality is in them, it will show itself, will find life. It is possible to look at the work of the most technically accomplished calligrapher and see that although the strokes are pleasant to the eye, they are ... soulless. But here—and you may not even be aware of it your-self, Master Shu—there is an *expressiveness* to the very strokes that perfectly matches the content of the words you were writ-ing! See," he said, picking up a proclamation having to do with the Empress's building projects and the renaming of the city, "in this one, the emotional content of the brushstrokes is light, crisp, joyous, celebratory. Whereas in this one"—he indicated the proclamation reporting the death of the unfortunate Crown Prince Jung—"the strokes fairly weep on the page. I can ac-tually feel your sorrow!"

Moisture glistened in Shu's eyes by now, so moved was he. "Yes," he agreed, "I was weeping when I wrote it. It is a miracle that my tears did not cause the ink to run on the page."

"The tears are there, Shu, in every stroke." Dee took a

deep breath and plunged forward. "If this is what you felt when you were writing of the death of a young man, I can only imagine your pain upon having to write of the death of a beautiful young girl."

"Oh, Master Dee," Shu said, shaking his head. "It was as if I had moistened my brush in my own salt tears rather than water." Dee held his impatience in check as Shu moved back to the cabinets and brought forth one more rolled parchment. He placed it before Dee, indicating that it was too painful for him to open it himself.

Dee unrolled it. It was the original draft of the proclamation telling the world of the execution of the nephews and the death of the Empress's niece, the Duchess's daughter, Holan. His eyes moved to the lower right-hand corner before the document was even flattened. He let his breath out.

"Oh, Shu," he said sympathetically. "How it must have cost you to even touch the brush to the page." Shu shook his head in wordless sorrow. "But what is this?" Dee asked, bringing forth a piece he had noticed earlier. "A poem? Are you a poet as well? 'Ode to the October Moon,' " he read aloud. "Yes," Dee said. "That was an exceptional moon. I nearly wrote a poem to it myself, and I can assure you, I am no poet. Look at the strokes here," he said hurriedly. "They speak to me of peace, serenity, inspiration." He looked hard at Shu. "And pure spontaneity."

"So true, so true!" Shu concurred eagerly. "Did you know, Master Dee, that I wrote that poem during the night, outside, with no light but the full moon itself illuminating my page? Ah! It was like a dream!"

"And your heart was still light and free. I see no indication of the sorrow to come. The sorrow I see in your later brushstrokes. You were as yet . . . untouched," Dee said, still watching Shu closely.

"What?" the historian asked, hesitating for only a moment. "Yes. Of course. That is right," he agreed then. "I was as yet untouched. My heart was still light and free, still capable of such frivolous pleasure. No," he mused, shaking his head. "I did not know of the sorrow to come. How is it that these things can approach us, and we do not feel them, sense them, smell them?" he asked Dee.

Dee shrugged. "Sorrow stalks us with the stealth and cunning of a beast of prey," he said, impressed with his own impromptu doggerel.

"I have heard the same thing said of inspiration, Master Dee," Shu said happily. "That it can leap at you like a tiger!"

Dee smiled, considering. "Yes, Shu. Like a tiger."

"The man is a capable extemporizer, I will give him that," Dee whispered. "The tales spin out of him with the ease of a spider casting her web."

"Or the ease of a rat chewing through paper," the monk whispered back. "Hold the lamp steady, Master Dee." He grunted a little, then Dee heard a metallic ping as the lock gave way and the door to Historian Shu's office swung open on its quiet hinges.

It was quite miraculous. Doors and locks were as nothing to the magician; they melted before him like phantasms at dawn. And to move with Master Hsueh was to be truly invisible; he could step into a pool of shadow and disappear, or stand perfectly still and become a piece of furniture. And always, unfailingly, he chose the momentary lapses in others' attention in which to move. The lone guard circling the building had never seen them.

"Your metaphor is much more apt," Dee agreed, holding up the lamp as they entered the room. He moved directly to Historian Shu's writing desk. He raised the hinged cover and held the lamp over the revealed contents: brushes, inks, grinding stone, handrest—and the ornate little box that was the object of his search. "There it is, Master Hsueh," he whispered. "Proof of murder that you could conceal in the palm of your hand. At least," he said, reaching in and lifting the little box, "that is what I believe we will find."

He set the lamp down and pulled a wrapped parcel from the purse on his belt and deftly unrolled it on the historian's desk. Inside was a piece of parchment, two small vials, a brush, and a small cloth. He opened the ornate little box he had taken from the writing desk and slid out the historian's carved jade chop. He held it under the light and examined it for a moment; then he opened one of the vials, dipped his brush in it, painted the printing surface of the chop, and made an impression with it on the piece of parchment.

He went to the various shelves from which Shu had taken his poems and proclamations. He gathered the papers up, brought them over to the pool of light cast by the lamp, and unrolled them carefully and quickly, one after the other, grunting with impatience, until he found the two he was looking for: the historian's poem to the full moon, and the announcement of the sad death of the Empress's niece. Close to the light, he held up the poem and the piece of parchment he had just stamped with the historian's chop; squinting with concentration, he examined them. Then he held up the proclamation of death and compared it with the first two. He picked up the chop, painted it again, made a second impression, and held it up next to the poem and the proclamation, staring hard for several long minutes. He heard the monk breathing behind him, just over his left shoulder. "Proof of murder you can hold in the palm of your hand, Master Hsueh," he repeated with satisfaction. "Do you see?" He pointed to the chop mark at the bottom of Shu's poem, and held up the parchments on which he himself had made impressions.

"There is a nick. A piece missing," Hsueh observed. "This was what you saw on the chop mark on the Empress's 'Daughter of Heaven' proclamation?"

"Exactly so. As if he had dropped it, and chipped it. But look at this," he said, holding the death proclamation under the light. Hsueh squinted.

"It is intact!" he whispered.

Dee superimposed the new impression over the old, holding both up so that the light shone through them.

"Yes. And you can see by the matching minute scratches, lines, and irregularities in the imprint that the mark was made by the same chop as the one used on the poem—*before* our clumsy historian dropped it, or stepped on it, or whatever he did."

"I think I am beginning to understand," Hsueh said.

"The poem was written in October. The girl died in November. The proclamation was released when it was nearly December. We now have proof that the proclamation was written before the nick appeared in. the historian's chop. Before the poem was written." He looked at the magician, whose sorrowful eyes already comprehended. "Weeks before her death," Dee finished.

"I do not like to think of it, Master Dee. A young girl consorting innocently with those three, the women and the historian, taking meals with them, talking and laughing with them, while words of her death were already on paper, hidden in a drawer somewhere. I do not like to think of it at all." In the next moment his attitude of sorrow was replaced by a hard-eyed shrewdness. "Master Dee, how can you be certain that the poem was written in October? That odious little charlatan is capable of anything. He could have written it last week, or day before yesterday."

"You are right, Hsueh. Through flattery, I caused him to babble about how he wrote it under the actual full moon and such, and not weeks later. I believed him. I believe I can distinguish between fact and fabrication with Historian Shu. But of course, that was not enough. Compelling, but not enough. I needed real proof. So I went through old copies of the poetry gazettes that are published regularly in the city, until I found his poem. It was indeed published in October." He laughed. "Right after that extraordinary full moon. I found that, and something else quite irrelevant to all of this but most revealing of our friend the historian, and very much in character."

"And what would that be, Master Dee?"

"He published the poem under an assumed name. Out of modesty, of course." They both smiled at this. Dee took the cloth he had laid out, moistened it with water from the second vial, and carefully cleaned all traces of ink from the historian's chop before replacing it in its box. "And then, in the next issue of the gazette, a commendation appeared for that very poem, a short paragraph gushing with admiration for the literary genius of this anonymous poet. And it was signed by Historian Shu."

Dee's smile did not last, though. A shadow had moved across his mind, a sad entreating shadow. "Ho-lan," he said softly, uttering the dead girl's name aloud for the first time. Such a beautiful name.

Two mornings after their excursion to Shu's office, Dee woke to his second cold gray sleepless dawn, and understood that the ghost of Ho-lan, though he had never seen her in life, had come to be as persistent as the ghost of the dead gardener had been years before.

So. You are not going to give me any rest either, he said, and rose from his bed, as weary as if he were rising from his tomb after one hundred years. He went directly to his writing table and drafted a note to a certain official whose name had been given to him by Wu-chi as one of the last of the just Confucians left at court.

He said very little in the note, which would be delivered by private messenger—just that he had a matter of some "delicacy" that he wished to discuss concerning the Empress's mother.

Dee was elated and frightened at the same time. He had an appointment with the man he had written to, the head of the Censorate—the highest Imperial legal body. Dee did not know if it would ever be possible to bring such an exalted person as the mother of the Empress to justice, but he needed very badly to talk about it with someone he believed to be a peer. The mother of the Empress: the thought caused him to shudder, there was no denying it. He felt like a man walking on a rickety wooden bridge swaying in the wind. And the Empress . . . ? He almost dared not think it. Madame Yang, he reminded himself as he walked, is merely a citizen. She herself is not royalty. She, as a resident of the city, is under your jurisdiction.

Under your jurisdiction, under your jurisdiction, he told himself with every step. But was she, if the truth be told, under *anybody's* jurisdiction?

He had evidence. Excellent evidence. If anyone came to him with such evidence, he would open a case immediately. First, the very interesting discovery made by the monk during his visit to Madame Yang's house: that she had a set of cookware, dishes, and utensils that were kept separate and carefully locked in a box in her kitchen. Madame Yang had told Hsueh that the reason they were kept separate from the other kitchenware was that they had been the last utensils used to cook the final meal eaten by her late husband, the last dishes to hold the food that he ate, and the last chopsticks to bear that food to his lips and to touch them. I could not, she had told the monk, possibly allow them to be used by anybody else.

But Hsueh had assured Dee that he had heard of just such utensils, impregnated with poison, that would kill anyone unfortunate enough to eat with them or to eat food cooked in them. Yes, he had told Dee, such things were not unheard of at all in the far west. He himself knew of more than one case; and of course, Madame Yang would have access to any such exotic ways and means.

Compelling, but not enough to make her a murderess, especially without the dishes themselves. Hsueh had offered to enter the house surreptitiously, open the box, and bring the dishes to Dee, but Dee had decided that it was far too risky. If she suspected anything at all, she would slip from their grasp like a cat leaping out a window and they would lose her forever.

You are merely going to make contact with this official, Dee told himself, trying to steady his racing pulses. You are not necessarily going to do anything rash and impetuous this very day. You are going to talk, that is all. To feel things out, discreetly and sensibly.

And the Empress? The question raised itself insistently again, and again he pushed it away. He was not at all ready to think about that yet. But uncomfortable images rose: he saw in his mind an infant, lying dead in its cradle. He shook his head, trying in vain to dislodge the pictures the way a housewife would shake hair and grit from an old rug. An infant lying dead in its cradle.

No, he told himself for the hundredth time. It simply is not possible.

"I am sorry, Magistrate Dee," said the clerk with the watery eyes. "But I do not know where the Censorate councillor has gone."

"Yesterday, you told me he was ill," Dee said with carefully checked impatience. "You said that I should return today. Is he still unwell? Is there no message for me from him?"

"I do not know," the man said, shrugging.

"Perhaps I could go to his home, then. Where does he live?"

"He is not at his home, Magistrate."

"He is not at his home. He is not at his office. Where is he, then?"

"He has gone on a trip."

"Gone on a trip! We had an appointment! Yesterday he was ill, and today he has gone on a trip! Where? Where has he gone?"

"To visit his aged mother, Magistrate Dee. That is all I know."

"Where? In this city? In some other city?"

"I do not know, Magistrate Dee."

"Is the mother dead, or is she alive?" Dee asked.

"Sir?" the clerk asked, confused.

"Never mind," Dee said, turning to leave. He stopped. "If you see the councillor, I would like you to ask him a question for me."

"Of course, Magistrate," the clerk said.

"Ask him for me if *he* is dead or alive," he said, and strode out of the office.

He gave the door another shake, still not believing what was perfectly evident to his senses: it was locked, and the office on the other side of it, that of yet another high Confucian official, was still and silent as a tomb. He looked up at its tall, solid, carved wooden length, and had a momentary childish urge to kick it and pound on it. Go ahead and do it, its ornate, dignified panels seemed to mock him. I will feel nothing at all, but for you, it will be very, very painful.

So, Dee told himself, wearily climbing the stairs to his quarters; we have always known that you are slow and thick-witted, but you do eventually learn. There are doors not even the magician would be able to open.

He had bruised his nose against four of them before he finally understood that there was not a single official in the city of Loyang who cared to listen to his sordid little tale. The mere mention of the name of Madame Yang had traveled like a vibration along a spider's web, and the officials vanished. And obviously, the word had spread among them—don't get trapped in your office with Magistrate Dee. Like the scabby beggar in his smelly rags raving on the street corner, he was shunned.

He sat in the pleasant glow of the lamplight, his brush poised, and thought about the last official he had tried to see. He had actually managed to get into his office, but had scarcely taken a breath when the man interrupted politely, saying that he needed to answer the call of nature, but that he would be back in a moment. After nearly an hour had passed and the man had not returned, Dee, feeling foolish indeed, finally rose from his chair and left.

 JOURNAL ENTRY ─────────────────────────

My experiences of the last two days have illustrated to me a few things concerning the nature of law—things which I understood only in the abstract before, but which now have the reality of the pavement under my feet: without concurrence, there is no law. A law may be written, it may be on paper and in the books, but if it does not have the force of many minds behind it, it does not exist. Elementary words, I know, but with meaning beyond my grasp until now. The monk, at least, has pledged his unwavering support. I am not entirely alone.

In the meantime, a torrent of sutras from the excavations at Tunhuang continues to pour into the city unabated. As I walked in the streets today, the theme of nearly every conversation that reached my ears was the nature of paradise and hell. At one point I actually stopped walking as the understanding hit me between the eyes that paradise and hell are not two different places, but are tangled, intertwined, ingrown and inseparable, and exist right here and now on this earth.

18

A.D. 669, February
Loyang

It could only have been the news of the severity of Kaotsung's latest sickness that had caused the bad dreams. Dee had felt his own internal sense of unease growing over the last several days, ever since the arrival of Hsueh Huai-i's letter. And why? What difference to the state, at this point, whether the Emperor was alive or dead? he asked himself. But he knew the answer. Ineffective and debilitated though he was, Kaotsung was a last vestige—a symbol, however ceremonial—of official Confucian constraint.

This time, Kaotsung had suffered a severe relapse, and yesterday Hsueh had written that the Emperor might not recover. Though Hsueh found the Empress's presence odious and always withdrew when she paid a visit to her mother, he said, he could not help but overhear her wailing, ranting, and complaining.

Dee thought that surely Ho-lan's death had proved too much for the Emperor. Whatever resiliency remained in Kaotsung's body must have collapsed with his will and his spirit. It was a wonder, the old Councillor Wu-chi had once remarked to Dee, that the Emperor had survived so long. A miracle, in fact, Dee added with his new firsthand knowledge.

Dee worried about Hsueh's safety, fretting over whether it had been altogether wise to allow him to undertake his covert mission. Two weeks ago, the monk had entered Madame Yang's household and was living under her roof, as many "holy men," scholars, and pilgrims often did. He was a guest of honor, the great "Lama" Hsueh, there to act as spiritual adviser to the Empress's mother, to instruct her kitchen staff, to help her with her plans for the construction of gardens and temples.

He had not laid eyes on the magician since he had gone in, but the clever monk had kept Dee well informed. Letters arrived almost daily, full of fascinating detail and information about life at the home of the Empress's mother. And what did they expect to do with any evidence they were likely to uncover? He had no answer to that question, either. But he was incapable, he knew, of turning his back now. He had no choice. He simply had to know.

Last night Dee had managed to fall asleep, but it was an unpleasant and fitful sleep, wracked with dreams of fires. At one point he was in the palace, talking to the Emperor while a fire sputtered and crackled across the polished floors. Then it leaped onto the tall bed so the corners of the bedclothes glowed. Dee had pulled anxiously at the paralyzed monarch's arms, but he could not get the poor man to move.

That was when Dee woke up. His feet touched the cold floor, and he ordered hot tea from the guesthouse steward.

With the tea came a new letter from Hsueh. Impatiently, he slit the seal and read. This latest news was interesting indeed.

Now far too weak to offer any resistance to his wife, Kaotsung had actually tried to abdicate—but she had not allowed him.

Not allowed him? An Emperor not allowed by his wife to abdicate? It was extraordinary.

A new morning. He raised the hot bowl of green tea to his lips, nearly scalding his fingertips. He blew lightly across the steaming surface, pondering the strangeness of it all, and wondered what news would come in the next letter from the Tibetan behind the walls of Madame Yang's compound.

* * *

He is an attractive boy, Kaotsung thought, looking at the handsome young Crown Prince Hung, now fifteen years old, who sat by his father's sickbed. Yes, he is a comely boy, soft-spoken and respectful. I do not think that he looks at all like me. Maybe around the mouth. The eyes, though, are definitely his mother's, dark and deep, but without her . . . intent.

The boy leaned close to the Emperor, sharing the same air with his stricken father's ragged breathing. Kaotsung was certain: the peculiar dark depth in his eyes was not his mother's madness. It was his vitality. A good and popular prince, he thought. The people love him as a humane and filial young man.

"Father . . . Father . . ." the boy whispered, leaning even closer to Kaotsung propped up on his pillows. "Father . . . do not try to speak." I must have tried to speak, Kaotsung thought, but I can only grunt and drool. I should know better than to try. Look at all those hands that wipe at my chin with the scented towels. "Father, I know that you can hear me," the young Crown Prince continued. "Just listen and nod your head. That is no problem for you, is it?" No, it is not, Kaotsung nodded.

"Father, I am afraid of my mother." The boy spoke in a hushed earnest tone. Kaotsung nodded again. "I am sorry that you are so ill and I pray that you will recover. But you must help me in any way possible. You must help me now, Father, despite everything." Hung paused and shook his head. "Your illness is poorly timed, Father," the Crown Prince said with a slight smile, a touch of humor in his voice. Despite everything, Kaotsung thought, and tried to return the smile.

"Because I am being sent north to the summer palace for my education," the boy continued. "I am to go in a week. That is what my mother wishes . . ." He paused, seeming to think about this for a moment. "That is what my mother commands. I am to further my study of the classics with your old tutor." Kaotsung nodded. That was not unusual. The Crown Prince was sent up every summer, Kaotsung thought; that was the tradition of my father and grandfather. "And it does not give me much time, Father. I fear that mother will remember something from the past, and order the deaths of the two hand-maidens."

Kaotsung shook his head and set his brow in a semblance of confusion. It was the best he could manage.

"Then you do not remember, do you, Father?" Hung

asked. "It was so long ago and they were of so little importance that they were simply forgotten. Forgotten by everyone, it would seem! Like all little people, Father, they can simply slip through the skeins of life. It all happened long before I was born." Hung must have seen the confusion in his father's eyes. "They were the unfortunate flotsam left over after Mother's predecessor's deposal. Incidental victims, locked away and forgotten. The personal household attendants of your first Empress," Hung added by way of explanation. "You are probably wondering how I came to know of this injustice."

Kaotsung shook his head as if he were curious for the answer. But the Emperor was not wondering how it came about at all. He knew all too well. Someone whose conscience could no longer hold quiet—a eunuch servant, a jailer who brought them food, even another handmaiden perhaps—had managed to leak word to the compassionate and intelligent young prince.

"It was well over a year ago, Father, but I did not have a chance with Mother so close and . . . " Hung's whisper trailed off; he said nothing for a moment. "But then there was your illness, and it seemed that there would never be a time. You see," the prince continued, leaning close to his father again, "there was a eunuch servant from the Inner Household staff who has seen to the women's care all these years. One of the women has been very sick, and he helped her by bringing in a physician, but of course, he feared for his life. . . . "

And who does not? Kaotsung thought. But he could only nod slowly as he looked unblinkingly at his son.

"Father, they have been detained for all these years. Free them before she remembers their existence. We have four days before I must leave. I will bring the Imperial jailers before your bed and I will bring your seal. If you are not yet talking, we shall carry out the Imperial decree by your nods of affirmation and I shall act as your intermediary. My hands upon the seal." The boy's eyes were lit with this thought of hope for the two innocent serving women and for his own ingenuity in the face of so many obstacles. "And we shall give them money and an escort to see them far off long before *she* will ever think of them again. I doubt that she has thought of them in years. She has been so busy. But my instinct tells me that she *will* remember them soon, for word of the physician's visits has leaked out. She will hear of it, and remember them, and . . . "

Kaotsung nodded. The boy was right; she never really

forgot anything. Like the Imperial librarians filing away long disused parchments, she might draw on them at any moment. One never knew anything about Wu. One never counted on anything. One no longer hoped for the best; one simply released oneself from hope. It saved the anxiety.

Kaotsung managed a smile as his son rose from his chair, placing a hand on his father's shoulder. Kaotsung's smile, though no one would have known it but himself, was one of pity for the boy. How could he explain it, even if he had a voice? Such strength of character, such meddling in his mother's affairs . . . but perhaps . . . We shall act quickly. No one will be the wiser. As for the jailers, the physician, and the informing servants, they too, will be sent away with pensions. Perhaps between all her rages and her vigilance the little people can simply slip through the skeins once again.

With the third letter from Hsueh that week, the nagging worry he had tried to push out of his mind as too fantastic to consider had grown into something ominous.

Hsueh's first two letters had outlined the noble young son's pleas for the lives of the two female servants before his father, and the subsequent release of the women, disguised and under cover of darkness. How Hsueh came to be aware of these secrets he did not tell Dee. There were the usual sources for such things—servants, someone passing in a hallway or pressing an ear to the wall, a few words of a whispered conversation overheard. But so many details were known. Far too many, and this fact was most disturbing to Dee. Because whatever the means had been by which these secrets had found their way to Hsueh at Madame Yang's home, it was more than certain that they had also found their way to the Empress.

With his third letter of the week, Hsueh included the substance of an interior palace proclamation. Because of various meteorological signs, compounded with fear for the Crown Prince Hung's wellbeing and the Imperial Family's problems with mutinous assassins hidden within the walls of the Forbidden City itself, it was necessary to send the Crown Prince's entourage north to the summer palace in Hopei Province four days earlier than planned and by a different route from the original one.

Dee raised his eyes from Hsueh's letter, the unwelcome image of an infant lying dead in its cradle rising in his consciousness again.

By the time Hsueh's fifth letter arrived, the Crown Prince's royal entourage was well under way with the blessings of Wu and Madame Yang. And the heavy gray skies that had been threatening rain for weeks but obstinately refused to break added to the uncomfortable sense of expectancy. Dee's private dread grew until it seemed as palpable as the pall of smoke that hung in the stale summer air of Loyang all the way out to the flaking whitewashed compound of his magisterial offices south of the city's central market.

Kaotsung sat up in his bed in the lesser throne room that morning awaiting audience with his special visitor. Elegant robes of state adorned him, and the quilts had been arranged around him in such a way so as to minimize his pallid, diminished condition. He blinked his eyes in the bright morning sunshine. He had decided to be an Emperor again, if just for the next few hours, but was painfully aware of his ravaged, wounded appearance in the merciless light. An uncomfortable heat fell on the left side of his face, the side that still dragged behind the other.

"The curtains," he whispered to the steward who stood attentively close; the man uttered a few terse orders, and the servants scurried about the high-ceilinged room closing shutters and pulling the curtains partway, softening the relentless glare. It was better, but still not right. He felt the good side of his face pull down in a frown of dissatisfaction.

"Shall we move the bed, Your Highness?" the steward asked solicitously.

"Yes. There," he whispered, pointing weakly with his nose, indicating a spot on the other side of the room.

"But the screens, Your Highness. They are in the way. They are massive and attached to the floor."

"Remove them," he said, and they jumped to obey, a little surprised, he thought; they were unused to their Emperor making commands.

Indeed, they were unused to hearing his voice at all. So was he, for that matter. It had returned to him quite suddenly two days before, breaking from his throat hoarsely and raggedly on the afternoon that the news had been delivered to him like a blow to the groin. And this morning, he was receiving a visitor. An important visitor, whose request to see him had made him struggle up out of his sickness and grief.

He was anxious to see the bold magistrate from Yangchou, who had requested a special audience with the ailing Emperor. Wu had gone to her mother's house in the city for several days, where she could weep in solace and privacy, she had said. And then an extraordinary thing had happened: no sooner had she left than the request from Magistrate Dee had arrived. It was as if the magistrate had known somehow that the Empress would be gone from the palace, Kaotsung marveled.

The day he had found his voice again, a wail of sorrow that had surprised him and everyone around him, was the day he learned the price his son had paid for his courage and compassion. The entourage, so it was said, had proceeded toward the palace in Hopei along an unannounced route. Despite the protection afforded Prince Hung in a closed carriage, surrounded by an elite cadre of lancers and bowmen, the young man fell to an assassin's arrow, which somehow passed through the carriage and then managed to pass through his temples. Word traveled quickly south by the fleetest horse bearing the most skilled messenger. By the time news of the death reached Kaotsung, some three days later, he had known something dreadful was approaching, for he had awakened that morning from a dream of galloping hoofbeats with clammy beads of sweat on his forehead.

"August Father, if you would allow this humble servant, I may be able to assist in discovering the nature of this calamity that has befallen the Imperial Family."

Dee delivered his formal request softly, squinting in the morning sun slanting between the curtains. The light caused Kaotsung's golden Imperial robes to gleam brilliantly, adding an unnatural yellow pallor to the Emperor's already sickly complexion. The last time Dee had seen Kaotsung had been by candlelight. There is nothing as merciless as daylight, Dee thought. The ravages of life with the Empress were plain on the Emperor's face.

"I cannot say how long it might take me to uncover the party that infiltrated the Crown Prince's entourage, August Father. But it is possible to find out." Dee paused. "Especially if we do not allow any more time to pass. We must not delay. Time is our worst enemy," he said, making an effort to control the rising tone of urgency in his voice.

"In all things," Kaotsung whispered.

"In all things, yes. And most certainly in such investigations, August Father," Dee said. Yes, and we both know where the investigations might ultimately point, Dee thought. But we play this delicate game of tiptoeing around, pretending.

"What is it that you want, Investigator Dee?" the Emperor rasped with effort. Dee leaned close so that he could hear and understand the stricken man. "There is no longer much that I am empowered to offer."

"Perhaps we might begin to remedy that situation," Dee said, afraid that his words would sound only like an empty promise.

The Emperor shook his head wearily. "Any investigation will fall short. Die before it can blossom." He shrugged. "No governing body to maintain it. No *sane* governing body," he corrected himself.

"That is one of the reasons I am here today, August Father," Dee said, lowering his voice and glancing around the large empty hall. "I wish to help reestablish that governing body, that sane government you speak of." The Emperor looked at Dee with weak, questioning eyes, as if Dee had suggested that they invite the gods down from the heavens. "The Council, Father. The Council of Six," Dee whispered, his voice now as soft as the Emperor's. His words caused a profound reaction in Kaotsung: his eyes widened and his nostrils flared, as if he were inhaling a wonderful fragrance. He released a thin stream of breath slowly through his teeth.

"You can do this?" he asked.

"I believe that I might be able to. With your help."

"Six good men . . . ?" Kaotsung began, then shook his head again. "You will not find them."

"I have talked to many," Dee said, but stopped. That was not a strong enough answer. He rephrased it: "I have heard the rising murmurs of disaffection. I believe that with your support I can tap this disaffection."

"Disaffection," Kaotsung murmured. "Nothing new. But fear is something else."

"Yes, August Father, but I believe sincerely that there are now a few willing to come forward after so many years. And these few will be the beginning," Dee said eagerly. "Others will follow when they know of your backing."

"And you?" Kaotsung said, raising his eyes to Dee's face.

"I would not think of sending any man into a place that I would not first go myself. I am willing to take up the vulnerable post of president of this reformed Council. If I am deemed worthy enough for such an undertaking." With these words, Dee felt light-headed, and the air was rare and strained. "I must be honest, August Father. There is much fear among the officials with whom I talked. Much fear. As you say. But I believe that *we* could win them over."

He wondered for a moment if the Emperor had heard what he just said. His face had gone dark and remote, and his eyes were ten thousand miles away. Dee peered at him uneasily, afraid that he had left and was not coming back. "You will consider this?" he asked anxiously, looking for some sign of response in those eyes.

The distance melted slowly from the Emperor's eyes, like a thin crust of ice on a puddle. The Emperor nodded slowly, then tucked his chin into his chest and took a deep breath before raising his head. He motioned with a single thick finger for Dee to come close. There was a long silence in which they studied each other. Then the Emperor spoke, his voice barely audible.

"I will consider your request. For an investigation into the death. Also your request for the reestablishment of my father's Council." He stopped again, breathing hard with the effort of so many words as if he had just climbed a flight of stairs. "But . . . " The Emperor paused again. "I must warn you of the true nature of my disease." Dee stopped breathing. "It would be a crime against man if the Son of Heaven cared and did nothing. But . . . " Kaotsung shook his head sadly. "But I am afraid that it is far far worse, Investigator. My sickness is a transgression against heaven itself. Because I do not even care."

In the guest quarters that night at the palace, Dee did not dare to put his head down on the pillow. He waited for morning and word from the Emperor.

At dawn, the household attendants came to his room with tea and fruit and pastries. They also brought an envelope bearing the Imperial seal of the Emperor Kaotsung and the T'ang House of Li. While an attendant stood and watched, Dee opened the missive. It was terse and clear:

To the Esteemed Magistrate Dee Jen-chieh:

The Imperial Family appreciates your concern at this time of great and dreadful tragedy, but this is to inform you that there are to be no further investigations into the matter of the Crown Prince's sudden and mysterious murder en route to Hopei. The Palace Department of Internal Security, the Yulin Palace Guards, will continue to carry out all such thorough and impartial investigations. And further, any future attempts to reorganize the retired organs of Imperial government will be looked upon as a heretical gesture both implying lack of confidence in the Imperial establishment and impugning the Son of Heaven's credibility. Therefore, these efforts could be considered treasonous, and treason, as you well know, is ultimately punishable by death.

There was the jangle of metal and leather. Four men wearing the armor of the Imperial Yu-lin Palace Guards and decorated with the symbols of Imperial livery appeared. Dee's escorts. Behind them, bearers brought a sedan chair. Dee stuffed his pockets with sections of fruit and doughy pastry and hastily gulped a mouthful of too-hot tea which burned a path down to his stomach. He motioned away the chair waiting to bear him to his carriage. He preferred to cross the inhospitable terraces of Wu's government on his own feet. He nodded to his escorts. The guards took up their positions around the honorable magistrate and they left the guest quarters.

With the four pairs of heavy feet clanking fore and aft as they descended the spiral staircase, Dee marveled at his luck in leaving the palace still alive and breathing. How had she known? She had been two days away, yet she had known everything—that Dee had visited and what he had proposed in a room containing only two people.

When they emerged into the pale winter sunlight, Dee took a deep, grateful breath of outside air and climbed into the waiting carriage.

LETTER FROM HSUEH:

Master Dee, I discovered that the great magistrate from Yangchou was most recently a guest within the walls of the palace, and that he sought audience with the Son of Heaven. I do not know the particulars, but I trust that you will reveal them to me when we are once again together over the wine cups.

There is news from the palace that may not have reached your ears. It could not have been very long since your departure. I do not give you that news here. I apologize for being cryptic, but I will share it with you tomorrow. Join me at the place where we first talked. Meet me at the end of the Hour of the Hare and the beginning of the Hour of the Dragon. Until then, Magistrate, stay safe.

Stay safe. The words whispered themselves in Dee's mind as he walked briskly across the marketplace, the city not yet fully awakened, the sky still pink and cold. It had been three weeks now since he had seen his colleague. Dee wondered why Hsueh had chosen those words, then told himself that they were merely words to close a letter, and that he should not read anything more than that into them.

Stay safe! The world was indeed a very dangerous place, he reflected, our destruction imminent from the moment of our birth. A cruel joke built into our nature, an inevitability, just as the moving gears of the water clock eventually bring the mechanism full circle. And in the face of that inevitability, to comfort themselves and to give meaning to their existence, men sought the ultimate safety—salvation, release from the cycle of suffering and death that is this world. But even on the subject of salvation, men could not agree, and divided themselves into disparate schools of thought. Since his association with Hsueh, Dee had these matters on his mind a great deal, and what he had learned from the monk was thought-provoking.

The older school of Buddhist thought, the Hinayana, held to the notion that salvation was a very rare and exceedingly elusive jewel, reserved for the few. It was obtainable only through lifetimes of rigorous application of highly esoteric knowledge and discipline. This form of salvation did not await with open arms the common plodder, the average sufferer stumbling through this grimy, hostile world, Dee reflected. And it was no coincidence that among the aristocrats of earthly society, Hinayana tended to be the form of choice. As always, such people preferred not to have to mix with the rabble. Madame Yang was a perfect example of this.

But at the center of popular schools of Buddhist thought such as the Mahayana was the very appealing notion that salvation was available to almost everyone, not merely an elite few. It was a very public party, with boddhisattvas everywhere—beings who had already obtained enlightenment and could, if they chose, leave the earth forever and dwell in eternal bliss in the Western Paradise, the realm of the Buddha Amitabha. Instead, these ascended beings stayed behind, roaming this sad, miserable world, striving to help even the lowliest of their fellow creatures attain salvation.

Moving through the quickening market with its smells and noise, Dee tried to imagine what it would be like to be one of these enlightened beings who voluntarily forfeited a world of perfection to wander amid the sickness and pain of this world like a sailor on primitive hostile shores.

This noisy, dirty, busy, complicated world, Dee thought, passing through the market's seething central square. In his years as a magistrate, Dee had seen virtually every possible manifestation of human deviousness, stupidity, cruelty, and ugliness.

Given the state of things, it was almost possible to believe in the Buddhists' Era of the Final Degenerate Law, in which the world supposedly dwelt at this very moment as it awaited the prophetic coming of the Future Buddha Maitreya: a time so removed from the moment of the Buddha's death that his teachings had decayed, deteriorated, suffered the inevitable attrition of time—with form and matter, full of deceptive, decadent vigor and vitality, coming inevitably to no good.

And how would he, Magistrate Dee, like a world free of temptations, defilement, desire, suffering, love and hate, women, old age, birth, death, and the rest of it? It sounded to him like a world devoid of challenge. He thought very hard about this. Without imperfection and incompletion, without the inevitability of death, without a man's finite allotted time as a backdrop, without pain, how would his life or any of his actions have meaning?

Salvation. For the wealthy and blessed, it meant further glory and aggrandizement. For the poor and toiling, it meant release from suffering after this life and aid and intervention during it. A mirage, a myth. A very marketable myth, this purchasable salvation. But quite unconvincing to him. As he entered the final alley before the teashop he became very conscious of the weight and solidity of the broken, uneven paving stones beneath the soles of his feet. As he did so, something inside him whispered that this was all the world that there would ever be.

And, he thought, it was quite enough.

* * *

The tea garden was already crowded early in the morning. Those who labored in the market shops before dawn had already put in much time. Dee preferred the anonymity of crowds, the noise and bustle. He had to lean close to the Tibetan to hear every word.

"Magistrate, you Chinese speak of the blessings of heaven," Hsueh began.

"*We* Chinese," Dee emphasized, reminding Hsueh that he had become as Chinese as himself, "also speak of heaven bringing its opposite."

"Then it is that opposite that I mean when I speak of *her*."

"Mother or daughter, Hsueh?"

"I no longer draw a distinction. They are simply two faces of the same entity." He sat pensively. "Two faces of Chamunda—the goddess annihilator. A vision of death and destruction in Buddhist and Tibetan Tantric lore. But her victims' faces are always serene."

Dee raised his eyebrows questioningly.

"Yes, Magistrate, serene. Despite the fact that she is often depicted in sculpture or painting ripping their arms and legs off and biting into their soft innards, her chin dripping with blood, entrails hanging from her mouth. But the artists are always careful to put the most placid and beatific expressions on their faces. Sometimes they are even smiling. Only the demon herself appears to be in any sort of agony."

"Serene and peaceful," Dee said, shaking his head.

"Supposedly because the idea of dying at the hands of the goddess is a *release*." Hsueh looked down into his tea as if gathering strength. "I told you that I have news."

Dee waited. The monk raised his eyes.

"Kaotsung has named the Empress Acting Regent."

"Acting Regent!" Dee breathed, unbelieving.

"Yes. It will be she who sits at Morning Audience now in his stead."

"Then the government is hers," Dee said quietly. "How long do you suppose Kaotsung will last now? The man is as good as dead."

Hsueh nodded. He held the bowl of tea to his lips, then paused and lifted it above his head.

"To Chamunda," he toasted before drinking.

19

"It is not right, madame."

"It must be. Look again!" Madame Yang demanded.

"Yes, do it again by all means. Measure the boy's head again."

"Yes, yes, of course, my Divine Empress. But I am certain of the readings. I cannot . . . " He shook his head with annoyance, cutting short his speech.

"With those things." Wu pointed to the odd calipers with the bowed arms on the low table. "Measure with those things."

"Yes, with the calipers, Nagaspa. Do it again. You did not mark the apex of the forehead properly." Madame Yang pressed her finger emphatically into the prince's scalp. The boy, who had just turned sixteen, batted the hand away irritably. Yang ignored his resistance. "The forehead does not begin there, Nagaspa. Here. Here." She pressed her finger hard into Hsien's scalp again, this time in a different place, making him wince. "That is where the forehead begins," she declared. "Not here." She jabbed the prince again for emphasis while giving Wu's short, muscular Indian lover a reproving look.

"Mother," Wu said. "Watch what you are doing. You are hurting the boy."

"Nonsense," Yang said. "Your Nagaspa is a barbarian fraud. That is the boy's hairline, not his true forehead. He has such thick hair," she said, tugging a handful of it.

"Watch closely this time, madame," the Nagaspa said with ill-concealed impatience, carefully manipulating the strange measuring device over the young Crown Prince's forehead. "I am putting this end of the calipers where you suggest, Mother Yang. You see . . . there . . . and there . . . and . . . " He pivoted the free arm of the calipers to a spot between the boy's eyes and just above his nose. " . . . there," he finished importantly.

Then he began to read off the measuring characters of the miniature geomancer's rule: "Ben . . . Bing . . . Li . . . I . . . There, as I have already said, madame, bad dimensions. Crown Prince Hsien has bad dimensions. Not at all those of his poor deceased brother Hung."

"But your numbers did not predict his brother's unfortunate death," Madame Yang said disdainfully. "And you expect us to believe your measurements now, Nagaspa."

"It is true," Wu concurred. "Your numbers did not speak well, priest."

"Crown Prince Hung's was an unfortunate and unpredictable death. A death outside the parameters of self-cause. Therefore, it would not show up in such calculations," the Nagaspa said indignantly. He paused and looked at Mother Yang with wounded self-righteousness. "Besides, I did detect an irregularity then, but I thought better of mentioning it. So slight. But this boy's numbers do not lie, madame." He looked to Wu for support. Wu shrugged her shoulders. He continued, "Brother Hsien is not fit to rule. I have shown you that the shape of his head, the planes of his face, and now the measurements add up to his absolute unsuitability ever to be a ruler. He can never take up the divine reins of earthly government." While he spoke, his fingers continued to explore the terrain of the prince's head through the hair.

The boy's hand came up sharply then and seized the Nagaspa's thick muscled wrist, twisting the arm down. "I have had enough of this babble, *priest*," Crown Prince Hsien said angrily. "Take your damnable hands off my head."

"Crown Prince, you are hurting me. You go much too far with that temper of yours," the Nagaspa said carefully, yanking his wrist free.

"I have had enough of *his* posturing nonsense," the boy said to Wu and Yang.

"And *I* enough of *his* childish insolence in the face of my irrefutable truths. He is not fit to rule," the Nagaspa said with flat vehemence. "Too much whoring with the serving wenches. Too many whoring expeditions into the city. He has far too little discipline and far too much freedom. If you wish my opinion—"

"Something of such little value is neither wished for nor wanted, you charlatan," the Crown Prince lashed out. Wu thought proudly that Hsien was the perfect mirror of his mother. This little session today with the calipers had been Wu's idea, a birthday present for the boy, but it was turning out to be quite different from the amusing pastime, the parlor entertainment, that they had all expected. It was obvious that the Nagaspa had decided to make a bold move to seize the opportunity to make himself important again, to reassert himself in Wu's eyes. How tedious, Wu thought. They all became tedious eventually.

"Quiet! Quiet, the two of you!" Madame Yang shouted, eyes darting back and forth between the Nagaspa and the Crown Prince.

"As I was saying, madame, in my opinion, the boy . . ." the Nagaspa continued, making no effort to quell the rising anger in his voice.

"Shut up, priest. There is no one who cares for your opinion. It is not your affair," Wu said. "The only thing that is irrefutable is your mouth."

"I did not hear that rude remark, my Divine Empress." The Nagaspa covered his ears and shook his head. "I will simply ignore it," he said with an arrogant peevishness which, lately, had been wearing badly on Wu. "But I was saying that the boy expels his vital forces without any concern for his inner balance. He is hardly the exemplary prince that his scholarly brother Hung was. Do not think that the rumors of this young Prince Hsien's questionable contacts outside the walls of this palace—in the plebeian city—have not attracted considerable attention." Self-righteousness and indignation struggled for the upper hand in the Nagaspa's voice. "The rumors fly—"

Wu cut him off with a rude laugh. "Who cares what the lowly think or say, priest?"

Madame Yang now watched the proceedings with raised, disinterested eyebrows while Wu took a motherly and solicitous position beside her son, displacing the Nagaspa, who moved to the far side of the table and began to scoop his array of instruments hastily and angrily into his bag.

"We will all feel better after we have had time to relax and think about what—"

"Shut up, priest!" Wu and Hsien said in perfect unison. They looked at each other and laughed.

"Dance your magician's dance and vanish from my sight," Hsien said, flicking his hand at the furious Nagaspa, who snapped his bag shut and stalked from the room.

Prince Hsien had an extraordinary memory. He could see clearly all the way back to his mother's coronation, and he could remember his nursemaid's hand leading him up the wide stairs to the throne. The image was clear and immediate, with all the attendant sensations of feel and smell; he could even remember the awkwardness of climbing the stairs on his short little legs. And he could still see his mother's bowed head, the coruscating gleam of her hair, and he could recall the cool, jeweled weight of the crown in his tiny hands.

Surely it was a curse to remember everything so well— he could even conjure the smell of the coronation's processional elephant and the fragrance of the blossoms, as if their odor lingered in the room now. And even at that delicate age of two years, he remembered thinking that something was wrong. He had felt foolish. He was a very little child, barely able to talk, yet somehow he knew enough to feel foolish for participating in one of his mother's performances long before he could possibly know just how absurd it really was.

And there were other things he remembered with perfect clarity from his first conscious moments—for instance, the way his mother's wild howls of laughter could metamorphose into wails of grief. And it could go just as easily in the other direction. When he was very little he used to watch her subject his father to these emotional twists and turns, pulling the poor man this way and that, and he knew that her manipulations had brought on his father's attacks and terrible deterioration. Many was the time he had watched as his mother made her defenseless husband laugh or weep so intensely that Hsien could not bear it. He remembered being a very little boy and believing that his poor father's head would burst like an overfull water sack. The fear was so real that he sometimes used to cringe when Kaotsung was near.

Was she, with her utter lack of conscience, not unlike a man who is born without sight, or arms or legs? Was it just something left out by nature, a cruel mistake of birth? Or was it something that had taken root and grown inside her soul? He truly did not know. Hsien and his brother had looked on, as they grew into young manhood, helpless to do anything, while his mother and grandmother disposed of aunts and cousins and distant uncles without a twitch. And the most terrible part of it was that neither mother nor grandmother had ever even known any of their victims. They were not even interested enough to know them and hate them. Hsien had watched it all. He had witnessed every deceitful posture that his mother and grandmother could effect, every self-satisfied wave of the hand, every huff of indignation, every mock-tear-filled roll of their eyes. And he knew, deep inside, that the reason he understood his mother so well was that he was the one most like her. Everyone had always said that he was his mother's true son, her heir, and he knew that it was true.

And now his brother was dead. An ambush on the way to the summer palace? He doubted it very much. Shortly after his brother's death, Hsien had overheard the famous Buddha-hunting magistrate Dee Jen-chieh talking to his father. He had been just outside the door. The eunuch servants had said nothing, because he had warned them to keep his secret. He said he was trying to help his father. The household servants were also on the poor man's side; they had witnessed Wu's tyranny for many years.

His father spoke so softly, and the magistrate leaned so close when he whispered to the Emperor, that Hsien could barely make out what they were saying. There were things that he missed. But he had heard enough to understand that an ambush would have been virtually impossible with the protection that his brother's entourage afforded. And it was certainly not a palace coup of any sort, because Hung was no threat to anyone. Hung had neither enemies nor power—he was never the chosen son. He had died only because he had dared to try to right a wrong from a long time ago—to free two poor serving wretches lost in his mother's shuffle.

And the worst of it was that though she had been indifferent to her other victims, Wu had truly loved Hung. His mother had lavished attention on him and had gone to great lengths to educate him, always praising his scholarship and seeking the finest tutors for him. She *had* loved him. Hsien was certain that his mother's affection for Hung had been real, just as it had been for his father, Kaotsung. And that was what made it so dreadful a crime: just as her laughter could turn to howls of pain, her love, in all its intensity, could turn to . . . to what? He had no name for it.

And so it chilled him to know that the affection she demonstrated for him was also real. How quickly she had sided with him against her lover-holy man, this Gandharan from northern India—her dancing, head-measuring fool of a Nagaspa. Hsien hated, despised, this "priest," far more than any other of his mother's collection of holy charlatans from the west. This muscular little Nagaspa was nothing but a leaping, prancing, pandering, pretentious, and by turns arrogant and

fawning sycophant. He hoped that his mother had finally
grown tired of this one. *He* certainly had.

Early one morning, at the end of the Hour of the Tiger,
the faintest sliver of roseate light illuminated the smooth shiny
wet cobblestones of the pathway known as the Way of Sanctity
and Transformation, which wended its way through the thick
stands of pine and bamboo. The path was part of a wild but
well-tended woodland within the high-walled enclosure of the
northernmost boundary of the Imperial Palace. Every morning
at dawn, pine needles, leaves, and animal droppings were assiduously swept from the path and its stones scrubbed so that
the monks and nuns and abbots who frequented the palace
might have pristine access to the temples, stupas, meditation
halls, and stony shinerooms Wu had created in the woodland
setting.

This morning, the usual team of five eunuchs was busy
scrubbing the winding stone path. One of the servants was
working some distance ahead of the others at a place where
the path became very tortuous before plunging steeply into a
leafy hollow. Just before the path began its decline, the eunuch
spied some thick dark drops of something that looked like
blood. Yes, it was blood. Animal blood? The blood of a deer
or roebuck, most likely. It was common. Animal as well as
human predators were not infrequent visitors to the more remote regions of the park. Dipping his straw broom into the
bucket of water carried by his assistant, the servant began to
scrub the stones, following the erratic trail of spots and
splashes as it led down the hill into an area of trampled brush
at the side of the cobbled path. Then he screamed the most
terrified old-woman scream imaginable. The assistant, who
had been walking a few paces behind the scrubber, rushed
forward, then dropped his bucket and stood paralyzed, unable
to take his eyes from the tableau in the thicket of brush at the
side of the path.

The gruesome scene before them was not the random car-
nage of nature. Rather, it was a meticulously created sculpture
of mutilation, arranged with the pure cruelty and ugly humor
that is solely the domain of the human heart.

Closest to the cobbled path was a man's body, minus the
head, propped in a perfect kneeling posture like a monk called
to prayer. A yard or so from the body lay the man's head. At
least, the immediate assumption was that the head on the

ground belonged to the supplicating body, unless there was another victim nearby.

It was the details of the wanton grisliness of the murder, rather than the murder itself, that was on the nervous contralto aunty tongues of every eunuch servant of the Inner Household staff. It seemed that those who had themselves lost a part of their bodies were always more grimly fascinated at the prospect of someone else suffering a similar misfortune.

The corpse had been quickly gathered up and dispensed with, so that only a very few had actually laid eyes on the horror. Secondhand accounts, embellished, passed around, and retold by the wagging tongues of so many jittery eunuchs necessarily lost some accuracy and objectivity—but the raw insidious cruelty of it emerged with hideous clarity.

All about the palace, the household eunuchs babbled about there being something on top of the severed head. When the others asked the obvious, if the head had been wearing a hat of some sort, those who delivered the juicy news said that it was clearly not a hat. They said that the eyes of the unfortunate victim had been open and rolled upward, their gaze forever fixed upon the last thing they saw—a most unusual two-armed measuring device that spanned the crown of the head.

A *what*? the curious eunuchs of the Household staff asked. An instrument. A device, the others who had heard the news "first-hand" responded, wagging their heads affirmatively. Yes, yes, certainly that was what it was, they answered enthusiastically. According to what they had heard, it was a measuring device, with odd calibrations of some sort marked on it.

Like a set of calipers? they asked incredulously. Yes, it was very much a caliperlike device. No other word would do so well to describe the dead man's incomprehensible headdress.

Guards flanked the Crown Prince as he was led quietly into his mother's chambers. Prince Hsien looked straight ahead before lowering his eyes to the cold black slate of the entry hall.

The Empress stood near the writing desk. With her gaze fixed somewhere far beyond the walls of the palace, she seemed to be looking through her son as he was brought into the center of the room. The boy's grandmother, Madame Yang, sat on a day couch in the far corner of the hall in front of an enormous cinnabar-and-mother-of-pearl screen depicting scenes from the young Buddha's early years.

With eyes discreetly averted, the diminutive figure of Historian Shu sat nearby behind the writing table, shuffling papers, his busy little hands officiously self-absorbed in their meaningless task. Shu had become very good at riding out the currents of Wu's rages; that meant knowing when to mind his own affairs.

"He will stand there," Empress Wu commanded. "Do not bring him any closer." She studied the Crown Prince carefully from head to toe, then began to speak in the calm tone that always gave Historian Shu a not unpleasant thrill of impending danger. "That is not the son that I raised. Is it?" She looked around the room as if asking for assent. Shu's eyes moved quickly between the boy and his mother before returning to his "work."

He thought that the Crown Prince looked as if he had been struggling with a demon or a ghost all night. His hair hung down in unkempt knots, and his eyes were sunk into dark sleepless pits in his haggard face. It was not the face of a divine sixteen-year-old boy, but of an exhausted frightened one that Shu saw when the Crown Prince was first led into the room. Young Prince Hsien had wrestled with something very dark, Shu thought. And he seemed to have lost.

"You, my brilliant son, whom I have helped to educate . . ." Wu continued. Shu lifted his eyes furtively to examine the boy, then returned to his pretend paperwork again. He recognized the dreadful calm in Wu's voice. It signaled something ominous. And the historian thought that it was especially ominous when he had no idea where she was going. He was there because she had called for her councillor and historian. She had not told him anything at all about where she would take things today, and that made Shu uneasy.

"You, Prince Hsien, the brilliant writer of history and poetry, the student with so much promise, have now chosen to write a bit of your own history." The boy did not move or look up at his mother. "You did not think that your place in history was sufficiently secure. You began to make history to your own liking, didn't you?" Wu asked, her voice soft and even.

The historian turned around and looked at Madame Yang. He thought he saw a sly glimmer of acknowledgment in her eyes. "You did not think that your place in history was secure enough," Wu repeated, a little louder. "So . . . ?" she started.

"My son . . . you are my son, are you not?" The historian saw the prince set his jaw, his eyes not moving from the cold stones at his feet.

"You are my son?" Wu asked, eyes widened, a pleading tone in her voice now. The historian inhaled a deep, silent breath and stacked the papers in front of him into useless piles.

"Why? Please tell me why!" Wu whispered, her eyes fixed intently on the boy's. "Why should you do this to me?"

Hsien stood, carved from stone. It must have cost him. The only movement Shu could detect was in the boy's throat, as if he were swallowing or suppressing words with a mighty effort.

"Why would you do this thing? Why would you betray *your own mother?*" Wu pleaded softly, lavishing great agony on the last three words. Shu, humming softly to himself, listened to the familiar practiced anguish in her voice. "I am your mother. I have given you life and nurtured you." Wu paused, and her face went an angry red. She forced something like a smile and stared at Hsien. After a long while she spoke again. "Just talk to me. Tell me anything. Make me understand. Perhaps I will understand."

Shu watched the muscles of Wu's jaw working, and imagined for a moment what it might be like to be ground between those strong white teeth of hers. He turned a "boat" of black ink into the water and idly prepared his writing brushes. This was it, he knew. This was the end of the quiet.

"TALK TO ME. YOU WILL TALK TO ME!" Wu bellowed, making everyone in the room jump, even Madame Yang. At the same moment she stepped up to the boy, yanked his head back by the hair, and slapped him hard across the face. Before he could drop his head she slapped him again, then again until blood trickled from one nostril and the corner of his mouth. "YOU WILL NOT BE QUIET TO YOUR MOTHER!"

She slapped him twice more, causing Shu to wince with each loud crack of her hand. With the third slap, the historian accidentally crumbled the ink stick into the well of the grinding stone. He had to fish around in the water for the pieces, the gluey lampblack staining his fingers while Wu continued to scream.

"YOU ARE A MURDERER! A MURDERER! DO YOU HEAR ME? You have killed the Nagaspa. You have murdered the wise and gentle priest. My son is a murderer. Not a brave warrior. No. Not my son, the Crown Prince. No. He is a murderer. He attacks them behind their backs, when they cannot defend themselves. MY SON, HSIEN, IS A COWARDLY MURDERER!"

"Mother, I am *not* a murderer!" Hsien said at last.

"SHUT UP! YOU ARE A COWARDLY MURDERER . . . YOU ARE A SKULKING COWARDLY MURDERER!"

"IT IS NOT TRUE!" Hsien yelled back, wiping the blood from his battered lip with his sleeve. "I have *not* murdered anyone! I . . . I was not even aware that the Nagaspa had been taking exercise along the path in the park so early." Hsien looked pale and frightened, but Shu saw a determination in him now.

Wu screwed up her eyes and fixed the boy with such a hard look that the historian was taken aback. "And how did you know that the Nagaspa had been along that path?"

"It is on everyone's tongue, Mother," the boy shouted. "Unless you are deaf!"

"Perhaps I am. Everyone's, you say? I did not hear that the Nagaspa was discovered along the path." She turned to Shu. "Did you?"

Shu pretended absurdly that his attention had been diverted until this moment. "I am sorry, my Empress, what is it that you ask? My thoughts were elsewhere." With a casual sweep of his hand, the historian indicated the papers in front of him.

"Had you heard that the Nagaspa made a habit of taking an early-morning constitutional along the path?"

"Mother, I did not say—"

"The path . . . ?" Shu asked.

"The cobbled path through the woodland, Shu. You know the one. The Way of Sanctity and Transformation."

"Yes, of course. A most beautiful path established for quiet contemplation and meditation," The historian prated irrelevantly. "But I was not familiar with the Nagaspa's habits. I do not make the business of others my own, you understand." He rolled up several of his papers and fastened them with a silken cord. "However, it does not surprise me that one so wise and solicitous of his physical well-being as your Nagaspa would take to the path so early—the air is particularly fine that time of morning, my Empress. No dust or haze from the city reaches the palace woods."

"Now I shall ask my mother the same question," Wu said.

In the back of the room, Madame Yang nodded, then shrugged her shoulders. "I did not know where the little wretch was found," she said, pronouncing her words with disdain as if she were referring to a mangy cur found stiff in the back alley. "I had heard nothing more than that he was murdered and his body compromised in some fashion."

"You see," Wu said. She turned around and faced Hsien. "We have no information. But you do, Prince Hsien. Why is that? Can you explain that?" The rage had left her voice.

"Mother, I did not know the Nagaspa's habits. I only knew where he was found that morning. Like everyone else." Hsien's pleading tone matched that of his mother's a few moments ago. How much like Wu Crown Prince Hsien is, the historian thought; not at all like his deceased brother Hung. Hsien was quick and resourceful, capable of dissembling without seeming to do so. He could twist and manipulate your emotions with his own. This one was truly his mother's reflection. And the historian knew that this was also what she saw in the boy—and the thing which, he was sure, most angered her.

"Enough, boy! Enough of this," Wu said. "You know why you were brought here. Forget about the Nagaspa. That is not so important as the other thing. I cannot forgive it, but I should have expected that you were capable of murder. But this . . ." Wu said with disgust, indicating the papers stacked on the desk in front of Shu. "I cannot believe that you would do this thing to me. I would not believe it, I refused to believe it. I told them all that it could not be true, that my own son would not be *fomenting a rebellion* against his mother. But what do my Yu-lin Palace Guard find when they enter your chambers?" Wu clenched a fist and pounded on the table with each word as if she were beating an enormous drum. "WHAT DO THEY FIND?"

The boy dropped his head and lowered his eyes to the floor again. Now he looked ready to surrender to his mother, Shu thought. Or perhaps it was that the prince dropped his head in readiness for the inevitable charges to be read against him. Hsien maintained an abject silence while his mother signaled the historian to withdraw the appropriate documents from the pile. When Shu had the papers, he looked up at her, careful to keep his eyes blank and impassive as he meticulously smoothed the pages set out on the desk in front of him. He awaited his cue from the Empress.

"Raise the traitor's head," Wu said to the guards. "Make him look at me." The two guards yanked the boy's head up by his hair just as his mother had done earlier, forcing it so far back he was looking at the ceiling. The guard who held on to the prince's disheveled braid then loosened his grip slightly while the other took firm hold of the boy's head between his palms and twisted it so that the prince faced straight ahead. The boy's nostrils flared out with anger. But still Hsien managed to keep his eyes averted, looking anywhere but at his mother.

"You will look at me now," Wu commanded. "The historian will read the charges," she decreed firmly and calmly. Shu straightened up officiously.

"For the most severe violation of the Civil Legal Codes of the T'ang-lu Shu-i," Shu began in his best pompously official tone, "Article Twenty, Chapter Sixteen, for the keeping and storing, for the maintaining and hoarding of military arms with intent to foment a coup, cause insurrection and rebellion against the rightfully established, legitimate, and heaven-decreed ruling house . . . In which regard . . . " Shu struggled to find his place on the next page. "In which regard, the discovery of some fifty broadswords, some one hundred rhinoceros-horn daggers, sixty-three pikes, a like number of war axes, one hundred and twenty-two bows, forty spring-loaded crossbows, three hundred iron bolts, thirty-two leather breastplates, Iranian and Sassanian chain mail in the numbers of . . . " Shu stopped, seeing the Empress's impatient eye upon him. "Madame does not wish for me to continue?" Shu sounded hurt, as if the compilation of the lists had been a great literary achievement.

"It is sufficient, Master Shu, to suggest the dangerous treachery abounding in this boy's heart." Wu spoke now as if she were referring to a complete stranger. "Read the final paragraph, Councillor."

Shu withdrew another bit of parchment, and took a deep preparatory breath.

"This cache of arms, providing sufficient weaponry to pose a risk to the Yu-lin Palace Guard and thereby the security of the Imperial Family and the stability of the Empire, was found secreted in the Crown Prince's apartments and in the Crown Prince's Imperial stables."

"Prince Hsien, have you anything to say for yourself?" Wu cut short the historian's proclamation. Her son stared at her now with unblinking eyes. "Have you anything to say for yourself?"

The boy's lips parted slightly. The formation of a word?

Shu wondered. Or a curse? In that way, too, he was like his mother. Dangerously strong-willed. He was her seed. But Hsien did not utter a sound. His tongue licked his dry lips. That was all. He continued to stare at his mother, as if he were trying to comprehend once and for all the phenomenon that had given him life. Surely the boy never considered his wan, pale shadow of a father as any part of that phenomenon at all.

Now Shu thought that he read something in the prince's eyes. Before this he had not been sure; in truth, he could never know for certain. But now he thought he saw murder. Not the murder of Wu's silly dancing Nagaspa, but a flicker of a more profound danger. Without a doubt this was what Wu saw as well.

What he saw, or thought he saw, was not even the first flame that would leap to life if given fuel and air. It was simply the first glowing ember of potential in the boy's dark unmoving eyes. An ember that could touch off a leaping flame, or vanish in a suffocation of smoke and ash. Maybe there was truth to the charges that he read. Maybe what he thought he saw in Hsien's eyes now was the truest essence of the murderer: the sixteen-year-old prince who could kill his mother.

It was a dire situation. With an ailing Emperor and another Crown Prince dead, another needed to be named. And that unlucky legitimacy fell upon the eldest of Wu's four remaining sons—a young man of only thirteen years named Chui-tsung, Heaven protect the unfortunate child.

Yesterday Hsueh had apologized for the sketchiness of the information he had to offer, but had made the daring promise that he would have more today.

While Dee waited in the pavilion, he poured himself another bowl of green tea and impatiently studied the faces of the crowd. Facts and questions tumbled about in his mind. Crown Prince Hsien had been banished for life to the isle of Hainan, but he had never reached his destination. He had committed suicide.

Were any of the extraordinary charges brought against Hsien real?

Had the young Crown Prince been fomenting a rebellion against his mother? And had he indeed done away with Wu's dancing Nagaspa? Or were Wu and Yang angry with the prince for some other reason? Had they made a discovery, perhaps that he had assisted his dead brother Hung in gaining

the release of the imprisoned serving women? And had Wu
and Yang, weary of the poor Nagaspa, dispatched him themselves, and then blamed the Crown Prince for it? Hadn't Hsueh
mentioned that Madame Yang had commented on the ever
more frequent arguments between the Empress and her Indian
lover in the last months?

Was the Crown Prince's death suicide at all?

Dee peered under the lid of the teapot, then poured the
cloudy, steaming remains into his bowl and sipped thoughtfully, straining the tea through his teeth to avoid the soggy
dregs. His eyes scanned the crowd, watching for the tall approaching figure of the monk-magician.

Outside the gardens, the market swelled with the
late-morning throngs. The yapping of alley dogs and the rhythmic chants of the vending hawkers made a strange music that
rode above the usual sounds of the crowd. Today, Dee relished
it, finding comfort in its normalcy. A song, a cry, that said that
while the world spun into disorder the market would always
remain the market.

Whatever I uncover, Dee thought grimly, I will at least
set down for posterity. Whether anything can be done with the
awful facts during my own life, I do not know. But the truth
will be known eventually, even if I am long dead. And the
monk had pledged his assistance. That was good. He would
not like to be in this all by himself.

He looked about, wondering what shape and form Hsueh
would take today. Yesterday, he had arrived with cages of
squawking birds across his shoulders. Noticing that his tea had
grown cold, Dee ordered a fresh pot, and waited, his fingers
worrying the fabric of his sleeves.

It took Dee a long time to understand that the monk was
not going to appear. Anticipation subtly gave way to fidgeting
impatience as the appointed hour came and then receded. By
the time the third pot of tea had grown cold and a chill had
crept into the air with the lengthening shadows, impatience
gave way to disquietude. The monk had never failed to keep
an appointment. Still, Dee waited, until the proprietor of the
shop began to light the lanterns and Dee's disquietude had
grown into the sure knowledge that something was not right,
not right at all, and he stood up from his hard bench and left
the pavilion.

* * *

It had been three days since the time of their planned meeting.

Yesterday, Dee had sent a runner to leave the disguised calling card of a "fellow devotee" at Madame Yang's Buddhist hospice. The gate steward had taken the card brusquely, saying nothing, not even indicating whether "Lama" Hsueh had ever been a guest there at all.

As Dee sat in his other offices at the National Bureau of Sacrifice, reviewing licenses and land counts for two new monasteries, he considered whether the monk Hsueh Huai-i might have become another victim of Wu's relentless hand.

But, he told himself firmly, perhaps the monk was onto something. He might have gone into an even more covert stage of investigation and discovery from which it was impossible to communicate with anyone. Dee knew that he had to hold on to his faith in the man's extraordinary abilities. It would be a disservice for him to give up on the monk.

A.D. 669, December

Even without the eyes and ears of Hsueh Huai-i, who had been missing for nearly three months now, Dee should have known right away what had happened within the walls of the palace. But the funeral procession along the Spirit Way out to the Li family tombs had been made under the secrecy of night, so that the world was not informed that it had happened at all until it was over. Only the immediate family and those servants and officials within the palace designated to carry out the barest form of ceremony were included. By the time the very modest flyers appeared throughout the city announcing the death, the body was cold behind the sealed doors of the tomb, deep within the tumulus. The people were given no opportunity to mourn their terrible loss.

Dee saw it as a clear indication of just how distorted the affairs between heaven and earth had become. It seemed that it had now become an Imperial requisite to shun official formality and the proper and decorous expression of Confucian government and ritual in favor of subterfuge and dark autocracy and whatever else suited Her Most August Majesty and Her Most August's mother. How Dee wished that Hsueh were present to talk with him on these things! He had not realized how much he had come to depend on the monk's insight, perspective, and friendship.

Emperor Kaotsung, two years shy of his fiftieth birthday, was dead, and the youthful, frightened, and inoffensive Chui-tsung had been named his successor. But Dee seriously doubted that the child would ever grasp the Imperial scepter in his hand, nor would he ever sit upon the Peacock Throne. The rumor was that the new "Emperor" of China found himself locked in an obscure wing of the palace, alone and friendless like so many other members of the Imperial Family before him. And while the crowned child Chui-tsung remained sealed off from the world—his meals served to him through a sliding grate, no doubt—his mother, the Acting Regent, was now sole ruler of the Chinese Empire.

Long live the Empress Wu Tse-tien, Dee wrote in his journal that night. And long live us all.

PART TWO

*So great was the wave of fear and terror that captured
the hearts of the people that they simply
marked time and held their breaths. . . .*

—Tzu-chih tung-chien
("The Comprehensive Mirror of History")

MARA'S ARMY

... But here, carved in all innocence centuries ago, were torsos turned into faces, eyes grafted onto trunks, whole festoons of eyes; there were also pigs' breasts, dogs' shoulders, beings with three bodies or four heads, polyphemuses and hydra-headed monsters, a whole fairground of triumphant monstrosity; forms which would be but toys if each one of them had not been endowed with a soul. Their expressions were often incomprehensible to us. What was moving them? What was disturbing them? Were they crying, laughing, screaming, lowing like cattle, grinning? Were they terrified or raving mad, passionate or vengeful?

—*SECRET TIBET* BY FOSCO MARAINI
(translated by Erik Mosbacher)

20

A.D. 670, spring
Loyang

Wu lolled in her bath as if she intended to stay there for the rest of her life. "Oh, Mother, it is as if I had been born for the second time. I am *alive* again," she declared, running her hands down her body in the steaming water. "I was imprisoned, *encased*, like some creature inside its horrid bony shell whose flesh has never seen the light of day."

Madame Yang, sitting nearby, merely smiled.

"Like some poor turtle trying to cross the road, and the wheel of a cart rides up onto its back and cracks it open."

"What a hideous image," her mother remarked pleasantly.

"Yes. The noise is dreadful, ghastly, and the pain almost unendurable—but somehow, the creature within survives, and behold! It emerges, renewed and reborn! Ah, it is an amazing thing, the way nature made women. We require the touch of a man so that we may be set into motion!" She caressed her hips and breasts as she spoke, savoring memories. "Yes. That is it. We require the touch of a man, and the greater his skill, the greater our motion, the greater the distance we travel. And to think that I believed I had encountered skillful men before. Oh, Mother," she sighed.

"Have I ever guided you in the wrong direction?" her mother asked her in a playful, conspiratorial tone.

Wu turned in the water to look at Madame Yang. "No. You never have. It is to you that I owe my first gratitude. You could have kept him to yourself, and I would never have known."

"Well, my dear, there *is* enough of him for both of us, is there not?"

Wu smiled while she considered her mother's statement. They looked at each other. "More than enough for us both," she agreed, and they both laughed.

* * *

And he was brilliant, too. When she compared him to the poor dead Nagaspa, the latter came up sadly short. The first, she saw now, with his pretensions to erudition, had been merely a pale antecedent to this one. The Nagaspa's masculine skills, too, though passably good, simply could not compare. Though of course, appearing at the time that he had, when her husband was so recalcitrantly sickly and difficult, and the odiousness of it had weighed on her very soul, the Nagaspa had seemed to be heaven-sent. It was a continually unfolding process, she saw now: as she entered each glorious new stage of her life, a man—progressively more skillful, more expansive, more able to encompass her growing needs—appeared.

She tried to remember back to the early days when she thought that Kaotsung would be all she could ever need or want. She was young then, a mere budding rose whose petals had barely begun to unfurl. Then when she had bloomed, opening more fully to the rain and the sun, as she liked to think of it, there had been the Nagaspa. It was all so clear. The others—the various incidental monks, mendicants, scholars, pilgrims, and the occasional servant, whose names and faces she could scarcely remember—the ones who did not fit so neatly into her pleasant picture of succession and destiny—she consigned to a category of diversion and entertainment. She did not let them interfere with the satisfying picture.

Kaotsung was gone now, and she could only feel relief. And the Nagaspa—well, it was difficult to admit to herself, but certain aspects of him had, of late, begun to grate on her nerves. His voice, for instance. A whining tone had crept into it in the last year or so, as if he had sensed that the natural progress of things was soon to leave him superannuated, and rather than retiring gracefully, his work done, he had been striving vainly and unbecomingly to retain his position. A position that had, after all, been a gift from her, and that he should have known he could not keep forever. Of course, she felt a little sorry for him—he was not a total charlatan. He had undoubtedly sensed the strong vibrations as his successor approached, riding in on the crest of fate. She herself had certainly felt it. She had known something extraordinary and awesome was already displacing the very air around her, closing in on her, coming to her.

Yes, this new one was brilliant as well. He had brought with him his work in progress, his own translation of a sutra that had never been seen or heard outside of its original Sanskrit. The way he had obtained it had been itself an exercise in the mysterious workings of destiny: he had encountered an old monk, he told her, a pilgrim who had traveled to India so many times over the last sixty years that he could no longer count the journeys, who had been challenging passersby on the street to purchase all of his earthly possessions—a bundle of ragged clothes, a begging bowl, a prayer wheel, a few utensils, a wooden box, and a broken-down donkey—for a single copper coin, for he was, so he announced to whoever might hear him, going to go off to die soon. When the Empress's new friend came along, he had made the purchase without hesitation, because, he had told her, he had seen a strange light around the old man.

And inside the tattered hide-covered box were the untranslated sutras. Naturally, he had set to work immediately. It was then, he had said to her solemnly, that I saw that it was my destiny to make my way to your side. It is too early to reveal what I have found, he had said. Too early. The translation is not yet complete. I must be absolutely certain of what I think I have uncovered. I need more time, he said, and she thought, I will give you all the time you want.

She had a fierce desire to honor him, herself, her mother, and every living thing she came into contact with. Something was definitely growing in her, some tangible manifestation of what had, until now, been mere abstractions. Only with the clear, penetrating vision that she now possessed could she understand how insulated and remote from these principles she had actually been, without true understanding. Her new friend explained that the living spirit of the Buddha was expressing itself through her. Challenging her to not merely think about it and talk about it, but to *be* it. It was Buddhism's most profound principle, manifesting itself in the world through her hands, eyes, and life. I am not at all surprised, he had said enigmatically. When my translations are finished, I shall know for certain, he had added, looking acutely at her, exciting her in a deep and thrilling way she had never experienced before.

Yes, she thought fiercely, she would set an example for every living creature in the Empire. She would *live* that principle which was the beating, breathing heart of Buddhism. It was her true calling, her own vital essence, her birthright asserting itself: pathos, compassion, reverence for life.

* * *

Dee had rarely experienced such frustration. If ever he needed the vanished Hsueh Huai-i, it was now, if for no other reason than to save him sheer legwork. He had tramped all over the city these last few days, and was footsore, weary, and vexed. He had been visiting the farflung sites of the Empress's newest multiple building project. He wished to see her latest extravagances with his own eyes.

He could have ridden in a carriage, of course, but to do so would have cost him the inestimable advantage of moving unnoticed through the crowds, mingling and listening. People on the street always had quite a bit to say, and if one listened with a discerning ear, valuable information could be gleaned. Somehow, he didn't fully understand why or how, the common folk always knew, if not the truth, then at least parts and pieces of the truth. Certainly he had learned more from them than he had learned from his colleagues, who had answered his queries with blank stares and infuriating vagueness. Everyone had heard of the Empress's massive new project, of course, but nobody connected with official channels seemed able to say exactly what she was building or why. If he still had Hsueh, he would know.

But he had made some fascinating, if discouraging and enigmatic, discoveries. The structures were unlike any built in Loyang before. Obviously Buddhist in origin, but unlike the stupas he was accustomed to seeing. These unmistakably foreign silhouettes against the sky gave Dee a distinctly uneasy feeling, as if the occupying troops of an invading army had set up camp in their midst.

When he set out that morning, he had not known how many of these oddities were being built around the city. He had only known that there were many more than one. But onlookers at the first site, right in the middle of one of Loyang's most beautiful parks, directed him to a forested reserve on the edge of the city. There the people had directed him to the next, and so on. At the base of each one he watched hundreds of conscripted laborers swarming like so many ants so that the things practically grew before his very eyes. And he had counted seven.

Ancestral temples, people called them. The Empress is honoring her ancestors while she expresses her faith. And when the structures were completed, there would be the usual celebrations, with food and gifts for everyone. Another rumor, exciting and strange, said that she would also induct at random one hundred of the common people into her family, bestowing her name upon them, making them honorary nieces, nephews, aunts, grandfathers, and so on, and these people would be the keepers of the family temples for the rest of their lives.

A dubious honor, Dee thought to himself as he prepared for sleep so that he could rise in the morning and journey to the monastery where Wu-chi resided. From what he had seen, to be a member of the Empress's family was as perilous as swimming in a river where crocodiles brooded beneath the water.

He felt it every time he stepped within the walls of the Pure Lotus: peace, sanctuary, tranquillity. If the true spirit of the Buddha resided anywhere, it would be here, he thought. The cool gray stones, the monks at prayer, the humble and pleasant welcome of the abbot all made him feel that the world had truly receded the moment the gates shut behind him.

Abbot Liao whispered to Dee with the solicitude of a mother speaking of her infant that Wu-chi was resting. He needs at least another hour, he said, but he will be glad to see you when he awakens. In the meantime, our library is at your disposal. And so Dee was seated in the pleasantly musty seclusion of the long, narrow room with its shelves of volumes, scrolls, documents, and sheafs of scriptures and holy writings, translated and untranslated. Today, it was the writings of pilgrims he was interested in—those who had gone to the far western and mountainous lands and had brought back vivid descriptions of what they had seen.

He did much better than he had thought he would. One volume contained original drawings of Buddhist architecture in various native locations. A brush painting of a stupa caught his attention right away by the familiarity of its outline and details of its ornamentation. And the inscription said it was Tibetan.

Dee read the accompanying text, but found nothing of significance. All he could see was that the Empress was choosing progressively more esoteric expressions of her faith—stronger, undiluted, *foreign* expressions: less and less Chinese. He gazed out the small, cobwebbed window at the top of the room. That fact in itself was disturbing enough. But he still wondered if there was some hidden meaning eluding him. Again, he cursed the absent Hsueh Huai-i. His vanished friend could have saved him a lot of time and trouble with this. *He* would have recognized the Tibetan origin of the design immediately. And if anyone would know if there were arcane secrets implicit in such a design, he would be the one.

"It is not so mysterious to me," Wu-chi said after welcoming Dee to his tiny private courtyard, where he sat in the sun warming his bones after his nap. "It is very simple. She is building ancestral temples honoring the Wu clan. There are seven of them. Seven is the number strictly reserved for use by the family of the Emperor." He spoke impassively, eyes shut, face raised to catch the pale rays of the sun. So calm was his tone that for a moment Dee failed to grasp the meaning of his words.

"Then we are merely seeing a display of extravagance and presumption?" he asked.

"We are seeing more than that," Wu-chi replied. "We are seeing the Wu family, all the way back to her earliest predecessors, elevated to royalty." Now he opened his eyes and looked at Dee's astonished face. "I can see that not even you would have given her credit for that kind of audacity. But you must understand—I *know* her."

Stunned, Dee could not speak for a moment.

"Yes," Wu-chi continued. "And I am even going to make a prediction. Soon, very soon now, we will be hearing from the redoubtable Historian Shu, that amazing little man with the uncanny ability to predict the future or alter the past."

"But the Li family, the family of the Emperor . . . " Dee began.

"Deposing the dead is a simple matter." Wu-chi shrugged. "And as we have seen, the living pose no particular problem to her."

"But what of all this . . . " Dee hesitated, lowering his voice self-consciously. " . . . overweening foreign spiritual imagery?"

"Her overt Buddhism?" Wu-chi asked. "Do not worry about what you say here," he reassured him. "There is no one here who will take offense. My good abbot deplores the chicanery and excesses more than you or I do, if that is possible."

"Since the Emperor's death, it is out of hand, running amok," Dee declared. "Tibetan temples in a Chinese capital! The halls of government renamed, with names unpronounceable by a Chinese tongue! I assume you have heard about *that*."

"I think I know the answer to your question. You have

heard, no doubt, that the Empress has not been . . . sleeping alone since Kaotsung's death and the murder of her charlatan lover?''

"No, I did not know that," Dee said in a flat voice. "I have recently lost my direct source of information. Left to my own devices, I seem to be many steps behind everything that is happening within the walls of the palace."

"I still have a few connections," Wu-chi said. "And besides, I would have recognized the signs. The Empress's fires are being stoked. The flames are rising to the very sky. She has," he said with ironic emphasis, "a new spiritual mentor."

They sat in brooding silence for a few moments, a bird chittering and scolding in a branch over their heads and the distant sound of the monks at prayer carrying over the high wall of Wu-chi's courtyard. "Yes, I heard about the name changes," Wu-chi said. "And there is to be another name change as well, or so I have heard. It is appropriate for a time of renewal and celebration such as we are experiencing now"—he smiled at Dee, who wanly responded in kind—"for a new Reign Title to be proclaimed. Soon, we will leave the period of Wen Ming* in the past and move into the glorious present of Kuang Chi.† " 'Uncovering Relics,' " Dee repeated gloomily. "I do not like the sound of that at all."

"Nor do I," Wu-chi agreed. "But I will wager that Historian Shu is delighted with it."

The ancestral stupas were completed as swiftly as something built in a dream. When Dee heard that the entire city was going to attend the Empress's ceremonies at the site of the first one, in the middle of Loyang's largest park, he decided to attend as well. Word had it that on that day the first lucky few were to be inducted into the Empress's family, and so people would be appearing dressed in their finest, hoping to appeal to the Empress's emissaries, who would be circulating anonymously in the crowd looking for likely candidates. Dee decided that he would go dressed in shabby, tattered garments, to deflect any possibility that he might be chosen. Perhaps I should rave and drool a bit too, he though grimly. He had no doubt that there would be other misfits there, mad people as well as beggars and thieves; an event of this scope always drew

*Illustrious enlightenment.
†Uncovering relics.

them out of their hiding places. He would simply be one of their brotherhood for the day.

When his disguise was finished, he was grateful that his wives were far away in Yangchou and could not see how completely and easily he had transformed himself into an example of the human refuse who inhabited every city.

The park and the streets and alleys leading to it were solid with humanity. Parents with children were everywhere—infants had been scrubbed and dressed in attractive colors, and were carried aloft like bright banners, as if to say, Look! Here is a princeling or princess if ever one lived! The atmosphere was more than festive; the air was charged with a peculiar excitement. He had to give the Empress his grudging respect. She had created it, accomplishing it by conferring on the common people, for one day at least, the magic possibility that each of them was potential royalty. Dee thought cynically that his own sons would make ideal additions to the Empress's family.

Unlike the families pressing forward everywhere, he had the advantage today of moving alone. People's eyes slid right over him, and everyone melted out of his way at his approach, plainly not wishing to come into unnecessary contact with his flesh.

He knew he was drawing closer. Delicious smells and strains of music were beginning to waft over him, and the crowd grew ever more densely packed. He noted that thieves aplenty had turned out. It would be easy pickings and quick disappearances today.

Dee watched their activities with interest, enjoying the detachment afforded him by his disguise. Today, he was under no obligation to call for a constable, to make an arrest, or to interfere in any way. He watched a scrawny young boy, no older than eleven or twelve, deftly slice a man's purse from his belt without the victim's ever noticing. For a moment, Dee was reminded of the little thug who had jumped him in his office so many years ago. The boy, sensing Dee's interest, glanced at him for a brief moment with his sharp rodent's eyes, assessed him, and calmly went on his way, slipping into the forest of humanity.

While Dee was looking at the place where the boy had been standing only a moment ago, he felt someone step on the hem of his tattered robe, straining the seams with a ripping sound and nearly pulling the garment off his shoulder. He turned reflexively and faced a very drunk, unclean man whose clothing was in even worse condition than his own. The man began to shape an eloquent and courtly apology, but Dee heard only the first few words of it. He was staring hard over the derelict's head.

About forty paces behind the man, someone very tall was moving against the current of the crowd's flow, the back of his head and shoulders presented to Dee's view, his drab clothing contrasting with the festive colors around him.

"Master Hsueh!" Dee heard his own voice call out. Dee tried to get around the drunk, who was still apologizing elaborately. The derelict stumbled, stepping on Dee's loosened robe again, this time almost pulling him down. The already weakened seam ripped and the sleeve partly detached itself before Dee could yank the fabric out from under the other's clumsy feet.

Cursing, Dee shoved his way rudely past the drunk, desperately craning his neck. He caught another glimpse of the back of the tall man's head in the distance, sailing away as if the surging crowd around him did not exist. Vainly, Dee fought his way forward. Where he had moved with relative ease before, the throngs seemed to close around him obstinately now, blocking his way so that he resorted to using his elbows and knees in an ungentlemanly way. This only increased the resistance, as people shoved him in return, cursing him. Dee raised himself on his toes and scanned the horizon in every direction, but it was as if the tall man had never been there at all. He stood, frustrated and infuriated, wishing he could find the drunk who had stepped on his hem and give him a good beating.

People were still staring at him with disgust. He remembered his clothes then, and realized what a sight he must present. Calm yourself, he muttered through clenched teeth. You are going quite mad.

A moment ago he had been so certain that it was Hsueh Huai-i he had glimpsed, but now he was not sure of anything at all.

Ahead, the stupa loomed against the sky, and a ripple of excitement was moving through the crush. People were repeating the words that were being spoken way up front, flinging them backward over their shoulders to be picked up and passed along. Historian Shu, they said, was giving a wonderful speech. Reluctantly, Dee gave up his vain search for the monk to listen to the historian's words:

"The Empress, in her infinite benevolence, and to cele-brate the New Age that is surely upon us now, to make life easier for the common people in the spirit of that New Age, to demonstrate that mercy and compassion are living things and not mere words, is instituting her Seven Acts of Grace. For you, her vast family, she decrees that taxes shall be lowered, land shall be redistributed, military conscription shall be limited, amnesty shall be declared in the prisons, slaves and servants shall be set free, each family shall be given six months' worth of rice, and capital punishment shall be abolished.

"Though only a few among you today will be selected, she wishes you to know that in truth, she holds each and every one of you to her heart as a member of her own family, the ancient and glorious Wu clan, which has been discovered by your humble servant Historian Shu to extend all the way back to the ruling family of the ancient Chou Dynasty at the begin-ning of the Empire's glorious history many millennia ago. In honor of these findings, the Empress and the young Emperor have declared that the dynasty shall henceforth be known as the Chou."

A tumultuous roar broke around Dee as he stood stunned and mute. Was this how it happened? Was this how dynasties ended? Could she simply declare that the T'ang was dead, and have it be so?

He felt like a scurrying little rat as he hurried along to his appointment. The mood in the halls of government today was one of averted eyes, uneasy gestures, and whispered conver-sations broken off abruptly. Dee nearly glanced down at his clothes, wondering for a moment if he had mistakenly put on his beggar's robes. It could easily have happened, such was his haste and excitement when he received a response from the head of the Censorate this morning saying that Magistrate Dee's request for a meeting had been granted. This was the same fellow who had suddenly decided to visit his mother the last time he and Dee had had an appointment. Dee hardly dared to hope it, but perhaps the man had been shocked back to his senses. He had only met this person briefly once, and so did not know his character. But he knew he had best hurry, before the man decided to lock his door, climb out the window, or take another trip.

He glanced with grim satisfaction at the ill-at-ease faces of the officials he passed as he started up the stairs. This was not the joyous, celebratory atmosphere that had prevailed yesterday in the park. Cowards though they were, these were men who had spent their lives close to the workings of government. They seemed to understand the terrible insult the Empress had dealt them all, the lies that threatened the very fabric of their lives. At least, Dee thought, some of them did. No doubt there were still those who moved about in a protective fog of complacency. As for the others, he muttered under his breath as he approached the outer door of the Office of the Censorate, I hope their discomfort grows like a bad headache.

Dee was ushered into the presence of two youngish men whom he took to be assistants of the man he was here to see. One was sitting at a desk, the other was standing to one side. The one behind the desk wore a pleasant smile.

"Welcome, Master Dee. We are most happy to see you! Would you care for some tea?"

"Yes, thank you, I would," Dee answered a little brusquely. "But first, tell me this: is the head of the Censorate in today, as he said he would be?"

The two men looked at each other for a moment. "He is most assuredly in," the one at the desk said. "And eager to see you. And so is the Lord Secretary, who heard that you were coming, and arranged to be present so that he too could meet with you. There are many important things to discuss!"

The Lord Secretary, too! Another man Dee had met once or twice. Dee had not expected this at all, but it was fine. All the better. It was time to protest, and protest loudly. If he could gather even a few men of conscience around him, he would draft a memorial and they would petition the throne.

"Excellent," Dee said, settling in his chair. "Please tell them that I am quite ready to meet with them."

The two men looked at each other again. Now the one standing smiled.

"But Master Dee," he said, "you are meeting with them at this very moment!"

Uncomprehending, Dee stared at the two.

"Precisely what do you mean?" he asked with care. The one at the desk shrugged.

"I am Censorate Chief Wu San-ssu, and this is Lord Secretary Wu Cheng-ssu. My brother," he added almost as an afterthought.

"Our predecessors have retired," the standing one said.

Dee stood abruptly, pushing aside a tray of tea proffered by a servant at that moment.

"May I ask," he said coldly, "what your relation is to the Empress?"

"Why, we are her nephews, of course," the standing one answered, as Dee turned to leave the office. "Master Dee! Please do not be so hasty! We have many important things to talk about!"

"I have nothing to discuss with you," Dee said, pushing through the door, but they were right behind him.

"The retirement of the Li princes!" one of them called after him as he strode down the hall. He stopped and turned. He looked at the two, noted irrelevantly that they looked very much alike, and waited for whatever else they were going to say. "It cannot be accomplished with the dignity and solicitude that they deserve without your help!" The one who had been sitting at the desk was smiling broadly now. "You are the only one who can do it, Master Dee! They need your help! The Empress would consider it a personal favor!"

"Exile and demotion, Master Wu-chi. That is what 'retirement' means in the Empress's parlance. There were twenty princes, cousins and nephews and so forth of the Emperor's family, incarcerated like common criminals, about to be sent to the steaming hell of the island of Hainan one thousand miles to the south, along with a large group of 'retired' scholar-officials who had complained that they could not work under the Empress. I intervened—or rather, I was allowed to intervene. I had to find a place for each one of them in a ridiculously short period of time or else it was off to Hainan with them. She knew that I would have no choice but to exhaust myself with the effort if any of them were to be spared. She must have enjoyed demonstrating to me that she could jerk the strings and make Dee Jen-chieh dance, just like anybody else. I made arrangements to send them to Yangchou to live on the estates of various wealthy friends of mine. I 'rescued' them, but it was all an elaborate mockery. Of them, and of me," Dee finished sadly.

"Conspiracy charges, I assume?" Wu-chi asked, and Dee nodded. "Stone by stone, she is dismantling the T'ang," Wu-chi said tiredly. "She removes the legitimate heirs of the Emperor's family. She replaces them with buffoonish pretenders from her own family and commoners from the street, and elevates her worthless ancestors to royal status. But the mockery you have suffered is mild, my friend, compared to what she subjected my colleagues to." Wu-chi sat quietly, remembering. "In fact," he continued, "I am surprised that she is being as merciful as she is. I am sure that she is filled with admiration for herself and her own compassion." He reflected for another moment. "It would seem that she is in a most excellent mood of late. I heard about the Seven Acts of Grace that her royal majesty has so graciously bestowed on her people. Her 'retirement' of the Li princes is no doubt an equal act of grace and mercy in her own mind. And she is quite right to think so! After all," he said, shrugging, "she could have merely slaughtered them. Yes, she is enjoying a most expansive and magnanimous temper these days. And of course, we know why."

Dee did not answer, but grunted. This was not a subject he cared to dwell upon, or to imagine in great detail.

"My abbot tells me that her 'spiritual mentor' wrote him a letter recently," Wu-chi said in his calm, offhand way, which never failed to catch Dee off guard. He looked at his friend.

"Do you mean her . . . " He could not find an appropriate word.

"Her holy man. Her lover," Wu-chi said succinctly.

Dee was instantly alarmed. "It had nothing to do with you, I hope!"

"No, no. It had nothing at all to do with me," Wu-chi reassured him. "I am dead, as far as she is concerned. No, this letter concerned a proposition for my good abbot. It seems that this . . . holy man, this priest, is founding a new sect, with the Empress's full support and blessing, to honor the great New Age we are all entering. It would appear that he is contacting and visiting a great many of the monasteries in and around the city. Recruiting them, so to speak."

"And am I correct in assuming that the 'recruitment' involves a large endowment?"

"Oh, yes. Most generous. And in exchange, we would be obliged only to receive within our walls the novices to the new sect. And of course, a gradual shift to a new order of existence, a new body of teachings. Not so very much to ask, eh?"

"And how did your abbot respond?"

"With his usual impeccable humility and grace, he declined the offer."

"No doubt others with less grace and humility did not."

"No doubt."

"And by what name, may I ask, will this glorious new sect be known?"

Wu-chi thought for a moment. "It was the most innocuous name. A name with a sweet, mild quality to it. Like a line from a lady's poem. Something that could easily slip right by. Let me remember. Ah, yes! The White Cloud."

"The White Cloud," Dee repeated slowly. "Well, Wu-chi it may sound to you like a bit of whimsy drifting by on the breeze. But to me, it sounds like the scream of an arrow released from the bow of a demon from hell, on its way to lodge itself in my beating heart."

21

A.D. 670, late summer
Loyang

"There is no mistake about it," he said, peering intently at her face. "I have been watching you closely for some time. But I am a cautious, conservative man. I do not rush forth with unsubstantiated statements. I wait until I am certain of a thing before I speak." He tilted her face toward the full sunlight coming through the window. "Absolutely certain," he repeated.

Her mother, sitting nearby, smiled fondly.

"I can see it, too," she agreed. "We both saw it some time ago, but promised that we would hold our counsel, until we were sure."

"Until we were sure," he said.

Wu waited, warm with flattery and smoldering with anticipation, drinking deep of the exquisite suspense to which her mother and lover were subjecting her.

"Now there is no more room for doubt," he continued, still appraising her face, standing so close to her that she could feel his breath on her skin. "You are getting younger."

"What nonsense," she protested, eager to hear more.

"No. It is true," her mother said. "Who could see it better than your own mother? I have watched you since the day you were born. I *know* you, as no one else possibly could. The years are reversing themselves, dropping away. It is gradual, just as the process of growing older is gradual. But I can assure you, it is quite real."

"Quite," he said. "And I think that I, too, am qualified to see it, hm?" he added with a suggestive grin. "Though, of course, there is no vision as clear as a mother's for her daughter." He turned his grin toward Madame Yang, who reciprocated. Wu felt positively suffused with warmth, vigor, omnipotence, and an impatient appetite for the future, fat with promise.

"Utter nonsense," she repeated, smiling along with them.

"Ah. But there is more," he said, allowing gravity to come into his voice and manner. He let his hand drop from her chin, then stepped back to gaze at her reverently. "There is much, much more. Soon, you will understand the reason for this phenomenon. And you will know that it is quite real. This, too, I waited to tell you. Your mother and I, I should say, for we have been working together for some time. It began on the day I saw the old monk on the street, toothless and shriveled, hawking his meager, shabby possessions, but shining as brilliantly as the sun."

"I refuse to listen to such rubbish," she said, happy and delighted.

"Shining like the sun," he continued, "and I, though blinded by it, my eyes hurting the closer I got, groped my way toward him. Because I knew I had to." He turned, head still bowed reverently, toward Madame Yang. "I saw the same light around your mother, my Empress. It was she, the great patroness, who was destined to provide the shelter and utter tranquillity without which I could not have achieved the sustained state of meditation necessary to penetrate the holy writings fate had brought to me."

"So that is what you have been doing," she said, flashing her smile in her mother's direction. "Penetrating holy writings."

"You cannot know the difficulty, my Empress. Imagine, if you will, a linguistic box-within-a-box-within-a-box. But each box within the larger box, if you will, is composed of progressively more arcane symbology, in a tongue which, even in its most direct form, is fraught with twists, turns, false doorways, and dead ends. Not only did I open each 'box,'" he said, straightening up to his full impressive height and squaring his shoulders with pride, "but I then fitted them all back together

again. So that I might be sure. There is good reason why the
years are peeling themselves away from your face and body."
He gazed at her. "It is time to reveal to the world the Great
Cloud Sutra."

Could there be a more glorious, tantalizing land than the
future? Desire and impatience flared up like a fire now, threatening to consume her. She wanted to sink her teeth into the
future, into the infinite banquet of possibility laying itself out
before her, into life itself, and into his flesh, which she now
hungered for acutely, and which, his eyes told her, she would
be feasting on very soon. She beamed at him unabashedly and
without constraint.

"Pure rubbish," she said.

Many months after the stupas had been completed, Dee
came to understand that they had been nothing, nothing at all
compared to the scope of the Empress's new project: a temple,
nearly as large as a wing of the palace itself, to be the principal
shrine and central locus of the White Cloud sect. As president
of the National Bureau of Sacrifice, he should have known
everything about the new sect: the name of its abbot, the number of monks it expected to have under its wing, its precepts,
its means of support. It should have been through him and the
Bureau of Sacrifice that its license was granted or not. But all
he knew was the name of the new temple—the White Horse—
and the fact that at least one thousand workers were participating in its construction. His repeated requests for a meeting
with the abbot of this new sect had been ignored; he would
have gone to him unannounced, but he did not know where
he would find this man, except perhaps in the Empress's bedchamber, and he knew that it would be impossible even for
the great Dee to gain access there.

He visited those temples in and around the city which
had accepted the offer to become part of the White Cloud sect,
but the various abbots—some of whom struck Dee as being
relatively honest men and some of whom did not—could tell
him very little, except that they had received a generous endowment and instructions to wait. To wait for what? Dee had
asked. For further instructions, they had told him vaguely, and
for the sutra of sutras, soon to be forthcoming.

The sutra of sutras?

Yes, they had replied; the sutra that would supersede all
others and would be a harbinger of a new world.

Later, when he stood and watched the construction, there was no mistake about it. The White Horse Temple was taking on an exotic aspect similar to that of the ancestral stupas. The same architect who designed the stupas must have designed the temple. He tried an experiment one day. He held his hands up so that everything surrounding the temple was blocked to his vision. It was not difficult to imagine this exotic building standing alone on a remote mountaintop in a foreign land. Yet here it was, growing incongruously out of the familiar municipal earth of Loyang, looking like an orchid in a garden of cabbages, an effect so obvious to him that he wondered how others could look at it and not see the same thing.

His visits to Wu-chi at the monastery were becoming more frequent. Here was true peace and respite, he thought, in a world growing daily and hourly more chaotic.

Today, Abbot Liao joined Dee and his friend. Dee was not the only one with the White Horse Temple on his mind. The usually serene abbot was plainly disquieted.

"An emissary of the White Cloud sect came to visit me last week," he said, frowning. "They do not give up so easily."

"But you made it clear with your letter that you were not interested in joining them, did you not?" Dee asked.

"Oh, yes," the abbot replied. "Quite. In no uncertain terms. I thanked them for their generous offer, but told them we were perfectly content to get along as we have for centuries. I said that we were a particularly simple, conservative order, and that change was not something we sought or desired."

"How had it been left, then?" Dee asked curiously.

"I was satisfied that I had conveyed my intent clearly and without giving offense. I did not expect to hear from them again. Certainly I did not expect a visit." He looked at Dee and Wu-Chi. "They made another offer this time, one they seemed to think I would find irresistible. The last time, they offered wealth. This time, they offered power."

"Power?" Dee asked, incredulous.

"Yes. They said that the Empress Regent and the abbot of the White Cloud had decided to reorganize the counties and prefectures throughout the Empire. The borders would be adjusted, and they would now be called 'parishes,' with each parish under the benevolent care of a local White Cloud temple. I was told that my monastery was propitiously located to preside over one of the most populous and productive parishes in the environs of Loyang."

" 'Parishes'!" Dee exclaimed. "What else did they tell you? How large are these parishes to be? How many people, how many farms would there be in each one? Would they be paying a tax in addition to their regular yearly taxes to the Empire?" The investigator in him was suddenly and sharply aroused.

"Master Dee," Abbot Liao said with a weak laugh, "you ask many astute questions. Alas, I do not know the answers, because I naturally refused the offer. I certainly did not allow them to get even that far."

"Of course, of course," Dee said. "And you were quite correct to handle it that way. Tell me," he said then, looking up sharply, "how was it left this time? Was your second refusal accepted with good grace?"

"They were pleasant," Liao replied. "But I did not get the impression that they were finished with me. In fact," he said, looking at Dee with worried eyes, "they said they would be back in two fortnights' time to discuss it again. And that during that time, the world would witness a miracle, which would dissolve any lingering doubts I may be harboring." Dee had never seen the good abbot's equanimity upset before. "A miracle, Master Dee," he repeated. "I should be glad, interested, and curious, but I only dread it." He sat pensively for another moment. "And the next time they come, the abbot of the White Horse Temple himself will be with them."

"The abbot himself!" Dee exclaimed. At last, an opportunity! "My good Father," he said enthusiastically, "will you consider allowing an errant magistrate to join your order for a short time?" The abbot looked at him, not understanding right away. "When this White Horse abbot with his White Cloud sect comes here, I want to be here too," Dee explained. "As one of you."

"But, of course," Abbot Liao assented. "In fact, I would be very grateful!"

"Excellent, excellent," Dee said, already planning.

Wu-chi had been listening quietly to the conversation. He spoke now, in the tones of a man remembering something from long ago.

"A miracle," he said. "I do not like the sound of that."

Dee looked at him, an uncomfortable feeling stealing over him as well. A miracle, indeed.

* * *

There was nothing to do but wait. And what could be more maddeningly vague than to wait for a miracle?

One afternoon about three weeks after his visit to the monastery, Dee sat in a wineshop situated along a busy thoroughfare reading a missive from one of the "retired" Li princes he had helped to relocate in Yangchou.

Away from the repressive atmosphere of Loyang, the scholars were becoming more courageous. They met often and talked. Quite naturally, the most frequent topic of conversation was the Empress. She was truly an inspiration to them. These men, who had never raised a sword or even their voices before in their lives, whose soft hands were more accustomed to parchment, tea bowls, and writing brushes than to cold metal and who probably did not even know the color of their own blood, were talking of rebellion. They wanted Magistrate Dee to be part of it, to be their contact in the capital. All of this had been communicated in veiled terms, naturally, written in the nearly incomprehensible vocabulary of the highly educated, which was virtually another language, but perfectly clear to Dee.

He wished that he could travel to Yangchou and speak with them in person. It was impossible to tell whether or not their planned insurrection was plausible or a pathetic delusion. Did they have a strong plan, a real chance? Or would the Empress be picking her teeth with their bones when it was over?

He looked at the letter again. The author of it was an acquaintance of his, Li Cheng-yeh, a middle-aged scholar who always breathed very hard after the smallest exertion. He shook his head in wonder. Tonight, he would draft a careful reply in the same symbolic language. He would tell them to wait, to be vigilant, to be quite sure of themselves before making a move of any kind. Some prudent part of him decided to write another letter, too: to his family in Yangchou, telling them that he was making arrangements to move them to Ch'ang-an. His wives would like that. That was where most of their relatives were, and some of his as well. He wanted them far away from a city that might explode in rebellion.

He rolled the letter up and paid the proprietor, and was about to step onto the street again when he became aware of a sound, familiar but utterly out of place, rising above the noise of the street. At the same time he became aware of a commotion. He stepped back to avoid colliding with two young boys running; when he stepped out again, he could see more people, mostly boys and young men, surging down the street ahead of a bobbing processional of shaved heads and saffron-colored robes. He saw immediately that these shaved heads rose well above the rest of the crowd; they belonged to men of unusual height. What he was hearing, which had, however, eluded his comprehension because this was the last place he expected to hear it, was the chanting of monks.

Rhythmic and assertive, the chanting grew louder as the tall monks, marching like soldiers, made their way down the populous main thoroughfare. As the monks approached, their height and their fearsome demeanor—faces grim and stern as those of a conquering army—caused people to fall back well out of their way. Only the youths and street urchins stayed with them, savoring the excitement, running and shouting, parting the crowd ahead of them.

The monks did not look left or right, as if the noisy, surging street did not exist. Fifty or so voices rose in practiced unison as if in a walking trance. When the monks were within twenty-five paces of where Dee stood, their words began to reveal themselves to him. He joined the pack of boys on the flanks of the processional and hurried along with them, not out of puerile exuberance, but because the monks were moving at such a pace with the enormous stride of their long legs that they would be gone in a matter of moments, and he wanted to hear every word of the refrain being voiced in cadence with one hundred marching feet:

"SHE HAS RETURNED TO THIS WORLD OF DAMNATION! THE LIGHT FROM HER BODY IS PURPLE AND GOLD! HER HALO IS FIVE THOUSAND BUDDHAS TRANSFORMED! HER LIGHT SHINES UPON THE FIVE PATHS OF EXISTENCE! ONE RAY FROM THE ROOT OF HER HAIR BLINDS THE WORLD! THE LIGHT OF HER WISDOM FREES US FROM CREATION! SHE COMES TO US FROM THE LAND OF WU-HSIANG! WU-HSIANG, THE LAND OF NO-THOUGHT COMES TO US! AVALOKITES-VARA REBORN! UNLIMITED LIGHT, THE DIVINE BODHISATTVA! UNLIMITED LIGHT, THE DIVINE BODHISATTVA! UNLIMITED LIGHT, CAKRAVARTIN REBORN!"

Dee stayed with them for several blocks before dropping out of the cortege, winded from the relentless pace. He stepped back into the crowd, astonished, breathing hard, watching the towering symmetrical column of shaven skulls advancing forward, disappearing, their dirge growing fainter as they moved out of earshot. Enveloped now by the excited babble of people around him, he turned to the nearest person, an old man standing just behind him, and while he was still trying to find words, the man answered his unspoken question.

"White Cloud disciples," he said tersely. Dee caught a last glimpse of the fiercely bobbing heads vanishing, then turned back to his informant. "Did you not hear?" the man said. "There was a miracle today."

"A miracle?" Dee asked, stupefied.

"Yes. It would seem that during a small dedication ceremony for a wing of the White Horse Temple, a sacred carving of the Buddha that had been brought in from India transformed itself into a flock of pure white doves. The birds flew up to heaven, and the carving was gone." The man shrugged. "There were dozens of witnesses. My brother happened to be there. He saw it with his own eyes."

Dee felt as if he had had a fever for a week. He had been jumpy with anticipation, expecting a tap on his door or window in the middle of the night, or a letter to be slipped into his hands in a crowd. The "miracle," which was on the tongue of nearly everyone in the city, could only have been a sign from Hsueh Huai-i that he was alive, and that he had infiltrated the White Cloud sect. It was exceedingly clever. A lot of information had been conveyed. Not only that he was within the sect, but that undoubtedly he had risen to a position of some importance if his skills as a magician were being employed to create miracles.

Excitedly, Dee reviewed the prospects. No doubt, Hsueh was acquainted with the abbot of the White Horse, the Empress's "spiritual mentor." Probably, Hsueh knew all there was to know about the inner workings of the White Cloud, its plans, its scope, its hierarchy of power; possibly, Dee told himself, Hsueh already knew the extent and location of its weak spots, its vulnerable underbelly. And possibly, he would be accompanying the White Cloud abbot tomorrow. No doubt he would penetrate any disguise Dee might assume. Possibly they could exchange some sort of wordless signal.

Tomorrow was the day he would be going to the monastery to assume his role as an anonymous contemplative. He wondered what sort of man the White Cloud abbot could be. Was he a mere minion of the Empress, like Kaotsung and the dead Nagaspa, or was he perhaps some sort of match for her?

Certainly she was flexing her claws and spreading her wings
in ways she had never done before. As Wu-chi had so aptly
put it, her fires were being stoked by this man. Whoever he
was, he was certainly audacious, with his spurious and bas-
tardized sutra, which anyone with any acquaintance at all with
holy writings would recognize as being rather clumsily drawn
from a plethora of sources. Audacious, and brave in his own
way, to be sure, Dee mused. What sort of courage did it take
to lie down in the Empress's bed?

It was late at night, and Dee had laid out a very sharp
knife, pea soap, and a bowl of hot water. As he picked up the
knife to begin what he had to do for tomorrow, he was grateful
for the second time in recent weeks that his wives were far
away, and would not again have to endure the sight of him
with his head shaved. As he took the first stroke, a faint memory came to him of the snickering, grinning faces of his sons
in the garden in Yangchou when they had seen his bald head
for the first time.

The poor good abbot of the Pure Lotus Monastery had
obviously not shut his eyes once. His normally cheerful countenance sagged with worry, and great blue bags had formed
under his eyes. Dee was indignant that such a fine and honest
fellow should be so disturbed.

Dee had arrived while it was still dark, and according to
the prearranged plan, had slipped in among the monks while
they were at their morning prayers. Wu-chi had gone into seclusion for the day; though he knew that the Empress was not
looking for him anymore, and did not know he was here, the
proximity of these representatives of hers made him uneasy.
No one knew what time of day the White Cloud delegation
would choose to arrive.

After the morning prayers, Dee shared the monks' simple breakfast and spent the morning working in the monastery garden. He found it most satisfactory to have the sun on
his back while he labored, watching the insects in the soil
and on the leaves of the vegetables, going about their own
tasks with industry and diligence. An insect's tiny life was all
work, he reflected. Other animals had their time of leisure
and relaxation. Even a busy squirrel took time off from his
labors to scamper in the treetops, and the buffalo had his
moments when the whip was not on his back nor the yoke

on his neck, when he could simply rest and chew. And he had seen birds splashing in puddles for the sheer pleasure of it. But insects knew no such respite. Designed by nature for unremitting labor, there was not a one among them who deviated or dissented.

He found a beetle lying on its back, legs waving helplessly while ants attacked it, and flipped it over with a small stick. It lumbered away with alacrity, as if it were not at all surprised to receive a helping hand from providence. He could just as easily have ignored it, or stepped on it. Dee mused that this was undoubtedly the way in which the gods, if they existed, intervened in men's lives—as the fancy of the moment struck them.

He had been working quietly for most of the morning. He wiped the sweat from his strangely bald head, and straightened his back for a moment to relieve the stiffness. At the same moment, he saw the figure of Abbot Liao's assistant approaching, hand raised in a wordless signal, his face as blank as a sheet of parchment. Without breaking his rhythm, Dee put down his hoe and moved, along with several others, toward Liao's quarters, where the guests were to be received.

The visitors were not yet on the grounds, so there must have been a lookout watching the road to the monastery. But Dee knew they were nearly at the gate, because he could hear them: the same aggressive, rhythmic chant he had heard last week in the city carried on the still pastoral air. The sweat on his brow chilled as he and his group passed under the shade of one of the enormous spreading trees. Dee kept his eyes downcast as the marching feet approached.

When he raised his eyes, he saw the battalion of about a dozen startlingly tall monks cutting diagonally across the grounds, their profiles to Dee's small group. The sun flashed off something shiny at the head of the processional. The momentary dazzle coincided with a flash of illumination for Dee. In that moment, he understood the enigma of the statuesque monks: they had been chosen to complement the great height of their leader, the abbot of the White Horse Temple, founder and head of the White Cloud sect and lover of the Empress, the man who marched at the head of the cortege, his simple abbot's robes adorned with a necklace of gold.

Dee fell back behind his compatriots and ducked into a

doorway, where he stood in the cool shadows catching his
breath and waiting for his hammering heart to slow. He did
not think Hsueh Huai-i had seen him. But with that one, you
could never know. It could truly be said of him that he had
eyes that could see through stone.

22

A.D. 671, spring
Loyang

I must listen to the voices, Wu said softly to herself. I must
learn to listen to the voices. I must trust in my ability to hear
them. She squeezed her eyes shut and told herself that she
must pay attention to what Hsueh Huai-i told her.

There would be very little difference at first, Hsueh had
whispered solemnly, between the sound of her own thoughts
and the Buddha spirit that now moved in her. He was adamant
about this. At some point, and she would know when, it would
be no mystery; the two voices that vied for attention in her
head would become as distinctly different as the deep resonant
sounds of a drum were from the clear and perfect pitch of a
brass bell. At that point, there would no longer be any confusion. The noise of greed and self—the voice of her own base,
worldly, and corrupt desires—would continue to hammer
away in her head, but there would be another. And this other
would ring far in the distance like a temple bell sounded from
behind mist-shrouded mountains. It would start small and
thin, perfect and high, almost inaudible at first, until its crystalline purity would pierce through all the rumblings of waterfalls and tumbling rapids, all the soughing of the pine
branches and the lonely echoes of the howling winds that ravaged the rocky distant peaks. The temple bell, clear and pure;
ping . . . ping . . . ping . . .

The Tibetan had mimicked the distinctive sound so perfectly, raising the pitch of his voice until it really did sound
like a metallic note, then humming deep in his throat the bell's
diminishing after-resonance, that she had almost convinced

herself that there was a perfect brass bell in the room with them.

It was today, this precise moment, that she had become certain that she could hear that voice. It was there, behind everything else, quiet, clear, alone, and persistent, like Hsueh's monastery bell. But it was there! The True Spirit of Buddhism, that pure voice, speaking through her. It would make everything that she must do very clear. But she must give it time, and she did not have time: the rebels had begun to mount their insurrection from the canal city of Yangchou. A minor insurrection, but it had raised her ire and made her recall her mother's remarks regarding irritating relatives. Only now they were somebody else's relatives—her dead husband's, to be precise— who were the irritants.

Five hundred demoted scholar—officials, most below the sixth level, had joined with the exiled minor princes of the Li Imperial Family. The princes had managed to raise an army of one hundred thousand men, but had yet to move away from the crowded junction of the Grand Canal and the mouth of the Yangtze and on to the north. The first observations of her spies stated that the leadership of the movement was already in disarray. Infighting among the princes was evidently rampant, but then the spies could not always tell the local Imperial militia from the rebel forces, and, so it seemed, neither could the common citizens.

But, Wu said, the whole affair, a minor challenge to her authority, amounted to nothing. She had resolved to deal with this crisis—the first of the rule of "Emperor" Chuitsung—with the quiescent calm that came from heeding that inner voice. With inner peace, tranquillity, and great largess, all answers would come to her, all questions become transparent. She chanted her own secret mantra, the one Hsueh had given her, its low hum filling her head. And in the sea of its echoing reverberation she visualized the seedling of Buddhavirtue bursting forth into the glorious blossom of Buddhadeed. . . .

Shu cleared his throat and continued reading. " ' . . . and so she has taken by malice and with intention both cunning and evil.' "

"No, no, no, no, no, no!" Wu said to the historian in a withering tone that took him aback. "Now you have *really* begun to annoy me, Shu." She narrowed her eyes in disgust.

"I am sorry, madame," Shu said. "Are you referring to the rebel leader Li Ching-yeh's proclamation, which I am reading faithfully?"

" 'Are you referring to the rebel leader Li Ching-yeh's proclamation?' " she mocked. "No, Shu, it is the set of your teeth, the crook of your nose, your nasty, tiny little eyes, your quivering chin," she ridiculed. "Stupid Shu, it is your *voice!*"

"Madame?"

"Shu?"

"I don't understand."

"Of course you don't understand, because you can't *hear* your own voice," Wu said.

"Well, I—" Shu began, but she cut him off.

"Oh, Shu, it is just that you read this Yangchou traitor's proclamation with such . . . such a tone of *respect.*"

"Madame does not like the way I read?" Shu asked in an injured tone.

"Madame does not like the way you give this nonsense such *credibility* with that pompously official tone of yours," Wu declared emphatically.

"Then it might be best for all concerned if I were to—"

"Feh!" she interrupted again. "You read this . . . this . . . *thing* as though you actually believe it!"

"—if I were to discontinue, and go home," Shu finished. "Until madame has rested, perhaps, or . . ."

"No, Master Shu," Wu said tiredly. "You will *not* go home. You will continue reading."

"Then how does madame wish me to read it?"

Wu slapped her palms exasperatedly on the tabletop. "Oh, I don't care! Just go ahead and read the damnable thing any way you please." She glared at him. "But just don't make it sound so bloody important."

Shu waited, to be certain that she was through.

"Shall I go on?" he asked with care.

"Yes, yes. By all means. Continue reading, Shu. I cannot wait forever for this . . . this . . . 'manifesto,' " she said with a sneer.

Shu cleared his throat and took up reading again from where his finger rested on the vertical row of blood—red characters:

" ' . . . this woman Wu, who has falsely usurped the throne, is by nature unyielding and dangerous. She is by family origin truly obscure—' "

"I *won't* hear any more." Wu rose from her chair, leaned over, and yanked the papers from Shu's hand. "It is nonsense, Shu. But your tone makes it sound as if you believe it." She gave him a look then. "*Do* you believe it?" she asked pointedly, then threw the papers on the table in front of him without looking at them.

"Madame . . ."

"Don't tell me, Shu." She put her hands to her ears. "I don't want to hear what *you* believe. It is inconsequential."

Shu did not try to respond. He picked up the papers and continued reading.

" 'Formerly, she was from among the lower ranks of Taitsung's servants and served him by changing his clothes. When she reached mature age, she brought disorder to the palace of the Crown Prince—the late Emperor Kaotsung—concealing her private relationship with him. She then plotted covertly to gain favor in the Inner Chambers . . . and concealing her mouth behind her sleeves, she skillfully slandered the other women—' "

"Because they *needed* to be slandered," she interjected, bringing her hand down hard again. "They were around him like so many stinking pigs dragging in their own muddy shit, Shu," she added, pleased at the reproving look her words elicited on the historian's face. "Why doesn't he write about *that?*" She folded her arms across her chest defiantly and looked coldly out of the window. Shu waited.

"Well?" she demanded.

"Uh . . . yes," Shu said, finding his place again. "Yes, ah . . .

" ' . . . skillfully slandered the other women. With cunning and flattery and perverse artfulness she deluded the ruler. She then usurped the pheasant regalia of Empress and entrapped our Kaotsung in incest as she betrayed his father, Taitsung, with her secret liaison—' "

"Oh, *shut up*, Shu! Just shut up!" she cried. She sulked for a moment before speaking again. When she did, her tone was one she might use with a slow child. "I did not *usurp* the 'pheasant regalia' of the Empress. I am the Empress because my Imperial husband, Kaotsung, *needed* me. He could not have gone on alone. The nation needed me. We ruled as the Two Holies, the Two Sages. There was no other way. Everyone knows what I have sacrificed for the heavy burden of kingship."

"Of course, madame. Indeed, we do know," Shu said obsequiously. "But . . . perhaps it would be better," he suggested, "if madame were to read the rest of the . . . the . . . ahh . . . 'manifesto' for *herself*."

"No, Shu. No, no, no," she said with infinite weariness. "I wish *you* to read it. Please," she added.

"Let me see then. Ah, yes . . .

" 'Then, with a heart like a serpent and a nature like a wolf . . . ' "

She sat calmly and stolidly now, listening. He picked up his pace, hoping to race past her objections and get to the end of the thing.

" ' . . . She favored evil flatterers while destroying her good and loyal officials. We suspect her in the murder of her own family members. She is hated by gods and men alike . . . ' "

He held his breath after these last words. When she said nothing, he forged ahead, scarcely pausing to breathe.

" ' . . . neither heaven nor earth can bear her. Still she harbors calamitous intentions and plans to steal the throne of the ruler. And the beloved Crown Prince, named Emperor Chui-tsung, son of the deceased ruler, she keeps locked away in a separate palace. And she banishes all members of the House of Li, and turns away her honest officials and has given the most important offices of state to her own group of scoundrels and bandits. . . . In the name of the orphaned princes and the Son of Heaven, the earth on his tomb not yet dry, we raise the righteous banner of rebellion for our ruling House of Li, in order to regain the trust of the whole world and to purify the empire of the baleful omens of disaster, and to restore tranquillity to the altars of soil and grain . . . to wrest the empire free from this illegitimate House of Wu. . . .' "

He was finished. He waited, the censuring words hanging uncomfortably in the air.

"And how does that make you feel, Shu? To learn that you are nothing more than a common bandit?" she asked at last, a wicked inflection in her voice.

"I do not feel anything, madame. I had not assumed that the odious rebel Li Ching-yeh was referring to *me*," Shu replied with dignity.

"Ah, my dear Shu. That is where you are wrong," she mocked. "In fact, I do not think he was referring to anyone *but* you."

"She has been this way since the news arrived," Shu said as the tall Tibetan pushed past him. "She just sits there. Her last words were something to the effect that everyone has betrayed her, that she can trust no one . . . that . . . that . . . " he called out after the monk whose long strides had already taken him halfway down the hall, " . . . that heaven itself has sent back its dead!"

Hsueh found the Empress sitting on her day couch and her mother on the edge of Wu's great canopied bed with a look of disgust on her face.

"Oh, Lama Hsueh, I am so happy to see you at last," Wu said, a light rekindling in her gloomy eyes.

"I, too, monk!" Madame Yang said with solemn gratitude. "I thought that they would never find you."

"I am sorry, madames, I made great haste as soon as I heard. I have been off in meditation and translation." He furrowed his brow in apology. "And just when did this latest . . .

ah . . . " He searched with great care for the proper words. " . . . treacherous proclamation arrive?"

"Late last night, Lama," Madame Yang said. "The missive arrived from the rebel outpost in Yangchou. But our Historian Shu did not wish to wake the Empress."

"Ah yes, Historian Shu. The little man was babbling something as I came into the reception hall about heaven betraying us, or something to that effect."

"Heaven sending back its dead," Wu stated, lifting her eyes and staring at him. "What I said was 'heaven sending back its dead'! That is what has happened, Hsueh."

"You see, Lama," Madame Yang said, rising from the bed and extending the papers, wrinkled and moist from being gripped in her hand all morning, "the rebels claim that they are being led by Crown Prince Hsien. Read it."

"But madame . . . poor Prince Hsien is tragically dead by his own hand. What is this?"

"Read on, Lama," Yang said.

"Yes, Hsueh. Now read this." Wu offered him a second page, which she had been holding tightly rolled in her fist. On it were only two single columns of bold oversized characters. "Even our own spies near the rebel encampments have seen this boy. They say that it is Hsien. The citizens that they have talked to have also seen him."

"These citizens of Yangchou would recognize him?"

"Yes. Hsien made a habit of traveling down there every year to see the great Tidal Bore. They evidently awaited his annual visit with exuberance and anticipation. His face was familiar to everyone," Wu said.

"They say that the Crown Prince has returned to avenge the House of Li," Madame Yang said. Hsueh studied the pages of the proclamation.

"There is, of course, an evident explanation here," the monk said, looking up. "That Prince Hsien simply never committed suicide at all. The body that was returned for interment in the Imperial tombs was, after all . . . how may I word it delicately . . . damaged beyond the point of certain identification." He looked to Wu and nodded his head deferentially. "You only assumed that you were burying your son."

"I am certain that it was my son." Wu snapped her head around and fixed Hsueh intently. "It was my son. I *know* that. There can only be one other explanation."

"You see, Lama Hsueh, my daughter convinces herself." Madame Yang threw up her hands and dropped herself back on the bed. "She will not accept the possibility that those sources in Yangchou are mistaken . . . that there *is* a double. Not dead and buried in the family tomb, but down in Yangchou serving as a rallying point for these traitors. She chooses instead the the impossible."

"There is no such thing as a perfect double," Wu countered. "They would have been able to tell that it was not really my son. They *knew* him! As well as I did!"

"Then all your generals must be plotting against us, child," Madame Yang said. "They themselves have spread this alarming story in order to undermine your very sanity. That is the only explanation your logic leaves us, short of heaven giving back its dead," she finished with a shudder of disgust.

Wu waved the unthinkable notion of treachery away with a gesture of her hand.

"Well, if treachery is an impossibility, and there is no such thing as a true double, we are left with only one other explanation—that Hsien *has* come back from the dead. You do not find that notion unthinkable, Empress?" Hsueh asked pointedly.

"I find the supernatural less unthinkable than the thought of being betrayed by my own handpicked spies and generals."

Hsueh held a hand up. His eyes lit as they always did when struck with inspiration. "The rebels are an ill-trained, undersupplied, ragtag army, and as of yesterday's reports, trapped on a small spit of land at the estuary of the Yangtze, correct? Victory is inevitable and imminent, is it not?"

"Of course it is," Wu answered irritably.

His wicked Tibetan eyes glowed even brighter as he spread the fingers of both hands and brought them together in a graceful summoning gesture.

"Well, then—here is my answer. To all of our questions. If indeed a demon possesses the undead body of our poor unfortunate Hsien, then I suggest a certain . . . old Tibetan *remedy* for stubborn cases of possession," he said enigmatically. "And if there is no demon, but merely a traitorous double posing as the dead prince, then madame's doubts will be laid to rest forever, I promise. One way or the other, you will know! As for the others, the leaders—the disaffected scholar-bureaucrats who have led this silly game of disobedience to the realm—I suggest the same treatment. Just for good measure." Hsueh clapped his hands, smiling with self—satisfaction. Wu and her mother, intrigued, looked at one another questioningly. What old Tibetan "remedy" did the monk have in mind?

"Do you trust me, madames?" he implored. "Do you trust my ascended magic? The gates of the White Horse Temple will become the locus of truth for all who gaze upon them. For the virtuous, and for the damned. And the truth will serve as an example, a deterrent to other, shall we say, wayward demons," Hsueh finished, and placed the pages of the proclamation neatly into Wu's hands.

Wu could now hear the inner voice speaking from that place deep inside her. It told her that the monk Hsueh Huai-i was the true leader of her army, the only viable force against the legions of demons rising all around them.

Yes. She trusted him.

Dee heard no more from his correspondent in Yangchou. Caution and restraint, he had advised, thinking as he wrote the words how absurdly inadequate and insubstantial they were, like a cricket in a windstorm. All he had to rely on for information was rumors.

The rebels have given up their campaign, one rumor said; they saw the hopelessness of their cause and sensibly laid down their arms. The scholars have turned into avenging warriors, others declared; they have raised an army of fighting mercenaries which has driven the Imperial troops back so far that they were practically dropping into the sea. Soon the rebel troops will be riding into Loyang to storm the palace. Others said that the Imperial troops were making short work of the pedants' pathetic "rebellion," squashing them like the upstart criminals and insects that they were. You are all wrong, said another faction. The true word is that the Empress, with the infinite mercy of the Divine Bodhisattva moving in her, has ordered the Imperial troops to show restraint and clemency, to demonstrate to the rebels that they had no reason at all to fight and to send them back to Yangchou severely chastened and grateful to be alive.

With this last one, Dee had allowed himself a small shred of hope. Left to her own devices, he was sure, she would drink the blood of her enemies, and bathe in it as well. Perhaps someone's influence was working against her rapacious temperament. Perhaps Dee had been wrong about everything he had felt when he saw Hsueh marching at the head of the column of monks. Perhaps he had given up too soon.

The twenty-six boxes were brought before the Empress by grim-faced guards. It was a bright and lovely morning, the sun shining after a night of gentle rain, making the world fresh and new. Wu watched the men place the boxes on the flagstones of her outer courtyard. Hsueh stood nearby; he and the Empress exchanged a smile. She felt benevolent and victorious, righteous and humble all at once. She felt life rolling up at her feet like the infinite waves of the sea breaking on the shore.

The monk made a gesture; a guard stooped and opened the lid of one of the boxes, which had been set slightly apart from the others. His face expressionless, the man reached in, lifted a severed head by the hair, and held it aloft. Wu peered at it intently. A few drops of dark blood dripped onto the stones.

"That is not my son," she said. "A remarkable resemblance. But it is not he." She turned to the monk. "Thank you, Lama Hsueh, for bringing me the truth."

The monk gestured again. The guard lowered the head into the box and shut the lid. Hsueh smiled at the Empress.

"And now, Madame, with your approval, I shall escort the 'prisoners' to the White Horse Temple."

"By all means, Lama," she said. "Let us not keep them waiting. I am sure they are eager to fulfill their destiny."

It began as a beautiful day after a night of rain, but with afternoon came clouds and a chill. Dee approached the grounds of the temple where a messenger had summoned him as he went everywhere lately, alone and on foot. Prisoners had been taken in the final battle of the uprising of the faction from Yangchou, the message said, and their fates had yet to be decided. There was to be a hearing of sorts. A temple did not strike Dee as the proper or customary place to hold a hearing—but then, nothing in the world was as it should have been these days. He did not believe that his presence would make any difference, but he would not turn his back on these prisoners, as so many of his colleagues undoubtedly would. He would appear.

Wind whipped along the paving stones and scattered debris around his feet as he walked; by the time he came within sight of the White Horse gates, little needles of rain dampened his face and clothing.

People had gathered there, and he quickly saw why—the gates had been decorated as if for a festival. Colorful streamers of silk, which were meant to flap gaily in the breeze, he supposed, hung wet and disconsolate. Flowers, too—garlands of them were strung between the iron spikes. Dee wore his magistrate's robe and cap today, so he was able to move to the front with little trouble. In his sleeve was a sharp double-edged dagger. He did not really think such a puny weapon could do him much good, but he had not wanted to come here completely unarmed.

He was gratified to see that he was not the only official who had appeared. At least ten or twelve others stood close to one another, wet and unhappy—looking. He nodded to them, and moved in their direction. When they open the gates to let us in, Dee thought, I will demand, in front of all of these people, that they be left open behind us. I refuse to be shut inside.

The rain grew steadily more determined, puddles forming under their feet. Just as Dee was beginning to decide that they had been the victims of a joke, some obscure exercise in futility, the door to the temple opened and a processional of monks emerged, chanting. Behind them, emerging from the same door, were Imperial guardsmen. Dee counted twenty—five of them. It was not until the guards were nearly at the gates that Dee saw that each man carried a box.

A monk pushed the gates open just enough so that the monks and the guards could come through single-file. The monks, still chanting, fanned out to either side while the guards, stony-faced, lined up twenty-five abreast directly in front of the gates, which then shut behind them. The crowd hung back as the chanting went on for many more minutes, the sound seeming to pull the rain down out of the sky. Then, at a signal from one of the monks, it stopped.

"We are here to give a fair and speedy trial to our prisoners of war," he announced. "The Empress in her infinite mercy will allow them to be heard before their fates will be decided." Dee saw no prisoners. And why this foolish ceremony in the rain?

Then the guards with the boxes approached the gates.

"The first to go on trial today will be Li Ching-yeh, prime fomenter of the rebellion against our Divine Empress," the monk said. Dee knew that name: that was the man who had written him the letter from Yangchou.

A guard stepped forward then, opened the box he had sent on the ground, and pulled out an object which, for a few strange and dreamlike moments, Dee's mind refused to identify. It was not until the guard placed it atop one of the cruel black iron spikes that he recognized the face of Li Ching-yeh.

Then the monk addressed the head.

"I will now read the charges against you," he said.

That night, Dee and the rest of the city learned the facts: the Empress had sent three hundred thousand of her fiercest, most experienced troops, hungry for battle and the taste of blood, to crush the rebellion with unnecessary force. Not satisfied that the scholars and their hired soldiers had laid down their arms, scattered, and fled in abject defeat, the Empress's army had pursued its quarry to the ends of the earth, killing anything that moved, storming the gates of Yangchou itself, and taking no prisoners. None except twenty-five.

JOURNAL ENTRY

I am leaving Loyang tomorrow, having written a formal statement declaring my wish to transfer to another city. I have chosen Ch'ang-an, the western capital, three hundred *li* from here. I have chosen that city because it is a city of government, and I intend to stay close to government, no matter how debased it may be, and because I do not think it would be prudent to return to Yangchou, the seat of the ill-fated rebellion. And of course, my family have been moved to Ch'ang-an. I am more than ready to be reunited with them.

Ill-fated? Those are mild words. And to think that I actually entertained the idea that the Empress might show mercy and restraint. Such is the extraordinary, undying, obstinate power of hope, even in the face of dismally mounting futility.

I recall the terrible confusion I felt when I ducked into the doorway at the monastery. When I understood that Hsueh Huai-i was not merely posing as one of the brethren, but was the very abbot of the White Horse, I hid myself in shock, thinking of betrayal, of danger, of the safety of my friend the Old Fool, thinking all of it faster than thought. I congratulate my quick instincts now. But in the ensuing days, I began to waver, and actually drifted back into hope. Well, I told myself, you must not assume that Hsueh is lost simply because he is the author of an outlaw religion and sleeps with the Empress. Perhaps he has attained a level of subterfuge of which you, with your silly superficial disguises, cannot even conceive. Perhaps, I told myself, you have completely underestimated him. Perhaps he has determined to make the ultimate sacrifice, to penetrate to the very heart of the malaise that holds the Imperial House in a deadly grip, and to destroy it from within, possibly losing his own life in the process. And with the rumor that the Empress was practicing the doctrine of mercy in her dealings with the rebels in Yang-chou, I thought: It is his influence. Now is the time he will show himself.

Now I know what a rumor of mercy is worth. And I have learned what might possibly be the cruelest fact of all: that those twenty—five prisoners were alive until they reached Loyang. Mercy and compassion? I think not. Indeed, my friend Hsueh Huai-i showed himself.

But of course, I did not know any of this when I went to attend the "hearing" at the White Horse Temple. It was there, standing in the rain, watching blood run down onto the flowers and streamers, that I had my moment of perfect, lucid understanding: there would be no more waiting for a message from Master Hsueh, because here it was, now, before my eyes. My instinct was to turn and run, to run and never stop. Most of my colleagues did. But I stayed, until all twenty-five heads were on the spikes and the "charges" had been read against each one. Why did I stay? For the same reason that I went in the first place—because I could not abandon them. And I stayed for a while after the monks and soldiers had gone. I looked upon the dead defenseless faces of men I had known, their poor mouths open, their poor eyes rolled up to heaven or staring fiercely at the ground and their wet bedraggled hair stuck to their skulls, and I understood something else: that if I did not leave Loyang, and leave quickly, it would soon be my own head gazing down from an iron spike in front of the White Horse Temple.

There is an interesting footnote to it all, which may or may not be relevant, and which in other times and places I would have considered to be merely an intriguing scrap of esoteric knowledge. I have done a bit of research, and I have learned that among the Tibetans, removal of the head from the body is, among other things, a way to ensure that the corpse will not be possessed by a spirit and rise from the dead.

Another message from Hsueh? I do not know.

23

A.D. 675, Late winter
Loyang

The boiling caldron of soup was rolled out on a heavy iron coal-fed brazier seated upon a small sturdy wagon. The dark oily roiling surface of the broth gave off a thick steam that released the odors of ginger and garlic, spring onion, leek, dark bean, and cloud mushroom. President Lai Chun-chen of the Empress's Agency of Secret Police inhaled the fragrance deeply, inviting his chief aide, Vice President Chou Hsing, to do likewise. President Lai smiled graciously in his colleague's general direction.

"Delightful!" Lai's nostrils flared accommodatingly for the appetizing steam. "Absolutely delightful. Wouldn't you say so, Master Chou?"

"Yes," Chou Hsing said without a great deal of conviction, taking a perfunctory sniff. "Yes. An excellent bouquet of aromas. But why so much broth in so large a pot?"

"Because my cooks are not yet done with the soup," Lai responded matter-of-factly.

Chou Hsing looked at the two large, burly men who had wheeled the caldron in and who now stood silent and unflinching in the steam from its churning surface. They did not look like chefs.

"I understand, President Lai." But he didn't. "But why so large a vessel?" Chou persisted, his curiosity really getting the better of him.

"Because we need room for the final ingredient."

"That being . . . ?"

"Yes." Lai nodded to his partner. "That being the meat."

"Then what have we? Pork? The entire sow?" He set down his rosewood-and-mother-of-pearl chopsticks and managed a toothy smile that presumed a laugh would follow.

Lai Chun-chen said nothing but tilted his head questioningly while looking at his colleague, as if appraising the unsuitability of his clothing. After a long uncomfortable silence in which Lai's smile faded to a wan shadow, the president asked:

"How presumptuous of me, Master Chou. You really don't know, do you?"

Chou Hsing shrugged. By now his smile was entirely gone. He was growing uncomfortable in a nameless way.

"You ask me to dinner to celebrate our mutual elevations in appointment, and then require that I must guess the ingredients of each dish," Chou Hsing said. "You certainly are making me work for every bite," he added, striving to maintain levity, but the effort had begun to tire him. They sat in silence, the only sound in the room coming from the boiling pot. "I am sorry," he said after a time. "But I cannot guess." His superior looked down for a moment, then raised his smiling face to him.

"*You* are that missing ingredient, Master Chou," Lai Chun-chen revealed flatly.

"I . . . ?" Chou cast a glance at the boiling caldron, then returned his eyes to Lai Chun-chen. "Very amusing, I am sure," he said. He noticed Lai's eyes flicking then, as if giving a signal. It had been in the direction of the two "pot watchers," who now slipped silently from behind the caldron, displacing wisps of steam with them.

"I am not joking, Master Chou," Lai said with a shrug of sincerity. "In fact, I have rarely been more serious." Lai paused and fixed Chou significantly. "But I have a question for you to answer."

"This is ridiculous," Chou Hsing said, trying to command dignity back into his voice. But it was trembling. "Ridiculous!" he repeated, trying to put some force behind it.

"Were you acquainted with the rebel leader Li Cheng-yeh before the Scholars' Rebellion?" Lai asked. "The man whose skull has adorned the gates of the White Horse Monastery these last four years with those of his comrades?"

Chou Hsing's eyes widened in disbelief. "Only distantly.

I was introduced to him but once. What is this all about?"

Lai Chun-chen motioned for the two men to approach the dining table and to take their place behind the little vice president of Her Majesty's secret police.

"I don't believe you," he declared, his voice still friendly. "The acquaintance was more than casual. How many times?" he persisted, as if asking after the other's health.

"Only once, as I have said. He is a distant cousin of the late Emperor's family . . . that is all that I know," the little man stammered indignantly, his voice rising several pitches. "A distant cousin. No one of consequence."

"Nor are we, Master Chou. Not until we revolt against the Empress's rightful Imperial government. But I still don't believe you."

"Believe me . . . believe me!" the little vice president said, pushing himself away from the table.

"Forgive me, Master Chou," Lai said with real regret in his voice. "I do not know why I do not believe you." He shook his head wearily. "But I do not. And unfortunately, I have not the energy to keep asking. We have already interrogated far too many of the leading aristocratic families whose highly educated members had occupied and hampered the upper levels of this bureaucracy. But I cannot continue with this game." President Lai looked down at his hands and released an exasperated sigh, then looked again at his colleague sitting unhappily in his chair.

"Strip him!" Lai said abruptly and forcefully to the two men.

The first put his hands on Chou Hsing's shoulders. Chou squirmed out from under them. White—faced with fear and incredulity, he attempted to rise from his dining chair, but the heavy hands now shoved him rudely back into his seat.

"I . . . I . . . don't know . . . anything about this! I . . ." Chou was breathing almost too hard to speak. The larger of two attendants, the one who had forced him back into his chair, took hold of the vice president's outer jacket and tore it free over Chou Hsing's head.

"Stop this insanity! His father did . . . did me a favor many years ago . . . that is all!" the vice president shouted in one ragged fragment of breath.

Lai Chun-chen was unimpressed with his colleague's words. He made no move to stop the two assistants.

The little man attempted to fight them off, but his thin

flailing arms were useless against their brute strength. The first
of the burly attendants still tugged at the outer jacket, which
hung on by only the failing seam of one arm. The other tore
his long robe from collar to hem as the vice president struggled
to get up. The first attendant, now finished with the outer
jacket, slid his arms under the little man's armpits, and locking
the fingers of his big hands together, pushed down on the back
of his neck, forcing his head down so that his chin was on his
chest. The other tore the light silk undergarments down over
Chou Hsing's ankles and took hold of the thrashing legs. Together they lifted the struggling vice president off the ground.

"His father helped me before my appointment to Her Majesty's secret police," Chou Hsing cried. He was naked. He was
breathing hard, his chest rising and falling violently with the
effort.

"So . . . so . . . " he huffed. The two men lifted him—one
torn leather sandal dangling from the big toe of his right foot—
to within a few feet of the boiling soup.

"So . . . so . . . so what are you trying to tell me?" Lai
asked.

"That I tried . . . that I tried . . . tried to . . . " But Chou's
dry mouth could not form the words. Licking his lips, he tried
again. "So I tried to help the son . . . a little. . . . "

The two men then hoisted the vice president so that he
was suspended directly over the caldron, the burning steam
caressing the bony wings of his back.

Chou twisted his head to face Lai Chun-chen, who remained placidly seated by the table.

"So I tried to return the favor! That is all! I sent agents
ahead to offer him a means of escape before the Imperial troops
trapped them on the levy! For Li only! Not for the others! A
banishment. He would have no power ever again. Just his life.
I am no traitor!"

"That is all?" Lai asked calmly.

"Yes . . . yes . . . the truth. I *swear* the very truth!"

"Well, now I believe you," Lai said, his voice friendly
again. "You are no traitor, Master Chou. I commend your effort to return a favor." He nodded his head at the two attendants. "Put him down."

Chou Hsing puffed heavily as he was placed unceremoniously onto his feet, legs shaking, wet, naked, and undigni-
fied.

"You see how simple that interrogation was? Not the

threat of long-drawn-out torture, nor the mind-confusing pain of undergoing the actual torture itself. But as you yourself suggested in your first treatise on torture and the extraction of information, the simplest technique: the certainty of a brutal and tremendously painful death!" Lai raised his eyebrows, his face beaming with success. "I was merely testing the efficacy of the technique."

The vice president, shaking and humiliated, now stood clutching a quilt that had been wrapped around him.

Lai raised his wine cup and saluted Chou Hsing. "Come join me in a toast to our mutual promotion to the Censorate's newly created Board of Punishments and Investigations." He lowered his cup. There was no response from Chou Hsing; the little man did not move. Lai continued, unabashed, friendly and chiding, as if it had all been a great joke. "Come, come! It is a fine time indeed, Master Chou. There is much to be thankful for. Under the Lord Secretary, Historian Shu Ching-tsung, and the spiritual counsel to our Empress, the great Lama Hsueh Huai-i, we are coming to see a new age in governmental efficiency. We shall not experience the futile and empty waste of any more 'Scholars' Rebellions,' now, shall we? It will be far easier to detect and prosecute those enemies of the state before they become an encumbrance. The urns! We are blessed to be so integral a part of that instrument for the stability and well-being of the realm. Don't you feel the vibration of that New Age that our Empress speaks of coursing through your veins, too?" Lai smiled again at his aide.

Still standing in the center of the room, clutching the quilt to his thin body, Chou Hsing turned his head at last and fixed Lai with a look of cold hatred.

"Now, now! Enough! Come back to the table, Master Chou, and sit down."

Chou Hsing's little body trembled with rage.

"You must be famished," Lai entreated, smacking his lips. "We have not even had the first course of soup yet."

"Bastard," the other whispered, and then made his way to the table and sat, for he was famished indeed.

Wu-chi put down his brush, rubbed his eyes, and in the soft evening light reread the letter he was going to dispatch to Ch'ang—an the next evening. He never used the state post for any of his missives, but relied exclusively on traveling mendicants and pilgrims introduced to him by Abbot Liao.

. . . Is it now that yin is yang and yang is yin? I do not know. But I do know that evil is rising to the top of this society like oil on water.

This is not new to you, I know. But since you wisely left the blessed "City of Transformation" nearly four years ago, it has grown relentlessly worse.

There is scarcely any quarter where one might find peace—even in this tranquil and overlooked bastion of true Buddhism. My good abbot has so far avoided becoming part of the White Cloud, but it costs him. Every month, an emissary from another nearby monastery, one that joined the fold enthusiastically, pays him a visit, and collects a hefty tithe for the privilege of "occupying" the land on which the Pure Lotus has sat for centuries. . . .

Criminals, my friend. Criminals are everywhere. They fill the upper echelons of Imperial government—men possessed of animal cunning and brute resourcefulness. . . .

Wu-chi raised his eyes for a moment. It was impossible to read or write anymore unless he rested them every few minutes or so. I suppose it is because they have seen too much in more than eighty years of life, he thought. I have simply worn them out. He squeezed them shut for a moment before returning his attention to the page.

The new officers of our fates are Lai Chun-chen and Chou Hsing, two minor thugs who once ran the Empress's secret police. But through the graces of the Empress's nephews in the Censorate (I believe you have had the pleasure of making their acquaintance), and, of course, Lama Hsueh, these two thugs are now the chief architects of a newly refurbished Board of Punishments and Investigations, an integral part of the Censorate's highest court. It appears that reason and mercy are the first victims of this "state-sanctified organ of government."

I will continue this missive tonight. By then, so my good abbot tells me, I will have had the privilege of seeing, with my own tired eyes, one of these blessed urns of which we have heard so much of late and will spare no detail in describing it to you. . . .

Tired eyes indeed, Wu-chi thought, hearing the tread of Abbot Liao on the stairs, bringing the evening meal, which the two had shared every evening for almost twenty years now. He put away his brush and inks and did his best to put a cheerful expression on his face for the sake of his friend.

Wu-chi gazed impassively at the proceedings before him. Not even this monastery was immune, it seemed. To the delight of at least fifty small, dirty, wide-eyed children who had gathered in the monastery's courtyard for the morning's meager but merciful meal, one of the Empress's urns was being installed outside the main front gates. Not just an urn, Abbot Liao had told him with weary irony, his equanimity wearing sadly thin, but a "Receptacle for Truth." That was what they were being called.

The urns were being placed at the pulse points of the world. They had been placed for the purpose of gathering information. Every person had become a possible source, a potential informant or enemy of the state.

Not only could one inform on one's friends, relatives, or neighbors, but one had an obligation to report other phenomena as well. The natural world of heaven and earth was no longer the basic interplay of yin and yang; there were no happenstance events. Everything was to be interpreted according to its relevance as an omen that pointed to Wu's Divine Destiny to rule in the Maitreyan Age. People were to be on the alert for such occurrences as oddly inscribed rocks found in rivers, birds flying in formations resembling ideograms, unusual weather, presaging rainbows, preternatural haloed moons, or even turnips resembling the Divine One himself. Blatant or covert, a thing or an event was deemed an omen if it was found to point to the proper, officially sanctioned conclusions.

I could think of a few omens myself, Wu-chi thought, watching the men grunt as they lifted the heavy brass urn into position. Oh, yes. Quite a few. Abbot Liao was clapping his hands, bringing the crowd of children to order in preparation for herding them into the monastery's dining hall to partake of a daily meal of rice cakes and vegetable broth to soothe their empty bellies. Wu-chi accompanied the abbot and the children inside, leaving the workers to their task.

"Mercy is such a tiring thing," the abbot remarked wearily to Wu-chi as they entered the dining hall. Wu-chi smiled at his friend. He knew how heavily thoughts of Loyang's poor and derelict weighed on the abbot at this time of year.

Later, when the children had gone and the workers had finished, Wu-chi and Liao examined the bronze urn more closely. The old abbot pulled his jacket tightly around his shoulders and shivered.

"Now we are all criminals of the state," Wu-chi said, looking at the vessel. It seemed harmless and even vulnerable sitting alone by the roadside on its little concrete pier, not resembling at all the forward-thrusting blade of an increasingly brutal government which both men knew that it was.

The top of it was divided into four compartments, inscriptions accompanying each. One of the openings was for receiving reports known as "self-recommendations," a second was for "criticism of the government," a third for "grievances and wrongs." The fourth and largest opening bore an inscription indicating that it was for "calamities, secret plots, plans, and omens."

"An interesting combination, don't you think?" Wu-chi asked at last, tapping the edge of the largest slot. "Plans, calamities, and omens. The government, if we may call it that, obviously sees no difference between interpreting plots against it and reading omens plucked out of the clear blue sky."

Wu-chi remembered Lai Chun-chen and Chou Hsing from their days with the secret police. Crude and brutal men, whose only identifying characteristic was their unremarkable ordinariness. Cruelty's lair almost always lay within the boundaries of the commonplace and mediocre.

Lai and Chou, for all their banality, were clearly men of action and ideas, Abbot Liao had remarked to Wu-chi only a few days before. They were the authors of a just recently completed and highly acclaimed volume called *The Science of Processes: The Instrument of Entrapment,* a clear and concise manual of methods of torture and the extraction of forced confessions. The work, drawn from their long personal experiences as the Empress's chiefs of the secret police, was replete with such poetic and ironic titles for the techniques detailed within its pages as the "Dying Pig's Rattle," the "Stop All Pulses," and the "Beg for Family Ruin." The central theme of this treatise, radically innovative and responsible for the fame and adulation now being heaped on its authors, was a new, experimental method of torture: the infliction of nervous exhaustion upon the victim.

With this technique, the victim had not a mark on him, yet he confessed to anything and everything. Lai and Chou had discovered that the dreadful anticipation of pain was far more effective than the pain itself. It was effective, and it was clean. And the urns had been their idea, too.

Wu-chi learned that the urns had another purpose besides that of "informing" Wu and supplying omens—they also offered the Empress and her thugs a way of meeting many useful men. They could present themselves at their "best" through the convenient means of the urns.

She began by offering jobs and appointments to the ones that she or Shu or "Lama" Hsueh Huai-i might take a fancy to. Most of these daring self-promoters, of course, proved to be criminals and liars. It did not take long for word to spread that if you possessed the courage and audacity to present yourself, and were able to impress Her Highness, she would give you a prestigious job. Before long the Court was thick in a poisonous vapor of competitive informing and counterinforming.

Most of Wu-chi's information came to him through one of his dwindling number of contacts with the Court. Through this contact, he had learned of a particularly foul case of attempted self-promotion and its dreadful consequences. Though this particular tale seemed hideous and nearly unbelievable—but not quite—to the old councillor and the abbot, it was only one example out of many. Apparently, the Censorate's Supreme Court had recently put to use a unique conveyance invented by Lai and Chou for the purpose of encouraging anonymous "reporting": Those who chose to make potentially damning statements could also choose to be wheeled into court under cover.

Specifically, as the elderly retired scribe who had visited the monastery a few days before had told his hushed audience of two, an "accuser" or an "informer" could be wheeled before the bench while hidden inside a rolling box. As the informant was asked questions by the "magistrates" of the court, he could view the officials through narrow apertures in the movable conveyance without being seen himself, or being identified by anyone. But the real stroke of genius was not merely the wheeled box, but the extraordinary "Voice of the Thunder Owl" that was attached to it.

The box was Lai and Chou's invention, but reliable rumor—all three men had smiled at that phrase—held that the inventor of the "Voice" was none other than the redoubtable Tibetan Lama Hsueh Huai-i himself.

The Voice of the Thunder Owl, the visitor had continued, was an elaborate device whereby the informer hidden inside the rolling box could disguise his voice not only from those he testified against, but also from the members of the court. There was always the possibility, after all, that the accuser might be pointing the finger at one of the court officials.

The Voice is nothing if not ingenious, the visitor had continued. It consists of an interchangeable series of reeded flute-like tubes and narrow bamboo baffles all contained inside a protuberance, attached to the outside of the wheeled box, resembling the beaked head of the Owl God. Those on the outside would be able to distinguish the words that were spoken by the accuser/informant within the box, but the voice emanating from the beak would be buzzing, humming, muffled, and distorted so that it was thoroughly unrecognizable. The pitch of the informer's voice could be raised or lowered as well by manipulation of the sliding fluted tubes from within.

It seems, explained the old scribe, that a particularly odious would-be informer thought that he might obtain promotion within the corrupt ranks of the new Censorate Supreme Court by revealing a traitor. The informer's mistake was in overestimating the degree of depravity that his superiors were willing to tolerate.

The informer was wheeled into court in the box fully equipped with the Thunder Owl apparatus. He told the court in his reedy, buzzing voice that his father had been a high-level official with one of the many departments or ministries of the Secretariat. As a Confucian official, the father had opposed the Empress's reign. Without openly joining them, the informer's father had given what moral support he could from the vantage of his high government post to the disaffected officials and the Li family leaders who organized the abortive Scholars' Rebellion.

At the moment of the informer's revelation, the entire hall of the Censorate Supreme Court became silent so that you could have heard a thimble rolling along the terrace bricks outside. The man said that it was his own mother who had hidden his father from the authorities for so many years.

This was more than even Lai and Chou's heinous court could stomach. The mother-incriminating informer was told that the court would have to recess for a short time until it reached a decision, and that he was to remain safely inside the box until then. The box with its miserable occupant was then wheeled into the courtyard and left there. After several weeks of deliberation, a verdict of guilty was returned. The crying and screaming from within the box, distorted by the Voice of the Thunder Owl, had lasted nearly ten days, so it was said. The informer himself was found posthumously guilty of transgression of the boundaries of filial respect, and both verdicts were entered in the court records. Such was the state of the Empress Wu's new courts.

And no doubt, the old scribe had gone on, you gentlemen have heard what has happened to our merciful and restrained T'ang laws regarding capital punishment. Now, under Lai's direction, circuit prosecutors anywhere can execute a prisoner on the spot without trials or hearings of any sort. This is also Wu's new court.

Wu-chi and the abbot had been looking at the urn for a long time when the abbot suggested that it was growing chilly, and that two old men had no business standing out in the cold. Wu-chi looked up from his distracted thoughts and was on the verge of complaining that he was quite capable of looking after himself when he saw that the afternoon was indeed almost gone. He still had a letter to finish.

Wu-chi took Abbot Liao's arm, and they started back, the abbot speaking of the delicious meal his cook would be preparing that evening for them, one of Wu-chi's favorite dishes, while Wu-chi thought ahead to how he would finish his letter to Dee. He meant to put in the details of the story the old scribe had told them; it was a grisly, horrendous tale, but not without a certain poetic justice that Wu-chi knew his old friend the magistrate would appreciate.

24

A.D. 675, early autumn
Ch'ang-an

For the first time in the four years since he had left Loyang, Dee wished that he could return. Not because he ever wanted to live there again, which would be tantamount to descending into hell, but because he burned with desire to expose the man who was perhaps the biggest charlatan he had encountered in his long career. To do that, he was almost willing to return to the city of purges, torture, and terror. He had considered the notion seriously, but thinking of the disharmony and upheaval it would cause with his wives, rejected it. A return journey to Loyang would exude danger with every step, every breath; he doubted that he would get away alive a second time. In fact, he was certain of it.

Something was happening in the streets of Ch'ang-an that many people seemed to think was jolly and festive, but that had an entirely different effect on Magistrate Dee Jen-chieh. Wherever one walked, in parks, on the broad boulevards, or in the back alleys, one could not avoid the knots of people gathered to witness the "miracles" that were now occurring with the frequency of sneezes.

Sometimes the crowds were quiet and awed, and sometimes they hooted and laughed, depending on the skill of the particular man at the center of their attention; the man, or the young ragged urchin, or—in more than one case, Dee was sure—the woman disguised as a man. Their peculiar affected mannerisms—a haughty demeanor, an otherworldly stare—set them apart from the usual Ch'ang-an street performers and marked them for Dee as being nothing other than stylized caricatures of their mentor and idol, the monk Hsueh Huai-i. Most of them, he was sure, had never set eyes on the monk himself, but were imitating each other or modeling their grimaces and stares after the descriptions of him in the popular poems and songs that circulated in the city. He was a hero, a legend—a god.

Today, Dee stood on a grassy knoll in the Serpentine Park

watching the conclusion of a young magician's performance. He had made coins appear out of the air, and had suggested to people that they would be too hot to touch—and Dee had watched as people yelped in pain and dropped the coins when the magician tossed them into their outstretched hands. A miracle! the people around Dee were exclaiming.

He had watched a variety of these performers in recent weeks. Some were clever and adroit, like this one, while others were merely pathetic. Like the old man he had seen earlier this morning in the middle of a public market with frogs and snakes hidden in his sleeves, trying to make the jeering crowd believe that the creatures were crawling forth from the orifices of his body. Or the young fellow with his cumbersome, dusty sword box, into which he contorted himself while he invited people in the crowd to impale him. Dee had seen the man yelp in pain and shed real blood as one of the blades grazed his leg, shoved in by an overenthusiastic spectator who did not give the performer the time needed to position himself.

Yes, the coin tosser's feats were certainly superior to the others'—but a miracle? He shook his head as he strode away. It was well and good to desire and even to expect divine manifestations on one's way to market in the morning, but to settle for such cheap, shabby, threadbare examples! The miracle, Dee thought, was that people could allow themselves to believe it, even for a moment.

And how had it come to be that street magicians were calling their stunts and illusions miracles, and getting away with it? Because that was what the monk himself was doing, on a grand scale, three hundred *li* away in the City of Transformation. Dee had listened to the tales, and knew that everything Hsueh had conjured, no matter how fantastic, no matter how strange and "miraculous," was well within the bounds of the Tibetan's extraordinary abilities.

He was awing the multitudes with huge feats of legerdemain. His specialty was levitation—giant, heavy statues of the Buddha rose from the ground as if made of thistledown. Buddhist saints and angels materialized from the clouds and flew through the air, singing the Great Cloud Sutra in high, eerie, otherworldly voices. Magic lotuses pushed their way up through the pavement and popped out from between dry stones, and bloomed, giving off sweet scents and music.

But strangest of all, people declared, were the temples. Several weeks before, the monk had declared that with the rising sun one morning very soon, certain of the temples around the City of Transformation would be marked, indelibly exposed as the nests of heretics that they were. Watch for the sign, he had said; there will be no mistaking it when it happens. And then one morning eleven temples in and near the city were found to be mysteriously painted in blood, from roof to foundation, completely coated with it so that the windows were opaque and it ran down the walls and soaked the earth the buildings stood on. The blood was fresh and sticky and only partially dried; it gave off a terrible smell and flies swarmed and buzzed over the afflicted temples while monks struggled to wash it off, crowds of silent, staring bystanders watching them accusingly. In every case, at every monastery, there had been monks awake all night and on guard ever since Hsueh Huai-i's warning—but no one had seen or heard anything. All had been peaceful, quiet, and deserted until the rays of the sun revealed the lurid sanguinary "miracle."

Dee pushed his shoulders into the annoyingly persistent Ch'ang-an winds, which picked up as the afternoon wore on, and wondered with a shiver of repugnance where Hsueh Huai-i had obtained that much blood. A part of his mind wondered if it was human blood, but he pushed the idea away. Even with the number of deaths occurring every day in Loyang, he and the Empress would have had a difficult time collecting the vats of blood that it must have taken to adorn the errant temples of Loyang, he told himself firmly; a human being was simply not a large enough creature, and the monk was nothing if not efficient. Surely the blood had come from animals. If Dee were in Loyang, the first thing he would do would be to visit every slaughterhouse in the city. He would get at the truth. Dee could feel his hands and feet twitching with the desire to begin an investigation; the call to action was nearly overwhelming.

Whatever the origin of the blood, Dee had been grateful to learn that Wu-chi's sanctuary had been spared. Probably, Dee surmised, because it was such a distance from the city. Effect, of course, was everything; without throngs of awed and staring people to appreciate the monk-magician's work, what would be the point? Covering the temples with blood in a single night must have been a mighty effort, a challenge even for the talented Hsueh Huai-i. He would not have wasted the effort on something so few people would see.

Dee entered one of Ch'ang-an's countless crowded market streets, alive with merchants shouting above the wind that pelted their stalls with grit and caused their curtains and banners to flap and snap. This was the cheerful, noisy bustle of daily commerce, undaunted by the famous vagaries of Ch'ang-an's weather. If only he could return to Loyang for just a few days, Dee thought, so angry that people moved instinctively away from him as he strode down the street. If only he could be present at one of these "supernatural" events that were making a living god out of the Tibetan, elevating him to a mythical status throughout the land so that an army of pale imitators paid him homage on every street corner in every city. Dee could not remember ever wanting anything as acutely as he wanted to turn his rational, empirical Confucian eye on the mechanics of the monk's illusions, to expose the greasy, dusty, and entirely earthly gears, ropes, and pulleys, as it were, behind his mirages. But he was impaled on a point of pure frustration: he knew he would not, could not, return to Loyang for a long, long time, if ever; like a prophecy, the uncomfortable vision of his own head atop an iron spike, gazing forlornly down on rain- and blood-soaked paving stones, had not left him.

Dee's life in the western capital had been quiet these past few years. He gladly performed his daily work of presiding over mundane civil cases, grateful for their soporific ordinariness, which served as a balm against the dreadful memory of his last days in Loyang. He allowed people to believe that the fire had gone out under the once-impassioned orator who had held forth so memorably against the excesses of the church at the Pai Debates eight years before. He was merely a magistrate now, shrewd and impartial, but the old ardor was gone. There was even a prominent Buddhist scholar and teacher who was known to make visits to Magistrate Dee's home; there were rumors that the great Confucian was taking instruction.

Dee did not discourage the rumors. He let people think it so that he could pursue his real work. In truth, the man was Dee's invaluable ally. Through him, Dee kept his hand in, but quietly, covertly, monitoring the activities of unscrupulous abbots and other sorts. He knew everything that went on in the city and its environs while keeping his own head down, attracting as little attention to himself as possible.

It was through his friend that Dee had recently learned that soon there would be a White Cloud Temple in Ch'ang-an, that it would simply appropriate the grounds of one of the truly compassionate orders here in the city, razing the old buildings and constructing extravagant new ones.

And the scholar had brought him something else, too— another manifestation of Hsueh's growing influence: a bit of the lama's latest literary masterwork, reciting the piece from memory. This was one of the scholar's great abilities—he could see or hear something but once, then speak it perfectly word for word. In this case, it was the only way Dee would have access to the piece, for Hsueh Huai-i had declared that his great work, entitled Commentary of the Precious Rain, was forbidden to be written down. It could only be disseminated by being spoken aloud. Dee had gone ahead and made himself a criminal by copying it down as the scholar spoke it.

As he listened, a sense of grudging admiration grew in Dee. Who would have thought that his old friend Hsueh would travel so far, or that his literary efforts would reveal such an uncanny mastery of popular myth and political expedience?

It spoke of the prophecy of the Devas—a direct reference to the Great Cloud Sutra. Dee recalled with a shudder the words chanted by the monks in the streets of Loyang, about a woman coming to rule the world and such.

The Commentary of the Precious Rain listed in painstaking detail all of the ways that Wu's actions as Empress, the circumstances of her birth, and even the color of the clothing she wore corresponded to specific references in the Great Cloud prophecy—thereby "proving" that she was none other than that preordained woman ruler.

It was a masterful second step for Hsueh—for the prophecy of the Great Cloud Sutra was, of course, the piece "discovered" by Hsueh Huai-i in the tattered old bag of a beggar.

By gradual degrees, with the help and encouragement of Lama Hsueh, the Empress was claiming divinity for herself. It was no wonder that the Empress was coming to be impressed with the notion of her own immortality. The scholar had informed Dee that the Empress, not satisfied with digging up the works of the ancients, was determined that her own work would stand with theirs. Work had begun, he said, on thirty-five Buddhas at the Lungmen Caves south of Loyang. So gargantuan would these Buddhas be that ten men would be able to stand with ease on one of their thumbnails.

And the scholar had looked ruefully at Dee. When a gesture of her hand causes the earth itself to be reshaped, then can one blame her for coming to believe that she is more than human?

Later, after his scholar friend had gone and he was alone in his study, Dee remembered what another learned man had said to him once regarding the nature of eternity: when the Himalayas are ground to dust by allowing a single piece of silk to waft against them one time every thousand years, and you multiply that time by the number of stars in the heavens on a clear summer night, you will have a fraction of the amount of time contained in eternity comparable to the fraction of the whole represented by the number of grains of sand composing all the deserts of the world.

How utterly useless, Dee thought. How irrelevant. What is the human mind to make of that? What possible good is such a concept of time to a man endeavoring to live his one small life, his minute allotment of that vast and empty stretch of eternity? It was no wonder that people grew impatient and wanted their deities among them here and now. And it was no wonder that someone sufficiently arrogant, audacious, and daring could step forward from their number and satisfy that need.

One morning as Dee was preparing to leave his house, there was a knock on his bedchamber door. He called out brusquely for whoever it was to enter. His back was to the door as he heard it open behind him; he was donning his jacket and cap and thinking of today's cases—some stolen farm animals, a dissolving business partnership, another wife-beating—as footsteps approached and a tray was placed on a table. He was looking forward to his tea and pastries and getting out into the day when a familiar voice startled him out of his thoughts.

"Will there be anything else, Master Dee?"

Dee turned in amazement to find his second wife standing over the tea tray, head bowed respectfully. That was quite strange enough. Neither of his wives had ever served him tea for as long as he had known them, nor had either of them ever knocked on his door before entering his chamber. But what was even more peculiar was his wife's attire: she was wearing the robe of a household servant.

"And what is this?" he asked, stunned.

"It is your morning tea, Master Dee," she replied without raising her eyes. For a moment Dee worried that perhaps he was finally losing his mind. Then she looked at him and smiled.

"It is such fun!" she declared. "Today I will go into the kitchen and scrub the floors. Then I will peel and chop the vegetables and skin and gut the fish for the evening meal, or perhaps carry the slop bucket out to the alley! There is furniture to polish, clothing to be washed and mended . . . " She paused and giggled. " . . . and perhaps there are even chamber pots to be emptied! I must do whatever I am ordered to do!"

"Ordered by whom?" Dee asked, mystified.

"Why, by the household steward, or the servants, or the cook, of course," she replied. He looked at her for a few moments before he remembered.

"Please do not tell me that you are giving credence to that charlatan's grotesque games," he said.

"You are stuffy and have no sense of fun," she declared, turning to go.

"I?" he asked in amazement. "It is not I who have no sense of fun. It is that bloodthirsty sham of an opportunist who has no sense of fun. Or, one might say, whose sense of fun is distorted in such a way that unless pain and fear are present, there is no amusement to be had."

"Pain and fear?" she said. "I see no pain, no fear. It is an exercise in tolerance. An experiment."

"For many, it will be an exercise in humiliation, an experiment in ignominy."

"It is only for a few days."

"Its effects will far outlive the few days of observance."

"You have no curiosity."

"I have great curiosity. I am most curious to see the effects of such a deliberate weakening of society's fabric."

"Weakening? It can only strengthen us to understand our fellow citizens better."

"That is a naive point of view, my dear," he said, putting his cap on his head.

"Why is it naive?" she demanded.

He exhaled in exasperation. "Because human beings are imperfect creatures who need rules, boundaries, and structure if they are to function with any semblance of productivity and dignity."

She shrugged. "As I said before, you are stuffy and have no sense of fun." He had no immediate answer to this, so he picked up a pastry and ate it while she turned again to leave.

"Wait," he said then in a sharp voice. "Did I dismiss you? Did I give you permission to leave?"

She turned and gave him a surprised, haughty, and indignant look. He was not the sort of husband who ordered his wives around, and neither of his wives was the sort who would tolerate it for a moment. He smiled and shrugged.

"Remember," he said to her. "An exercise, an experiment." She gave him a withering stare and marched out of the room, shutting the door behind her with a bang. He sighed and finished his tea.

On his way out of the house, he heard the voice of the steward emanating from the kitchen, telling Dee's wife that she was clumsy with the delicate tea bowls, that she handled them as if they were farm implements and not irreplaceable heirlooms hundreds of years old. He heard his wife's voice murmuring an apology. The last thing Dee heard before shutting the door behind him was the steward's voice listing Dee's wife's tasks for the day, including taking all the chamber pots in the household outside, scrubbing them, and leaving them in the sun to be purified.

Dee was grateful to have left the house before his mother appeared on the scene. He knew that her tolerance for such a distasteful escapade would be nil. No power on earth could have compelled him to stay at home today.

Today, of course, was the first day of three of the "No-Barrier Rites," a supposed ancient festival "uncovered" by Historian Shu and promulgated by the glorious monk Hsueh Huai-i. For a short time, prescribed roles would be reversed and social barriers let down. Servants would give orders to their masters. Children would reprimand their parents. Chambermaids would sit and have their nails manicured and their hair brushed by their mistresses. Stable hands would ride fine horses, and cooks would sit at long, polished tables eating from fine china, and perhaps send the food back to the kitchen if it did not please them. We will all learn humility, flexibility, and tolerance, the monk had proclaimed.

It was not that Dee had forgotten about the monk's proclamation, precisely; he just had not expected it to occur in his own house. Obviously, his knowledge of humanity was far from perfect; he had not counted on the perverse enthusiasm of the sort displayed by his wife this morning.

He saw nothing out of the ordinary during the first few blocks of his walk. Eventually, though, a fine-looking carriage rumbled down one of the large avenues. A very fat, elderly man with sweat running in rivulets down his face rode alongside on a horse. Dee guessed that inside the carriage, lolling on the cushions and watching the world go by from the small curtained window, was the man's strong, lean young servant, the outrider who usually sat on the horse while the fat man rode in the carriage's satin interior. No doubt. Tonight, Dee imagined, the fat man would sit in a hot bath soothing the pain and soreness from his backside, and contemplate the day's lesson in humility.

And the young servant? What would he learn? That silk cushions suited his own backside in a way that a hard leather saddle never could? When the exercise was over, would he relinquish pampered luxury with philosophic detachment, grateful for the knowledge the experience had afforded him?

As Dee approached the marketplace, he found his step quickening. His curiosity was getting the better of him. The food vendors and farmers had been out since dawn, hawking every variety of edible plant and animal known to mankind. This was the time of morning when the servants were out making the day's purchases for the household, haggling, bargaining, arguing, declaring the food unfit for decent human consumption, while the vendors argued and haggled in return, raining friendly insults on the prospective customers, telling them that they were ignorant fools and barbarians from the frozen north who did not know the difference between buffalo dung and rice pudding.

Dee always enjoyed all of it thoroughly, appreciating the tacit understanding between vendor and customer as they went through the time-honored rituals of the marketplace. He headed for the busiest part of the market. It did not take him long to spot a delicate, aristocratic lady with a basket on her arm who appeared to be nearly in tears over something that had been said to her by a wizened old crone selling chickens. Nearby, a young girl, obviously the aristocratic lady's servant, shouted from the window of a sedan chair she had been riding in. She directed a few expert, well-aimed insults at the crone, the transaction was completed, and the lady with the basket trudged off dejectedly behind the sedan chair, which had been lifted into the air and carried away by two grinning young men who, Dee surmised, were the sons of the household, probably the woman's own progeny, enjoying their mother's discomfiture.

Of course, Dee thought, the young would adapt better to such a reversal. He doubted that the lady he had just seen would make it through the day before giving up. He breathed his silent thanks that his own sons were still far away in military service in Szechuan and not here in the city participating in Hsueh Huai-i's No-Barrier Rites. Heaven only knew what sort of gleeful advantage they would have taken of the situation, what sort of inventive destruction they would have wrought.

But no, he told himself; that was not fair. He was not giving them credit for the exemplary lives they had been leading for more than a decade—exemplary, at least, when compared to what they would surely have become if their careers in Yangchou had not been interfered with in a timely way. While the sons had not distinguished themselves particularly during their service in the far western province, neither had they been arrested, demoted, discharged, beheaded, or hanged. It had been a long time since Dee had been visited by the vision of himself sentencing his own sons in his court.

He hurried on through the marketplace. He saw a few more interesting sights, including a husband and wife who had imaginatively carried the No-Barrier Rites a step further. The woman wore her husband's robe, jacket, and cap, and her husband wore a flowered, richly embroidered gown, his face heavily painted with cosmetics. A few scraggly beard hairs hung from his chin, lending a ludicrous finishing touch to the whole effect. The pair were thoroughly enjoying the looks, laughs, and stares from the people around them. Dee turned down the side street that led to his office. Perhaps his wife was right. Perhaps it was true that he was stuffy and had no sense of fun.

At the end of a long, forgettable day during which Magistrate Dee had interceded in the petty details of a dozen people's lives, he turned his thoughts to the evening ahead. His household would undoubtedly be in a state of chaos. There would surely be a long list of complaints served to him along with his dinner. Already he could feel his stomach rumbling and gurgling. Though he was ready to concede in a tentative, grudging sort of way that perhaps the monk's great social "experiment" was a relatively benign diversion—no more, no less—he had no wish to see any more of it. Certainly, no profound revelations or great spiritual insights would come of it.

Conversely, there would most likely be no lasting damage to society, either. Mainly, it was an annoyance, mostly to older conservative Confucian officials. More than an annoyance to some. Several of the older fellows Dee had encountered today—one senior magistrate in particular—were convinced that it was the final end of order and rationality and that the world was sliding irrevocably into nattering, jibbering chaos. Dee looked at the elderly magistrate's worried, watery old eyes and his expression of outraged propriety, and asked himself if this was how he had looked to his wife this morning.

The older man had told Dee that he was not going to return to his home that night. He said he did not care to see the servants sitting at his dining-room table eating off his plates and drinking from his cups, and he did not care to watch his daughters pouring their wine and carrying their dishes.

Therefore, he said, I shall simply withdraw for the next few days. I shall take my food and my rest at a very pleasant little inn I know of. My household will see me again when this infernal buffoonery is quite finished. I shall not dignify it nor breathe life into it with any more of my attention.

Dee had thought that that was an excellent idea. He knew of a very fine little inn overlooking one of the city's many green parks. How pleasant it would be to take his dinner there, and retire early, without any further discourse, debate, or altercation. How peaceful and civilized. My own attitude of forbearance can only be enhanced by such a respite, he told himself as he left the office.

At the inn, he was happy to find that all was as it should be. Peace and order reigned. The proprietor welcomed him, served him an excellent meal on the open-air veranda with its view of the peaceful manicured park wearing its autumn colors, and Dee was able to sit undisturbed in the fading evening light for as long as he pleased without the burden of conversation.

He thought of his time in Loyang, where he had been without his family. There, he had all the solitude he could possibly have wanted—but the memories were not of peace and seclusion. They were of uneasy, enclosed isolation, an aloneness that he sincerely hoped he would never experience again. There had been times, usually on a crowded street or in a courtroom full of people, when he had acutely yearned for his family. And strangely, it was not sustenance and nurturing that he missed, not visions of warm and cozy domesticity that pulled at him, but the familiar comfort, like broken-in shoes one slips into with effortless practice and ease, of well-worn contentions and old arguments. There, he remembered feeling, was where true solace was to be found—safe within the borders of one's tiny kingdom, snug within the parameters of its utterly predictable internal squabbles. And now that his aged mother resided with him, there was certainly no shortage of squabbles and discord.

In years past, his widowed mother had always refused to live with Dee and his wives. She had chosen to live in Ch'ang-an, with the family of her deceased husband's much younger sister. Nothing could make her leave the city where she was born, raised, and married. Her husband was buried here, and she would die here, she declared, and lie beside her noble husband under a substantial stele. And so it was that she would not leave Ch'ang-an and come to Yangchou for the wishes of her son. Besides, she had always said to Dee, "that" woman, meaning Dee's principal wife, clearly did not want her in her house. In *his* house, Dee had countered, making an effort to summon his patriarchal authority, a weak and ineffectual stance that she had dismissed with a flick of her bony wrist. Feh, she would say; men do not run the household. It is not their domain. And he had not been able to counter her.

But now that Father's youngest sister had died suddenly, the old woman, a shuffling and obdurate eighty-seven, had consented finally to move in with Dee and his wives and little adopted daughter now that he had moved them to Ch'ang-an. Fortunately, the house was large, so that the often strained atmosphere could at least spread itself out.

There would be no shortage of familial bickering and griping this evening, of that he was sure. But tonight, he did not need it. He took that to be a healthy sign—it could only mean that the unease that had hung over him in Loyang had lifted its oppressive influence, leaving him free to seek solitude again. It was barely twilight, but already he could feel sleep coming over him. He stood and stretched, looking forward to the luxury of a long, deep, dreamless sleep.

The morning was fine, and Dee was full of a well-being he had not experienced in years. It had been infinitely pleasant to wake up in the little room at the inn and gaze toward an unfamiliar configuration of branches framed in the window.

On the street after an excellent breakfast, he allowed himself a mild feeling of benign superiority toward the people he encountered. No doubt there had been voices raised in homes all over the city last night; he felt very wise for having sidestepped it all. He would be in a cheerful, tolerant mood when he returned to his house tonight.

He passed a vendor's stall selling fine ripe peaches; on an impulse, he stopped and bought several, envisioning himself presenting them to his wives, daughter, and mother. As he put the coins into the vendor's hand, he thought briefly about the abstract concept of family: people who may have nothing in common and who might not even like one another particularly, but who were inextricably bound by blood, lineage, or marriage to share the space under a single roof. Since he had no basket and his purse was not large enough to carry them, the peaches were folded into a large square of cloth, and he was on his way.

He was not halfway up the stairs leading to his office when the figure of one of his assistant magistrates appeared on the landing above. The look on the man's face instantly dispelled all thoughts of family, peaches, wives, pleasant mornings, branches framed in a window with sunlight streaming through. Dee stopped. The assistant started quickly down the stairs to meet him.

"Where have you been?" the assistant asked, breathless, his words spilling over one another as he took Dee's arm and hustled him down the steps. "We have been searching for you since dawn. Your household did not know where you were. We have touched nothing. We have sealed off the house and grounds. We were beginning to worry that you, too, were dead. Your wives are convinced of it."

Dee halted and seized the man's arm harshly.

"Has something happened at my house?" he demanded.

"No, no, no," the other answered. "Forgive me. Not at your house. Not at your house at all. Another house, a fine big house in the northern suburbs."

"What?" Dee demanded again. "What has happened?"

The assistant magistrate shook his head as if he did not believe the word about to come from his mouth.

"Murder," he said.

Murder? Dee was almost relieved. He dropped the man's arm. Murder was hardly an unusual event. He wondered for a moment if the man was simply a novice.

"But it is not . . . an ordinary murder," the assistant

added. Dee looked at him, waiting for more, but the assistant seemed quite unable to find the words. "You will simply have to see it yourself." He pointed weakly toward the door at the bottom of the stairs. "There is a carriage in the rear awaiting you." He went down a few more steps, Dee right behind him, and turned and spoke again. "A family," he said. "An entire family."

25

There was simply too much of it. He turned back to the open doorway behind him and gazed outside, pressing his hands to his temples. When he turned around to reenter the house, he was surprised to discover that his legs were shaking like an old drunk's.

Somehow, he would have to make sense of it. There were five adults—mother, father, grandmother, grandfather, and another older man, an uncle, most likely—and one child, a boy of about eleven, dead, and with the exception of the child, facedown on the floor in a row, their arms wrapped about their heads in the manner of schoolboys dozing at their desks. The adults lay in pools of blood. They were all fully clothed. The boy was naked, with one half of his body painted green with broad, crude brushstrokes. There was no blood on the child, or any other mark of violence. He lay face-up, eyes open and gazing at the ceiling. The family's two lapdogs lay nearby, side by side, their throats neatly slit. The floor and carpets were a welter of crisscrossing bloody footprints made by bare feet; the room was torn to pieces.

"Remember my instructions," Dee cautioned his constables, a swarm of them squatting here and there on their haunches or picking their way carefully about as they worked over the room and the victims for details. "Do not disturb anything. Be very careful. We do not yet know what is significant and what is not. Until we do, everything is significant."

Dee's chief constable, a tough little man with a pronounced hump on his back, came and stood quietly next to the magistrate.

"What do you think? Have we an act of sheer, meaningless brutality on our hands, or . . ."

"I think not," Dee remarked.

"No. I do not think so either," the hunchback said. "If I did not know better, though, I would say that a pack of hungry leopards had come through here." They looked at the chaos of overturned furniture, scattered and smashed vases, books, flowers, screens, and shredded curtains. "Leopards," he repeated, and allowed his hands to drop uselessly to his sides.

"But of course, there are no leopards in Ch'ang-an," Dee answered distractedly. "What of his servants?" he asked.

The constable shrugged.

"All alive, all untouched. They saw and heard nothing, they say. They woke up this morning to find the household slaughtered." With those words, an unpleasant idea presented itself to Dee.

"Find out whether or not this household, or anyone in it, participated in the No-Barrier Rites," he said to his assistant.

The hunchback looked sharply at Dee as the implication of his superior's words hit him. "Yes," he agreed. "An excellent idea."

Dee fixed on the body of the dead child, naked and half painted. Then he looked at the damage to the room with a shrewd, appraising eye. At first glance, one might surmise that the wreckage was a result of the death struggle. But now that he had a chance to really look at what was before him, he was thinking that this was not so at all. There was a forcefulness and depredation that looked . . . vengeful, orgiastic. As if killing the inhabitants of the house had not been sufficiently satisfying, as if the room and all the innocent objects had to suffer, too. What he found particularly chilling was the contrast between the frenzy of the destruction and the deliberateness with which someone had treated the bodies—the child's, most notably. The boy looked as if he had been carefully prepared for some obscure funeral rite. He made a mental note: funeral rites. A place to start, at least.

"And what of the other rooms?" Dee asked.

"Nothing," the hunchback replied. "Nothing. No damage. Nothing out of place. As neat and scrubbed as if the matriarch herself had just prepared for a tea party."

"Nothing I have seen before compares to this," Dee said. "I have seen robbery, and acts of revenge between families and clans—but nothing resembling this. Nothing."

"Nor have I," the constable offered.

Dee stepped forward, knelt, and began to meticulously scrape a sample of the odd green paint from the boy's body into an earthenware jar. He carefully set the jar aside. Then, to each of his constables, Dee passed out brushes, cups of water, and small boats of black and red ink. While he painted a general sketch of the room showing the relative positions of the bodies, his constables began to trace with ink on the wooden floor or the carpets the exact outline of the bodies as they lay. It would not be long before the corpses would have to be removed, and Dee wanted as many aids to memory as possible.

When the outlines were finished, Dee gave the order that the bodies could now be taken away.

Two of the constables reluctantly approached the body of the old grandmother. When they attempted to disengage her arms from about her head, they found them quite stiff. Dee surmised that the time of death had been many hours ago—possibly the night before. He turned away as the men began to lift her. She was as stiff as if she were a statue carved from wood. He had always particularly disliked the pitiful sight of rigor mortis; it seemed to him an unnecessarily cruel mockery on the part of nature. Dee was aware of a silence, a pause in the activity going on behind him, as he busied himself with his sketch of the room.

"Magistrate. You must look at this," the hunchback said, his voice strained with incredulity.

Dee turned. The men stood looking down at the old woman, who had been turned so that she lay stiffly on her back. Her arms still framed her face. Her eyes were open, and her gaze glared upward, her mouth contorted in a terrible grin that stretched, quite literally, from ear to ear.

"What is this?" Dee whispered, and knelt down. "This is hideous," he said gratuitously.

Someone had sliced the corners of the old woman's mouth on both sides all the way back to where the molars began, and then rolled and carefully stitched the gashed flesh with fine black silk thread in a parody of lips to create the hellish smile. If the poor old witch had smiled any wider, Dee thought, her head would have simply separated in two.

"The others," Dee said then, rising to his feet. The constables turned over the next body, and the next. It was the same for all of them. Only the boy had been spared. Gods, Dee

thought; just a moment ago he had been contrasting the formless frenzy of destruction with the care taken in painting the
child's body. These stitched mouths represented hours of
painstaking work. A message, obviously.

But what?

After the bodies were taken away, Dee and his men
scoured the grounds, the gardens, and the outbuildings for anything they could find. But the oddest finding of all, the one
that was literally right under their noses, was discovered quite
by accident only moments before it was about to be swept
away forever. How could the swarm of constables and deputies assisting the investigation have missed it? Worse, how
could it have nearly escaped the "inimitable" eye of the famous magistrate from Yangchou?

It had been a question of the angle of light. The thing had
been right there, on the floor of a corridor that led from the
opposite end of the murder room to the rest of the house, mingled with the bloody prints that went in every direction. It was
only because of one last, obsessive look down the corridor that
Dee happened to see it.

When he had first examined the bloody corridor, the
morning light that slanted through the shutters had been glar-
ingly bright. There did not seem to be any discernible pattern
in the dried mess: it was smeared about, and appeared to be
no different from the pattern of bare footprints within the main
room.

But when Dee returned to examine the area one more time
before closing the investigation for the day, the light had
changed considerably and the sun no longer glared off the polished wooden floor. And there he saw what he had failed to
notice before: a staggered row of bloody crescents, half-moon-
shaped prints moving out of a main puddle of dried blood.
Dee moved closer and stared down. These were not just random circles or the odd vague crescent shapes such as might be
formed by the heel of a boot edged with blood. No, they were
clear, complete prints. Something had walked through the
blood, but that fact was not what was unusual. They had not
been made by a human.

They were hoofprints. Too large for a goat, but . . . He
looked around him. The narrow corridor was too small to accommodate any animal much larger. He came all the way into
the corridor then, threw open every shutter in the now fading

light, and lowered himself to his knees in a lighted rectangle of mahogany floor.

Yes. There was no doubt. They were certainly hoofprints: of a horse. An unshod horse.

Ch'ang-an, the western capital, was the greatest city on earth. With its teeming millions and thriving commerce, the city was the point of confluence for highways, canals, and rivers that went for two thousand *li* in every direction. It was an enormous vortex of peoples, native and foreign, a city where the cosmopolitan and urbane existed alongside customs and superstitions as exotic as anything found in the deep jungles or high mountains of other lands. Ch'ang-an was a many-faceted jewel fragmenting the infinite light of human inventiveness and imagination into a palette of colors that was its strength and magnificence.

Human fear, too, came in many colors and textures. Unchecked fear was a ripe breeding ground for the misunderstandings that arose wherever diverse nationalities coexisted. Now, fanned by rumors concerning the nature of the bizarre and brutal murder of one of the wealthiest households in Ch'ang-an, innuendo and xenophobia raged through the city like a poor man's fire.

Each tribal nationality, each group of immigrants, feared and suspected the other. The northern Turkish Mongolian nationalities—Sogdian, Khitan, Juchen, Uighar, Hsi—hated the southern Hua, Man, and Miao peoples of Lingnam and the uplands of Nam-Viet. Among the southerners, the Miao were distrustful of the Hua peoples, but even more distrustful of the diverse "barbarians" from the jungle gorges of Lingnam. And to each, the other's magic was black and evil. Added to this great churning broth of humanity were the recently arrived Sassanid immigrants from the faraway Persian Empire, with their strange Zoroastrian dualities of good and evil.

The imagination of the city had been stimulated. Details from the murder scene had leaked out, and were exaggerated and distorted even beyond their true gruesome proportions. Tales of unclean magic proliferated and flew about; no one was exempt, and everyone was suspect.

In one retelling of the event, it was not the mouths that were slashed wide but the bellies that were opened, and the intestines wound around the bodies like a bloody rope, or draped like garlands of flowers, or stretched and curled along the floors in the forms of recondite Dark Taoist scripts, their bloody curves spelling out secret words. In another story, the heads were missing, separated so neatly from the necks as to suggest that they had not been severed but had simply taken leave of the bodies on their own. And the word was out that the bloody tracks of animals had been found on the walls and ceilings.

Dee was helpless to stop the hideous fantasies that were scaring the city to death. Although it was never clear where rumors began, it seemed to Dee that fingers were first pointed in the direction of the mideastern sector, the Persians in particular—the most foreign and strange. The Sassanids with their peculiar Zoroastrian beliefs were reputed to have among their number dark sorcerer magicians—the Yatus—who could conjure up evil demons of the underworld at will.

Within the Zoroastrians' richly populated pantheon was the demon Azhi-Dahaka, a foul entity possessing three heads, six eyes, and three mouths, with serpents emerging from his shoulders. It was probable, so certain factions maintained, that in some act of vengeance for personal motives, a Persian sorcerer had conjured him. Did it not fit? Because among his many vices, Azhi-Dahaka had to feed daily on human brains. And were not the brains missing from all the corpses? And once sated on his dreadful meal, did he not simply vanish through the same portal of smoke, created by his summoning Yatus' magical command, through which he entered? It would explain many things for which the civil authorities seemed to have no answers.

The rumors had their own logic. Some factions implicated the Jews and their stern-tempered, jealous, and sacrifice-demanding god. Didn't he insist that the true devotee forsake all others for him—and wasn't a human sacrifice required as proof of that unwavering faith? And of course, there were the Tibetans, bringing their strange mountain ways with them, their mockery of death and mortality. The murders, some parties declared, were the Tibetans' idea of an elaborate joke.

The rumors persisted precisely because the civil authorities had nothing better to offer. The office of the chief magistrate was at a loss. Dee's questioning of the many friends and associates of the deceased family turned up nothing. No revenge motive, no trouble, no shady dealings for which the murder may have been retribution. There were no clan rivalries. There had been no robbery. He could not discern that they had any enemies at all. A fine and generous Confucian household of excellent lineage. That had left him with the only other possibility, one that had seemed strong to him at first but had faded as he looked into it more deeply: the No-Barrier Rites.

He could envision some buried resentment surfacing when roles were switched. But there was no evidence at all that the household had even acknowledged the ritual, and nothing at all to indicate that the servants were anything but loyal and happy. His questions turned up nothing, except the fact that the servants had not heard anything at all, were unaware of a disturbance, and could scarcely remember any details of the evening preceding the murder. After closely questioning every member of the staff, Dee was satisfied that none of them was covering anything up. But he was utterly puzzled by an odd vagueness among them, as if perhaps they had all drunk too much wine: how had such a bloody, brutal killing taken place under their roof and escaped them entirely?

Where Dee could come up with nothing, the people of Ch'ang-an were infinitely resourceful, hardly so barren of ideas; with astonishing vigor and inventiveness, new tales rushed to fill the void of the chief magistrate's investigations. Losing interest in the round-eyed Persian and Jewish populations, the theorists moved on to other more compelling territories.

The immigrant jungle tribesmen of Nam-Viet believed that runs of ill fortune could be reversed only by the hiring of shaman masters to perform appropriate sacrifices. Although the victims of these particular shaman sacrifices were usually nothing more than a pig or a cow, the Chinese people did not believe that the practices stopped there. The question of human sacrifice rose again, more strongly than ever. The Viet shamans vigorously denied any such thing. Never do we touch human blood, they said.

So if it was not the shamans, people said, then it must be the practitioners of *ku*, unquestionably the darkest expression of the Viets' sinister ritual magic, born out of what was barely human civilization, a hot, distant world where the black starless night swarmed with nature spirits as diverse and venomous as the creatures that hopped, slithered, crawled, and flew there. The demons of *ku* were conjured from the deepest fevered delirious abyss of the human mind.

Among the vivarium of *ku* magic were the dreaded reptile ghosts of calamity. Though no one knew why such forces should have been released on the devastated family, anyone could see that this was the answer to the mystery. It all fit. Once released, the phantom reptile ghost entered the victim and bit him from within, paralyzing him. This would explain the lack of anything seen or heard by the servants. Then the victim remained fully conscious, but helpless, as the reptile-ghost ate his innards and squirmed around inside him, its spiky tail raking the inside of the throat and abdominal cavity and finally the skull, which it licked as clean inside as a river polishes stones. And once the host-victim had died the creature took form and burst out through the aperture of the mouth. And weren't the mouths of the victims *ruptured*, people whispered to one another?

Then an unshakable rumor began that the victims had all been headless. And from this distorted truth came the most horrifying myth: the flying heads. This hideous image kept Dee awake at night, wondering at the depths of the human imagination. And the worst part was that this was not a story that has come from some distant and barbaric foreign land. It originated within the "civilized" borders of the Chinese Empire itself.

According to the people of the mountain jungles of Lingnam in South China, a small red line, almost unnoticeable, as slender as a fine silk thread, would appear on the neck of an afflicted person. If this first warning sign was not heeded by some member of the family and proper remedial magic applied immediately, then the wound would widen until the head separated from the neck, and sometime before early morning the ears would metamorphose into enormous webbed wings, and the head would fly silently out into the night through an open window and forage over the jungle with the great birds of prey. It soared above the lush forests and whistled under the foaming torrents of rivers and the sea. Faster than the swiftest hawks and eagles, the head raced the winds through precipitous peaks, narrow gorges, and rocky grottoes while it hunted, and ate and ate throughout the night. Then, sated, it would return before light to join the body. The victim's stomach would now be bloated as if it had participated directly in the magical feasting.

And the stomachs of the murder victims, so the gossip in the streets and teahouses and markets went, had been found to be burst open, glutted on carrion. Proof, pure and simple!

Of course the traditional Chinese Taoists and their dark

practitioners filled the back streets with plenty of goblins and bewildering creatures of their own, some of which could never be seen directly, but only in reflection. Many people began to carry small pocket mirrors with them at all times; there were some who walked backward everywhere while peering into their mirrors, ever on the lookout for the hidden presence of lurking invisible demons revealed in the truth of reflection.

The city had gone quite mad with superstition and xenophobia, and Dee had nothing—no clues, no workable theories, nothing—with which to counter it. Gloomily, he would reflect on how far they had sunk from the rational society so dear to the Confucian heart.

Even his own mother insisted on a chair to take her to market twice a week so that she might update and add to her jingling, jangling collection of beads, charms, mirrors, disks, coins, pouches, roots, claws, powders, and talismans. And although Dee argued with her over the embarrassment caused by such an indulgence in blatant superstition on the part of the dignified and revered mother of Ch'ang-an's Confucian chief magistrate, she merely waved his objections away in her infuriating fashion and pointed to her own advanced age as proof of the efficacy of her system.

Then his old mother would bring up the matter of her son's total ineffectuality as a crime solver. Inevitably, she did this in public in a typically loud mother's voice while her dutiful son was accompanying her on her shopping trips into the foreign west market. And poor Magistrate Dee, chagrined, would be left to smile at the bowing passersby who discreetly pretended not to hear.

None of this, of course, improved the atmosphere at home. Frequently, he would take an early supper and go back to his office with a thinly contrived excuse involving unfinished business. Of course, there was no shortage of unfinished business, but Dee found himself sitting in the dark, thinking, doing nothing, looking out at the streets below his window.

There was only one thing that kept him going: he knew that he could never solve the first murder unless a pattern revealed itself, and a pattern could only emerge with a second mass slaying. Dee was waiting for the unthinkable.

And so he waited.

Dee entered his office one morning after a long night during which his worries and the continual buffeting of Ch'ang-

an's strong winds had conspired to rob him of any semblance
of rest. The old magistrate welcomed him with a look of exasperation and reluctantly dropped a very official-looking
Imperial envelope onto his desk. It had come by early-morning
runner.

Dee studied the envelope's elaborately embossed wax
seals with misgiving and looked around among the disorderly
piles of papers for the silver-and jade letter opener.

He felt a similar tug of apprehension. But why, he asked
himself, did he react so strongly to an as yet unopened envelope? Was it the way it felt in his hands? It was thick, heavy.
But that was not unusual for official communiqués. Was it the
way it lay on the desk, perhaps? Neat, orderly, and distinc-
tively out-of-place and dangerous-looking in the midst of Dee's
comfortable chaos? Was it the way it smelled? It had no odor
other than the smell of silk and parchment. Any smell of ink
had long since disappeared. Nevertheless, he could smell it. As
he slit the envelope cleanly with the sharp decorative blade,
the thin distinctive resonance of expensive paper tearing put it
all into focus for him: three hundred *li*, the distance from the
City of Transformation to Ch'ang-an, was no longer far
enough.

It had been two days since the moment of first unfolding
the pages of elaborate instructions and plans, but Dee was certain that the original expression of bewilderment still showed
on his face.

An enormous pillar of "white iron" topped with a magnificent orb or crystal quartz was to be erected at the exact
center of Ch'angan, two hundred seventy-five gleaming feet
soaring to the greater heavenly glory of the Empress Wu and
the coming of the Age of the Future Buddha Maitreya.

How was that much iron and silver to be raised in so
elaborate and flawless a form? How in the world was that
much ore to be found, mined, and processed in so short a time?
And who was to do this work? Was she planning to send an
army of skilled workers to assist them in this project? If so, it
would have to be an army already experienced in the erection
of these pillars. He envisioned White Cloud monks, hundreds
and hundreds of tall, shaven-headed, dead-faced anchorites,
descending on the city, obsessive and disciplined, wordless but
for the ceaseless chanting issuing from their throats as they

smelted and polished, carved and raised, driven toward some new and perverse metaphysical goal.

But no. The reality was far worse. The burden of assembling the work crew rested on *him*. Like the great corvée work projects of old, it was incumbent upon the city's chief magistrate to raise that army. But this time, he was to draw them not from the common pool of overworked citizenry, but from the prison work gangs—with the purpose, so the instructions had read, of elevating the criminals above the debased plane of earthly sin through this sacred task.

But here was another possibility. There were no longer enough prisoners in the camps of Ch'ang-an and the outlying areas to even begin to realize such an undertaking. Dee's zealousness in returning most prisoners to their families would now prove his undoing. Where was his pool of labor to come from?

Late into the evening of the twentieth day after the murders of one of Ch'ang-an's most respected families, Dee was busily at work in his office on the formation of a plan to gather the workers to raise a ludicrous pillar of white iron to the sky. He had seen that his only option was to work with the Ministry of Defense and the Board of Tribute to acquire captured soldiers from the recent Tibetan and Korean campaigns.

Given the pressured circumstances, it was all he had to work with. He would study the tribute lists and in the morning dispatch a messenger to the prefectural commandery. He did not go home and go to bed until very late that night.

Early in the morning of the twenty-first day after the murders, a shy young servant took hold of Dee's upper arm and shook it as gently as if it were made of paper.

"Master Dee . . . Master Dee . . . " the young servant whispered. Now the boy shook Dee's shoulder with a bit more pressure. Dee grunted, split an eye for a second, then rolled over. He was hard asleep again instantly. The reluctant young servant reached tentatively forward again. He was aware of the impatient little group of people in the hallway behind him, including Dee's two wives. Nobody, it seemed, had been willing to wake the magistrate, and so the task had been assigned to the lowest-ranking houseboy, who had no choice but to obey.

"Wake him!" the senior steward hissed from the doorway. "They are coming upstairs now!"

Dee's wives clutched their robes around them in the chill. The heating fires had all gone out. Three deputies, led by the hunchbacked constable, talking loudly among themselves, tramped into the outer foyer of Dee's room, but stopped short of entering the bedchamber when they realized that their superior was still asleep.

"Why is he still asleep?"

From outside the hallway, coming from behind the deputies, in the corridor to Dee's bedchamber, a stentorian old voice enunciated sternly, its owner unmistakably taking charge. "Let me pass. Let me see him."

"Dee Jen-chieh, wake up NOW!" she said, standing over her son, unassailable in her ancientness.

Then she reached down with her spotted old hand, grabbed a handful of Dee's unraveled braid, and gave it an unrestrained motherly yank, speaking directly into his ear as she did so.

"They are murdering your town," she pronounced.

With a yelp, Dee woke abruptly and completely to a pair of fierce black eyes inches from his own in the lamplight. Startled, he jerked his head backward and knocked it painfully against the headboard.

"Damn!" he said, then looked beyond his mother's reproving face to see the deputies and his wives standing behind her.

"Sir, Magistrate Dee," the hunchback constable said. "We apologize for this inexcusable intrusion on your privacy, but ..." He lifted his hands helplessly. "We did not know what else to do."

"They are murdering your town, that is what I told you," Dee's mother repeated. "So what are you going to do? Sleep, Magistrate Dee?"

"My poor husband gets no sleep at all anymore," Dee's first wife said.

"And he will get even less now, it seems," Dee's mother countered.

"I am quite awake," Dee said, sitting up, all traces of sleep vanished—this time forever, he was sure.

The houseboy reappeared with a tea tray and set it on the magistrate's bedside table. Dee was now sitting on the edge of the bed, his arms pulled into the sleeves of his robe and his feet pushed into slippers while the little group stood around the bed watching him. In the chill air, he saw their breath hanging about their faces like clouds of awful thoughts that had not yet formed themselves into words.

"They do not want to tell you, Dee Jen-chieh," the old woman said, pronouncing his name with a mother's hardened familiarity, "because they are all to blame. I warned everyone the last time that this would happen again if you did not see to the barbarian Persians."

"I know, Mother," Dee said placatingly as tea was placed into his hands. He blew on the steaming bowl and took a cautious sip, looked past his wives and mother to his deputies. "Will no one tell me anything? How many were involved?"

"There were five in the Ch'en household," the hunchback said after waiting deferentially for a moment to see if Dee's mother would speak first. "And we—"

"There were more than that, deputy," the old woman interrupted brusquely. "Tell the magistrate how many the Persian necromancers have killed. There was a visiting wedding party of six members of the Lao family. Two of Ch'ang-an's best and oldest families."

"Persians?" Dee asked sharply.

"There were no *Persians*," Dee's first wife said scornfully. "Your mother's imagination is riddled with Persians."

"Pah," the old woman spat. "What would you know of it, girl? You are too young and foolish to know how things have changed since the foreigners have come to live in Ch'ang-an."

"I know much more than you think," Dee's wife returned. But the old woman's attention had returned to Dee. She was no longer listening to Dee's wife.

"None of this would be happening if my son had listened to his old mother. I warn him every day of these barbarians and their witchcraft."

"Quiet . . . please!" Dee implored. "Gentlemen, I beg you. How many dead, and what of this mention of Persians?" Dee said, addressing his chief constable directly.

"All told, eleven people, including the Lao family, who were staying in the guest quarters."

"And the servants?" Dee asked. The hunchback shrugged and looked unhappy.

"The same as before. Nothing. They saw nothing, they heard nothing. They found the household slaughtered before dawn this morning."

Dee took this information stolidly.

"Is everything sealed off?" he asked sternly, on his feet now.

"It is being tended to, Magistrate, by the Investigating Tribunal of the Serpentine Ward. The assistant is a most competent man."

"Good. Very good. And the . . . the condition of these bodies?" Dee glanced quickly at his wives. They stood their ground. Apparently, they wanted to hear. Certainly, his mother did not budge from where she stood.

"Mutilated," the constable said reluctantly, embarrassed, as if speaking of some sexual aberration in front of the ladies. "In a bizarre and horrid manner. Beyond recognition. We have many details. . . . "

"Of course the poor people were mutilated in a bizarre and horrid manner," Dee's mother declared. "What do you expect, Dee Jen-chieh? The Goddess of Mercy, perhaps? When you summon forces from hell, this is what you get. Invoking evil! Hah! You see! I warned you, Dee Jen-chieh. You call me a silly old woman. But I told you about these Persians and their dark shamans!"

"Mother, I thank you for your invaluable help," Dee said politely. "Forgive me now, but I must get dressed."

The old woman huffed in indignation and stalked from the room. Dee's wives withdrew as well as the steward approached Dee with warm clothing and a bowl of hot water.

"Were there any witnesses at all?" Dee asked his men while he hurriedly splashed water on his face. "Tell me that there is something that we might use this time. How was the crime discovered?"

The hunchback chief furrowed his brow and rubbed his chin with his hands.

"The neighbors summoned the ward constables because the old household steward was found running hysterically through the streets speaking gibberish. That is how the massacre was discovered. Other than that . . . " he trailed off.

"Yes. Just like the last time," the second deputy offered, and the third nodded in agreement. "No one else heard or saw anything. Anyone who might have been a witness seems to have slept through it all."

"And did the screaming old steward reveal anything at all?" Dee persisted. "Something? Anything?"

"Well, he saw one thing . . . that is . . . " the hunchback chief began hesitantly. "That is, he says that he saw something before he leaped from the balcony. His fall was fortunately broken by the carp pond. It was not particularly deep there, but it was soft and muddy."

"What did he see?" Dee said impatiently, struggling into his clothing, which fought him at every turn. Was he going to have to drag the information out of his constable?

"He saw ... he saw a seven-taloned claw come through his wall, he said. The rest was gibberish."

Dee stared at the constable for a moment, then finished pulling his outer jacket on. He indicated the door.

"Shall we go, gentlemen?"

26

Loyang

The processional began at dawn four days after Historian Shu's private meeting with the twenty-five geomancers. Printed gazettes containing an elaborate announcement by the historian had been released in vast numbers the same day of the meeting. The ancient art of Feng Shui, the infallible science of geomancy that divined the most harmonious, propitious site for the placement of houses, buildings, and tombs, was to be put to the ultimate test. Fully twenty-five of the most distinguished practitioners of the art had been chosen from hundreds of eager volunteers all clamoring for the privilege, Historian Shu had been happy to announce, to locate the most consecrated spot in the universe.

The historian's gazette reiterated the progressive stages of the inexorable revelations of Wu's divinity: how the Great Cloud Sutra suggested that a great woman ruler would preside over the coming Age of the Future Buddha Maitreya, and how the Commentary of the Precious Rain, divinely inspired writings for which Lama Hsueh was the channel, emerged from the Great Cloud Sutra like a baby dragon from its egg— revealing that the divine female bodhisattva prophesied in the Sutra was among them here and now in the person of the Empress Wu.

The world knows, Shu said, that at the center of the holy

land of Jambudvipa is Wu-hsiang, the land of No-thought. At
the center of Wu-hsiang is our own precious City of Transformation. We are at the center of the center of the center. But we
must be even more precise than that. The geomancers' job will
be to designate the center of the center of the center of the
center. When we find that point, we will have found the center
of heaven. And there, at the very pivot of the universe, we will
begin construction of a megalith that will stand for all time.

No one knew where that point might be—it might be in
one of the city's great parks, it might be in the middle of a
river or in the middle of the offices of government, or even in
the midst of the poorest, most crowded part of the city, the
historian had said. But it *would* be found, with the concentrated
powers of the twenty-five working in concurrence. It would be
a great and memorable day in the history of the glorious Chou
Dynasty, a day that would be remembered forever, a day that
would commemorate the coming of the great bodhisattva herself. And just as a geomancer's right choice according to the
considerations of location, surroundings, water, and the eight
directions augured a propitious future for the dweller in a
house or a comfortable afterlife for the inhabitant of a tomb,
so would the Empire, and every person in it, benefit by the
concentrated efforts of the chosen twenty-five.

A crowd was waiting when the geomancers emerged
from the palace gates in the thin early-morning light. Geomancer Ling-shih, a man in his sixties who had practiced his art
for over forty-five years, looked neither to his left nor his right
at his fellows walking next to him. Each solemn-faced man
held his *luopan** like a talisman in front of him. They walked
in loose formation, their faces set, their eyes not seeking the
crowd. They were followed by a drummer beating out a leisurely, monotonous walking cadence, and a group of seven
praying monks, heads bowed, who chanted in a low, languid
drone. They did not hesitate when they left the gate, but proceeded directly toward the west, causing people to murmur to
one another that the pull of the dragon veins must be strong
indeed, for they did not even pause before proceeding.

Down the broad main boulevard they went, the crowd
following, the drum marking time, and the monks praying.
Behind them the rays of the rising sun fanned out from be-

---

*Geomancer's compass.

tween the buildings, casting long golden shafts of light. They had gone about one hundred paces in that direction when a voice from their ranks cried out, "The water pulls now!" The processional veered to the right down a small diagonal side street so that they now walked northwest, the sun warming their right shoulders. "The pull of the water grows stronger," the voice called, and they veered again so that they walked directly north, the sun on the sides of their faces, the drummer speeding up his rhythm just a bit, the monks scarcely looking up from their prayers or opening their eyes, the geomancers maintaining their stoic faces and still avoiding all eye contact with the surging crowd on their flanks and with each other.

Ling-shih did not have to look at the faces of his colleagues to know the shame that he would see there, for he wore the identical shame like a wet heavy coat across his shoulders. Today, all twenty-five of them would bring dishonor to themselves, their long careers, and their profession— but there was not a one among them who had had the courage not to appear this morning. Eyes straight ahead, they moved in the direction that the shouting voice told them to move, as if the motion preceded the voice, and not the reverse.

We are the twenty-five honored enough to be chosen from the "eagerly clamoring" hundreds, he thought bitterly. In truth, it had been an "invitation" to a meeting with Historian Shu Ching-tsung from President Lai Chun-chen and Vice President Chou Hsing of the Censorate Board of Punishments and Investigations—delivered directly into his hands one chilly, windy morning at dawn by two Imperial guardsmen—that had brought him reluctantly forth from his home. Within an hour, he and the others—a silent, grim, bleary-eyed, incredulous group—sat in a room, Imperial guards at every door and around the perimeter, awaiting their "meeting" with the historian.

Geomancer Ling-shih, out in the street now at dawn four days later, could hear the crowd around him speculating loudly. They had turned away from the direction that would have carried them eventually into the poorer part of the city; if they kept going north as they were now, they would find themselves wading into the great canal. Was that the water that pulled them? Everyone knew that blessings proceeded from the north, but a flowing body of water cutting across from east to west might compromise the benefits, some said, while others declared that just the opposite was true; the proximity of any water was always a blessing.

But soon their speculation was moot, because the voice from within the ranks of the geomancers called out again. "Water turns to wood!" it cried, and the cortege made an abrupt right-hand turn down the next street so that they marched due east, directly into the rays of the rising sun, their eyes squinting and the light flashing from their *luopans* with their bobbing, whirling lodestone-needles. "The dragon advances!" the voice said now, and people in the crowd looked ahead and saw that indeed the hilly horizon to the west, glimpsed now and again between the buildings, closely resembled the humped, sinuous back of a dragon. Now real excitement began to spread, while the drummer increased his tempo and the monks' praying voices rose. The sun climbed higher in the sky, warm and glorious, and the crowd pressed forward around the processional with the growing urgency of the hunter closing in on its quarry.

Inside his house within its locked gates old Prince Li I-yen, eighty-four this spring and cousin to the late Emperor Kaotsung's father, Taitsung, lay in his morning bed and began the ritual he performed every morning. Cautiously, he raised his right leg and flexed it at the knee, wincing at the pain and stiffness. He held it in that position for a few moments, lowered the leg, and repeated the process with his left leg. The left leg was stiffer than the right this morning. He could barely tolerate the pain. He held the leg in its flexed position, eyes squeezed shut, counting, thinking of ancient rusty hinges left out in the rain, groaning and grating in protest when forced by a callous hand. Finally he let the leg down, lay for a moment, and lifted the right leg. Like the old rusty hinge, his ancient joints would prefer, given a choice, to be left alone, to fuse peacefully into uselessness. But he did not give them a choice. He forced himself through his ritual of pain each day when he awoke. It was the only way he could get out of bed in the morning.

He was lowering his right leg, much loosened now, and was about to force the recalcitrant left into action when something made him pause and listen. He lay still. It had been little more than a vibrational disturbance of the air, a small window of incongruous sound that had opened for just a moment, jostling his concentration. All he could hear now was the familiar noises of an awakening household: a barrow being wheeled across the courtyard, the creak of footsteps in the hall. He glanced down to where his little dog, old as himself in dog-years, looked back at him with filmy black eyes, begging permission to come up. Prince Li bent stiffly and picked his friend up under the rib cage. The jump to the bed was too much now. And to think that he himself had already been a grizzled old man when the dog was a puppy.

He was preparing to raise himself up, for he knew hot tea was imminent, when the animal stiffened, eyes and ears alert. The small head turned sharply to the west, the pointed ears raised and quivering.

"What is it, Thief?" the prince asked, scratching the dog's muzzle.

Thief did his best to turn his loyal attention back to his master, lowering his ears and wagging his tail for a few seconds, but then he stiffened again, and emitted an anxious little whine that flattened into a growl.

The crowd was giddy with excitement. Most of the people following the processional had never in their lives ventured into this part of the city, where vast rolling estates were cloistered in serenity behind tall gates. Now here they were, boldly marching down the quiet streets, their presence sanctioned by the Empress herself, on a divine mission that could not be stopped!

The monks' praying had grown to a dirge, the drum was beating a brisk meter, and the geomancers strode forward unerringly. "The dragon stirs!" the voice from within their ranks called out. People craned their necks, looking to see if they could discern in the profile of the gentle hillocks where these estates resided something resembling the neck, the ear, or the head of the dragon, that most potent of creatures in the geomancer's menagerie. The angle of approach that caused the landscape to suggest most vividly the contours of the dragon was what they were seeking now, though the followers could not see much more than trees and walls and an occasional sweeping, elegant roofline beyond one another's pushing, jostling bodies. But the geomancers, they knew, were far more sensitive and observant than they.

"The dragon retreats!" the voice called out, causing the

processional to correct its trajectory, veering now, heading down a left-hand fork in the street. Past tall gates they went, the nervous faces of servants visible through cracked portals and sliding hatches that snapped shut as the marchers went by.

"The heartbeat of the dragon deafens us!" the voice cried out, urgent now, as they stood in front of what must have been the tallest, finest set of gates in the entire city. The drummer kept his tempo; though it was no faster than it had been, the rhythmic pounding was loud and forceful, purposeful and irresistible, the sound of impending fate itself. But still they moved forward, pausing at the next gate. Did the pounding of the drum soften just a bit? people asked one another. "The heartbeat of the dragon grows fainter!" the voice declared. The parade moved on until they reached the farthest gate on the street. The drumming slowed and softened. "It grows fainter still! The dragon retreats! Stand back and out of the way! We must breathe!"

The crowd obeyed, pulling back. The geomancers and monks reversed their direction, the drum beating ever more loudly now as they moved back the way they had come. Geomancer Ling-shih felt his heart constricting with dread. They were back in front of the tall, fine gate where the drum had beat its loudest and most insistent cadence. They had found it: here was the center of the center of the center of the center, the pivot of heaven itself.

The gate opened then, and a little dog darted out. A haggard and very elderly man emerged as well, still in his nightclothes, his hair and beard as yet uncombed, his face affronted and agitated.

"Thief!" the old man called out to the dog, then bent and scooped the animal up and held him, barking frantically, against his chest. A monk signaled, and the drumming abruptly ceased.

"What is your name?" the monk asked the old man.

"I am Prince Li I-yen," the old man answered in a quavering voice. "State your business!" he demanded then.

"A great honor is being conferred upon your house today, Prince Li," the monk said. "For it has been found to lie at the divine holy center of the universe. By decree of the Divine Empress Wu, the bodhisattva Kuan-yin incarnate, this shall be the site of the greatest structure ever built by human hands,

which will mark that divine axis for all time. In her infinite
wisdom and mercy, she will allow you a full ten days to remove yourself and your possessions from the premises."

The little dog, making a sudden leap, took the flabbergasted old prince by surprise as he stood in outraged, blinking,
speechless consternation. The dog sprang to the ground and
hurled himself against the monk, sinking his teeth into the
bare, spindly leg so that the monk let out a howl. And no
matter how hard the monk kicked and flailed his leg, Thief
hung on grimly, all four feet lifted off the ground, his body
flapping like a regimental banner being carried into battle.

In less that two weeks' time, no one would have known
that a house had ever stood on the site. Two hundred workers
had swarmed onto the structure like beetles onto a carcass. The
public had been invited to watch, of course, and it was to them
that the pieces of the house went—with so many thousands of
eager hands carrying away bricks, stones, roof tiles, carved ornamental doors, beams, slats, railings, floorboards, and window shutters, as well as furniture, statuary, carpets, clothing,
antiques, dishes, kitchen utensils, and even plants and shrubbery from the garden, it did not take long for every vestige of
Prince Li's household to vanish neatly, thoroughly, and forever.

There was a festival atmosphere to the proceedings, with
people making daylong excursions to the site, bringing food
and often a sturdy wagon or barrow for carrying away a prize.
They watched the work with great interest as the site was
cleared and excavated. And what of the old prince? some asked
one another. Word had it that he had retired; he had been
happy to move to a warmer climate. His bones had been aching a lot in the last few years, they had heard.

It was exciting, too, because various officials representing
the Empress herself often visited the scene. Up on a high platform, removed from the crowd of onlookers below and beyond
their earshot, long important-looking conversations took place
between the official and the head architects and engineers in
charge of the project. Maps and plans were unrolled and discussed at length. People watched, rapt, knowing that they were
witnessing a moment in history.

On this particular day, there was more excitement than
usual, because it was rumored that the official in the brightly
colored robe who had appeared this morning was none other

than Historian Shu Ching-tsung himself. He had smiled and
waved to the people below lining the edges of the site, and
some of them had waved back. Workers were digging busily,
making a deep, deep hole. Long trudging lines of men with
barrows carried dirt and rocks out of the excavation. Up on
the platform, the usual lengthy conversations were taking
place.

Heads were upturned, watching, as if the sight of important people talking were some rare form of theater—which it
was, of course—when there was a shout from the pit below.
The head engineer, who had been up on the platform conferring, excused himself and was soon scrambling down the rocky
embankment. People pressed forward, trying to see. There
were more shouts. Something had been uncovered. What was
it? people asked eagerly. A stone. A slab. A carved stone, as
long as a man is tall. But not just a stone.

A stone with writing on it.

People grew nearly delirious with excitement at what
happened next. Historian Shu descended from the platform,
and hiking up his brilliantly colored robes, picked his way
carefully down into the rocky hole. Workers cleared the last of
the dirt off the stone with their hands, and the historian knelt,
examining it, for many long, suspenseful minutes. Then he
stood, and gave an order to the engineer standing next to him.
The man scrambled urgently up out of the pit, shouting as he
did.

Translators, he said to his aides waiting above. Dispatch
a messenger to the palace that translators are to come here at
once. Historian Shu has declared that the writing is not Chinese. Not Chinese? people asked.

No, not Chinese. It is Sanskrit.

"And what will you do if they accept?" Madame Yang
asked her daughter as Wu stood with her arms upraised while
the Imperial seamstresses measured and snipped. "What will
you do if they arrive, expecting to be fed and entertained?"

"Then I will feed and entertain them. Though you know
perfectly well that they will not," Wu replied. "But read it to
me again." Her mother sat at the small writing-table and flattened the sheet of parchment.

" 'Her Divine Highness the Empress Wu Tse-tien extends
a gracious invitation to your household, an invitation she

fondly hopes you will accept. It is her wish that you attend a ceremony, the likes of which will not occur again for another hundred years, to mark the beginning of the new and glorious Reign Title . . . ' "

Madame Yang paused here. "Have you decided what the Reign Title will be?" she asked her daughter.

"Oh, what does it matter?" Wu replied, lowering her arms, while the seamstresses carefully rolled and pinned the brilliant piece of blue embroidered silk. "Call it the Reign of the Precious Dragon Droppings, if you wish." Her mother smiled. "Or the Reign of the Shriveled Old Scrotum."

"No, my dear," her mother laughed. "It is the Reign of the Shriveled Old Scrotum that is *ending*. You seem to forget. We need something entirely new."

"Let Historian Shu come up with the name," Wu said with a wave of her hand. "That is his job, is it not? It is immaterial to me. Keep reading."

" 'The Empress wishes for you and your family to spend a glorious day in celebration and feasting—' "

Wu interrupted her mother. "Celebration and feasting. That is very good. Perhaps we should put more emphasis on the feasting. Perhaps we could say something about the Imperial chefs wishing to prepare a special meal, just for them, the likes of which the world has never seen. That sort of rubbish. Historian Shu puts such things so well."

Her mother made a small mark on the page with a dainty little brush she had in readiness, and continued reading.

" ' . . . as the Empire and the world enter an era of unprecedented heavenly indulgence and grace. Such a celebration will not be possible, plausible, desirable, or indeed complete without your esteemed presence, where the old and the new shall converge in peace and harmony beneath one sky, to feast together, to toast the future, to make peace.' "

"Oh, that is very good—'not possible without your presence,' 'to make peace,' " Wu said approvingly, her voice temporarily muffled as the unfinished garment was drawn up over her head and arms. "Also 'beneath one sky.' Excellent. That, and the emphasis on the food, should certainly do very nicely." She stood in her dressing gown, her hair mussed, and looked at her mother. "What would *you* think if you were the recipient of such an invitation? Would it inspire confidence? Would you send a messenger scampering back immediately with an enthusiastic and grateful letter of acceptance? Or might you just possibly ... demur? Might you be perhaps just a bit ... *hesitant?*"

Her mother considered for a moment.

"Do I look like a fool?"

Prince Li Cheng-i, seventy-six years old and cousin to Prince Li I-yen, held in his spotted, trembling hands the missive that had arrived that morning. He put it down and looked at it with loathing, as he would at a letter he knew would tell him the precise hour and place of his death.

His poor cousin Prince Li I-yen had vanished, along with his house and beautiful gardens, as if he had never existed at all, as if his eighty-four years had been merely a brief dream, his life a flimsy apparition. Where his fine house had stood there was now rising, like a gigantic ugly lance mortally impaling the earth, an iron-and-silver pillar, the tip of which would disappear into the clouds when it was completed. Prince Li Cheng-i had heard only one rumor about the displaced old prince, but he knew it instantly to be true: his elder cousin, it was said, would never have to worry about the cold creeping into his aching joints again, would never watch his brittle fingers turning blue as the chill of winter stole the diminishing warming *ch'i* from his limbs.

No, he would never have to worry about the cold again. Instead, the stinging sweat would roll down from his scalp onto his face while clouds of biting insects sucked his blood. Green and black fungi would grow in his slippers overnight, and he would learn to shake out his robes morning and evening lest he surprise some hairy, venomous, spiky-legged creature that had taken up residence in the sleeves or hem. And he would learn to converse with the chattering monkeys and their brothers the grinning savages if he did not wish to suffer the jungle in total isolation. And when the fever had him, which it inevitably would, he would lie on a mat and toss and sweat, unable to recall whether he had lived anywhere but there, on the green and fevered island of Hainan, three thousand *li* to the south, the Empress's favorite retirement ground for inconvenient old men.

That is, of course, if he survived the journey there. An interminable jolting ride in a crude wooden cart—or worse, on foot.

It would be a miracle if the old man survived the journey, another miracle if he survived more than a month on the island. Prince Li Cheng-i thought bitterly of the word: "miracle" had taken on a bad flavor of late, like tainted meat. These days, whenever the word "miracle" was heard, some sort of suffering was sure to follow. The repugnant antics of the monk Hsueh Huai-i were quite sufficiently atrocious, but they were put to shame by the Miracle of the Talking Stone. And of course, it was real. Scores of people had witnessed the discovery of the slab, at the center of the universe, in the earth beneath where the house of the one of the last T'ang princes had stood, and had seen the expert translators, three old holy menscholars, scramble down into the hole, there to confer in hushed voices full of reverence. And of course, everyone had been listening when a shout rose from the pit. An extraordinary divine relic had been found, a stone buried for at least a thousand years. There were words carved in the stone—words that miraculously reiterated, almost character for character, the prophecy of Hsueh-Huai-i's Commentary of the Precious Rain. Heaven itself, it seemed, had revealed the Empress's mandate to rule.

If humiliation and degradation followed small, everyday miracles, then what catastrophe would follow one such as this?

The letter that lay on Prince Li Cheng-i's table before him, and that caused his old hands to tremble when he so much as touched the fine parchment, bore the Imperial seal. It was from the Empress herself.

Sitting in the pool of soft light cast by the lamp over the desk in his bedchamber, Prince Li Cheng-i dipped his brush and regarded the blank parchment before him. His hand shook so badly that he doubted that he would be able to write. That afternoon, the day after the letter from the Empress had arrived, he had received a letter from Prince Li Chu-tao, his distant cousin. Reading it, he had detected a certain tremor in the brushstrokes, a distinct unease and unsteadiness that could not be solely attributed to the man's age, which was eighty-two. It had been a simple message, an inquiry, but it had started his own shaky hand dancing as if strings were attached to it, being jerked by an invisible and malign puppeteer.

"My cousin," the letter had read, "I have received a most unusual invitation. My curiosity has been aroused, and I wish to know if you, too, have received a similarly unusual invitation. I also wish to know if any other members of our scattered and diminished clan have been so honored."

What he was going to write in his reply, but which seemed a virtually impossible task at this moment because of his hand, was that it was indeed a fact that others in the family had received the invitation. His own brother, for one, who had also contacted him immediately, asking him if he thought it wise to attend such a celebration. And his brother had told him that he, too, had received a letter from yet another cousin expressing his own doubts.

Late the next afternoon, he found himself listening expectantly for a sign that a messenger had arrived at his house. He had written his letter and dispatched it at dawn. The letter told his cousin that he knew who else had received an invitation, and had ended with questions: Was there a way to gracefully decline? Or did they, indeed, have any choice but to attend?

For the rest of the day, he paced, he stopped and listened, he tried vainly to distract himself, but no messenger came, either that afternoon or evening. Resigning himself to having to wait until the next morning, he went to bed.

By midmorning the next day, his patience ran out, and he seized his brush and wrote another letter, begging a reply to the first. His hand shook, but two cups of wine steadied it. After he had dispatched the second letter, he decided that he needed more wine. It was not only his hands that shook now, but his entire body.

Late that afternoon, he was startled out of a doze by the sound of knuckles rapping softly on his study door. He raised his head up off the writing desk and looked around for a few startled moments, trying to remember where he was, and who he was.

"Of course, of course, of course," he whispered, hastily rising and adjusting his clothing. He bent to pick up his cap, which was lying on the floor, as the knock came again.

It was his cousin, Prince Li Chu-tao, with a face so worried and agitated that Prince Li Cheng-i might have been looking into a mirror.

"I could not wait any longer," Prince Li Chu-tao said in his weak, elderly voice when the door was shut behind him. "When I did not receive a reply to my letter, I became uneasy. And when you did not respond to my second one . . ." He did not finish, but looked at his cousin, his face a sagging mask of fatigue and apprehension. Prince Li Cheng-i wondered for a moment at the fact that old men such as themselves, with only a few years left to them under the best of circumstances, should feel the fear of death as acutely as any youth with fifty years ahead of him.

"But . . . but I did reply," he said to Prince Li Chu-tao. "Immediately. And I have been quite ill with misgivings for the very same reason that you describe."

They looked at each other, their disquietude of the past two days shrinking into insignificance as a new one, darker and infinitely more disturbing, moved into its place. They stood there, ancient creaky limbs trembling and syncopated old hearts pounding with the vain directive to flee, to run, to fly.

The Empress and the monk Hsueh Huai-i lay naked, a breeze from the open balcony doors drying the sweat from their bodies. She felt beyond words, beyond talking. Her mind and heart were open, just like the doors to her garden, and she could feel infinity moving through her like the breeze wafting through the room.

When the monk began to talk, she did not open her eyes, but let his voice move on the current that traveled in and around her.

He was chuckling softly, incredulously.

"I would not have believed it possible," he said, "unless I had experienced it myself." And he laughed again. "Where did you come from?" he asked her in a reverent whisper, running his finger from her forehead down her face and neck. She lay still, not answering, as if she were in a faraway trance. "You cannot hide it from me. I know who you are," he said then. She felt a little smile pulling at the corners of her mouth, but she fought it and kept her face impassive. "And so does your mother. And," he said, dropping his voice even lower, "I think that you know, too."

His finger moved down her body; in her mind, she saw

a little trail of light marking the finger's path. That was the way it was whenever he touched her. She was suffused with light and heat. The more of his flesh touching hers, the more light, the more heat. Yes, he was right. She did know who she was.

"And I think," he added, "that there are some others who know who you are." His finger lifted off her body, and she was aware of him leaning to one side. She could hear the rustle of papers, then she felt his weight settling back down next to her. "I have a gift for you," he said.

She lay still, waiting. And when he began to read, in the cracked voice of an old, old man, she had to fight harder to keep the smile from her lips.

" 'My cousin,' " he read. " 'We are not alone. There are indeed others of us who have been so "honored." My brother Prince Li Cheng-yu has written to me asking the same question and informing me that Cousin Li P'ie had conveyed the identical query to him. I believe that it is of urgent importance that we meet, as many of us as possible, in one place at one time. And I defer to your greater experience in such matters: does protocol provide us with a means by which we might decline, or are we left with no choice?' "

The monk spoke the last sentence with a voice of such convincingly quavering senescence that Wu could have sworn that if she were to open her eyes at that moment, she would find not the long muscular body in its prime that she had seen suspended over hers only a few moments ago, but a gray and sagging grandfather with sunken chest and shriveled flanks.

" 'My cousin,' " the monk continued, in a different voice, still that of an old man, but lower and not quite so thin as the other, as if the second old man were possibly a few years younger than the first, " 'perhaps I did not properly convey the urgency which grows upon me, and which compels me to beg you for an expeditious reply. I do not feel that we can afford to be profligate with time under these grave conditions.' "

Then it was the first old man speaking again, the voice strained with worry and fatigue: " 'I can only trust that my first letter found you in your usual excellent health, and that your lack of response is not due to any infirmity or misfortune that I have been unlucky enough to intrude on. I cannot stress to you enough the importance of immediate discourse in this matter.' " Wu swore that if she were to open her eyes now, there would be two old men sitting on the bed, not just one, their brows knitted with apprehension.

Then a third voice, slow and measured, full of ponderous dignity: " 'I wish to declare here and now that I most firmly and positively decline offers or invitations of any sort from within the gates of the Palace City. I stand obdurate and immovable in my position, and I urge others of our clan to remember who we are and to maintain a staunch and unambiguous mutuality, without which I believe that neither the Li clan nor the Empire itself has the smallest hope of survival.' "

She heard the rustle of papers being rolled, felt him leaning as he put them on the floor or the table. She waited, full of pleasant anticipation, for his finger to touch her body again and continue its journey.

Heavy footsteps reverberated in the hallway leading to his wing. Prince Li Cheng-i understood that this was the last day of his long life. It had come, as all anticipated days finally do, carried to him on the steady river of passing time. Now that the day was here, all of the queasy terror, the heavy dread, had dropped away, leaving him encapsulated in calm, in a place where nothing could touch him. He carefully adjusted his cap. Nature provides, he whispered, repeating the words his father had once spoken to him, and let his arms sink slowly down from his head. He straightened the front of his robe and turned toward the door. He was ready. He only hoped the others were, too.

Many of the people had witnessed executions before. But somehow, none of the people watching today had expected to see what was before them now. No one had ever articulated it exactly, or indeed even brought the idea to the level of conscious thought: execution was properly a younger man's death, a death for those in their prime or middle years.

But some of the men kneeling on the ground on this damp morning had needed help to bend their knees, and then had had to be lowered down to the paving stones by the guards. What was normally done with a shove and a kick was done almost decorously. Some deeply buried sense of propriety was emerging, causing the guards to handle the old men with something resembling deference. Their brawny arms hung at their sides, and their closed, cruel faces wore expressions of unease. Perhaps they were thinking of their own grandfathers.

The people watching were almost contemplative: eleven old men, some of them in their ninth decade, who had lived for so many long, long years, who had successfully navigated the countless dangers of living, were about to come abruptly to the end of those years. An official stepped forward to read the charges.

"Decrepit and superannuated princes of the fallen House of Li," he read, addressing the old men. "Today is the day that you pay for your transgressions, which are grievous and which offend the sensibilities of the Empire and heaven itself. For the crime of conspiracy with intent to foment treachery and rebellion, the proof of which you yourselves abundantly provided with your exchange of foul missives, the all-merciful and all-seeing bodhisattva incarnate purges you, the enemies of the Dharma itself, from her realm."

One of the old men half rose on his feeble legs and spat in the direction of the official's feet. The crowd braced itself for the swift retaliation by the guards that usually followed such a display. But there was none. The official, temporarily nonplussed, continued.

"As the house of the old prince had to fall in order that the stone that lay under the earth could come to light bearing its great and mysterious truths," the official intoned, "so must the House of Li and the Dynasty of the T'ang fall to make way for the House of Wu and the Dynasty of Chou." He looked at the old men on their knees. "And so you must fall," he finished. He turned and hurried away, robes flapping, as if he had an urgent appointment elsewhere and was already late. The crowd pressed forward as the executioner raised his gleaming sword over the first white head.

The Empress, Madame Yang, and Historian Shu walked in the Empress's private garden on a beautiful day of warm sunshine and sweet breezes. Ahead of them, its little hoofs ticking smartly against the flagstones and its small rump moving with purpose and importance, trotted a small gray pig. They were all smiling at the amusing sight, for the pig not only seemed to know exactly where it was going, but it was dressed in a little robe and cap, perfect miniatures of the vestments of a high Confucian official.

The pig hurried on along the path until they were in the

uncultivated woods of the park that bordered the garden, the vegetation growing thicker and wilder.

"Where are we going?" the Empress asked as they moved along at a brisk pace, twigs snapping under their feet, keeping up with the pig. There was no path here at all, but the pig did not seem to notice.

"Do not ask me," Shu replied, smiling mysteriously at her. "Ask him," he said. When at last the historian pulled a low branch out of the way so that the Empress could pass and they stepped into a clearing, she inhaled sharply with delight.

It was a little meditational rockery, an exquisite grotto of tranquillity and retreat completely surrounded by trees. Child-sized stone Buddhas of ancient and exotic origin sat in timeless repose, moss creeping along the legs and arms as if they had been in these woods through the centuries. A diminutive stone temple, with just enough room for a person to kneel in prayer before an altar, stood atop three marble steps. They stood in silence, hearing only the song of birds and the timeless mantra of water purling over rocks. The Empress gazed about her, her eyes glistening.

"Do not thank us," the historian said quickly. "Thank him." He indicated the pig, whose snout was rooting in a determined way at a spot of ground near the little temple. The Empress looked at the two again; they both smiled, and she put her head back and laughed with pleasure.

The pig was turning something up out of the soil. When the object was out of the ground, the pig nosed it around, snorting and grunting. It was a little ornate box. The pig worried the box this way and that until it fell open; inside was a flat rock about the size of a man's hand. The pig sniffed it and pushed it along the ground. The historian knelt and examined it for a moment.

"There seems to be writing on it," he said to his companions with a serious air, and extended the rock toward the pig, which responded by delicately taking the rock in its teeth and trotting up the steps into the temple. "I think he wants to read it to us," Shu said to the Empress as he straightened up. "It may be something important." The pig vanished inside the little building.

Then a voice seemed to issue from within the temple walls, high and oddly inflected, singsong and formal, with a strange little lisp. It was a voice one might imagine issuing from the throat of a pig speaking human words.

"The rich black earth reveals the intent of the airy blue heavens," said the voice. The Empress's eyes glittered with anticipation. "So perfectly do heaven and earth concur that the very rocks push their way to the surface, seeking the light of day. The truth presses in on us, rains down upon us, rises from the ground like flowers in the spring. The golden age is upon us now, for in our midst is a divine creature, the bodhisattva who embodies the male and female aspects of creation, Avalokitesvara and Kuan-yin inhabiting the same form, a female creature of surpassing and excellent beauty with the powerful male entity dwelling within. The Holy Spirit Divine Sovereign is among us."

With that, the pig put its face through the doorway of the temple and trotted down the stairs, where it stood looking at the Empress, the historian, and Madame Yang, flicking its tail comically, clearly expecting some sort of reward. The Empress crept stealthily around to the rear of the temple, planning to take the monk by surprise—but in the few moments since the pig had finished its "pronouncement," he had already vanished. She raised her eyes sharply to the low boughs of the trees bordering the clearing a few paces from the rear wall of the building. Though she saw no motion, no disappearing hem of a robe, and heard not so much as the rustle of vegetation or the snap of a twig, she was sure she detected a vibration of the leaves along the branches, a barely perceptible quiver, as if they had just snapped back into place in the moment before she looked at them.

She stood, the sun on her back, suffused with joy, in a magic world of talking pigs and mystic rocks inscribed with her own name by the hand of nature. Though she could not see him, the monk was everywhere—in the living air, in the sound of water splashing on the rocks, in the carved stone faces of the Buddhas serenely contemplating eternity with their hands upraised in the *mudra* of peace and compassion, in the graceful curve of the miniature temple's roof, in the fat white clouds sailing in the sky, in the fierce hunger possessing her limbs and innards.

"A most excellent pig," she called out to the still woods. "I think that I will marry him!"

Abbot Liao of the Pure Lotus Monastery stood facing south, the direction of the city. His expression was pained; Wu-chi thought that he looked like an entirely different person from the man he had met years before, whose face, it had seemed then, was wholly unfamiliar with the configurations of anger, despair, or even mild unhappiness. The new aspect sat like a disfiguring mask upon his features, turning him almost into a stranger. But when he sighed, and spoke, his voice restored him somewhat to being the man that Wu-chi knew, though his words were those of a stranger.

"I swear that I can smell blood," he said to Wu-chi. "It carries on the wind from the city. Can't you smell it?" They stood on a knoll near the edge of the monastery grounds; they had been taking their customary evening walk when the abbot had stopped and put a hand on Wu-chi's arm.

"And I am not just speaking figuratively," the abbot said. "I mean that I can truly smell it. *I know* the smell. From when I was a boy. My father worked as a slaughterer of animals." He tested the breeze in a way that Wu-chi had seen dogs and horses do: head tipped back, nostrils lifted and flared, concentrating intently. It was a peculiarly unnerving sight for Wu-chi; he turned his eyes away and gazed out at the hills.

"It is a sharp smell, almost like the smell of the sea, but saltier," the abbot said. "Metallic. Pungent. It is . . . " he trailed off. "It cannot be described. You must experience it."

Tentatively, furtively, Wu-chi smelled the air, but all he could detect was a trace of smoke from a farmer's field nearby, cow dung, and cut grass.

"I confess that I cannot," Wu-chi said. "Though I know I should be able to."

Indeed, he was surprised that blood was not lapping at their feet where they stood. Every day brought more news of spurious trials, purges, executions, and families being marched toward the steaming jungles of the south, never to be seen again. When he thought of the Empress now, he thought of a fat leech, or a tick, engorged with blood, torpid and slit-eyed. When, he wondered, would she be sated? And there had been a ceremony in the city today. A coronation. The two men had received that news after the evening meal. Neither had been able to speak of it, so stunned were they. But it was the abbot who broke the tacit silence.

"She is nothing if not resourceful. She has overcome the final barrier." He shook his head. "The very last one, the seemingly insurmountable one. The only one that held her back from absolute dominion—the fact that she was a woman. Now that it has been announced to the world that she is a male

entity occupying a female instrument, Avalokitesvara and
Kuan-yin in one body, that little impediment has been vanquished. She is no longer a mere Empress. She is something
else altogether." He paused and shuddered, as if he had just
caught a fresh whiff of the sanguinary wind. "She may have
named herself Holy Spirit Divine Sovereign today, but that is
merely another name for what she really is."

They looked at each other. Abbot Liao could not bring
himself to speak the words aloud. Indeed, he whispered
them:

"She is the *Emperor* of China."

There was something else the two men who stood smelling the wind from the city were reluctant to speak about. It
was a piece of news which arrived with the announcement of
the coronation. The Empress, after the ceremony, had issued a
decree. In keeping with the doctrine of compassion and mercy,
she had banned the slaughter of pigs throughout the Empire.

27

A.D. 675, autumn
Ch'ang-an

 JOURNAL ENTRY

Today, I searched out friends and acquaintances of a dead
man, the patriarch of yet a third murdered family. I had
been called to the home at dawn, and gazed upon the man's
corpse and those of his family. And though I looked at them
all—wife, sons, old father and mother, young daughter—
for a long, long time, I do not know what their faces looked
like, because their heads had been removed and replaced
with the heads of pigs. The limbs and clothing had been
arranged with care, and the corpses propped in sitting
positions on the furniture in a ghastly caricature of a family
gathering. The father, the head of the household, sat with
his robes slit open in the front so that his large belly was
displayed, resting on the table before him, painted with a

profusion of red spots. I was glad that the man's head was missing, so that his eyes, even though lifeless, were spared having to gaze upon that scene. I noted the facts down, feeling obscurely once again as I did so that the forces of Chaos were cackling softly over my shoulder, thoroughly enjoying the joke.

After the first murder, the thought had crept into my mind and stayed like an unwelcome visitor that only a second murder might provide me with something useful. Something would emerge—some fact, some clue, some pattern, some error on the part of the perpetrators. When I got my "wish," and was dragged from my bed to preside over murder number two, what did I find? Another slaughtered family, of course. But this time, instead of having their mouths slit into hellish grins, they were all stark naked, with their heads shaved quite perfectly bald and their noses removed. Again, no witnesses, nothing tangible left behind, such as a weapon or an item of clothing. And apparently, nothing taken.

And my "wish" has been granted in abundance. Now I have a third murder. There are common patterns, to be sure, but I seem to know less than when the nightmare began. All of these families were wealthy, and lived in the same suburb of the city. In each case, the entire household was put to death. There have been no signs of forced entry, and selected rooms in the houses have been devastated. And in each case, a multitude of naked footprints. And of course, the hoofprints. I am beginning to think of them as the hoofprints from hell.

When the hoofprints of a horse emerged from the mess, I was astounded, but after careful consideration I decided that the hallway where the prints were found was large enough after all to accommodate a horse, though just barely, as were the doorways at either end. Very well, I thought; someone rode a horse through the house. After everything else I had seen, why not this? I checked the hooves of the family's carriage horses, and found them to be without traces of blood and also much too large to have made the prints in the house. So, I concluded, the horse that made the prints was brought by the killers.

In the second murder, there was not quite as much blood as in the first, but there were the usual naked human footprints here and there. At first, I did not see any hoofprints, but then I found them—not in the room where the corpses were found, but in the dining room, crossing it widthwise, from one garden to another. Here, I noted that there was indeed abundant room for a horse to enter through the large double doors on either side. I went outside, looking to see if there might be soft earth carrying impressions, but discovered paved paths of stone leading up to both the doors. I found a puddle of blood outside one of the doors—and the hoofprints beginning at the puddle and leading into the house. The puddle was a lone one, with no drips or spatters leading up to it, forcing me to the odious conclusion that the blood had been deliberately poured there and the horse led or ridden through it and then into the house. Whoever did it *wanted* those prints to be seen, and went to some trouble to make sure that they would be. When I went back into the room, I realized that this could not have been an ordinary horse: the room was densely furnished with many tables and shelves laden with delicate knicknacks—statuary, vases, carvings, and the like—yet the animal had negotiated these obstacles without breaking or disturbing anything. The horse, I could only conclude, had to be a very well-trained one, possibly a performing horse of the sort seen in traveling menageries.

In the third murder, there was blood aplenty, and no evidence that it had been necessary for it to be premeditatively poured before the horse walked through it. The prints were everywhere, winding in and out of the others. And this time, it was apparent that the horse had not confined itself to a single room: the prints led from the first room to virtually every room in that wing of the house—again, leaving those rooms undisturbed—and doubling back to the murder room after each foray in order to walk through the blood again, in order, I am forced to conclude, to ensure visible prints.

I have, of course, looked into the spiritual affiliations of these families, but I have found nothing of obvious significance. In one, the elderly grandmother had a small Buddhist shrine in her bedchamber, while the rest of her family were Confucian. In the other two families, various members dabbled in Taoism or Buddhism while others appeared to have no affiliations at all. This does not offer me a great deal.

The city is in an ever more furious frenzy of speculation. I have observed a new and rare animation permeating people's activities and conversation. When they talk about the crimes, their eyes shine, their voices rise, and their hands shape the air around them in their enthusiasm. There can be no mistake. They are enjoying the spectacle. And since the vast majority of them are unlikely victims, they eagerly await the next one. The exceptions to this, of course, are the wealthy people living in certain sections of the city. For them, it is a slightly less abstract concept, and they are frightened, angry, and more than a little impatient for the killers to be apprehended. But I sincerely believe that most people would be disappointed if we were to announce tomorrow that the mystery is solved.

Of course, they have never lived in such times nor had so much to talk about. Neither have I, for that matter. With the news that the Empress has found a way around the last obstacle standing in her path, and that we may at last speak of her and think of her as our "Emperor," we know that we are not living in ordinary times—nor, it appears, in an ordinary place. It is the Empress's monstrous pillars that have demonstrated this last to me, and that provided me with a chance to prove to myself that my powers of deduction have not grown completely flaccid and useless: the pillar being raised here in Ch'ang-an will not be standing alone. I heard, of course, of the one just like it being erected on the site of poor old Prince Li I-yen's demolished home in Loyang. And when I heard of yet a third being built in the far eastern city of Pienchou, I consulted a map of the Empire, and saw that the three cities—Ch'ang-an, Loyang, and Pienchou—form an east-west axis. I studied the map carefully, and chose two more cities—one north of Loyang and one south—as probable sites of additional pillars. Inquiries by messenger proved that I was quite correct. Although construction has yet to begin in those places, orders have already been received by city officials to begin to assemble the men and materials. The purpose of the pillars was so obvious that it nearly escaped me. There is repeated mention in scriptural writings of the Buddhist realm of Jambudvipa, with four corners and a center. The Empress—or should I say the Holy Spirit Divine Sovereign—is simply defining her realm here on earth.

Did I say we were living in a strange world? Let me revise that: we are the denizens of a world gone quite mad.

An hour after he had left his house, Magistrate Dee's head still reverberated with the voices of his wives and mother, raised in shrill fury. His mother knew, knew for a fact, that the next family was going to be wiped out to be themselves. She had seen it in a dream. Our bodies will be shrunk down to the size of dolls through evil magic, she had said. I am packing my things and leaving this very morning. Tiresome old woman, his first wife had shouted; all you are capable of is spreading agitation and turmoil. Go ahead and leave! I will help you pack your hampers! Do not speak to an old lady that way, his second wife had said then. She is your husband's mother! Your disrespect is revolting and abominable!

Please, Dee had interjected; this does not help us in any way at all! We must treat one another with respect! We have armed servants on guard night and day! And what if the servants are killers? his mother had snapped back at him. What if the weapons with which we are supposed to preserve our lives are the ones they will use to put an end to them?

That is precisely what I mean, his first wife had said with exasperation. You cannot satisfy her. You cannot appease her.

That is no reason to drive her out into the street, his second wife had retorted.

And you, his first wife said, addressing Dee. When are you going to catch these murderers so that we may sleep decently again?

And when, said his second wife, are you going to take the time to be a good filial son, to sit down with your old mother and calm her fears? Have you no respect for the old?

He had brought in the armed servants, had asked his mother to look into their eyes and tell him if she still thought they were murderers, had placed the servants back at their posts with strict orders not to let his mother leave the house, and had left, the sound of the three women arguing still audible as he closed the gate behind him and stepped into the street. Only his adopted daughter, a quiet child of almost fourteen, had stayed out of the altercation, whispering to Dee as he left that she would stay with Grandmother and try to calm her fears.

Sons, Dee thought; other men have sons, level-headed and filial, to help carry the load. Where were his sons? Far away, obscure military men in the western wilderness, the last he had heard. Alive, as far as anybody knew, but silent for these last several years. Certainly they were not here to help their father, he reflected as he joined the morning foot traffic along one of the city's great boulevards.

The streets, which usually cheered him with their life and bustle, gave him a tired feeling as he pushed his way among the thousands and thousands of people and thought of the minutes, hours, days, and years of each of their tedious lives, all to be got through somehow.

Well, he told himself, you are certainly in a fine frame of mind this morning. At least your head is still attached to your body and your blood is not being mopped up by constables' assistants. There are a few things to be grateful for.

He caught a savory whiff of food on the wind as he approached the vendors' district, and felt a little surge of something faintly resembling hope, or cheer, or interest.

He had bought a spicy dumpling and had taken the first bite when he heard the chanting of monks. With the new White Horse Temple in Ch'ang-an, this was not an unusual or unexpected sound. He was taken by surprise only because he had forgotten about it for the moment. He waited, the food in his mouth turning into a greasy and flavorless lump, which he dutifully chewed and swallowed. Reflexively, he raised his hand up and took another bite, because he was truly hungry. Then he caught a glimpse of the chanting processional.

Instead of the tall, fierce, chiseled monks he had expected to see parting the crowd, there appeared a column of the most misshapen specimens of humanity he had seen anywhere, awake or dreaming. He and people around him stared, hands and arms frozen languidly in mid-gesture, transfixed, as malformed skulls, bulging foreheads, sloping shoulders, twisted legs, asymmetrical faces, and jutting, protruding jaws passed close by, chanting the dirgelike rhythms of the Great Cloud Sutra.

When they had gone by, he swallowed the food that had been in his mouth and felt it move slowly and disagreeably down to his stomach, as if it were a rock with sharp edges. It was one thing to see the deformed singly or even in pairs—

but it was altogether a different thing to see sixteen of them at once, and with the spurious doggerel of the Great Cloud issuing from their ragged mouths. Well, he told himself, here is a concession that you have to make. There is one discernible redeeming factor to this religious schism: at least the pathetic misborn have a refuge.

28

Loyang

Without stopping, Chou Hsing ran up three long flights of the vast stone steps of the Censorate Hall of Justice. He was not a strong man. He was weak and tired quickly, but today he raced a good distance along the Secretariat terraces past stunned guards and amazed Supreme Court officials before he even began to ascend the stairs. Today, he was a different man.

He was shot through with an excess of animal strength and power, his legs carrying him nimbly up the steep marble incline.

"He possesses not only the mind of a bird but its frailty and lightness as well." President Lai Chun-chen had said that about him. It certainly fit. They sounded like words that Lai would use if he were to condescend to describe Chou to the other members of his little clique. And just who were they? Chou wondered. Probably the Empress's unctuous and petty nephews high up in the Censorate. Those nephews had never much liked him. And certainly they would be the kind of slime with which President Lai would consort and conspire against him. In fact, hadn't he seen them together quite often lately in the gardens? Heads always together, murmuring furtively? Especially with the elder nephew, Wu Cheng-ssu. He was the dangerous one. But they had not counted on Little Chou Hsing. He would show them all.

"And by that lightness, how easily and naturally he will soar in the heavens above the earth," Lai was also to have said about Chou. "At least he will serve that purpose well. Yes. The little fool will fly. That is one way he may prove his worth . . .

prove that he is, at least, a useful fool!" Chou could easily imagine Lai's haughty and self-satisfied demeanor as he spoke those words. So that was how he would treat his most trusted assistant, Chou thought, his anger surging anew. I shall prove to him how much of a fool I am!

With jumps of three and four steps at a time, Chou Hsing ascended the final flight in a matter of seconds. He felt young and strong as a soldier, and all because of the words that ate at his innards like ten thousand gnawing worms. The anger rushed through him and caused his heart to pound thickly in his throat. He felt for his dagger, clutching the carved handle through the thick brocade fabric. With that gentle but sinister touch, Chou Hsing was reminded that he could never trust his superior. He never had.

"I have no doubt that the silk and parchment wings stretched over their bamboo frame will lift him like a feather on the breeze. . . . We shall send his tiny insignificant form aloft with the bugs and the birds . . . " And then Lai had added, so Chou had been told, these final insulting words: " . . . where he might finally hold court with others of equal intelligence."

Chou Hsing shoved his way through the big studded doors that led into the reception hall of the office of Lai Chunchen, president of the Censorate's Board of Punishments and Investigations. Then Chou entered the main office. President Lai was exactly as he expected to find him at this late time of day—reclined on his day couch with his back to the doorway, his gaze drifting thoughtfully out onto the darkening manicured courtyard.

As usual, Chou would be addressing the back of his superior's head. This was how they always conversed. But all at once his mighty exertion caught up with him; his chest burned, he was out of breath, his heart was pounding wildly against his ribs, and he could no longer feel his feet touching the floor.

Despite weeks of preparation, Chou was appalled to find that he was losing his nerve. He stood paralyzed in the entrance way, some forty paces from the day couch. He desperately needed to collect himself before attempting to speak to President Lai Chun-chen in a normal voice. After a long moment Lai nodded his head slightly in that annoying way he had, indicating that he was aware of Chou's presence in the room and wished him to get on with whatever it was. He could not delay anymore.

"I have . . . I have something . . . something for you, Master . . . Master Lai," Chou managed to mumble, infuriated and humiliated by the stuttering lack of force in his voice. But Lai did not seem to notice anything amiss.

"I . . . I . . . I . . . believe," Chou said, struggling for control, "that you will find it most important, most instructive." The president nodded again, slowly and thoughtfully. It was his custom to speak little, if at all, while listening to Chou. Perhaps Lai was only feigning interest in what he had to say, Chou reflected now. Perhaps he had only been feigning his interest in his words from the very beginning of their association. That was at best. At worst, perhaps Lai had been mocking him under his breath and behind his back all the while. Yes, that was probably how it was. It was a thought that maddened poor Chou all over again.

Seeing that Lai did not intend to speak or acknowledge his presence beyond the nods of his head, Chou Hsing approached the president's day couch and stopped about six paces behind him. For a long while he just stared at the back of Lai's head, observing that his superior's hair still possessed the clear, smooth silkiness of his youth while his own was thinning and flecked with white. Only Lai's topknot was visible, the nape of his neck and his shoulders concealed by the high ermine collar of his jacket. But that would present no problem. Chou looked carefully around the room. There was no one present but the guards in the outer hall.

"Yes," he said in a quiet voice. "I believe that you will find this most interesting." Lai's head tilted back ever so slightly as he waited.

"I have here . . . something most unusual that has just come to us today." Chou reached deep in his robes, growing confident again. Did Chou detect a certain attentiveness in his superior's posture? He smiled to himself, and extracted a thin coil of gold jeweler's wire from an inside pocket. Unwinding the bright strand, he stretched it tautly between his hands, anchoring the ends around his wrists and palms. Among other things, he had, in fact, practiced this motion at least a thousand times this past week, Lai's infuriating words about himself running through his mind as he did so.

"And here it is, Master Lai Chun-chen," he said, bringing the taut wire quickly over Lai's head and under the man's chin and pulling it upward with all the force he could muster before the other could cry out or even make a gurgling sound. "An old discovery, a very old discovery," he panted exultantly, "but as good . . . as the day . . . it was first used!"

Teeth clenched with the effort, he twisted the wire tightly around Lai's neck and pulled back with every ounce of strength remaining in him. In a moment, and without a sound, Lai Chun-chen, president of Her Majesty's Censorate Board of Punishments and Investigations, would be dead. Then Chou would place the dagger in Lai's own hands and thrust it deep into the dead man's neck, slashing it vilely, wiping out any marks left by Chou's strangulation. An apparent suicide, the court officials would all agree. Perhaps the Empress had been about to demote him, they might think.

A mere few seconds had passed and Lai's neck hung limp. There had been no fight, no resistance. Chou twisted the wire tighter. Something was not right.

It was not flesh that his deadly wire encircled. He dropped the wire and stepped around to face the figure on the couch. The jointed features of a mannequin stared back at him with a ludicrous little painted smile.

Then he saw the delicate black silk thread hanging from "Lai's" chin. His eye followed it down to the floor, where it passed through a metal eyelet, traveled along the carpet, then rose back up through another eyelet and disappeared into a decorative slit in a screen. As Chou stared dumbly at the screen, the cord tightened, and released. The head dipped and rose. Nodded!

"Master Chou, I am surprised at you," came a familiar taunting, singsong voice from behind the big teak-and-jade-inlay screen. "Tsk, tsk, tsk! Is that any way to greet an old friend?" The voice chuckled. "From Chapter One, Volume One, of *The Science of Processes*: I quote: ' . . . one sees only what one expects to see.' End quote. Again, Master Chou, you have proved our observations and joint authorship valid. I am so sorry this promising partnership must end. But I am even more sorry that the rumors of your plans to murder me turned out to be so unfailingly accurate. You are *such* a predictable little man!"

Chou was about to say something cutting, or was trying to think of something, when he heard a metallic *click* and felt a sting in the back of his neck. He reached around and felt the rounded fins of a crossbow bolt protruding from the flesh. His other hand rushed upward to meet the dripping warmth of his throat and caught the barb emerging just below his chin. He pulled his hand away quickly and looked at his fingers. They glistened with the thick crimson of his own blood.

"And I was told," his voice rasped hoarsely, "that you had planned to make me fly like a bird. . . . " He dropped to his knees.

"What?" Lai exclaimed.

"That you planned to . . . to send me up in one of your . . . man-carrying kites . . . to let me be dashed upon the ground," Chou rasped in his dying voice.

"Master Chou!" Lai's voice sounded genuinely hurt and perplexed. "I said no such thing, Master Chou. I had no such plans for you! And that is the truth, my friend!" Lai paused in thoughtful silence.

Chou Hsing slumped forward, a terrible harsh gurgling issuing from his violated throat. His forehead hit the floor with a thud. Lai spoke after a moment.

"I do believe that we have been set one against the other like . . . like so many greedy little monkey demons in the Buddha's colorful Jataka tales. Indeed, that is the regrettable explanation for what has happened, Master Chou. Someone has taken great pleasure in watching us tear at each other's throats. Someone . . . and think I know who it is." There was no mockery in Lai's voice; he was serious, thoughtful, and irritated.

Chou Hsing raised his head up with his last strength. His mouth was working like a fish's as he tried to speak. But Lai spoke first.

"I did not think that I would say this, but I shall miss you. But I will not blame myself. In truth, it was not my hand that slew you."

Chou dragged himself along the floor a few feet toward the screen from behind which President Lai stepped. He gulped air with the effort to speak. But it was too late for speaking, and whatever it was he was going to say was lost forever.

The new garden stupa blazed in the bright late-autumn sun. Wu watched with distracted interest as a handful of workers put the final touches to the construction project. Behind the stupa loomed Hsueh Huai-i's enormous warehouse—a vast building that hid a secret that Hsueh said he would not reveal until the day of a great and spectacular celebration. Despite the fact that a hundred artisans sworn to secrecy passed in and out of the great structure every day, neither Wu nor her mother pressed the Lama for details. They were happy to let him surprise them. Besides, Wu had other things to think about.

The upper offices of the Censorate Supreme Court, Wu's ultimate organ of government, were beginning to rot from the inside out. She had not believed it when Hsueh had first suggested it to her, so he said that he would prove it by putting on a little demonstration for her. Ambitious, gnawing little rats are what you have on your hands, he had said, and I will show you just how easily they can be made to turn on each other. The instruments and personalities that once served you have outgrown their usefulness, he had said. If they are capable of devouring each other so easily, it will only be a matter of time before they will turn on you. And Hsueh had proved that the first part of his thesis was quite correct.

Hsueh had scarcely to turn the nest, and Lai and Chou had fallen upon each other like two hissing, scaly, tongue-flicking vipers. How pathetically easy it had been. And Lai Chun-chen and Chou Hsing had once been the best of friends! Plainly, things were out of hand. Now there were rumors to the effect that Lai was forming an unwholesome alliance with her two nephews in the Censorate. But Wu and Hsueh had come up with a remedy for the creeping illness, an idea that had surprised them both with its simplicity and obvious merit.

Now that the cleansing of the old regime was complete, now that the last traces had been scrubbed away, now that she was a secure, loved, and established ruler, she could afford to place here and there, in carefully selected positions, some of the honest Confucian officials she had removed years before. It was an excellent strategic move. She and Hsueh had discussed every aspect of it, and it made quite good sense. Certainly, there was no danger of another Scholars' Rebellion. She had more than demonstrated the consequences of that sort of folly. No, Hsueh had said; these are exactly the men we need. They will be conscientious and practical servants, quiet and hardworking, so overwhelmed by the fact of being returned to government that they will not even dare to think of making any sort of trouble for us. Of course, we will have to make our selections carefully, and they will have to be watched, but it is the obvious solution to our problem, he had said. We are capable of disciplining Confucian officials. But men like Lai Chun-chen and the deceased Chou Hsing and your nephews cannot be disciplined, let alone trusted. Certainly, they are not the sorts upon whom great government is built. Your ungrateful nephews have *ambitions*, Hsueh had said pointedly. We must build for the future.

And so Wu had devised something, a new and wondrous plan. Aside from recalling certain key officials, she ordered the Ministry of Civil Appointments to overhaul the Imperial Civil Service Examination system. The exams would be even more rigorous than before in order to facilitate the selection process of the best, most useful servants of her government. Both the Chin Shih and Ming Ching—the two highest degrees of candidates—were to be screened with more emphasis on their academic excellence and far less on their family backgrounds.

That, however, was only the first part of the plan. She would now add by decree a third exam: in addition to the rigorous testing of candidates' knowledge of classics, politics, and prose through the Chin Shih and Ming Ching, there would now be the Jataka, a test of excellence in the field of Buddhist texts, philosophy, ethics, art, architecture, biography, Sanskrit, the sutras, and so forth.

Traditionalists would carp and complain. But they would get over it eventually, and the Jataka, like the other Confucian civil service examinations, would last for centuries and would become just as much a part of the world order. Wasn't Historian Shu always telling her that traditions began with individuals?

The Empress informed the delighted Hsueh Huai-i that he was to be the cofounder and organizer of this new Jataka: an exam that would test the government official on his knowledge of the Buddhist texts.

Hsueh had got down on his knee then and, kissing her hand worshipfully, said that this exam would herald Wu's new age, the Coming of the Future Buddha. The Empress's forethought, he said, had brought about a gradual accommodation of China's ancient institutions of government to her new moral and religious climate. And the fundamentals of this new age, which would always be associated with her name, would be practicality, humanity, and reason.

Wu had felt that deep, ancient, satisfying glow that had heated her blood in her youth. She had pressed his hand suggestively, thinking that it had been a long time since they had enjoyed one another, but now he returned only a distracted look. It seemed that he was always tired lately, what with all of his secret projects, celebrations, and other pursuits. Of course, she understood. She hid her annoyance for now. Another time. Soon, she promised herself.

The decisions were handed down from the Empress the following week. A Palace Decree said that the sentences reflected the new age of mercy and stern but just punishment. The Wu nephews were exiled to life terms of hard labor within one of the northern border provinces *fu-p'ing* military units. There was to be no chance of pardon. But theirs was the gentle sentence.

For the crime of excessive cruelty, Empress Wu had ordered Lai Chun-chen demoted to former president of the Censorate Board of Punishments and Investigations, a title he would wear for the rest of his life, along with an accessory personally fitted to him by the Imperial blacksmiths: a mask of iron, designed so that the inside was lined with ingeniously placed protrusions that dictated a limited number of positions that the wearer might assume. The least comfortable of these positions were those conducive to rest, reclining, and, of course, sleep.

It was an easy assignment for the palace blacksmiths, as Wu pointed out; Former President Lai had already provided them with everything they would need with his own detailed plans and schematic drawings for the construction and application of this implement in the pages of his multivolume treatise *The Science of Processes: The Instrument of Entrapment.*

Worse than the mask itself, though, would be the guards attending him at every moment, night and day. Ironically, this had been Chou's contribution to the concept of the mask, his own excellent idea: in addition to seeing to those functions necessary for his survival, the guards were there to prevent the wearer of the mask from ever taking his own life.

But Wu revealed to Shu, Madame Yang, and Lama Hsueh that Lai Chun-chen's extreme punishment was really for the most inexcusable of all crimes. Though for the sake of public decree "excessive cruelty" was the official name given to his crime, he was really sentenced for a crime far more heinous. Lai Chun-chen had transgressed the most inviolable rule that Empress Wu had ever set down. He had crossed the uncrossable bounds of Wu's Imperial Palace propriety and decorum. In murdering his friend and colleague, he had dared to spill blood within the sacred walls of her tranquil Palace of Peace and Mercy.

It is such a shame, Wu commented later to her mother, that they all inevitably try to make themselves important. But don't they all? Madame Yang asked.

How tedious, they both agreed.

"Mother Yang, have you guessed what I am going to do with this magnificent holy effigy?" Hsueh asked playfully, his eyes bright and smiling with his secret.

"So this is the monument to the Buddha that you have been working on for so long under such clandestine circumstances, with such stealth and secrecy that you would not even talk to me about it. It is extraordinary, Lama. Positively extraordinary. It will bring great blessings upon us." Madame Yang stared up at the enormous carving, hardly able to believe her eyes. It was for this that the enormous special warehouse had been constructed, a building of staggering proportions. Inside it for the first time, she looked in awe at the soaring scaffolding and great vaulted ceiling.

Hsueh folded his arms and stood back proudly. "One hundred feet long and fifty feet high, madame," he said. "The great Buddha reclining on his right side, his legs outstretched, laid out at length, as you can see, one upon the other," he pronounced, his deep voice reverberating in the vastness of the warehouse. Then, with both arms spread wide above his head in a gesture meant to encompass the entire statue, Hsueh expounded further. "This was the Buddha's meditational position as he awaited his earthly death. It has taken over five hundred of the Empire's finest craftsmen one entire year to complete." He laid a loving hand on the burnished laminated wood and let his gaze drift slowly upward to the great Buddha's knees hanging out over their heads like the ledge of a *cliff*. "Teak, mahogany, rosewood; with silver, jade, gold, and mother-of-pearl inlay."

"It is . . . fabulous . . . beautiful . . . extraordinary . . ." Madame Yang fumbled for the words. "I can scarcely believe my eyes, Lama." She was truly confounded. "No, Lama, in all honesty, I *cannot* believe my eyes." She began to circle the base of the statue.

"We shall have to construct a palace of marble and jade to house it for posterity," she said. "Right here. We will build it around the warehouse, and then dismantle the warehouse from within."

"That will not be necessary," Hsueh said, politely, interrupting her rapturous vision. He paused for a moment. "Do you know why I had this effigy commissioned, Madame Yang?" he asked. "It is called 'The Buddha at the Moment of His Earthly Demise,'" he said, with special emphasis on the final word.

There was a silence from the other side of the statue where Madame Yang had gone. Then, with a startled little gasp and the quick patter of her slippered feet on the boards around the far side of the statue, Madame Yang hurried back and stared at Hsueh, her features aghast.

"You cannot mean that you would destroy this . . . this deathless work of art . . . this incredible act of homage to the Buddha!"

Hsueh inclined his head in wordless assent, raising his hands toward the vaulted ceiling like an offering.

"It is precisely out of our devout homage that we destroy so great an effort, madame," Hsueh said then. "It is quite simple. It is very simple. What use would the Buddha have with earthly wealth of any kind, including great art? Hm? Wealth in his name? Ah! But the *sacrifice* of our earthly efforts? That is another matter entirely. A demonstration that we have heeded his teachings, that we understand the transitoriness of all things, of life, of all earthly desires and attachments! The 'death' of this Buddha will symbolize the death of the Sakyamuni—the historical Buddha himself—his moment of enlightenment, his entrance to nirvana and his making way for the arrival of the Age of the Future Buddha! It is all quite scriptural. And I have decided that the day the historians consider to be the day of the Buddha's death shall be marked by a great public conflagration!"

The doubtful look on Madame Yang's face had softened into a glow of approval.

"A splendid idea, Lama. Most inspiring. But we have come to expect no less from you, our brilliant instructor."

"Madame, I am nothing without my esteemed and brilliant patron," Hsueh declared. "But of course, all of my inspiration is owed to the Blessed One himself, as you know."

"Of course."

"Although I do expect that most of our symbolisms will be lost on the unenlightened, they will take what benefit they can. There is much more to our day of holy conflagration. It is a day that will mark the beginning of our new age of enlightened government. But that is not all," he said, eyes afire as if they already gazed upon the sacred flames. "Think, madame! The first earthly departure of the Buddha also heralds his return in his many and varied incarnations, as all manner of strange animals and earthly rulers! This is the most important part! Hm?" he said in a delectably mysterious tone.

He placed his hand lovingly on the smooth wood. "With the death of *this* Buddha, the way will be cleared for the Future Buddha Maitreya and the coming of the New Age."

DEATH OF THE BUDDHA

Ananda, the Blessed One's cousin, had made ready the Buddha's bed between the two sacred *sala* trees. And she wept. It was not yet the season of flowers, yet the sacred trees were draped in the magic colors of their heavenly blossoms like great skeins of transparent silks and ten thousand times ten thousand gems and diadems. And the petals of those heavenly blossoms, a rainbow of fragrance and light, shed themselves upon the Blessed One's body as if they, the sala trees, were weeping like Ananda, having forgotten the Master's teachings: "Do not cry, do not lament my death. For my earthly bonds are broken. I am released. My soul flies." And above, the *apsarases* and *gandharvas* made the skies resound with sweet melodies. . . .

The Buddha meditates and from his trancelike state passes into nirvana. He dies lying on his right side; his legs are stretched out at length, one upon the other. He is surrounded by his disciples who also weep despite the Blessed One's final admonishments. But no one weeps more bitterly than the Buddha's cousin, whose faithfulness and unfailing affection is far removed from the state of detachment. . . .

29

A.D. 675, late October
Environs of Loyang

Dee stood in the shelter of the branches of a tall pine tree outside the little postal station twelve *li* south of Loyang. Stray drops of rain spattered down from the lowering gray sky. He could have waited inside, but he wanted to avoid unnecessary contact with people. Besides, he was far too impatient and eager. His eyes were fixed on the place where the road emerged from the woods. At any moment, the donkey cart carrying Wu-chi and Abbot Liao would appear.

Months ago Wu-chi had written Dee that he and Liao were planning a discreet expedition to the Lungmen Caves outside the city to see for themselves the Empress's monumental works in progress. They had suggested that he disguise himself and join them. He had been tempted. As the head of the Bureau of Sacrifice, he had an obligation to get himself to the caves and view the Empress's works with his own eyes and record what he saw for posterity—but then the murders and the infernal pillar came along to occupy his attention.

Now, with no leads in the investigation and the pillar nearly complete, Dee had decided to go. He had been waiting for murder number four, if there was going to be one; some part of his mind told him that if he stayed, nothing would happen, but if he went away, something was sure to happen. He would be back in Ch'ang-an in just a few days, and he was hungry for a distraction and consumed with curiosity to see Wu's giant Buddhas, which would stand for eternity—but these were minor reasons compared to the one that had decisively made up his mind to go, and go now: in Wu-chi's most recent letter, he had issued the invitation again, and mentioned that he would soon attain his eighty-third birthday. It had been more than four years since his departure from Loyang and the last time Dee had seen Wu-Chi. If I do not go, he said to himself, I might never see my old friend again.

* * *

Dee and Wu-chi, dressed as mendicants, sat facing each other behind Abbot Liao, who held the reins. Their knees rattled together each time the donkey cart jolted in the ruts.

"Whenever we see each other, we are dressed as monks," Dee said with a smile. "I am beginning to believe that we do belong to some religious order or other."

They had already discussed the Ch'ang-an murders, Dee expressing his frustration and bewilderment. They had talked about the pillar, Abbot Liao describing the progress of the similar pillar going up in Loyang. Dee told them what he knew about the other pillars going up in the Empire, and his conclusion that Wu was marking off the boundaries of her imaginary Buddhist realm. It turned out that the pillar in Loyang was complete; the one in Ch'ang-an, he told them, was only three-quarters complete, and when he left, the engineers had still been awaiting further instructions.

"I must confess," Abbot Liao said, "that aside from the obvious fact that the pillar is a waste of money and labor, I am actually beginning to like it."

"You always were an old fool," Wu-chi remarked. "Naive and easily impressed. It is for you and those like you that the Empress works her wonders."

The abbot laughed. "Strictly from an aesthetic standpoint, I mean. It is rather an attractive addition to the city's skyline."

"I am just grateful that the old Li prince whose house was torn down to make room cannot hear you saying that," Wu-chi said.

They discussed the fates of Lai and Chou and the Wu nephews, and agreed tentatively and with great caution that the dreaded reign of terror might be running out of momentum. They told Dee what they knew about Lama Hsueh's great performances, from what eyewitnesses had told them, especially the conflagration of the gigantic reclining Buddha and other "miracles" that had sprung up around the capital. Dee could only shake his head at the absurdity and expense of it all.

"I wonder when Her Majesty will grow tired of Lama Hsueh," Wu-chi said suddenly and darkly.

"Perhaps these extravagant performances are a mighty effort to keep that from happening," Dee suggested. "But if ever there was a man sufficiently resourceful to offset the royal ennui, it is Hsueh."

"You should see what *I* have to do to keep our councillor

here from growing bored with my company," the abbot remarked over his shoulder, and they all laughed. That was
something Dee had forgotten how to do of late.

The abbot dropped one of the reins then, and bent over,
grunting, fishing around to retrieve it. The donkey plodded
steadily along, oblivious.

"What do you even need reins for?" Dee said. "The donkey is obviously a good Buddhist. He knows his way to the
caves without any help."

As they watched the work on one of the largest seated
figures of Buddha—the Buddha Vairocana, symbol of creation,
presiding over a court of attendant bodhisattva disciples, heavenly kings, celestial demigods, and fearsome Lokapala guardians—it was hard to believe that the sculptors could achieve
such delicacy of form on such a gigantic scale in the flowing
drapery of the Buddha's gown. It was as though the limestone
of the great cliffs, carved into a niche one hundred ten feet
high, had been transformed into soft and luxuriant folds of silk
and linen raiments.

There was a powerful difference in styles between the old
and new sculptures, Dee remarked to Wu-chi and the abbot as
they passed by row after row of niches filled with carved Buddhist figures. The earlier statues seemed broader and much
stiffer, whereas Wu's most recent additions were far more elegant—elongated and curving. No doubt Wu's vanity played
a direct role; she wished to mirror herself. Perhaps the Tibetan
had a hand in orchestrating these sensual and feminine
changes as well, Dee concluded. The others agreed.

By the time they reached the cave shrines, the sun had
gone permanently behind an ominous mountain of clouds and
the few remaining pilgrims, anticipating rain, had huddled into
several of the thousands of tiny low niches. The walls of these
tiny niches—no bigger than a doorway or window—were
lined with rows of figures, miniature versions of the giant ones,
each a hand's span in height. Aside from Dee, Wu-chi, and the
abbot, only a handful of other mendicants could be seen still
strolling beneath their umbrellas along the promenade at the
base of the great expanse of carved cliff. There were now some
sixty or seventy thousand carvings of seated and standing figures. The Empress had already added tens of thousands to the
vast array, filling every niche and slot. But today the work was
practically at a standstill. Here and there one or two craftsmen

still hammered and chiseled away, but that was all. Under the threatening skies even the hundreds of vendors with their colorful stalls of figurines, medicinal herbs, and healing potions and magical recipes had closed up, packed their wares, and disappeared. Only a few banners still flapped at the entrance gates.

Overhead, the low darkening sky blackened and the iron-white light that squeezed through the towering thunderheads bathed the limestone cliffs in weird color. Sublime faces and gracious gestures were subtly transformed, becoming disconcerting, even somewhat sinister, Dee observed. Like the thickening clouds, the sculpted foreheads and elaborate crowns towered about eyes at once distant, contemplative, and mysterious. Now, in the changing light, those eyes seemed to become immediate, harsh, and judgmental.

As far as he could see, row upon row of frowning celestials stared out in bleak and uncompromising attentiveness. The cliff face and its thousands upon thousands of sublime carvings offered nothing transcendent to him. There was no mercy here. It was too much all at once, and Dee felt the superstition of the unenlightened wash over him with an oppressive metaphysical weight.

He was relieved when the sky-promised heavy drops finally began to spatter the paved pathway. Distant rumbles of thunder confirmed heaven's commitment. Dark spots appeared on the dry yellow stone. The patter of droplets on the paving bricks increased as the distant sounds were joined by a closer volley. There was another faraway rumble. The air smelled rich and anticipatory. Then the dragon spoke as a crack of thunder split the sky and the boughs of the pines blew silver in the wind. The sky blazed with flashes of brilliant light and the random drops became a solid sheet of gray.

They pulled their hoods over their heads. Through the gray torrent it was now almost impossible to see any distance in front of them. Dee could make out two or three figures on the path ahead, racing for the cover of a small carved niche in the cliff. The abbot, shouting above the roar of the cloudburst, told Dee and old Wu-chi that they were most lucky to have such a good guide with them. Not only would he bring them to shelter, but he would take them into one of the most celebrated cave shrine rooms. They were almost there anyway, he said. He had been slowly guiding them in that direction before the storm hit.

They were thoroughly drenched by the time they made it into the abbot's favorite cave shrine, but they quickly forgot about their soaked clothing. For a few moments the three men stood in awe, dripping water onto the smooth rock floor. A small thin monk was present. The little man greeted them and told them that he tended to the lamps and the votive candle offerings so that even on overcast days the room's special works would always be visible to visiting guests, mendicants, and pilgrims. Especially those works in the inner rooms. Abbot Liao nodded in knowing agreement, then turned to Dee and explained that some unique and wondrous works awaited him inside the innermost sanctum. They were images, the abbot said, delight creeping into his voice, that could be seen nowhere else.

In the center of the entrance hall to the inner cave shrine, dividing the space into two narrow aisles, were row upon row of delightful little figures of sensuously curved *apsarases* set amid a bewildering array of carved blossoms, palmettes, Yakshas, Devas, musicians, nimbuses, scrolls, dragons, birds, and beasts of every imaginable type.

On the walls to either side were magnificent frescos depicting processions of Buddhas, horsemen, palanquins, and courtiers moving through a sky strewn with heavenly flowers, clouds of flowering ribbons, and angelic creatures.

"It is all quite lovely, my good attendant," Abbot Liao said to the caretaker, "but we have come here to see the art of the inner sanctum."

"Yes, Your Grace." The slight, baldheaded attendant bowed dutifully and handed the old abbot an earthen oil lamp as they passed through the narrow doorway into the interior of the cave. The inner sanctum was dimly lit with rows of votive candles that flickered in the altars set in the cave walls. The air was still and cool. Aside from the dank odors of water and stone and their own drenched clothing there was a suggestion of incense, as if something had been burned a long while ago and still lingered. It was far different from the cloying, overpowering scent of most temple offerings, and Dee found the smell remote and pleasant. The abbot had walked ahead of him, and was now standing by a grouping of carved figures against the center of the rear wall of the great room.

The figures were in various positions: arms raised, bodies crouching, running, and leaping. Bodhisattvas, raging demon slayers, Dee assumed as he approached. Perhaps a soaring angel or celestial king or two, he guessed, waiting for the abbot to raise the lamp.

The old abbot passed behind Dee with the oil lamp casting elongated shadows of Wu-chi and himself on the rear wall. Dee caught a flicker of light glinting off the varnished shoulders of one of the figures.

"There now ... let me set the lamp here," Abbot Liao said, placing it on a ledge near the raised bases of the statues. "And bring me a few more candles from that altar," he said to Wu-chi. "These are most splendid works. It is the whole effect that is so impressive. All sixteen figures should be seen together. In fact, *must* be!" He heaved a sight of admiration as he rose to his feet again to take more candles from Wu-chi's hands.

"The artist would not wish us to miss the total rhythm of this masterpiece," he continued. "The way his wonderful Arhats or Lohans, or disciples, call them what you wish, work together." Dee went and gathered more candles to help illuminate Liao's favorite figures. The abbot and Wu-chi were arranging the candles in a semicircle on the floor while the abbot happily continued his lecture, warming to his subject. "The manner in which the artist has depicted this grouping of sixteen figures—I believe that is the correct number according to the sutras—so that all the space utilized is most harmonious: where one Arhat—disciple twists to the right, another is depicted twisting to the left. Where one is short, another is tall, so that the forms mutually fill the space. One might say they appear to be ... *cooperating* in some strange heavenly business that we can know nothing about." The abbot smiled, "There, Master Dee. Very good. Place those candles here in front and join us."

Dee knelt and placed the candles in the place where Liao indicated, then stood and made his way around to the front of the figures, where the abbot stood admiring the work, as if it were his own and just completed.

"What is most wondrous, Magistrate," Liao said, whispering Dee's title, "as I was explaining to Wu-chi, is the grotesque, the wonderfully mythic, fantasy quality of their features. They are each quite bizarre."

Dee stood and faced the sixteen magnificently carved polished black stone statues. He looked at the faces, seeing them clearly for the first time now, and could not quite believe what was before him. He stood, transfixed, paralyzed. He was aware of his breath whistling in his nose and his eyes so wide that they must have been starting from his head, but he could not speak. Liao and Wu-chi looked at him curiously. The abbot had obviously not expected these works to have quite such a profoundly moving effect on the magistrate.

"As I was saying . . . " Liao began, trying to pick up the thread of his lecture again. But he was unable to take his eyes off Dee, whose initial surprise now appeared to have changed into shock. "Ah . . . these sixteen most bizarre and delightful figures represent the Arhats . . . " He broke off, genuinely alarmed now. He squinted and leaned toward the magistrate, who still had not moved or spoken. "Are you quite all right, Master Dee?" Now Dee was moving his head from side to side. The abbot and Wu-chi looked at each other in alarm, thinking perhaps he was having a fit or a seizure of some kind.

"Yes, indeed," Wu-chi said, "Are you sure you are not feeling unwell, Magistrate?" He put a solicitous hand on Dee's arm. Dee's hands came up fast, startling Wu-chi badly, seizing both of Wu-chi's arms in an urgent grip.

"I am afraid . . . " Dee turned to the abbot. The old man shrank back from the blaze in Dee's eyes in the candlelight. "I am afraid that I must get back to Ch'ang-an." He released Wu-chi's arms. "Immediately."

Without so much as another glance at the carvings, he turned and walked out into the downpour.

He had expected opulence. Instead, he was surprised to find an ascetic, almost spartan quality to the atmosphere and surroundings at the new White Horse Temple in Ch'ang-an. And it was not merely because the monastery was so new, the grounds still raw from recent construction and the gardens as yet unfinished.

It was quiet here, as it was at every monastery whose paths Dee had ever trod. But it was not the contemplative quiet he had experienced at the Pure Lotus, walking with the abbot, enveloped by the peaceful hum of life in the absence of talk: wind in the leaves, the song of insects and birds, the swish of the abbot's robes as he walked, with the distant rhythmic ringing, perhaps, of the monastery blacksmith's hammer, and at different times of the day, the soul-soothing dirge of the monks at prayer. More than once he had lain beneath a tree there, eyes closed, and luxuriated in the sound of his own heart thumping lazily against his ribs.

No, this was a different quiet, an enforced silence, he thought. Monks hurried past him in groups or singly, eyes to the ground. With its spare, utilitarian look and its disciplined monks marching smartly, the White Horse Temple looked like a military installation—or a prison. He knew that the temple in Loyang was an oasis of indulgence. But this was an outpost, in every sense of the word. He had the distinct feeling of trespassing on enemy territory. Which, he reminded himself, was precisely true.

As the monks passed him, he kept a wary eye on them. Many of the faces he saw were youthful, with a look to most of them that suggested backgrounds of hardship, poverty, deprivation. He knew that look, because he had seen it on the faces of young soldiers. Life had offered them little, and so they had sought the austere solace of the military, where there would be—at the very least—food, clothing, and direction. And some of the monks were older, with a hardened look, their faces closed, like the faces of prisoners. It was not difficult for Dee to imagine what other lives some of these men had escaped from, seeking sanctuary within the White Cloud sect.

And he was certain that he perceived a certain system of rank. Most of the monks who passed by were of ordinary stature. The tall ones, the statuesque counterfeit Hsueh Huai-i's, were also in evidence, but they moved about in their own groups, not mingling with the others, with an air of arrogance and unmistakable privilege rising off them like an odor. Even their robes were different: Dee noted that they were made of a better fabric that contrasted with the rough cloth of the lesser monks' garments, and had been cut and sewn with care and attention. In their hauteur, the tall monks did not so much as glance at Dee, and for that he was grateful, while the others rushed by with their eyes to the ground. So far, no one had spoken to him or impeded him in any way, as if he did not quite exist.

He was making his way along the broad central walk, hoping that he would be able to find the monastery library without having to ask anyone for directions, when he saw, among the ordinary faces of a small group of approaching monks, a now familiar countenance with a grotesquely bulging forehead that protruded like the lip of a snowdrift about to slide down a mountain. The rest of the man's face was compressed and embryonic beneath the overhang, his tiny eyes peering out from the shadows. Like the others, the man passed by Dee without looking at him, while Dee quickened his step, making a mighty effort to keep his own features composed.

He proceeded in the direction of the main temple, scanning the faces moving by. He saw frowns and expressions of blandness; he saw flat noses, long noses, and crooked noses, eyes far apart and close together, scars, lines, white teeth and black ones, full lips and thin, wide faces and narrow ones, faces with prominent bones and others smooth and fleshy, foreheads low and flat or high and rounded—none beautiful, but all normal faces, all within the bounds of ordinary human homeliness.

He was about to pass through the doorway of the main temple when it swung open and a monk emerged, passing Dee so closely that the disguised magistrate barely kept himself from recoiling. The man's face looked as if the two halves of it, left and right, belonged to two different people and had been joined together by the gods indulging in a malign joke. And each side of the man's face seemed to be searching for its rightful missing half: one eye was two finger widths higher than the other and gazed off in a completely different direction besides; the poor nose started out as if it were going to point to the left, but changed its mind partway down the man's face and veered sharply to the right, while the jaw jutted sharply to one side, pulling the mouth with it. Right behind him was another man whose face had obviously once been horribly burned: the eyelids were gone, leaving hideously staring eyes, and the tightening scar tissue had pulled the mouth open so that the yellow teeth were permanently exposed in a fearful grimacing smile. Stunned, Dee held the door for them as they walked by him without a glance. His heart was pounding as he entered the cool darkened hall.

Now he was certain: he had seen the three monstrous men twice before. Once in the flesh, and the second time carved in stone. And he also knew that if he stayed on the grounds of the White Horse Temple all day, he would eventually find thirteen more—and each would be a match for one of the fearsome Arhats he had seen at the caves.

It was as if the figures in the cave had had life breathed into them, had climbed down from their niches, and had followed him to Ch'ang-an. But he knew that in truth, it was the other way around. The men he had seen today were three of the sixteen he had seen and pitied in passing several weeks before as they marched and chanted in the streets of the city.

And all sixteen of them, he was now sure, had been painstakingly handpicked by somebody for their uncanny resemblance to the carved mythical figures. Sixteen such perfect likenesses could only have meant that there had been literally hundreds—possibly thousands, he thought with revulsion and fascination—of aspirants.

Leaving his discreetly following constables to loiter within earshot, he hoped, he had found the library, but discovered quickly that within its walls he was no longer invisible as he had apparently been outside. His unrestricted wanderings had come to an end as the monastery librarian materialized out of the shadows to ask if he required assistance.

Abbot Liao had advised him what to ask for, and how to do it. He bowed his head and spoke his carefully prepared words.

"I am on a pilgrimage. I am searching for my vocation," Dee replied. "I have been looking for an order to join. I have been drawn here from a distance of many hundreds of *li*. I have heard that this temple possesses one of the finest collections of relics and texts in the Empire." Which was true; the collections of almost every other temple in Ch'ang-an had been plundered, their most valuable treasures appropriated. Dee paused for a moment and bowed his head again humbly in preparation for his request. "I have come on what may be a fruitless search. It is my heart's desire to gaze upon that rarest of treasures, the leaves of the sacred *bodhi* tree."

The librarian looked at him, considering.

"Let me see your hands," he said then. Hesitantly, Dee raised them. "I am sorry," the man said with a sniff, "your hands are not clean enough. You may not touch anything. But you may look. I will accompany you. I will answer your questions." With that, the man turned, indicating that Dee was to follow.

It was true; his hands were not particularly clean, and it was intentional. As a finishing touch to his impersonation of a traveling mendicant, he had rubbed black grime into his fingernails and palms. It was a detail too easy to forget. No wandering ascetic sleeping wherever he could find shelter and dependent upon the generosity of strangers would have the soft clean pink hands of a bureaucrat or clerk. Dee thought of asking if he might perhaps wash them, but decided not to. He was fortunate to have got this far, he reminded himself. He knew he was not as famous in Ch'ang-an as he had been in

Loyang, and was confident that his disguise had not been penetrated—but he had best not push his luck. He walked politely behind the librarian.

"I appreciate that *bodhi* leaves are rare, as rare almost as a glimpse of the living Buddha's face," he added fulsomely, speaking to the man's back, for the librarian did not acknowledge his words, but merely kept walking. "I have visited several temples already that did not have any. Perhaps you do not have any either. That would be quite understandable. Certainly, no one could hold the White Horse Temple in any less esteem because of it," he babbled. Still the librarian did not indicate that he had even heard.

He led Dee down cool, dark, newly varnished corridors, past countless books stacked on shelves, their colorful silk markers hanging down, stirring in the faint breeze raised by the two men's passing. Dee was impressed to see a particularly ancient Kanjur, the extremely rare one-hundred-four-volume set of the words of the Buddha. He recognized it because his friend the abbot of the Pure Lotus had a set; the distinctive characters of its title stood out boldly on the yellow silk marker above it. He wondered what shelf sat empty somewhere else, bereft of its greatest treasure.

The librarian halted abruptly so that Dee nearly ran into him. He pointed to a desk.

"Stand there. Please keep your hands in your sleeves," he ordered. Dee did as he was told, while the man unlocked a tall cupboard and removed several large, flat silk-bound folios. He laid them reverently on the desk, raising his eyes for a moment to reassure himself that Dee's hands were out of sight. Perhaps you should simply tie them, Dee thought, though he said nothing.

The man removed the cover of the folio. Again, Dee wondered what collection had been plundered: inside, pressed between pieces of heavy silk, were the graceful curved shapes of the leaves of a *bodhi* tree, the same kind of tree under which the Buddha had found enlightenment. And on each leaf was an exquisitely rendered painting, a portrait of a face, as Dee had known there would be, from what his friend the abbot had told him. It was the paintings Dee had wanted to see, and the short accompanying text, not the leaves themselves, which was why he had not mentioned them directly.

The portraits were of the sixteen Arhats of Buddhist myth and legend. Where their stone counterparts were nightmarishly hideous, these were merely fierce and grimacing, stopping short of deformity—but the specific resemblances were there. There was the man with the bulbous forehead, and there was the man with the jutting jaw. There was the Arhat of the fearful eyebrows, and there was the fellow with the bulging, staring eyes, and another with a thin face like the blade of a knife. And their specific function, so the text had said, was the slaying of the enemies of the Dharma—the Devadhatta. Now, studying the painted leaves, taking in every detail and reading the minute inscriptions, he assiduously avoided any mention of the portraits. Instead, he behaved as if he did not even notice the faces looking back at him, as if only the leaves were of any interest to him.

He asked the librarian a few irrelevant questions about the climate of the places where the *bodhi* tree grew, how long such a tree lived, whether it was at all possible that the leaves in front of them now had come from the original tree, how the leaves were gathered, and so forth. The librarian responded to his questions in a measured, pedantic tone. All Dee heard was the drone of the man's voice, not the words themselves, for his attention had been distracted: he was gazing at an ancient *tonka* painting that the librarian had incidentally uncovered as he leafed through the folios.

It was a depiction of the metaphorical continent of Jambudvipa, showing the four corners of the Buddhist realm. He had only a few moments to look at it, for the librarian soon covered it with another page. But he had had time enough to see the tortuous black line in the upper left-hand corner, resembling a vein standing on the forehead of an angry man, and to read the inscription: the dark river of danger, it said, which flows from the realm of the Devadhatta.

"So, Master Dee, you have decided to come out of 'retirement,' " said his friend, the Buddhist scholar and teacher with the extraordinary memory, as Dee escorted him into his study in his Ch'ang-an home and shut the door behind them. Dee did not sit, but paced restively, a sense of urgency breathing over his shoulder as it had every moment since he took his leave of the White Horse Temple library that afternoon.

"It is not that *I* have decided," Dee replied. "Rather, it has been decided for me."

"Indeed," his friend said sympathetically. "It seems at times as if we are in the grip of forces much larger than ourselves, beyond our human scope, but that use us—our lives, our minds, our bodies—for their purposes."

Dee looked at his friend for a few brief seconds without speaking. It was as if he were gazing through a window that had opened momentarily onto the infinite black mysterious universe. In that moment, he had felt that the man's words were perfectly true. He blinked and returned his attention to the page of notes and scribblings on the table. Somehow, he had to pull it together. Even if we are being used in such a way, he thought, the responsibility is still very much ours, and presses upon us mightily.

"I have need of your extraordinary memory and your knowledge," Dee said. "I could flounder for weeks and months through the holy writings, and I might eventually, possibly, find what I am searching for. Or I might not find it at all. But my feeling is that I do not have a great deal of leisure. The Arhats and the Devadhatta," he said, uttering the words aloud for the first time. "Aside from being the protectors and enemies of the Dharma, who—and what—are they?"

"The Devadhatta," his friend said slowly and thoughtfully. "You could say that they are a metaphor for human frailty. As the enemies of the Dharma, they will arise, it is said, during the period of the Degenerate Law, the period following the Era of the True Law. In the Era of the True Law, which began at the moment the Buddha attained enlightenment, the sage's teachings were fresh and men were pure and faithful. In the Era of Degenerate Law, the teachings of the sage have been corrupted by time and human fallibility, and the influence of the Devadhatta will have gradually spread. It is in this period that the Maitreya—the Future Buddha—is to return, and the Arhats are to rise up and destroy the Devadhatta."

"And how long are these eras?" Dee asked.

"One thousand years apiece. It has been twelve hundred years, approximately, since the Buddha's nirvana." He shrugged. "That puts us, now, at this point in history, about two hundred years into the Era of the Degenerate Law."

"And the Arhats . . . ?" Dee asked, peering anxiously at his friend's face as if he were an oracle, as if all questions and answers lay there.

"This could very well be their time, according to law and prophecy," he replied, and paused pensively. "If we accept that the Maitreya's coming is imminent," he said with a raised eyebrow, "then the Arhats should also be among us, destroying the enemy, assisting in the cleansing of a corrupt world."

"*If* we accept that the Maitreya is coming," Dee repeated.

"The Arhats have undergone a complex evolution historically," his friend went on. "They were once depicted as beautiful, graceful creatures, sublime recluses. True disciples of the Buddha. It is only very recently—within the last sixty years—that they have emerged as fearsome, ugly avengers. In fact, I once met the man whose work solidified that vision. Do you remember Hsuan-tsang?"

Hsuan-tsang, the celebrated pilgrim-translator who carried countless thousands of arcane holy words back from the distant reaches of India and Tibet. It was a name Dee would be unlikely to forget as long as there was breath in his body. He could close his eyes at almost any time and see the ancient monk, frail and bent, nearly at the end of his long, long life, exhorting the masses from the podium at the Pai Debates, the voices of the faithful challenging the very heavens.

"It was Hsuan-tsang who promulgated the notion that the Era of Degenerate Law was upon us, and who translated certain obscure writings that definitively depicted the Arhats as twisted, deformed creatures," his friend went on, "but exalted and elite in their ugliness because of the way it set them apart from the masses. It was from his specific descriptions that the artists who painted the portraits on the *bodhi* leaves and who carved the figures you saw at the caves drew their inspiration. There were eighteen in all, and each was distinct from the other, and each flaunted his hideousness as if it were beauty."

Dee remembered the air with which the misshapen monks had carried themselves: proud, arrogant, aloof—as if, after lifetimes of absorbing the disgust and pity of everyone they had encountered, someone had conferred royal status on them. It was not a comfortable thought.

"Eighteen?" Dee remarked, almost as an afterthought. "I have never counted more than sixteen in each case—the carvings, the portraits, the living men."

"The Chinese have always embraced the number eighteen for Arhats," his friend said. "Sixteen is the number of Arhats we associate with more esoteric schools of thought. Specifically, the Tibetans."

Dee walked from one end of the room to the other. The Tibetans. By all the gods, the Tibetans. He turned abruptly toward his friend.

"Do you remember a discussion we had some months ago? We were debating the extent to which the Empress and the monk and her mother actually *believe*. You said that earthly power assists in fostering delusions of immortality, of divinity. That because one experiences a certain omnipotence, one comes to believe that an omnipotent force occupies one's life. And you said that we would never know the extent to which they actually believed in their divinity. That in all likelihood, they themselves did not know. I think that we are being given at least some answers to our questions. I think that we are seeing the way that the monk Hsueh Huai-i is feeding illusions of divinity to the Empress, piece by piece, dainty tidbits prepared just for her by him who knows her so well, knows her tastes, her appetites, her peculiarities. First he lays a base with his forged Great Cloud Sutra, with its nonsense about a woman ruler. Then he elaborates shamelessly with the nonsense of the Commentary of the Precious Rain. Then he tells her that she is Kuan-yin and Avalokitesvara incarnate, and then arranges the world around her to support that illusion. He has practically told her that she is more than just the bodhisattva disciple— why, he is allowing her to believe that she is the Future Buddha Maitreya himself!"

"But the Great Cloud Sutra is not a forgery," his friend said. Dee looked at him, not understanding.

"Of course it is," he said. "The nonsense that the monks chant in the streets. The words that Hsueh Huai-i 'found' among the possessions he bought from an old beggar."

"Oh, he is very inventive," Dee's friend said. "He can come up with a good tale for dramatic effect, to draw belief from men's minds the way a wick draws oil, and he can rearrange words to suit his purposes, so that they will root themselves in the popular consciousness. But the truth is, the words chanted by the White Horse monks are but a derivation of a genuine sutra. A very, very old sutra. A sutra that has existed for centuries. I assumed that you knew. I recognized it as soon as I heard it. Probably there are only a few others who similarly recognized it. It is very obscure—but it is quite real."

Astounded, Dee watched while his friend closed his eyes as he always did before delving into his vast memory. Then he began to recite. Dee lowered himself into a chair and listened, rapt.

" ' . . . The Venerable One has said that when Bhagavat is reborn he will eliminate all evil. If there are arrogant and recalcitrant men, young Devas with rods of gold will be sent to punish them. The Venerable One wants Maitreya to build for him a City of Transformation with a pillar of white silver above and an inscription below. On top of the tower will beat the Golden Drum to proclaim this message to all disciples. It will be heard by all who believe, even if they are ten thousand miles away, but for those who do not believe in this Law, they will hear nothing though they be in the adjoining room.

" 'A holy mother will rule mankind and her imperium will bring eternal prosperity. She will truly be a bodhisattva, and will receive a female body to transform all beings. A Buddha will stroke her head and prophesy, and she will teach and convert all the places she rules. She will destroy the heterodox and the various perverse doctrines. She will obtain one quarter of the realm of the Cakravartin. She will obtain the greatest sovereignty and be self-existent. The people will flourish, secure from desolation, illness, worry, fear, and disaster. All the lands of Jambudvipa will come under her sway and there will be no opposition from far-off places. Wherever in the world there is sedition, it will come to naught.

" 'She will rule from the land of Wu-hsiang, also called No-thought. In that state will be a river called the Black River. In the time of the decline of the True Law there will come an army of demons, riding in on the ill wind generated by the waters of that river, and Mara will attempt to destroy and confuse the True Law.

" 'It is an inferior man who will discover this inscription. But she who reads it will be the sage ruler.' "

Dee's friend opened his eyes at the end of his recitation with a look as if he were emerging from a trance. Dee himself had felt as if he had been in a trance while he listened to the words of the sutra. Here was the source of all of Hsueh's inspiration: the pillar, the "discovered" inscriptions, Wu's apparent destiny as a divine ruler. A thousand questions rose to his tongue as he opened his mouth to speak, but one rose faster than the others.

"Mara?" he asked. "Who—or what—is Mara?"

"Mara, or Kamadeva. He is the leader of the demon army, the destroyers of the Law. It is another way of speaking of the Devadhatta: the demon army of Mara."

Dee's other questions were swept away in the next moment as he felt something nameless and shapeless moving in his mind. He stood abruptly, upsetting his chair and hitting his knee on the underside of the table in his haste.

"Demon army," he said. "What are the references in the holy writings to this demon army?"

"They are very brief. Very obscure. It is going to be difficult even for me to recall them. It will be necessary for me to perform a certain exercise designed to stimulate the memory. I must reach in, to the exact right spot. The corridors of my mind," he said with a smile, "are like the corridors of a musty old library. The writings are there, carefully stored and intact, but pressed under their own weight. One could spend a great deal of time tramping up one corridor and down another looking for a particular piece of writing. But there are more efficient ways to do it."

It was an extraordinary performance. The man shut his eyes and became as still as death; then he rose from his chair slowly and moved into a half-crouch, rotating slowly, as if he were scanning the landscape of a world visible only through his tightly closed eyelids. Watching him, an image bloomed vividly in Dee's mind of a dense forest, alive and crowded with creatures flitting this way and that in every direction, stealthy and silent, breaking cover now and again, moving across a patch of sky or a bit of exposed ground for a few seconds, daring the eye of the hunter to find them.

The man paused in his motion every now and again, as if he had seen or heard something, but then would resume his slow movement, peering into his invisible forest. All at once, he gave a shout which made Dee jump, so sudden and loud was it in the quiet dark room.

" 'THEN HE SAT IN A POSTURE IMMOVABLY FIRM, WITH HIS LIMBS GATHERED INTO A MASS LIKE A SLEEPING SERPENT'S HOOD, EXCLAIMING: "I WILL NOT RISE FROM THIS POSITION ON THE EARTH UNTIL I HAVE OBTAINED MY UTMOST AIM!" ' " he bellowed. Then his voice dropped to a whisper, as, still crouching with eyes shut, he continued his recitation, pulling it from his memory, Dee thought, like a knotted rope from a barrel. " 'Then the dwellers in heaven burst into unequaled joy . . . the herds of beasts and the birds uttered no cry; the trees moved by the wind made no sound when the Holy One took his seat firm in his resolve . . . ' " Dee's friend reached out with one hand, located his chair behind him, and sat down again. He had found his way to the words he had been looking for.

" ' . . . and when the Great Sage, sprung from a line of royal sages, sat down there with his soul fully resolved to obtain the highest knowledge, the whole world rejoiced; but Mara, the enemy of the good law, was afraid. . . . ' "

Dee had moved to his writing desk and taken up his brush. Characters began to move down a page of parchment as he strove to keep up with the recitation.

" ' . . . he whom they call in the world Kamadeva, the owner of various weapons, the flower-arrowed, the lord of the course of desire, he whom they also call Mara, the enemy of liberation. His three sons—Confusion, Gaiety, and Pride—and his three daughters—Lust, Delight, and Thirst—asked of him the reason of his despondency, and he thus made answer unto them. He answered: "This sage sits yonder, wearing the armor of resolution, intending to conquer my realms. If he succeeds in overcoming me and proclaims to the world the path of final bliss, all this my realm will become empty." Then Mara called to mind his own army, and wishing to work the overthrow of the sage, his followers swarmed around, wearing different forms and carrying arrows, trees, darts, clubs, and swords in their hands.' "

Dee's brush was just keeping pace. He put down the last hasty characters of the sentence and waited while his friend drew another great breath.

He began to describe, in lurid, minute, living detail, so that they began to take rustling, breathing form in the shadows of the room where Dee and his friend sat, the demons who made up the legions of the army of the Lord of Desire. For a moment, Dee neglected to write, so stunned and entranced was he. But in the next moment, he had returned to his senses, and his brush flew down the page.

Hours later, Dee sat alone in his study, sunk in thought. When his friend left Dee that night, he had looked at Dee for a long time before stepping out the door and delivered some words Dee had not been able to get out of his head. The tone of his voice had been such that thinking of it afterward, Dee could hear the words in his mind as either literal or ironic, or a dozen shades in between. It would seem that there is an aspect to all of this, the scholar had said, that none of us has anticipated. It would seem that the true Arhat—the true protector of the Law in this era of decline—is you, Master Dee. And he had smiled, and stepped out the door, leaving Dee with his papers, his hasty scribbles, ten thousand questions, and the nameless, shapeless thing that was now beginning to take definite, uneasy form.

The evening after the scholar's visit, Dee had requested absolute solitude and quiet in his house so that he could concentrate, and he put little wads of cloth in his ears for good measure. Before him was a schematic drawing of the city of Ch'ang-an. He had rewritten and organized all of his notes, and had laid out the sutra he had written down the night before. He had fresh blank parchment as well, and his brush and ink in readiness.

He picked up the brush, dipped it, and idly applied it to the upper left-hand corner of the page while he ruminated. He watched as a snaky, sinuous black line flowed from the bristles. He looked up for a moment, imagining that he had heard a faint scratching on his study door. He must have been mistaken. He had been more than clear about his wish not to be disturbed. He returned his attention to his line, letting his thoughts flow along as if they rode on that symbolic river. The dark river of danger: the river of passions, of birth and death.

He raised his head sharply. Now he was certain that someone scratched on his door. Why couldn't they respect his wishes? Why did he always have to negotiate when it came to peace and quiet, solitude and concentration? He would have been better off saying nothing, merely retiring to his study and shutting the door. By informing them of his need for quiet, he had practically guaranteed himself at least one disturbance. Well, he would ignore it. He began to read the Demon Kirita Sutra aloud to himself in a low whisper, which filled his head because of the wadding in his ears.

In the next instant he was up, pulling the wads from his ears, blazing with exasperation. They had left off scratching and were now tapping, steadily and insistently. He strode to the door and pulled it open.

His mother stood in the hallway. The look on her face made him swallow the sharp words on his tongue. And just behind her, looking as apologetic as a dog who has done something egregious before his master, was his chief constable, his loyal hunchback. And behind him, two brawny guards.

"There has been another murder," he said to the constable.

"No, Master Dee. There has not been another murder," the constable assured him. Dee quickly saw his mistake. For the two guardsmen were Imperial guardsmen, not constables.

Dee did not need to be told. He knew that the two guards would not be present unless he was about to be arrested. He considered: the dash for the doors to the terrace behind him, the chase through the garden, the pursuit over the wall and down the dark streets outside. There was a time, in younger, stronger years, when he would probably have done it. But he could already feel the fruitlessness of it. Besides, the miserable, pleading expression in the hunchback's eyes told Dee that it would be, quite literally, the little constable's head if he returned emptyhanded.

"I am sorry," the hunchback began, but Dee cut him off.

"Never mind," he said tersely, stepping forward and shutting the door behind him, mindful now of the papers on his desk. "You can tell me about it later," he added in a more kindly tone, allowing the guards to take his arms. "Let us go now."

30

Dee had expected to see his friend the constable at his desk when the door squeaked and stood slightly open. The constable usually thought nothing of letting Dee's cell door hang open. It made the magistrate feel more comfortable, less trapped. After all, there were ward policemen just outside, and he knew well enough that Dee would never endanger his position by attempting to escape.

But it was not the friendly hunchback at his desk. Where was the constable this morning? This was someone else entirely—a thick and somewhat ugly man with small suspicious eyes set a bit too close in a broad flat face. The thick man lifted his tiny black eyes from the ward reports on his desk and glowered into the cell at Dee.

"So you are awake, Magistrate." The man's voice was deep and hoarse, but not at all as unfriendly as his features had suggested.

Yes. Now Dee remembered the man. Maybe. His memories of the evening before were fuzzy and confused, as if he had drunk too much wine. Maybe that was it. Maybe the man had plied him with wine to get him to talk. No, he would be feeling the aftereffects this morning. But this was the same one who had questioned him last night before he fell asleep. Wasn't he? And he had been questioned last night, hadn't he? He would not have forgotten this thick ugly man.

"Have you thought more about cooperating with us this morning, Magistrate? You were not very helpful last night. Your recalcitrance will only hurt you, you know." The man was casual and unforceful. His voice, though hoarse and gruff, was still calm and patient.

"What was it that you wanted to know?" Dee asked, unable to remember the questions. He rubbed his eyes and looked through the open door to the desk.

"Just your full family name, Magistrate. Nothing more," the man said perfunctorily, before lowering his eyes and returning to his paperwork.

"My name?"

"That's all. A simple question."

"Yes. I am called . . . I know my name. Give me a moment. My name is . . . is . . . "

"Oh, come now, Magistrate," the thick jailer said without looking up from his papers. "We can do better than that, can't we?"

"My name." Dee was exasperated, struggling, trying to push the simple memory up through the layers of his mind. It was a physical effort, but he could not bring his name to his tongue. "I can almost remember it. My name is . . . I am Magistrate . . . damn . . . I can't think . . . "

"The act won't do you any good, Magistrate. Either you give us your name now, or we begin by killing one member of your family for each day you 'cannot' remember."

"But the city has my name . . . "

"No good unless it comes from you," the man said, his voice so casual and offhand he might have been telling Dee to sweep the floor of his cell. "Tonight we start with your mother. It's up to you, Magistrate."

"Not my mother."

"Who would you prefer we start with? One of your wives?"

"No!"

"One person at a time until we have finished the entire household." The man shrugged sympathetically. "It's all up to you."

Dee woke from the unpleasant dream to find his constable's unhappy face looking down at him.

"Another one, Magistrate?" his hunchbacked friend said sadly, giving him such a long sorry look that Dee felt he had to say something pleasant to counter it. The poor man worried more about Dee than about himself.

"It was nothing at all, Constable." He lifted his head and smiled, then pulled himself up on his mat so that he leaned against the rough wall. "I have forgotten it already. In fact, I am feeling more refreshed this morning than yesterday." He rubbed his scratchy, tired face. "My tea in a moment, if you please." He stood up shakily at first, and as his waking senses returned to him went to the washbasin.

"Indeed, tea, right away, Magistrate." The constable went over to his desk and brought the steaming pot and bowls on a tray back to the cell. He had the preparation of the tea well timed. Dee always woke at the same time, bad dreams or not. He walked back into the cell and put the tea on the table behind Dee, who was splashing water on his face. "Is there anything else you might need?" he asked. "Perhaps something from home. Some special foods. Something to make you more comfortable." Dee heard an all too evident embarrassed solicitousness in the other's voice. He knew that the man shared his own sense of rising urgency, and unfortunately, the same rising sense of hopelessness, too. But the constable was making a valiant effort to conceal his unease, to spare his superior.

The hunchback was aware that Dee had made some crucial discoveries, but it was an unspoken understanding between them that they would not discuss the details. Their silence over this subject was not only because of the very real possibility that they might be overheard, but also because of a tacit agreement between them that to put theories into words at this point might cause the fragile structure Dee was striving to build in his mind to evaporate like one of his bad dreams. Although Dee had most of the pieces of the brutal puzzle in his hands, his work was incomplete, leaving them, theoretically, as much in the dark as they ever were. That, of course, was the source of this morning's unpleasant dream—a deep anxiety that *all* knowledge, even his own name, could slither from his hands in the span of one short lapse of attention.

"I don't believe the governor-general of Shensi Province disallowed anything to you in his arrest orders," the constable said. "That is, anything in the way of small comforts."

Most generous, that good fellow, Dee thought. No, indeed; he didn't even inconvenience us with an explanation of the charges against me.

"I thank you, Constable. You have already been most considerate and helpful. In fact, I cannot thank you enough for seeing to my family," Dee said graciously, but his thoughts had turned to the governor-general. He knew that if the man was behind the vague charge that had been read perfunctorily to Dee—that he had been declared an enemy of the state—then his hand had clearly been forced by someone else. His seal had been neatly applied to the papers, but that was all. A useful pawn. "But there is one great service that you *could* do me, Constable," Dee said then, a mischievous, conspiratorial note in his voice that caught the constable's attention immediately. The little man learned attentively close.

"Of course, Magistrate. Anything. Whatever you need. That is, anything within my powers. I feel helpless, limited. Powerless."

"Of course, my friend. We both are." Then he lowered his voice to a whisper. "But only for the moment. Let us not forget that." Dee tried to sound uplifting. He was not very convincing, especially to himself.

"But I will do whatever I can," the constable said, a trifle hesitantly, as if Dee might be about to ask him to perform some impossibly daring and heroic feat. But his manner told Dee that whatever it was, he would try.

"Bring me a bowl of that excellent fish broth you gave me last night. I will also be needing another blanket, if that it not asking too much. A comb, a writing brush, and . . . please arrange for a personal audience, here in this cell, with the good governor-general of the province. I should like very much to speak with the man," Dee said.

The constable looked worried for a moment, then smiled in obvious relief. "So should I, Magistrate." The man gave a dry little laugh. "So should I."

*   *   *

The days passed. They were long, slow days filled with every nuance of emotion and tedium, days crowded with feelings and memories that Dee had not confronted in years. And he could trace every one of them to its source as easily as his eyes followed the series of hairline cracks in the walls and ceiling that all led to a big discolored blotch in the corner over his head. Dee knew that the helplessness he was feeling over his false imprisonment was as nothing compared to the helplessness that the murder victims had probably felt on their fateful nights.

At least he could think here. It was ironic that he had finally found the peace and quiet that had eluded him at home. By concentrating in the silence of his cell at night, he had been able to recall almost every detail of the notes and drawings he had been forced to leave on his desk. He remembered his scholar friend's exercise, the one the man had employed to retrieve stray fragments of memory. Though he knew he was untrained in the technique, he tried his own crude version of it, shutting his eyes and visualizing until surprisingly detailed pictures presented themselves to his mind's eye.

Whoever put him here should have moved more quickly. If he had been separated from his notes any sooner, he would not have assimilated them sufficiently to recall them now. And who had recognized him, and when? He could not help but think that it had to have been someone either at the caves or at the White Horse Temple. As long as his investigations had been confined to the secular—gangs, shamans, robbers, and the like—he had been left alone. As soon as his attentions had turned in the direction of the White Cloud sect, he found himself apprehended. This fact alone certainly provided him with a strong affirmation of his most dire suspicions. And they had saved him some time, too: he could have been a long time conjecturing on vague theories with little assurance that he was on the right path, like the logician who drew circles that touched but were never quite confluent. But now he knew for certain that the circles overlapped.

But why, he asked himself, had they merely had him arrested? Why had they not had him killed? He had several possible answers to that question, all of which tended to point him, once more, in the direction of the very worst of his hypotheses.

And this was the most maddening part of it: he believed that he had what he needed to predict *who* was to be the next family to fall victim.

What he did not know was *when*.

But it had to be soon, he thought, turning uncomfortably on his hard cot. It must be getting very close to the time for another murder, he concluded, because somebody wants me locked up, confined, but alive—alive to hear about it, and to suffer helpless torment because of it. And that is probably why they have not moved me yet, either. They want me right here, in the same city, when it happens.

As the second week of his confinement drew to a close, Dee found his spirits sagging dangerously. Like the false rush of energy after a sleepless night, the initial vigor that had sustained him when he was first locked away was quickly disappearing. He woke in the morning feeling as if he had been sleeping on rocks all night, so tired that he could barely summon the strength to raise himself to a sitting position. More and more, he was finding sleep to be an easy, available escape route. The rumor persisted that he was to be moved at *of* some indeterminate time. He had tried to press for details, but none were forthcoming. His constable had no more information than he did.

He thought about his long walks through the city, the way they used to clear his head, invigorating him and putting a delicious healthy fatigue into his bones at the same time. A tonic for body and soul. It was really the one thing in the world that he wanted; locked in a cell, deprived of all the comforts to which a man of his wealth and position was accustomed, the only thing that made him feel that he truly was a prisoner was that he could not take his walks. To walk and think seemed to him, at this moment, to be life's greatest, most unattainable luxury.

It had been a very windy autumn. He remembered being buffeted about on many of his walks, and the extra effort it had taken to bend his shoulders into the wind, but he had never let it keep him indoors. With no windows in his cell he could not tell if it was raining or if the sun was shining. This lack of contact with the weather was contributing to his melancholia too, he was sure. One morning when the constable brought him his tea, he delighted the man, who had not heard him speak very much at all in the last few days, by asking him a question.

"Tell me, Constable, what has the weather been like?"

"This past week? Today?" the constable asked eagerly.

"Yes, Constable. Today and the last several days."

"Well, Magistrate," the constable began, his face gladdening with the promise of renewed conversation with the man he most admired. "It has been quite comfortable and unusual for so late in autumn. Usually we are badgered by dreadful winds. Much worse than what we have had."

Dee was listening, making an effort to move about briskly. He splashed icy water on his face.

"Actually, Magistrate, a better word would be *driven*. We are usually driven by winds at this time of year. But the last of the really heavy winds was several weeks ago. Before your . . . detainment. You probably recall. It has been relatively calm since then. At least for this time of year. Breezy, brisk, but no great winds."

"Then I would probably enjoy a walk today, would I not?" Dee asked, rubbing his face vigorously with a cloth.

"Yes," the hunchback answered, enjoying the little game. "Yes, you probably would. As long as you got out early. The sun is shining. There was a stiff breeze at my heels when I came in this morning. Nothing very formidable at all. But I believe it is going to pick up. By this afternoon, or tomorrow, it may be too windy for a walk."

"Ah," Dee said, pulling a cap on his head. "Yes, So today is good, this morning at least. But by tomorrow, perhaps I might not want to take a walk."

"Possibly not, Magistrate. But . . . " He thought a moment, engaging in the pleasant fantasy that Dee maintained. "One can never tell. It is possible that we will be pleasantly surprised, that the weather will improve. Tomorrow could turn out to be excellent walking weather." He shrugged. "But the winds are unpredictable. It could get much worse."

The old monk had to cover his face with his hood to shield it from the blasts of grit and debris kicked up by the wind. These occasional walks out across the courtyard of Ch'ang-an's enormous new White Horse Monastery were annoying interruptions to the pleasant task of sutra-copying within the warm, snug gatehouse. He checked the wind calibrator high upon its decorative perch atop the roof of the Great Hall, and grumbled to himself. The more the wind rose, the more frequent his trips outside. He could see that he would be making many more trips that day.

When the northwesterly wind reached a certain intensity, the first of the calibrator's three weighted figures of the Buddha's faithful disciples would flip over. As the intensity of the winds increased, then the second figure with its heavier weight would follow. And if the winds managed to flip the third and heaviest of the ornamental disciples, it meant that Ch'ang-an's mountain winds of full force and duration were due from the northwest.

On the monk's fourth visit to the courtyard that morning, the second disciple had fallen. He was nearly back to the gatehouse when a short intense blast raced through the gates and into the monastery courtyard, creating a little dancing whirlwind of debris. He turned, shielding his eyes, and studied the roof of the Great Hall: the third disciple had not yet fallen.

He had his instructions: when it happened, he was to scribble on a small piece of parchment the date and time that the strength of the wind had been sufficient to overturn the third disciple. He would blot the note, fold it and seal it, and hand it neatly and efficiently to a courier, who would race away with it. He did not know or care about the purpose behind it all. He merely followed his instructions, and was left in peace to do his beloved copying, the thing he had done all of his life.

He was just settling back into his seat when he felt another shuddering blast. He raised his eyes. No, not yet. Sometimes the winds teased him, he was sure of it. Carefully rinsing his brush, he smoothed the bristles to a delicate point before dipping it into the ink pot. He returned to his sutra and his waiting.

The constable had been right. The wind did pick up. Rising up out of his fitful sleep from time to time during the night, Dee became aware of its insistent, steadily growing intensity. He had thought that he might not be able to hear it inside the walled prison compound, but he was wrong. It caused the building to shudder from its foundation, and he fancied that he could feel a constricting in his chest. He remembered what his mother had said about the Ch'ang-an winds, that they roared through the city, coming out of nowhere, like vengeful spirits, shaking the buildings and turning proud trees into hunched old men, sometimes pulling them up by their roots or splitting them in two, and ripping the tiles from the rooftops. If this kept up, he thought when he woke sometime before dawn, it would soon turn into just such a wind. He shut his eyes and tried to drift back into sleep, covering his head with his jacket.

With a start, he brought his head out from under the jacket moments later. What had he heard? He listened intently. There it was again. A new sound, something inside the wind, it seemed; a deep, low, mournful wailing note, as if all the banished hungry ghosts in the underworld had put their sorrow into one voice.

He sat up and looked around his cell. Everything familiar; all of the meager little objects in his present existence were in their proper places. Reassured that he was not dreaming, he set his feet to the cold floor. He shivered, and listened. The single note wailed again, longer and more sorrowful than before. And real. Very real.

Dee was on his feet in the next moment and at the sliding window in the cell door. He moved the wooden grate all the way back so that he could see down the hallway and into the outer office. There did not seem to be anyone about, so he rattled the wooden grate back and forth, calling out the constable's name. The hunchback appeared from around the corner, bleary-eyed and only half awake himself.

"What is that wretched sound?" Dee demanded.

The hunchback rubbed his eyes.

"It is ghastly, is it not?" he said, standing and listening. "We were just discussing it now. The word is that it is a . . . a horn."

"A horn?" Dee asked incredulously.

"Yes. A huge horn, from what the men this morning have told me. Enormous. As long as three men. Something from the mountains of Tibet, they are saying. I cannot remember the name for it."

"A *thungchen*," Dee said.

"Yes! That is the word!" the constable said.

"Constable," Dee said, "why are we hearing a *thungchen*?"

"The work on the pillar has been completed. The infernal device has been installed at the top, just below the place where the orb will be. It has been placed at an angle so that it sounds only when the wind has reached a certain velocity and comes from a certain direction. Apparently, the conditions are quite perfect now," he said regretfully. "We do not know why it was put in place there. But we are sure to be in for a noisy winter. . . . " He trailed off. He could see that Dee was not listening to him anymore.

"Constable," Dee said slowly and pensively, "from what direction is the wind blowing this morning?"

The hunchback thought a moment, and shook his head. "I am not certain. Let me ask one of the men." He vanished around the corner for a few moments while Dee, his hands gripping the bars, strained his ears, a thousand desperate pictures moving in rapid succession through his mind. The hunchback reappeared in a moment.

"Northwest, Magistrate. It is blowing from the northwest."

"Constable," Dee whispered. "Constable, come close." Dee put his arm through the slot and gently took hold of the constable's clothing, pulling him right up against the door. "Listen to me." Outside, the wailing changed volume and pitch, becoming softer and lower for a moment. He fixed the constable with his eyes. "I must get out," he said, pronouncing each word distinctly and firmly. Then, in a softer voice still: "I know when the next murder is going to take place."

"There is nothing I can do, Magistrate," the constable whispered back desperately. "I wish there were something that I could do. I would do anything if it were possible. I would do it even at my own risk. But now it is too late." He looked especially regretful as he spoke his next words. "I am being transferred this morning."

"What? Transferred?"

"Yes. I am to oversee the wards in the western market. I will have to leave shortly. My replacements are already here. They are the ones who brought the news about the horns."

"Who are they?" Dee asked. "Why are there so many of them?"

"I do not know them." His voice was still barely above a whisper as he spoke.

Dee cursed in his frustration.

"Constable," he whispered again with renewed urgency. "I must . . . get . . . out."

The man looked back at him helplessly. The voices of the others were approaching now, forcing Dee to let go of the hunchback's clothing. The Tibetan horn atop the Empress's pillar moaned.

Then the hunchback spoke in a normal voice, for the benefit of the approaching deputies.

"Magistrate Dee, we have received other orders as well. Tomorrow morning, you are to be transferred to a larger magisterial office compound in one of the southern wards. You are to be escorted on foot. These deputies will be accompanying you." He paused, looking pained. "From there you are to wait transport to Loyang."

Later that afternoon, after the constable was gone, Dee thought only about escape. The meaning of everything had come together for him, and it was so shockingly bizarre that it mocked even his own nightmares. But it was not a nightmare. It was quite real, and it was happening in a city where for a once-privileged few sleep had become a fearsome gamble. He calculated that he had only a day—two at the most—to get out of his cell and be present at the scene of the crime to catch the murderers at their work. All of the work he had ever done in his long career was nothing compared with what he believed he had uncovered.

The great trumpet was quiet now, thank the gods. The winds had diminished in the courtyard outside and the building had ceased its infernal shaking. His mother was right; the winds were like vengeful spirits. The day passed into late afternoon, moving inexorably closer to the time of dark dreams, into another of Ch'ang-an's nights of sleep without sleep.

Early that evening, only a few hours after the constable's reassignment, a visitor appeared at the jail. It was a child selling sweet sesame, fruit, and bean curd rolls. Dee heard the youthful voice in the outer office describing the quality of the wares he had to sell. The deputies were laughing good-naturedly and evidently partaking; Dee heard their exclamations of pleasure as they ate the pastries, the boy's little voice prattling away all the while in a most charming manner.

He heard the child's voice approaching along with the footsteps of one of the deputies Evidently they were going to let the child try his luck with their distinguished prisoner. Dee heard the boy telling the men that the two copper coins they had paid him was a very good price indeed, that usually he received only a single copper coin, and that he was glad he had taken his father's advice, because he had told him to go to the offices of government workers, because men of importance were more likely to pay commensurate with the worth of his exceptional goods.

The boy said in the precocious and disarming manner that marks an intelligent child that his father did not cheat on ingredients. And men of quality were the only ones capable of truly appreciating the extra effort. Here is a young fellow who will go far in life, Dee thought. He is already a master of technique, applying kind flattery to his dullard customers, coaxing the coins right out of their pockets.

As they walked with him to Dee's cell, one of the deputies remarked that it was late for a little child to walk home by himself. The boy responded that his father was out selling close by in the eastern market until curfew. He also told them that the streets that he would walk on were always crowded and well lit from all the shops. This seemed to be a good enough answer for them, because they nodded happily, obviously pleased with themselves for showing such concern for a child.

"Master," the boy said, bowing, as the deputies opened the cell door, "my father has asked that I bring you something very special and very delicious. It is an unusual doughcake. It will make us rich and famous, he says. Because there is not another in the bakers' guild in Ch'ang-an who can make cakes like these." The child entered the cell. The deputy stood outside, watching, smiling. "He has filled the pastry with sesame paste, bean curd, honey, crystal ginger, and plum wine. But . . . " The boy widened his eyes and looked at Dee, who sat on the bench in his cell in his dressing gown. The child lifted his basket to Dee's table. "But, master, they are expensive. Three copper coins for one. Because the ingredients are so expensive for us to purchase," the child apologized. "But they are much bigger than the others."

"Ah. *Three* coins for these!" Dee said. "They must be special indeed." Dee brightened momentarily. "Perhaps they are worth more, though. Perhaps they are worth four!" With that, he extracted five copper coins from his purse. The boy's eyes lit up at the sight of the small fortune. Dee laid the coins on the table while the child tilted the basket toward him so that he could view the selection. They were startlingly beautiful cakes, Dee saw immediately, with decorative icings on their tops in the form of characters for luck, good health, prosperity, long life, and the like.

"It is my father's specialty," the boy said, seeing Dee's admiring look. Then the boy looked at the coins. "I cannot read, master, but I can count. You have given me five coins instead of four." He counted them again, then held out the extra coin to the magistrate.

"So I did," Dee said with feigned dismay. "Hm. How could I have done that? But for your honesty, child, I shall give you one more." He dropped a sixth coin into the small up-turned hand. The boy's eyes grew wider. Neither protesting nor thanking Dee, the child quickly put the coins into a little wooden box in his basket. Dee smiled over the boy's head in the direction of the watching deputy, who nodded and laughed. The child, meantime, was lifting a cake from the basket.

"See, master, it is such a beautiful cake. It is iced in white. My father says it is like a mountain in winter with snow." He placed the cake, sitting on a piece of parchment, on Dee's table, taking elaborate care not to crack or disturb the delicate icing-writing on its crest. "A poem," the child said. "My father tells me that he has written something for the winter. He has in-scribed a poem on top about falling snow."

Dee leaned over to examine the poem. As he did, he saw a serious look in the boy's eyes; the innocent child was mo-mentarily absent. Dee raised his own eyes furtively to the cell door. The deputies were talking to each other, paying little heed to the transaction. The boy put a finger to his lips. Dee looked down at the cake, moved his lamp closer, and read the "poem." It was a five-character line:

Help. Escape. Ling family. Thanks.

"Ah, yes," Dee said, recovering his composure. "Beauti-ful. 'The falling snow turns trees to white-bearded old men,' " he improvised quickly, looking up and nodding to the child, who smiled with understanding. The magistrate had received his secret message.

He had no doubt that the jailers were illiterate, and so would anyone else be who might wander in from the ward tonight. But he took no chances. He seized the cake as if he were a very hungry man and took a big bite.

"Superb," he said, his mouth full of sweet pastry. "A shame to ruin such a work of art, but that is what it is for, is it not? Wonderful!" he pronounced, his words muffled. "You must tell your father that he is a most excellent baker. This is truly the best I have tasted." He took another large bite, fin-ishing the cake completely.

The boy, consummate actor that he was, beamed with pride at his father's achievement. "Cakes like these will keep me going during my imprisonment. They will keep my strength up. I will need it, as I am to be moved tomorrow." Dee turned to the opened cell door and called down to the deputies, who were busy speaking with constables from a neighboring ward. "I am to be moved early tomorrow morning to the Serpentine Ward. Is that not right?"

The deputies said that that was correct, and returned to their conversation.

"Tell your father," Dee said, "that the cakes are excellent and I hope he will have some brought to me after I am moved to the Serpentine. Tell him it is a *long walk*, and I shall be tired afterward, and in need of sustenance. Tell him I would be especially pleased if the cakes are so stuffed with paste that it will fairly *run out* of the sides when I bite into them. Do you understand?"

The boy nodded. A bright child, Dee thought, thinking of his sons for one or two seconds and patting the sweet bean paste from his lips with a damp towel. The deputies were still talking among themselves. The boy was looking hesitant now, as if something had occurred to him.

"That was superb," Dee went on, concerned, trying to sound nonchalant, still patting his lips. "I have never had a sweet to compare."

"Master, I may not be permitted to walk so far as the Serpentine. Perhaps it will be my elder brother who will bring you cakes there. Tell me what you will be wearing tomorrow when you leave, so that I might be able to describe you to him." Dee understood the child's meaning immediately. Either he was a very bright child, or he was very good at remembering his father's instructions.

"Why, now, let me see. . . . " Dee turned to the rack where a few garments hung in the corner by his cot. "I should guess that gray hooded winter cloak with the ermine collar for the winds," Dee said, pointing.

The boy glanced at the garment while he crumpled the oily parchment and swept the crumbs off the table. When he returned his attention to his basket he noticed Dee's heavy purse sitting on top of his wooden coin box. He looked questioningly at Dee.

"The Serpentine is a good long walk from here. That is for your father's troubles," Dee said. "Perhaps he might wish to buy a new cloak for you for the winter." The boy took the purse, gathered up his basket, bowed, and backed politely out of the cell. A fine child, Dee thought. "I look forward to your visits," he said to the boy. "Tell your father that I cannot afford to miss my cakes. . . ."

Then the boy was gone.

It was cold that morning. Though Dee couldn't see the frozen blue of the cloudless sky from his prison cell, he could imagine it. When he first awoke, he felt the chill in the air despite the coal-fired brick *kang* heaters along the walls and under the cots in the ward jail. Their heat was comforting, but scarcely adequate. Their meager warmth was quickly sucked away and dissipated by the cold damp masonry of the walls.

The jailers had said that they would give him a few moments' warning before he was marched out. Time enough to wash, dress, and gather his necessities. Why, he wondered, was he to be walked to his destination? Usually prisoners were transported in a cart. There were two possibilities that he could think of: either the walk was supposed to be some sort of public humiliation—the great Magistrate Dee Jen-Chieh marched through the streets like a criminal—or else the hunchback, remembering what Dee had said about the pleasures of walking, had obtained permission for it.

He washed himself with the freezing water, gingerly, as if he were blotting stinging wounds. This was the day. Either he got out, or he was dead—he and who knew how many others. Washing was more brutal this morning than on other mornings, but that was good. He was as awake and alert as it was possible for him to be. And that was a good thing, because he had no idea what the baker's plans were. They are depending on me to recognize the plan and be ready when it happens, he thought. I only hope I am equal to the occasion.

He dressed, doing his best to make himself presentable. There was no sense in resembling a beggar on the morning of his freedom. If indeed this was the morning of his freedom. He looked at the long gray hooded winter cloak with the ermine collar and cuffs, the only remaining sign of his status. Or, he reflected, is this the morning a too-eager guard runs me through on the end of his lance? With that thought, he combed out his sparse beard, deciding that the more he looked like a respected official, the less likely would that last eventuality be. He placed his cap carefully on his head and straightened his clothing.

*   *   *

Out in the cold morning air, Dee's senses were nearly overwhelmed. The nervous anxiety and expectation that had been consuming him were displaced for the moment. He marveled at what a mere two weeks of incarceration had done to him. He had never been so grateful for color, noise, smells, and motion as he was today. He tried to imagine how it would be for a man being released from prison after ten or twenty years, but he could not. His legs felt stiff and slightly weakened from disuse, but he walked eagerly, filling his lungs, glad for the great distance that lay before him. He did not make a good prisoner, he knew. All his life he had resisted being at the mercy of anyone else's whims.

He saw people he recognized here and there, market people whom he had spoken to in passing during his frequent forays here. But they kept their eyes strangely averted. Was it embarrassment? Did they perhaps believe that he truly had become some sort of criminal?

He stole looks at the faces of the four ward policemen escorting him. Were they a part of the plan? If so, he saw nothing in their solemn faces. Dee and his little processional trudged in grim silence. He reviewed his conversation with the lad. Had there been something he had missed? He tried to stimulate his memory; as he walked, he whispered to himself the exact words they had exchanged. And he saw the words atop the cake, their message of hope swirled in sugar and honey: Help. Escape. Ling family. Thanks.

The Ling family, he whispered to himself. He still could not place the name.

They were not far along in the back alleys of the eastern market when they heard the distinctive sounds of a street brawl. From somewhere behind the row of market stalls to their right there came a commotion of invective and the crash of breaking pottery. Dee's guards paid no attention, and Dee's first instinct was to walk straight ahead without even glancing around, as he was accustomed to doing in order to avoid being drawn into the fracas as an official mediator. But the commotion was moving along with them, it seemed, invisible behind the screens and curtains to the rear of the vendors' stalls.

The feuding voices grew louder, the fight more intense. Now Dee's curiosity was aroused. Just ahead at a baker's stand it appeared that things might break out in the open at any moment: curtains swayed and bulged with the scuffle just behind them, and then were torn down as two figures locked in combat flew through them and landed on the floor of the stall. Shelves, pans, utensils, bags of flour, and pots of dough crashed down upon the man and woman who rolled about, howling with fury, pulling at each other's clothes and hair.

The baker's stall was collapsing, sending cakes and rolls and sizzling vats of hot oil spilling and hissing into the street. Now the guards were interested. They exchanged smiles, and slowed down their determined marching so that they might have a look at the entertaining diversion.

The couple rolled out into the street now, covered with flour and bits of dough, while people shouted and jumped out of their way. The angry baker stood over them with a long wooden spoon in his hand, cursing them and all their ancestors for destroying his shop; a crowd quickly formed, jeering, laughing, offering encouragement, taking sides. Dee could see that the woman was young and extremely pretty, even with her features distorted by anger. The attention of the guards had been quite drawn away from their prisoner as they found themselves unable to take their eyes from the sight of the woman on the ground whose clothing was coming off in shreds in the hands of her combatant. Since they were not on their regular ward duty, they were under no obligation to stop the fight. And it was plain that they had no desire to stop it.

The woman was slapping the man hard across the face and chest, and the man was jeering and insulting and yanking and tearing at her threadbare clothing, inadequate enough in the cold to begin with. When her shirt was torn away completely and she was battling her opponent bare-breasted, Dee saw that the four guards had virtually forgotten his existence. By now, the crowd was in an uproar of enthusiasm over the spectacle, with other vendors joining in the melee, until the whole north side of the narrow cobbled alley was in chaos and pandemonium. The woman's breasts, smeared with dough and flour, had the attention of every man on the street.

Dee stood where the guards had left him, looking around desperately for a signal. Was this it? Was he to make a dash for it? What was he to do? Where was he to go?

Just then, the soulful laments of a myriad of *hsiao* flutes and *sheng* reed pipes and the wails of dozens of hair-tearing mourners' voices filled the narrow cul-de-sac thirty or so paces down the alley from the baker's stall. Dee swiveled his head in the direction of the new sounds. Briskly flapping white banners could be seen snapping their brightly painted characters against the cold cloudless blue of the sky: a funeral procession, an enormous one, of a person of obvious immense wealth and importance. And the cortege was bearing down directly on Dee where he stood.

By now, his guards were thoroughly involved in the melee. Their hands were quite literally full as they grabbed this person and that, separating adversaries, struggling to take hold of dangerously swinging arms and getting hit themselves, only to have five or six more combatants roll out of the crowd and start it all over again. Food was flying, as well as utensils, stools, tables, screens, and curtains. And all that Dee could think about as he was shoved this way and that into the crowds of jeering, teasing, taunting, shouting onlookers was how he would compensate the good merchants of the street for all the expense they had incurred.

Then the funeral procession was upon them, sweeping everything out of the way before it, and Dee found himself literally carried along, quite unable to stand his ground even if he had tried to. Looking back on this strange morning, Dee could not recall being aware at what point his feet were no longer touching the pavement, but he would always remember the moment that his distinctive great gray ermine cloak, the unmistakable mark of his rank, was torn from his shoulders and trampled beneath a hundred feet and twice that number of great wooden wheels of ox carts festooned with flowers and trailing billowing clouds of incense. A celebration to end all celebrations. And Dee would always remember the sounds. How could he ever forget the cacophony of the street fight mingling with the wails of one hundred mourners and the sweetest, lightest, prettiest funeral dirge he had ever heard? The sounds that bore him away became, in his memory, the heavenly sweet voices of angels.

By afternoon, Dee sat in a small anonymous room somewhere near the southern gates of the city not far from the vast, wealthy suburbs that surrounded the sprawling Serpentine Park. He looked up at his hunchbacked friend. The constable stood over him as Dee unrolled his ward grid map of the city. As Dee traced down with his finger the lines representing the southern wards, trying to get his bearings, his constable wordlessly placed a hand on his superior's shoulder. It was a gesture that Dee found almost fatherly. It made him understand how close he had come to his own end, and how much they relied on him now.

Though each of the twenty or so men in the room had worked with Dee before and held him in respect, none of them had faced anything resembling the unknown they were about to enter. They understood that Dee could do little to prepare them, and that he himself did not know what to expect. They knew the details of the previous murders, of course, and Dee had sketchily outlined his fantastic theory to them and told them what they would do once they arrived at their destination, but they knew little beyond that, and he did not offer them anything resembling bravado or even encouragement. It would have rung false, and there was no time for that sort of thing anyway. They could see that he himself was strained to the limit, going over his calculations one more time at the eleventh hour, checking and rechecking his notes and maps, which had been rolled up and hidden for safekeeping by his mother when he had been arrested, and retrieved this morning from his house.

Though their knowledge was incomplete, each of the men was here for his own reasons, and each knew that he could very well die tonight. But each had sealed his fate, and there was no question now of backing out or losing heart. There was little talk, just the sounds of preparation—blades being honed, bowstrings tested for tautness, the creak of hard leather sheaths. It was enough for them to know that they were about to confront a singular enemy: the darkness that had held Ch'ang-an in its grip of fear.

Presently, Dee raised his head from the papers and rubbed his weary eyes. Something seemed to occur to him as he brightened and turned to the hunchback standing over his shoulder.

"Constable," he said. "Who is the Ling family?"

There were a few smiles and laughs around the room. A voice spoke up behind him.

"I am Ling Ming-lo," someone said. "I am repaying a favor from a long time ago. You did my family a great service once, in the city of Yangchou. You saved our name from disgrace."

Dee turned. "You know me as the baker," a man in his early thirties was saying. Dee looked hard at him. He had seen him before. Yes: he was the man who had stood over the battling couple, cursing and waving his wooden spoon. The man whose stall had been destroyed. "My father was a gardener in Yangchou," he said simply. Dee started to speak, but the man continued, "Some of your men objected to my coming on this . . . expedition, but I insisted." There were a few grumbles and protests around the room. "But I have done some military service. I know how to fight and how to defend myself. I also know how to follow orders."

"I have no doubt," Dee said. "And I am indebted. But how . . . ?"

"Suffice it to say for now that your good constable enlisted my services."

"Very good," Dee said. "And I am returning the favor by giving you the dubious honor of entering our motley force, led by a senescent general." There were more laughs as Dee's little joke alleviated the tension a bit.

"I have acquired many friends along the city streets in my years of service in Ch'ang-an," the constable said. "But you have been here only a few years, and though you thought yourself quite anonymous as you moved about the city on your daily walks bestowing good will and various kindnesses on the people you encountered, the people did not forget you. It was not necessary to tell them why you were arrested. The details were unnecessary complexities. Suffice it to say, Magistrate, that they trusted you. They do not trust much else. They are aware that great corruption hides in high places. Very high places."

"But such an enormous crowd of people," Dee marveled, thinking of the fight, the throngs on the street, the funeral cortege. "And at such short notice!"

"You have many, many friends in the eastern market and the alleys," the hunchback said. "Besides, isn't it true that it is a condition of humanity that any break from the tedium of the day is most welcome? Any opportunity for frolic and celebration, especially at the expense of the authorities!"

"Don't tell me that the funeral was play-acting too," Dee said. "It was much too real."

"No," the baker said sadly. "You are right. It was quite real. You have already met my youngest child—the one who brought you the pastries."

"No!" Dee said. "Please do not tell me . . . !"

"No, no, Magistrate. He is quite well. I had to promise him the Rabbit in the Moon to prevent him from sneaking from the house to join me. No. The funeral was for his cat. A gray-

and-white alley cat with six toes on each of his front paws, so
that they resembled nothing so much as an oarsman's paddle.
A rangy, singularly intelligent and personable beast with dark
piercing green eyes. An extraordinary companion. An animal
with countless friends among the shopkeepers down the very
alley that came to your rescue. So you see . . . ?"

Dee laughed and nodded, thinking of a little dog many
years ago.

"I do indeed understand, Master Ling. We wish his soul
a happy journey." Then he turned his attention back to the
papers on the table. The hunchback bent forward attentively
while Dee ran his finger along one of the Serpentine Park's
winding roads and stopped it abruptly at a small circle indicating a cul-de-sac not far from an area near the southern gate
of the Vermilion Sparrow.

"This is where we are going, friends. Here." He pointed.
"The estate of the Sung family. I believe we will be receiving
our visitors there shortly." He lifted his head. No one uttered
a word. "Arm yourselves well. Isn't that what a general would
tell you now?" He shrugged apologetically. "I wish I could tell
you what you are arming yourselves against." Dee pushed his
bench back and stood as the room filled with murmurs and
purposeful bustle. "All I can tell you is what you already
know. We are probably in for something . . . ugly."

31

Loyang

The Empress lay beneath the inert body of the monk Hsueh
Huai-i and listened as his breathing slowed. He had been
breathing about as hard as if he had made a short dash up a
small flight of stairs. It was very different from their early days,
when he had first been enamored of her, and used to howl and
pant in his ecstasy while tremors shook his whole body, after
which he would grow miraculously hard again, and start all
over, relinquishing himself to her as a plaything with which
she could toy for hours if she wished, satisfying herself time
after time at her leisure.

A small flight of stairs, she thought with disdain, or perhaps across a modest courtyard. A not very impressive dash, barely enough to quicken his breathing. Her two pug dogs sat on the divan across the room panting noisily through their flattened noses; they had watched the proceedings with interest, long pink wet tongues curling from their open mouths. The whole thing had taken no more than a few minutes from beginning to end.

He had been absent from the palace for several weeks, and she had found herself anticipating his return with a growing appetite. During the evening meal, he had seemed a bit fatigued and distracted, but she had felt certain that she was making her desires known, and she had thought she had detected a gleam of response in his eye at least once. She had prepared herself with great care, anticipating his arrival with sly pleasure, but as soon as he had come to her chamber, he had begun to complain unbecomingly about the dogs, Spinning Top and Dragon Jaws.

I cannot stand the way they sit and stare like that, he had said. They are not staring, she had answered, they are merely interested in human activities. They are preparing for the time when they will be born as humans, she had added, trying to introduce a note of levity. Well, I do not like being *watched*, he had said coldly. And besides, their snorting makes me quite ill. It makes me lose my appetite. They are not snorting, she had snapped then; they are merely breathing. They cannot help the way they sound. It is the shape of their noses. Well, said he irritably, I cannot help that it makes me ill. They do not have to be in the room. Forget about them, she had said, and had begun to go to work on him with her tongue.

But he did not seem to be in the mood for subtlety tonight, and now she lay in a quiet fury at the entirely perfunctory manner in which he had attended to her. It had happened just a few times too many in the last year or so. She waited for a sign that he was going to stir, to rouse himself to further action.

His breathing grew suspiciously shallow and regular. Still she waited. Then his limbs twitched in the unmistakable manner of a body drifting into sleep, down into dreams; she felt his full relaxed dead weight lying on her now, heedless, unconscious, inanimate. She gave a mighty heave, pushing him off her, startling him to sudden wakefulness.

"What do you think I am? A chaise?" she said. "A piece of furniture?" One of the dogs gave a single excited yip, responding to the sharp anger in her voice. "Hush!" she shouted across the room at the animals.

"What is the matter with you?" he said groggily and irritably. "I am very tired."

"I am sure that you are," she said. "What with your travels and all. I am sure that you are quite worn out." She raised herself up on an elbow and spoke into his face. "But I am scarcely satisfied!"

Her face was close to his, but indistinct in the dim light. She waited for a response, but was annoyed to hear, after only a few moments, a gentle snore. Disgusted, she rolled over, extinguished the lamp, and prepared herself for sleep. It took her at least an hour to drift off, the dogs rooting and rustling on the divan across the room, while next to her, the great magician and holy man Hsueh Huai-i snored and smacked his lips, undisturbed, and far, far away from her.

"It is the women who are doing it to him," she said to her mother the next day as she sat at her dressing table.

"Yes," Madame Yang agreed. "I would venture to say that they are playing a role."

"Young women, eager maidens. I am sure that to him they resemble veritable orchards of peach trees groaning with dewy, unplucked fruit." She stared down into the black foreshortened muzzle of Spinning Top, who sat at her feet gazing up at her, brow wrinkled with incipient anxiety at her unhappy tone. The graphic image of a peach, pinkish, vulvate, and juicy, rose to her mind and freshened her anger.

She was speaking, of course, of the young women Hsueh Huai-i had been busy recruiting throughout the province for the newly rejuvenated Kuan-yin nunneries. It had been his special project, begun some months before. It had been his wish, he had said, to honor the Empress by increasing the ranks of the female faithful. He had given quite an impressive speech about his theories pertaining to the focus of divine energy through the feminine instrument in this era of the Holy Sovereign Mother, and how her position and authority would be exalted and magnified with each new female convert he brought into the fold. His name was known far and wide, of course, and wherever he went, to small towns or into the rich or poor enclaves of the city, daughters were offered—pressed upon him, actually—for his nunneries. Some parents, the more well-to-do ones, even offered "dowries" with the girls.

"And to them," she said to her mother, "he is godlike, infallible, irresistible."

"As he was to you once," her mother said.

"To me!" Wu cried. "You mean to you! Let us not forget who it was who first partook of his 'talents.'" She looked closely at her mother. "And how long has it been since he has paid *you* a visit?"

Her mother returned the look.

"I am much less concerned with such matters than you are," she replied. "I am nearly sixty-five years old, please remember."

"Feh," Wu snorted. "You say that when it is convenient for you to say it, when it is useful. But there is nothing in your manner or looks that would make you appear to be any older than I. In fact," she said, still looking closely at Madame Yang, "you appear to be younger than I. Yes, if anyone who did not know us saw us together, they would assume that I am the mother and you are the daughter. Whatever 'youth potions' he may actually have he must be using on you. I remember when the two of you stood there before me nattering on about how I was growing younger by the day. You know, of course, that I never believed any of it."

"You say that now, because it suits you to say it," her mother retorted. "But at the time, you gloried in the conceit of it. I know you too well." The rising perturbation in their voices caused Dragon Jaws to yip and whine. This set off Spinning Top, who joined in excitedly.

"Hush! And I mean it!" Wu cried admonishingly to the animals, who cowered and stared at her with their bulging eyes. "That was a performance only for your benefit," she said to her mother. "Yours, and his. I know *you* too well." She glared at her reflection in the glass. "I know *him* too well."

She picked up a sponge and began to dab cosmetic on her face from one of at least one hundred jars. She thought of the dead Nagaspa from so many years before; she even thought of her husband, Kaotsung. She remembered her gratitude when each of them had disappeared from her life at expedient moments, leaving her free to move into the embrace of whatever wondrous thing was being carried toward her by Fate, which had once seemed ever solicitous of her satisfaction.

That was the essence of what it was to be young, was it not? Fate moved toward you. Fate initiated the effort, carried the presents to your door, sought you, courted you with per-

sistence, stealth, charm, and determination. Never mind what
her face looked like in the mirrow now—that was not the true
measure of how old she had become. The true measure was
the extent to which Fate solicited her with gifts. Or, to put it
in a harsher sense, the extent to which she now had to entice
Fate, to remind it of her existence. Now the game was reversed,
there could be no denying it. She wondered abstractedly if this
process of Fate's losing interest was strictly a function of time.
What if, for instance, she could live for several hundred years
and show no outward signs at all of physical age? Would Fate
remain interested in her? Or would it move on to fresh prospects regardless of her appearance? Or had Fate lost interest
in her as soon as her flesh began to sag?

She smoothed the cosmetic over her cheeks and down her
neck, tilting her head so that her most favorable angles presented themselves. She could not recall the exact moment when
she had begun to do the "courting," but it had been going on
for quite some time now. All things were accomplished by
minute degrees, she knew, each gradation imperceptible. But
when enough of them had accumulated, worlds were transformed. Mountains were shaped, canyons carved in the earth,
or a young woman's smooth flawless face was transformed
into the face of a crone, and she was no longer desired by men,
and no longer drew the interest of Fate. She looked hard at
herself. She did not yet qualify as a crone. She would try, for
a while at least, to see if she still had the ability to entice Fate.
It might prove to be an interesting stage of life.

She looked at her mother's reflection in the glass, sitting
behind her, watching her impassively.

"Do you know, Mother," she said to Madame Yang, "that
I sincerely believe that you are a younger woman than I, and
that you will outlive me?"

"Nonsense," her mother replied, but Wu thought she saw
something in the older woman's eyes that contradicted what
she spoke aloud.

With her mother assisting her, she had applied her cosmetics with the care of a performer in a Po-t'o dance panto-
mime. The wrinkles around her eyes and mouth had been
filled in and smoothed over like cracks in wood; then a layer
of fine white was applied over her entire face, with a dusting
of soft powder over that. She finished by painting extraordinary moth-brows on her high forehead, with deep blue shad-

ows between the brow and her eyelids and delicate black lines
edging her eyes. Her hair, still gleaming and dark, was swept
back and piled high.

She had arranged the lamps around the room for the
softest, most flattering light. Velvety shadows filled the corners, while the golden pools illuminated her treasures and exquisite little objects, all of it strategically placed and designed
to enhance the centerpiece of all of this rare beauty, her own
person. Spinning Top and Dragon Jaws sat on the chaise with
anxious expressions of canine solicitude while their mistress
went about the finishing touches to her face, her clothing, her
room. She shooed the dogs into the anteroom and shut the
door.

The monk was due at any time. He had drunk a great
deal tonight, but had agreed to come and visit her. She felt
strong, like the vessel of Fate that she had always been. She
looked at her reflection with satisfaction, adjusting the lamps
on either side of the mirror. No. Fate was not through with her
yet.

"You *hide* under these paints," Hsueh Huai-i said, sweeping an unsteady hand along her dressing table, knocking over
row upon row of bottles and jars. Some clattered and crashed
noisily to the floor, scattering their spiky shards across the tiles;
others spilled their contents onto the polished rosewood surface of the table, sending forth their exotic commingled odors.

"Hiding the creeping age that crawls across your face . . .
woman." He had never used such a bold form of address before. "All of this . . . *detritus* is quite useless, hm?" the monk
said, swaying drunkenly, then folding his hands as if there
were nothing more to be said. He stumbled backward against
the table, upsetting it further. "Excuse me," he said gallantly
to the piece of furniture, righting himself and it and regaining
his balance.

Wu made no response to the stinging insults. She kept
her back to him. Carefully, she picked up an unbroken bottle
of Hsueh's own famous cosmetic from where it had rolled to
her feet across the floor. She watched him in the mirror as he
stretched his arms and turned toward the door, as if he were
quite finished and about to leave. She turned and flung the
bottle with force and accuracy, hitting him solidly between the
shoulder blades. He flinched and stopped where he stood, but
did not turn around. She knew that it must have hurt.

"You are a pig," she said quietly. "A lying, fornicating, charlatan pig."

"And what was that little childish outburst for, my dear?" Hsueh's tone, even in his slurred drunkenness, balanced precariously between hurt and insolence. He faced her now with his hands raised in a gesture that indicated either appeasement or that he was prepared to ward off more flying bottles.

"And what was *that* little childish outburst for, my dear?" Wu said, mocking him, pointing to the mess he had just made of her dressing table.

"I was only doing you a favor," Hsueh said, his gaze drifting down to the mess of broken bottles and spilled paints and creams. "I was only ridding you of useless products. Why distract yourself any further from the truth, Madame Emperor, Avalokitesvara-Buddha Maitreya Incarnate?"

Wu threw something else. The monk stepped aside. It crashed against the far wall.

"Useless, are they? It was *you* who gave them to me, *you* who promised me that these 'secret' preparations could reverse age."

"I lied," he said flatly.

"Yes, of course," she said. "I already know that. Thank you."

"You are a god. Or is it goddess? I cannot remember. . . . In any case, you shouldn't need cosmetics." He raised his eyebrows. "Your life spans infinite *kalpas* of time." He made a broad, splendid arc in front of him with his hands, nearly losing his balance. "Another birth, another incarnation, and . . . it is magic! The lines vanish! Or have you forgotten how to do it?"

"I have forgotten nothing that you have told me," she said calmly. "How could I? You rant incessantly. You are the great inflated Hsueh Huai-i. Monk! Teacher! Magician!" She pronounced each name with increasing disdain. "Lama from the mysterious mountainous west! How could you possibly be wrong?" Her voice was mocking, dangerous, haughty.

"Alas!" The word dripped off the monk's tongue. "How could I?" He paused and rolled his eyes to the ceiling, shaking his head in chagrin. "I failed. I did not predict that you would age so quickly."

She ignored him. She had no intention of letting the drunken fraud get the better of her.

"Or so badly," he added. Still she ignored him. "Such

remedies, such palliatives," he went on, pointing to the shattered bottles, "can reverse, figuratively speaking, the course of streams, madame." He spread his hands and fluttered his fingers lyrically. "And perhaps the flow of rivers. But stem the tides of *oceans*?" he said, making a sweeping gesture of defeat. Pleased with himself, he squeezed his eyes shut, swaying while he contemplated the simple beauty of his metaphors. "Madame is . . . over fifty now," he said almost as an afterthought. "Tsk . . . tsk . . . tsk. Time certainly has not been good to her."

"No, Lama. Time has been very good to me, and it is about to get better," Wu said after a moment. "It is you who have aged. What you press against me is as limp as all of your ideas. Limp and dribbling is the very best that you can manage. Of course, it is understandable, overtaxed as you are these days, doing the work of a much younger man—"

"Enough!" he said, holding up a warning hand. It seemed that she had struck a sensitive nerve here. "Enough of that. Do you want to know what it is, what our . . . problem is?" he asked, approaching her, loomingly and menacingly. "Do you? I will tell you." She waited. He stopped in front of where she sat. He knelt down and leaned close, moving his nose about and wrinkling it in disgust. "It is the smell," he whispered. "It is the smell that puts me off."

"The smell?" she said, incipient rage at the nature of his implied insult beginning to move through her. "What smell?" she enunciated, glaring back at him, challenging him, their faces inches apart.

"You know what smell," he said. "I have told you many times. Have you noticed that I have been giving you more and more perfumes lately? Well, this is why," he said, putting his hand down into the sticky mess of a broken bottle. He lifted it to his nose and inhaled deeply. "Even with all of this on my hand, I can still smell it everywhere in this room."

"Smell what, Lama?" she said dangerously. Hsueh rubbed his hand on the back of Wu's couch. He then lifted his fingers to his nose, pretending to inhale, and grimaced. "Smell *what*?" she repeated through her clenched teeth.

He sighed and exhaled.

"The dogs," he said at last. "Your snorting, bug-eyed dogs. I cannot stomach the stinking dogs. They leave their odor everywhere . . . like soiled clothing." She relaxed a degree or two and leaned back. He smelled his fingers again. The dogs were barking and growling outside the bedchamber now, excited by the raised voices within. "They leave their sour smell on everything. The bed. The couches. The chairs. The quilts. The rugs. And on you, madame," he said. "I cannot put a bit of food into my mouth anymore without being choked by nausea. And madame expects an excited lover."

"Considering the possibilities, Lama, madame expects nothing." She smiled, her anger giving her strength and clarity, like a tonic. She was his complete and equal adversary. "But may I suggest that this nausea you claim to experience is most probably the result of an illness known as *gluttony*? You are catching the ill scent of your own carrion-filled guts, Lama. Of course it is everywhere. Of course you smell it on the furniture, and on your hands. Of course you cannot escape it. And it is not mere gluttony of the mouth," she said, lowering her eyes to his groin. "I can smell something on you," she said, curling her lips back and inhaling. "Something that makes my dogs smell like jasmine blossoms. I smell *women* on you, monk."

"Madame will get rid of her repulsive dogs and she will have her lover back."

"Madame will not get rid of her dogs. And perhaps madame does not *want* her lover back."

Wu could see that Hsueh pretended not to hear her last remark. She continued, "My dogs are faithful little friends. Quite unlike one arrogant charlatan who deludes himself that he is a holy man. They do not pretend that they are learned masters of divine wisdom—though if *you* were able to become a great lama, then so perhaps will they—*Dog Boy*," she said, taunting him with his childhood Tibetan name, which he had divulged to her once in an unguarded moment long ago—the name he had spent years living down, he told her. She laughed. "Perhaps you and my dogs are brothers under the skin."

She was touching raw nerves. She knew it, and it felt good. She loved to tell him that he was a sham. Despite all of his native cleverness, he was sensitive on the point of his legitimacy, his credentials. She watched him struggle to let her ultimate insult go for the moment.

"I do not know of a single animal, either domestic or wild, that makes such awful noises when it eats," Hsueh said, trying to keep his own line of insult going. "Even a tiger, or a bear, ripping its prey apart, could not produce such sounds as those dogs. But I suppose that is why they are such perfect companions for you, madame."

"They are better sounds than the ones coming from *your* mouth, monk."

"Of course, it is your Imperial prerogative, madame. If you wish to maintain such repulsive pets in the Imperial throne room over my guiding presence . . ."

"Thank you, monk. You make my choice so very easy."

"It is, of course, your Imperial prerogative . . ."

"And it has also been my Imperial prerogative to maintain a vainglorious fool by the name of Hsueh Huai-i," she snapped bitterly. "Isn't that true, monk? The man who claims to be the mouthpiece of the Buddha, wallowing in his conceit and self-delusion. If I am the Bodhisattva Avalokitesvara-Kuan-yin, and also the Future Buddha Maitreya reincarnate, the bearer of the New Age," she challenged, fixing him with narrow ominous slits of eyes, "then just *who* in the name of *hell* are *you*?"

Hsueh stood and turned his back to her. She had got at his vanity, the weakest point in his character. Good! Let him cook in his juices, she thought. Now that she had him, it felt wonderful. She had never known a feeling quite so wonderful. He had become a nuisance, really, a vainglorious nuisance way out of proportion to his usefulness. They all did eventually, she thought with some regret.

Hsueh turned suddenly and fixed her with a look so fierce and alien that it made her draw back. This was not even the same person. He had changed from the vile, sloppily drunk, rude and insolent monk into something else. Though his entire face reddened with anger, the pits of his eyes conveyed nothing. They were black and expressionless—empty holes to a soulless interior. It was by far the worst aspect of him that she had ever seen.

"I will tell you just who I am," Hsueh declared in a hoarse and menacing voice. "I will tell you." He took hold of Wu by the shoulders. When she attempted to break his grip and rise from the couch, he pushed her back down. She forced herself up again, prying his grip from her shoulders, but he slid his hands down her arms and took hold of her wrists and twisted them behind her. He pushed her over so that she was bent backward, but still not all the way down. He gave a brutal push. She fell backward onto the couch and he lay on top of her looking into her face.

"Yes, I will tell you who I am." He raised himself up so that he was leaning on his long arms. He was very serious now. What he was about to tell her was no longer part of their game of hurled invectives and insults, she knew. His menacing tone told her that he wanted her to believe what he was going to say.

"I am the pathway, the guide that brings *Them* through *you*. That allows *Him* passage to incarnate in your inferior female form."

He was smiling again. He bent his arms now, partially lowering his weight down onto her. "Is *that* what you want?" He pressed his hardness against her thighs. She seemed to yield for a moment, relaxing her hips and letting out a deep breath. "You would not insult me as you have been doing," he said, "if you only knew."

"If I only knew what, Lama?" She moved her leg up slightly to accommodate him.

"You would not say these untrue things to me, madame . . . you would not make these pathetic accusations." The danger in his eyes was gone, replaced by sadness and hurt. It was too late for that to be convincing, Wu thought. "If madame had any idea whatever of what I have done for her benefit so that she might rule as the glorious Avalokitesvara incarnate, the protector of the Dharma . . ."

"What you have done for my benefit?" Her voice was soft now, and responsive, her words delivered in the cooing tone of a lover. She stretched her other leg out as he pushed his hardness onto her belly. She brought her knees up on either side of him, pressing, closing around him.

"You could not possibly know . . ." he said. He smiled, looking like his old fulsome and self-satisfied self. He bared his teeth in an obnoxious way. Wu's knees pulled back ever so slightly as Hsueh teased her with his secret. " . . . what I am doing for your benefit so that you, Avalokitesvara reborn, might rule in the New Age of the Law." He lifted himself up from her a little bit and shifted his weight, preparing to settle himself into a more advantageous position. Wu could feel that the monk had gone very hard now. He had stiffened like an eager young lover for the first time in many months. That was good. His passion would throw him off his guard. His breathing was shallow and ragged, full of sexual urgency.

"And I will tell you what *I* have done for *you*, monk," Wu said softly. "Are you listening?" Propped precariously on one arm, Hsueh squinted at her. He had begun to drool slightly, unconsciously, from the corner of his mouth with the effort of struggling with one hand to yank free the drawstring of his silken trousers and to push them down. He was huffing unpleasantly now. Wu could smell the sticky sweet wine on his breath as he thrust his pelvis at her in quick unromantic jabs while still clumsily attempting to free his member, whose stiffness had snagged itself in his trousers.

He was now two minds that would not cooperate, she thought. Monk and cock were not part of the same person. They were two drunken lusting partners fighting for the same prize, forcing their way rudely through the bedroom doorway in the same crowded moment. His stupid urgency would make it that much easier for her. He arched his back, spanning above her like a canal bridge; he tore at his trousers and they gave at last. Wu looked down between their bodies; the glistening stretched purple head had finally emerged over the waistband—but he was already in full ejaculation.

The boisterous, pompous, arrogant, stupid fool, Wu thought. He dripped onto the satiny fabric of her dressing gown; he had not even attempted to raise her clothes above her knees. Then he began to sink down onto her in spent satisfaction.

Wu's target was clear. With speed and accuracy she kicked up with her left knee. Hsueh howled, doubled over, and rolled to the floor. It was too much for the dogs; the door flew open and in they raced, adding their high-pitched barks to the monk's outraged song of pain. Hsueh writhed about on the floor, hands lovingly cupping his middle, moaning invectives, as the dogs surrounded him, leaping, bounding, barking in a frenzy of excitement while Wu laughed and laughed until the tears rolled down her face.

"You see, monk, they only want to join the fun," Wu said, weak with hilarity, leaning over from her couch to study the spectacle. The dogs bounced and bounded, their yapping and yelping building to earsplitting pitch. It was the sound the monk most hated. And precisely for that reason, it was music to her ears at that moment.

"Aren't they cute, monk?" She watched as he struggled to his feet, kicking at the dogs, who charged, feinted, retreated, and barked and barked and barked. "*Now!*" she bellowed, silencing the dogs abruptly. "*Get out of here, Monk. I have had quite enough of you!*"

"If you knew . . ." he gasped, but she did not let him go on.

"OUT, YOU DAMNED FRAUD!"

Then he was gone, the door slamming behind him. She put her hand to her throat. It was raw from shouting. She realized that it had been many, many years since she had shouted, without restraint, with the full force of her fury behind it. It felt good.

And she realized that this was the first time she had ever shouted at him.

"But it is natural for men to be . . . forgetful, inattentive," her mother said. "You should not assume that his behavior is a reflection upon *you*."

Wu did not answer. She bent down and tickled the upturned belly of one of her dogs.

"It is their nature," Madame Yang added. "You can scarcely blame him for it. Do you blame your dogs for barking and scratching?" This made Wu smile. Madame Yang smiled, too. It *was* a good choice of words. "His . . . dalliances with the young nuns are of no concern to me. I do not think that they should be of any concern to you, either." She waited for a reply.

Wu continued to rub the dog's stomach. She picked a flea from the hair with her long nails, examined it briefly, crushed it, and flicked it away. She resumed her rubbing and stroking. The dog writhed ecstatically, its long tongue lolling.

"Perhaps his sexual performance *is* sagging," Madame Yang said. "Perhaps it is the weight of responsibility. Responsibility *we* have put on him." She waited. "It is a delicate thing for a man," she continued. "Far more delicate than women think. Women think a man should be always ready, always able. It is not such a simple thing. And you—you should be less concerned with such matters yourself, at your age."

At this, Wu shot her mother a look. Madame Yang sighed.

"I agree that he has been headstrong of late," Madame Yang said then. "And his behavior less than exemplary. And his sense of self-importance perhaps a bit overinflated. But he is amusing and innovative. He is inventive. He keeps us aware of the infinite possibilities." Wu raised a thoughtful eyebrow at this. "And he works so well with Historian Shu," she added.

The second pug had come around to Madame Yang, plopping itself down and rolling over, hoping for some of the treatment its brother was getting. She bent over and tickled it while its legs flailed in the air.

"You have just named it, Mother," Wu said, speaking at last. "The one aspect of the Tibetan I cannot excuse," she declared, shaking her head, using the disdainful term that had lately taken the place of his name in her vocabulary. "He works well with Shu only when it serves him to do so. In private, he tells me that he merely tolerates the 'little dog-faced bastard.' He makes fun of Historian Shu. He mocks him, and holds him in contempt."

"Could this not be seen as a matter of personalities?" Madame Yang offered. "The inevitable friction between the energies of two highly creative men?" Her daughter merely looked at her.

"It is Shu who has reestablished the glory of this family," Wu said flatly. "Not the Tibetan." She sat back, ignoring the dog that still rolled imploringly at her feet. She stared down at the animal. The dog righted itself and looked intently back into her eyes. "If the Tibetan speaks in such a way about Shu," she said, still looking at the dog, "then what do you suppose he says about us?" Now she looked at her mother. "Father would not be pleased. Not pleased at all."

Madame Yang sighed resignedly and nodded. Lovingly, she tucked the second pug's wrinkled head between her knees and began to scratch it vigorously behind the ears.

Daughter was right, of course. Her husband was not pleased-and had, in fact, already expressed his displeasure to her. Madame Yang had not said anything, but had waited. Now she had done what she could to defend the Tibetan. She had carried out her obligation, for the sake of their old association, their old friendship. But it was out of her hands now.

Her husband had put it well and clearly. Having transcended the limitations of the corporeal state, he was able to see, simultaneously, the beginning and the end. Some ends, he had said to her, were simply more inevitable than others.

32

The family, with the exception of the old grandmother, had not offered Dee and his deputies the slightest resistance. When the famed magistrate Dee Jen-chieh had presented himself at their door with the news that they were almost certainly the next wealthy Ch'ang-an family to be exterminated, they had hastily packed a few possessions in hampers, and under cover of early darkness, withdrawn for a relative's home in the mountains, taking the argumentative old lady and their servants and gardeners and groundskeepers with them.

Dee, with heavy padding under his robes to make him resemble the portly departed head of the household, sat in the man's chair at the dining table raising a ladleful of soup to his lips. To his left sat a man who could only have been his elderly father, and next to him, the old man's brother accepted food from a tray offered by a servant. Farther down the table, the son of the household and his wife picked at their plates; opposite them, the son's mother and bent, ancient grandmother ate, the elder woman displaying an appetite uncharacteristically robust for an old lady.

Dee gave his hunchbacked constable an admonishing look.

" 'Mother,' " he said in a discreet voice, "your excessive appetite is most unbecoming. I have never known you to display such ill manners at the table." The old lady gave a weak smile and selected a daintier portion with the next dip of her chopsticks. Dee looked at the others, trying to offer reassurance with his glance after his one attempt at levity on this tense evening; the constable seemed to be the only one with any enthusiasm for his food tonight. The "steward" moved around the table, offering the tray.

"Eat," Dee encouraged them. "You may as well enjoy it. It will help to calm you."

"I would eat," said his "father" to his left, "if the food

520

were not scorched and greasy." Dee took a mouthful, considering.

"I find it edible, if uninspired," he said. "I am sure our lieutenant and his assistants are doing their best in the kitchen. Let us not criticize them too harshly, or they may become disheartened."

"We do not want them to become disheartened," said the hunchback. "Because if they become disheartened, so might we," he said, ducking his homely head to take another bite. There were a few wan smiles from the disguised men around the table.

In other parts of the house and grounds, Dee's heavily armed men, in the guise of servants, gardeners, and even lady's maids, moved about with studied nonchalance, passing occasionally in front of a lit window or doorway, ostensibly carrying out the normal business of running a large home. At the gates and here and there within the walls of the estate, Dee's men also posed as hired guards patrolling the grounds, a precaution taken by virtually every wealthy family now in this suburb of Ch'ang-an. More men were sequestered—in the servants' quarters, in the gardener's shed, in the kitchen area. The people in the dining hall ate, hands and heads gesticulating and moving conversationally, their silhouettes visible through the silk shades over the windows.

After the meal, Dee retired to the householder's study. Dee and his men had found themselves becoming strangely formal with one another as the night deepened and the roles they were playing seemed to grow around them and they knew that soon they would be going to different parts of the house. As the hunchback in his old grandmother clothes had bade the other good night and prepared to withdraw, Dee had found himself looking solicitously after the diminutive bent figure retreating down the hallway, for all the world as if there were a frail elderly lady beneath those embroidered robes and not a hard little weasel of a man with eyes and ears as sharp as an animal's, and quite capable of looking after himself.

In his host's study, which was separated from the rest of the house by a long hallway, Dee shut the door most of the way, leaving it ajar behind him as a precautionary measure. He stood in the semidarkness for a moment, listening, breathing the interesting smells of another man's private world. Those he discerned were similar to those of his own study, but the proportions were different: sandalwood, lamp oil, old furniture, paper, a not unpleasant hint of mildew and damp. He stood for another moment more. The room was quite uninhabited, he was sure; he felt no other presence displacing the air around him. If this were his own study, he would know his way in the dark; his desk would be over there, he thought, visualizing in the darkness, and his chaise over there, with a window behind it.

He groped for a moment and found a lamp and a flint. The vision in his mind's eye of his own study was immediately displaced in the flare of light. He saw right away that this man, a landed aristocrat, was much more orderly than he. The desk was neat, without the jumble of papers and brushes apt to be found on Dee's desk. There were volumes on the shelves, but they had a disused look about them, as if perhaps the man had inherited them from a dead relative and had put them up out of sentiment, but never took one down to look at.

The rugs, Dee noted, were rare and of an exceptionally fine quality. So were the brush paintings on the walls. Dee moved the lamp closer and inspected these works. He recognized the watermark of the great painter Ku K'ai-chih, and was more than a little bit impressed. The man had excellent taste. He moved to the shelves to look at some objects there, and smiled. There was a small, but obviously genuine, temple carving of an *apsaras*. Without a doubt, the piece had once been part of the contraband that had flowed into the Empire by way of the canals of Yangchou. No doubt it had been through many hands since then on its long journey to Ch'ang-an and this wealthy man's study, where it now resided as a curiosity. Quite possibly, this very piece had once been held in the hands of the old Transport Minister himself, murdered so many years before, whose death had occupied so much of the young Dee Jen-chieh's time, energy, and thought.

Dee carefully picked up the *apsaras* and looked at her delicately carved face. He brushed his fingers over the swelling curves of her breasts and hips, trying to conjure the spell that had come over him so long ago. He remembered how the carved wood had practically turned into smooth brown skin under his touch; he remembered the exotic foreign smell of the packing material in the crates. He remembered how the carved ornaments the *apsarases* wore had seemed to come to life too, like their skin; he remembered how his heightened senses had all but perceived the flash and refraction of rubies and emeralds. And he recalled the stirring and gathering heat in his own body.

He looked at her. She was exquisite, but she was only wood. The power and spirit of the artist who had made the piece were definitely there, but locked in repose, reserved for now in the smooth, still wood, to be released again, Dee supposed, by the heat of a much younger man's hand.

And it was just as well, he thought, replacing her on the shelf. He also remembered how that moment of bewitchment, that minuscule lapse in attention, had nearly cost him his life. And what became of you? he thought, recalling the malignant child with whom he had grappled in such deadly ernest. Are you still alive? Musing, Dee picked up some other small pieces. He had never forgotten the feel of the boy's hard, dangerous little bones, impressed on his memory forever during their few seconds of contact. He remembered how it had been, feeling those small child's bones, like those of his own sons, and holding himself back because of it from using his full strength. That, of course, had been his mistake. It seemed at this moment that he could remember those scrawny bones even more clearly than the contours of his wives' bodies.

He glanced behind himself at the still room. The circumstances were awfully similar, and he had vowed not to make the same mistake twice in one lifetime. But the room was quite empty, and Dee was alone. He went and sat in the wealthy man's chair, and allowed another fantasy a bit of free play. This one was only for distraction and amusement, hardly strong or compelling enough to qualify as a spell.

Dressed in the man's clothes, sitting in his chair, and looking at his possessions all around him, he felt himself become the man. He imagined that he felt his well-worn attitudes of complacency and satisfaction, duty and honor, and all the rest of it. But another feeling made him stand abruptly and resume his pacing about the room: it had been a sense, very definite, but lasting for only one or two heartbeats, or something approaching, something moving toward him. He recalled the readiness with which the man and his family had vacated their home; it was as if Dee had just now caught a whiff of some premonitory sense that had been in the air in this house for some time. Quite abruptly, he did not wish to be alone anymore tonight. He wanted the company of the others. He lit a small candle before extinguishing the lamp's flame, and left the study.

On his way through the house, Dee spoke in a low voice to the men he knew were posted here and there, greeting them, making little jokes; he did it to encourage them, but mainly, he wanted them to know who was approaching.

He found the little grandmother-constable sitting in the darkness of the old lady's quarters with one of the other men. The lamps were extinguished so that any eyes watching from outside would see nothing out of the ordinary. The hunchback had heard him coming, and was waiting for him in the doorway.

"Walk with me," Dee said.

They moved down the corridor, guided by the dim flicker of Dee's candle. They were silent for a few moments before the constable spoke.

"It was most disquieting," he said. "Sitting in the old grandmother's room, I imagined that I felt what it was like to have lived for eighty-seven years. I felt light and frail. I could imagine what it was to need only two or three hours' sleep and a bird's portion of food to sustain me. And I knew what it was to sit awake deep into the night while the rest of the household slept soundly. I understand now why old people do not sleep much; it is a waste of time to them, for there will be sleep enough in the tomb, so close at hand. And I felt . . . quite unafraid. Unafraid of death in any form."

Indeed, the old woman of the house had expressed her desire to stay in her own quarters, and would have, had her son not insisted that she leave with the rest of the family. Let them kill me in my bed, I do not care, she had grumbled. I welcome it. Quite different from Dee's own mother, with her tenacious grip on life, her lurid imagination and ready apprehension.

"Quite so, Constable," Dee said. "Wearing this man's clothes has been almost like stepping into his spirit. He, unlike his mother, is not at all ready for death."

Walking through the dark, quiet house, Dee wondered what the others were experiencing—the men playing the roles of the old father and his brother; the young "husband" and "wife," his own "wife." Dee had an odd sensation, almost of impropriety—as if they were intruding on people's lives, sniffing about in their closets and cupboards, handling their personal effects. He had had to suppress an urge, while in the householder's study, to go through his papers.

Dee and the hunchback moved through the entire house,

acquainting themselves more fully with its layout, murmuring greetings to the men waiting in the darkness. Earlier, Dee had done his best to inform them of what they might expect, and had watched their faces as he explained his theory to them more fully; their eyes had told him that if he had been anyone else but Magistrate Dee Jen-chieh, they would have dismissed him as a madman, and his theory as a malign tale. And he knew that with darkness and the peculiar pervasive spell, there was little danger of anyone's falling asleep tonight. Eyes and ears in every corner of the estate were open, awake, alert. They had become the quarry.

Dee and the constable retired to the drawing room after they had walked the house and grounds. With only the one candle burning, they sat and talked into the night hours. Dee was fascinated to learn something of the little hunchback's life, of his impoverished boyhood in the western wards of the great city. "I was a comely child," the constable said, "with a straight, strong back, until I was about eight years old, when my spine began to grow in on itself like the shell of a snail. The hump pulled one leg up with it," he said, indicating his short right limb, "and seemed to use up all the vitality left in my body for growth—for after the age of twelve or so, I scarcely grew any larger, as you can see. I spent my childhood thieving and living by my wits. When my hump was finished growing, when it had twisted and fused itself, I found it easier to earn a living, for now I could simply beg on the streets.

"One day when I was about eleven years old a gentleman invited me to come to his home; out of curiosity, and because my parents had abandoned me, I went. I stayed for three years. During that time I was fed well, and clothed; all I had to do in return was be an entertaining little monkey for the man's guests, for he was very rich. Occasionally, he and his wife would have me take my shirt off so that his guests could examine my hump and touch it if they wanted to. My body may have been small, but I was growing into a man inside, and I soon tired of the gentleman and his wife, so one night I simply left. After my return to the streets, I received a reward from a constable once for furnishing him with a clue that helped him solve a killing in the neighborhood. That was when I understood what my vocation in life was. I apprenticed to that constable, found that I was quite brilliant at insinuating myself into the fringes of a crowd, a small hiding place, or a conversation. And so, here I am, privileged to work with the great Magistrate Dee. I even found a woman who was not bothered by my hump. I have a son who is a full two heads taller than I."

"I have sons," Dee said, "though I have not seen them for many years."

"They must be fine young men," the hunchback said.

"I hope that they are," Dee replied.

Dee told the constable about his life in Yangchou. "There are moments in our lives we never forget," he said, "which we can recall in perfect, living detail, no matter how many years elapse. I can, right now, at this moment, remember perfectly the taste of the canal water that filled my mouth and nose and that I swallowed in copious amounts one dark night. Never mind that the false abbot's arm was locked around my neck and his full weight trying in earnest to push me under. The *taste* of that black, foul, stinking water in my mouth is what comes back to me. I think that I have retained a permanent touch of queasiness from that moment on. I do not think that since then I have ever quite enjoyed my food as thoroughly as I might, for instance, or taken a sip of wine without tasting canal water in it."

They talked for many hours. At a certain point, Dee stood up to stretch. Though no light was visible yet, the heavy darkness of night seemed to have thinned. He noticed his limbs aching in an irrelevant way, and he knew: no one was coming. This had not been the night.

Unless they were in the wrong house.

The constable was saying something about a day and a night he had had to spend hiding in a crate in order to apprehend some particularly vicious criminals, but Dee scarcely heard him. He was thinking of the terrible possibility of the dawn revealing a slaughtered household elsewhere in this suburb. Had another family died while Dee and his men, close by but oblivious, sat awake all night in their borrowed clothes?

He excused himself. He went down the hallway. Now there was a definite graying of the blackness visible through the high windows. Another possibility had occurred to him—absurd, crazy, implausible—but he had to satisfy himself.

He found one of the rooms where men were stationed, waiting. Softly, he called out names.

To his relief, they answered immediately. It was the same with the other rooms he checked. The impossible thought that had come to him was that perhaps while he and the hunchback had sat talking, the killers had entered the house and silently put all of his men to death. Of course, they could not have done it. His men were not old grandmothers and overweight aristocrats. But the possibility had been real enough to Dee to send him to each room to see for himself. The killers possessed what seemed to be preternatural stealth. Had they not done their work in the other houses without disturbing the servants?

He found his notes and papers where he had carefully cached them the night before. He took them to the householder's study for a careful review. Now he had to satisfy himself that his calculations had been correct.

An hour or so later, during which time the room filled with washed-out light, Dee had exhaustively pored through his notes again, the census map of the city, the sutras, and the rest of it. He had found nothing to suggest that this was not the right house. And it had to be at least close to the right time. That was the more indefinite factor—the time. They had best summon their reserves of patience, and prepare themselves for more waiting.

Of course, the news of Dee's escape would be all over the city. He had thought of the possibility that the killers' plans might be altered because of it, but decided that that was unlikely, for two reasons—one having to do with the nature and purpose of the murders, the logic of which he believed he had penetrated. The second reason was a simple matter of time and distance: it was unlikely that orders to cancel or change the plans would be coming from anywhere but Loyang. News of his escape would have to travel the three hundred *li*—at least a day's journey by the fastest messenger—and the response would take the same amount of time to travel back to Ch'ang-an.

Despite the review of his calculations, he discreetly sent out at dawn one of his men, posing as a servant on his way to the market, with instructions to wend his way circuitously to the magistrate's offices and ask if there was any news. The man went, and returned in an hour.

Nothing, he reported. No news.

Dee told his men that they would have to sleep, at least for a few hours. It was morning now, the time of day he deemed least likely for a visitation. We will rest in shifts throughout the morning and afternoon, he said to them. I and some others will stay awake until midday. The rest of you sleep. Then it will be our turn. At least we will be refreshed enough so that if we see anything, we will know that it is real and not some figment our exhausted minds have manufactured.

It was a fine morning, clear and sunny, but Dee felt quite immune to its pleasantness. His night of wakefulness had left his senses raw; he felt that he was seeing how insubstantial was that phenomenon which people called a sense of well-being. A fragile thing, really, a palliative provided by our brains so that we might cope and not go mad every single day of our lives, he thought; one night without sleep, and the thinness of the illusion becomes quickly and unpleasantly apparent. He felt defenseless against his regrets, at the mercy of his fears and sorrows. They were being turned loose like a pack of hungry dogs who have found the gate carelessly unlocked.

But now, of course, was not the time. He stood in the double doors leading from the householder's study. It was chilly this morning, but considerably milder than it had been yesterday. The garden lay before him, tranquil and beautiful even though brown and dry from the recent cold. Undoubtedly, the master of this house would be likely to take a walk through his garden on such a morning, so Dee stepped outside.

The sun warmed his shoulders and back. The combination of his fatigue and the bright light made him feel oddly disconnected from what was around him. He moved slowly, conserving his energy, following the stone pathway. The morning sun shone through ragged leftover spider webs strung with drops of dew; the ground was still damp in the cold shady spots. The temptation to crawl into one of these little bowers and curl up and sleep like an animal was strong indeed, but he kept walking. Like the house, the garden was laid out with taste and elegance. Here, a graceful curved archway invited one to step down another path; in the other direction, a little carp-filled pond and a stone bench beckoned.

He looked at the archway. A motion, as slight as a peripheral thought, had caught his eye. At first, he thought that he must have imagined it, but as he was about to turn away, he saw it again. He stepped forward. It was a single very long black hair, being lifted by the breeze, catching the light intermittently. He detached it from where it had been snagged on an irregularity in the surface of the curved wood of the archway. It was of medium coarseness, and very, very long, much longer than he had thought at first. Holding one end in each hand, he had to spread his arms wide in order to extend the hair to its full length. He rolled the shaft of the hair between his fingers, testing it. He had never seen a hair this long.

His fatigue and distraction had vanished. He looked down at the flagstones under his feet, but they were dry and devoid of footprints. He looked at the meandering path leading away from him through the archway; if one followed that path, it would circle all the way around through the garden and eventually lead back to where he stood now. He began to walk.

When he had gone most of the way around, and had seen nothing more, he found himself approaching the vicinity of the decorative little carp pond with its bench. He went down the steps diverging from the main path. He meant to sit on that bench for a moment and gather his thoughts. He still held the hair pinched between his fingers.

He sat, and gazed into the water, but he did not remain sitting for long. There, only a few paces from him, at the point where a little stream fed the pond, the moist ground held an impression. He crouched down, and bent over it intently. The size and curvature were unpleasantly familiar to him: it was a single hoofprint, and it was fresh. He looked down at the hair in his fingers. No, he had never seen a hair that long before.

Except from the tail of a horse.

But this hair was not of sufficient coarseness. Or was it? He rolled it again between his fingers.

A disagreeable sensation that the back of his neck was exposed and vulnerable made Dee rise slowly from his crouching position and survey the bright garden around him. The tranquil landscape was transformed—what had been peaceful and inviting only moments ago was now dense and foreboding. The pleasant autumnal colors of the garden preparing itself for winter, alive with birdsong and the fresh scent of morning, may as well have been a dark, urine-smelling alley in a questionable neighborhood of the city in the dead of night.

With the chilly, exposed feeling on the back of his neck prodding him at every step, he hurried back along the path to the house.

He knew there would be no sleep for him at all today. He had told the hunchback what he had seen in the garden, and they had conferred in low voices in the householder's study. They have been here, and have determined that we are imposters, Dee had declared to his friend. They have changed their plan and are going to strike somewhere else tonight.

Not necessarily, the hunchback had said. Who knows? Perhaps they are in the habit of making a preliminary foray before they strike. No doubt they were watching us through the windows, just as we thought they might. A family, going about its business.

But I only saw the one print, Dee had said. There were no others, human or animal. Someone came alone, on a horse. If there were others, they were most careful to stay on the dry flagstones. Why would they take the risk of entering the grounds, and then not do what they came to do? And how did they do it, without being seen or heard? Our men were awake all night. No one reported anything. There could only have been the one. And why would he come on a horse?

The hunchback had sat pensively for a moment or two.

All of our questions, he had said, must be considered in the light of your theory. Only then do answers even begin to present themselves.

Quite so, Dee had said. Quite so. Disturbing answers, but answers nonetheless.

Disturbing was scarcely the word for it, Dee had thought to himself. It was the first time he could remember wishing that one of his theories was not bearing itself out.

By early afternoon, the constable had urged Dee to rest, at least for an hour or so. I will be your eyes and ears for you, the little man had said. I am not tired in the least. I will sit right here in this chair in the anteroom. Among my many talents, he had said, is the ability to go for days without sleep. It is the one advantage to being small and stunted, he had joked.

Dee had accepted the offer. He lay on the chaise in the householder's study, forcing his fluttering, twitching eyelids to shut, and breathed deeply several times. Yes, it would appear that his theory was bearing itself out, like it or not. But there was a piece of the enigma that had never fit in anywhere. He had found nothing in his research to connect it to any of this, had never even come close to penetrating the logic of it: the hoofprints. Their incongruous presence had a profoundly disturbing and sinister effect. Much more so, he realized, than if the prints of an overtly frightening, predatory animal had appeared—say, a tiger, a wolf, a jackal. Somehow, that most noble of beasts, the horse, the servant of mankind, had been transformed.

Transformation. The word itself had been transformed. The whole world had been transformed, he thought as he drifted, lying very still so that the current might take him.

He dreamed that he was a huge, predatory bird flying at night in heavy rain. He could see nothing at all, but it didn't matter. His enormous wings stroked the blackness with inexhaustible power. He knew there was a wild, rugged landscape below him, and mountains ahead of him, all invisible in the darkness and rain, but there. He flew, exultant in his power, lord of the dark invisible world below him.

He rose most of the way to the surface. Like a man swimming beneath the ice of a frozen lake, he searched desperately for an opening. He had a sense of having slept much too long; he had to find the way out. Looking up at the soft, blurry, diffuse light glowing through the barrier he could not penetrate, he found that it was not the ice of a lake he was peering through, but the floor of the house where he and his men waited. Something was walking around above him, and there was a sound, deep and pulsing, that seemed to come from the center of the earth, as if all the dead lying in their graves murmured the same continuous note. Above him, footsteps. No, not feet: hooves, walking directly over his face now so that he could see the dark crescents appearing, disappearing, and appearing as the hooves were lifted and placed down, lifted and placed down. The murmuring enveloped him, the way the voices of his colleagues might during a recess in official proceedings: muttering, discussing, conjecturing. No, not talking or discussing. Singing. Droning.

Chanting.

He woke abruptly. Oblique late-afternoon shadows cast themselves across the ceiling, and branches whispered against the walls of the house. How long had he slept? Too long. He shook his head in an effort to clear it of lingering remnants of the dream: the low drone, like the heavy lazy buzzing of insects, almost below the level of hearing.

Behind him, he heard a sigh, as of someone wearily releasing his breath. My faithful constable, he thought, and turned to speak. But he did not speak. He could not have spoken, even if he had words to say. A naked man stood facing the window. A hunchback.

He stared in rapt fascination at the line of the vertebrae, coiling like a snake beneath the skin, and the hump, formed of the ribs pulled with slow steady inexorable force up and out of place by the traction of the sinuating spine. For a brief strange moment he wondered why his constable would remove his clothing and stand with his back to him. Then he understood that this was not the constable at all, but someone else.

The figure turned, and Dee recognized the face he had seen coming through the door of the temple at the White Horse monastery: the man with the burned flesh, the tight fearful mask of scar tissue. Dee thought fleetingly that he had failed to notice, that first time, that he was also a hunchback.

He leaped up from the chaise, pulling his long knife out from under his robe. Dee thought he saw a look of astonishment on the frozen, immobile features. A householder taken by surprise was not supposed to be armed. But the surprise did not last for more than a heartbeat.

The man hurled himself at Dee with terrible force, catching him in a tight embrace before he had even finished drawing his knife. They hit the floor, Dee's arms immobilized in the other's grip, the scar-tissue mask with its permanent grimace inches away from his own face. Each time Dee exhaled, the grip tightened so that he could barely expand his rib cage to get his next breath; he was unable to utter a sound as the air was squeezed out of him with crushing force. Like a pig in the coils of a constricting snake, he thought dreamily as he began to black out. The dark bloodshot eyes peered into his own, and the fetid breath was warm on his skin; he noted the configuration of the long yellow exposed teeth rooted in pink gums, grinning at him, and thought that this was not a man in whose arms he languished, but some other creature, a demon, not a demon from hell but from his own mind and heart, given life, force, form, and substance and coming forth now to embrace its creator.

His field of vision shrank until there was nothing in the world but the two dry protruding eyes, yellow where they should have been white, with their fine network of angry red veins. Around the edges of his vision, in the encroaching velvety blackness, little white lights were shooting like tiny comets in a darkening evening sky. His ears buzzed. Far, far away, through the buzzing, he heard running footsteps; he felt the body of his attacker stiffen as it was struck with something; the demon grunted and released its grip. Dee rolled to one side, consciousness fading, found himself rolling over and over and over down a steep hill, the world spinning and tumbling out of control, sick and nauseated, until he came violently to rest against something hard and flat.

His body against a far wall, he opened his eyes to a scene from hell: a naked demon and a bent old woman circled each other; a knife protruded from the demon's hump and blood ran down the length of its body. A moaning growl issued from its mouth. The old woman held a long sword with the sure grip of a seasoned warrior; old woman and demon, eyes locked, moved in the slow formal dance that heralded the imminent death struggle.

With the speed of a ferret Dee's constable lunged with the sword; with equal speed the demon grabbed the blade with his bare hands and held on. They stared at each other for a fraction of a moment, the demon's moan rising in pitch, mouth open, hands bleeding, the constable momentarily astonished into nonaction. With superhuman force, the demon, gripping the blade, jerked the weapon so that the constable lost his balance.

Then Dee found his strength. He was on his feet in the next moment and bringing a heavy brass figurine down on the demon's head with all the force he had in him. The demon dropped. The constable regained his balance. Together, they fell on him, and before he could recover from the blow to his head they bound him hand and foot with the heavy braided cord from the householder's silk drapes, hurriedly and frantically tying him with much more force and many more knots than were necessary to restrain a human being, because they did not feel as if this was a mere man they subdued, but something else.

But when they were finished, and dared to lean back for a moment to catch their breath, their hearts thumping in their chests and their limbs quivering, they looked at the creature on the floor before them, helplessly bound, bleeding and shaking his head as he regained consciousness, and saw that he was nothing more than a man after all.

"I . . . I am sorry," the constable said. "It seems that I did fall asleep. I do not know how he got past me."

Dee and the constable looked at each other. Now that the

noise of their struggle had subsided, they realized that there had been a sound, steady and pervasive, surrounding them throughout. It was a sound one could easily mistake for the roaring of one's own blood, a vibration, a whisper. It was the low buzzing drone of Dee's dream, distant and nearly inaudible, but seeming to come from every direction at once.

"Come," Dee said softly, rising to his feet. Leaving their bound prisoner where he was, they crept to the door and peered down the long hallway that separated the study wing from the rest of the house.

It was empty. If there were others, they had not, apparently, heard the sounds of the struggle in the study. Dee signaled to the constable to follow. They crossed back through the study, weapons ready, the directionless muttering just below and behind the noise of their thudding hearts. Dee pointed to the bound creature on the floor; the constable understood his meaning, and together they picked their prisoner up by the shoulders and feet. Dee's legs felt weak, his strength sapped; he had to will himself to take every step. When they got to the door, Dee lowered the man's feet to the ground; silently, though his hands shook as if he had a chill, Dee opened the garden door and he and the constable stepped outside with their burden. They hid the man in the bushes, then stood for a moment and listened. The murmuring was here, too, pervasive and directionless. If they turned their ears one way, it seemed to emanate from inside the house; if they turned their ears just slightly, they thought that they had been mistaken, that it came from outside. For a moment, Dee fancied that it was coming out of the ground, vibrating up along his bones. At that moment, Dee's peculiar sense of weakness intensified; he felt purpose and energy flowing out of him like water from a cracked bowl. He looked at his constable, whose heavy-lidded eyes betrayed the same feeling. It was all Dee could do not to sink to the ground then and there, cover himself with leaves and grass, and sleep.

He gripped the constable's arm hard enough so that he knew it would hurt. The constable's eyes opened and cleared and looked steadily back at him. He gave the arm a twist and a pinch for good measure, making the constable wince, then pinched his own flesh, hard, on the tender undersides of his arms. The pain cleared his head. They looked at each other. Dee pointed, indicating that they should proceed, staying close to the outer walls of the house. They moved through the cover afforded by the elaborate ornamental plantings until they moved along the exterior of the long corridor that led to the householder's study. They were approaching the large central drawing room, adjoined by the dining room.

When they reached the drawing room, Dee crouched next to a set of double doors, inching over with infinite caution. The blinds were not drawn, so if he put his face against the swirls and ripples of one of the ornate panes he had a good view of the room in the dimming afternoon light.

He was aware of stepping back hard in clumsy shock onto the constable's foot and the constable yelping involuntarily with the pain. Dee lost his balance. The constable caught him. Dee clutched at the man's clothing, regained his balance, and pulled his friend urgently toward the door.

"Tell me I am not dreaming or mad!" he hissed.

They peered in. Dee did not know what the constable's thoughts could be, but for his part, he thought that he must still be asleep and in his nightmare.

Naked demons, their images rendered even more distorted by the heavy rippling glass, prowled the elegant drawing room, hideous and out of place as if a crack had opened in the floor and released them from their domain in the underworld. There was the fellow with the great overhanging brow like a snowdrift, and there was the one with the jutting jaw like the prow of a ship. There was the unfortunate with the mismatched, warring halves of his face. There were others Dee had not seen up close before, but who were familiar to him nonetheless, for he had seen their likenesses in the caves at Lungmen. And on the carpet, sprawled and apparently helpless so that the demons stepped over them as if they were pieces of wood, lay several members of Dee's "family"—the disguised "grandfather," the "brother," the "son." Dead, Dee thought in a panic, but quickly saw that they were not—their arms and legs moved languidly now and then, their heads rolled from side to side. As if they were asleep. Not as if they were unconscious from a blow to the head, but . . . asleep.

Dee almost stood up and shouted as another demon with a face and ears that resembled a bat's entered the room from the far doorway, leading by the arm one of Dee's most hardened lieutenants. Dee restrained himself and watched, unbelieving, as the lieutenant shuffled along, docile as a child, his chin resting on his chest. The bat-headed demon pushed him down gently so that he sank to his knees near the others on the floor, then lay down among them as if falling into his own bed.

The naked deformed men moved about slowly, in no hurry, their mouths moving, but they were not conversing. Dee thought he was beginning to understand, and he knew that they had little time to spare. He pulled the constable harshly down to the ground.

"The guards, the sentries," he whispered urgently, squeezing the man's arm painfully. "We must get to them. We have almost no time. Hit them. Pinch them. Kick them. Do what you must do!" The constable nodded his quick understanding and rose to go. Dee grabbed the other's clothing. "Move fast. Stay under cover where you can. Keep your weapon ready. And . . . " Groping on the ground around them with his free hand, he found what he needed: moss. He seized a wad of it and thrust it toward the constable. "Plug your ears with this. Make the others do it, too."

The constable crammed the moss into his ears, Dee released the handful of fabric, and the little man shot away like an arrow released from a bow. The enervation in Dee's limbs made him stumble as he rose to his feet, stuffing his own ears and thrusting a handful of the moss into his pocket, but he pushed himself forward like a dreamer willing his legs to move.

In a crouching, stumbling run, staying close to the walls of the house and its cover of ornamental shrubbery, he made his way to the servants' wing. Branches raked his face and poked at his eyes as he approached the door to the kitchen area, found it standing ajar, and put a cautious shaking hand forth to push it farther open. He crept through. Stillness reigned within. His plugged ears made his heavy breath and thudding heart the only sounds in the world.

He entered and came around the long central worktable, and nearly stumbled over the bodies of two of his men, one of them the heroic baker, sprawled on the floor. Dead, he was certain, until be bent close and saw their ribs rising and falling peacefully. He knelt and put his hand over the mouth and nose of the one nearest him, causing him to wake. His eyes opened and looked at Dee from far away, without recognition. Keeping his hand over the man's mouth, Dee seized a healthy handful of the flesh of his arm and pinched with brutal force. This time the man's eyes flew wide open while Dee tightened the hand holding his mouth shut, preventing him from crying out. Seeing recognition in the baker's eyes in the next moment, Dee lifted the hand off his mouth. Dee put a warning finger to his lips, and woke the other man the same way.

He pointed to his ears and thrust a wad of moss into each man's hands. They understood and stuffed it into their ears, and the three of them crept from the kitchen area to the nearby servants' quarters.

In each room they found men in chairs, collapsed forward onto the floor, or leaning against walls as if they had been standing or sitting when sleep overcame them. When each man was awakened with a painful pinch or a pull of the hair, he was silenced with a fierce admonishing look, his ears stopped up with moss or with cloth hastily torn from a sleeve, and directed to follow the others.

They crept from room to room, each man enclosed in his own muffled heart-thumping silence, until there were nine of them aside from Dee. Still feeling the peculiar weakening vibration in his bones, Dee anxiously pulled the wad of moss from one ear and put his head cautiously into the gloomy hallway, but drew it back out immediately. Someone was approaching, with a loping, shuffling walk. Dee waved the others back. They crouched, retreating into the shadows. Dee listened. The steps drew near. Now he could hear breathing; moist, noisy, slobbering breathing mingled with a low, inarticulate muttering that seemed connected with the vibration in Dee's bones. Dee could not see the nose and mouth that would make such sounds, but the picture in his mind was clear enough.

The deformed man stopped at the door, paused, breathing and mumbling in the half-light, then stepped in. In a moment, a cord was around his neck from behind, cutting off the muttering drone with harsh abruptness, and with scarcely so much as a grunt and a scuffle, he was down, subdued, bound, and a heavy cloth stuffed into his mouth. The men stared with shock and fascinated revulsion at the creature on the floor: it was the bat-faced man, his gagged mouth little more than a snag-toothed slobbering aperture. Dee had tried to warn them the day before of what their eyes might look upon, but he could see that mere words had fallen far short.

Dee thought of the creature he and the constable had left in the bushes outside the householder's study. It would only be a matter of time until his compatriots missed him and went looking for him. And now this one, too. He grabbed the baker's arm, gestured, and together they rolled the captive into a far dark corner of the room behind some furniture.

"Outside," he mouthed to the baker, who signaled the others. Forcing their gaze away from the helpless blazing-eyed demon on the floor, they moved in a crouching run, unwilling to look behind them. They went back through the kitchen, Dee leading the way, and exited through the open door. Outside, Dee stopped, catching his ragged breath, and pulled the plug of moss from his other ear. He listened. The sound, the vibration just below the level of hearing that had started in his dream and had seemed to come from everywhere, had become faint and was no longer directionless. He shook his head to clear it, tilting his ears this way and that, but heard only the quiet of the early-evening garden outside. The low murmur was now coming only from inside the house.

Leaves crunched behind him. His head turned. His breath rushed out in relief and deliverance: it was his hunchbacked constable, and he was not alone. He had the sentries with him, their faces still groggy, their eyes confused.

"We have no time," Dee hissed. The hunchback looked at him uncomprehendingly for a moment, then snatched the moss from his ears. "No time," Dee repeated. He looked around desperately, stooped, picked up a rock and hefted it, though he had no idea what he would do with it. "The central room! Hurry!"

They had started to move, awkwardly and clumsily jostling each other in their haste in the fading light, when a new sound carried across the still air from another part of the garden, a sound that struck such deep dread into Dee that he thought he must have been waiting for it all of his life: hooves, clattering down the flagstone path where he had walked earlier that day, approaching the house at a brisk, measured, stately canter. With the poor light and the dense trees and bushes obscuring their view they could not see whatever it was that made the sound, but they heard it reach the end of the walk, and with a drumming of hooves on the wooden floor, enter the open door of the house and thunder down the long hallway from the study to the central room.

Now Dee and the men were running. They came to the double doors where Dee and the constable had peered in earlier. Dee pressed his face to the pane, and saw at last, its image distorted by the glass, the maker of the bloody hoofprints, the creature who had walked above him in his dream and who had afflicted his thoughts these past many weeks. He stared, but he still was not sure what he was seeing.

In a grotesque parody of a trained dancing horse, the creature pranced about the room, stepping nimbly over and around the prone bodies on the floor. It veered, came close to the glass, and Dee caught a glimpse of a long horse-face, shriveled and desiccated, and a row of snarling blunt horse-teeth. And he saw one of the men on the floor raise a feeble arm as a naked demon began to crouch down over him with a thin wire taut in its hands, while the hideous horse danced in uncouth glee and the other demons stood watching, mouths moving as if in prayer.

Dee stepped back, took aim, and heaved the rock in his hand with all his strength through the thick glass. He reached, jagged glass making a long deep slice in his arm, unlatched the door from the inside, and in the next moment he and his men poured into the room. The demons' prayer had ceased with the crash of breaking glass and started again as a howl of rage and surprise.

There were five demons and fifteen of Dee's men; then there were two more demons as the horse separated into two men with the severed dried feet of an actual horse attached to their own feet, a horsehide draped over them with a long, luxuriant black tail attached, and carrying a mummified horse-head with empty eyesockets and bared teeth. One of them threw the grisly head, hitting Dee directly in the stomach. He went down, heaving the dreadful thing off him in horror, while someone practically flew over him and attacked the demon head-on: the constable, Dee saw, as he struggled to get his breath.

The demon and the constable rolled on the floor. Dee could see that the demon was endeavoring to get the constable in a deathly snake-embrace like the one that had nearly finished Dee in the study, but someone else dealt the demon a blow to the back of the head, which barely slowed him down, but made it possible for the other man to pull the demon off the constable so that together they were able to subdue him. All of the creatures fought as if they didn't care if they lived or died. They howled and moaned, clawed and kicked and bit, but they were greatly outnumbered, and seemed to have no weapons. Dee's men had nets and ropes, knives and armor; in a few terrible minutes, they had subdued them all, and held them down, some of them netted and squirming, with knees and heavy feet pinning their backs, arms, and heads.

Dee saw that they had only one weapon: a long knife, lying on the floor, near a bloody sack. He crawled over, looked inside, and saw the severed limbs of animals. He knew what purpose the severed limbs would have served, and the knife as well. He closed the sack and sank back down onto the carpet, his strength spent.

Barely able to speak, Dee turned to his constable.

"Are there not more of them . . . ?" he gasped. "There should be . . . sixteen." He scarcely got the words out, so winded and shaken was he. The constable shook his head, gulping for air himself.

"Seven here," he panted. "One in the house . . . one outside . . . and . . . seven in the garden. We got them all." He bowed his head and breathed, making a concentrated effort to get himself in hand, then looked up at Dee again. "Seven outside in the garden, surrounding the house. Chanting."

"Chanting," Dee repeated.

"It was most curious, Magistrate," the hunchback said. "The ones outside. Even they had no clothes. In this cold, they had no clothes at all," he said, shaking his head with bewilderment. "And no weapons."

"No," Dee said, his breath coming more easily now. "No. They did not think that they needed any. Only that one." He was pointing to the knife on the floor.

A.D. 675, December

JOURNAL ENTRY ———————————————

It will not be the first time that I have acted on a wager, but it will certainly be the largest wager of my entire life when I begin my journey tomorrow. And will they who might read my words believe that I am not completely deranged when I add that I am traveling to Loyang for a personal audience with the Empress, that I believe she will extend a warm welcome to me, and that I plan to put a singular proposition to her?

No, they probably would not believe it, so I may as well go ahead and tell a bit more of the story so that they will have plenty of substance to add when they tell the sad tale of my madness.

It was a letter from Wu-chi that ultimately led to my

decision to return to the City of Transformation. A letter, and a long black hair.

In the days following the arrest of the sixteen White Cloud Arhat-monks, when honors and approbation were being heaped upon my head by a grateful citizenry of Ch'angan, and when it appeared that I at last had all the pieces of the puzzle, I came to understand that my troubles had just begun. Because now I had confirmation of what I had suspected ever since I stood and gazed at the carved stone figures in the caves at Lungmen: that my old friend Hsueh Huai-i had traveled very, very far indeed—so far that he was above and beyond the reach of the law. After my moment of truth in the caves, in the days when I was making my discoveries and my dreadful theories were taking shape in my poor obsessed mind, I scarcely had time to think ahead to how I would bring him to justice. What made me think that it would be possible to prosecute Hsueh Huai-i once I determined that he was behind the series of terrible murders in Ch'ang-an? And what made me think that he would not have me hunted down and killed before very long? There is not a constable in Ch'ang-an who would arrest me now, nor a magistrate who would jail me, but technically, I am still a wanted man and an escapee. Surely Hsueh would not hesitate to use this against me mercilessly, or failing that, simply have my throat cut in an alley and my corpse dumped in a canal.

This is why I have not told the world about Hsueh Huai-i yet. I am allowing everyone to think that the sixteen monks were acting on some impulse of their own. And I have released none of the details. They are for the Empress's ears alone. She will learn all of it from me—how the Arhats committed murder practically in broad daylight, why they did it, who taught them the skills that allowed them to do it, and my desperate deductions that brought me face to face with them.

This is the point where someone reading my words will undoubtedly decide that I have gone quite mad. Perhaps I have. But let it be known: I am the victim of my own logic.

In the days following the arrest of the monks, I received a letter from old Wu-chi. He told me many interesting things, as he always does. But one thing he mentioned, which I am sure he included only as some sort of comic relief for my overburdened senses, was that Hsueh Huai-i had embarked on a most curious pursuit—another of his apparent efforts to win himself a place in the immortal annals of history. An attention-getting device, designed to outlive him, rivaling his most audacious antics of public chicanery.

It seemed that Master Hsueh was manufacturing unique "relics" that would, he hoped, be forever associated with his name. Great numbers of these relics were being distributed to all of the monasteries around Loyang, the Pure Lotus among them, to be placed with their treasures, so that in a hundred or two hundred or three hundred years' time, pilgrims could gaze upon them and ask one another: who was Hsueh Huai-i?

The relics, Wu-chi told me, were luxuriant "horse's tails," symbolizing and honoring the role of Hayagriva, the mythical horse-assistant to Avalokitesvara and protector of the Dharma under the Holy Mother Divine Sovereign, the Empress Wu. Of course, I immediately thought of the long, long hair I had found in the garden on the morning of the visitation. I had saved the hair, finding it compellingly curious and enigmatic, rolling it up and wrapping it in a piece of silk. As soon as I read Wu-chi's letter, I took the hair out and examined it. I made some comparisons, and saw then that this was most definitely a human hair, and not of animal origin at all: a bit coarse, and very, very long, but human. Undoubtedly, a specimen from one of Hsueh's horse's tails, this particular one having been attached to the demon horse assisting the Arhats.

What else did I conclude? First, that the hair, judging by its length, could only have come from the head of a woman; second, judging by its strength and luxuriance, the head of a young woman. Then, judging by the number of such long, luxuriant hairs that it would take to manufacture such a number of tails, I concluded that Lama Hsueh Huai-i had to have access to a great number of young women. And under what circumstances would a great lama have access to the hair of vast numbers of young women? It was an obvious inductive leap from there: it would have to be something connected with a nunnery and the ceremonial removal of the hair.

A bit of checking revealed that I was quite correct. In recent months, Hsueh had dedicated himself to a new pursuit, at the expense of almost everything else: the revival and rejuvenation of the Kuan-yin nunneries, long a repository for old, unwanted women, a useless vestige of another age. Under the tutelage of the great Lama Hsueh, the Kuan-yin nunneries were to be given new life, new purpose. They would honor the role of females in the great and glorious new age of the Holy Mother Divine Sovereign. They would define the invaluable contributions of womankind in the propagation of the new order. They would serve humanity with works of mercy.

And they would, I was sure, provide fresh, tender, young female flesh for the delectation of the lama.

I sat down one evening not long after and worked out a formula, an equation, if you will, based on known factors: the monstrous egotism of the Empress; her well-known insatiable appetites; her present age, which is fifty; the age of Hsueh Huai-i, which is thirty-six; the number of years that the two of them have been involved with one another, which is nearly six; the monk's appetites and his own monstrously disproportionate sense of his importance in the universe. I concluded that unless I was a very poor judge of human nature, there could be little doubt that disenchantments had grown between them like weeds in an untended garden. And now might well be the perfect, most expeditious and propitious time for me to present myself to the Empress with my tale.

And so, I leave tomorrow for Loyang. And since I will be leaving the sanctuary of Ch'ang-an and entering a perilous venue where I am still a wanted man, I will be disguised, but not as a monk this time. No, I have drawn inspiration from recent events; I believe that this time, I will be disguised as a woman. An old, homely woman, long past her prime, perhaps not completely right in the head—the sort that will be left alone, ignored, unhindered in her journey.

Am I mad? We will know for certain in a very short time.

33

It was one of those freakish days in early December when the sky was blue and still and the sun was hot. Dee leaned against an ancient garden wall of the Pure Lotus Monastery, eyes closed, face bathed in warmth and light and his mind floating free.

It was not that he had experienced a change of heart about what he had come to Loyang to do. It was not that he was shrinking from the task at hand or having doubts or second thoughts. But if he knew how to do it, he would have stopped the forward progression of time, just for a while, so that he could merely sit here in the warm sun, free from thought, free from pressing exigencies.

Upon his arrival the night before, he had found the Pure Lotus untouched and unchanged, still the haven of tranquillity that it had always been. It was with extreme gratitude and gladness that he had drawn his first breath within its walls, and felt light and clarity enter him and soothe his weary body and soul. He had dined with Wu-chi and the abbot, had told them everything while they listened in awed silence, and had gone to bed and slept as peacefully as a child. Now, with his head resting lightly against the dense, cool, stolid rock of the old monastery wall, his mind, for the first time in countless months, ceased its anxious, relentless searching, calculating, and probing.

Instead, his contemplations drifted toward nothing more important than the notion of the yellow mossy bones of dead monks lying in the monastery burial ground not far from where he sat. He thought that it must be a very pleasant state of existence indeed, to be resting peaceably in the black earth, all work, trouble, passion, regrets, and urgency finished, done with, accomplished—written; indelibly, irreversibly written. How wrong people were to think of the grave as cold and desolate, he thought; at this moment, it seemed to him to be a cozy place—warm, dark, and snug as a bed on a winter night.

And no one will come there and shake you by the shoulder, demanding that you rise and tend to business.

He sighed with pleasure and rolled his head gently from side to side on the stone. As it was, he knew his idyll could end at any moment. A message had been dispatched that morning to the palace via a trusted contact of Wu-chi and the good abbot. Now he sat, the sun in his face, the light brilliant through his eyelids, and waited for a reply.

He pulled back the curtain of the closed carriage rumbling its way through the Loyang streets. He peered out at the City of Transformation, and thought to himself that it did not appear to have been particularly transformed; whatever its name, it was the same city that it always had been, serene and gracious with its network of rivers and parks and its countless graceful arched bridges, each different from the next.

He had not had to wait long for a reply to his message. It had come in the late afternoon of the day he had sent it. It said that a carriage would be dispatched to call for him at any place of his choosing; Dee had sent a return message with explicit instructions, and the next morning had traveled into the city in his disguise, not wishing, even at this late date, to draw any attention to Wu-chi's hiding place. The coach had picked him up at a little teashop next to a park, the very place where Hsueh Huai-i had failed to keep their last appointment. The stony-faced driver and the outriders acted as if it were nothing unusual at all to call for strange old women at teashops. Dee climbed in, and in the private interior of the coach, unrolled the bundle of clothing and other items he had been carrying, with the intention of transforming himself back into Magistrate Dee Jenchieh. He was about to place his cap on his head when he paused, reconsidered, then rolled the clothing back up. Why not, he thought, smiling.

He would not do this if he were going to the palace—but he was not. The coach was taking him somewhere else, a place he had specifically requested—a place where it would be harder to trap him, if indeed it was a trap. But he did not think so. He believed he had, in a manner of speaking, sniffed the wind and made an accurate reading of the coming weather.

He peeked out of the curtained window again. They were entering the quiet, muffled graciousness of one of Loyang's wealthiest suburbs.

The irony of his destination was not lost on Dee. He was

going to the place where Hsueh Huai-i had made the first fateful contact destined to open the door to his new life, the place where Dee himself had sent him, a place where Dee believed at least one heinous crime had been committed, and which, for all of those reasons, had always aroused Dee's intense curiosity, for it was a place where Dee himself had never set foot: he was going to Madame Yang's house.

But now, he was not going with the intention of snooping for evidence or to reopen old murder cases. He was going in order to strike a bargain. The carriage leaned slightly as it turned into a drive. They had arrived.

Dee had a moment of genuine confusion, when he was not at all certain whether the woman before him was the Empress or Madame Yang. Years ago, the resemblance had been strong, but circumstances had always left little question as to which was which. Now, in this particular setting and with the passage of so many years, the distinctions had sufficiently blurred so that he found himself staring dumbly at the strong, handsome face, for a strange interval entertaining the notion that the two women had finally, somehow, merged into one.

She regarded the strange homely old woman who shuffled into her presence in the reception hall. The two studied each other for a moment; then she put her head back and laughed heartily.

"Dee Jen-chieh," she said. "You are most welcome. You have made me feel young and beautiful again."

As soon as he heard the voice, Dee's confusion lifted. He removed the tattered black scarf from his head, and bowed.

"Madame Empress," was all he could say.

He could not remember ever having such an appreciative audience. The Empress was an excellent listener, rapt and fascinated by his strange tale, drawing the words out of him, imbuing him with a rare sense of drama and animation.

He had told her about the trip to the caves, his moment of recognition, his rush back to Ch'ang-an, his imprisonment and escape, and the hasty evacuation of the aristocratic family from their home so that Dee and his men could take their places. He had reached the point in his story where he had thrust the moss into his ears, and had had to pinch and hit his constable in order to keep him from sinking to the ground and falling asleep. He had described his bad dream, and the low muttering that had permeated it and had continued after he awoke to find the creature in the room with him, the weird enervation spreading in his limbs and head, and the sight of his men being led docilely by the arms as if they were sleepy children.

"It must have been the chanting," she said intently, leaning forward, eyes large and dark.

"Indeed, madame, you are quite correct. You can imagine what a stunning revelation it was for me. I was filled with terror and urgency, fighting to keep my head clear and to save my men from certain death, with the realization dawning on me all the while that here was the answer to the mystery that had taunted me for so many weeks. Ever since the first murders, we had been quite unable to even come up with a theory as to how the killers seemingly entered the houses, unnoticed by servants and staff, murdered the families, and then withdrew as easily as they had come.

"I realized that the men on sentry duty around the estate could only be asleep, put under by the chanting, and that the Arhats had simply walked right past them. Then, several of the intruders had remained stationed here and there on the perimeter of the estate, where they continued to chant. The others, the ones who went to the house, were chanting as well, so the sound was everywhere at once, as if it were coming from the ground, the trees, the walls of the buildings. As I have said, madame, it was not so much a sound as a vibration, precisely pitched and modulated, inducing such a state of torpor and lassitude that it was as if we had been fed a potion. It can even cause odd hallucinations in certain highly susceptible types." Dee was thinking of the old servant from one of the previous murders, who had seen a taloned hand come through the wall.

"But how did it happen," the Empress said, "that you and the constable awoke from the spell while the others did not? What prevented you from being led to the slaughter like the rest of them?" Now her eyes had narrowed. Dee felt his own eyes narrow as he leaned forward to reply; he was aware of himself mirroring her spirited gestures and expressions as he acted out the story.

"Ah!" he said with emphasis. "An excellent question. One I was asking myself even as I scrambled through the bushes in the garden while the murderous Arhats prowled about inside the house. The answer was simple and obvious. I figured it out afterward, when it was over, when I had time to think. My surmise was correct, and was corroborated for me later by one of the Arhats when I questioned him." He paused, took a sip of wine, and glanced surreptitiously over the top of his cup. He saw by the expression in her eyes that he would not be able to keep her waiting longer than a heartbeat or two.

"You see, madame," he continued, placing his cup back onto the table, "the chant is very effective, virtually irresistible—but *only* if the victim is in a state of wakefulness when he hears it." He looked at her. There was a wordless moment as she took in his meaning.

"Of course," she said then, slapping the table. "You were asleep! You were taking a nap!"

"Correct. And so, apparently, was my constable. He had, shall we say, overestimated his powers to remain in a wakeful state after having been a night without sleep."

"And since the others were all put under by the chant . . . " she began.

"Quite right again. We can only conclude that they were doing their duty as promised, and had remained awake, and had been awake when the chanting began. You see, the Arhats did not come in the dead of night as we had assumed from the other murders. Not at all. They came in the late afternoon, when households would be quite awake. This, of course, had never occurred to us."

She leaned back and released a long, incredulous breath.

"No," she said. "Of course. They would not have expected anyone to be sleeping at that hour. But you were, because you had been awake for the entire night."

"Yes. If we had been a normal household of victims, the Arhats would have entered at a time of activity and wakefulness, put us all into a trance, including the servants, and then killed the family at their leisure, with the rest of the night to accomplish their . . . arrangements of the corpses and such, and leave. The servants would have awakened with no memory of having gone to sleep the night before. You see, the killers were very specific about who their victims were to be. Those who were merely employed by the families were never touched."

"But did the intruders not realize that you and your men were not the actual family members? Did they not notice that the women, for instance, were actually men in disguise? Surely they must have known something was not right as soon as they saw them."

"I am sure that they did. But then, what would be the logical thing for them to do under those circumstances? Kill us, obviously, which was precisely what they were going to do. Think of how that story would have raced through the city—Dee Jen-chieh and his men the latest murder victims."

"Tell me this, then. How did your constable manage to wake the sentries and get back to the vicinity of the house without becoming entangled with the ones outside?"

"Well, there were a great many more of my men than there were of them. There were, in fact, only seven of them outside. They were subdued, quietly, one by one, from behind, while the sound of their chanting filled their own ears. My sentries were well equipped, with garrotes, cords, blades, and the rest of it. The intruders had virtually no weapons, and they were naked." He shrugged.

"No weapons, and no clothes," she marveled. "As if what they were doing was some sort of . . . " She shook her head, groping for the right words. ". . . disciplined spiritual exercise!"

"You are quite correct, madame," Dee said, with admiration for her quick intelligence. "Almost ritualistic. The only weapons they believed that they needed were their hands and their voices."

"Hands and voices," she repeated incredulously. "But what sort of stealth did they possess, to be able to walk onto an estate in the daylight? And naked, in the month of November! How could they be human, and do that?" she asked, challenging him.

He looked into his wine cup, then at her face.

"They had training," he said simply. "From an expert. An expert in Tibetan Tantric magic. The same expert who taught them the Drone of Forgetfulness."

Her reaction surprised him. She put her head back as she had done earlier, and laughed. As she did so, Dee could not help but see her upper molars all the way back, strong and white, with nary a one missing. His tongue inside his own mouth gently and enviously probed the numerous gaps.

"Yes," she said. "He is not a total charlatan. I believe that I have come to know the difference, Magistrate. From time to time, our household has hosted various holy men of differing degrees of talent and learning." That was surely an understatement, Dee thought, but maintained an air of polite interest.

"Years ago our court was 'graced,' " she said, a bemused smile on her lips, "with an Indian from the Gandharan region. He called himself a Nagaspa, one in touch with certain supposedly powerful Tibetan magics. He was a fraud. Nothing more. But not Lama Hsueh. He surely possesses certain ... esoteric skills."

"I can certainly attest to that," Dee said. "I worked with him for a time. There were moments when I would have sworn that he possessed the ability to transform himself into a phantom. It was all in the timing, he used to tell me. You only move when the other person's attention is diverted, even if it is merely to blink an eye. But there was much more behind it; I sensed it even then. We were not together long enough for him to teach me his techniques, but I know what he can do." A question occurred to him then. "Did he ever tell you that he and I were colleagues for a while?"

That I sent him to this very house to search for evidence of murder, he thought, but did not say it out loud, watching her face closely.

"He mentioned that he knew you," she answered with an enigmatic smile. "And I often got a feeling from him that he harbored a certain admiration for you, and perhaps even a bit of envy." She arched her brows. "The perfect combination of characteristics to make him an adversary."

"I believe that it was our old association that prevented him from simply having me killed," Dee said. "When I was in jail in Ch'angan, this was one of the factors that helped to solidify my suspicions as to who was the mastermind. You see, when I found myself arrested, and not done away with entirely, I came to suspect that he did not want to waste the opportunity to challenge me. Later, of course, when I had the chance to gather information from the Arhats themselves, I found that my theory that he was behind it all was quite correct."

She looked at him with much the same expression as she had when he had first met her years before. She had known then who he was and what his life's work was, but had taken a liking to him, with a sort of perverse fascination with him as a worthy and respected adversary. He had counted heavily on that feeling still being intact, after all these years, and after all that she had become in the interval.

"But Master Dee," she said, regarding him steadily, "what made you so certain that ... others were not involved as well? I, for instance, might have spared you for similar reasons, might I not? What gave you the courage to come and lay all of this before *me?*"

He understood her meaning immediately.

"Madame," he said, returning her frank, unwavering look, "I knew that you were much too pragmatic for anything like this. You see, there was no, shall we say, *practical* purpose behind these murders." He shrugged. "Except in certain very specific, very obscure terms, the logic of which I have finally penetrated. And that logic . . . " He chose his next words carefully. " . . . simply did not have your mark on it. Besides, I have been watching you closely during our talk today. I am more than satisfied that what I have told you about the killings was entirely new to you."

"And if it had not been?"

"I daresay that I would still believe our friend to be the prime instigator. And I daresay that I would still be prepared to ask for your assistance in bringing him to justice. You see," he said, glancing down at his hands for a moment, "it is my feeling, my belief, that he has outgrown his usefulness to you."

Now the look she gave him was particularly hard and searching. Dee knew that they were beginning to tread on territory even more delicate and dangerous than the topic of murder. He had a moment of misgiving as her face darkened, but the storm cloud apparently decided to pass over without breaking open. Her expression relaxed, and she spoke in a nearly bemused tone.

"You are quite correct," she said. "But how did you arrive at that conclusion?"

"I have a gift for you, madame," he said, bending to retrieve his bundle of clothing. Unrolling it hastily, he produced a wrapped parcel; she watched as he undid the string, then slowly pulled from within the folds of cloth a swatch of long, luxuriant black hair. He laid it on the table before her with a flourish, smoothing it out to its full extraordinary length. He could see that she recognized it immediately. Again, her reaction surprised him. She reached forward and stroked it, smiling. He watched the hand languidly smoothing the hair, and thought of poor dead Kaotsung, and of others who had undoubtedly felt the caress of that same hand. An infant daughter, dead for so many years now. A son. He raised his eyes from the hand and saw her watching him.

"One of his priceless 'relics,' " she said. "Master Dee, your powers of deduction are without parallel. But tell me—where did you get this particularly fine specimen?"

"It came from the tail of Hayagriva."

She raised her eyebrows questioningly.

"He is the horse deity. He assists the Arhats in the protection of the Dharma; he is a most terrifying router of its enemies," he replied, watching her face. "Hayagriva is, more specifically, a deity of the Tibetan Lamaist tradition."

"Master Dee," she said decisively, rising from her chair and walking to the window, "I am going to allow you to proceed. And I will provide you with assistance. But you are going to have to agree to certain rather specific terms."

She turned to face him. The hardness had returned to her aspect now. Whatever it was she was going to propose, he knew that she meant it. Sitting before her at that moment, he had a strong feeling that if he were to violate the agreement they were about to make, the longstanding prophetic vision of his head grinning atop a spike might at long last come true.

"Very well, madame," he said simply, for he also had a very good idea of what it was she had in mind. He had, in fact, been counting on it. And when Madame Yang glided into the room at that moment, startling Dee rather badly with her silence and her uncanny resemblance to her daughter, he was certain of it. Madame Yang did not speak, but settled herself in a chair at the table and looked at him steadily, one long-nailed white hand resting on the other in her lap. Some white hairs at her temples and a somewhat more veiled, hooded look to her eyes were all that distinguished her from Wu.

"But first," the Empress said, sitting down again, "I want to see more of your extraordinary deductive abilities at work. I want you to tell me exactly how you solved the riddle of the murders."

"Of course," he said, recovering from his moment of discomfiture, and bent to his bundle on the floor. With an acute awareness of Madame Yang's eyes upon him, he pulled out his papers, unrolled his map of Ch'ang-an and an accompanying drawing, then took out his own handwritten copy of the Demon Kirita Sutra and smoothed it onto the polished tabletop.

When Dee returned to the monastery late that evening, Wu-chi was hungry for details of his audience with the Empress. It reminded Dee of nothing so much as a jilted former lover inquiring about the once-beloved. With an almost morbid curiosity, old Wu-chi wanted to know everything about her face, her voice, her appearance, the color of her hair. He walked in brooding silence alongside Dee, listening to every word of his description.

"She is still beautiful," Dee said. "Compellingly so. One senses a core of some sort of hard, woody vitality in her. Like an old tree. It was not difficult for me to imagine her in very different circumstances—say, living a life as a tough old peasant woman in the far provinces. You know that she would be the most influential person in the village. She would have been a queen of some sort no matter what the circumstances of her birth."

"Of course she has excess vitality," Wu-chi remarked. "She has fattened herself on the life force of her countless victims. She should live for at least five hundred years."

"It is interesting to sit in the presence of a true killer," Dee said. "One feels . . . oddly exposed. It was as if my life, my still-living, breathing body, were a gift from her. Which is quite literally the truth. By all rights, she should have made a corpse out of me years ago for my meddlesomeness. But she did not. So, I suppose I do owe her my life. There was a palpable awareness of that fact in the air between us." He thought for a moment. "She is going to allow me to proceed. But she drives a very hard bargain."

"Let me guess," Wu-chi said gloomily. Dee had been unhappy about telling Wu-chi this part of the story, but there was no way to avoid it.

"It was the only way, Wu-chi," Dee said, sincerely sorry.

"I know, I know," Wu-chi said with a philosophical wave of his old hand. Dee saw in that gesture all of old Wu-chi's years of quiet, patient hope for vindication consigned to the wind.

"She will allow me to arrest and try the monk Hsueh Huai-i. She will even assist me. But I had to agree to certain terms. And this was where her mother entered the room and sat gazing at me. I find the mother a much more disturbing presence than the Empress." He looked at the ground, remembering. "The terms I agreed to were simple. I will refrain from any revival of my investigations into Madame Yang, or herself, or any of their associates for old 'indiscretions.' In return, not only may I proceed, but I may do it through a restored Censorate." He had saved this piece of news for last, hoping to offer it to Wu-chi as consolation, pale and insubstantial though he knew it to be. "Perhaps you would consider coming out of 'retirement,' Wu-chi," he said shyly and tentatively.

But Wu-chi merely shook his head.

"No, Master Dee. I think not."

Dee began to say something else, something meant to convince him, something encouraging about how he belonged at the vital beating heart of government and all the rest of it. But the old man's look was so distracted, his thoughts so obviously far away, that Dee's unspoken words seemed inane to him and he quickly swallowed them.

"I too have held on to certain hopes over the years, Wu-chi," he offered. "It was painful for me to give them up. I would almost rather cut off my arm with a dull knife. But we must face the facts. The Empress and her mother are simply out of our reach. You know that it is so," he said. "But the monk is not. Not now." He shrugged. "She was going to have him killed soon anyway. I am convinced of it. Then he would have been beyond our reach as well, never brought to account for his crimes. What a dreadful waste that would have been. While I was traveling between Ch'ang-an and Loyang, I entertained the worry the entire way that when I got here, I would hear the news that the monk was already dead. You know that when the Empress strikes she is both swift and accurate." He held his hands up imploringly, as if trying to convince the bare trees and the cold darkening snow-laden sky. "I have spent my life opposing the adulteration of religion. I have seen charlatans, and I have seen manipulators, criminals of every description exploiting the pathetic vulnerability of the human heart. He is by far the worst offender I have encountered."

"And he was once your friend," Wu-chi remarked.

"Indeed he was."

"And he was once the lover of the Empress."

"Yes."

"And she is going to assist you in apprehending him."

"Yes."

"Oh, how he is going to fall. I very nearly feel sorry for him," Wu-chi said.

"Don't," Dee said. "He is every bit as much a murderer as the Empress herself."

"Not quite," Wu-chi said. Dee understood his meaning. Both of them were thinking of the dark rumors from so many years before, the words that were uttered but not quite believed: *her own children. A son, an infant daughter.*

"But you are right," Wu-chi said then. "You are quite right. The monk must not be allowed to go through this life without answering for his atrocities. By the way, a message arrived for you today from Ch'ang-an." Before Dee had left the western capital, he had set up a system of trusted message carriers between himself and his constable. "Some of the monk's accomplices have been arrested as well—the runners who carried information back and forth between the White Horse Temple here in Loyang and its counterpart in Ch'angan. Apparently there was an altercation at the temple in Ch'angan over payment for services rendered. These were hired thugs, you see, not monks. The monks at the White Horse had them arrested. They are being held by the civil authorities, awaiting your word as to what is to be done with them."

"Excellent. I shall have them transported here," Dee said. "No doubt their testimony will be useful to me. It will not be long, Wu-chi, before Master Hsueh finds himself in custody like a common criminal, and facing trial for his transgressions. But it will not be a common trial, I can assure you. That would scarcely be worthy of someone of his stature. I have many surprises in store for him."

"You mean that you and the Empress have many surprises in store for him," Wu-chi corrected him.

"Yes," Dee said. "She and I have become accomplices. I suppose you could call us bedfellows now."

"It is a strange world, Master Dee."

"That it is, Master Wu-chi."

It was getting dark. They knew that the old abbot would be awaiting them with a good dinner. Wu-chi began walking purposefully in the direction of the abbot's quarters. Dee experienced a moment of insight then, and believed that he understood the real reason that Wu-chi would never leave the monastery to return to government and his old, long-ago life. Aside from age, and resignation, and the other obvious reasons, Dee knew that the truth of the matter was that Wu-chi simply did not want to leave his friend the abbot. They had been together too long.

Historian Shu tried one more time, momentarily squeezing his features into an intense knot of concentration before releasing them again. He shook his head. No, this just won't do, he muttered under his breath.

The sun that had earlier touched his face with pleasant warmth was now uncomfortably hot. The room, which had been kissed with just the right amount of inspirational morning light an hour or so ago, now glared brightly and distractingly. No, it would not do at all for him to be sitting down to what would most likely be the masterwork of his career without perfect concentration. He had the servants close the shutters.

This was no ordinary morning, and last evening had been no ordinary evening. It had been a good long time since he had had such an important a document to create. And seldom, if ever, had he relished taking on a writing task as much as he did this one. And that he should now be working for both the great Empress Wu and the brilliant magistrate from Ch'ang-an was an incalculable honor that caused a fevered tickle of anticipation to rush up his spine and down his arms to his fingertips.

It had been good to see his old friend Dee Jen-chieh again. Shu had almost forgotten how much he enjoyed the company of the great official and scholar and how closely he had identified with him. Weren't they both, after all, civilized men who enjoyed a good puzzle, and wasn't Master Dee, like himself, quite at home amid the subtleties of literature, from the great flowery prose poems to the rigors of clean classical essays?

It had been some years since the great magistrate had visited the palace and honored the historian with his delightful and unexpected visit to his office, but Shu had never forgotten that day. He polished and embellished the memory of it in his mind's eye until it shone like a cherished piece of rare family jewelry. Shu still recalled with fondness the details of their conversation—they had talked about the grueling Imperial Triennial Exams of their youth, and they had also discussed some recent poetries that Shu had written to the full moon. Yes, it had been a memorable day indeed.

Now it was to be Shu's pleasure to compose, in part, for the great man himself. They shared a mutual mission of great importance. Rarely had Shu felt so honored.

With the shutters closed the room fell into the sort of dim cavernous half-light conducive to Shu's best thinking. He held the brush poised over the parchment, prepared for the flow of inspiration he knew was coming. He was not going to disappoint Magistrate Dee or posterity. History needed correcting, the Empress had enlisted him, Dee had given his approval, and Shu was going to put his very best into the effort. There was no one else qualified to do the job. Master Dee had said so himself.

Shu rang for the household steward; another stimulating cup of green tea and he would be ready to set brush to paper, ready to do what was required to put the offensive and arrogant Tibetan in his place. Of course, Magistrate Dee and the reinstated courts would take care of the holy man for the present. But Shu's job was to take care of him for the future. Perhaps for all time.

There are strange forces at work in the universe, Dee reflected, often best left unexplored—such as the forces that had drawn the Empress and himself into collusion, and now himself and the little historian. The Empress had expressed her desire for a bit of retaliatory public humiliation for the magician, who now resided behind the closed doors of one of the Kuan-yin nunneries. The historian had jumped at the chance to implement it, and Dee, knowing that it would serve to distract and draw out the monk, making his own job a bit easier, had given the project his approval. Besides, there was an element of grim humor to it that Dee could not see any reason to spare the monk. In fact, he found it irresistible. And so the three of them were conspirators. And Shu had readily accepted some of Dee's suggestions, working them into the piece, allowing Dee to contribute to the "restoration" of the monk's place in history. Since he is supposedly an enlightened, transcendent being, he had said to Shu, there should be no difference for him between the highest and the most lowly of earthly tasks. In our biography, let us grant him suitable employ. And he had watched over Shu's shoulder as the little man, giggling ecstatically, had written Dee's idea down.

It was impossible for Dee to define the attraction, and he certainly did not approve of it, but he found himself to be rather fond of Shu. That was why Dee so easily agreed to another of the Empress's demands: that her faithful historian, official court slanderer, chronicler of her reign, and detractor of her enemies should also be immune to prosecution.

This project would differ from all the others. Shu hated Hsueh Huai-i. That much was plain to Dee. Years of the Tibetan's contemptuous treatment had sunk deep into the little man's soul and left its sediment there. Because the historian had kept his true feelings carefully contained, it only increased the amount of scorn the magician heaped on the historian. He knew that the Tibetan assumed that he was simply too stupid, or too self-involved, to notice it. But it was a sacrifice necessary for the sake of Shu's relationship with the Empress and Madame Yang, whom he worshiped and adored. But now that the sacrifice was no longer necessary, the historian was at last venting his soul, both for Hsueh's treatment of himself and his treatment of the Empress. Now it was no longer an exercise of words. Whether he was consciously aware of it or not, the full force of years of the historian's affronted pride was behind the words that now flowed from his brush. The results made Dee grateful that he himself had never been on the wrong side of Shu Ching-tsung.

THE LIFE OF A PRETENDER

Wherever there is Greatness, there will Inevitably be parasites, sycophants, exploiters, opportunists, and those who have a Mistaken Belief in their Own Greatness. It is a Law of Life, an Inevitability; but of course, the Truly Great have Full Knowledge of the phenomenon and are perfectly Equipped and Endowed by Nature to Absorb and Accommodate.

It is as an illustration of this Truth that the life and exploits of an obscure monk named Hsueh Huai-i are mentioned in these Histories; in and of themselves, his works are of No Consequence and could scarcely be said to have earned themselves a place in the Annals of Immortality. It is only as a Testimonial to the Perspicacity of the great Empress Wu Tse-tien that he is even given Space on the page.

It can be said of this man that he possessed a certain crude Prowess and Cunning, if nothing else. His origins are more than obscure, but it is thought that he came from the Far West, the issue of a family Plagued for Many Generations by Drunkenness and a tendency toward Criminal Behavior. Apparently wishing to better himself, or at least to experience a taste of life beyond what the Meager Circumstances of his Birth promised him, he set out at an early age and began his journey to the East. Along the way, the lands he traveled through being Rife with Every Variety of the breed just as the Sea is rife with Fishes, he had Sufficient Contact with Men-

dicant Holy Men and Ascetics of Every Description to
Equip himself in a Perfunctory sort of way; it could be
said of him that his Cunning enabled him to Acquire a
Dilettante's Tools, an array of Stunts, Illusions, and
Clever Argot, so that to the Naive and Easily Led he was
able to present himself as a Learned and Enlightened
Sage.

His Overweening Ambition left him no choice but
to attempt to make his way to the one position on Earth
which is only a Degree below the Position of Heaven: to
the side of the Holy Mother Divine Sovereign herself, the
Empress Wu Tse-tien. Plainly, Fate meant to demonstrate
to him his Limitations. And so It did.

Giving the monk Credit where it is Due, it should
be said that he gained Entrance to the Palace through
clever and inventive means. He presented himself to the
Palace kitchen staff by posing as a Purveyor of Rare
Herbs; it did not take Long for him to Inveigle his way
into the Imperial Kitchen, assuming a lowly position as
Slops Carrier, gradually rising in rank until he was allowed to Slice the Imperial Vegetables. It was at this
point, knowing of the extreme Devoutness of Her Royal
Highness, that he let it be known to the Empress's Personal Chef that he had learned in his travels what had
been the Last Meal eaten by the Enlightened One before
he entered Nirvana, and that he wished to prepare the
same meal for the Empress. The Empress, in her Wisdom
and Compassion, and out of Divine Curiosity, accepted
the offer. Leaping at the opportunity presented to him,
the monk proceeded to try, with his usual Voluble
Tongue and his Tricks and Illusions of Legerdemain, to
convince the Empress that he was nothing less than a
Holy Man, a Seminal Buddhist Scholar and Teacher.

In her Infinite Perceptiveness, the Empress sensed a
Fraud in her Midst immediately. Nevertheless, exercising
her reknowned Restraint and Fairness, she decided that
she would allow the monk an opportunity. She devised
a way by which she could extend to him the Benefit of
the Doubt and by which he would be able to prove himself if he was by some Obscure Chance what he claimed
to be. At the same time, if he was the Vile Pretender, the
Unprincipled Charlatan, which She sensed him to be,

then he would find himself Suitably Humbled for his Supreme Audacity.

He was granted an Audience with Her Highness, during which she bestowed upon him an Imperial Appointment: he came away from the meeting bearing the title of Keeper of the Imperial Matriarchal Inner Household Chamber Pot. In her Infinite Wisdom, the Empress had recognized that if he was truly the Evolved Buddhist being that he claimed to be, then such a lowly task should for him be No Different from being King of the World while gathering Armloads of Sweet-Smelling Flowers in the Spring. On the other hand, if he was a mere charlatan, than what more appropriate Punishment could there be for such a foul Deceiver of the Masses?

Just as the Empress suspected he would, he endured his Imperial Position for a few short days before complaining. No sooner had the First Grumbling Dissenting Word fallen from his Deceitful Lips than the Empress banished him from the Palace forever. Like the very Slops he had once hauled and like the very Contents of the Imperial Chamber Pot he had been granted the Honor of Carrying, he was tossed out and quickly sank into Well-Deserved Obscurity, surfacing only occasionally on the Periphery of some great Public Event or Celebration, with his Threadbare and Much-used Repertoire of Old Tired Stunts. Befuddled by Drink and Dissolution, the monk Hsueh Huai-i was apparently incapable of perceiving that those few who forbore to watch his Feeble Performances did so out of Pity or else to Laugh at him. He was arrested more than once on petty charges involving Thievery and Disturbance of the Public Peace. It was Rumored that his Decline was due not only to over-indulgence in Wine, but to the Debilitating effects of progressive disease. It is Widely Believed that he died quite insane of a Wasting Disease as a ward of the merciful Kuan-yin nunneries, raving to the Very End about his Enlightenment.

These words have been officially entered by Historian Shu Ching-tsung into the official biographies of the T'ang Histories on this date, January 676, so that posterity may know the Truth.

Hsueh Huai-i tossed the pamphlet to the floor disdainfully. The young nuns who had brought it to him suppressed a giggle as he rose from his chair and stalked to the center of the room, jaw working and eyes blazing. He stood there, glaring down at them where they knelt, though they knew it was not they he was seeing at all. He bared his teeth in a grimace of disgust, causing the young women to cover their faces in giddy, delighted terror.

"A ward of the merciful sisters of Kuan-yin, hm?" he said, turning away from them. "She does not know it, but she has given me an idea. An idea!" he pronounced with fierce suddenness, whirling about so that the two nuns jumped. Now he was looking at them, and seeing them. He crossed the room slowly, walking toward them, nodding his head, a sly smile replacing the fearful grimace of a moment ago. One of the nuns backed up on her knees, both fists pressed to her mouth, tittering with nervous laughter, while the other simply put her head to the ground and covered it with her arms.

Now he stood over them, so close that they could hear his breath in his nostrils.

"Are you ready to receive the divine inspiration of Avalokitesvara?" he whispered. "The scribe!" he called out then in a loud voice to the servant in the hall. "Send me the scribe!"

Dee raised his eyes cautiously from the page, thinking that the Empress had been altogether too quiet. Her face was expressionless in a blank, menacing way that made Dee think of something a man who trained bears had once told him. Bears are the most dangerous of the animals to work with, the man had said, because they have no expression, and give no warning. A dog displays its teeth when it is about to attack; the tiger snarls; the horse flattens its ears and shows the whites of its eyes. But the bear's face shows nothing at all right up to the moment it turns on you and sinks its fangs into your skull.

The Empress looked at him, her eyes and face communicating nothing. One hand caressed the arm of her chair. Dee shifted uncomfortably.

"Do continue, Magistrate," she said in a voice as neutral as her expression. Dee cleared his throat, found his place on the page, and resumed reading:

" ' . . . it could be said that because of an inherent weakness in the female vessel, questionable to begin with, and unresponsive to the remedial masculine essence, the dual male-female essence of Avalokitesvara/Kuan-yin no longer finds expression through the person of the Empress Wu. . . . ' "

He stole another look at the Empress. Now one hand caressed the underside of her chin and her throat while she still looked at him.

" 'Instead, and of necessity, it has migrated, like the bird that finds the climate unsuitable and must move on. It has returned to the place where it first manifested itself on this earthly plane, its point of origin, its doorway to this world, where it may reside in an untainted and hospitable environment, uncompromised and unsullied, until such time as it is called forth. . . . The physical person of the Lama Hsueh Huai-i, maintained through rigorous meditation, abstinence, and purity, like a humble hut cleaned, swept, and scrubbed to receive a royal visitor, is honored to be the vessel of the Divine Essence. . . . Recognizing the grave responsibility entailed by this Divine Residency, the Lama has pledged to maintain a constant meditation, even as he goes about his daily tasks, so that the Divine Essence will feel welcome, and stay in this world to benefit humankind. . . . ' "

The Empress snorted.

"Shall I . . . ?" Dee asked deferentially. An impatient wave of her hand told him to finish the thing.

" 'Undiscouraged by the first failed experiment, the Divine Essence has communicated a desire to find expression once again in a female form. . . . The requirements are better understood now. . . . A female form uncompromised by base ambition, unmuddied by lustful indulgence, with the vigor and purity of youth. . . . ' "

Dee's eye jumped ahead; when he saw what was coming, he stopped, cleared his throat, flicked his eyes upward, then pushed on.

" ' . . . and with a virgin womb, untenanted and unused.' "

With this last, Dee did not quite dare look at her; he heard only the crisp rustle of her silken robes as she changed her position in her chair.

" 'Therefore, let it be known that the Lama Hsueh Huai-i has graciously consented to bestow the Infinitely Divisible Divine Spark upon the female devotees of the Kuan-yin nunnery, in as many selfless acts of Divine Insemination as will be required, with each novice who wishes to partake, in a cere-

mony to be held on the third day of the second week of the
current month.' "

Dee had an interesting few moments of believing that the
Empress was about to put her fangs into his skull, figuratively
speaking. He watched her face uneasily; she still had not
frowned, smiled, spoken, or moved. He wondered briefly what
could ever have possessed him to place himself at the mercy
of this woman; her opaque black unblinking eyes, which held
the sure knowledge of having killed, were trained upon him
as he sat fidgeting with the monk's proclamation. The peculiar
naked feeling that he had first experienced when he met her
at her mother's house came over him again. Sitting in her gaze,
he had an insight into that feeling: as a killer, she possessed a
form of carnal knowledge that he did not. She was experienced; he was an innocent.

"Magistrate, are you ready to move?" she asked him in a
cold voice, bringing him abruptly to attention.

"Very nearly so, madame."

"What do you need to do?" she asked, and he felt her
impatience like a hunger behind her words. He thought for a
moment. He had in fact taken full advantage of the Empress's
decision to let him prosecute the monk, accomplishing a great
deal toward the eventual restoration of the government above
and beyond the pursuit of this one case. He had been very
busy doing what he could to strengthen the revived Censorate
and to obtain appointments for honest officials wherever he
could. But he still thought it would be wise to understate
things to her.

"I have only to place a few more good men in position to
set up a court, to organize my evidence, and . . . " He shrugged.
" . . . to make the arrest."

"I think the monk himself has chosen the time and the
place, Magistrate. Don't you agree?" Now she was smiling,
conveying her idea as clearly as if she had spoken it. It was a
wicked idea; wicked, but very, very fine.

The monk did not know that Dee was in Loyang, or that
he had met with the Empress. Dee was sure that as far as
Hsueh Huai-i knew, the magistrate was still in Ch'ang-an trying to think of a way to come after the monk. No doubt the
monk still believed in his immunity. He would never have anticipated Dee's bold move to confront the Empress directly. He
thought about the Empress's idea. Aside from its aspect of
grim humor, it held a distinct advantage—the monk would

never expect it. He would be off his guard, to say the least, and totally, thoroughly surprised. Not merely surprised, but stunned.

"I do agree, madame," Dee said.

"And Master Dee," she said, leaning toward him, putting a hand on his wrist, "I want him brought to me *naked*."

Dee nodded dumbly, unable to think of a response. Her fingers had rested on his skin for only a second or two, but the place where they had come into contact was marked, he was sure, for the rest of his days.

Would he have thought of it on his own, or had the Empress infected him with her peculiar insidious deviltry? He was not certain. But the idea had come to him on the night after his last meeting with her—while the place on his arm where she had touched him still faintly itched and tingled—and had not left in the ensuing days.

Today was the second day of the monk's Divine Insemination ceremonies. Apparently he had not been making mere empty promises to the Empress when he declared that he would satisfy all takers; according to the regular bulletins issuing from the nunnery—for the Empress's benefit, Dee was sure—he had already transferred the "Divine Essence" to nine women, replenishing himself through rest and meditation between sessions. Dee was certainly impressed. Though the monk was scarcely senescent at thirty-seven, neither was he in the first blush of youth. But then hadn't the Empress herself conceded that he was not a complete charlatan?

Dee had organized a group of armed Imperial deputies to accompany him. Their plan was to go to the Kuan-yin nunnery in the evening, when the light would be poor. Dee decided that today was the day. Even if it was the Divine Spirit that was providing Hsueh Huai-i with his unnatural endurance, he was, after all, only made of flesh and blood, and it was important that the monk not call the rites off, or drop from exhaustion, before Dee had a chance to pay his respects.

Dee and his entourage found a considerable crowd gathered at the gates of the Kuan-yin nunnery. Most were women, young and not so young, and girls, some of them mere infants, with their mothers and fathers shepherding them. The word had certainly got out, Dee thought as he picked his way among the standing and sitting bodies. Some of them appeared to have been there for a good long time, obviously hoping that they might somehow gain admittance and receive divine "inspiration" from the monk. Dee was particularly disgusted by the parents with little children. What could they be thinking?

Dee was wearing the clothes he had traveled in to Loyang, transforming him back into the odd old woman with her bundle and her head scarf. The difference now was that she was accompanied by an impressive contingent of armed guardsmen. People stepped aside at the bewildering sight of the plainly dressed, stern-looking old lady in the lantern light at the head of the column; Dee knew that he must take advantage of the momentary confusion and move quickly and decisively before anyone had time to think or react. He would only have this one chance. He led the men right up to the main door, where two eunuch attendants gazed at him uncomprehendingly; before either of them could utter a syllable, Dee stopped, stood in front of them, and spoke the words that caused them to fall back in unresisting consternation, just as he had thought they would.

"I am the Lama's mother," he said, his voice in his own ears sounding much like that of his own mother.

In the next moment he and his men were through the door and walking quickly down the dimly lit corridor toward the prayer room. It was not difficult to ascertain just where the monk might be; a long row of waiting nuns chanting prayers in attitudes of devotion led to a set of double doors. Startled from their meditations by the intruders, they lifted their eyes in confusion; as he passed their astonished upturned faces, Dee murmured glib, placating phrases, lightly touching a shoulder or the top of a head here and there as he proceeded.

"Never mind, it is quite all right, he is expecting me, I trust I am not late," Dee said soothingly, reassuringly, moving directly to the doors. He placed a hand on the latch and pushed. The door swung quietly inward, and he stepped into the prayer room, his guardsmen behind him.

The smell of sweat and incense nearly overpowered him. The air of the room was heavy with the mighty effort that had been put forth there. Dee looked at the rows of flickering candles and the disarranged furniture, and understood that the monk had truly not been merely issuing idle threats and empty promises; he meant to carry out his self-assigned task of Divine Insemination with utter thoroughness.

Two female musicians who had been playing a monoto-

nous four-note melody on stringed instruments fell into startled silence at Dee's entrance.

The altar had been curtained off. Dee sensed a momentary
cessation of activity behind the brocade tapestry, an attentive
listening stillness. He had the distinct sensation that the monk
knew exactly who it was that had entered the room. The silence
from behind the curtain lasted for a scant moment longer before the fabric was pulled aside forcibly, and there stood Hsueh
Huai-i, naked and glaring.

Dee stepped forward so that the monk would be able to
see him clearly, and bowed.

"It was most thoughtless of you to keep me waiting for
so many hours that day at the teashop, Master Hsueh," Dee
said. "I grew quite chilly and discouraged. It was hardly
proper treatment for an old friend."

"My apologies, Master Dee," the monk enunciated. "It
could not be helped. As you know, I had important business
to attend to."

"Indeed you did."

The two regarded each other. The monk seemed taller and
more gaunt than Dee remembered, with a strange sunken look
to his eyes that Dee did not think had been there before. He
thought fleetingly of the picture he himself no doubt presented
to the monk: grayer, older, his odd clothing. And what did his
own eyes betray?

Behind Dee, people had begun to gather at the door—the
eunuch gatekeepers, the nuns, some of the braver souls from
the courtyard. Dee remembered the Empress's request: I want
him brought to me naked. He signaled the guards, who strode
forward and seized the monk's arms. The monk stiffened at
their touch, clenching his fists and glaring at Dee, his face
twisting into a haughty snarl.

"Do you believe that you can hold me?" he sneered. "You
have no authority here!"

Dee pulled out the document he had been carrying. The
monk, seeing the paper, rolled his eyes up into his head and
began to chant loudly, determined to drown Dee out.

"Silence him!" Dee ordered, and one of the men put a
heavily gloved hand over the monk's mouth from behind
while the others tightened their grip. The hand muffled his
words, but could not silence him altogether; head thrashing
from side to side, he continued to howl and moan behind the

straining hand of the guard while Dee read his document aloud.

" 'Her Imperial Highness Empress Wu Tse-tien does hereby declare the erstwhile Lama Hsueh Huai-i to be an enemy of the state, and does direct, desire, and fervently wish for his detainment and incarceration for the despicable crime of murder. . . . ' "

Despite the noise he was making, the monk appeared to comprehend Dee's words. He ceased howling and looked at Dee with burning eyes. Dee nodded to the guard, who removed the hand.

"Murder!" the monk snorted. "That is not at all unlike the crow berating the hyena for its carrion-eating nature!" He bellowed, "YOU KNOW WHO SHE IS, DO YOU NOT?"

Dee continued to read.

" 'The following shall be duly entered into the T'ang Histories so that posterity shall know the truth. The record of the monk Hsueh Huai-i's life, chronicled herein by Historian Shu Ching-tsung, stands amended in these few but vitally important details: he was arrested in the year 675 for the crime of murder, was successfully tried and prosecuted by Magistrate Dee Jen-chieh, and suffered the worst, most painful and extreme form of execution it is possible to inflict on a living man: death by slicing, the appropriate punishment as it is put forth in T'ang code for the crime of multiple murder.' "

The monk was chuckling quietly now, his head hanging as if the weight of so much irony were more than his neck could support.

"You do know who she is, do you not?" he asked again, looking sideways at Dee, shaking his head, laughing. "You know just who it is that you conspire with, do you not? Murder!" he said incredulously.

"Take him," Dee ordered, and the guards began to drag him toward the door. Dee stepped back as they brought the monk by the place where he stood; as he passed, the monk spoke to him in a harsh whisper that imposed itself on his senses and would remain with Dee for a long, long time, just as the touch of the Empress's fingers on his wrist had remained with him.

The monk glanced down at Dee's right sleeve and grinned.

"We are older friends than you think. Tell me, Magistrate—do you still carry my tooth marks on your arm?"

At first, Dee did not know what the monk meant; but then Hsueh Huai-i's grinning face contorted itself into an expression of surprise and terror; they stared at each other, and for a fraction of a heartbeat, nearly twenty-three years fell away and Dee was looking into the face of a fourteen-year-old boy, a murderous child with wild eyes and bristly hair, pinned and struggling against the wall, the child who was about to disappear over the balcony after very nearly ending the illustrious career of the great Dee Jen-chieh when it had scarcely begun.

Then the monk relaxed his features into a grin again and the guards pulled him away through the parting crowd.

Dee found himself quite unable to reply. For now, the monk had had the last word.

The day before the trial dawned gray and oppressive. Excellent, Dee thought, as he made his way to the Censorate offices. I hope that the weather holds. I hope that the sky will be low and ominous tomorrow, pressing down on us poor mortals like the lid of an iron pot, robbing us of hope, of spirit, of all memory of light, blue skies, and cheer.

The way the sky had been on the morning of the gardener's execution so many years ago.

You were quite right, Lama Hsueh, Dee thought. We are older friends than I had thought; older, in fact, than even you had thought. Though we had yet to meet until that evening in my office, I had been searching for you since the moment that the gardener's outraged and wounded spirit left his broken body. And now, after all these years, the great Dee Jen-chieh finally brings his man to justice. Never mind that nearly a quarter of a century has passed, and that while you were at large immeasurable quantities of blood were spilled and mopped up and spilled again—the great magistrate has finally run you to earth.

We will, of course, have to bring in Historian Shu to perform one of his expert patch-up jobs; it just wouldn't do for posterity to glimpse the worn, shabby, threadbare fabric of Master Dee's life and work, the unraveled corners, the gaping holes. No, that would hardly be appropriate or decorous. Go to work, Master Shu; clothe me in resplendent silks and magnificent robes of virtue, skill, and competence. Dress me for my journey into the future. Make me presentable.

Dee had been thinking all night of his association with Hsueh in Loyang before the monk's disappearance, dredging up minutely detailed memories of conversations they had had, wineshops they had sat in, places in Loyang where they had walked, even what the weather had been on particular days when they had talked and worked together. And all the while, during every moment of every exchange, the knowledge had been right there, right behind Hsueh's eyes, and Dee had failed to see it, smell it, or sense it in any way: the knowledge that he had once very nearly killed Dee Jen-chieh, and the knowledge that he was the killer of the Transport Minister of Yangchou, the one who had stood over the corpse and finished the man's afternoon snack, letting the crumbs rain carelessly down. The one who had let an innocent man die in his place.

So, in my own tardy, blundering fashion, I have finally found you. Never mind that you slipped through my fingers repeatedly, that I practically conspired with you and promoted you to become the man of influence you became. Know this, Master Hsueh, Dee thought as he began the ascent of the long staircase leading to the Censorate offices. When the trial begins tomorrow, the world will believe that it will be for the murders in Ch'ang-an. And of course, that will be partly true. But you and I will know the truth: that you will be paying a long-overdue and greatly compounded debt to the ghost of a dead gardener.

The offices of the Censorate were a hive of activity this morning. The exhaustive preparations for the trial were nearly complete. Evidence and reports had been organized and set down, appropriate excerpts from the T'ang legal code had been researched and copied by the Censorate scribes. Magistrates and officials reappointed by Dee were conferring. Everywhere there was a sense of repression lifted, of men looking around themselves and understanding that at last they could speak freely, that the siege was over, that they need not fear reprisal for the crime of speaking their minds. The hum of voices filled the many rooms as men who had not spoken to one another in years, or who had not seen one another at all, conversed the way hungry men eat when they have been deprived of food to the brink of starvation. Despite the gloomy skies outside, the feeling was of the sun breaking through the clouds after a long, cold season.

As Dee passed through the offices, men smiled and bowed deferentially. Dee waved a diffident hand, and avoided eye contact, willing them to refrain from breaking into applause and adulation. He did not think he could tolerate that.

It was scarcely what he deserved, he thought, and quickly ducked into the main office before things got out of hand.

He shut the door behind him and nodded to his assistant.

"Good morning, Magistrate," the man said, glancing up from his desk for a moment, then returning his attention to the paper he was inscribing. Dee was grateful for his straightforward manner. He treated Dee like a colleague, as someone worthy of a normal amount of respect, but did not embarrass him with fawning praise or obsequious adulation. Dee poured himself a bowl of tea and sat. When the man had finished what he was doing, he looked up again.

"We are fairly well organized, Magistrate. I think we will be ready by tomorrow. I have taken care of the special details and preparations you requested. The work is under way at this moment."

"Good," Dee said, still preoccupied.

"Also, the prisoners whose transport to Ch'ang-an you ordered have arrived. They are awaiting you."

"Ah, yes. The runners. The hired criminals. The messengers of death. I'd like to interview them. Have we a scribe in readiness?"

"We have."

Dee rose to his feet. He wanted to get this over with expeditiously so that he could see to the other preparations. He was going to make sure that this was no ordinary trial. Not even Historian Shu with his rich imagination could have invented something to surpass this. This would be Dee's gift to "history."

The prisoners were being held in an office on the next floor up. Dee, the scribe, and the assistant climbed the stairs discussing some of the surprises that tomorrow would hold for Lama Hsueh. The Empress herself had contributed much to the idea. It had been educational for Dee to watch the way her eyes blackened and enlarged with the sheer pleasure of dreaming up retribution for her former lover; he had almost felt sorry for Hsueh.

They reached the office door.

"In here, Magistrate," the assistant said, and stepped aside. Dee went in. The two prisoners sat in chairs, heads bowed, their feet hobbled by the leg irons they wore. They raised tired, sullen faces as the door opened.

Dee stood, hand on the latch, and thought that surely this was Hsueh Huai-i's ultimate piece of work. This put the levitating Buddhas, flying angels, clouds of magic doves, and blood-covered temples to shame. The Arhats, the Drone of Forgetfulness, the Voice of the Thunder Owl, the Jataka tales, and the giant burning effigy of the Enlightened One with the flames licking the sky were as nothing compared to this.

He stared at the faces of his sons for a moment longer, then turned and left the room, shutting the door behind him. His assistant said something, but he could not comprehend the man's words, or remember at which end of the corridor the stairs lay. He was aware of the questioning faces of his two companions, looking at one another wordlessly.

"There will be no interview" was all he could manage to say before he hurried away from them down the stairs.

34

A.D. 676, spring,
Five months after the trial of Hsueh Huai-i
Environs of Loyang

Today, it was almost possible to believe in the existence of a perfect world. As he gazed out over the rippling water, the dropping landfall's sweet smell of blossoms filling his nostrils, Dee thought that it was possible to not merely believe in such a world; for the narrowest of moments, aboard this heavenly vessel, he could believe that he actually inhabited that perfect world.

The upswept eaves of the great dragon boat's multistoried golden pavilions shimmered in the dazzling reflected light. Before the graceful dragon-scaled prow, thick fragrant carpets of lilies yielded gently and disappeared, only to spring up again, pure and unsullied like a thousand Buddhist lives reborn, in the foaming, churning wake of her tail.

They glided out through the lilies and past aquatic fields of swaying weeds as the big boat made for the center of the lake. From the balcony high above, twenty flutes exhaled their gentle whispers into the spring air, and wind chimes made music over Dee's head, the dainty melodic tinkling playing off the dazzling crystal of the water as it parted before them. The shore receded until the cliffs and the thick piney forests at their base lost definition as the settling mists softened forms away like a brush painter's ink wash.

As they entered the deeper waters of the enormous lake, the boat began to pitch and roll, gently at first, but then with increased motion as they met the river's currents and the winds that entered here. Dee was startled from his reverie by the sudden roll of the deck beneath his feet; he slammed his elbow into the railing and nearly slipped before recovering his footing. There were whitecaps toward the middle of the lake, foamy white lace blowing off their sharpened crests.

He did not dare massage his throbbing elbow, because it would mean taking his other hand from the rail; when he looked down at the deep black waters of the lake, the pain in his elbow made him think of the black purple of blood. With cautious steps, he turned away from the rail, away from the disturbing vision; he no longer wished to gaze into the water.

Behind Dee, with an urgent little gasp of exasperation, Historian Shu clutched his small writing table and quickly lifted the pages of his poems—written on this seventh day of May, 676, on the occasion of the great Madame Yang's sixty-fifth birthday and the annual Dragon Boat Festival—from the path of the water of his overturned brush pot. Then they were hit again. The row of colorful lanterns swayed and Dee braced himself against the carved doorway while Shu struggled to right himself in his chaise and keep his precious papers dry.

The little man, Dee noted, no longer needed to involve himself in her scandals. Free of politics at last, he seemed happily absorbed in the innocent art he loved best—poetry. Dee thought that this was, perhaps, the real Shu Ching-tsung: the happy man indulging his poetic sensibilities.

"This rough weather is awfully sudden, is it not, Master Shu?" Dee said, bracing himself against the carved lintels.

"Oh, no, Magistrate. It is not at all unusual for us to feel the ocean toward the center of this great lake. Lake Tai is noted for this unique feature. As we sail into the deeper waters, it is almost always surging and quixotic." Shu was enjoying his role as poet. "It is quite inspirational, don't you think? The forces of nature, I mean. And this is quite a calm day by comparison, Magistrate. We are all so vulnerable, are we not?"

Quixotic and unpredictable, yes, Dee thought. Vulnerable,

oh ... very much. But then I have had enough of those forces of nature for one hundred lifetimes.

"Then you have sailed here before, Historian?" Dee asked, feeling very much the inexperienced sailor.

"Oh yes. Many times, Magistrate. It is the Empress and her mother's favorite. But that is why the Imperial boat is so large. One would not want to subject oneself to the vagaries of the lake's currents on anything less," Shu said. "And we always sail here for the Dragon Boat Festival and Madame Yang's birthday. It is a considerable effort to move the Imperial Household, but it is always worth it."

While Shu was evoking these pleasant images of Imperial domesticity, Dee could not help but think of the poor men in the decks below who pedaled furiously to spin the wide screws that pushed the heavy boat through this rough water. Was it merely some chance of existence that put him on top of the deck and the others below, he the privileged, and they the toiling? Or were the Buddhists right about the endless wheel of life, and would he someday, in another incarnation, perhaps change places with those men?

Dee noted that the sweet music of the orchestra from the balcony above had faded as the celebrants moved inside. Now the wind snapped the banners and blew the icy spray of the waves across the decks.

Dee wedged himself with his foot and back pressed into the doorframe. The shoreline had disappeared, dissolving completely into the distance and the mists. Out here in the middle of the lake, there were no carpets of blossoms, only rolling swells and foaming whitecaps. Cold wet air, devoid of pretty fragrances, entered his lungs. On either side of the great dragon boat, some distance away, the Imperial war junks that flanked them rode up and down, their ribbed sails strained against the stiff breezes.

"I, for one, Magistrate," Shu sighed in mock exasperation, "have had quite enough of this wind." Decisively, he rolled his papers up and stuffed them under his arm. He made no attempt to gather up his brushes and bowls, but left them to roll about. "I am going inside. Perhaps you will join me. The Empress and her mother await us, I am sure."

Inside, the orchestra had reassembled and had begun to play a bold and striking melody appropriately entitled "The Play of Wind and Wave," a delicate two-part piece wherein the breathy "wind" of the *hsiao* flutes and *sheng* pipes was answered by the echoing "waves" of strings and chimes and clappers. On a calm sea of brightly colored satin pillows, beneath the gay light of the swaying mica lanterns, a dozen young, handsome men fawned over the Empress and her mother. The two women reclined on opposite sides of the room, feasting from jade and silver dishes arrayed on low, wide rotating tables.

Madame Yang celebrated her sixty-fifth birthday with lavish ministrations from the young men, who alternated between massaging her feet, hands, neck, and temples and plying her with tasty morsels. The young men, of course, belonged to Wu, but she was always most generous when it came to sharing with her mother.

The motion of the boat sent Shu stumbling into the pillows near Madame Yang, upsetting a serving table and one or two bowls with it. When Shu realized that everyone was laughing, a small embarrassed smile spread itself tentatively across his face while his eyes flicked uncomfortably around the room. But when he saw Madame Yang laughing harder than anyone else, he joined in, apparently happy now to play the buffoon for her birthday party.

He stretched himself out comfortably upon the pillows, and reached into his sleeve and brought out the papers he had saved from the wind and water on the deck. His announcement that he wished to read his newly composed ode to Madame Yang's celebration met with a round of approval.

From her position across the long narrow room, surrounded by her sycophantic boys, Wu caught Dee's eye with a significant look. Dee observed the Empress lolling in the midst of her swains, and thought how much the world had changed in the past months. For years, the only man at Wu's side or in her bed had been the Tibetan, Dee knew. Hsueh allowed for no competition, and Wu, to the best of Dee's knowledge, had been completely in thrall—but willingly so, with no desire to break his hypnotic hold over her. She had always been the one in control, of course—Dee understood that now. She had been under his spell only because she chose to be. And when she decided she was through, the spell was broken, completely and thoroughly, cut through cleanly and suddenly, with the same unsentimental pragmatism with which a lioness walks away from her cubs when the time comes and never thinks of them again. Hsueh's influence was gone, as if it had never been.

As Dee approached her, Wu's significant look softened to an inviting smile. Rising to her feet, she unceremoniously shook off the young men who had jumped up, supporting her, holding her arms. She steadied herself against a wall, and motioned for Dee to join her in another part of the boat, the topmost, graceful pavilion reserved just for her.

Dee followed the Empress up the stairs, holding carefully to the rail. They entered the pavilion, and she gestured for him to make himself comfortable.

"Shu gave me this today. He is particularly proud of the work he put into it," she said, settling herself on the cushioned chaise. "He wanted you to see it. If you approve, it will be entered into the official histories."

She handed him a document with Shu's now-familiar seal upon it.

Dee bowed, and steadying himself against the railing, read Shu's piece to himself, aware all the while of her eyes upon him:

The Execution of Hsueh Huai-i will stand as a Remarkable Lesson for All Time. Dreadful though it was to watch, it provided. This Chronicler with the very rare opportunity to witness the Carrying Out of the sentence of Death by Slicing, an excruciatingly Slow and Painful end. He corrupted the Divine Ruler of China and the Soul of an Empire. So such an end was Fitting. There are times when Heaven proclaims that such an execution is the Only Way to resolve a dire Imbalance in the Universe. This was just Such a Time.

Death by Slicing is an end to be reserved only for the Worst that a Universe that has lost its Harmony can produce, a soul irredeemably Foul and Corrupt. It is such a Slow method of Death that it has been noted that the *ch'i* essence of a victim actually Oozes from the Gaping Wounds. Of the duality of souls—*hun* and *p'o*—that which escapes—the higher Superior Soul of man's Spiritual Nature—is cut off in its Flight from the Body and Ascension to Heaven when one experiences Death by Slicing. It is for this reason also—aside from the Physical Agony—that it is a most Cruel and Dreadful method of Torturous Death. But so evil was the charlatan, the Cor-

rupter of the Good Buddhist Faith Hseuh Huai-i—only
Heaven knows his Real Name—that he utterly deserved
it.

The Slicing of Hsueh Huai-i began in the First Moments of the Appointed Day and lasted until the middle
of the Hour of the Horse—midday—when the sun was
directly overhead. That is when Hsueh Huai-i Breathed
his Last Earthly Breath. He Screamed Out in Terrible Agony as the executioner's blade Drew Across his Flesh. He
was sliced in One Hundred different places along his
chest and back and legs while he hung by his wrists, his
feet Fastened Firmly by leather thongs to the lower rack.

Hsueh Huai-i cried out with Wails of Agony that
Pierced the Air and Shook the Hills and chilled to the
bone Anyone who Heard him. He no longer Laughed;
he no longer talked of his Fortunate Incarnation. He only
suffered the Worst that Any Man can Imagine and then
More. It would have been Better had his body Given Up
the ghost far sooner. But such was Not in the Stars for
Hsueh Huai-i. Hsueh Huai-i is No More, and all around
us, we can hear the Earth Itself release a Deep Sigh of
Relief.

And, on this Same Day, Magistrate and President
of the National Bureau of Sacrifice Dee Jen-chieh has led
us back on the Path of Confucian Reason and Humane
Righteousness: he has outlawed all White Horse Temples
throughout the Empire and has banished their Clerics to
a distance of one thousand *li* for life.

Recorded on this Final Day of the Dismal Winter of
675–676 By the Chronicler of the Reign of the Empress
Wu Tsetien, Official Historian Shu Ching-tsung.

Dee sighed, and in an entirely unconscious act, began to
crease and fold Shu's account of the execution of Hsueh Huai-i.
He placed it back on the table in the Empress's upper deck
pavilion. He said nothing. He had tried in vain to distance
himself from all that had happened in the last months. Now,
with this, he understood just how futile his efforts had been.
Everything that he had seen had carved itself indelibly into his
soul, and now Shu's writing followed that incised course as
flowing water followed the weathered cracks in a stone.

"Then I was correct in assuming that you had not seen

that yet, Magistrate," Wu said. "Master Shu composed it just a few days before we traveled here to sail. That is how it ends, Magistrate. We celebrate the Dragon Boat Festival. Retired officials return to high office, and the evil that Lama Hsueh so often spoke of is dead."

She rolled her sentences off so matter-of-factly that Dee felt a weakening in his knees, which he knew was attributable to something other than the pitching of the vessel, and which forced him to drop down into his chair. The lama would have been nothing, nobody at all, without his willing and corruptible accomplice. And now Wu sat before him, calmly discussing the lama's end without registering any more emotion than if she were discussing the death of a distant relative. It was the lack of emotion that Dee found particularly disturbing. Hsueh Huai-i had been some sort of aberrant monster, yes; but what had he been to her, aside from a source of carnal gratification and a force that squeezed out the deadly poison deep inside her, the way the venom milker squeezed poison out of a serpent's fangs? She did not even make a pretense of emotion; all he heard in her voice was the flat sound of finality and conclusion. And now her eyes, skimming over the papers on the table as if looking for grammatical errors, then back to Dee, then out the window to the great lake as if it, too, were just another thing.

For the briefest instant Dee felt that he had entered her heart and mind like those drifting spirits he had read about in folklore, who join you in your flesh because they wish to experience human emotion again. And he imagined that he felt nothing but an empty coolness in her heart, like an ancient cave uninhabited for centuries, a stillness and emptiness occupied only by the sound of the water and the roll of the boat. Perhaps this peculiar void was only Dee's imagination, or perhaps it was a true insight into all she had ever really felt. Nothing. Was it possible? If it was true, it was a deeper, darker void than he had ever peered into before, and he drew back from its edge as he would from a sheer precipice.

"A writer of extraordinary talent," Dee managed at last, looking back onto the page he had just read. For the moment, that was all he could think to say. He felt as if his own ghost had only just returned to his body.

"Yes . . . quite extraordinary. I believe he must have captured the monk's final moments very well."

The thing that had made Dee sit down, that made him

doubt his legs could support him, was an image of what Hsueh had been to the Empress: some sort of grotesque magic mirror that reflected and reinforced her, and that she had looked into with the vanity of a great beauty admiring herself in her looking glass; he was also something that she had nurtured, and something that had nurtured her, too. Something that had breathed abundant life into everything that she already was. And this included the enormous charitable acts of mercy that had characterized her rule over the common man. This was also a part of Hsueh's legacy. She had been at once the punishing deity, the avenging angel, and the compassionate savior. But didn't it seem as if Hsueh had known that all along? And was she not genuine in some terrible, unnamable way? Had not the monk uncovered prophetic sutras, writings going back centuries, that predicted her coming? And now, as she handed Dee the account of Hsueh's death, it seemed to him as if she had severed a hand from her arm. A hand that had murdered, her own hand. And now she looked down on it dispassionately as it lay still warm and twitching in a pool of her own blood, mutilated but still recognizable as having once been an intimate part of her.

After a long pause, and against all caution, Dee forged ahead. There were few hesitant games of diplomacy left between them.

"And no doubt, madame, Historian Shu has been a powerful instrument of your reign." Dee was now determined to continue past his faltering start.

Wu was quiet for a while, appearing to study the motion of the waves that slapped against the bow far below. As her eyes played over the black churning surface, one of her hands drifted unconsciously to her mouth. She began to stroke the flesh above her upper lip with her forefinger. Dee recognized it as one of the Tibetan's many little cosmetic massages that had become a part of her unconscious mannerisms now.

"You are still beautiful, madame," he said, and it was true.

"Thank you for your most kind remark, Magistrate. But age is such a harsh mistress." She ceased her stroking and dropped her hand. "This is no longer the dewy skin of youth."

"Nevertheless."

"I say 'mistress' because only a woman could be so mean-spirited."

"Oh?" He waited, fascinated to hear what she was going

to say. He always found her commentary on the sexes to be revealing, to say the least.

"If age were to be given symbolic form, it would have to be portrayed as a woman. It has all the female characteristics. Men are so much more forward and decisive with their mischief. Even for the most innately deceptive men, cruelty serves such a far different purpose. It arises from an altogether different part of the soul. Do you not agree?"

Dee did not reply, but with a noncommittal lift of his shoulders encouraged her to continue.

"Women are insidious. They are cruel for vengeance." She closed her fingers and looked at Dee as if expecting confirmation.

"It is really all the same, I think."

"Oh, Magistrate, for a man with the most acute understanding of the human heart"—the asperity that entered her voice here was cool—"you disappoint me."

Wu crossed her arms and turned back to the rail, where she gazed far out at the cold water and the sunlight that had now begun to break through the mists and sparkle on the wet sails of the colorful escorting junks rhythmically riding the waves.

"If I am the one you describe as having the most acute understanding of the human heart," Dee continued, "then humor me. I am also the one with a great need to solve all extant puzzles. Surely you are aware of that weakness in me."

Wu's eyes drifted over Dee and returned to their contemplation of the water. The boat was rolling less now as they moved into shallower waters. He stood and walked to the rail. The blood-black water had lightened with the emerging sun, foaming emerald-green now in the great boat's wake.

"Curiosity is the force that drives me. I should simply like to compare notes. Puzzles left unfinished, madame, are such infuriating things; they are like buildings put up by sloppy masons. They are full of holes through which the wind and rain impinge. I have always done my best, but to be bluntly honest, madame, my motives were not always selfless. I did much of my life's work for myself—for the simple reason that I cannot tolerate an unsolved riddle. So I will accept the honor you have generously bestowed upon me . . . if you will return a simple favor. You know that I have promised not to look into your . . . past affairs in any *official* capacity. I have already told you that. But help me patch my drafty house. Resolve a few unanswered questions for me."

She leveled an amused look at him.

"But Magistrate—why should the great sleuth Dee Jen-chieh need *my* help?"

"Madame, the term 'great sleuth' is yours, not mine. The fact is, I do need your help if I am ever to know the truth."

She appeared to consider his proposition for a few moments.

"My mother and I would love nothing better than to hear of your legendary days in Yangchou, Magistrate. Over dinner someday soon, perhaps." She smiled. "But I am afraid that I can offer no stories from *our* past in return."

The golden light of the afternoon sun cast a glow of incongruous innocence over the Empress. Dee studied the outline of her face.

"Dee Jen-chieh," she said decisively, "I have a responsibility that surpasses even my duties as Empress of China. I am, first and foremost, Madame Yang's daughter. And I am far too filial a daughter to reveal any of our secrets. Not yet. I will not allow anything to be revealed until my mother has passed on to heaven, Magistrate. Surely a good Confucian like you can understand that. The missing pieces of your puzzle cannot be put into place yet. Unfortunately," she said, rising to her feet, "you must endure your 'drafty house' a bit longer. At least as long as my mother lives."

Dee's importunate effort left him feeling slightly chagrined.

"And ten thousand years to the Imperial Matriarch, the Divine Madame Yang, mother of the Empress, on her birthday," he offered with appropriate cheer, recovering quickly, while his mind was busy calculating. Madame Yang was sixty-five, eight years older than Dee and fourteen years older than her daughter.

He had appeased the restive ghost of the gardener, but lately some other troublesome shades, insubstantial at first but gathering strength and volubility now with every passing day, were clamoring for his attention. The Duchess. Wu's niece. Her own sons. The unfortunate Nagaspa. And the smallest voice of them all, but the one that whispered the most urgently in his ear at night, the frail wisp of a spirit that had barely existed at all—Madame Wu's firstborn infant daughter.

How long would he have to wait?

Very well. I must wait. I must cultivate the patience of the most disciplined ascetic, and with no idea of the duration. Although my impatience and curiosity burn inside me the way a thirsty man's tongue burns for wine, I know that I have no choice. The Empress will be the one who decides when that wait is over, and if I have learned anything at all, it is that she will make her decision in her own time.

I know too that Master Shu, the esteemed historian, is assiduously busy recording for posterity the exchtraordinary events of recent times. I have no intention of attempting to interfere or to influence him in any way. Now that I have learned that truth is a relative, flexible thing, I shall certainly allow him to set down the truth as he sees it. I, in the meantime, feel obliged to record my own version of things as I saw them; certainly, anyone reading the two histories side by side in one or two centuries' time should have an intriguing riddle on his hands. Very well: here is the order of events and the words spoken by the principal players as seen through the eyes and heard through the ears of one Dee Jen-chieh, who, though he may have failed at a good many other things, always tried to tell the truth.

The high officials of the court had begun to gather early at the gates of the Censorate Hall of Justice on the day of Hsueh Huai-i's trial. They understood that I had a plan, that I intended to show them something out of the ordinary, a bit of mystic Tibetan symbolism that I believed would get the lama's attention.

When the large crowd had assembled and finally come to order, I could feel the anticipation building at the sight of my mysterious curtains at the far end of the room. The hall hummed with speculation. I was pleased. Small pockets of anxious conversation broke out here and there as the attention of the court shifted between the monk Hsueh Huai-i, kneeling at the dais and laughing quietly to himself, and the curtains and the enigma waiting behind him.

I certainly did not expect to witness remorse on Hsueh Huai-i's face, nor did I expect that the formal, official proceedings, as they would be conducted for the first part of the trial, would have much effect on him. I surmised that if Hsueh thought anything at all, it was probably that his arrest and all the rest of this were nothing more than inconveniences or obstacles to his further "work."

In fact, the monk showed no interest at all in his surroundings. He was gone, into his private world, untouched by all that went on about him. Hsueh was clearly exempt from the fragile agreements of conduct called morals and ethics that govern other men.

There were times during the trial when I allowed myself to think that the monk was becoming involved in the proceedings, moments when he seemed somber and almost attentive. But I had also learned not to be so easily fooled. Because quite unexpectedly, and at altogether inappropriate moments, a wild smile would sweep across the monk's face and a peculiar fire would light in his eyes, as if one demon entity had departed and another had come to roost within Hsueh's carcass. I had seen the same crazed smile on a mad-man once, long ago; it was a self-satisfied smile that implied that it was we, not he, who were the deluded ones.

I had much opportunity to observe him closely. In fact, it was difficult not to watch him. From time to time Hsueh's shoulders shook with soft silent laughter. At other times he withdrew into himself, his eyes cast down to his pillow, kneeling there as still and serious as one of his statues. He would retreat completely, unseeing, inspiring me to try to imagine the interior of his mind; what I glimpsed was a labyrinth, like a dark, haunted, crumbling palace with ten thousand windowless rooms filled with decayed and perverse treasures. At those times, the dry proceedings of the trial—the drone of the readers, the court's rhetorical questionings, the complex issuing of statements and decrees that accompanied so far-reaching a crime—went on as if they had nothing to do with Hsueh. The court could not touch him. He was a smooth rock in the center of a raging river.

I must confess that I preferred the monk when he was outright abusive, when he yelled foul insults to the questions and to the officials, and even tried to spit on my slipper once. At those times I felt that he was at least present, occupying the same room as everyone else, affected by what was happening to him. When he became removed, laughing and talking softly to himself, I felt that he was, in a sense, escaping. And I saw no reason why he should be spared.

But his raging moments never lasted very long before he was restrained. The guards had to gag him more than once to stanch the flow of foul invective, and bind his arms to his thighs to prevent him from rising from his kneeling position.

But Hsueh was no more helpful gagged or ungagged; he ignored each pointed question, answering either with silence, more invective, or irrelevant ranting. I could only guess what effect my final spectacle would have, but I hoped that my "performance" might speak directly to the monk. I knew that it would be a gamble, though, for I was about to intrude on the monk's private symbolic game.

In the end, Hsueh Huai-i was convicted of the most heinous crimes against man and the state and heaven itself. Now the readings and declarations and all of the formal proceedings of the Censorate were over. It was time to pass sentence. My moment had arrived.

Conjecture rose to the gilded squares of the ceiling over our heads. Voices rose, and conversation became louder and more animated until the room echoed with the excited din as, in the far corner of the great hall, the tall curtains hiding my secret were pulled open.

There was a moment of stunned silence in which not even a single cough or clearing throat could be heard. It was as if everyone present in the Censorate Hall of Justice was trying to understand what was now revealed before them. The mirror was especially large because what it needed to reflect, given its iconographical significance, was enormous, large beyond comprehension. So I was not surprised that many in the hall were startled when they discovered themselves looking into their own reflections.

I ordered the recalcitrant Lama Hsueh brought, or should I say reluctantly dragged, across the hall and placed on the kneeling pads facing his own reflection. My assistants fitted a heavy wooden cangue over his neck and arms. It was an appropriate part of the Buddhist and Tantric symbolism that I had contrived to put to use that day. Now that the monk's corporeal, earthly self had been sentenced, it was time to sentence his soul according to his own twisted imagery. I began, in as loud and authoritative voice as I could muster, to enumerate the various degrees of the Eight

Hot Hells of the Abhidharmakosa Sutras—a symbolic
reference that I was most certain would not be lost on our
lama. I was playing at his own game:

"... The hell of equivalent life, for those sinners
destined to return to their same forms and repeat their sins
for five hundred years ... the hell of black bonds, where the
sinner is bound and cut apart and his wounds lined with
salt for one thousand years ... the hell of being crushed
beneath mountainous rocks for two thousand years ... the
hell of ear-bursting wailing for eight thousand years ... the
hell of great heat, where the sinner suffers burning and
searing flame for ten thousand and sixty years ... the hell
of ultimate heat, the hell of suffering under molten lead for
eight million four hundred thousand years ... as for you,
Hsueh Huai-i ..." I stopped. In the entire hall, no one
breathed.

The monk's face was no longer empty and
expressionless; he tightened the muscles of his jaw and
clenched his fists within the confines of the cangue. If I read
the man correctly, this was more out of embarrassment that
his own secret instruments and symbols had been turned
against him than from any fear for his own life. He was,
perhaps, too far gone for that.

"Those are but a few of the hells that open their
beckoning arms to you. Now it is time to pass sentence." I
paused for eight or ten heartbeats and gazed significantly
around the silent hall before my voice rang out again.

"For the heinous crimes of your long career, I absolve
you."

A great rush of consternation rose from the hall, a sea
of whispers and groans. It was necessary to raise my hand
to quiet them.

"You are absolved of the murders in Ch'ang-an. You
are absolved of the deaths and misery, which cannot be
calculated, which you caused in your years of ascension.
You are absolved of other crimes that are known only to
you. You are absolved for every murder you ever
committed."

I paused again. Angry murmurs rose. I raised my hand
again, my voice cutting through the commotion.

"Except one. You are sentenced, Hsueh Huai-i, for a
long-ago and obscure death at which you were not even

present, a death of which you may not even be aware." Now the hall fell into abrupt silence.

"You are sentenced, Hsueh Huai-i, for the wrongful execution of a gardener in Yangchou, many long years ago when you were but a child. The gardener could not be saved, nor his family kept from the shame and public disgrace of his death for his erroneous conviction of the murder of the Transport Minister. You were that murderer. And for the death of the gardener, Yama, the King of the Underworld Death Lords, shall see you pass into the ultimate hell of Avici . . . the hell of uninterrupted torments, to last for sixteen million and eight hundred thousand years.

"You, Monk Hsueh Huai-i, shall enter the gates of Avici the day following tomorrow. The Divine Emperor Wu Tsetien has decreed absolutely that there shall be no postponement and that there shall be no Imperial appeal. Therefore, Monk Hsueh, prepare yourself for the most painful death that can be suffered upon this earthly plain." I paused again to draw breath for my final pronouncement.

"But before you are taken from this court, you will look upon your sin." I lifted my hand to indicate Hsueh's reflection in the great mirror.

The guards had been prepared to force Hsueh to gaze into the mirror, just as the unfortunates in the esoteric writings had been forced to do, to see the specific sins for which they would suffer eons of torment. But the monk had already turned toward it without coercion and was studying his reflection. He had begun laughing softly to himself. This time, it seemed, Hsueh's laughter was directed toward something he saw in the mirror. The guards were about to gag him when I raised my hand again.

Instead of protesting his innocence, or cursing me or the court or the Empress, Hsueh giggled absurdly, rocking back and forth with the burdensome cangue across his shoulders.

"I won," he whispered. "Dog Boy won the wager, old Left Foot!" He laughed and trembled with hilarity. "I know you remember the terms, you old rascal! Start counting your heartbeats, or whatever it is that will thump in your hard little chest. That is, if there is a number high enough to measure them. You have plenty of time, Left Foot. Immeasurable lifetimes. Lifetimes and lifetimes. And just to start with, one thousand lives as a cockroach. A filthy . . .

little . . . shit-covered . . . cockroach,'' he said, dissolving in mirth at this last. After a few moments he regained his composure and became quite serious again. ''Whereas I . . .'' He closed his eyes and smiled sublimely, speaking in a soft voice just above a whisper, shaping the words with the tenderness of a poet. ''I shall be borne on golden feathered wings. A soaring eagle that will live for two thousand years, sailing above the clouds and the lofty pinnacles dressed in their emerald-green gowns of pine forests and adorned with their diamond necklaces of ice and snow and sparkling waterfalls. . . . ''

Then the monk turned away from the mirror and looked at me. His face was placid, content. It was not until that moment that I believed I was finally looking upon Hsueh's madness; all the rest of it had merely been noise and camouflage. Now I was truly seeing it. My hand was still upraised to silence the hall; I wanted to hear every word that Hsueh might be about to say. He smiled pleasantly, and was once again my old friend of the teashops and the long afternoons in Loyang.

''Hm! I thank you for my death, Magistrate-King, for hastening me toward the next incarnation.'' Hsueh turned from the mirror and bowed, for all the world as if the heavy block of wood across his shoulders were a mantle of the lightest silk.

Master Shu has told me that he intends to allow himself the luxury of poetic self-expression in his later years; he has already hinted to me that he is at work on a series of pieces honoring my life and work. He has even coyly shown me a snippet or two. I read them politely, and nodded my head approvingly, but saw that I would have to retire to my rooms immediately and set brush to paper. If Shu's work was going to continue in the direction in which it appeared to be going, then I was obligated to see to it that it did not travel through the centuries unescorted. Like the plain brown little donkey that plods along beside the long-maned, brilliantly caparisoned horse with its polished hooves and flying streamers of colorful silk, my humble, unadorned, and prosaically factual account of how I came to solve the Ch'ang-an murders must plod along beside Shu's poetic fancy. The piece he showed me hinted at portentous dreams, extraordinary visions, and heroism of mythic proportions; in truth, it was dumb luck, blind coincidence, the invaluable assistance of a brilliant friend, and sheer dogged persistence punctuated by secret moments of dread and self-doubt, which would simply have no place in Shu's glorified vision. So be it. I suppose there is no way to stop him, and I have pledged not to interfere with him; but he cannot stop me, either. So once again, posterity will have to choose.

Murder, of course, was as common in the land as rotten apples on the ground in autumn in the days when the Ch'ang-an incidents took place. Execution, torture, and exile were the order of the day in Loyang, but I did not connect the Ch'ang-an deaths with all of that. In Loyang, the murders were plainly of a political, expedient nature. Shocking, deplorable, hideous, frightening, yes; but not difficult to understand. Plain, forthright, strategically performed murders. Murders with a purpose.

What we had in Ch'ang-an was different. What struck me full in the face right away and left me trembling was the amalgam of method and mayhem. The killings were an orgy of careful, painstaking, systematic destruction and chaos. There could be no better symbol of what I am speaking of than the ghastly stitched smiles of the first dead family. Whoever had made those tiny stitches in black silk thread did it with the care of a royal seamstress.

Each new murder reaffirmed that something systematic was being acted out before us, but the specific mutilations carried us farther and farther from anything resembling logic as we knew it. Very well: I understood that I had to penetrate someone else's logic. Someone's perverse, alien logic.

When I set eyes upon the carvings at the caves, I still knew nothing—but when I saw rendered in stone the faces that I had once seen chanting in the streets of Ch'ang-an, I felt the cool hand of fate resting on the back of my neck. I was not even sure what I was looking at, but I knew I had to get back to Ch'ang-an without wasting even a heartbeat. I needed to look at those faces again. I needed to see if I was perhaps finally going mad. But when I went to the White Horse Monastery and saw the deformed monks again in the flesh, moving about with an aloof and arrogant purposefulness—not at all the poor miscreants I have naively adjudged them to be the first time I saw them—I understood that I was not mad, that they were indeed the faces carved in stone, and that they were an elite corps of some sort, there could be no doubt, painstakingly handpicked.

Still, though it was bright broad daylight, I was a man moving through a dark room filled with obstacles. In the library, I looked at the *bodhi* leaves with their painted portraits, and again saw the startling resemblance—and the inscription: Arhats, slayers of the Devadhatta. Slayers. My heart was pounding, though I gave no outward sign, when I caught a glimpse of the ancient *tonka* painting showing the mythical realm of Jambudvipa, with its four corners marked, and the dark river of danger flowing from the realm of the Devadhatta—the extreme northwest. I believe that it was at that exact moment that I had my first taste of a madman's logic.

I still knew nothing, and felt that if anything I knew less than when I had walked through the door—but I did know that with the pillars rising at the four corners of the Empire, the realm of Jambudvipa had been marked, and Ch'ang-an, the site of the murders, was the site of the northwest pillar.

Was it possible, I asked myself, that those poor dead people, who did not even know one another, who had no connections with the underworld or with any peculiar religious sects, and certainly not with the ruling aristocracy of Loyang, had somehow come to represent these Devadhatta, from whose realm flowed this dark river of danger? Were those deformed men appointed Devadhatta-slayers?

By now, of course, though I had not said it out loud or even articulated it to myself, the madman whose logic I was tasting was beginning to have a face; a name was forming on my reluctant tongue. Someone had had to exercise his considerable influence to handpick those sixteen men out of hundreds or even thousands of aspirants; someone had gone to a great deal of trouble. The sixteen ugly monks seemed to be the pride of the White Horse Monastery in Ch'ang-an. And who was the leader of every White Horse Temple in the Empire, founder of the White Cloud sect, and inspirational "leader" to thousands?

It was in the comfortable privacy of my own study that the extraordinary memory of my good friend the Buddhist scholar laid open a dark world, a veritable feast for an ill mind. Our discussion of the Arhats, the Devadhatta, and the doctrine of the Era of Degenerate Law led to the uncomfortable discovery—for me—that the Great Cloud Sutra was not a total forgery. Here, set down centuries before the Empress was born, were words seeming to prophesy her rule. It was all there—everything Hsueh Huai-i needed to forge in his own mind a powerful, literal belief in what was usually taken only metaphorically. Did I say before that I had had a taste of a madman's logic? Well, now I felt as if it had me by the ankles and was about to pull me under. And it was there, toward the end of the recitation of the Great Cloud Sutra, that the name of Mara was spoken for the first time, and the door swung wide.

Mara, leader of the demon army, the destroyers of the Law and enemies of the Dharma—also known as the Devadhatta.

And this, of course, led to the Demon Kirita Sutra. So vivid was my scholarly friend's recitation of this obscure piece of sacred writing that the demons seem to swarm and gibber in the shadows around me. No doubt its original intent was that it should serve as a strong symbol meant to discipline those who waver in the purity of their faith, who succumb to the fleshly desires that keep them trapped in the world of birth and suffering; but the images chosen to represent these desires draw on a particularly dark and frightening part of the mind. One could go quite mad if one allowed oneself to take the demons as fundamental truth— as literal representations.

I will never forget how the verses flowed from my colleague's tongue, without hesitation or error. I did not even perceive that he paused to breathe. Here were the creatures of evil temptation who assaulted the serenity of the Enlightened One, while he sat in their midst in an attitude of perfect repose, resolute and immovable: " . . . and the swords and spears of the demon legions of Mara shall become as so many garlands of flowers strewn at his feet, their rocks and arrows as so many white doves flying about his sacred head . . . "

The scholar recited, and I wrote feverishly:

Then Mara called to mind his own army, wishing to work the overthrow of the Sakya saint;* and his followers swarmed around, wearing different forms and carrying arrows, trees, darts, clubs and swords in their hands . . .

Having the faces of boars, fishes, horses, asses, and camels; of tigers, bears, lions, and elephants; one-eyed, many-faced, three-headed, with half-mutilated faces, half their bodies green, and with monstrous mouths . . .

With disheveled hair, with topknots, with arms reaching out longer than a serpent, some the size of children with projecting teeth, with knees swollen like pots, carrying headless trunks in their hands, with no noses, and no hair . . .

Copper-red, bearing clubs in their hands, some as tall as trees and carrying spears, with triumphant faces or frowning faces, wasting the strength or fascinating the mind, with protuberant bellies or speckled bellies and the faces of grinning pigs . . .

Armed with tusks and with claws, with yellow or smoke-colored hair, with long pendulous ears like elephants, clothed in rancid leather and smeared with dung, girdles jingling with rattling bells, blended with goats and assuming many forms . . .

Some as they went leaped about wildly, others danced upon one another, some sported about in the sky, others went along on the tops of the trees . . .

One danced, shaking a trident, another made a crash, dragging a club, another bounded for joy like a bull, another blazed out flames from every hair . . .

By the time my friend finished his recitation, not only had the door swung wide, but I had stepped through.

There, at the end of each verse, were my poor murdered families: bodies half-green, monstrous mouths, protuberant speckled bellies, no noses and no hair, faces of grinning pigs, their poor corpses mutilated into the images of Mara's demon army and offered up on an invisible altar of sacrifice. This was a grim, serious battle someone was waging, utterly apart from the world of earthly politics. The

---

*The Enlightened One
The Buddha

power of twisted belief behind it nearly knocked me to the floor.

I asked my friend to repeat the fifth verse. Its final line left little to the imagination: " . . . blended with goats and assuming many forms . . . " It was not difficult to envision what was planned for the next family of victims; my mind, now accustomed to horrors, it seemed, had no trouble in presenting a picture to me. A picture I had to stop from ever coming into being.

So far, the war against the demon army had been waged in a rigidly sequential way. There was a terrible order to it, and I had a piece of it by the tail—but only a piece of it. I knew what was going to be done to the next family, but I had no way of predicting who that family would be, or when it would happen. I had risen from my chair and paced helplessly. "Three families have died," I told my friend. "Three. Soon there will be a fourth. Are there any other references to this demon army?" I implored. "Something else that might tell us something? Anything!"

"Let me think," he said.

When a man with a memory such as his speaks those words, one keeps one's mouth shut. He closed his eyes and thought for a long time; I could feel him moving back into those long dusty corridors of his mind that he had described to me. I waited. All at once he gestured for my brush and some paper; I pushed them across the table and waited, filled with anticipation.

He began to sketch. Once the images in his memory started flowing, he moved with extraordinary speed. He sketched a great Buddha at the top center of a square of paper. Then he began to draw a series of fine vertical and horizontal lines, like a grid, with the space occupied by the Buddha making a large rectangle in the midst of the smaller rectangles formed by the intersecting lines. Then, within the various smaller rectangles, he began to draw tiny figures. I moved around and stood quietly behind him, looking over his shoulder: tiny demon figures—beast-headed, half-human, distorted, cavorting, leering, one for every space. By now, I recognized the army of Mara as if they were old friends.

I did not interrupt him, but as I stood looking over his shoulder, I saw something. Carefully, quietly, so as not to break his concentration, I tiptoed back to my place at the table and retrieved my map of Ch'ang-an. I went back to my place behind my friend, and held the map in front of me so that I could look at it and his sketch at the same time. I scarcely dared breathe; I felt that my excitement at that moment was a palpable thing.

When he finally put down his brush, he had before him an extraordinarily complex sketch. His brushwork was very fine, even in his haste. "Mara's army," he said. "This is from an ancient painting depicting the Enlightened One under siege. A very rare piece, which I saw once many years ago in my travels, and which I studied and committed to memory." He laughed. "Even I don't know what I am carrying about in the recesses of my mind."

I laid my map on the table next to his painting. He looked up at me sharply, then back at the map and the drawing. Looking at the two was like looking at the same person dressed and undressed.

My grid map showed the city of Ch'ang-an and its division into rectangular wards formed by a series of intersecting lines, with a larger rectangle in the center at the top of the page. Where the Buddha sat in repose in the drawing, the palace complex sat on the ward map. I counted the horizontal and vertical lines on both, and with a shaking, unbelieving hand, found that they matched: eleven vertical, ten horizontal.

"Find me the demons who fit the descriptions in the final sentences of the first three verses of the Demon Kirita Sutra," I said quietly.

He studied his drawing with infinite care for a minute or two, then dipped the brush again and made several tiny marks in a group of squares in the vicinity of one another in the lower right-hand section of his drawing. "These are all possibilities," he said. "We will have to find a way of narrowing down the choices."

"I do not think that is impossible," I said. If he had been making his marks on the corresponding sectors of my map, they would have fallen on the part representing the wealthy southeast suburbs.

The southeast suburbs, where the murder victims' homes had all been.

Marked on my map, of course, were the exact wards where the particular homes were located. I counted up and across carefully so that I would have a numerical reference point. Doing the same on the squares of the drawing brought me, in each case, to a demon that not only satisfactorily matched the demons of the sutra, but satisfactorily matched the mutilations performed on the victims in the corresponding ward square.

I saw a problem immediately, though. Each square in the drawing contained but one demon; there were many more families than just one in the corresponding ward squares, which were a good one and one-half *li** in length and width, and the particular locations of the murdered families within those ward squares revealed no common pattern. Very well, it was not their location within the square that singled them out as members of Mara's demon army. It had to be something else, something less tangible.

We found the square on the ward map corresponding to the square on the drawing containing a demon with the furry arms and legs of an animal—"blended with goats," the fourth verse had said. "Here," I said, putting my finger on the map. "This may well be the ward where the next murder will take place. There are seven estates in that sector. We must decide which one it is going to be."

Possibly the murdered families had been the highest ones on the national registry, the most prominent families in their particular wards. We consulted the registry, and our surmise appeared to be correct, so we chose the most highly listed family in that ward. "This has got to be it," I said.

"Yes," my friend said. "We may have discovered who is next. But there is another problem. We don't know when."

I had come to learn that the sleuth and the fanatical believer have a great deal in common. They are both possessed by a drive for order. I had discovered the chilling extent to which orderliness lay behind the Ch'ang-an murders. Now I needed to rely on Hsueh Huai-i—by now, I was certain that he was the author of it all—to maintain that order. As it turned out, of course, he did, and that is why he ultimately fell into my hands. But at the time, I could only hope that he would not deviate even one, single, obsessive step from his strictly laid scheme. If he had, I would have been lost.

---

*A "Li" is a third of a mile.

When my friend left me that evening, I began my desperate review of all that we had uncovered, looking for something in the order of it all that I had missed, something that would lead me to the timing of the next killing.

And that was precisely what I was agonizing over at the moment that I was arrested. And it was while I was imprisoned, of course, that I finally discovered the "when" that would go with the "who," and the darkest, strangest convolution of madman's logic of them all.

The arrest, of course, was a virtual shouted affirmation that Hsueh was the one; anyone else would have had me killed. For reasons relating to our old association and his inability to resist having a bit of fun with me, he had me arrested instead. I believe that his plan was to keep me incarcerated until the next murders happened so that he would have the pleasure of knowing that I watched, helpless, from my cell. After the murders, no doubt he would then have finished me off.

The timing of my arrest made me strongly suspect that someone had recognized me when I was snooping about. At first, I thought it had to be either at the caves or at the monastery. But there had been very few people at the caves that day because of the rain, and we had our heads covered most of the time. Inside, there had been only Wu-chi, Abbot Liao, the fellow who showed us around, and myself. No. It had to be someone at the White Horse the day I went to the library. This turned out to be precisely the case, of course; after the White Horse in Ch'ang-an was closed down by the National Bureau of Sacrifice, a certain little man came forward, protesting vociferously that he did not like being put out of a comfortable position. I recognized him after only a few moments of looking at his face and hearing his voice. He was none other than the man I knew as Diamond Eyes, whom I had punished years before in Yangchou. He had found himself a pleasant, easy job with the White Horse in Ch'ang-an as keeper of relics. Exactly where he saw me he never would reveal, but I suspect that it was at a moment when my attention was riveted to the Arhats. Old friends meet again. . . .

In retrospect, I think that I must have worried over the missing piece even more than I did over my own fate. That is how obsessed I was. But it was Hsueh's weakness for showmanship on a gigantic scale that ultimately gave him away. He had me, and I would have been utterly baffled if he had only been able to keep quiet; but then quiet and modesty were never his strong suits.

The great *thungchen* atop Wu's Ch'ang-an pillar marking the northwest corner of her metaphorical Buddhist Realm was perhaps his ultimate public performance. A device that became significant only with the blowing of the particularly strong northwest winds could not help but draw attention to the significance of those winds.

The morning that I and all of urban Ch'ang-an were startled from uneasy sleep by that dolorous sound and the shuddering winds, I lay on my hard cot, my eyes still unopened, and thought of a later verse from the Kirita Sutra that I had virtually forgotten, so intent was I on the descriptions of the demons: " . . . a wind of intense violence blew in all directions, spreading a deeper darkness of night around . . . And such were the troops of demons who encircled the root of the *bodhi* tree on every side, eager to seize it and to destroy it, awaiting the command of their lord . . . "

Awaiting the command of their lord. Winds. Of course, winds, I thought, scrambling to my feet. I thought hard, and seemed to recall, to the best of my ability, that there had indeed been strong winds in the days preceding the murders. And what had the interval been between the winds and the murders? A day? Two days? I could not recall with any certainty or exactness, only that in retrospect I remembered experiencing the unpleasant and persistent winds always in the days prior to the crimes. When my constable confirmed that the winds were blowing from the northwest—from the direction of the mythic realm of the Devadhatta—and that the horn sounded only when the powerful northwest wind reached a certain intensity, then I knew.

I believe I mentioned earlier that with the discovery of when the next murder might take place came my encounter with the darkest and most convoluted aspect of the madman's logic. Ch'ang-an's infamous winds that blow each late autumn and winter through the gritty passes of her outlying hills had become the Dark River of Danger depicted flowing so copiously from the northwest in the paintings of the Buddhist Realm. That much I understood on my own, before I left the jail. I was to acquire an even deeper understanding later—and it would come from the ragged mouths of the Arhats themselves, after our struggle with them was finished.

The Arhats, after they were overpowered and captured, gave up their information slowly, reluctantly at first. That was when I decided that a forged message from their spiritual leader claiming that their lives were no longer useful was in order.

This faked "message" from Loyang that I conveyed to them when I questioned them later that evening in prison— evidently with sufficiently convincing detail—went on to explain that their souls, having become equally corrupt by the evil that they battled, must also be extinguished from this life and from the cycle of a rewarding rebirth, or something to that effect. I prided myself on stepping into their belief system so well, convincing them in a way that spoke to them directly that their lama had no further use for them, and indeed considered them a detriment. So, fearing for their lives and believing that I might be merciful with them if they cooperated—because they were nothing if not obedient to their superiors—they revealed more to me than I could have hoped. They confirmed my most dire theories, and more.

By their confession, I came to understand many things according to their particular highly specialized system, taught to them by their lama. Under Hsueh's auspices, they had become proud of their ugliness. By contrast, the Devadhatta demons of Mara's army always sought to inhabit normal, comely flesh. It was the work of the demon-slaying Arhats not only to seek out those who had been "inhabited" by the invading demons, but to kill the possessed bodies so that they could not be possessed again. The mutilation of the corpses was simply a way of identifying which particular demons from the Kirita Sutra had been vanquished. And it was the wind, the Dark River, that carried evil into the hearts of the murder victims—an ethereal river, howling down from the northwest, hurling the demon spirits into their bodies, with the wailing trumpet announcing their coming. And, unwitting and comfortable in their homes, the unfortunate souls of the hosts would soon be displaced to make room for their new occupants. I learned all of this shortly following our struggle with the deformed men, when such was my state of mind that I could very nearly believe that it was all true.

The bloody bag they had brought with them, which I gazed into in the moments immediately following the struggle, confirmed that the fourth verse of the sutra had been their inspiration for that day's work, just as I had believed it would be: the bag contained the pathetic severed limbs of many goats. With the help of the Arhat's one weapon, the long wicked knife, the innocent people of that household—or ourselves—would have become the Devadhatta of the sutra, "blended with goats and assuming many forms."

The Arhats did truly believe in their mission and that they had been divinely ordained. I can recall, in vivid detail, as if they were sitting before me this very moment in their horrid nakedness, the first session in which I was able to question all sixteen. I was exhausted and should have been barely able to stand, but I quite forgot my fatigue in my excitement. Many of my deputies were in even worse condition; I, at least, had had an hour or two of sleep, the sleep that had saved me from the Arhats' drone.

I recall the vague smell of incense mingled with the odors of sweat and effort that hung about their bodies. I remember that when we gathered them together in the reception hall, before wrapping their odd forms in quilts and linens, I was surprised to see a faint shimmer of reflected light on their bodies. Despite the extreme cold and their nakedness, they glistened with perspiration. This was a vivid indication of the self-induced trance state that gave them their inhuman strength and imperviousness to cold, and that made it possible for them to carry out their assigned deeds. The redolence of temple incense emanating from their bodies spoke of ritual ceremonies, no doubt performed in the White Horse Monastery just before they set out on their mission.

As they stood there in the reception hall of their intended victims' home, naked and subdued, the strangeness of their beings seemed all the more intense. The chaos of their features made it difficult for me to focus my eyes on any one face.

I noted, however, that the Arhats' spell upon themselves was beginning to break—because as they were escorted from the house, they had started to shake with the cold. They pulled the quilts and blankets tightly around themselves, and their teeth—if they had any—chattered audibly. As they filed past me I could see that the flesh of their faces had lost the high color that had been visible only moments ago, and their lips had gone blue as if they had been tinted with an artist's colors.

The Arhats were bound together tightly with ropes in such a way that just progressing slowly along the alley on foot required great concentration and cooperation. More than a few of them walked with an odd rolling gait, a halting limp, or a dragging foot. Their processional, moving forward a few staggering steps at a time, the ropes stretching apart to their full length and then bunching together, presented a sight I will not soon forget; they resembled nothing so much as a huge and hideous caterpillar. Despite the heavy guard surrounding them, the occasional neighborhood observer backed away as this grotesque lantern-lit assembly passed by.

Although I was so extremely tired that my legs trembled and went weak and nearly collapsed beneath me more than once, my wits had been hardened by the desperate efforts of the past several weeks. So even as I struggled to stay on my feet, I had already determined the nature of their punishment. The idea had come upon me suddenly as I watched the Arhats, bound together, struggle forward down the lane.

It was when our little parade finally reached the walled compound of the southern ward's prison that I undertook to question them, and learned about the nature of the evil wind.

But when I asked them on what basis the timing of the spiritual "invasions" after the winds was calculated, they all fixed me with the same expression of disbelief, or perhaps it would be more accurate to say that the odd mechanics of their facial features conveyed dismay in sixteen unique expressions of the same emotion.

"You mean you do not know?" the one who appeared to be their leader responded at last. His voice dropped away with such a sorry note that one would have thought he was responding to a slow-witted person wanting to know on how many legs a dog walks.

"Do you mean to tell us that you do not know the length of time that it takes a peripatetic demon soul to seat itself within its host?" he said in his slurred speech after considering me for a very long and uncomfortable moment in which I was determined to reveal nothing. This man's mouth was particularly malformed, so I had trouble understanding everything he said, but I responded as best I could, hiding my surprise at his unmitigated arrogance.

"I must confess that I am ignorant about such matters," I said in what I hoped was a calm and evenly collected voice. With that, their expressions—such as they were— changed to pity. That is, I believe that that is what I saw in their strange eyes, some veiled and hooded by odd shrouds of flesh and protuberances of bone, others unevenly placed upon their faces. They turned to each other and shook their ugly heads, mumbling beneath their breaths. No doubt they had not intended for me to overhear any of what they were saying, but I did manage to catch just enough of what passed between them: "Poor unenlightened fools"; and "They will find themselves unprepared for the coming Age of the Law." And of course, the questions I heard repeated most often in their sad, regretful voices as they shook their heads back and forth: "How can they ever expect us to protect them?" and "What will they do when we are gone?"

"It is quite all right, gentlemen. Your vigil is over. Your labors are no longer needed here. From now on we shall simply have to watch out for ourselves." By now, of course, I had already decided where they would be going, having been inspired by watching them struggle along the street tied together. I would banish them high up in the great Tibetan mountains, where they would remain joined to one another forever with chains. In this fashion they would work, under the command of a military garrison, to build a great wall, atop the mountains, to prevent "evil spirits" from descending into China.

I am pleased to record that this is where they are today, having just completed, I am told, some several hundred yards of brickwork. There in the clear crystal air, five *li* above the earth, there will be work for them for a lifetime, and many thousands more yet to come, I hope.

At first, I was foolish enough to be proud of myself for my quick retort. The Arhats must have assumed either that I could not overhear their private conversation or that I could not understand them, because they seemed taken aback when I responded so readily. By then I believed that I had become fairly adept at interpreting their expressions;

I was sure that I read looks of chagrin on the faces of at least eight of them. That is when I chose to surprise them, to disarm them further, with all that I had learned about their plans, to show them that I was a step ahead of them.

"We are already in the Age of Degenerate Law, gentlemen. Perhaps that is why the unenlightened are yet the victors." But now they did not seem at all surprised. They acted as if they expected that I should be aware of these sorry circumstances as a matter of course. And, to their way of thinking, I was quite correct: the ignorant and unenlightened *were* the victors.

They mumbled their weary agreements and nodded sadly to each other as they were led away. Their reaction to my final statement was not exactly what I had anticipated, but it was what I should have expected. Never doubt the conviction of madness, I thought.

In conclusion, I am forced to consider the tragedy of how these sixteen men came to be where they were on that cold evening. I do not have the individual stories of all sixteen, only scattered bits and pieces here and there. But although the details for each man will differ and are sketchy at best, they have been sufficient to provide me with a general picture—a picture of the lamentable state of the human condition. The Buddhists (and now I refer to those followers of the true faith) are indeed correct when they tell us that to be born in the flesh is to be born to suffering.

It is difficult if not impossible for those of us blessed with normal appearance, whether comely or homely or somewhere in between, to imagine how it must be to go through life as an outcast gargoyle. Can we imagine how it would be to be unable to do something as simple as move through a crowd without being an object of revulsion, pity, and cruelty? How would we live with the constant knowledge that all people, whether they stare rudely or avert their eyes, are thinking the same thing? They are thinking that the misborn would be better hidden away, locked in basements and such, so that we do not impose upon their sensibilities or ruin their appetites. And yet we would have to go on from day to day, occupied with the same thousand and one ordinary tasks necessary for life as anyone else.

Some of these creatures were disfigured by a crippling accident sometime during their lives, like the fellow who had been burned. Others were born as they were. Regarding the latter, it is difficult to imagine the circumstances in which the parents allowed so hideous an offspring to live. But somehow the child, fully conscious and sentient in the way that all children are, was allowed—no, forced, because that is what the world imposes—to live, aware of his condition among men, forever reminded of the untouchable that he was. In such a state, I can well imagine that it would be difficult not to embrace an order that exalted you for what you were, honored you, and explained away the outward meaning of your wretched existence with tantalizing intimations of a higher purpose. An order that you could believe in with an unwavering heart, because it was told to you by another creature, one who understood the true nature of monsters upon this earth.

Would they not have been better off, Hsueh Huai-i, as cold twisted bones in their graves?

I learned much from my sixteen friends, including a piece of information that changed the fates of at least three of the participants in this saga. The Arhats had asked me pityingly if I did not know the time necessary for a peripatetic demon soul to migrate and seat itself within its host; out of curiosity, I did eventually ask them how long it took, because I had done a bit of research into the recorded weather patterns in Ch'ang-an for that autumn, and still could not perceive a consistent time lapse between the peak intensity of the winds and the murders. It had always taken at least a day, but sometimes it had been longer. I knew, of course, that a sealed message was carried by runners on swift horses between the monastery in Ch'ang-an and its counterpart in Loyang whenever the wind reached a certain pitch; then a message was dispatched back to Ch'ang-an, containing explicit instructions as to the precise moment that the Arhats should begin their work. It would seem that the timing of the invading Devadhatta demons was somewhat arbitrary, and there was only one man astute enough to calculate what that timing might be, and that man was, quite naturally, Lama Hsueh Huai-i.

I had remarked to them that the time lapse between the fierce winds and their arrival at the estate was longer than it had been in the case of the previous murders. It had been two and three-quarters days from my moment of realization in the jail cell until their appearance in the house. "Well, we were there earlier," one of them told me, "but only to perform the cleansing rites." I recalled the long hair and the hoofprints I had found in the garden after our sleepless first night of waiting. "But you are right," the Arhat told me, "it was a slightly longer lapse than usual. Certainly it was longer than we had expected it to be; our master had led us to believe that this next mission would take place almost immediately after the winds."

Indeed, I thought; that would be because Hsueh Huai-i had known that I was imprisoned, and he wanted to taunt me.

"But you see, our instructions from our master in Loyang were delayed," the Arhat said. The runners whose job it was to carry the message as swiftly as possible had been diverted along the way. "Drinking and whoring," he muttered with distaste. "They were many, many hours late. We would have been there a full day earlier if not for those faithless, weak-fleshed fools," he finished with disgust.

In other words, they might very well have arrived before my men and I did. We could easily have got there to find the family already dead, were it not for those weak-fleshed fools the Arhat spoke of with such disdain. Those weak-fleshed fools, my sons. Let history note that it came to pass that Dee Jen-chieh sentenced his own sons in his court. The comparative lightness of their sentences—twenty years in the far west, guarding the border between the Empire and Tibet—had nothing at all to do with the fact that I am their father. It was because they had unwittingly saved the lives of the fourth family.

Another sentence was lightened, as well. The famous death by slicing so vividly recounted by our master historian Shu Ching-tsung, with Hsueh Huai-i's screams of agony echoing down through the ages, was, of course, nothing more than a fanciful little gift to the Empress. We do not know for certain if she believes it or not; we go on the assumption that she does. We do not ask her, and she does not offer. She is satisfied that he is gone forever, and that as far as posterity knows, she dealt with him without mercy or compromise. She did not ask to witness the execution, and she did not ask to examine the head afterward, as was her prerogative.

Hsueh Huai-i was banished from the Empire forever.

At this moment, according to my calculations, he should be many hundreds of *li* along in his forced march under guard back to Tibet. It will take him at least two years of walking every day, winter and summer, spring and autumn, to arrive in his homeland. In his case, the leniency I showed him had nothing to do with our old friendship, but everything to do with the fact that his two hired thugs were none other than my own sons. How could I sentence Hsueh Huai-i to death, and spare myself? Am I not equally guilty for all that happened? My daughter, the infant I purchased from the Indian years ago, argues with me passionately to the contrary, placing herself firmly between me and my terrible conviction like a tigress guarding her young. At times I almost believe her, and then I remember that her own nobility did not come from me, but is the legacy of two anonymous peasants. But she is my only solace.

Certain parts of this journal will be deleted after I finish writing them. I record them now as an exercise for my weary mind, but that is all. Historian Shu's account of the execution will stand. And I shall allow him to indulge in another bit of fancy, for the sake of the eyes not yet born that will read his glorious histories.

I have asked him, when writing about my life, to make me a good father.

35

A.D. 706
Loyang

Retired Magistrate Dee Jen-chieh had received the message only a few hours before. The Empress, so the letter said, was ready to keep an old promise to the magistrate, and he was to come at once to the palace.

There was only one old promise that Dee could think of. He had not heard that the Empress's mother had died or was even unwell; but she had, after all, celebrated her ninety-fifth birthday that spring. With each successive year, Dee had watched old colleagues and friends die off. Wu-chi had gone twenty-eight years before; his comrade the good Abbot Liao had lived a scant year beyond that. Historian Shu had died ten years ago, and there had been others, so many others. But Madame Yang seemed incapable of dying. She simply grew older while everyone around her fell like trees in the forest.

It was with gratitude that he made his way to the palace on this pleasant morning, refusing the carriage that the Empress had offered, choosing instead to walk. Twenty years ago, he would have covered in half the time the distance he walked today. Though he did it considerably more slowly than he once did, he still walked the streets of the city when his bones did not ache too much and the weather was fine. Today, anticipation quickened his step and he nearly forgot his own eighty-six years.

The Empress, now eighty-one, had gradually retired from active participation in government, content, apparently, to leave things in the hands of the Council of Six and the Censorate. He tried to recall the last time he had actually set eyes on her: it had been at least five years, he was sure, since he had seen either her or Madame Yang. He himself had moved his family to Loyang and had been living here for almost thirty years now. There were no more public celebrations of birthdays and such; the two women had gone into virtual seclusion. The only visitors admitted to their vast wing of the palace, so it was rumored, were various Taoist shamans. It had been a long, long time since a lama or any other Buddhist practitioner had paid them a call. With the departure of Hsueh Huai-i, it seemed that the Empress had experienced a slow but steady decline in her interest in things Buddhist; now, in her late years, she drew diversion and succor from a source as Chinese as the broad flat feet of the peasants who had plowed the land for the last four thousand years. The name "City of Transformation" had fallen away as well; it had been at least ten years since Dee could remember hearing anyone even utter the words. The Empress's great pillars still stood, but only as architectural curiosities. There was talk of dismantling the one in Ch'ang-an; it was the opinion of several of the city engineers that it was becoming a hazard, and that the valuable metal in it could be put to other uses. Wherever in the universe the invisible realm of Jambudvipa lay, it was no longer over the Chinese Empire.

His pace quickened again. The one thing that had not

died, changed, or faded away with the years was Dee Jen-chieh's curiosity.

Dee was ushered into the great bedchamber by a hand-maiden who then withdrew and shut the doors silently behind her. He walked forward and stood looking at the ancient woman lying quite still in the great bed, her eyes closed. He stared intently for a moment, then experienced a moment of disappointment when he saw the woman's chest gently rise and fall. She was not dead; she was merely dozing. He looked at the lined flesh, the sunken eyes, the sparse white hair, and the unpleasantly apparent outline of the skull under the skin. Some care had been taken: the hair had been brushed and care-fully pinned up, and white powder had been applied to the face. But ninety-five years, Dee thought, cannot be disguised by any earthly artifice.

A ragged little snore escaped the partly open mouth. Just as Dee was catching a glimpse of a set of incongruously white teeth behind the shriveled lips, another door to the chamber opened, and a woman stepped through; a woman older, if pos-sible, than the one in the bed. Dee understood his error in that moment. This was not the Empress's mother whose head rested on the pillow before him, but the Empress herself. The other ancient woman, the one walking through the door very much under her own power, was Madame Yang.

Before Dee could say a word, Madame Yang raised a si-lencing hand, and indicated a chair at the foot of the bed. Obe-diently, Dee sat, and she herself took a seat in a chair near the head of the bed and lovingly stroked the face on the pillow.

The Empress opened her eyes; her mother propped a pil-low behind her, helped her sit up, and held a bowl of hot tea . to her lips. Dee knew that he was looking upon the most ex-traordinary sight of his long life: a mother tending to her daughter who was dying of old age. He gazed at Madame Yang, and understood that she would outlive both the Empress and Dee himself.

Presently the Empress opened her eyes and focused on the figure at the foot of the bed. She smiled in recognition. Now Dee had an unhindered view of the amazing strong white teeth in the ruined face. Teeth and claws, he thought. Once these words were synonymous with the Empress's name, but her claws had been sheathed for so many years now that people had almost forgotten. But Dee had not forgotten, nor had he forgotten a single small detail of the questions he had carried with him for all these years.

"Magistrate," the Empress said, extending a bony hand. "Bring your chair closer so that I may see and hear you." He obeyed, and she looked at him quizzically. "I detect . . . questions on your lips," she said then. "You look a trifle impatient."

He shifted uncomfortably, wondering if it was so obvious. "You needn't look so stricken," she said. "I know what you are thinking. And you are quite right. I have asked you here because it has become plain that if I attempt to keep my promise to my mother to wait until after she has passed from this world before divulging our little secrets, then I shall not be able to keep my promise to you. And you are wondering if I am going to slip away before your very eyes, before I am able to answer all of those questions that are racing this way and that across your features."

She shifted, closed her eyes for a moment, took another sip of tea. He watched her with a hard, appraising look. He decided that she was not going to die this afternoon, nor even tomorrow. Nonetheless, he had best not waste time. But he found himself at a loss for words. After thinking for so many years now about what he wanted to ask her, he found himself unable to find a delicate way to frame his questions. But it was the Empress who took the initiative.

"You know, Magistrate, you are not the only one with questions. My mother and I have always been curious ourselves as to the astuteness of your deductions. We cannot help but wonder just how close you came to the truth in the days of your—how shall I say it?—*interest* in us."

Interest, indeed, Dee thought. How well she put it. But he was grateful to her for making it easier for him.

"Well, madame," he said with elaborate deference, "I think it only fitting and proper that you ask the first question."

She and her mother exchanged a look, and Dee sensed the current of wordless empathy that had flowed between them for as long as they had known each other.

"Very well, Magistrate," the Empress said. "There is a question my mother and I have often asked ourselves. We have even argued over it." The two women glanced at each other again. "To which of us did you attribute the demise of my young niece?"

"Ah," Dee said, lowering his head momentarily, remembering how he had so easily manipulated Historian Shu into inadvertently revealing that the poor child's death had been a premeditated, calculated thing. "Well," he began, "according to our ..." He paused, remembering the tacit injunction against mentioning the name of Lama Hsueh Huai-i or even referring to him in the abstract. "According to my findings, there was no question as to whether or not her death was a planned death."

He told them about his visit to Historian Shu, the fatuous poetry, the shameless way he had flattered the little man, the broken chop, and his subsequent nocturnal visit to Shu's office. He told his story with great care, elaborately avoiding any mention of the monk, thinking ahead as each sentence of the story formed in his mind.

"And since her death so closely resembled her mother's, both in circumstances and location," he said, referring to Madame Yang's house, "I could only come to the conclusion that you, madame,"—indicating the Empress's mother—"were the ... *author* of the event," he finished.

They both looked at him with identical faint smiles.

"But Magistrate ... you know that the Duchess had a delicate constitution. She had been known to suffer severe attacks of indigestion throughout her life. And her daughter was so much like her," Wu said innocently.

"Yes. So much like her," Dee repeated with only a touch of irony in his voice. "Of course. Indigestion. And the Duchess died shortly after eating, just as her daughter was to do not long after. But ... I seem to recall something about a set of dishes and cups in Madame Yang's house. A special set, kept in a locked hamper." He raised his hands imploringly. "I could not help but conclude that there was some significance to those dishes other than their ..." He paused and raised his hands a degree or two higher. "... their sentimental value." The last dishes my late husband ate from, Madame Yang had told Hsueh Huai-i.

"Very astute, Magistrate," Madame Yang said, speaking for the first time, her voice just a shade lower than her daughter's, and with a rusty, unused sound to it, as if she did not bother to speak much anymore. "Although it was quite true that the dishes had great sentimental value to me. They were indeed a gift from my husband. He told me to keep them until they were truly needed. But he himself never ate from them," she added with a small smile.

"No," Dee said, momentarily entranced by that little smile

on the lips of a ninety-five-year-old murderess speaking of her transgressions as if they were so much bygone mischief. "I am sure he did not."

"But Mother," the Empress said petulantly, "it is not at all fair that you should leave Magistrate Dee with the impression that you were entirely responsible. After all, *I* was the one who thought of it in the first place. You know that quite well."

"Yes," her mother replied, "but please remember whose ingenuity was responsible for removing those two tedious cousins who came snooping about. A little bit of credit where it is due, please."

The unfortunate cousins. Dee recalled the two young men executed for the murder of both the Duchess and her daughter. The entire performance had been a masterpiece of efficiency, no doubt about it. He sat quietly, not wishing to interfere with the remarkable spectacle before him of the two old women vying for preeminence as the grisly details of their past were finally brought to light.

"I give you full credit for that, of course, Mother. But we must share certain accomplishments if we are going to be entirely fair. Those other two troublesome boys, for instance."

Other troublesome boys? Dee asked himself. Was it possible for her own dead sons, Hung and Hsien, to be spoken of in such a dispassionate way? He held himself very still, afraid that Wu and Yang might remember his presence and shut the door through which a crack of light shone after so many years. But Wu was looking at Dee, and speaking directly to him.

"My mother forgets that I know a thing or two about efficiency myself," she said. "For instance, that travel always provides auspicious conditions for taking care of certain exigencies."

Dee remembered Prince Hung, who had pleaded for mercy at the sickbed of Kaotsung for the two serving women of the Empress's predecessor, and the assassin's arrow that had lodged itself in the young man's head on the trip to the summer palace. He had not thought of it for years, but now minute details of his visit with poor grieving, dying Kaotsung came back to Dee. He recalled the unspoken knowledge, dark and dangerous, that hung in the air between them as they spoke, Dee offering to assist in uncovering the identity of the "infiltrator" to the royal entourage—and then his abrupt dismissal from the palace the next morning.

That, of course, Dee thought, looking at the Empress in

her bed now, was the moment when I knew whose hand had actually slain the youth. And now, so many years later, she is tacitly telling me that I was exactly correct.

And what about Hung's brother, Hsien? The one who killed himself in exile after being accused of fomenting a rebellion against his mother? He had been accused of other crimes as well.

Dee and Hsueh had argued over it repeatedly. The Empress, they both knew, had turned on the boy in a fury, blaming him for the death of her erstwhile lover, the Indian Nagaspa. He had been found dead with the calipers on his severed head.

"The Nagaspa," Dee said aloud. "What of the poor Nagaspa?"

"*You* tell us," the Empress said with a wily look. "What did the great Dee Jen-chieh surmise from his astute observations?"

"Very well," he said, joining in the game now. "Frankly, madame, it has always been my belief that you yourself did away with the fortune-teller. My theory was that you wished to initiate action against Prince Hsien; possibly he had been involved, along with his brother, in the freeing of the serving women. At the same time, you had grown weary of the Nagaspa." He shrugged. "Your admirable efficiency, I assume." She watched him, obviously enjoying this. She wanted to hear more of his theory. "Of course, there was always the possibility that the boy himself had in fact killed the Nagaspa. There *was* enmity between the two. But there is the matter of the cache of arms found at the prince's residence, which was the official charge brought against him. Either he was truly planning a coup, or the weapons were placed there to give that appearance."

Still she waited, wanting to hear his final verdict.

"I believe," Dee went on, "that there were not really any significant weapons at the boy's residence. I believe that the charge of fomenting an armed rebellion against you was brought against him for convenience. Though I admit I have never quite understood why it was necessary to create such an elaborate scheme. You could simply have charged him with the murder of the Nagaspa, and that would have been that. Possibly you wished to set a stern example. And I have always wondered if his death was truly a suicide. Others," he said, again avoiding speaking Hsueh Huai-i's name, "theorized that the boy had indeed killed the Nagaspa, and that he had been planning a coup in earnest, angered and saddened over the death of his brother."

The Empress heaved a great sigh then. Did he detect a note of sentiment? Regret?

"I am surprised that you never guessed the truth, Magistrate," she said. "No, it was not I who put an end to the Nagaspa. Nor was it my son, as I had believed at first. I had seen with my own eyes the ill feeling between them, the ridiculous remarks the fortune-teller had made regarding the shape of the boy's head. But tell me: who was it who argued most vigorously in favor the the prince's being the killer of the Nagaspa?"

She had left him no choice but to speak the forbidden name. He hesitated; she saw his consternation and came to his rescue.

"The monk Hsueh Huai-i, of course," she said, pronouncing the three syllables as if perhaps Dee had never heard them before. "Do you mean to tell me that you never even thought of it?" she said. Dee could only look at her. He still did not know what she meant. She shrugged. "Well, I did not think of it either. It was not until many years later that the Tibetan told me the truth. He himself did away with the Nagaspa."

Dee sat back. She had taken him utterly by surprise. He remembered his long afternoon at the teashop, waiting for Hsueh Huai-i, innocent of the knowledge that the monk had moved on forever to other, more important business. Of course: investigating murder, the monk had been tempted by it. Dee imagined the moment when Hsueh understood that here was his ultimate opportunity—kill the Nagaspa, implicate Hsien by placing the calipers on the head, create a vacancy by the side of the Empress, and step into a new life. And he had not hesitated: he had done it. His new life and his old one had overlapped for a short while; the Nagapsa was already dead by Hsueh's hand while Hsueh still met with Dee, relayed information, and discussed theories. And what had been the decisive event that took place on that afternoon when Dee sat with his successive pots of cold tea in the fading light, the precise occurrence that prevented the monk from keeping that one last appointment?

Dee was surer of his own answer to that question than he had been of anything in his life: the monk had been in the Empress's bed that afternoon. He had stepped through into his new life. And though it would not know it for some time yet, so had the rest of the world.

"Hsien," the Empress said, pronouncing the name of her long-dead son. "It was true, Magistrate, that he was planning a coup. Although it may seem to you like something I might have created, it was not. Nor had the monk fabricated it. He was telling you the truth there. Hsien was my true son, the one most like me. That, of course, was why he could not be allowed to remain at the palace." She was quiet for a moment. "My true son. And yes, he did die by his own hand."

The three old people were silent. It had not taken very long for the exchange of words to be spoken, and their voices had scarcely risen, in excitement or regret or passion. There were no more mysteries now, except for one small one that Dee did not quite have the audacity to broach, and not very much time left to any of them, though Dee had his doubts when he gazed at Madame Yang. He swore he could see at least another ten years on her face. As for the Empress, he gave her a few months at best. He was less sure about himself; trying to prognosticate there was a bit like feeling about in a dark room for an object one knows is on the table, but cannot place for the moment. Two years, possibly three. That was what he felt.

While he was looking pensively at the toes of his slippers, Dee was startled to see the Empress, on the edge of his field of vision, lift a hand to her eye. A tear from the eye of Empress Wu Tse-tien was as rare as a tooth of the true Buddha, he thought, lifting his head and looking at her. For an instant, he entertained a fantasy of catching that one lone droplet in a little bottle, sealing it, and adding it to a collection of impossibly rare artifacts.

And for whom, or what, had she wept? So far, neither her sons, her niece, her sister, her lovers, nor her husband had been able to elicit even a glint of moisture from her black eyes.

Madame Yang seemed to know. Saying nothing, she reached forward with a silk cloth and wiped her daughter's eyes and nose.

"There was another one, Magistrate," the Empress said. "One you probably do not know about at all." Dee held his breath. The very small ghost he had carried in a dark quiet corner of his mind was still and attentive as well.

"My daughter," the Empress said, and her voice broke. She raised her wet eyes to her mother's. "My firstborn." Ma-

dame Yang shook her head reprovingly from side to side, as
if admonishing her not to upset herself unnecessarily, not to
waste her waning strength. And Dee saw a wordless agreement pass between Wu and Yang. No more was to be said
about the specifics of that small death. It was to remain their
secret.

"It is just that I sometimes cannot help but wonder, Magistrate," the Empress said, composing herself and looking at
Dee, "who she would have been."

A.D. 706, autumn
Ch'ang-an

 JOURNAL ENTRY ————————————————

There was a last bit of business with the Empress, which I
left for another day. It was a risk, because I knew how little
time was left, for her and for me, but it was a matter of such
delicacy that I did not want to make the mistake of pushing
her too far all at once. And yet it was vital. I let her rest for
a few days before returning to her bedside.

In the years following the departure of Hsueh Huai-i,
the Empress became a different woman. Her play took on
a frivolous quality, her interest in government waning to
virtual nonexistence. For a while after the monk was gone,
she had her "Stork Institute," her harem of pretty young
men, the Chang brothers being the most notable members.

The Changs were two gentlemen who preferred
intimate contact with each other to contact with anyone else;
whether they were actual brothers or not we shall never
know. It is irrelevant, and only noted here for its passing
historical interest. Like all the men in her life, the Changs
appeared to control her, the usual flimsy illusion brought
about only because she wished it.

Like the other men, the Changs influenced her
government, but not in the fashion of their predecessors.
They imbued our Empress and her government with a
lively penchant for things magical and mystical, things
Taoist, and refreshingly enough, native and Chinese. Once
again she built halls and pavilions, decorated fairy gardens
and magical palace retreats, for no other ostensible reason
than the pursuit of pleasure. And though I repeatedly
advised her to limit the burden of spending that fell upon

the people, I was happy that there was no hidden, ominous meaning behind these projects.

So great was my relief that her pastimes were free of dangerous religious overtones that I was able to concentrate instead on important business—cutting back on unnecessary military expenditures, useless campaigns, and border expansions at the expense of the welfare of the common people, and so forth. And I met with a modicum of success for such an old amateur statesman as myself.

But there was one problem that weighed heavily on me, one last bit of business that kept me from sleeping the full, sound sleep of an old man at the end of his life. It was a problem for which I could find no solution. It was the matter of succession: the matter of restoring the lineage, of returning the T'ang to its rightful stewardship.

The Chou Dynasty was dead, and had been for twenty years now, dissolved into the mists of legend. But as yet, no Crown Prince had been named, no successor to mount the throne after the Empress's death. Her surviving sons, living in exile, had not been designated. An oversight? Perhaps. But I believe it was more likely that Wu, though largely ineffectual now, had never completely abandoned her plans for the Wu family's place in the royal lineage. In the end, she meant to leave the Empire with a line of succession that did not possess the mandate.

No longer a despot, she retained much of the resolute obstinacy of her younger years. Though Wu's nephew Wu Cheng-ssu—the Censorate collaborator with the infamous Lai Chun-chen—had been banished along with his brother, the less ambitious Wu San-ssu, I knew from conversations with her that she was actually considering including the latter as a possible candidate. Her old obstinacy was rising, reasserting itself. Never mind that there were four living rightful heirs to the House of Li, sons of Kaotsung himself. I saw a hard reminder of the old Wu of decades past.

This was my little problem, my last small obstacle: how to return the throne to her sons, how to avoid the bloody conflict that would inevitably arise with Wu family fools upon the throne. I was plagued by the question, the final obsession of my long career.

One morning shortly after my revealing meeting with the Empress, I awoke, and there was my answer, like a gift, complete and admirable in its simplicity. With a few well-

placed words, I would be able to persuade the dying
Empress to bring her sons—specifically, Chung-tsung, for
he was the brightest prospect—back to the palace.

I knew that she reclined on the very brink of death,
and would naturally be increasingly concerned with her
position in the afterlife. So I took it upon myself to question
her at her bedside—one old artifact to another—and to
remind her of a simple rule of the cosmic plan: only the
mother of an Emperor—not an aunt—could be guaranteed
permanent worship and a secure position forever in the
ancestral shrine. Restoring the rightful lineage of the T'ang
by making her son the heir to the throne was the only way
to assure that an Emperor's constant, dutiful prayers would
rise to heaven, her only insurance against becoming a
wandering, hungry ghost.

My strategy, as history now knows, worked; from her
deathbed, the Empress signed the proclamation naming her
son Chung-tsung Crown Prince.

As I watched her affix her seal to the page that I held
before her with my own shaking hands, I thought that she
might even now change her mind, tear the paper in two,
and throw the pieces on the floor. But she did not. I had
touched something deep in her. She made her mark on the
paper with no arguments or hesitation, and it was done,
and I breathed my own silent prayer of thanks. The T'ang
was restored. Now, perhaps, I would be able to sleep.

EPILOGUE

One hundred years later
Near a *gompa* in the high Himalayas of Tibet

The monk hummed in a low, nearly inaudible resonance that
vibrated deep inside the two boys' heads. Out of this formless
sound, the words of a song gathered shape:

> " . . . lowly myself, above my head . . .
> Carpet of moon on lotus white bed.

From Hum springs Lama Dorje Sem
White-shining in Enjoyment Form . . .
A vajra-bell with Nyemma . . ."

Then his voice fell back into the deep wordless drone of his chant. He hummed this way for a while before words emerged again:

" . . . be thou my refuge; purge my crimes
Which I with sharp remorse lay bare
And henceforth, cost it life, forswear . . ."

The monk snapped his string whip above the oxen's thick necks while his eyes carefully watched the stony path before them.

"Why do you sing the words of the sacred Vajrasattva recitation to them? They are just dumb oxen," the taller of the two young novices said, an impertinent little smile on his face. "They are all the same." The monk merely continued walking and chanting, snapping his little string whip and looking straight ahead.

Taking the monk's silence as encouragement, the boy continued, "Except, of course, for the stupid little differences that arise in temperament from one dumb animal to the next." He caught a warning glance from his friend—another novice close to his own age—that said he was getting himself in deeper with each foolish remark he made. But the first boy, the bolder one, ignored him.

The monk said nothing, appearing to take no notice of the child's remarks. But he had stopped singing to the laboring beasts pulling the heavy cart. His eyes had caught their first glimpse of the bright string of the *gompa's* prayer flags just now visible over the crest of the ridge. They were nearly there. Now and again he shook his little whip and made a clicking noise with his tongue to spur the team. But still he did not respond to the boy.

They were a tiny grain of color and motion against an infinity of towering stone and sky. They moved slowly up the steep rocky hillside toward the brilliantly painted *gompa*. The ornaments and little bells hanging from their wooden yokes tinkled and jingled while the breeze played with colorful bits of rags and prayer flags and peacock feathers attached here and there to their horns and harnesses as the beasts strained against the cart laden with stone and timber beams for the *gompa*'s new prayer hall.

His eyes flashing mischief, the monk turned at last to the outspoken young novice.

"You are quite a knowledgeable boy, are you not?"

The first boy searched for an answer while the second shot a furtive glance at the monk and then to his bold friend. I tried to warn you against speaking out so stupidly, his look seemed to say.

"You are a foolish child," the monk continued. The outspoken boy, embarrassed, watched the muscles of the animals' straining haunches. "But that is a good way for a child to be," the monk said good-humoredly. "You cannot be a ready receptacle for knowledge any other way."

The boy's eyes brightened with these words. The monk snapped his string whip and took hold of the harness straps by the rightmost ox's jaw and shook them gently. The beast's big, moist brown eye rolled back and looked at him, annoyed. The animal snorted. The monk made more clicking sounds with his tongue; this was the steepest and most difficult part of the path. The final steps to anything were always the most difficult, he had said many times.

"You say all dumb beasts are the same, but then you do not listen to scriptures very well," the monk continued, with a mild chiding tone. "For some, incarnating as an ox would be a step down, for others it is a step up in the cycle of birth and rebirth."

"But what has any of that to do with why you sing to them?"

"Singing is a way of easing their burden."

"Surely they cannot understand you. They are merely soothed by the rhythms, the humming," the brazen boy said. "That is all."

"Is it? Are you certain they are not soothed by the words as well? The words are ones of encouragement, praise, and instruction," the monk said, his eyes following the dancing strings he raised over the animals' heads. This time the boy who had been silent drew up his brow questioningly and looked at the monk. The older man continued, "Oh, yes—they understand all the words. I am certain of it. Old Scholar here, with the big brown patch on his nose, becomes very angry if

I make a mistake. You can tell when he is angry, he snorts loudly . . . and there are other things about him, too." He had the boys' attention now. They looked at him with doubting eyes, and the one who had been so outspoken now smiled back at the older man.

"The other," the monk continued, dangling his string whip over the head of the ox on the left, "Old Sage, there, actually knows a thousand different prayers by heart. But grouchy Old Scholar here, with the brown patch, why . . . " The monk raised an instructive finger to his face, then lowered it and tapped the animal on the soft flat inviting furry space between the huge curled horns. " . . . why, he knows *all* the sutras by heart. If he could hold a brush, I think that he might even compose a few himself."

Both boys laughed and said that they did not believe this. The monk was going too far now, the cautious boy said.

"It is true. Every word of it. I swear," the monk said, moving around them so that he now walked next to Old Sage. He leaned over close to the animal and began to recite a prayer to the ox. It flicked its big, furry ear in response to the monk's tickling whispers, but plodded on unperturbed.

"You see, Old Sage pretends not to listen to me. He prefers to pretend that he is just an ordinary ox; he will not so much as even glance in my direction when I speak to him. He will always maintain the dumb animal air about him, as if I did not know otherwise. But this one," and he shook his string whip over the other beast's head, "ornery Old Scholar, here, will give me the meanest look or even try to trample me if I am impudent enough to recite a sutra into his ear while he is working." The boys' eyes widened in amazement and disbelief. "Old Scholar definitely does not want to hear the sutras. He does *not* like the joke."

"What joke?" the quieter boy asked.

"Yes, what joke?" the bolder child challenged. "And how do these beasts know so much?"

"Ahhh . . . " The monk rubbed his chin and pointed his finger at the bolder boy. "Now you have finally asked the worthwhile, pertinent question, child. The oxen know so much because it is actually the souls of two men who dwell in these animals."

"What two men?" the boys asked in unison.

"Many years ago two men made a wager. A boy and an

old man, actually. The boy was as young as you are now, and the man was just a few weeks from death. One of the two thought he won. He laughed to the heavens with his victory. But . . . '' The monk shook his head and patted Old Scholar between the horns. ''He had not won. In fact, neither of them had won. They both lost. You see, they were both very vain men. They interfered with people's lives. But I will tell you all about it later. Tonight, perhaps, instead of scripture study, we shall have a true story that should serve as an excellent example to young men like yourselves.'' The monk smiled. ''But for now, we have work to do.''

The boys smiled to each other at the thought of another of the monk's stories. That was why they goaded him, of course. They knew that the monk's stories could not be true, but they were very good.

The monk snapped the string whip over the animals' shoulders and began to sing to them again, his eyes on the colorful flags that snapped and furled against the vast empty blue of the sky.

> '' . . . Whereby, I pray, may be erased
> All karma, klesa,* seeds of woe . . .
> Distempers and all demon plagues,
> Of sin's dark shadow, evil's sow—
> Both mine and in all realms
> below . . . ''

NOTES TO THE READER

Given the unusual nature of the subject matter of this book, the question must certainly have arisen in the minds of our readers: How much of this tale is true?

Although *Deception* is a work of fiction, it is an extrapolation from the truth, much of that truth far stranger than any

---

*Karmic accretions, defilements upon the soul.

fiction we might have dreamed up. The Empress Wu was in fact the first and only female Emperor of China, usurping the legitimate ruling house of the T'ang Dynasty in the seventh century and creating the shortlived Chou Dynasty. She ruled through the appointment of such cruel and unprincipled men as Chou Hsing and Lai Chun-chen, the chief orchestrators of her brutal reign of terror, who created in their wake vast bodies of information as well as departments of torture and punishment. Her excesses resulted in the massacre of thousands of officials and members of the legitimate aristocratic houses, not to mention many members of her own immediate family— infants and children being no exception (including those members of the Imperial Family cited in our own story).

It is a fact that the Empress Wu achieved a certain internal peace and beneficence for the common people, a revamping of the national clan system and advancements to the great Chinese Civil Service Examination system. But the price in thousands of lives purged, exiled, tortured, ruined, and extinguished was far too great. Yes, rebellions were put down and many heads did appear on stakes; the infamous boxes—or urns, as they are more aptly described—held the land in a long siege of fear and terror through their use by the Gestapo-like Bureau of Internal Securities. Centuries before the many technological marvels put to use by the brutal dictatorial regimes of the twentieth century, the walls did indeed have ears—and eyes as well.

In her ascension, the Empress Wu did in fact use her own unauthorized "interpretations" of traditional respected Buddhist texts. More specifically, these unique interpretations were fabricated and then fostered upon the world by Hsueh Huai-i, her chief holy man. Master Hsueh has been compared to another famous cleric and royal adviser, the Russian monk Rasputin. Hsueh created for his Empress and her Chou Dynasty a great fiction in his Precious Rain Commentary to the Great Cloud Sutra. This Hsueh Huai-i did indeed live, and even within the context of his strange times, history records that he was a bizarre and awesome man responsible for innumerable "miracles" and phony scriptural "discoveries" and the establishment of the White Horse Temples. It was he who foretold the coming of the great savior boddhisattva and/or the Future Buddha Maitreya in female form. However, Hsueh Huai-i's ultimate insanity after the Reign of Terror and his fate at the hands of Magistrate Dee is our creation.

China's only female ruler in an aeons-old Confucian male society had to struggle fiercely to establish her legitimacy. In constructing our novelized version of her well-known difficult temperament and disposition—mercurial, quixotic, dangerously whimsical, and terrifyingly female—we have drawn on many sources, fictional and nonfictional, living and dead, known to us and distant from us. History tells us that she was a menacingly powerful and obsessively impassioned individual. One seldom reaches such heights against such odds without these characteristics. It was upon this base that we built our fictional character.

Into the fray comes our hero, Magistrate Ti jen-chieh—or Judge Dee, as he came to be known through his immortalization in the mystery fiction of Dutch Sinologist Robert Van Gulik in the late 1950s. But what is the truth? Professor Van Gulik created a fictional composite of a scholarly, astute detective of enormous personal integrity. Van Gulik then placed this man in a time resembling the China of a much later dynasty, rather than in the seventh-century T'ang Dynasty of the Emperors Taitsung and Kaotsung and the Empress Wu Tse-tien, which is when he actually did live.

But Van Gulik was certainly quite correct about one thing: In actuality, the real Magistrate Dee was a rather severe overseer of the spread of "foreign" religions and superstitions. In his capacity with the Bureau of Rites and Sacrifice, the real Ti Jen-chieh was responsible for the shutting down of some tens of thousands of illegal temples, shrines, and monasteries. He also remonstrated against the parasitic nature of the Buddhist establishment—its wealth, its existence outside the law, and its vast, unproductive, and not always scrupulous clergy. An original translation of the actual words of Magistrate Dee as they were recorded in the T'ang Dynasty follows this note.

Magistrate Ti (Dee) Jen-chieh rose to become the paramount minister of the seventh century, enjoying the Empress's complete trust and ultimately restoring the legitimate succession while steering the nation away from its costly foreign military adventures with the Tibetans, the Turks, and the Koreans. Our fictional presentation of his character was based on the few facts that have come down to us: the various towns and regions where he lived and worked, the rigid literary degrees he took, the antireligious memorials he delivered, the civil appointments he held, and ultimately his service on the highest ministries in the land—including the Bureau of Sacrifice (as it came to be known in the latter part of the century) and the great Council of Six. And in Van Gulik's wonderful tradition, already known to millions of readers, we kept him a sleuth, and developed the major part of our story around him as a sort of seventh-century Sherlock Holmes.

Of all the facts that we were able to obtain and use in the interest of fiction, none intrigued us more than the knowledge that the good Magistrate did have several sons. And two of these sons, history records, were an embarrassment to Dee. They became corrupt and incorrigible officials. Although it was now several years ago, we remember with astonishingly clear detail the day and even the moment of that discovery. This was when we at last put down the big overwhelming books of facts, lifted our brows, and smiled. We knew that these unexemplary sons were going to play a rich background role in our portrayal of the life and times of Magistrate Dee. But we wonder: If these incorrigible sons had not existed, would we have created them anyway?

AN ORIGINAL TRANSLATION OF MAGISTRATE TI JEN-CHIEH'S MID-SEVENTH-CENTURY MEMORIAL AGAINST THE EXCESSES OF POPULAR AND CHARLATAN BUDDHISM

BY DANIEL P. ALTIERI

In speaking of the ills that attack the root of government and law, I must first address the state of human affairs. I beseech our August Imperial Father to have pity on the multitudes of his subjects who are, at this very moment and even while I speak, being deceived and deluded by the tens of thousands. Their lives sink into oblivion without the act of death; they are united solely in their foolish desire to follow the dictates of this Buddhist religion and its idols in their infinite forms.

Is it not so that these elaborate pagodas and halls, rivaling the grandest imperial structures, that these establishments must by their very natures demand great veneration and extravagant and wasteful spending for their support? And is it also not so that these monks and nuns must have benefactors and must have bestowers to these Buddhist monasteries and to their convents?

In order to obtain the Precious Teachings of Buddha—The Precious Raft that shall ferry its believers to their hoped-for Land of Bliss—the people are summoned to honor this religious establishment with bestowals of alms, thereby augmenting its profit and strengthening its very existence. As for these Buddhist monasteries and nunneries, they are outside the law;

they escape the regulations of the Palace and its rightful, Heaven-appointed government. They deem themselves beyond repute or remand.

In their desire for luxury—a desire that is, at times, boundless—these members of the Buddhist establishment have, without conscience, exhausted the already strained labors of the nation's artisans and craftsmen, and in these works display all manner of precious gemstones in elaborate idols and ornamentations, which in turn use up enormous quantities of the nation's precious raw materials for the construction of great edifices to house them.

There is no magic involved, although there are such members of a clergy who might, at times, wish us to believe that there is. And if not magic, just where does the labor come from to support so elaborate and nonproductive a structure? Just where does the labor come from for such great edifices? It is not the labors of spirits which is utilized, if such exist. Rather, it is the exhaustive utilization of the employment of the masses. And if the wealth and materials are not Heaven-sent, then just where do they come from? Just where does the land necessary for these temples and great monastic estates come from? It comes out of that share of equal-field land allotted to the simple peasant farmer. To enrich the few, they must impoverish the many. Is that not the case?

If these Buddhists do not wish to injure the masses, and I am certain that they do not willingly wish to do so, then what is it that they seek to do? There is only so much time granted a human life upon this earth, but there seems to be no limit to the expenditure demanded of it. Households—and often the poorest households, although the rich are by no means exempt from the mass delusion that steals our nation—serve this establishment, offering constant effort. And yet they are unable to satisfy the boundless greed of the Buddhist church. The masses, the poor deluded masses, push their worn bodies to the painful limit and do not shirk from suffering for this elusive cause . . . never refusing one additional burden in its name.

And as for those who willingly have chosen this monastic life, these so-called pure-of-heart mendicants who claim to have detached themselves from any notions of earthly failure or success, going about with shaven heads to free themselves of the vanity of hair, giving up the secular folly of the distinguishing marks of clothing for the simplicity of their priestly robes . . . I, in my many encounters, have not witnessed a change in their inner natures. They are still concerned with the petty things that obsess us all and are still ashamed for their weaknesses. They are still the same on the inside.

Moreover, among these priests and mendicants and monks and anchorites, there are those who willfully sow discord among flesh-and-bone relations, treating stranger and relative alike, taking liberties with others' wives and daughters ... regardless of the price, all in their part entrusting themselves entirely to the codes of their own Dharmic Buddhist Law, while deceiving others, while misleading others.

Look around you. Walk the streets of this grand city. Wherever you go, the neighborhoods and wards, the streets and lanes and alleys are crowded with every manner of Buddhist shrine. Along every wall and beneath every market gate lies the innumerable variety of odd little temples, little houses of the spirits. Those who are pulled under the veil of Buddhism, too often seduced and misled, hastening to retire from secular life, rush to separate themselves, to sever themselves from all respect and adherence to Imperial Law. And yet these very same ones rush just as quickly toward the all embracing arms of the Buddhist regulations of the Sangha, strictly adhering to its every word.

And what of the temples, and the farmlands needed to support them? Such establishments remove from the common good so much useful property and fertile land and so many grain mills and village plots that the extent of it cannot even be guessed. And there is another problem, one that has thrust itself upon me far too often: The monastic establishment, in providing a refuge for the pure, also provides a refuge for the criminal. Those people fleeing the law, criminals, thugs, and miscreants of all sorts wishing to escape punishment, all rush through the welcoming gates of these Buddhist monasteries, secure in the fact that they are safe. How many tens of thousands of nameless criminals have escaped into the waiting arms of this establishment? Close investigations from magisterial offices in the capital and the provinces below have already seized many thousands of those seeking to evade the law in this way. How many others are there as yet unapprehended? And posing as priests and abbots and monks, these criminals—these charlatans—appeal to the baser desires of men's bodies and not to the loftier metaphysics of their hearts and minds and souls.

And there are further problems. What of the man who does not work, but receives his sustenance at the expense of others? Is this not fraudulent? And what of those whose means far surpass the multitude's, yet who still choose their course of openly robbing others of their valuables and properties? And acknowledging also those selling false sutras and relics, false hopes and promises, I can only reflect that this realm is indeed a place of pain and suffering as the Buddhists tell us.

Wherever you go the evidence tells us that Buddhism in all its infinite forms is flourishing. Flourishing, growing, multiplying. Can the dispensing of alms and charities by the Buddhists possibly match the amount of the people's wealth taken? Is the return to the people equal to what is taken from them in its name? Everywhere rows of monasteries and temples line the roads to overflowing, more numerous than the roiling waves of San Huei, more ubiquitous than the mists that cling to the sacred peaks of Wu Tai.

We see a nation now in crisis, plunging steadily into a darkening shadow of superstition. About us the great roads and byways are darkened by the black silk of Buddhist robes. And it seems that there is no one left to assist the Emperor and the State in its time of crisis—because all about us good men are falling prey to this disease of the mind, good men whom we had once relied upon for rational counsel.

In recent years past, in parts of the west-central provinces, the dry, eroding winds have covered everything with dust, and elsewhere, the constant disturbances of floods and droughts have gone unchecked and there is little chance of these troubles diminishing. Everywhere the peasant farmer is continuously reduced to the extremes. This is the nature of our world. His sorrows and pains, his distress, are boundless and his sufferings unendurable. I bow before the greatness of our court and regard its measureless merit . . . but how can it be bound to manage so great a problem? How can it allow such a waste of labor and effort and wealth? A single monk hoards money—wealth that might support a hundred is barely sufficient for the one.

If, as it is said, in preserving the wealth of a nation, you will preserve its people, then what is it that these Buddhists seek? If these good words are taken as truth, how is it that they willingly steal the wealth of this nation and exhaust the loyal and faithful? They tell us that earthly wealth is an illusion and that they seek a higher wealth. Why, then, in the transcendent name of compassion, can they . . . no, why *do* they *aggrieve* the common suffering?

If Buddhism is a religion of compassion, then they must take that compassion as their universal guiding principle. And they must bring that ideal of compassion down as an example, a paradigm of righteousness for the common people. This compassion must be at the root of their hearts and conduct. If they followed its dictum they would not sway from it. But they do not. They follow a law of greed. Otherwise, how can they possibly desire the labors of our peoples to be used to support these vain and insubstantial adornments? Buddhism as a compassionate religion should not be the cause of imposing labor upon the people. But Buddhism is the cause.

If we do not sow the proper seeds now, then we shall bring famine upon ourselves and upon the future. Without the loyal and diligent assistance of our officials, righteousness will not succeed. If we waste the official wealth and if we allow the labors of the people to be exhausted, then no corner of this nation shall escape the dire consequences. And it will be too late to save us. Historians will only speak of the lost glory of the past—the past that was us.

—Hsin T'ang Shu
(New T'ang History)

POSTSCRIPT

May the world never forget the nobility and heroism of all those who stood up and those who died in Tian An Men Square.